THE SILENCER SERIES
BOX SET

THE SILENCER SERIES BOX SET

BOOKS 1-4

MIKE RYAN

WWW.MIKERYANBOOKS.COM

Copyright © 2020 by Mike Ryan

All rights reserved.

No part of this book may be reproduced in any form or by any electronic or mechanical means, including information storage and retrieval systems, without written permission from the author, except for the use of brief quotations in a book review.

Cover Design: The Cover Collection

THE SILENCER

1

London—Nobody could remember exactly when or how long the unidentified man had been waiting in the hospital lobby. It was a busy night, and he never checked in at the desk or asked for assistance. It wasn't until he fell off the chair and laid unconscious on the floor that anybody really paid much attention to him. His long trench coat had covered up the gunshot wound to his stomach, but his white shirt had now turned red thanks to blood soaking into it for a few hours. They immediately took him to the emergency room and put him on the operating table. The doctors needed to take the bullet out and stop the bleeding as soon as possible. After an hour of surgery, the doctors successfully removed the bullet. Luckily for the man, no major organs had been damaged, other than a very minor graze to part of his liver. Once he was stitched up, they wheeled him to the fifth floor and a private room for his recovery.

A couple of hours after the surgery, the man had awoken in a considerable amount of pain. He was holding his side and feeling where the bandages now were. He grimaced as he looked around at his surroundings, not remembering how he got there. A few minutes later a nurse came in to check on him.

"Hey!" The smiling nurse greeted him. "Nice to finally see you awake."

"Hi."

"How are you feeling?"

"I've had better days."

"Yeah, I bet. My name's Kelly. Can I get you anything?"

"Yeah. My release papers."

She laughed. "That might take a little while."

"I can't stay here," he said.

"Why? You in some sort of trouble? Is that what the gunshot was from? Somebody after you? I can get the police here for you."

"No. Don't call the police."

Kelly looked at him a little strangely. The police would be there anyway, but usually the people that came in there that didn't want the police involved were in most cases running from them. Not that it mattered to her in how she treated the patient. Law-breaking or law-abiding, she did her duties the same way no matter what.

"You didn't have any identification on you when you came in," Kelly said. "What's your name?"

The man thought about it for a minute, knowing what would happen if he revealed his true name. At least the one he was going by now. If he gave that, his name would ping up in somebody's computer and they could come back to try to finish the job.

"Uh… it's John. John Smith."

Kelly raised her eyebrows as she looked at him over the top of the clipboard that she was writing on. She knew it was a fake name right away, but being an experienced nurse of over ten years, knew not to take issue with it. If that was the name he wanted to use, that was his business.

"John Smith, huh? That's what you're gonna go with?" She scribbled on his notes then hung the clipboard over the end of his bed.

"Yeah."

"You remember how you got here?"

"Umm... no, not really."

"Apparently, you were waiting in the lobby and you suddenly passed out. Nobody could remember when you came in or if somebody brought you in."

"I came in on my own."

"So, you remember. Anybody you want me to call to let them know you're here?" She knew what his answer would be.

"No."

"Friends, family, anyone?"

"I don't have any friends or family here."

Kelly stayed with him for a few more minutes, asking him some more questions that he mostly evaded. She checked his vital signs, all of which seemed to be OK. As she wrapped things up, she let Smith know that a doctor would be in to see him in a few minutes. That doctor wound up walking in about ten minutes later.

"Mr..." The doctor picked up the chart and examined it, "Smith. I'm Dr. Karlson. How are you feeling?"

"Fantastic."

"Well, considering what happened, I'd say you're a very lucky man. We removed the bullet. Luckily it didn't hit any major organs... well, it did hit a very tiny piece of your liver, but it was such a small piece it really wasn't much at all. Most people with a gunshot to their stomach or abdomen don't fare quite as well as you."

"No kidding. So, what's my recovery timeline?" Smith said.

"You should be up and about and out of here in two or three days I'd say."

"Long-term effects?"

"Difficult to say right now. Full recovery will be anywhere from three to six months if you don't do anything too strenuous. No climbing mountains or obstacle courses or anything like that. You never truly know whether someone will ever get back to a hundred percent after something like this. Some people will get to eighty or ninety percent and that's as far as they'll ever go. Now, you seem like you're in decent shape so I would imagine you'll get there, if not, then pretty close to it."

After Smith's conversation with the doctor, he worried about what might happen next. He knew that the law required the hospital to notify the police of a gunshot injury. Since gunshot wounds were not very common in England, Smith knew the police would be there soon, and with questions he didn't want to answer.

He hit the button for the nurse's station to get Kelly. She came in just a few seconds.

She poked her head around the door. "What can I do for you?"

"Is there any way I can get a shirt or something? Kind of cold just laying here like this."

"I should be able to find something. Give me a couple of minutes."

"Thank you." Smith smiled.

He was going to have to speed up his recovery time and exit the hospital sooner than the doctors had planned. He couldn't risk the police asking questions and poking around. It only took five minutes for Kelly to return with a plain black shirt.

"This OK?" She held it up for him as she walked in.

"Should do fine. Thank you."

"Got you a large. You don't quite look like a medium."

"Just my size," Smith said, slowly putting the shirt on.

"Better?"

"Yes. Any idea on when the police will be here?"

"The police?"

"Yeah. They're coming, right? Gunshot wounds have to be reported, right?"

A little taken aback by the questions, Kelly wondered why he was inquiring. It seemed strange to her. "I believe they were just called. Thirty minutes ago? Everything OK?"

"Everything's fine. Just wanted to know when to expect company. Could you just give me a minute or two's notice when they get here? I hate surprises."

"Sure thing."

It took a few minutes for him to come up with a plan, but Smith knew anything was better than staying there. He unhooked all his monitors and gingerly got off the bed, walking over to the window where his trench coat was draped over a chair. Just as he was putting it on, Kelly came rushing into the room.

"What do you think you're doing?" She stood in front of him, hands on hips.

"I'm afraid I have to go."

"Oh, no you don't. You're gonna lay right back down," she said, gripping his arm.

Smith resisted and gently removed her hand from his bicep. "Thank you for patching me up and everything but staying here isn't an option."

Kelly objected again, but he shrugged off her attempts to keep him there. Smith walked out of the room and down the hall, right past a team of doctors and nurses, all of whom were wondering what was going on.

"You still need attention." Kelly stayed two steps behind him.

"You've done enough," Smith said, not even bothering to turn around.

He kept walking until he found an elevator, Kelly running after him. Once the doors opened, he stepped in and pushed for the main floor, Kelly just barely getting in before the doors closed again.

"What do you think you're doing?" Kelly said, watching the brightly lit numbers count down.

"Leaving."

"Can I ask why?"

"Already told you. Can't stay here."

"Who are you running from?"

"You don't wanna know."

"The police? Or a criminal?"

"Neither."

"What else is there?"

"There are people looking for me more powerful than either of those. And once they know I'm here, they'll come looking for me," Smith said.

"We can try to protect you while you heal."

"Afraid not. Not from these people."

"How do you know?"

"Because I used to be one of them."

"Used to be?"

"Up until last night."

The elevator doors opened and Smith walked out, Kelly following for a few steps. Eventually she stopped without saying another word, knowing that there was nothing else she could do to prevent him from leaving. A couple of police officers entered the hospital and walked right past Smith on his way to the exit. As soon as he passed the officers, Smith looked back at Kelly, wondering if she'd inform them of his presence. Kelly looked at the officers but let them pass by her without a word, watching them get into the elevator. Smith looked at the nurse and gave a smile, nodding slightly as if to say thank you to her.

"Take care of yourself," she said.

Philadelphia—It'd been six months since his shooting and he figured he'd spent enough time laying low. After arriving at Philadelphia International Airport, Smith had just picked up his bags and started walking through the corridor when he stopped suddenly. There was a man standing there, holding a placard with his name on it. John Smith. There was a second man standing next to the one with the sign.

He sighed, resigned to the fact that they had finally found him, ready to submit to what had started in London. He knew it would be futile to resist, knowing that agents were watching from several locations. He took a quick glance around to see if he could spot any guns with him in its sights, though he couldn't pick anyone out. The man put his hand out, indicating to Smith that he should follow him.

Ready to accept whatever was coming, he followed the man over to a restaurant. Smith was instructed to wait there while the man walked over to a table where another gentleman was sitting. Sitting with his back to him, and dressed in a nice black suit, Smith couldn't make out the identity of the person. From behind, it didn't appear to be anyone that he'd ever met before. The man waved Smith over to have a seat with the gentleman that was sitting, who never turned around to look at him. Smith walked leisurely over to the table, not keen to hear whatever the person had to say to him. Smith sat down across from the well-dressed man, still unsure who the hell he was. He wasn't the type of person

Smith expected to see if he was ever caught. The man was eating tomato soup but stopped when Smith sat.

"Mr. Smith, it's a pleasure to meet you," the man said, putting his hand out.

Smith wasn't sure about shaking hands, but decided to do so, anyway. "Wish I could say the same to you but you seem to have the advantage of actually knowing who I am. I can't say the same about you."

"You can call me David," the man said in a quiet, unassuming voice.

"Got a last name?"

"Just David will do for now."

"How'd you know my name?"

"Which one?"

"Either."

"I have ways. Though I would think a man such as yourself would be able to come up with a better alias than Smith."

"I was in a hurry. You work for Centurion?" Smith said.

"You can put your mind at ease, Mr. Smith. I can assure you I'm not with the CIA, or any other government agency for that matter. I'm not here to harm you in any way."

"Then how do you know who I am? How'd you know I would be here?"

"There are many things that I'm aware of that I probably shouldn't be. That's something we can discuss at another time."

"What do you want from me?" Smith shifted slightly on the hard, plastic seat.

"Well since you seem to be in transition at the moment with regards to your work, I wanted to offer you employment."

"Doing what?"

"Similar to your last line of work," David said. "Only hopefully without all the killing."

"Listen, I'm not sure what this is all about but you seem to talk without really telling me anything. Why don't you just tell me what you really want?"

David opened his mouth to start talking, but hesitated as he tried to formulate what he wanted to say. "My... goal, my aim, what I hope to accomplish... is to prevent bad things happening to good people. To do that, I need someone I can trust; who has your particular set of skills."

"Bad things happen to good people all the time. You can't prevent it."

"But you can. I can. And if you choose to help me in this pursuit... then we can."

"What're you, a detective or something?"

David grimaced, "Not quite."

"Well then I'm not quite interested," Smith said, standing up. "Am I free to go?" He looked at the two men sitting a few tables away.

"If you like," David nodded. "But I think it's safe to say that if I could find you, I'm pretty sure Centurion would be able to as well."

"Let me worry about that."

"What you need is a friend who can help you in that regard."

"I'm all out of friends. Besides, you look like you should be working in a library or something. I doubt you can help me against Centurion."

"Looks can be deceiving, Mr. Smith. For instance, it's a good thing you left the hospital in London when you did. Not only did you manage to just barely avoid the police, but Centurion agents came about two hours later to check on the man with a gunshot wound to his stomach who had no ID on him."

Smith sat again, wondering how he knew all that. "How'd you

get that information if you don't work for Centurion? You're not British, so you're not MI6 either."

"Let's just say I'm good with computers and finding information that others can't."

"Which means you're either a hacker that's on some type of government radar or you've worked for one of the agencies before. So, which is it?"

"A little bit of both I would say," David picked up his spoon. "I'd also like to let you know that it's a good thing you had this unscheduled layover here. There were several agents waiting for you at your original destination down in Orlando. I'm quite sure they would not be giving you the courtesy of this conversation that we're having." He dipped his spoon in his bowl and slurped a mouthful of soup.

Intrigued, Smith was now interested in finding out more, though he was still suspicious. Six years in the CIA had that effect on people. "If you want me to join this crusade that you got going on, then you're going to have to spill a whole lot more information. Like exactly who you are, what you do, and how you get all this information you have. You seem to know everything about me but I know nothing about you. For all I know you're just setting me up for a hit later."

"I assure you, Mr. Smith, that is not the case."

"I'm sure you can understand my suspicions."

"I can. Fine," David said. After a little deliberation, he continued. "I'll tell you a little about myself. How I get my information, well, I should keep that a little more guarded. At least until I know you're as invested in this as I am."

"I'm all ears. You can start by telling me your name."

"My name is David Jones."

"Jones? You gave me crap about Smith and you're using a name like Jones?"

"I'm not supposed to be as creative as you with this alias thing. You should be better at it."

"It is an alias?"

"Yes."

"So, why do you need an alias?"

Jones pushed his bowl of soup aside for a moment as he thought of where to begin. "I, at one point, worked for the NSA. I had the highest level clearance as an analyst and consultant."

"OK?"

"At least, until several months ago. I'd become disillusioned with the agency over the way they process and act on the information that they acquire."

"In what way?"

"As you're well aware, the NSA keeps tabs on everyone. They have mountains upon mountains of data and information, most of which the public is never aware of. In addition to trying to track terrorist activity, as well as gaining foreign intelligence, they track everything that normal people do. They have access to emails, phone calls, voice messages, almost anything you can think of, they are privy to," Jones said.

"And you take issue with this?"

"Not in its basic context. They're looking for items in reference to national security and I believe in that regard, nothing should be left to chance."

"So, what do you have a problem with, then?"

"That they have access to millions of documents, emails and the rest that they do nothing with. Normal, everyday people, that have real problems, whose lives may be in danger, and the NSA does nothing to help them."

"And if the NSA were to act on that information, or forward it to local authorities, that information couldn't be used in court or else it would be learned where that information came from," Smith said.

Jones nodded his head. "And there'd be a public outcry, more than there already is about the use of the NSA's methods in acquiring such information."

"And how do you propose on helping these so-called normal people?"

"I've devised a program where I have access to some of that information," Jones said, sliding his bowl back in front of him.

"You're hacking the NSA?"

Jones scooped up soup as he considered his answer. "Uh, well, I guess you could put it that way. I prefer to think of it as piggybacking to get the proper information that I need."

"Do they know this yet?"

"Not that I can tell. It's only a matter of time, however, that they do. But by that time, by the time they've located the source, the signal will be bounced around all over the country. I'm not particularly worried about them finding me. At least not yet. What I'm more concerned with, is acting upon the information that we acquire."

"Just what information is that? What kind of help do these people need? And how are you finding people who need it?" Smith said, eyeing the bowl of soup. He was hungry after his flight and it smelled great.

"The NSA has software programs that scan every email sent, every phone call made, every voice mail, every post on Facebook, every tweet on Twitter, that looks for certain words and phrases to indicate potential problems. Now, what they currently do, is if it's related to terrorism or foreign intelligence, they act upon it. If it's just Mary Sue, afraid for her life from an abusive boyfriend, they ignore that information and file it away. They don't care whether this normal, everyday woman who's just trying to get by lives or dies. I do. I want to make a difference."

"You can't save the entire world, Jones. Trying to is a futile effort. Take it from me. I've been all over it."

"I know that. I'm not trying to save the world. I have no illusions about trying to change the planet or how its people look at each other. I just want to make a difference on my end of it."

"So, what do you need me for?"

"Because I can't do the things you can do. You have a particular set of skills that I can't duplicate. I am good at certain things... computers, finding information, things of that sort. I've always been in the background doing what needs to be done. What I need... is a partner who is good in the field who can do the things you do."

"What makes you think I'm your guy?"

"I've read your file. I know everything about you. You went into the military straight out of high school, became a member of Delta Force, spent eight years in the military, then when your enlistment ended, wound up at the CIA. I know you've been there the last six years, the last four of which you were in a top-secret project called Centurion in which you were a foreign assassin. I also know that Centurion knew you were growing tired of your role in the agency and were seeking to get out, but with all you know about the organization, couldn't just let you leave and sought to terminate you in London six months ago."

"Well then you also know that most of the people that come across my desk have a tendency of ending up dead," Smith said.

Jones shifted his eyes back and forth, "That is something we would have to work on."

"It sounds like you have a noble cause, and I'm all for it, but I'm not sure I'm your guy."

"On the contrary, I believe you're the perfect guy," Jones swallowed more soup.

"I'm a little set in my ways. Violence tends to follow me around. I'm not a wallflower who believes in turning the other cheek."

"That's where we could benefit each other. I've read your files and reports. You certainly don't run from a fight, and at times seem to embrace it, but it seems like you do it for the right reasons. You don't especially like killing but you will if you have to."

"What are you looking to do? Save people? Send them to the authorities? Jail? What?"

"Whatever the situation calls for, Mr. Smith," Jones replied. "Whatever the situation calls for."

"I have a feeling you're looking for someone who's gonna swoop in and save the day, get the girl, and leave the bad guy tied up and waiting for the police to arrive to take him to the slammer. That ain't me. It's not how I operate."

"I'm fully aware of that. And I'm not naïve enough to think everything we work on will be simple and easy with no grey moral boundaries to cross. I would prefer to do things as quietly and non-violently as possible. In saying that, there will be times when I'll disagree with your methods. And I'm sure there'll be times when I think you're being too violent for the task at hand and I'll be right and you'll be wrong. Just like I'm equally sure they'll be times when I think that… and you'll be right and I'll be wrong and that's exactly what the situation calls for and I just can't see it. But I believe that together we'll complement each other. We won't agree on everything, no. But I think we could be an effective team. If you're of the mind to be one."

Jones stood up, putting on his hat and coat. He motioned to his two bodyguards that he was done, and they walked over to him.

"Where are you going?" Smith was surprised he was leaving.

"I have other business to attend to."

"I thought we were going over your business."

"It's a lot to take in, I know. I really wasn't expecting to go into so many details with you on our first encounter. I had merely planned to make this an introductory meeting. But things rarely go as planned, don't they?" Jones said.

"How will I contact you if I agree to this venture of yours?"

"Don't worry, Mr. Smith, I'll contact you."

Jones reached into his pocket and took out a piece of paper, putting it down on the table in front of Smith.

"What's this?" Smith smoothed out the slip as he read it.

"I took the liberty of arranging accommodation for you at a nearby hotel. That's your check-in information and room number."

"What makes you think I'll go there?"

"Curiosity. If you're interested in this operation, I assume you'll be there when I check in with you tomorrow. If you're not, then you're not, and I wish you well in your future endeavors."

Smith sat there for a few moments, watching the stranger walk away, followed by his two bodyguards. Once they were out of sight, he glanced down at the piece of paper given to him and thought about the offer. Though he still wasn't sold on the idea, he was intrigued. It would interrupt his plans in Orlando, but Smith knew what he was planning down there wasn't likely to go over well. Jones wanted Smith to help with whatever little crusade he was planning, but if he was as good with computers as he said, and as he appeared, Jones could help Smith as well.

2

Smith was sitting on the bed watching TV when he heard a knock on the door. He went over to the peephole and saw that it was Jones, standing there with a briefcase in his hand. He opened the door and popped his head out, wondering where Jones' guards were.

"Where's the muscle?"

"I didn't feel I had a need for them today,"

"You mean, you no longer feel I might be dangerous to you."

Jones shrugged. "You never know how a first meeting will turn out. If it doesn't go as predicted or planned, precautions must be taken."

"And now you're satisfied that I'm not a sociopathic killer who doesn't care about anything?"

"You're here."

Smith allowed Jones to come in and they sat down at the small table near the window to continue talking about Jones' business proposition.

"One of the first things we have to do is get you a new identity,"

Jones stated. "Even if one person inside the CIA knows your Smith alias, it's one too many. Luckily I've brought along several new identities for you to pick from and you can take whichever one you'd like."

"Not necessary. I already have one." Smith smiled in response.

"A new one?"

"One of the things my mentor taught me when I just started out was to create a new identity that nobody else would know, even him, in case things went bad."

"So, nobody else knows it?"

"Only me. And now you."

"What is it?"

Smith went over to his bed and picked up some papers, then placed them in front of Jones for him to look at. "Michael Recker." Jones nodded. "Looks like you have the bases covered. Passport, driver's license, credit cards. Very impressive."

"We're taught to be resourceful."

"So I see."

"I was wondering, how'd you know what plane I was flying in on?" Recker said.

"Flight manifests are rather easy to hack into. The bigger question is why you used one of your known aliases? You must've known the CIA would've been waiting for you down in Florida once your plane arrived."

"I did."

Jones gulped, not knowing how he'd receive his next statement. "The only thing I can deduce is that you were expecting a welcoming committee and weren't actually planning on ever leaving that airport."

Recker smiled. "So how do you plan on financing this operation of yours?"

"I've already taken care of the finances. Money will not be an issue."

"Detective work, security work, vehicles, guns, supplies... all that can add up."

"Believe me, the amount of funds we have at our disposal will not be an issue. I've secured enough money to operate for several years I suspect," Jones said.

"How? Your own money? Or do you have a financial backer in this enterprise of yours?"

"Why does it matter?"

"If you want me to join this operation, I need to know who all the players are. As you can imagine, I don't like surprises."

"There is no one else."

"How much money are we talking? How about my salary?" Recker didn't like to be so mercenary but while the subject was on the table...

"Our starting capital is in excess of five million dollars. Is that enough?"

"To start with. You'll be surprised at how fast that goes. Supplies get expensive. Guns, cars, equipment, payoffs, it adds up quickly."

"I understand your point, Mr. Recker. If the situation arises that we need more capital, I'm quite confident in my ability to acquire it."

"Are you that wealthy that you have nothing else to do with your money?"

"Why are you so interested in the money?"

"Like I said, I need to know all the players. You want me involved in this operation, then you need to let me know all the details. I'm not just gonna be some hired muscle to do your dirty work and get left out to dry when things go bad," Recker said.

Jones sighed and nodded, realizing he needed to be more

forthcoming with the former assassin. "The money has been acquired from some, shall we say, less than reputable citizens."

"You're in bed with criminals?"

"I wouldn't put it quite that way."

"Then how would you put it?"

"The money's stolen," Jones said.

"It's what?"

"I identified some individuals known for criminal activity, mostly drug players, and hacked into their bank accounts. I took around a million from five different people."

"And you think they won't come looking for you?"

"It's not likely." Jones smiled, this was right up his street. "I engineered it to look like the money went into accounts held by their rivals, and sent anonymous messages stating that fact. Meanwhile, the money was siphoned through several other accounts before finding its final resting spot in mine. I used some hacking skills to conceal the final whereabouts of the money. I then went into the rivals' accounts and made it look like they had additional money that they didn't really have."

"So, you're sure they can't trace it back to you?"

"Yes. Each account has a different name on it, in four different countries, so I'm reasonably sure they'd be unable to trace it back to me. As for your salary," Jones reached into his inside pocket which earned a raised eyebrow from Recker. He took a couple of credit cards slowly out of his pocket and put them on the table in front of him. "I've taken the liberty of establishing a bank account for you with an initial amount of one hundred thousand dollars. In addition, on the first of every month, you'll draw a monthly salary of twenty thousand dollars that will automatically go into your account. So, you see Mr. Recker, your salary is also not an issue." He slid the cards across the table with one finger.

"Sounds reasonable enough," Recker said. "How are you going

about picking out people that you deem of needing our help? Gonna grab an office building and put up a neon sign?"

Jones grinned. "Not quite what I had in mind. I get the same information the NSA is getting. It's up to me to decipher it. Some people that we'll look into might not actually need the help. But some will."

"I have one condition if I come in on this thing," Recker said.

"OK?"

"I don't help criminals. I won't protect them. I won't save them. If you get something on your computer about one criminal intending to kill another... I won't help them. And I won't get in the way."

"Is that a blanket statement about every person who has a criminal record, Mr. Recker?" Jones raised an eyebrow this time.

"I'm not talking about some twenty-year-old college kid who just got busted for smoking a joint. I'm not talking about someone who got busted for shoplifting once ten years ago. I'm talking seasoned criminals who've got bad rap sheets. Assault, rape, murder. If one gangbanger's trying to kill another one... I'm staying out of it. If you decipher that someone's trying to kill them... let them."

Jones quickly nodded his head, agreeing to Recker's conditions. "Agreed. So, I take it this means you're on board?"

"Let's just say I'm willing to give it a shot and we'll see how it works out."

"Fair enough."

"How many more people do you plan on recruiting on this endeavor?"

"No one. As far as I'm concerned, the less people we have the better. Too many people involved and we risk exposing ourselves. I wish to remain as low key and inconspicuous as possible."

"Probably won't be possible for very long."

"Regardless, let's try to keep it that way."

"When do you anticipate starting this little gig?"

"Oh, we've already started, Mr. Recker," Jones answered, reaching down to the briefcase on the floor and putting it on the table.

Jones unsnapped it and removed a bunch of papers and laid them on the table, looking at them briefly. He then moved the briefcase aside and handed one of the sheets to Recker.

"What's this?" Recker asked, looking the paper over.

"I believe that would be what you call our first...," Jones hesitated, struggling to find the proper wording. "What would you call it exactly? Assignment?"

"Our first person in need?"

Jones smiled, "That'll do for now, I suppose. But yes, that's our first victim or target... neither of those sounds quite right. Anyway, that's who I'd like to help first."

"Why her?"

"Seems like a rather straightforward case. What appears to be a decent woman who's being abused and threatened by an ex-boyfriend. I intercepted several emails, texts, and phone calls indicating he was quite unhappy with the termination of their relationship. Well, as you can see, it's all there for you."

"Why hasn't she just gone to the police?"

"It's a little further down there," Jones said, pointing to it. "But, anyway, she has. She has a protection order out on him."

"They're not worth the paper they're printed on. All it takes is one time for him to violate it and she could be dead by the time the police get there."

"Exactly. She appears to be a good person, no criminal record, works as a nurse at a major hospital, and volunteers for a dog adoption organization. She's in fear for her life from this man and she needs our help."

Recker continued reading the paper on her. On subsequent pages, Jones had included some of the e-mails and texts the boyfriend had sent. Mia Hendricks was twenty-eight years old and worked at St. Mary's Hospital as a pediatric nurse. Three months prior, she'd broken up with her boyfriend of six months over his physical and abusive nature. He had a propensity for drinking too much and caused several bruises on Hendricks' arms, as well as a couple on her face, including a black eye. It was after the black eye that Hendricks' co-workers, fearing for her life, convinced her to get away from him. In the three months they'd been apart, her ex, Stephen Eldridge, hadn't quite gotten the message. He told her that he'd change and not drink anymore, but he was still verbally abusive and threatened to kill her if she didn't get back with him.

"What got her on your radar?" Recker dropped the paper back onto the table and leaned back in his seat.

"Well, anything the software deems a physical threat is noted. Words like kill are an automatic red flag. There are other words and phrases that start sounding alarms, but that's the gist of it. And as you can see, he used that word several times, both in emails and texts."

"Seems like he's not getting the message."

"No, he's not. She keeps rebuffing him, but with each subsequent contact, Eldridge's replies are getting more dangerous and indicating he won't stop no matter what."

"So, what do you want me to do? Throw him off a rooftop?"

"Uh... while I have no doubt in the effectiveness of such a strategy, I was hoping for something a little less... noticeable," Jones said.

"Would you rather me whisper sweet little nothings in his ear?"

Jones opened his mouth to speak, then closed it again as his eyes danced around, thinking of a proper reply. "I was hoping you could get him to realize the error of his ways and divert his attention to a different path."

"I thought you'd let me work things through my way?"

"Merely a suggestion, Mr. Recker. Maybe try my way first..."

"And then throw him off the rooftop?"

"I'd prefer our first case to not wind up with a dead body."

"Well aren't we picky?" Recker smiled at his own joke.

They discussed Hendricks and her situation for a few more minutes before Recker stood up, ready to start moving. He put on his long, grey trench coat.

"Where are you going?" Jones said.

"Need guns and ammunition. Have to be properly equipped in case something happens." Recker shrugged the coat onto his shoulders and patted his pockets.

"How much money do you think you'll need?"

"Not sure. Have to find someone first."

"Can't you just get them from a dealer?"

"Not the kind of dealer I'm looking for."

"You mean criminals? The very same people we're trying to put away?"

"Well, buying the stuff we'll need, you can't just walk into a store and ask for a bunch of guns and put it on the credit card," Recker said. "Those stores have cameras. I think it's a good idea if we try to avoid video surveillance. Plus, you need to fill out forms, and the guns are registered. If you want to stay under the radar, you need guns that are untraceable and avoid putting your name to anything."

"Sounds logical."

"Plus there's only so much you can learn from computers and emails and such. Sometimes you need good old-fashioned intelligence. Eyes and ears on the street. Connections. Most decent people won't have the kind of information we'll need sometimes."

"Well, I'll take your word for it I suppose. Although I do appreciate your thoroughness, I did establish new identities for us to use so that wouldn't be a problem."

"Trust me. I've tracked people down for a living for the past eight years. If you leave a paper trail, eventually someone will find you. No matter how careful and deceptive you think you are. If you leave a crumb, someone will eventually find it. It's best to stick to using cash, staying out of cameras, and not filling out forms that can leave a trace."

"I will agree with your judgment on the matter."

"How will I contact you?"

"I took the liberty of acquiring phones. They're prepaid to avoid detection," Jones said. "I already programmed my number in yours."

"Good. One other thing… we're gonna need a base of operations to work in. Don't tell me you're planning on doing this out of a hotel room or a bedroom or something."

"On the contrary, Mr. Recker. I've acquired a little business just outside the city where we can set up."

"A business?"

"A legitimate business on the first floor and office space on the second."

"Are you sure that's wise?" Recker didn't want this thing to fall at the first hurdle.

"Of course. It wouldn't look good if two men were seen going into a vacant warehouse or building all the time, would it?"

"I suppose not."

"I'm the legitimate owner of a business and I have every right to use that office for whatever purpose I see fit. Who'd think twice?" Jones said.

"You're probably right. What kind of business is it, anyway?"

Jones wrote down the address on a piece of paper and

handed it to Recker. "Here's the address. You'll see when you get there. There's a private entrance in the back with steps leading up to it."

"OK."

"Oh, Mr. Recker?" Jones said, remembering something.

Recker had just gotten out the door when he heard Jones call for him. He came back into the room and saw Jones taking keys out of his pocket and holding them in front of him.

"I almost forgot," Jones said, handing the keys over.

"What's this for?"

"Well it's tough to get around the city on foot or by public transportation. So, I took the liberty of acquiring a car. An SUV to be exact. A brand new black Ford Explorer with tinted windows is in the parking lot."

"Company car?" Recker said with a smile.

"On the contrary, it's yours."

"Mine? Gonna take it out of my salary?"

"No. Consider it a signing bonus."

Recker nodded. "Thanks, Jones."

"I'm gonna stay here for a few more minutes and check a few things on Ms. Hendricks. After that I'll head back to the office. There's still a few more things that need to be settled there."

"All right. After I've... done what I need to do, I'll meet you over there."

"Sounds like a plan."

"By the way, you can save me a little time. Where would you suggest I go to meet some rough-looking characters who might, by chance, have some guns?"

"There are several areas. You could try Hunting Park, that's North Philly between second and ninth I believe. Or you could go a little farther until you hit Germantown. Or there's Kensington. Or..."

"Basically, what you're telling me is just drive into the city and park anywhere."

"There are a lot of good parts to this city, Mr. Recker. Most areas are good. But there's a few that's not. You asked for the not so nice ones."

"Do me a favor and lock up when you're done?" Recker said. "Unless you, by chance, took the liberty of acquiring a house or an apartment for me as well?"

"Oh, thank you for reminding me," Jones said, grinning. He tossed another set of keys toward Recker that he snagged out of the air. "It's a nice little apartment, quiet community, you should like it."

Recker returned the smile and continued out the door. He went to the parking lot to find the new truck that he'd just received. He hit the alarm button on his keypad, saw the lights blinking on a truck parked on the far right of the lot and heard the horn sound. He walked over to it, got in, checked out the interior and fiddled around with some of the controls.

"This gig might not be so bad after all."

3

Recker drove through the city for a couple of hours, just trying to familiarize himself with his surroundings. He'd been in Philadelphia before about five years prior to this, but only for a few days, and he really didn't get to see much of the city. He'd have to rely on Jones, at least for a little while, to get him familiar with the place.

He did take Jones' advice and drove around through Hunting Park. It was a rough-looking area. He turned onto sixth street near an elementary school, a three-story brick building with a raised basement. He parked near the curb as he saw several youthful looking guys in the school playground area.

Recker watched them for a few minutes, looking like they were buying and selling drugs, as money and small bags passed between the parties. He waited until they finished their business until he made his move.

Recker fixated on one guy and as the group broke up, he got out of his car and started walking towards him. The other four guys went separate ways. Recker looked back to make sure they were still going in the opposite direction. He started closing in on his target and picked up his pace. The guy he was following had a suspicion he was being tailed and turned his head back, seeing Recker coming towards him. He darted across the street towards a mini-mart, Recker running after him. Recker anticipated he'd run and had already begun in that direction before the guy even took off. Recker grabbed the collar of the man's jacket and pushed him into the wall of the building.

"Yo, man, what'd you do that for?" the man asked, turning around to face his attacker.

"Just want some information, sonny."

"What're you, a cop?"

"Nope."

"You look like a cop," the man said, noting Recker's hairstyle and the way he dressed. "You in narcotics or somethin'?"

"I'm not a cop." Recker tightened his grip.

"Well if you're not a cop then what you want with me? You're in the wrong neighborhood, pal."

"Looking for some information. I figured you were the guy that could give it to me," Recker said, taking his hands off the guy.

"Got the wrong guy, dude. I don't know nothin'."

Recker smiled. "Oh, I think you do."

"If you ain't a cop then what you want information for?"

"What's your name?"

"Why should I tell you?"

"Because I'm asking."

The man looked at Recker, wondering what he was up to. He didn't look like the usual kind of guy that was in that neighborhood.

"I need to do some business," Recker said when the name wasn't forthcoming. "You look like the kind of guy that can help me do that."

"That all depends. What kind of business you talking about?"

"I need weapons. Unregistered and untraceable," Recker said, looking around to make sure nobody else was nearby.

"What you need weapons for?"

"That's my business."

"How do I know you're not a cop just looking to set me up or something?"

"If I was a cop, I'd have busted you and your friends back there for dealing. I'm not a cop. Now can you help me or not?"

"Maybe. Whatcha need?"

"A few handguns, assault rifles, maybe a few grenades, a missile launcher'd be nice," Recker told him.

The man's eyes widened, surprised at the request. "What're you, trying to start a war?"

"Nope. Just like to be prepared."

"Prepared for what?"

"Like I said, that's my business. Can you help me or not?"

"Uh... yeah, I might know some people."

"I would like to have it within the next few days if you can arrange it."

"You got the money ready if I can?"

"Money's not an object. If you can get something set up for tomorrow, I'll give you a little something extra for your troubles," Recker said. "I also prefer Glocks and Sig Sauers if you can get them."

The man moved his head around like he was thinking. "Aight. I'll let you know."

"Give me a call on this number when you're ready," Recker said, handing him a paper with his number on it.

The man nodded, "A'ight."

"One more thing... I don't do business with people I don't know. So, what's your name?"

"Tyrell."

"Tyrell what?"

"Gibson. You didn't tell me your name yet."

"You can call me Recker."

"Recker? That a nickname or something?"

Recker shook his head, "No."

"That's a fitting name then, 'cause it seems like you're the kind of guy who likes to wreck things."

"Yeah. Almost like I picked the name myself or something."

"You like a mobster or somethin'?"

"If I was a mobster, do you think I'd be here asking you about guns?"

"No. I guess not."

"I'll be waiting for your call."

"Just to warn you, these guys I'll talk to about the guns, they're not the kind of people you mess with. You better not be yanking their chain or try to cheat them with money or anything. You better have it. Or else. You don't wanna mess with them."

"Same could be said for me." Recker smiled.

"I dunno man, you're like all calm and shit, but there's something crazy about you."

"Glad you noticed."

Recker ended the conversation and went back to his truck. He looked at the address that Jones gave to him and plugged it into the GPS in the truck. It was in Bensalem, a large suburb located just outside of the city. He took the I-95 highway to get there, arriving at the strip center business in about half an hour. There were five businesses located in the shopping center, a pharmacy, a pizza place, a self-serve laundromat, a real estate office, and an insurance office. Recker stood there by his truck, looking over the small complex. He looked at the address on the signs of the businesses until he saw the one he was looking for. He wasn't sure what to make of it. The type of business they were running was sitting overtop of a laundromat?

"This is a new one," he said to himself.

He made his way around to the back of the building and walked up the wooden steps to the second floor. Recker turned the knob, but it was locked. He knocked on the door and heard movement inside. The door opened just a sliver, with only one of Jones' eyes visible. As soon as he saw it was Recker, he opened it further and let him in.

"Glad to see you made it," Jones said. "Find the place alright?"

"Yeah, no problems. You really think having this place over a laundromat is appropriate?"

"Why not? It's a perfect cover. A legitimate business. People coming and going all the time. But it's not something that needs hands on management to run, letting us focus our attention on the more important matters that we have to attend to."

"What if a machine breaks down? You doing the repairs?" Recker said, his question dripping with sarcasm. He didn't think Jones liked to get his hands dirty... in any sense.

"Don't be silly, Mr. Recker. I've hired someone to look after the place every couple of days, clean, make repairs and such."

Recker was walking around the room, sizing up the office. He was a little surprised at how it looked. He anticipated some dingy lit room with an antique desk, maybe a lamp, and one or two computers. What he found was what seemed like a very high-tech establishment. Brightly lit, a huge L-shaped desk that had six computers on it, three of which were laptops. There were maps of the area on a wall, a big whiteboard on another one, as well as two microfiber couches.

"How do you like it?" Jones wondered.

"I'm impressed. I wasn't picturing something so involved. When you first told me about all this, I thought it might be some rinky-dink operation out of your mom's basement or something."

"Hardly."

"I'm gonna need something to house the guns and weapons we'll need."

"About that... do you really think it's going to be necessary to have all these weapons you're talking about?"

"If you wanna help people, then you're gonna have to be prepared for whatever we might come across. What if I'm protecting someone? Bullet-proof vest would be nice. Night stake out? Night vision goggles would sure do the trick. It'd be easy to come back here and grab what's needed for the assignment. If not, you might not always get the chance to go out and acquire those types of things," Recker said. "They don't just sell that stuff at the local supermarket you know."

Jones nodded. "Your point's been made. What size will you need?"

Recker walked over to the desk and found a pen and some paper. He jotted down a few ideas and drawings and handed it to his new partner. Jones looked at it for a few minutes.

"I'll see what I can do," Jones said.

"The sooner the better. I'll probably be able to start stocking it tomorrow."

"Have something lined up with whoever you were seeking earlier?"

"We'll see. Looks promising though," Recker said. "Can you run a check on a Tyrell Gibson?"

"Should be able to. Might take a few minutes," Jones said, sitting down at one of the laptops. "I'll run the name through the DMV so we can get a photo so you can verify."

"You can hack the DMV?"

"I can get into just about anything. Some things are easier than others, of course. Is this the guy you're getting your equipment from?"

"More like the third party connecting two interested people together."

They waited a few minutes before a match popped up, showing Gibson's driver license photo and information.

"That's him," Recker stated. "Let's get whatever else we can on him."

"Why? For what purpose?"

"He might be of some use to us. If he's got eyes and ears on everything happening on the street, he might be someone I can pump for information if the need arises."

"I'll tap into police records."

"Seems a little sketchy, Jones. Hacking into all these databases. Some might say you're no better than the people you're trying to put away."

"Hardly, Mr. Recker. You could scarcely compare a rapist, a child abuser, a murderer, an assault perpetrator, or someone of that ilk, to me, who's simply acquiring information."

"Sounds like the rationale of a criminal, spinning whatever lawbreaking thing you're doing to suit your own tastes and needs." Recker was taking his chance to shake Jones' chains.

Jones sat back and spun his chair around, a little perturbed at what he deemed to be ridiculous accusations. While he knew he was breaking multiple laws by hacking into private government databases, he felt since he was doing so with good intentions; it wasn't as egregious an offense as it looked, though he knew others would not have the same outlook as he did. He said as much to Recker.

"I am not doing anything that the NSA hasn't done, or won't do. They've done the same things that I'm doing, only on a much larger scale," Jones said.

"I'm just messing with you. With the things I've done, I'm hardly in a position to be critiquing other people's judgments," Recker said holding up both hands in submission.

Jones spun his chair back around and focused on his work again, pulling up what he could find on Gibson. He appeared to be a small-time criminal, no major offenses to his name. From what Jones could gather, Gibson didn't appear to be a part of any gang that he could trace. He seemed to operate on his own.

"Here's what you're looking for," Jones said.

Recker pulled his chair alongside the computer genius. "How's he looking?"

"He appears to have a modest record. Nothing major though. Mostly petty crimes. Shoplifting, robbery, theft, receiving stolen property, pick pocketing, fraud, and smuggling. Longest he spent in jail was twelve months. No hard time, just local facilities. No known gang affiliations."

"That's good."

"Why?"

"If he's affiliated with a gang, it's unlikely he'd be any help to us at all. If he's a loner, or just small time, it's more likely he'd be willing to talk," Recker concentrated on the details on screen.

"When do you expect to deal with him?"

"He's gonna call me later if he has a deal set up. Hopefully for tomorrow."

While Jones continued pouring over the information that was on the laptop, Recker looked over at one of the other computers, which had a picture of Ms. Hendricks on it. He reread some of her information, before going back to her picture. He stared at it for a few minutes; her face reminding him of someone he once knew. As he looked at it, his memory went back to London, six months ago, replaying the events in his mind.

"Centurion Six, are you in position?" The voice crackled in his ear.

"I'm just outside the office building now. Going in," Smith said into his sleeve.

"We got word his assistants left an hour ago so he should be alone."

"Roger that."

"Check back in when the job's finished."

Smith entered the building through a side entrance, which was left unlocked by a security guard, just as was planned. The guard unlocked it just five minutes prior to that, right before he took a coffee break. Smith glided through the hallway until he reached the stairs in the middle of the building. Roger Coleman was supposed to be the intended target, one of the more influential members of the London Assembly.

Just like every other mission, Smith had no clue why his victim's number was up. Didn't know what Coleman did, or why he was chosen to be eliminated. All Smith knew was the job at hand. He went up to the fifth floor where Coleman's office was located and went down the hall to the fourth door on the left. Smith couldn't see through the frosted glass door but did notice that a small light was on in the office. He took a quick look around, double checked his gun, a Sig Sauer 1911-.22 caliber pistol, took a deep breath, turned the handle, opened the door, then burst through the entrance. He quickly found the desk and was ready to fire, but found no one sitting there. Smith looked around the room, not seeing a sign of life anywhere. He walked around the other side of the desk and looked underneath. It wouldn't have been the first time he found his victim hiding under one. He didn't hear a single sound, unusual from someone who was either hiding, or trying to get away. Usually he'd hear heavy breathing, footsteps, or something breaking accidentally from trying to run. It was eerily quiet. The lamp on the desk was on but Smith took a closer look at the desk. It struck him as odd. It was very neat. Too neat for someone who was working late. There was a file folder on the top left corner of the desk but that was it. No disheveled papers all thrown about, no scattered pens or pencils, nothing that'd indicate someone was there.

"Alpha One, we have a negative on our target," Smith said. "He's not here."

Smith waited about thirty seconds before trying to repeat the message. Once again, it went without a reply. He looked around the room again, alarm bells going off in his head. He quietly walked over to the door, listening for any sounds in the hallway. Thinking he may have been set up, he had a feeling someone was out there waiting for him. But he had no other options, he had to take the chance and leave sometime. Smith slipped out the door and started walking down the hallway, paying careful attention to his surroundings. He believed a person could just as easily run into trouble by going too fast and not paying attention, as you could by maintaining a steady pace. He thought it was more beneficial to know what was around you as it was to go quickly.

Just as he passed one of the other offices, he heard the elevator chiming. He snapped his body around as the elevator doors opened, ready for someone to step off. Nobody did. He took a few more steps toward it when the door by the stairs swung open, a man immediately opening up and firing. Smith instantly went down from the blow of the first bullet, lodging into his stomach. He rolled on the floor and returned fire, hitting his attacker several times as they each emptied their pistols. Holding his stomach, blood soaking his hand, he reached around and grabbed another magazine to reload his pistol.

Smith got to his feet, grimacing in pain as he slowly walked over to the other man lying on the ground. With the gun laying close to the man's hand, Smith kicked the gun down the hall. Smith nudged him with his foot a couple of times, and after satisfying himself he was dead, checked his pockets for some ID. He had none on him. He saw he had an earpiece, the wire going into the back of the shirt down to back of his pants. Smith turned him over and took the earpiece out and listened to see if he could pick up anything. After a minute, a voice spoke out.

"Centurion Twenty-One, have you finished your assignment?"

It was the same voice that gave him his own orders. Smith thought about whether he should answer, and all the different things he could answer with, or just ignore it. If he didn't reply, they'd know the agent failed. If Smith replied in the wrong manner, they'd also know they failed to eliminate him. He picked up the earpiece and waited for them to ask again.

"Centurion Twenty-One, is your assignment complete?"

"This is Twenty-One, mission successful. Target's been eliminated."

"Good job. Go back to your hotel and wait for instructions."

"Roger that."

Smith went down the stairs quickly, knowing he didn't have a lot of time, but also knowing that there may have been more than one agent sent there for him. Once he reached the bottom of the stairs he slowed down, hearing what sounded like someone pacing just outside the door. He knew it wasn't the guard since he shouldn't return for another hour. Holding the side of his stomach, still bleeding profusely, he closed his eyes and took a deep breath. Smith pushed the door open, his gun already raised and in firing position. He immediately saw another agent standing there and began firing, three shots landing in the agent's chest before he could get a shot away. Smith did a three sixty in the lobby just in case anyone else was there waiting, but without having to duck any other bullets, assumed it was just the two of them. He ducked back out the side entrance and made his getaway through some bushes and trees, not knowing what was on the other side of them.

Knowing he couldn't go back to his hotel room in fear that the agency had someone watching it just in case, Smith wasn't sure where else he could go. The agency had contacts everywhere, and anyone that he knew of, could burn him. He didn't know who he could trust, if anybody. After about ten minutes, he walked out of the clump of trees. Suddenly, his thoughts turned to his girlfriend, Carrie.

Worried that they might not have been satisfied with just taking him out and might try to eliminate anyone close to him, he got out his cell phone and tried calling her. She was the only person who really mattered to him, who he thought they might try to take out. He had no other close friends. His parents had both passed away several years ago, and being an only child, was never close with any other relatives.

Smith dialed Carrie's number, desperate to reach her and hear her voice, letting him know she was OK. With the time difference, Smith figured she should've gotten home from work about a half hour ago. Her phone kept ringing, eventually going to voicemail. Smith kept walking, trying the number again. This time, after four rings, the phone was answered. She didn't talk though or greet him with the usual warm hello that she usually did, heightening Smith's fears.

"Carrie?"

A man's voice answered back. "I'm afraid Carrie will not be able to come to the phone right now."

"What have you done to her?"

"I wouldn't worry about her so much as I would about yourself."

"I swear if you hurt her, I will hunt you down and kill you," Smith said, his heart racing.

"Big threat from a man who won't make it through the night."

"Let Carrie go. You have no beef with her. If it's me you want, come and get me."

"It's not really necessary at this point. I'm afraid you'll never see her again."

"Don't do this to her. She's a good person."

"She seems that way. Too bad she fell for a man like you. That was her undoing."

Fearing for her life, Smith was ready to bargain. "I'll give myself up for her."

"How chivalrous of you."

"I mean it. My life for hers. Let her go and I'll turn myself in to whoever and wherever you want. Just tell me where."

"If only you had called ten minutes ago. I would've made the exchange in a heartbeat. I'm afraid now... it's not possible," the man said cryptically.

"Why not?" Smith asked, stopping in his tracks, afraid of what he was about to hear.

"Because five minutes ago... I killed poor, sweet Carrie. Don't worry though. I gave her the professional courtesy of making it quick and painless. She never saw it coming."

Smith hunched over like he was about to throw up, though he didn't. He straightened up again, though still wincing from the pain of the gunshot wound.

"You didn't have to do that! She was innocent!" Smith yelled.

"Nobody's innocent."

"She didn't have to die! If you wanted me, come get me!"

"Oh, we will. We will."

"Who are you? I'd like to know so I can make your death extra special when I look into your eyes."

The man laughed, amused by the threats of a man he assumed would soon be dead. "Seventeen," he said then the line went dead.

A whirlwind of thoughts swirled around in Smith's head. Carrie was dead. Because of him. If she'd never have met him, she'd still be alive. Smith eventually got to a sidewalk and continued walking along the street, not really having a destination in mind. He closed his coat tightly to prevent his wound from showing to passers-by. For more than two hours he wandered around the streets of London, putting his head down, and not going anywhere in particular. He knew Centurion had people on the ground looking for him by now so he couldn't go to anyone he already knew. Even if there were people he could trust, which there wasn't, he wouldn't put anyone else's lives at risk. Not for him.

He knew he left a fair amount of blood at the shootout at the office so he figured they'd check hospitals and any underground doctors in the area first. When the third hour after the shootout had passed, Smith finally picked his head up and looked around, amazingly finding himself standing in front of a hospital. He debated whether he wanted to go in. He wasn't sure if he should go in. He wasn't sure if he even wanted to go in. With Carrie gone, he thought maybe he'd just give up and join her wherever she now was. He thought maybe it was better if he just kept moving, or creeped off down some dark alley, knowing eventually he'd collapse.

Then he thought about Carrie and knew she'd want him to carry on. His legs began moving, and he walked through the hospital doors, taking a seat. He wasn't sure if he was doing it for Carrie, or for himself. Thoughts of rage and revenge flowed through him. If he gave up, he wouldn't be able to extract the punishment that Centurion and especially seventeen had coming to them. He found the waiting area for the emergency room and saw an empty chair towards the back and sat down.

～

"Mr. Recker? Mr. Recker?" Jones said, touching his shoulder.

Recker broke free of his stare, the combination of hearing his name and feeling Jones' hand, woke him from his trance. He snapped his head towards Jones, still in a little bit of a haze.

"Are you OK?" Jones' face showed his concern.

"Yeah. Yeah. I'm fine," Recker replied, getting the images out of his head.

"I'm sorry. I hope I didn't interrupt anything important for you. You seemed to be in some sort of trance."

Recker shook his head, "No, it's fine. Just thinking about something."

"Anything you'd like to talk about?"

"Uh... no. No, I'm good."

Jones had a feeling he was replaying the events of something terrible in his mind. London, or one of the other couple of dozen assassinations he'd been involved with. Or something unrelated to any of them. Jones couldn't be sure what it was, but whatever it was, it had to be something traumatic for him as he seemed troubled by whatever he was thinking about.

Recker and Carrie had been dating for a little under two years. They met in Orlando, where Carrie lived, running into each other in a hotel lobby where Recker was staying. It was just a layover for him, in between jobs, whereas she was there for a conference for her job. While she was on a break between sessions, they sat next to each other on a bench and began talking. Well, she did most of the talking. He was hesitant to talk and get to know anybody, knowing he wasn't likely to see them again. Eventually, with her pleasant personality, she got him to open up a little. He told her he worked for the government and went overseas often. After that conference, they exchanged phone numbers and agreed to see each other again.

Every chance Recker got from that day forward, he traveled down to Orlando to be with her, usually for one or two weeks a month, though a couple of times he had as much as four weeks to spend with her while he waited for an assignment. He tried to shield her from what he did as much as he could. It wasn't until three months before London happened that he sat down with her and explained exactly what he did and who he was. Up until then, he felt like he was leading her on and thought she was going down a path with someone that wasn't real. He fully expected her to be done with him after he told her the truth about him and was hoping she would be, wanting Carrie to find a nicer and more stable guy than he was that could really make her happy. She deserved at least that much. Her response wasn't what he envisioned.

She'd always known he was hiding something about his work but she never wanted to pry. From her vantage point, he was a handsome, kind, considerate, caring guy who she wanted to spend the rest of her life with. Whatever he did for a living, it wasn't the person that she knew. It wasn't the person that he was when they were together. She understood that he did things for the government that weren't pretty, that most people wouldn't understand, or couldn't stomach.

From that moment on, Recker questioned his role in the agency. He expected, and had fully accepted, the fact that he was likely to spend the rest of his life alone and would die in a hail of gunfire. But her love changed his perspective. He now had something, and someone, to live for.

Recker and Carrie had discussed him leaving the agency, and

though she never forced him to do so, he wanted to quit. Though Carrie was happy that he was making that decision, she didn't want him to do it on her account. She wanted him to do it because he was ready to, and not because he felt like she was forcing him to. But now that he had her, Recker wanted to give it all up and just settle down to spend all his time with her.

He'd approached a couple of his superiors a month before the London assignment and expressed his feelings to them, telling them that he wanted out. Though Recker expected to hear some objections to his leaving, and wondered about how they would take it, they never expressed any negativity to him. Not one bad word, leaving him to think they were OK with it. They led him to believe that he would be able to leave the agency behind and have a normal life.

Obviously, he was wrong, and as far as he was concerned, was likely never to forgive himself for leading Carrie down the path that eventually got her killed.

4

Recker had just walked into the office, two empty duffel bags draped over his shoulders crisscrossed. Jones was sitting at the desk working and turned around. His eyes widened, wondering how much equipment Recker was bringing back.

"Just how many guns are you planning on purchasing, Mr. Recker?"

"Huh? Oh. These aren't both for the guns. One's to put the money in. You have it ready?"

"Twenty thousand dollars. Just as you requested. It's over there in the corner in the briefcase."

Recker walked over to it, shuffling the money from the briefcase into one of the duffel bags. Gibson called Recker first thing in the morning to let him know he had a dealer ready to deliver if he was still interested in purchasing the weapons. Jones had a medium size safe in the office, holding about fifty thousand dollars. His goal was to have a large amount of cash on hand to avoid frequent trips to the bank. Since banks had cameras, they thought it was best not to be seen there much, if at all.

Gibson said the deal would happen along sixty ninth street. There were some vacant stores in a strip center where a McDonald's was located. The deal would happen on Barrington, the street behind the center, inside a vacant, boarded up row home. They'd have a red flag or bandana on one of the boarded-up windows to let Recker know which house it was.

"Do you need me to accompany you or help you in any way?" Jones offered but hoped the answer was no.

"Thanks. But I don't think you'll be much help in this instance."

Jones breathed a quiet sigh of relief. "You don't think it's a trap do you? Nothing could go wrong, right?"

"Something could always go wrong. Could be they just decide to try and kill me and take the cash and forget about the deal." Recker shrugged. "Wouldn't be the first time that happened."

"Maybe it's best if you try to acquire the weapons in some other manner then?"

"No, I don't think that'll be necessary."

"Why not?"

"Because once they see that I could become a long-term customer, the possibility of future, larger payments should outweigh this one smaller transaction," Recker said with a grin.

"You call twenty thousand dollars a small transaction?"

"It is in this instance."

Recker stewed around the office for another hour, just passing the time until he had to leave. Once the meeting time started creeping up, he grabbed his gun, tucked it inside his pants and put his coat on. He put his earpiece in so he could communicate with Jones if he should have to.

"Please be careful," Jones said.

Recker stopped as he reached the door and turned around. "You almost sound concerned." He smiled.

"I am. I'd hate to have to go through this process all over again if something happened to you."

Recker smiled at his sense of humor, dry as it was. Like his own. It took him about forty-five minutes to get to sixty ninth street. This area was technically in Upper Darby but it was only a few minutes outside Philadelphia. He found the McDonald's and turned onto Barrington. It wasn't a large street and only had a dozen or so houses on it. It only took him a minute to find the one with the red bandana pinned to a boarded-up window, even though it wasn't necessary, as there was only one house on the street with any boarded windows at all. The other houses appeared to be well maintained. Recker parked on the street along the curb, seeing several other cars in the driveway. He grabbed the empty duffel bag, as well as the one with the money, and slung them over his shoulder as he got out of his truck.

As Recker approached the house, the front door swung open, with a young, rugged looking man appearing in the frame of the door. Recker stopped for a second then continued toward the door, walking past the unfriendly looking man. Recker immediately saw a large table in the middle of the room with a few folding chairs surrounding it. There were six other men around the edges of the table on the far side, a few of them Recker could see with guns tucked in the front of their pants. One of those men was Gibson. Recker couldn't see if he was armed. Gibson walked around the table and stopped halfway between Recker and the man who'd be selling him the guns.

"This is Recker, the man I was telling you about," Gibson said.

"Before we get started, if I hear a siren outside or anything, I'll be gone long before they get inside. I got men upstairs lookin' out," the leader said.

"I don't want the police here anymore than you do," Recker said.

"Whatcha want the guns for?"

"That's my business," Recker stood his ground, alert to what was happening around him.

"If you intend to use them in my city, then it's my business too."

"Oh? Did you get elected mayor recently?" Recker just couldn't help himself sometimes.

"Don't be cute. You know who I am?"

Recker shrugged. "Haven't a clue. Does it matter?"

The leader looked at Gibson, not sure he believed him. The man at the door came into the room, standing a few feet behind Recker, just in case anything went down.

"Vincent send you here?" the leader said.

"No idea who that is."

"The Italians?"

Recker shrugged again. "Still no clue. Look, if you don't wanna sell me the guns, that's fine. I'll just be on my way, and I'll do my business elsewhere. Maybe I'll look up this Vincent you're talking about."

Recker turned as if he was about to walk away when the leader stopped him. "Alright man, just calm down. I gotta take precautions as to who I do business with. If you don't know who those other chumps are, then you must not be from around here."

"I'm not."

"Where you from?"

"Around."

"What are you planning on doing with the guns?"

"My business," Recker said, repeating his answer with a shake of his head.

The leader pulled one of the metal folding chairs out and sat down, sizing up the stranger in front of him. "You're not like the usual people who come in here."

"Is that a compliment?"

The man shrugged. "Somethin' different about you. Somethin' dangerous. How do I know if I sell you these guns you ain't gonna use them to come after me or take out my crew?"

"Well... stay out of my way and you got nothing to worry about."

"You got the cash on you?"

Recker opened up the duffel bag and lowered it so he could see it was in there.

"I could just kill you and take the money and keep the guns for myself," the leader said, the threat clear.

"Maybe. Big gamble for you though."

"How's that?"

"Well, if I hear so much as a twitch from that guy behind me, or anything that sounds like he's pulling that gun out of his pants, the first thing I'm gonna do is blow a hole through your head. Then I'll turn around for him. I should be able to take out one or two more of you before you get your wish though." Recker smiled at the man opposite him.

The man smiled back, impressed with Recker's confidence. "You're very sure of yourself. I like that. You come in here, someone who's not from around here, and you have the balls to make threats about killing me and my men."

"I don't make idle threats. I back them up," Recker said, beginning to get aggravated.

"I believe you. You're very calm for someone in a difficult situation. Lot of money, guns, outnumbered, but you don't seem worried at all. Your life could be in danger and you don't even look like you're breaking a sweat."

"The only people who fear for their life when it's in danger... are the people who have something to lose."

The man nodded, understanding what he was saying. "You a cop?"

"Nope."

"Ex-cop?"

"No."

"Well you somethin'. Military?"

Recker sighed, still weary of the questions. "Used to be."

"So, what are you now?"

"Nothing. Look, we doing this deal or not? Because if you ask me one more question I'm gonna walk out that door."

The man nodded to one of his men, who left the room with another member of the gang. They returned a couple of minutes later, bringing with them several large bags containing weapons, dumping them on the table for Recker to see. There must have been close to a hundred guns laying on the table, pistols, revolvers, rifles, of all different makes and models.

"I charge a little less than double retail on most. The Glocks are a thousand each. Sig rifles two thousand each. Sig pistols fifteen hundred, except the 250's which are a thousand," the leader informed. "Even got an AK-47 at the end there, that's fifteen hundred."

"Sounds fair," Recker said, throwing him the bag of money.

"Just take whichever ones you want. Gibs'll count the cost. I won't get picky if you're a little over."

Recker looked the pile over, picking a few up to get a feel for each weapon as well as test the sights out on them. After a few minutes of deliberating on which ones he wanted, he finally decided.

"I'll take the full and subcompact 250's. Three Glocks," Recker said, putting them in the empty duffel bag. "The AK-47..." he looked over the rest of the guns laid out before him. "Three of the Sig pistols. And four of the rifles. What's that come to, Tyrell?"

"Uh... nineteen thou," Gibson answered.

"Got a thousand left to play with," the leader said as he rocked back in the chair.

Recker looked up and down the table before noticing a couple of silencers toward the end, nestled in between a pair of guns. "How much are the silencers?"

"Normally a thousand each. Because we're getting off on a good foot here, I'll let you take two if you want, one for the rifle and one for the pistol, and we'll call it even."

"Generous of you," Recker said, grabbing the two silencers and shoving them in the bag.

"With a haul like that, I'm assuming I'll be hearing about you in the coming weeks."

"Maybe," Recker said. He turned to leave then did an about face. "Oh, uh, one more thing... I like to know the names of who I'm doing business with. I never did get yours."

The leader hesitated, unsure if he should give it, though he finally relented. "Jeremiah."

"Good," Recker said, turning to leave again, and again turning back. "I guess it's two more things. I have a few other articles for my wish list. Can you get some grenades, maybe an RPG, night vision, tear gas, tasers... oh..." Recker laughed. "And a bullet-proof vest."

Jeremiah looked at him like he was a little crazy asking for all those items. "What're you, trying to start a war or something?"

Recker smiled. "One might think so."

"I'll look into it."

"Good. If you get something, let me know. Gibbs has my number," Recker said, walking out the door.

"I told you, Jeremiah, somethin' ain't right about him," Gibson said.

Jeremiah went over to the door and watched Recker get into his truck and drive away.

"We'll try to keep tabs on him if we can," Jeremiah told his crew. "If anything happens to any of our boys over the next few weeks, and it's done by someone matching his description, we'll know what's what."

Once Recker got back to the office, he put the duffel bag of guns down in the corner of the room. Jones broke free of his computer work and was a bit concerned about the bag full of weapons.

"I do hope you plan on putting them in a more secure location," Jones said.

"Yep. Soon as I get some type of safe or cabinet constructed."

"I assume all went as expected?"

"Yep."

"Get all you need?"

"Not quite. Still a few more items I'd like to have around," Recker said.

"How much did you get?"

"Let's see... there was eight pistols, four rifles... and an AK-47."

"Oh, dear."

"And a couple of silencers."

"And you still need more?"

"You wanna do this right, you need to be prepared. We're good with guns for the moment. Just accessories that we need."

"Oh."

Recker sat down at one of the desktops and started looking at gun cabinets. After a few minutes, he decided on which one he wanted. It was a large steel one that could hold up to fifty guns, plus shelving for some of the accessories, such as ammo, cameras, tasers, and such. Plus, there were pouches on the inside of the door that could hold the pistols, as well as the silencers, scopes, and other small items.

"Find one to your liking?" Jones' eyes never left his screen.

"This one should do."

"When do you plan on acquiring it?"

"No time like the present," Recker said.

"At the risk of seeming to be impatient, when were you planning on working on Ms. Hendrick's case?"

"Oh. That. Yeah, I guess I should get started on that."

"It might be helpful. Especially considering I intercepted his latest text message about two hours ago, telling her that if he couldn't have her, then nobody else would either," Jones said.

"Have you any idea where Eldridge is at right now?"

"Should be at work. He's done in about an hour."

"I'll let you know how it goes. Get me that safe."

Recker immediately left to meet Eldridge before he left work. He worked in construction, for a large company, and was on a job in the northeast part of the city in Mayfair. As Recker was driving, Jones texted him Eldridge's exact location. It only took Recker about half an hour to get to the construction site. He parked on the street and stared at the site, watching different workers come and go. Jones sent him a picture of Eldridge to make sure he recognized him. He patiently waited for an hour and a half for the crew to finish work. They worked a little later than usual since they were behind schedule on the building. Though there were still some guys working, it looked like Eldridge had finished for the day since he had his coat on and keys in hand. As he walked toward his pickup, he hit the button to unlock it, flicking the lights on and off. Recker looked at the picture on his phone to confirm it was him. He quickly exited his car and walked in his target's direction, making sure he didn't get away from him. Recker timed it just right. As soon as Eldridge got in, Recker opened the door to the passenger side, hopping in beside him.

Surprised, Eldridge wondered what the guy was up to. "What the hell you doing?"

"We're gonna have a little chat," Recker said, calmly leaning over and taking the keys out of the ignition.

"Who are you?"

"Just call me a concerned third party."

"Get the hell out of my car!"

"Now that's no way to get acquainted."

"Dude, get out of my car! If you don't..."

"Then what?" Recker asked. "You'll beat me up? Like you beat up Mia?"

Eldridge was taken aback. "What? You know Mia? How do you know Mia? She send you here?"

"She doesn't know I'm here."

"What're you? Her new boyfriend or something? Is that why she won't see me or return my calls or messages?"

"She won't return your messages because she's afraid of you and that you might beat her up again."

"I've never laid a hand on her," Eldridge said it again.

"Oh, stop. Let's not play games here."

"What do you want?"

"I want you to leave Mia alone. She's done with you. You need to accept that and move on." Recker held Eldridge's gaze.

"Yeah, well, I love her. And she loves me. We're just having a rough patch right now. We'll get through this."

Recker rolled his eyes, knowing this talk was going nowhere. "Listen, idiot. She doesn't love you. She doesn't want anything to do with you. And if you don't move on, and I find out that you're still threatening her, you're gonna find yourself in a lot of trouble."

"Oh yeah? With who?"

Recker stared at him with his menacing eyes. "With me," he said, clenching his jaw. "Keep it up and you're gonna wind up with another visit from me. And I guarantee our next one won't be so chummy."

"Are you done?"

"No. I'm giving you two options. Leave her alone... or wind up in the hospital." Recker then smiled. "I kind of hope you pick the second." Recker tossed back the keys.

He got out of the car and walked back to his own, Eldridge peeling out of the street, leaving tire marks and smoke in his wake. Recker started driving back to the office but got Jones on his com device.

"Jones, just got done having a chat with our friend, Eldridge."

"And how did it go?" Jones asked.

"Tough to say but I don't think he got the message. I'm pretty sure we're gonna have to deal with him again."

"I had a feeling that would be the case. I don't get why she doesn't just contact the police and have him arrested. Surely the text messages and phone calls are a violation of the restraining order."

"That's why it's a worthless piece of paper. It does nothing to protect the victim. Doesn't stop the perpetrator from showing up and a lot of times the victim's afraid to go further. It's only a six-month to a year stay in jail for a restraining order violation. Some women, certainly not all, but some feel that if they send the guy away, he'll come back madder than ever and hurt them even worse than before."

"Well we can't let that happen," Jones said.

"We won't."

"Where are you heading now?"

"Back to the office, I guess."

"Maybe it'd be wiser for you to head to the hospital where Mia works to keep an eye on her."

"Think Eldridge is going there?" Recker checked his rearview mirror. After so many years it was like a tic now.

"Possible. I don't know for sure but I don't think we can adequately protect her from a distance. I think you need to have eyes on her at all times from now on."

"I'm on my way."

Recker drove to St. Mary's Hospital and parked in the lot. Jones had told him that her shift ended at seven, so he had some time to wait. He kept his eyes open just in case Eldridge showed up though he saw no indication yet that he was there. After a half hour of patiently waiting, Recker attentively sat up straight, noticing Eldridge's brown Chevy pickup roll into the parking lot.

"Jones, I just saw Eldridge's pickup come into the parking lot."

"Uh oh. Any sign of Ms. Hendricks yet?"

"Not that I see."

"She should still have at least thirty minutes left on her shift. He might be waiting as well."

"No doubt."

"Do you need assistance?" Jones asked.

"I got it."

Recker kept an eye on the brown pickup as it coasted through the parking lot looking for a spot. Once the truck settled into a spot, Eldridge sat there, apparently doing the same as Recker... waiting. He had parked in a spot that Recker could keep an eye on, so he didn't have to change positions or get out of his car. After about twenty minutes, Eldridge got out of his car and walked toward the entrance of the hospital, waiting in front of a brick wall, out of sight from the entrance doors. Half an hour later, twenty minutes past when her shift was supposed to be over, Hendricks walked out. As soon as she got near the edge of the brick wall, Eldridge stuck his hand out and grabbed her arm, pulling her over to him.

"Let go of me!" she yelled.

Eldridge did let go of her and put his hands up, letting her know he wasn't going to hurt her. "I'm sorry. I'm sorry. I just wanna talk."

"All the talking's over."

"You won't return any of my calls or texts." He shrugged. "I don't know what else to do."

"There's nothing else you can do. We're done."

"C'mon, Mia. You don't mean that."

"I absolutely mean that," Hendricks said, looking around nervously, trying to keep her voice down so nobody else would hear them.

"I just wanna make things right with us. Why won't you give me another chance?"

"I gave you another chance, remember? You blew that one too. And the third one."

Eldridge sighed, looking away from her. "I'm different now."

"Oh really?" she said, "I don't believe you."

"I haven't had a drink in a couple of weeks."

"Good." She nodded. "Maybe another girl will find that appealing."

"I don't want another girl. I want you."

"That's not happening anymore. Ever."

Eldridge was starting to get frustrated at his lack of progress. "Is it that other guy? Is that why you won't give me another chance?"

Hendricks shook her head and shrugged. "What other guy? There is no other guy."

"The one in the trench coat. He paid me a visit today and told me to stay away from you," he told her, sounding a little angrier.

"I don't know what you're talking about. There's no other guy."

"So, you're just gonna lie to my face like that?"

Frustrated herself, Hendricks was also starting to lose her cool. "I don't know what to tell you, Stephen. There is no other guy. I don't know who you talked to today. I don't even know what you're talking about. The reason we're not together anymore is you. And that's never gonna change so please leave me alone. No more texts, no more calls, no more anything."

Eldridge grabbed her arm again, squeezing it tightly. That was a big enough sign for Recker that he needed to move in. He got out of his car and started running for them.

"Stop it! You're hurting me!" Hendricks yelled before breaking free of her ex's grasp.

"I'm sorry... I'm sorry," he told her, wanting to move closer and hug her, but then stepping back.

As soon as Recker stepped on the sidewalk, Eldridge noticed him coming closer.

"There a problem here?" Recker shouted.

With him still remembering Recker's threat from earlier, he completely forgot about Hendricks and kept his eyes fixed on the stranger walking toward him. Thankful that someone was coming, and with Eldridge's concentration elsewhere, Hendricks turned and jogged over to her car. She immediately drove out of the parking lot, not looking back at what was happening behind her.

"You again," Eldridge said.

"I think I warned you already about what would happen if you didn't leave her alone."

"I'm not afraid of you."

"Probably should be," Recker grinned.

Eldridge took a swing at him. Recker ducked the blow, countering with a shot to the left cheek. Eldridge tried another punch. Recker blocked it, countering with a short left to the bridge of

Eldridge's nose, blood appearing from a small cut. Eldridge, though stunned and wobbly, tried one more time, this time successfully getting through Recker's defenses, punching him in the side of the stomach. Right near the scar from where he got shot, Recker grimaced in pain, still not a hundred percent healed from the injury. Not wanting to continue the fight any longer, Recker put all of his might into his next shot, punching Eldridge in the face as hard as he could. Eldridge was knocked to the ground, another cut opening up just above his eye. He put his arms down as if he was trying to push himself up but he just couldn't do it. He didn't have the strength. A couple of onlookers rushed over, but still stayed a healthy distance away, not quite sure what to make of the tough-looking stranger standing over the fallen man.

"Think he must've slipped or something," Recker said, moving between the crowd.

Recker went back to his truck and drove away, letting Jones know what happened as he drove. He immediately went to Hendricks' apartment to stake it out in case Eldridge was stupid enough to eventually make his way over there.

5

Recker had been tailing Hendricks for the last three days. He followed her to work, back to her apartment, to the grocery store, even to the gas station. Not a single sign of Eldridge. According to Jones, Hendricks hadn't received any communication from her ex-boyfriend in the three days since Recker had worked him over. Though Jones was hopeful that his encounter with Recker had finally helped Eldridge wise up, Recker was skeptical that it made much of a difference. In his experience, very few people changed who they were or how they behaved. He expected that he'd run into him soon enough.

It was just after nine o'clock, and Recker followed Hendricks to a large two-story bar that also doubled as a nightclub on the second floor on the weekends. A couple of her friends from the hospital had invited her, and even though that really wasn't her type of scene, she reluctantly agreed to go, hoping it might clear her mind somewhat. Recker followed her into the bar, making sure he kept some distance from her. He stayed near the end of the room as Hendricks and her friends sat at a table in the corner, sipping on a drink slowly as he kept his eyes on them. The trio of women kept to themselves for the next couple of hours, talking and laughing the night away, though they did rebuff the advances of a few guys who tried hitting on them. Ten minutes after eleven, Recker noticed a very attractive woman, dressed in a short skirt, walk out the front door. Coincidentally, three athletic looking guys who appeared to be in their mid-twenties followed her out the door. Recker thought that he had just assumed the worst of people, but he found it a little too convenient for his tastes. Seeing as how he still hadn't seen Eldridge anywhere, he decided to follow the others out the door.

Recker hadn't stepped outside for more than a few seconds when he heard a woman screaming from the side alley of the bar. There was a small parking area there, only enough for about ten cars lined up against the side of the building. Recker rushed around the corner and saw two of the guys trying to force themselves on the woman while the other stood there as a lookout. Recker ran over to them, the lookout yelling something at him, then started swinging. Recker blocked the punch, then gave him a shot in the kidneys, making the preppy looking guy hunch over. Recker forcefully kneed him in the face, then punched him as he laid on the ground holding his broken nose. He then raced over to the two guys and pulled them both off the girl, ducking one of their blows. Recker took the back of the head of the first guy and drove his head through the passenger side window of the car next to them, half of his body sticking out of the car. The other guy stood there in shock before getting the courage to throw a weak-looking punch that Recker easily sidestepped. Recker gave him a left cross, flooring the man without too much effort. Recker looked back at the woman, still standing by back of the car, stunned by everything that just transpired.

"You OK?" Recker asked, walking over to her.

"Uh, yeah, yeah, I'm OK," she replied. "Thank you so much," she said, giving him a hug. "Are you a cop or something?"

"No. Go inside and tell the bartender what just happened and to call the police."

The woman did as she was instructed and went inside. The first guy that Recker decked started to move around like he was going to get up but Recker gave him a good, solid kick that put him down permanently. Knowing he couldn't stay there too much longer to be questioned with the police on the way, he went back to his truck and just sat there, waiting for Hendricks and her friends to leave the bar. Quite a few people started coming outside to look at the carnage after the woman told her story to the people that worked there and to make sure that the three men didn't go anywhere before the police arrived. Hendricks and her friends came out with the rest of the crowd but didn't stick around much longer. They each got in their separate cars and went their own way, with Recker following Hendricks. She went straight home and appeared to go to bed as Recker waited outside her apartment for another hour to make sure nothing happened.

The following morning, Recker walked into the office, breakfast in hand. Coffee for both of them along with bacon, egg, and cheese sandwiches on a croissant. Just the way he noticed that Jones liked it. With his trained eye, he noticed that Jones had one several days in the past week. Jones was sitting at the desk and working on a computer, not paying much attention to his partner. Recker walked over to him and set the coffee and sandwich on the desk, next to the keyboard.

Jones was a little surprised at the breakfast offering. "What's this?"

"What's it look like? Breakfast," Recker said.

"Yes, I can see that. I mean, at the risk of sounding ungrateful, I don't recall asking you to bring me anything."

"Well, being the sharp fellow that I am, I noticed that you had one of those three days this week. Figured you liked them. Coffee... milk, no sugar."

"While I do appreciate the kind gesture, you must've missed the pattern," Jones said in his usual measured tones.

"What pattern?"

"I try to stick to Monday, Wednesday, Friday for them and filter in other breakfast items on the other days."

"Oh. Sorry about that," Recker said, picking the sandwich back up.

"What're you doing?"

"Well, since today's Saturday, and not a croissant day... I figured I'd eat it for you."

Jones playfully slapped his hand and took the sandwich back. "Since you already took the trouble of getting me one, I suppose I could at least do you the favor of consuming it."

"Kind of a weird thing you got going on there, Jones."

"Yes, well, I suppose we all have our little quirks, don't we?"

Recker took a seat next to him as they ate breakfast together.

"See the morning papers?" Jones said, laying them out in front of Recker.

"No. Not yet."

"It seems that you've made them."

"Me?"

"It would appear that your escapade of helping that young woman at the bar was newsworthy. Story in the Inquirer read, 'Mysterious man in trench coat saves woman from getting raped'."

Recker just listened as he sipped on his coffee.

"Daily News says, 'Woman saved from rapists by trench coat man'. Publicity we could do without, Mr. Recker."

"Well, you hired me to save people. I saw a woman in trouble and I helped."

"Don't misunderstand me, I wasn't criticizing you. You obviously did what you had to do to save that girl. Without you, she almost certainly would've been raped. I just wish it didn't make headlines."

"Well, it's most likely just to be the first. If we're successful in this, we're probably gonna make a lot more. A couple of people out there in the city saving people from bad guys, who aren't law enforcement... is bound to make headlines. That's a big news story," Recker said, trying to see what Jones' point was.

"Perhaps. And perhaps it wouldn't have been if one of the perpetrators hadn't had his head thrown through a car window."

Recker opened his mouth to say something, then closed it as he thought about what Jones just said. "Did you just criticize me?"

"Not at all. Just openly wondering if there could've been another way the situation could've been handled other than... so violently."

"Jones, when you're in a fight against three men at one time, you don't worry about anything other than disabling them as soon as possible. Whatever way is necessary. I don't think talking them to death was much of an option."

"As I said, Mr. Recker, you're probably completely right in how you handled it."

They stayed sitting there, eating their breakfast and drinking their coffee, browsing through the newspapers. Recker figured he'd try to get to know Jones a little better. His employer seemed to know quite a bit about him, but Recker knew very little the other way around. All he knew was that Jones once worked for the NSA.

"So, why'd you pick this city?" Recker said.

Jones picked his head up from reading the paper and looked at him quizzically. "I don't follow your question."

"Well you're not from around here so I was just wondering what made you settle here."

"What makes you believe that I wasn't born here?"

"Because you're obviously too smart for that. Anyone intelligent enough to work for the NSA, smart enough to create new identities for himself and others, and crafty enough to hack into government files and databases, as well as banks of criminals and filter money into a secret account... isn't dumb enough to go back to the city he was born in, or for that matter, any city which he was ever associated with prior to this," Recker said.

Jones grinned, though not surprised that Recker would come to that conclusion. He would've been disappointed in his abilities if he didn't. "Very astute deductions, Mr. Recker. You are correct. I've been here approximately two months, and before that, never stepped foot in this city before."

"So... why here?"

Jones shrugged. "I don't know. I guess I figured it was a large enough city to blend in and... large enough that it had plenty of problems and issues where we could help and make a difference."

"So where are you from originally?"

Jones took a deep breath, unsure if he wanted to divulge any more information. Recker tried to set his mind at ease, knowing they had to trust each other if the partnership was to work and be effective.

"If you want me to go on with us, then I need to be sure I can trust you," Recker said.

"Why would you not trust me already? I've told you I worked for the NSA. I told you I diverted your flight from Florida, where Centurion agents were surely waiting for you to finish what they started in London. I believe I saved your life, whether you wanted me to or not. I've given you employment. What else can I do to gain your trust?"

"You can start by telling me who you really are. What you're about?"

"I've already done that."

"No. No, you haven't. You've told me what you want to accomplish and how you acquire the information that you do. But you haven't told me who you are."

Jones just looked at Recker for several moments. "I guess it's just... I just fail to see why that's important."

"How am I supposed to trust somebody that I don't really know? Something comes up on that screen of yours and I'm supposed to follow it without asking questions?"

"So when you worked for the CIA, you knew exactly everything and didn't work in the shadows with only snippets of information?" Jones said.

"This isn't the CIA. Or the NSA, for that matter. I knew I was working for the government and I'd be doing highly questionable things that I had no clue the reasoning behind. That didn't end so well for me and I'm not about to make that mistake again. If I work for someone, anyone, then I need to know all the facts. No more games, no more guesses, no more secrets."

"That is a two-way street, Mr. Recker. I could say the same thing for you."

Recker's head snapped back, unsure what he was talking about. "How's that?"

"Well, I know quite a bit about you already. But there is one thing that has been puzzling me though."

"What's that?"

"You were ambushed in London. Nearly killed. But you survived and spent six months in hiding."

"What's so strange about that?"

"That you used a known alias to book a flight to Orlando, surely knowing that alias would pop up on the CIA's radar."

"You already figured that out. I wasn't planning on leaving that airport."

"So, you were planning on going down in a blaze of glory?" Jones' eyebrows raised.

"Sure."

"No. No, I don't think so. I don't believe that a man who survives an attack and nearly dies, then hides out for six months, suddenly plans on going down in a hail of gunfire. If that were the case, you would've decided to do that days, if not minutes, after getting out of the hospital. Or you never would've gone to the hospital to begin with. Your reasoning for doing so eludes me, but you had a reason for choosing Orlando. I just haven't figured it out yet. Of course, if you'd like to share, then perhaps... perhaps we both can divulge some of our inner secrets."

Recker thought about it for a minute, staring ahead but not looking at anything. He really hadn't planned on spilling the beans on why he was really going to Orlando, but he figured that if he did, maybe Jones could actually be useful in helping him track down the man he was looking for. If Jones could find him, he should be able to find Agent Seventeen. Eventually, he knew he'd have to turn to someone for help. Since he didn't know if he could trust any of his former contacts, he'd have to find someone who was on the outside. Maybe Jones was that guy.

"OK," Recker said, finally making up his mind. "You're right. I wasn't planning on going there just to meet my maker. I was looking for someone."

"But you had to know Centurion would be there waiting."

"I was counting on it."

"It's still not making much sense yet. Who exactly were you looking for there?"

"One agent."

"Who?"

"I don't know his name. I only know his codename. Agent Seventeen."

"Is he a friend?"

"Hardly. I've never met him. But when I do... I will kill him," Recker said.

"Why would you want to kill someone you've never met? Do you think he's the one responsible for what happened in London?"

"No." Recker shook his head. "He's just a regular operative... like me. You know, I'm not even angry about what happened in London. It's a secret world full of people in the shadows. You kill, people try to kill you, and it goes around and round. When you live in that world, you learn to expect things like that."

"I'm still not connecting the dots," Jones said, his eyebrows now furrowed.

Recker's eyes became glossy as he thought about Carrie and what happened to her. "I made the... uh... unfortunate mistake of meeting a woman."

Jones could tell by Recker's manner of speaking that it was uncomfortable for him. He seemed to be deeply moved and there was an intensity in his eyes that seemed to consume him.

"And I fell in love with her," Recker said, the words starting to tumble out. "And she had the misfortune of falling in love with me."

"So, that's who you were going to Orlando to see?" Jones paused for a moment, getting the picture straight in his head. "None of that information was in any of your records."

"Usually isn't."

"So, what does this Agent Seventeen have to do with her?"

Recker clenched his jaws as he described what happened. "He killed her."

Jones closed his eyes, having a feeling that's where he was heading with the story. "I'm very sorry for your loss."

"So am I."

"What happened? When did it happen?"

"The night I was attacked in London. They came for her too."

"Why? What harm could she be?"

"No loose ends. If they got rid of me, they couldn't risk her living to tell anything that I might have told her in confidence. After I killed the two agents sent to kill me, as I walked to the hospital, I called her just to make sure she was all right. A man answered the phone. He told me he killed her."

"How do you know it was this Agent Seventeen?"

"He told me his codename. It was like he was taunting me, not expecting me to live the night. He probably assumed the attack on me wouldn't fail and I'd never live long enough to remember his name," Recker was gripping the edge of his desk.

"Are you sure she's dead? Maybe he was only telling you that to provoke you for some reason. It wouldn't be the first time that..."

"She's dead," Recker said, releasing his grip and holding one hand up. "While I was recovering in London, I searched online for any news that I could find on her. And I found it. Her obituary. They covered it up by making it look like a house fire. Carrie Brodin, twenty-nine years old, the only victim in a fire that engulfed her home, burned it down to the ground." Recker could vividly remember every word of the article.

"Carrie, she was why you'd grown weary of the agency, wasn't it?"

Recker nodded. "I never expected to meet someone like her. After I left the agency, another year or so... I probably would've asked her to marry me."

"Was she aware of what you did?"

"Not at first. I kept it from her to protect her. And probably because I was sure she'd want nothing to do with me if she did know. But, after a while, once things got more serious, I told her. I expected that'd be the end of us. That she wouldn't want me anymore."

"But that wasn't the case?"

"No. I think it might've made her love me even more. The hardened killer whose heart she softened. I think she found me a challenge. She always liked a good challenge." Recker smiled.

"So, what was your intention in Orlando?"

"To kill whatever Centurion agents came looking for me and get the information I needed. Unless Seventeen was one of them."

"You mean, you were just going to keep killing agents until you found the one you were looking for?"

"That was the plan."

"While I sympathize with your loss, Mr. Recker, you can't just keep killing whoever's unlucky enough to be in your path until you find the one person that you're looking for," Jones said.

Recker shrugged. "Seemed like a good enough plan at the time."

"Well if that was your plan then why did you agree to my offer?"

"I'm not sure exactly. I guess it just struck a nerve."

"I don't know if I believe that. You don't strike me as the type who does things on impulse. You're usually already thinking several steps ahead."

"Well, it certainly wasn't what I was thinking when I agreed to this little enterprise of yours, but now? Now I'm thinking maybe you can help me."

It didn't take Jones long to realize what Recker was implying.

He knew what he wanted. "You mean you want me to help you locate this Agent Seventeen."

Recker made a face and shrugged, which was as much of an acknowledgment as Jones was getting. "It occurred to me."

"What makes you think I can find this... mysterious agent?"

"You found me. You can find him," Recker said.

"So, what you're asking, is to help you find this man so you can execute him?"

Recker nodded. "If that's how you want to interpret it. I look at it as finding the man who executed the woman I loved."

"I'm not sure I can do that." Jones rubbed his eyes. "To have someone's death directly tied to my hands, albeit one of questionable character, is not something I'm sure I want to be a part of."

Recker looked a little disappointed, but certainly wasn't going to beg for help. "That's your call. But know this... I'm going to look for him on my own, and when I find him, I'm gonna leave you and this place the moment that I do."

"And if you do, when that happens, even if it's a year from now, you'd risk leaving behind and throwing away everything we might have built up?" Jones said, becoming more animated.

"Listen, this is your project, not mine. If you were to help me, maybe I could be persuaded to stick around when I was done with him."

"Assuming you'd come back from whatever predicament you were running into."

"I'm gonna do what I have to do. The rest is your call."

Recker stood up and walked around the room for a few minutes, finally stopping by the one window in the room, overlooking the laundromat. He watched a few cars pull out of the lot and onto the main road. Jones watched his newfound companion as he gazed out the window, thinking about their predicament. After about five minutes, Jones finally broke the silence.

"If I were to agree to this plan of yours, I can't guarantee a specific time frame of finding this man. It could take weeks, it could take months."

"That's OK. My hatred will still burn no matter how long it takes," Recker said, turning back around to the desk area to face his partner. "How exactly did you find me?"

"I had stumbled across your situation during some of my... well, let's just say, some of the files I happened to come across."

"So how did you know where I was when Centurion didn't?"

"I didn't. I wrote down a list of several agents who were of interest to me. Yours happened to be one of them. I left the NSA about a month after your situation in London. I spent the next three months looking for you, not physically, but on the internet with any crumbs of information I could find on you. But I couldn't turn up a thing."

"Yeah, it was a pretty good spot I found," Recker said, walking around the desk.

"So I put you, and all of your aliases on my watch list. Two months later, John Smith popped up as buying a plane ticket to Orlando. I thought you'd made a grave error in deciding to use a known alias and used a rather clever hack to change the plane's destination. So, whoever was waiting for you, believes that you actually got off the plane in Virginia, then rented a car to St. Louis. From there you went on to Texas."

"I was wondering about that. About why they wouldn't see that I came to Philadelphia."

"Little did I know that it wasn't a mistake on your part. If I'd known it was intentional, well, maybe we wouldn't be having this conversation today."

"If you're feeling a little too uncomfortable with my situation, Jones, feel free to hire somebody else. I won't think bad of you for it. And I give you my word I'll never say a word about this to anyone else," Recker said.

Jones gave a half smile. "Thank you, Mr. Recker, but that won't be necessary. And though I believe you in that you would keep all this quiet, I don't feel the need to hire anyone other than you. You see, I do trust you. I do believe I hired the right person for this. So if I want you to help me... then I need to help you."

Recker sat back down on one of the chairs by the computers. He spilled his guts, let his heart down on his sleeve and revealed his innermost feelings to Jones, just as he'd wanted. Now, it was Jones' turn to reveal his.

"So, now that you know what my true endgame was and is out on the table, why don't you do the same?" Recker said.

Jones squinted at him and nodded, agreeing. "You are correct in that my motivations, though honorable, are not completely just about saving humankind. Much like yourself, I've had to deal with a personal loss, which is a big reason why I'm here today."

"What happened?"

Though Jones was still a bit hesitant to divulge information about himself, he knew he had to in order to further gain Recker's trust. "You're right. I'm not from Philadelphia, or even this state. I'm originally from Chicago. Well, a suburb just outside of Chicago. As for my real name, that's something you'll never know. As far as I'm concerned, the person I was before is dead. He will never return. Much like you're now known as Michael Recker, for me, from now on, my name will only ever be David Jones."

"So what got you into this?"

"Though I obviously knew and was aware of the NSA's ability to filter information from multiple sources from everyday people, I never really thought much about the consequences, or lack thereof the same. They do a very good job of identifying and tagging people who are a national security threat."

"But?"

"But the amount of information they receive that they just let slip through their fingers that could help regular, normal people is staggering. I believe we've already discussed the reasons why, and they're valid, but I just couldn't keep watching good, valuable intelligence be thrown away."

"What happened to change your mind?" Recker said, swiveling in his chair to face his partner.

"My brother. He died last year in a robbery," Jones said, remembering the event like it was yesterday. "He owned a bar. One night, he was closing up, just him and one of his employees. As they walked out the door, they were both shot and killed."

"I'm sorry to hear it."

"The men who did it were caught and apprehended rather quickly. But several months later, I read something about how the men sent texts to each other about the robbery before it happened, planning it. So I went back into some of the NSA archives, found their names and phone numbers, and there it was. The NSA had data that the bar my brother owned was going to be robbed by these men." Jones shrugged his shoulders. "And they did nothing. It didn't pertain to national security, so it didn't really matter in their eyes." Jones' eyes flicked back to his screen for a moment, then back to meet Recker's gaze.

"That's pretty rough."

Jones sighed as he continued. "So, it was then that I decided I needed to break free of the NSA and branch out on my own. I wanted to help others and try to prevent something like what happened to my brother. I spent the next several months working on a program that sends the information the NSA gets to my own personal servers. Then I figured out how the rest... how to finance this operation, how to operate, where to go."

"And who to hire."

"I have many skills, but I lack certain traits. Those are the traits that you have."

"How is it possible to grab the information from the NSA without them knowing it?" Recker said, his eyebrows screwed up emphasizing his question.

"It's a very complex formula of which I'll spare you the technical details. Suffice to say that the NSA receives such huge packets of data, and once it's logged into their servers, that even if the smallest amount was diverted to me, they'd be alerted."

"So how do you do it?"

"I developed a program that takes a very small amount of data, only from this area, copies and redirects the copy to my computers at the very same time as it's uploaded to the NSA's servers."

"So they're not aware of it being taken from them?"

"Correct, because as far as they're concerned, nothing is missing," Jones said, leaning back on his chair, hands behind his head. "They're still getting the data that they're supposed to be getting. I'm just pilfering a small amount of it and concealing the whereabouts." He smiled a self-satisfied smile at his achievement.

Recker hoped that Jones was as good as he seemed to be but he still had questions. "What if they did some type of system check and noticed the data being redirected?"

"In that event, they would find the information going to a server in Washington... the state, not D.C. Further investigation would find them following the trail from there to Texas, to North Dakota, to Maine, and so on and so on, even with a couple of stops in Canada and Europe thrown in for good measure."

"How are you able to do that?"

"As I said, I'll spare you the technical details. Unless you have years of programming knowledge, it's unlikely you'd understand anything I told you. Just understand that what I've done is not really supposed to be possible." Jones was shaking his head slightly.

"So how is it that you were able to find me?" Recker said.

"The NSA has tools that make it possible to also lift the layers of other United States government agencies' private and secure files. While I was still there, though on the verge of leaving, I thought it might be a good idea to look at potential candidates who I thought could help me on my endeavor."

"Who had my experience?"

"I was, in particular, looking at certain agencies who specialized in clandestine operations and were experts at multiple activities. In addition, I was looking for people who had at least five years of experience, and in my view... limited time left at their then current location."

Jones turned back to his screen and clattered at his keyboard seemingly finished with his story but it occurred to Recker that Jones might already have the name of Agent Seventeen when he was initially searching through the CIA's records. "Do you have those records or files from when you found me? Maybe the guy I'm looking for is in there."

"I'm afraid not," Jones said, shaking his head. "All I have left are the files and information from the final five agents I was considering."

Recker sighed, figuring it was just his luck that Jones didn't already have the information he was looking for. "Figures."

"I'm sorry. I didn't think I'd need it. I didn't think I'd ever have use for all of that information anymore. Besides, the man you're looking for might not even have been in my search, anyway."

"Possible."

"Might not have been on the job for the five-year requirement I was looking for," Jones said.

"Maybe." Recker rubbed his clean-shaven chin prompting a

burst of the smell of his aftershave to waft gently over him. "How soon can you start looking for him?"

"I can start within the next couple of days. It could take some time, though. First, I no longer have the NSA program that hacks into the CIA database. So that means I'll have to create my own. That will take time to make sure that it's invisible to them, or in the event they notice, leads them on a wild goose chase to Timbuktu."

"I understand. I know one thing though, no matter how long it takes..." Recker said, his voice trailing off.

"Yes?"

"He's on borrowed time."

6

The following morning, Jones was already in the office by eight, as seemed to be his trademark. Recker came in a few minutes after eight to get instructions for the day. As soon as he walked in, his phone started ringing. Considering he hadn't been in town very long, and he only had two phone numbers programmed into his phone, one of them being in the same room with him, he knew who it was before even looking at it. Unless it was a wrong number. It wasn't.

"What can I do for you, Tyrell?" Recker said into his phone.

"I wanted to meet up with you for a few minutes if you got the time."

"Why? Did you acquire those other items on my wish list yet?"

"Nah, not yet. That'll prolly take a little time. There's a couple of other things I wanted to talk about."

"Such as?"

"Rather do it in person. One thing I've learned over the years is not to discuss business over the phone. Never know who's listening," Gibson said. From what Jones had told him, Recker knew very well.

"All right. Time and place."

"Art museum. Make it an hour."

"I'll be there," Recker said, ending the conversation.

"Who was that?" Jones said.

"That was our friend, Tyrell."

"You have a curious opinion on what constitutes a friend."

"Can't all be peace lovers and churchgoers."

"I suppose not. What was it about?"

"Oh, he wants to meet up for some reason."

"Has he located the rest of your merchandise?"

"Says no," Recker said, looking at the wall trying to figure out what he might want.

"You don't suppose it's a trap of some sort, do you?"

"I doubt they'd set a trap at the art museum."

"The art museum?" Jones thought about that for a few seconds. "Yes, you're probably right."

Recker went over to the new steel gun cabinet that adorned the far wall by the corner. He took out two of the pistols, a Glock and a Sig, and put them in their respective holsters, one in the back of his pants and one on his left side.

"Do you really think you'll need both of them for some reason?" Jones said, peering up at him over his laptop.

"Never know. Always have to be prepared. Just in case." Recker smiled back at the slightly worried look on Jones' face.

"Well, I understand that, but why are you taking two?"

"Always carry a backup weapon," Recker said, he felt like he was an instructor on a rookie agent's first day. It wasn't far off the truth. "Just in case something happens to the first one. Misfire, lost, stolen, taken... whatever the case may be."

"You certainly are thorough."

"You know, I was thinking, how exactly did you go about finding Ms. Hendricks? Or anybody else for that matter?"

"I thought we already discussed all that?"

"No, you told me the process for how you get the information. You didn't exactly say how you get a name. I mean, she must not be the only name in that little system of yours."

Jones felt like he was an instructor on some green computer geek's first day as a spook. That wasn't far off the truth either. "Well the names don't just fall out of the sky, Mr. Recker. I actually have to do some work to identify the potential victim. This isn't like a TV show or something. I don't just get a name or a number and hand it over to you. I get snippets of information I already told you about then I go to work. I cross reference the code phrases that alarmed the system and match them up against phone numbers, emails and such, then try to get the names of the particular parties involved and assess the threat levels, figuring out who exactly is in need of our assistance. It can be quite involved and doesn't happen in a matter of minutes."

Recker raised his eyebrows. "Sounds reasonable to me. I was just wondering." It actually sounded deadly dull. Give him some jerk to deal with and he was happy. Fiddling around with data felt as if it would be like a slow day in hell to him.

"And no, Ms. Hendricks is not the only victim on our radar. She just so happens to be first on our radar. The others will be coming shortly."

Recker smiled and nodded. "I'll catch up with you later." He was glad to be out of there for now.

Recker walked out of the office and down the wooden steps. He stood there for a moment and pulled out his phone, contemplating dialing a number, the one person on the planet he knew he could trust. Although he believed everything Jones had told him to that point, after everything that had happened to him, trust wasn't something that came easy for Recker. His gut told him that everything Jones had said was honest and accurate, but if Recker was to keep on going with this arrangement, he needed to be a hundred percent sure that his new partner was completely trustworthy. Recker walked around the building to the parking lot and started to punch in the number he knew by memory.

"Hello? Who's this?" A man's voice.

"Alpha Two One Seven, Delta Six Four Three," Recker said on autopilot.

"Oh, it's you. Didn't recognize the phone number."

"Well, considering everything that's happened, I figure I'll need to change them every few months."

"How are you holding up?"

"Pretty good. All the injuries have basically healed."

"Where you at these days?"

"Cleveland." Recker lied without the slightest hesitation.

"How's the weather there?"

"Harsh."

"I know you didn't call to chat about the weather," the man said. "What's up?"

"I need a favor."

"Another one? Already? After what I did for you in London?"

"You owed me that one in London," Recker said.

The voice hesitated for a moment. "Yeah, I did. What do you need?"

"Information."

"What kind?"

"The kind you can't get from a simple internet search through the white pages."

"You don't say." The voice chuckled.

"I need anything you can dig up on any NSA agents, consultants, anyone that has left the agency over the past eight months or so."

"Looking for anything in particular?"

"Yeah. If you see one from the Chicago area, that's the one I'm interested in," Recker said as he started to walk toward his truck.

"What's the connection?"

"He might be able to help me in finding Agent Seventeen."

"I see six months hasn't changed your appetite for that."

"Never."

"I'll call you in a couple of days with anything I come up with," the man said then hung up.

Recker got in his truck and drove down to the art museum, one of Philadelphia's biggest tourist attractions. He parked on nearby Pennsylvania Avenue and walked over to the building. The museum was famous for its steps. Used in the movie Rocky when the character ran up them, many visitors tried doing the same. Recker, not being Rocky or a tourist and not seeing Gibson at the bottom of the steps, walked up to see if he was waiting by the entrance. He looked around for a few minutes but still didn't see him. He went back down about halfway then sat down on a ledge on the outer edge of the steps. About five minutes later, he noticed Gibson walking toward him.

"Few minutes late," Recker told him.

"Traffic."

"So what's up?" Recker asked, watching people walk past.

"Jeremiah asked me to meet up with you."

"What for? He got my other merchandise?"

"Nah, man, it's not like that," Gibson said, looking around constantly. "He's a little... worried about you."

"Why?"

Gibson dropped his voice as a couple of tourists ran past them, cameras swinging. "Cause you're new, and a wildcard. You come in like some sort of badass buying guns, looking like you're James Bond or something."

"I'm an unknown."

"Yeah. He wants to know what you're up to and whose side you're on."

"I told you already. What I'm up to is my business. Whose side I'm on would depend on who we're talking about," Recker said.

"Men like you don't just pop up out of the blue usually, unless you were brought in by somebody."

"And Jeremiah thinks I'm here to start some type of turf war or something?"

"I think he's more worried about you being here to finish a turf war."

"Well, you can tell Jeremiah that I'm not. I wasn't brought here by anybody and I'm not interested in whatever war he's got going on. I'm not a player in it."

"Then why are you here?" Gibson said. "You obviously got something going on."

The two tourists walked back past them on the way down, trying to laugh and pant at the same time.

"Let's just say I was brought in for security purposes for certain individuals... none of which should be of any concern to Jeremiah."

"I'll let him know."

"That should put his mind at ease a little bit."

"Maybe. He hates new wrinkles though."

"Tell your boss I'm not one of them," Recker said.

"Well, I'll tell him, but he ain't my boss."

"Then why are you here?"

"He asked me to talk to you. Figured you'd be more willing to talk to me than someone in his crew that you don't know."

"Makes sense. If you don't work for him, how come you always seem to be around him?"

"I didn't say I didn't work for him. I do some jobs for him here and there but I ain't part of the crew. I'm my own guy, do my own thing, sometimes I'll do something for him if I need some bread real quick."

"Well if you're not part of his crew, then maybe you can explain a few things for me."

"Depends," Gibson said.

"Tell me what all this stuff Jeremiah's worried about is."

Gibson scouted all round to make sure nobody was listening in.

"I'll break it down real quick for you. There's three factions fighting for control of this city."

"I take it all of these factions are of the illegal variety."

"Depends on what you mean by illegal, man. There's some cops in this city who are worse than the people they lock up."

Recker laughed. "What about these factions? I take it one of them is Jeremiah?"

"Yeah. Jeremiah runs the north and west side of Philly. Vincent controls the northeast. Then there's the Italians, they run everything downtown," Gibson said, resisting the temptation to swing his arms around pointing in the various directions.

"Who's in charge of the Italians?"

"Man named Marco Bellomi. Man, if you do get mixed up in any of this, stay clear of him."

"Why is that?"

"Violent guy. Quick temper. Not somebody you wanna cross."

"How do you figure in all of this?" Recker said, keeping his eyes fixed on Gibson.

"I don't."

"But you know all the players?"

"Like I said, I'm my own guy. I've done work for Jeremiah. I've even had business with Vincent. I only know of Bellomi by reputation."

"And these guy's trust you? Enemies, fighting against each other, but they both employ the same guy."

"Listen, they both know I ain't spying for nobody, ain't killing nobody, ain't setting nobody up to get killed, nothin' like that. I do small jobs for them but they know they can trust me and I ain't up in their business."

"So, why is that?"

"Why you wanting to know?"

"You asked me a bunch of questions. Figured it was my turn. I've seen your file, no major arrests."

"How'd you get my file?" Gibson said, turning to look directly at Recker with a surprised look on his face. "If you ain't a cop, how'd you get that?"

Recker smiled. "I have my little ways. Listen, if I feel I can trust you, I may have some work for you in the future."

"If you mean snitchin' on anybody, that won't fly. I ain't no snitch, man."

"Good. Don't need one. Cops use snitches. Since I'm not a cop, I got no use for one. I'm just talking if I ever need some information, you seem like you're... well connected," Recker said.

"You mean for your... security firm?" Gibson said. He still sounded like he needed some convincing.

Recker looked over at him and smiled. "Yeah."

"I dunno, man. We'll see. Depends on what you're looking for."

"Well, when the time comes, I'll let you know."

They sat for a few minutes, neither saying anything, just watching the people go by and more tourists running up the steps.

Finally, Recker opened up, intrigued by the underworld factions fighting for control of the city.

"Tell me more about this upcoming war, what's behind it?"

"What's any war about? They want what they ain't got, and more of what they do," Gibson said.

"What about the players? Who do you think has the upper hand?"

"That's a tough one, man. I don't even know. They all got their pros and cons if you know what I mean. Bellomi, he's a shoot first, ask questions later type of guy. He don't wait around for trouble to find him. He looks for it first. He even got an inkling of something bein' up, you're knee deep in it."

"What about the others?"

"Jeremiah and Vincent are pretty similar, actually. Smart guys. They sit back. Watch. Observe. Wait for the right opportunity, then strike."

"They're not impulsive."

"Nah. But they ain't weak neither. Don't think they're the kind of guys you wanna cross cause you don't. Not unless you're prepared to eat some lead. They don't go looking for trouble, but they won't back down from it neither."

"They'd rather fly under the radar," Recker said. He understood that strategy.

"Yeah. That Bellomi, though, he's a different type of cat all together. He don't care about nothing. Don't care if you know he did something."

"So how'd you escape getting caught up in it?"

"Whatcha mean?"

"You say you're a solo operator. How come you didn't get recruited into one of their organizations?"

"What, just cause I'm a black man from the streets, you think I gotta be caught up in a gang or something?"

"No, because you do business with all of them. How come none of them tried to put you on the payroll?" Recker said.

"Hey, I only do business with two of them. I don't mess with Bellomi."

"So what's your story?"

"Whad'ya mean?"

"Well, if you're working with all these guys, then they obviously respect you enough to keep you on board. I'm sure they've tried recruiting you at some point. Why not fall in?"

Gibson shifted on the hard ledge, shaking his head. "I like doing my own thing. Don't have to answer to nobody, don't have to follow nobody's orders, just my own."

"And they're OK with that?"

"Like I said, I've built up trust with them. They know I'm not out to screw nobody. Just looking out for me."

"Got a family?"

Gibson hesitated before answering, not sure if he wanted to reveal anything. "Yeah. Got my mom and a little brother."

"How they feel about what you do?"

"Mom worries. But that's what moms do, right?"

Recker smiled. "Yeah. I guess so. What about your brother? He caught up in all this too?"

"Nah. He's only fourteen right now. In ninth grade."

"Let me guess, you're the breadwinner, right?" Recker said.

"Yeah. It's all good though."

"Hopefully your brother doesn't follow your footsteps... no offense meant."

Gibson laughed. "You're crazy, man, you know that?"

"May have been told that once or twice before."

"Nah, my brother ain't following my footsteps. He's the reason I keep doing this."

"How's that?"

"My brother's smart. Smarter than me. He loves reading, loves to learn, likes those graphic novel type books, you know what I mean?"

"Yeah." Recker nodded. He'd seen them on the newsstands but never read one. All that superhero stuff? Not his cup of tea.

"I do what I do so I can get enough money to put him through college so he can make something out of himself, so he's not on the streets, hustling like the rest of us."

"Noble of you."

"Just looking out for my brother. He's too nice for this type of stuff. Don't got the personality for it."

"So how come you never went?"

"Went where?" Gibson said absentmindedly, watching a long-legged blonde with her boyfriend as they walked up the steps toward them.

"College."

"My mom barely had enough money to put food on the table, man. College was nothing but a dream for me. Didn't have good enough grades for scholarships or nothing like that."

"What about a regular job?" Recker eyed the blonde as she passed them by. She reminded him of... Gibson's voice brought him back.

"What? Working at McDonald's? Not for me, man, not for me."

"There's other stuff. Construction, truck driver, warehouse... there's other things."

"I dunno. Maybe. Not an option anymore. I'm already in what I'm in. And I'm gonna make sure my brother has enough money to go to whatever college he wants to go to."

"So that's why you don't get involved in anything heavy?"

"I ain't getting involved in no killin' or robbin' or any of that. My brother ain't going to college if the money ain't there. And it won't be if I'm dead or locked up, y'know what I mean?"

"You seem like a decent guy, Tyrell."

"I dunno about all that. I've done stuff. I'm just looking out for me and my family."

The two sat for a while, shooting the breeze, more at ease with each other as the minutes passed by. Both of them could tell that the other wasn't there under false pretenses or trying to put something over on the other. Just two regular guys having a talk.

"So you gonna tell me what you're really here for?" Gibson asked. "Who you really are?"

"I already did."

Gibson laughed. "Man, you ain't told me nothing. Just ran around the subject a bunch of times."

"Can't tell you any more than I already have. For my protection... and yours."

Gibson leaned back for a second, wondering what he meant by that. He thought he had it figured out though. "You on the run from somebody? Cops?"

Recker smiled, shaking his head. "Maybe someday I'll tell you. For now, all you need to know is that I'm not in law enforcement, I'm not working for criminals, and I'm here to protect people," Recker said. "I'm one of the good guys, that's all you need to know."

They talked for a few minutes more, then went their separate ways.

Recker wanted to check back in on Hendricks. When she was on the night shift, she usually stopped by a diner and had lunch there before going off to work. If he timed it right, he could get there just a few minutes before she did. As he was driving, his phone rang. This time, it was the only other number that was in his phone.

"What's up, Professor?" Recker said with a sarcastic edge.

"Professor? You do realize who this is, right?" Jones replied.

Recker chuckled, "Yes, don't you like your new nickname?"

"I didn't realize I had one."

"You kind of remind me of a professor."

"Are you insulting me?"

"Of course not. I mean it in only the most positive ways and with the utmost respect."

"Hmm. Not sure I believe that."

"You're kind of like a professor. You're smart, seem to have all the answers, you even dress like one."

"Be that as it may, I was just calling to find out about your meeting with Mr. Gibson," Jones said.

"Oh. Went OK."

"What was he after?"

"Seems as though there's a turf war on the verge of happening. Jeremiah's one of the players and wanted to make sure I wasn't going to turn up, gunning for one of the other sides," Recker said.

"Perhaps it would be wise to avoid all the players in this game for a while. I don't think it'd be in our best interests to get mixed up in it."

"Well, I agree about not taking an interest in it, but we may not be able to avoid them altogether."

"Why do you say that?" Jones sounded concerned.

"Well, that depends on where our cases take us, doesn't it?"

"Yes, I suppose you're right."

"Plus, no matter what happens, it's always beneficial to know the players in the game, even if you're not in it."

"Why is that?"

"What they do, at some point, even in a roundabout way, may have some consequence on what we're doing," Recker said. "In any case, I'll stay in contact with Gibson so we have ears on what's going on. Plus, he may be someone we can turn to for information on the street if the need arises."

"It sounds as though you made a new friend. Are you sure you can trust him?"

"Not yet. But I don't think he's a bad guy. He seems like someone who's not interested in hurting or killing people. Just looking out for his family. Wants to send his younger brother to college to get him away from this life."

"Hmm, seems to be an honorable and worthy choice on his part even if he had chosen an unorthodox route."

"Yeah. I'll tell you more about it when I get back to the office. Right now I'm on my way to the diner where Hendricks usually goes before work. I'll tail her for a little bit before she goes in."

Recker arrived at Joe's Diner a little after noon, and was sitting at a window booth near the rear of the establishment. He sat facing the door so he could see Hendricks when she came in. He didn't have much of a wait as she came walking in about ten minutes after he did. As soon as she walked in, Recker put his head down like he was reading the menu so she didn't notice him. It didn't work. She was being shown to her own table when she saw Recker sitting in the corner. Though she didn't get a great look at the guy that intervened at the hospital, she recognized his haircut and coat. She also remembered seeing someone similar at the bar where the woman was attacked.

"Actually, I see someone over there that I know, I'll just sit with him," Hendricks told the waitress.

Recker kept his head down for a few moments until someone sat down across from him. He smelt perfume. Without picking his head up, he raised his eyebrows to see his visitor. Seeing it was Hendricks, he closed his eyes for a second, mad at himself for getting made.

"Hi," Recker said, pretending not to know who she was.

"Hi," she said, flashing a smile. It was a nice smile Recker thought.

"Can I help you with anything?"

"Yes, you can. You can tell me why you're following me for starters."

Recker cleared his throat then coughed as he stalled while he thought of a reason. "I'm not sure what you're talking about, ma'am."

"Is this really how you wanna do this?"

"Do what?" Recker said, pretending not to understand.

"The stupid act doesn't suit you," Hendricks said.

"It doesn't, huh?"

Hendricks shook her head. "No, it doesn't."

Recker grabbed his drink off the table and took a sip of the soda. "So what can I do for you?"

"You can tell me who you are and why you're following me."

"Why would you think I'm following you? I was here before you, remember?"

"Let's see... oh yes, you showed up at the hospital and beat up my ex. I couldn't really see your face too well then, but I noticed the close shaved military haircut and nice trench coat of yours. Then there was some trouble at a bar a couple of days ago where a woman was almost raped. Some guy in a trench coat saved her," she said, tilting her head and looking at his coat. "Kind of like yours."

Recker smiled. "A lot of guys wear trench coats."

"You know, I thought I saw a guy leave the bar a few minutes before that girl was attacked. I didn't quite see his face, again, but his hairstyle reminded me of that guy at the hospital. Kind of like yours."

"I hear this look's all the rage these days." Recker laughed.

"It's a nice look," Hendricks said. "It's uh... quite a coincidence that I find you here, I mean, fitting the description of those other people and all."

"Isn't it?"

Hendricks took her phone out of her purse. "So are you gonna make me do it or are you gonna tell me the truth?"

"Do what?"

"Call the police. If I feel I'm being followed, especially since I have a restraining order out, I'm very jumpy, I should call the police, don't you think?"

Recker knew she was playing him, trying to bluff him into revealing his true intentions. He could just get up and leave and not say another word, but that seemed like it might be counterproductive at this point. He figured that she knew he was there, and at least had some indication of who he was, or what he was doing. If he just left, and she saw him again at another time, it might lead to the same conversation all over again, or maybe even worse. Also, the fact that she was there and approached him, as well as initiated a conversation with him, meant that she didn't feel threatened by him. That was a plus on his side. After thinking about it, he decided the best course of action was to let her know that he was there to protect her. Maybe that'd even make the job easier for him. If she was in on everything, it would help him if she advised him on everywhere she was going or planned to be.

"Well, what's it gonna be?" Hendricks asked, tapping her thumb on her phone.

"How about if we just leave it at, I'm here to look after you and make sure you're safe?" Recker said, knowing full well that wouldn't satisfy her.

She shook her head. "Who are you?"

"My name's Recker."

"Interesting name."

Recker grinned. "I've heard it before."

"What's your first name?"

"Michael."

"I'd reciprocate but I have the feeling you already know mine."

"Kind of ballsy, coming over here, talking to a stranger who you think is following you."

Hendricks made a face, scrunching her nose. "Not really. You stepped in and took on my ex, you stopped a girl from getting raped… it didn't really occur to me that I had much to fear from you. You seem like you're from the right side, I just want to know why. Though it seems you're not the talkative type."

"I usually let other people do the talking. I'm more the action type," Recker said.

"So I've noticed. So, Michael Recker, why are you following me? Did my father put you up to it?"

"What's that?"

"My father. I figured it must've been him. The last time I talked to him a couple of weeks ago and told him about Stephen, he indicated I should do something about it."

"You did. You got a restraining order."

Hendricks rolled her eyes. "That thing? Hardly worth anything."

"Why do you say that?" Recker wondered.

"I work in a hospital. You know how many women I've seen walk, or wheeled in, that had restraining orders?"

"Then why'd you get it?"

"I don't know. Everyone kept telling me what a good idea it was, friends, family, people I work with… I guess I figured it was better than doing nothing, even if I didn't really think it was worth it," she said.

Recker nodded, understanding her reservations. "You know, he's already violated that order, you could just call the police if he goes near you again."

"Why? So they can put him in jail for a couple of months. Then I have to worry about it all over again. It's like, why bother? It just keeps prolonging everything and it's never settled."

"I understand."

"So is it my father that hired you?"

"Uh, I'm not at liberty to reveal that kind of information. Why don't you ask your father about it?"

Hendricks groaned. "Yeah, like that would be any better. He would just deny it too."

"You two don't get along, I take it?" he asked.

"We get along fine as long as we don't see each other more than once a month," Hendricks said, smiling. "He's a big business executive. He's always been more concerned with his stock portfolio, or his vacation house, or the three BMW's he owns, than his own daughter. Money cures all problems according to him."

"I know the type. Don't confide in your mother much either, I take it?"

"She died when I was ten."

"Oh. I'm sorry."

"Yeah. She had cancer."

"And you and your father haven't been close since."

"Not really. I mean, I guess I understand, you know... what's a man who's not there most of the time know about raising a daughter on his own?"

"Sounds like he struggled."

"If he ever tried. All he did was hire babysitters and nannies to watch me all the time, most of whom he probably slept with," she said, reminiscing.

"Sounds rough."

Hendricks shrugged. "Wasn't so bad I guess. I guess I turned out all right."

"So it seems."

"So what are you gonna do, just follow me around all day?"

"Not while you're at work," Recker sipped his drink.

"How long do you plan on doing this for?" she said.

"Until I'm sure your ex is no longer a threat to you."

"I'm sure he'll go away in a few days."

"Considering the threats he's made, I kind of doubt that's the case," Recker said.

"How do you know he's made threats? I didn't tell my father that. I just said I was having trouble with him."

Recker smiled. "I have my sources."

"Did you hack into my phone or something? Can you do that?"

Recker put his finger in the air, trying to deflect the question. "Uh, did you order yet?"

"Oh, no, not yet."

The waitress came over and took her order as the two continued discussing her situation.

"It doesn't seem like you're afraid of him," Recker stated.

Hendricks shrugged. "I'm not, really. I mean, he makes idle threats and all, but I don't really take them seriously. It's just him talking a big game like he always does."

"You know, a lot of women who end up dead or in the hospital... they probably said the same thing."

A more concerned look overtook the pretty nurse's face. "So you really think he means it then?"

"I think he's dangerous and I think you shouldn't overlook what he's capable of."

"Gee, I'm so glad I talked to you and put my mind so at ease," she said, faking a smile.

"I'm sorry, I didn't mean to scare you. But I just want you to understand how serious this is and not to underestimate him."

"So what if he doesn't do anything for a while, or just keeps up doing this for months? Are you just gonna keep following me?"

MIKE RYAN

"I don't think it'll take that long. It's escalated for him. I'm pretty sure it's gonna come to a head soon enough."

"That doesn't sound appealing for me," Hendricks said.

Recker tried to give her a warm smile to reassure her. "Don't worry. That's what I'm here for. I'll protect you."

"Well, I'm sure you can't be near me twenty-four hours a day. What happens if he shows up when you're not around?"

Recker had a feeling about what she was intimating and thought it probably wasn't a bad idea. It certainly made his job easier if he didn't have to operate in the shadows. He took out a small notebook from his coat and tore out a piece of paper. He wrote his name and phone number down and slid it across the table to her.

"If you feel threatened, any time, day or night, you call me. Chances are I'll be nearby anyway," Recker said.

Hendricks looked at it and nodded, smiling at him. "Thank you." It wasn't the warm smile she gave earlier though. It was more along the lines of "I can't believe I have to go through all this."

Hendricks continued talking about her situation for a few more minutes. Even though Recker could hear what she was saying, he wasn't really listening intently. He was looking at her, thinking of how pretty she looked. She was pretty, not a bombshell, but she had that cute, girl next door vibe going on for her. She talked softly, had sexy eyes that could melt any man's heart who looked inside them, and had soft, jet black hair. She seemed to be pleasant and have a good personality, though not afraid to be bold if she had to be, evidenced by her approaching him to begin with.

Another time, another place, and Recker thought she was the kind of girl that would interest him. He could imagine getting lost in those eyes. He couldn't believe there was a man out there lurking around with the intention of hurting her. The more he talked to her, the more she spoke, the more he found himself liking her. After about an hour of conversing, Hendricks looked at her phone.

"Oh my gosh, I lost track of time," she said, making sure she had everything in her purse. "I'm gonna be late."

"Well this was fun," Recker said.

Hendricks grinned, picking up the playful sarcasm and looked at him funny. "Really? Was I that bad company?" She gave as good as she got.

"Not at all," he said, shaking his head. "This will probably be the highlight of my day."

Hendricks stood up at the edge of the table. "Do I need to give you my itinerary?"

Recker smiled. "No thanks. I already have it."

She returned the smile. "I'm sure you do. Should I give you my plans for the day or the rest of the week?"

"I already have your work schedule."

"Why does that not surprise me? Well, after work, I'm going straight home, not stopping anywhere."

"Good to know."

"So will I see you again sometime? Or only if I look at the end of a parking lot and see you lurking in a car somewhere?" she said.

"Never know."

"Well, I guess I should say thank you for looking after me."

"There's no need."

She gave him that sweet smile of hers before leaving. "Well, hopefully we'll see each other again."

Recker smiled and raised a hand to say goodbye.

7

Recker and Jones had just had dinner in the office, fast food, as they'd often had in the past week. After finishing, they each went to different computers, working on different projects.

"Do you think it was wise to engage Ms. Hendricks in conversation?" Jones asked, typing on his keyboard.

"Well I didn't have much choice, David. She'd seen me on three different occasions and approached me. Not much I could do."

"And here I thought someone with your expertise and experience could avoid detection by a simple pediatric nurse,"

Recker didn't really have a comeback, "Hey, you made a joke." He gave Jones a look of mock annoyance. "I'm a little rusty OK! It's been a while."

"So it would seem."

Recker laughed. "Ouch!" He sat quietly tapping away at the keyboard before he spoke again. "It might work out for the better. It's always easier to keep someone under surveillance who knows what the stakes are and willingly knows and allows it."

"I just worry about your cover."

"It's fine. She thinks her father sent me to look after her. That should hold up since it doesn't appear that they're very close and don't talk often."

"I hope you're correct."

"Don't worry about her. She's fine."

"I'll take your word for it."

"Besides, she may come in handy for us after her case is over," Recker said.

Jones stopped typing and swiveled his chair around to look at his partner. "What do you mean?"

"She's a nurse, right?"

"I'm failing to see your point."

"At some point, a nurse might be a good idea to have around in case of emergencies."

"I don't know about that." Jones sounded worried.

"I dunno. I figure at some point, if we wind up doing this for years, it's a decent possibility that I might get hurt eventually, or even shot."

"And you think it'd be wise to bring Ms. Hendricks into the fold for that purpose?"

"Not bring her into the fold. She doesn't have to be in on what we're doing. Just keeping her as a contact in case of emergency. After all, me going to a hospital in such a case is risky business."

"You've gotten out of there before."

"How many times you think I can do that?"

"How did you do that in London, anyway?"

"Found a contact with a less than reputable reputation. I'll tell you about it another time. Let's just say he trusted the CIA even less than I did, which made him the perfect contact."

"Well, as far as Ms. Hendricks, I'll follow your lead. If you think she's necessary."

"Not necessary. Just someone we can trust. One thing you learn as a CIA black op is that if you don't have a few people you can trust when your life's in danger... you won't last very long."

Jones turned back to his computer and continued typing away, alternating between the laptop and the desktop. They kept banging away at their respective computers for several hours. Just as the time reached nine o'clock, Jones stopped, seeing something on the screen that stopped him in his tracks.

"Oh dear," Jones said suddenly, sounding deeply concerned.

"What's wrong?" Recker swung round on his chair to face him.

"It appears we have another situation on our hands and it looks gravely serious."

"What's up?"

"It would seem there's a woman whose life is in danger. A man too for that matter."

"What's going on?"

"Listen," Jones said, hitting the play button on his software program.

"I'm telling you right now, if I find her at that hotel tonight with her boss, I'm gonna kill them." The strange voice sounded angry.

"That was the message that Martin Gilbert left on the voicemail of a friend of his," Jones said, filling in the first bit of detail.

"I take it the her he's referring to is his wife?" Recker said.

"That would be correct." Jones was feverishly typing away on the laptop. "His wife's name is Lorissa Gilbert."

Recker looked at the screen as Jones pulled up the DMV information of the husband and wife, picture included.

"Who's the boss?" Recker said.

"Hold on, getting that information now," Jones said, pulling up Lorissa's job info.

"Advertising agency secretary." Recker read the details off the screen. "Boss is Kevin Fitzpatrick. Where's that hotel Gilbert's talking about?"

"I'm trying to locate it now. But it sounds as if Mrs. Gilbert's having a late night rendezvous, perhaps not work related."

"You don't know that. Don't jump to the obvious conclusion," Recker said. "Maybe it is work related and this husband of hers is the super jealous type who also jumps to the wrong conclusion."

"Perhaps you're right. Maybe I am being too hasty with my judgment."

"How's that location coming?" Recker grabbed his coat, checked his weapons and was ready to go.

"Just about got it," Jones said, taking another minute to find the spot while Recker hovered impatiently knowing that sometimes seconds can mean the difference between life and death. "There it is. Sheraton Hotel in Society Hill."

"What room number?"

"Three twenty-one. Registered to Kevin Fitzpatrick. And it looks like Mr. Fitzpatrick has already checked in."

"I'm on my way. Call me with whatever else you come up with," Recker shouted as he rushed out the door.

Recker drove the half hour it took to get to the hotel. As he pulled into the parking lot, Jones called him with more information.

"Mr. Recker, have you reached the hotel yet?"

"Just got here."

"I've come up with a few more details, one of which being that Martin Gilbert purchased a gun two weeks ago."

"What kind?"

"A Smith & Wesson forty caliber, it's…"

"That's all I need, I know it. Nice weapon."

"Yes, well, regardless of your fondness for it, I would imagine he's carrying it with him tonight."

"Gilbert have a record?" Recker asked.

"Not that I can find."

"I don't think I have to worry too much about him. Sounds like a novice."

"Just be careful with him. Anyone with a gun can be dangerous, especially if you take them lightly."

"Yeah, thanks for that." He cut the call. Like he needed telling.

Recker got out of his car and went inside the hotel, immediately going to the elevator, stopping at the third floor. Without seeing anyone else in the halls, he walked down the hallway, stopping at three twenty-one. He stood there at the door, listening. He heard several voices. A man's voice was talking loudly, and somewhat incoherently, as well as a woman's voice, though it was mostly crying from her.

Recker tapped his earpiece. "Jones, he's already here. Sounds like something's about to go down. Looks like I'll have to step in."

Jones responded, his voice distorted in Recker's ear. "Do what you must."

Recker carefully turned the handle so as to not make any noise to alert the subjects in the room. He opened the door a hair, peeking inside to gauge where everybody was. The bed was in a small room to his right, and Gilbert's back was to him. He had a gun out and pointed at his wife, naked under the bed sheets next to her boss. They were holding each other, afraid for their lives. Recker slowly walked into the room, hoping the floor wouldn't creak underneath him and give him away. Amidst her crying, Lorissa looked over and saw Recker walking closer. Recker put his hand up to his face and moved it around, hoping she wouldn't give away his presence. Gilbert kept yelling at his nude prisoners, trying to get up the nerve to pull the trigger on the pistol he'd never fired before. He waved the gun around, taking turns on which person he pointed it at. Once Recker got within a few feet of him, he rushed him. Gilbert didn't realize he had company until Recker was right on top of him, the former CIA agent throwing him into the wall with a body block any NFL tight end would be proud of. Anytime you surprise someone who's holding a gun, and there's physical contact, there's a chance of the gun going off by accident. Luckily, Gilbert's finger wasn't on the trigger and the pistol flew out of his hand without incident. As Gilbert laid against the wall, stunned, and holding the back of his head which hit the bottom of the wall, Recker walked over to the gun and picked it up.

"Oh my God, thank you so much!" Mrs. Gilbert said, as her and her lover scrambled to put clothes on.

Recker looked away to one side. "If I were you two, I'd be more careful next time."

"We will."

"Or better... you... you might wanna see a divorce attorney. I might not be around next time," Recker said, smiling.

"Are you a cop or something?" Fitzpatrick asked.

"Not quite. You, call the police and tell them what just happened," Recker said, pointing at the boss.

Recker noticed Gilbert starting to move around and went over to him, punching him in the face, temporarily incapacitating him again.

"What are you doing?" Lorissa asked. She didn't seem upset that Recker was beating on her husband. Maybe the divorce attorney was a good idea.

"Making sure he doesn't wake up again," Recker replied.

He picked Gilbert up from behind, grabbing him underneath his arms, and dragged him along the floor across the room.

"Open up that closet," Recker told them.

Lorissa did as the stranger instructed and opened the closet door as her boss was on the phone with the police. Recker threw Gilbert into the closet and closed the door, locking it. He looked around and saw a chair, maneuvering it in front of the door to prevent it from opening, just in case Gilbert had a fit of rage and tried to plow through it.

"What are you doing now?" Lorissa asked again.

"Making sure he doesn't escape."

"Is that really necessary?"

"He was about to kill the both of you," Recker answered. "Do you really want to be here by yourselves when he wakes up?"

"Uh, no, good point. Aren't you staying with us until the police get here?"

"Sorry, don't have the time. I've got other things to attend to."

"Poor Martin," his wife said.

Recker rolled his eyes. "He was going to shoot you. Too late for pity now." Her reaction, belated as it was, made no sense to him and was beginning to aggravate him. "Listen. If he wakes up before the police get here, don't you even think about opening that door, no matter what he says."

"Don't worry about that, I'll make sure of that," Fitzpatrick replied, walking over to them. "Police should be here in a few minutes."

"Good. Next time you wanna screw one of your employees, you might wanna make sure their husband isn't the violent type," Recker said.

"Noted."

"Who are you?" Lorissa asked.

"Oh, just call me the silencer."

"What?"

"I'm just someone who silences problems."

Recker then left, eager to get out of the hotel before the police arrived. Once he got to his car, he stayed for a few minutes and watched to make sure none of the parties disappeared before the police got there. The cops arrived a little over five minutes later, Fitzpatrick and his lover still waiting in the room for the police. With the police being there, Recker's work was done. He drove out of the parking lot with the intention of going home. He figured he'd let Jones know he was finished as he drove.

"Jones, mission accomplished."

"Excellent, Mr. Recker. How did it go?"

"No problems. Gilbert's subdued, the wife and boss weren't harmed, police are there now. I'd say everything went off without a hitch."

"Excellent. What are your plans now?"

"I figured I might go home for the night. You know, get some sleep," Recker said.

"What about Ms. Hendricks?"

"She's still at work. She's going straight home after her shift is over."

"Do you think it'd be wise to cruise around her apartment just to make sure that Eldridge isn't waiting for her?"

"Why, is there something indicating he might be?" Recker said.

"Nothing specific. But his threats lately have been escalating. You already had a physical altercation with him and alienated him."

"And you're thinking it's gonna come to a head soon."

"That would be my guess. He thinks you might be her new boyfriend, or something along those lines. I would think you'll be seeing him again sooner rather than later."

"All right, I'll head over there for a bit. Once she comes home, I'll wait there for a couple of hours to make sure everything's safe and sound. After that I'll check out for the night."

Recker then proceeded to drive the forty-five minutes it took to reach Hendricks' apartment. It was a group of four-story buildings that housed a couple of hundred apartments. He drove into the lot where her building was and was startled to see her car parked there. She wasn't supposed to be home for another two hours or so. He got out of his Explorer and walked over to her car and felt the hood. It was still warm so she couldn't have been there long. She must've finished work early. Recker just casually turned his head, not looking at anything in particular, when more alarm bells started going off. Eldridge's pickup was there. Recker quickly ran over to it, hand on his gun, just in case Eldridge was in there and decided to make some trouble for him. Once Recker got to the truck, he looked inside. It was empty. Recker sighed and got Jones on the phone.

"Looks like my night's not over yet, Jones."

"What's the matter?"

"Mia's already here. Must've got done work early," Recker said.

"Why is that troubling?"

"Cause I also see Eldridge's truck… and he's not in it."

"Oh my. You better get up to her apartment," Jones told him.

Recker was already running. "I'm on my way."

Recker ran towards the apartment entrance and rushed down the hallway until he got to the stairs. It'd be quicker than waiting for the elevator. He quickly ran up the steps, skipping several at a time until he got to the fourth floor. He ran down the hall, stopping in front of Hendricks' door. From the commotion that was coming from inside the apartment, it appeared as if she was in trouble.

It sounded as if Eldridge was roughing her up.

She was pleading with him to stop.

Recker turned the handle to the door, but it was locked. He took a step back and kicked the door open with a loud crash as it opened and another as it smashed into the wall inside. One step inside Recker saw Hendricks laying on the floor with Eldridge standing over her, lunging down as if he'd just hit her.

When he saw the stranger who'd roughed him up once already, Eldridge jumped up and stepped back from his ex-girlfriend.

He had a gun in his waistband and reached around for it. He never got the chance to use it though, as Recker rushed into the room and speared him shoulder first in the gut, slamming him into the floor. The gun flew from Eldridge's hand as his body hit the ground.

The two of them wrestled on the ground for a minute, exchanging a few punches. Once they got back to their feet, Eldridge attempted to land a couple of shots on Recker's face, though the former CIA agent blocked them. Recker returned the favor and had better luck, landing several punches to Eldridge's face, bruising him around his eye.

Hendricks had gotten back on her feet and went to the kitchen, standing by the counter to observe the action. She would've called the police if she had her phone but she didn't have a landline, and her cell phone was in her purse, which was on the other side of the room and there was no way she was going to interfere in the tussle between the two men.

After a few more minutes, Recker felt he was getting the upper hand and Eldridge was looking to escape. He fainted and dodged past Recker out through the smashed doorway and into the hallway. Recker took off in pursuit and followed him down the hall. He caught up to Eldridge as he reached the door to the staircase and the two of them scuffled as they burst through the door onto the stairs. Recker was the first to his feet and delivered another blow to the side of Eldridge's face, knocking him down the steps. Eldridge was dazed and struggled getting up. Recker slowly descended the steps, knowing he was now in full control of the situation.

He grabbed the back of Eldridge's shirt and helped the beaten man back to his feet, only to smack him around a few more times. Eldridge fell again, his back on the steps, and though he was woozy, came to the conclusion that the man in front of him had the intention of killing him. Since Recker stood in front of him, blocking his access to the bottom of the stairs, Eldridge stumbled away from his attacker, going up to the roof in hopes of somehow getting away from him.

Recker kept following his victim up the stairs, though he didn't think it was necessary to hasten things, walking methodically up each step. Recker assumed his target had nowhere to go, unless there was some type of ladder on the side of the building to allow his escape, and knew Eldridge couldn't get away from him. Even if he did, Recker hoped the beating he had giving the man would be enough to teach him to steer clear.

As soon as Recker walked through the door to the roof, a big right hand from Eldridge caught him in the face sending him back a couple of steps. Though stunned for a split second, Recker shook his head and shrugged it off, going back on the offensive. He caught Eldridge with several more blows, the amount of punches now taking their toll on his body as he crawled along the floor. Once he got to the end, he pulled himself up by the concrete ledge that lined the rooftop.

Eldridge was able to turn himself around, breathing heavily from the punishment he'd absorbed, to face his attacker. He put his hands out, hoping to stop Recker from coming closer to him.

"Just wait," Eldridge pleaded, wiping blood off his forehead. "I have some money."

"Not interested," Recker replied, taking a step closer to his subject.

Eldridge coughed and looked around, hoping for something he could use to fend off the man who seemed to be intent on killing him. There was nothing that would save the day for him. He looked over at the building next to them and knew his only chance would be to jump onto the roof next to them. It was a big gamble though. It was about eight feet away and he wouldn't be able to get a running start. With his injuries, he wasn't sure if his body was strong enough to make the jump. But he knew that without taking the chance, he was as good as dead anyway. He was positive that the man who'd beaten him so severely was going to kill him. His only chance at surviving was to jump to the adjacent roof and escape down the stairs.

Eldridge quickly mustered enough strength to get back to his feet, clambered up on the ledge and faced the neighboring building.

Recker stopped walking toward him, wondering what the man was planning. It looked as if he was thinking about jumping, but Recker didn't think he could make it. Recker stood and watched, deciding to let him take the risk if he was so inclined. Eldridge turned around to take one last look at Recker, who took a step forward. It was now or never. Eldridge took a step back, then hurled himself off the roof. He just barely reached the neighboring building, his fingers grazing the concrete ledge, unable to take hold of it. His nose was broken as his face smashed into the brick building and he fell the momentum of the jump turning him over mid-air. The back of his head and neck were the first parts of his body that hit the ground, and he died instantly, unable to survive the brutal impact of a forty-foot fall.

Recker looked on from the roof, staring down at the lifeless body of the man he'd just beaten to a pulp. He sighed and shook his head, unconcerned about Eldridge's death, but he knew it would complicate matters. Now, the police would come in and do an investigation. He wanted to grab a minute with Hendricks before the cops arrived to make sure she was OK. Recker rushed back down the stairs and down the hall, going into Hendricks' apartment. She was sitting on the couch, holding her head.

"You all right?" Recker asked, trying to close the door behind him the best he could.

Hendricks took her hand off her head, and looked up at him, relieved to see him. "Uh... yeah. Yeah, I think so."

"What happened?"

"I got done early from work. When I got here, I got to the door, and as I was unlocking it, he grabbed me. I didn't see him. I don't know where he was. I guess he was waiting for me." She looked down at her feet as she spoke.

"What then?"

"We started talking, and I told him to go and I didn't want to see him again. That made him mad. Really mad. He shoved me inside and started yelling at me and hitting me."

"That's when I walked in."

She nodded. "Yeah."

"Well, you won't have any more problems with him."

"You don't think he'll come back?"

"Not likely."

"How can you be sure?" she said.

Recker sighed, knowing there was no good way of telling her. "He's dead."

"What?" Hendricks said, jumping up in disbelief.

"As we were fighting, he went up to the rooftop. I guess he figured his only chance of getting away was to jump to the next building. He didn't make it," Recker explained.

"Then you didn't kill him?"

Recker shook his head. "No. Can't say I didn't want to, but no. He did that on his own."

Hendricks looked disappointed, not that she wasn't happy to have Eldridge out of her life finally, but she didn't want anybody dead, even him. "So what now?"

"Police will probably be here soon."

"So what do we tell them?"

"You just tell them the truth and what happened. You'll be fine."

A peculiar look came over her face, as it sounded to her like he wasn't planning on sticking around. "You say that like you won't be here too."

Recker made an agonized face of his own. "I can't, really."

"Why not?"

He sighed, not wanting to get too involved. "It's complicated. The police can't know anything about me, even my name."

"Why?" Hendricks fixed him with a look. "I don't understand."

Recker knew he was in a difficult spot. He risked compromising himself whether he told her the truth or not. "Let's just say that the police may not believe that someone like me didn't throw him off the roof instead of him jumping."

"Is that really what happened? Did you throw him off the roof?"

"No. What I told you is exactly what happened."

"Then I don't understand why you can't stay."

"I don't expect you to understand, but I can't."

"I'm scared," Hendricks said. Shock was starting to kick in now the adrenaline high was wearing off.

Recker put his arm around her to try to comfort her as best he could. "I know. Just tell them when they arrive that you don't know who the man was that helped you."

Still looking quite nervous, Hendricks still tried to get him to stay. "I just don't know what to do."

"You'll be OK. He can't hurt you anymore."

"Are you wanted by the police for something?"

"No. Not for the reasons that you'd think. I'm not a criminal or anything. There are bigger things at play that I don't have time to go into right now though," he said.

"What if I just tell the police that I fought him off and he left despondent? And that he went to the roof and jumped."

"Mia, you don't need to lie for me. You can just tell them what happened," he smiled. "Just conveniently forget my name."

Hendricks nodded, agreeing to his terms. Recker took his arm off her and started towards the door when Hendricks asked for a favor from him. "If I do as you ask, would you be able to meet with me tomorrow and explain what this is all about? Please?"

Recker sighed, knowing it was against his better judgment to agree to her request. But there was just something in her voice that he couldn't deny it. Plus, he was in a no-win situation. If she told the police his name it'd be just as bad as if he stayed and talked to them himself. "OK," he said.

"Can I call you in the morning?"

"Why don't I just meet you again for lunch at Joe's Diner at noon?" Recker said, "and don't mention that number to the police."

Hendricks nodded again. "OK. Thank you."

Recker left the apartment, making sure nobody saw him exit, and went down the stairs to the main floor. He walked out of the main entrance and noticed a crowd starting to gather around Eldridge's body. He went to his truck and just sat in it for a minute. His hands were scraped and bloody and when he looked in his rearview mirror he had marks and abrasions on his face. He didn't want to be there when the police showed up so he didn't waste any more time in staying there. He started driving to his apartment, calling Jones along the way.

"Jones, doesn't look like Eldridge is gonna be an issue anymore," Recker said.

"Why is that? Did he finally get the message?"

"Well, yeah, in a way. He's dead."

"Oh no. What happened?" Jones said. He sounded genuinely concerned.

"Fell off the roof."

Jones was temporarily stunned. "Fell off or was thrown off?"

"Fell off. Well... jumped to be precise."

"Excuse me for my apprehension, but didn't you say something about throwing him off a roof when we first started this case?"

"Oh, come on, I was only joking when I said that," Recker said. "Well, sort of."

Jones sighed, knowing this wouldn't help them to remain inconspicuous. "How is Ms. Hendricks?"

"She's fine. A few bumps and bruises from Eldridge before I got to him."

"Well, I'm glad she's not more seriously hurt. Why don't you go home and get some rest?"

"Thanks, I will. It's kind of been a long day."

"We'll discuss your methods further in the morning," Jones said sternly.

"Can't wait... Professor," Recker said.

8

Recker came into the office the following morning, breakfast in hand, hoping it'd help to smooth things over with Jones. He knew Jones probably wasn't happy with him in regards to Eldridge's death.

"Is this supposed to be a peace offering?" Jones said, taking his food.

Recker shrugged. "If you like."

"I can't be bought with food, you know."

"So what can you be bought with?" Recker couldn't resist trying to find out more.

"Nothing," Jones said, not taking his eyes off the computer screen. "Have you seen this?" he said, handing over a copy of the newspaper.

Recker sighed, sure he was about to find himself in there somehow. He immediately saw the headline of the situation that happened at the hotel involving the Gilberts.

"It appears the man in the trench coat has been nicknamed

The Silencer," Jones stated. "Wonder how they came up with that."

Recker looked away from the paper and at his employer, chuckling to himself that the name stuck. "You know these media types. Just throwing names at the wall to see what sticks. Helps to sell papers. God knows where they get these kinds of ideas from," he said, rolling his eyes and pretending to know nothing about it. "Nothing about Mia in here?"

"Her situation was too late for the morning edition," Jones replied. "It is on the online version though since it's updated throughout the day."

"What's it say?"

"Here, you read it," Jones said, backing his chair away to let Recker read the article.

The article gave the account of what happened, with Eldridge forcing his way into Hendricks' apartment and roughing her up. It then stated that a man who was visiting someone else in the building walked by and intervened, leading Eldridge to become despondent and go up to the rooftop, where he then chose to end his life. The article gave a brief physical description of the stranger that interrupted the attack, though it didn't match Recker at all. It listed the stranger as being around 5'9, a hundred and eighty pounds, in his forties, slightly husky, a beard, and black hair that ran down past his shoulders. That was as far away from Recker's description as it could get. After he was finished reading, Recker stepped back from the computer, letting Jones get back in there.

"It would appear that Ms. Hendricks covered for you," Jones said.

A grin came over Recker's face. "Seems that way."

"Thank goodness for that. You've had a lot of publicity the last several days. We don't really need more of it."

"Better get used to it. Gonna be a lot more of it by the time we're through."

"Isn't there a better way to end these conflicts without being compromised?" Jones said.

"Sure there is."

Jones' face brightened. "Then why don't we do that?"

"Because that'd involve a sniper rifle and me killing the targets from a distance," Recker said through a mouthful of food. "Now, I don't personally have a problem with that, and actually would probably prefer it, but I assume that's not what you're going for."

Jones' face was a picture of disgust. He wiped imaginary crumbs off him as he spoke. "I was hoping to avoid killing... as well as making you a household name."

Recker shrugged and took another bite. "So, what's next on the agenda? Have another target?"

"I think I should have one by this afternoon," Jones replied, sliding his food away from him. He'd lost his appetite.

"Good. Need me for anything until then?"

"No, I don't think so. Why do you ask?"

"I told Mia I'd meet with her for lunch," Recker said.

"Mia. We're on a first name basis with Ms. Hendricks now, are we?"

"She wanted some answers about what happened last night. Considering she covered for me and lied about me being there, I figured I owed that to her. Don't worry, I won't tell her about you or this place or our exact business."

"I'm not worried about that," Jones said, skeptical about Recker's newfound relationship.

"What then? I can tell it's something." He screwed up his wrapper and threw it at the trash bin. He missed.

"I wonder if perhaps you're getting too close to her. She does have a pretty face."

"I tried that once before," Recker said with a shake of his head. "I won't make that mistake again. Maybe she's a friend, maybe she's a contact, maybe she's someone we can use in case of emergency. But that's all she is and all she will ever be. Even if I wanted to, I'd never let another woman make the mistake of loving me. She deserves better than that. You not going to eat that?" Recker pointed at Jones' rapidly cooling breakfast and smiled.

Knowing it was still a touchy subject for him and noting the change of subject, Jones simply gave him a warm smile and nodded. He knew Recker was still hurting over what happened to Carrie and could tell it was a pain that wasn't likely to go away anytime soon. He just hoped it'd be a pain that didn't consume him. Since he had a few hours to kill before meeting Hendricks, Recker fiddled around on one of the computers, helping Jones to identify future victims for them to aid.

Once eleven o'clock rolled around, Recker excused himself and slipped out of the office for his lunch date. He got there about fifteen minutes ahead of schedule and waited in the same booth they met at the day before. While he was waiting, Recker ordered drinks for the both of them. Two cokes. That was his usual choice of drink during the day and he noticed that was what she had the last time they met. Mia came right on time, exactly at twelve, punctual as usual. As soon as she entered the diner, she immediately found her lunch date in the corner of the restaurant and sat down across from him. She flashed him that sweet, innocent smile of hers, though behind that smile was a boatload of questions that she wanted answers to.

She took a big breath before starting to talk. "I had fears, or visions, that I'd come and you wouldn't be here."

"Why would you think that?" Recker said.

"I don't know. Just had this thing where I thought you were gonna blow me off."

Recker shook his head. "I wouldn't do that. Not to you."

Hendricks smiled again. "I have so many questions," she said, not quite knowing where to begin.

"I know. Before we get to all that though, how are you?"

It looked like she was struggling to find an answer. "I'm uh... I'm OK, I guess."

"It's not an easy thing to have to go through."

"It's weird, you know? Umm, I'm glad, relieved that I'll never have to worry about being stalked, or followed, or hit, or anything like that."

"But..."

"But I feel... kind of sad. I once really cared for him and to know that he's no longer alive, it's just..."

"It's a lot to process." Recker finished off the thought.

"I guess so. I don't wish death on anybody, no matter what they've done. I just wish there'd been another way and things would've worked out differently," she said, feeling down.

"It's important to know that it's not your fault for what happened to him. He chose the path that led to his downfall. Nobody chose it for him and nobody else is to blame for the choices he made."

"I know. And I don't feel guilty or responsible or anything. I just wish things went a different way."

"That's because you're a good person. Only an idiot would want bad things to happen to people."

"Well, I don't know how good a person I am, but thank you anyway. By the way, what do you prefer to be called? Mike? Michael? Don't tell me you're one of those people that prefers to be called by their last name. That really irks me when people do that," Hendricks said.

"Mike or Michael's fine. Only my enemies call me Recker." He smiled.

"Good. I like Mike. Michael sounds too formal, not very personal."

"Whatever you prefer."

The waitress came over and took their order, both of them ordering burgers with fries. He ordered his without onions, drawing a comment from Hendricks.

"How do you eat a burger without onions?"

"Are you kidding? I don't know anyone who eats that stuff," Recker said, pulling a face.

"Uh, hello? I do!"

Recker smiled, amused at her sense of humor.

"So are you finally gonna tell me who you are?"

"You already know that."

"No. I know your name. But I don't know *who* you are," she said.

"What do you wanna know?"

"You can start by telling me who hired you to watch over me, and don't say my father because I called him this morning and he was quite convincing in telling me he had no idea who you were. I kind of believed him when he mentioned hiring a bodyguard for me after what happened last night. Now, I doubt he'd mention that if he had already hired someone, don't you think?"

Grinning, Recker thought of how he could explain the situation to her. "I work for a very secretive security firm."

"Why didn't you tell me that before?"

"You didn't ask."

"Yes I did."

"You assumed your father hired me and I just went along with it. I never confirmed it was true," Recker said.

"Kind of a dirty trick."

Recker didn't reply and just tossed his hands in the air, not disputing the charge.

"You know, I read something in the paper this morning about a man who thwarted an attempted murder at a hotel last night," Hendricks said, looking at Recker's attire. "He, uh, happened to be wearing a trench coat. I'm sensing a pattern."

"I think I told you this before... there's a lot of trench coats out there."

They concentrated on their food for a few moments.

"So, what can you tell me about this security firm of yours?"

"Nothing."

"Let's see... you saved me, a girl who was almost raped, someone else who was almost murdered, robberies, how do you get around so fast?"

"I get good intel."

"You have to tell me something. Anything."

"I work for a security firm who wants to help regular, everyday people with certain problems."

"If I use myself as a guide, I'd say you're not hired by those people. So how and why do you do it?" she asked.

"We have a sophisticated computer system that indicates when people might have certain problems then we act on it."

"But why? What do you get out of it? Money? You're disappearing from every scene so I know it can't be notoriety or fame."

"The owner of this security firm is very wealthy. We don't get anything out of it except for the satisfaction of helping people who need it," Recker said.

"So why are you hiding from the police?"

"I'm not really hiding from them, per se."

"Then what?"

Recker sighed, not really sure of another way to tell her without saying the truth. Hendricks could see that he was struggling to come up with an answer and was getting frustrated with the cloak and dagger act that he put up.

"Why won't you tell me anything?"

"Because anything I tell you could put you in danger." Recker gave her the only reply he could.

"How?"

"It's complicated."

"Do I need to go to the police? Or start my own investigation?" Hendricks said.

"Why do you need to know?"

"Because I find you interesting. And I'd like to know something about the person who helped me. Is that so wrong?"

"No, it's not wrong."

"Then please just tell me the truth. Would it put me in more danger if I tried to find out on my own?" She was trying hard to wriggle it out of him.

"Probably. And me along with it."

"Then why don't you just tell me so I don't have to go through all that."

"You know, behind that pretty face and innocent smile of yours, you're a very stubborn woman," Recker said.

Hendricks laughed. "You're not the first person who's ever told me that before."

"Why does that not surprise me?"

"So are you going to tell me? Or do I have to find out on my own?"

Recker put his hand over his mouth and rubbed his face a couple of times as he decided how much to reveal.

"So why all the secrecy?" Hendricks said again, leaning forward in anticipation of the answer.

"If I were to tell you the truth, you probably wouldn't believe it. If someone told it to me, I probably wouldn't believe it either."

"Let me be the judge of that."

"The real reason I don't want to have any type of police contact is because once I do, my name goes into the system. Once that happens, radars go off everywhere," Recker said.

"What's that mean exactly?"

Recker sighed, figuring it was easier to just tell the truth than continue to dance around the subject. Well, at least as much of the truth as he could divulge, which still wasn't much. But he figured if he'd give her a little snippet of information, that'd hopefully be enough to satisfy her curiosity. He looked up to the ceiling for a second before his eyes danced around to the rest of the restaurant. He knew there was a risk in telling Hendricks anything about what he once was, but he also knew that if she was being truthful in that she would try to find out on her own, it was safer for her if she found out from him. At least he could control what she knew. He'd just have to hope she was as trustworthy as he thought she was.

"I used to work for the United States government," Recker revealed.

"OK?"

"That's about all I can tell you," he said, not really expecting it to suffice.

"Seriously? You think that's going to be enough?" Hendricks responded.

"No, not really. Was kind of hoping though."

"Why are you so secretive? I'm not trying to give you the sixth degree. I just want the truth about who you are."

Recker took a deep breath as he continued remembering his past. "There are things that are happening that I just can't tell you. Not right now."

"You don't trust me. Do you?"

"It's got nothing to do with trust. If I didn't, I wouldn't even be here right now," Recker said.

"What is it then?"

"It's about keeping you safe."

"From what?" Mia's eyebrows raised.

"From people a lot more dangerous than Stephen Eldridge."

"Are you on the run or something?"

"It's a lot more complicated than a simple yes or no answer," Recker said.

"Try me."

Recker leaned forward and started talking more softly, looking around to make sure nobody was listening. "I was involved in a top secret government project."

"Was?"

"My involvement in that project didn't go exactly as planned. Someone decided that I was no longer necessary in that project and decided to terminate me."

"By terminate you mean..."

"I mean kill. Someone tried to kill me and now I'm here... trying to make a difference. While at the same time trying to stay out of the crosshairs," Recker said, leaning back.

"Wow."

"I'm not a criminal or a bad guy, but I know a lot of things that certain people would be worried about me revealing. Once my name goes into an official government system, alarm bells start going off, and it pops up on the CIA's radar."

"The CIA?" Hendricks asked.

Recker just nodded.

"So that means they would know where you are and would come after you again?"

"That's it." Recker nodded. "Crazy, huh?"

"Wow. I'll say."

"Now that I've told you I'm afraid I'll have to kill you," Recker said, stony faced.

"What?"

Recker let out a laugh, "Sorry, an old secret agent joke. Always wanted to say it one time."

"Oh," Hendricks said with a look of relief on her face.

"I've taken you into my confidence. For your protection and mine, you can't say a word about me to anyone. They've already killed people that were associated with me before. They won't hesitate to do it again. If they even knew we had this conversation right now, they'd kill you just for sitting here, regardless whether you knew anything or not."

"Nobody will ever learn about you from me." She looked a little worried now.

"Good. I'd hate to move to a new city already."

"Why would you move?"

"If you told anybody about me, I'd ditch my phone, pick up a new name, new city, start all over again. That'd all be done by tomorrow morning." He grinned.

"You don't have to worry about me," Hendricks said.

"I know. I pretty much knew that when I read an article this morning about the mysterious man who helped fend off your attacker. Didn't seem to fit the description of me at all."

"Well, you said to keep you out of it. I figured the best way to do that was to say it was someone else."

"Police believe it?"

"Seemed to. I told them I didn't know who the man was. Must've been visiting someone else in the building."

They continued talking for another hour as they ate their lunch, Hendricks still ribbing him over his lack of an appetite for onions. She was fascinated by his life, or former life, and sought to hear more stories from his past, a past he wasn't as anxious to delve into. Luckily, he wouldn't have to duck the questions any longer. Still wearing his earpiece, Jones' voice came booming in.

"What's up, Professor?" Recker said.

"Back to that again, are we?"

"Don't forget, I have company right now." Recker fake smiled at Hendricks, who was listening to every word her companion was saying.

"Oh yes, I almost forgot. How is that going, by the way?"

"Just fine."

"Good. Well, we have a new situation developing and it is urgent," Jones sounded slightly flustered.

"What's up?"

"I've intercepted several text messages indicating a robbery is about to take place."

"How soon?"

"Two o'clock."

"Where?"

"Albert's. It's a small convenience store over on fifth. Can you get there in time?"

"Why not just call the police with an anonymous tip?" Recker asked.

"Because we act on the information we uncover. We don't pass it along and hope. What if they don't act or they don't get there in time?"

Recker nodded his head, agreeing. "OK. I'm on my way. How many people am I dealing with?"

"Three that I can definitely pinpoint."

"Armed?"

"I can't say for sure. Looking at their backgrounds, I would say that there is a distinct possibility," Jones said over the clatter of fingers on the keyboard.

"OK. On my way."

Recker was already done with his meal and asked for the check, which he promptly paid. "I'm afraid I have to go," he said.

"Off to save the day somewhere else?"

"Something like that."

"Will I see you again soon?" She hoped she would.

"I don't know. I'll call you."

"Well, wherever you're going… be careful."

Recker smiled and walked away. He sped out of the parking lot and drove as quickly as he could to get to Albert's. He got there about ten minutes before two. It was a small family owned store. Recker walked in and was immediately greeted by an elderly man, probably in his early sixties. He was standing behind the register, no glass or bars separating him from the customers he checked out. He was slightly overweight, wore glasses, and was mostly bald except for a small patch of gray hair on the sides of his head.

"You Albert?" Recker asked.

"Just like the sign says." The man replied with a cheerful laugh.

Recker took a quick look through the aisles to see if anybody else was in the store, either regular customers, or the three crumbs that were about to knock the place over. After going through the six small aisles, Recker went back to the front of the store, where the register was located.

"You might wanna take a break," Recker told him.

"Excuse me?"

"You're about to be robbed."

"What? Are you drunk or high or something?" Albert asked.

"Nope. You keep a gun under there?" Recker asked, his eyes pointing to under the register.

"Maybe." The storekeeper was getting a little uneasy about the stranger's questions.

"Three young kids are coming here in a few minutes with the intention of robbing you," Recker informed.

"How you know this? You a cop?"

"Close enough. You got a place you can hide out till this is over?"

"Uh, there's a bathroom and an office in the back. What are you gonna do?" Albert came out around the counter.

"I'm gonna pretend to be you," Recker said, stepping behind the register.

He looked down under the counter and found Albert's gun, a Sig Sauer 9mm. Recker picked it up and handled it for a second, aiming it toward the wall. He smiled and handed it over to its rightful owner.

"Nice choice."

"What do you want me to do?"

"Go back to the office or bathroom and hide out there. Take the gun with you just in case."

"You want me to take them out from back there?" Albert asked.

Recker smiled, impressed with his willingness to get in the fight. "No, I'll take care of them. If shooting starts, just make sure you're not in the line of fire. But just in case one of them gets a lucky shot off, be prepared to defend yourself if the need arises."

"You mean if one of them shoots you then searches the store for other people?"

"You got it."

"OK. If that happens, where should I shoot them? I know how to use it but I never had to fire a gun before. Wing them in the arm or leg or something?"

"If you have to shoot, shoot to kill. Center mass," Recker said, pointing to the middle of his chest. "Or, if you're close enough, right here." He showed him, putting his index finger in the middle of his forehead. "A winged or injured man can still kill you. If you ever fire that thing, you shoot to finish the fight."

"Gotcha," Albert said, walking to the back of the store. Just

MIKE RYAN

before he got to the office he turned around. "Is the backup team coming soon?"

Recker smiled. "It's just me. You're the backup team."

Five more minutes went by. It was a minute after two o'clock. Not a single customer entered the store in the time Recker had been there. Then the door swung open. Three young kids, probably in their late teens or early twenties, walked through the door. They all had sports caps on and baggy clothes, with a gun most likely nestled in the waistbands of their pants. Recker closely eyed them up as they all came in. As soon as the first one saw Recker, he stopped and did a double take, then nudged the second man in the arm to alert him. They weren't counting on anybody else other than Albert being there. They'd been in the store a few times before and never saw anyone else working there. Recker was a new wrinkle in their plans.

"Yo man, who you?" One of the kids spoke up first.

"Just an employee," Recker said.

"Where's Albert?"

"Oh, he took a lunch break."

The three men separated and walked throughout the store, making sure they were all alone. Recker could tell they were the three that Jones was talking about. A common technique of criminals that worked in pairs or teams was that they would spread out, especially in smaller stores or places without a lot of eyeballs on them, knowing you couldn't watch all of them at once. One of the kids walked up to the register and started talking to Recker, while the other two moved around the counter.

"I'm sorry, you two aren't allowed back here," Recker said, facing the pair.

While he was talking to the others, the one in front of the register pulled a gun, pointing it squarely at Recker's body. Recker faked being surprised and began putting his hands in the air.

"Get the cash," The one with the gun gave out the instructions. Must be the brains of the outfit.

They started to move but quickly stopped when Recker brought his left hand down and kept it in the air in front of the two, directing them to stop.

"You guys don't really wanna do this, do you?" Recker knew what the answer would be.

"Yo dude, shut up and move out of the way and you won't get hurt," the gun toting man said.

Recker gave a half smile, "Well, I just wanted to give you a fair warning."

"Fair warning for what?"

Recker quickly reached into his opened coat and grabbed a pistol with each hand. He brought his hands out of the insides of his trench coat, pointing a pistol in both directions that the robbers were standing in. "Like I said, you really don't wanna do this?"

"Hey man, we ain't armed." One of the two to Recker's left spoke up.

"So why don't you guys just pack up and move on out of here before someone gets hurt?"

"We will. As soon as we get what we came for." The one with the gun was back in charge.

"Well, I don't think that's happening."

"There's three of us, man. There's only one of you."

"You got one gun, I got two," Recker said calmly.

As soon as Recker took his eyes off the two to the left, one of them reached into his jacket and pulled out a pistol. Recker looked back at him as he was removing it, shooting him in the chest. He turned back to the man in front of the register and blew a hole through him before he got a chance to do the same to him. Both men were dead as soon as they hit the ground. The third man in the crew really wasn't armed and hadn't made a single motion in any direction as he froze himself the moment the action started, not wanting to make a wrong move.

"I really ain't armed," the remaining robber said, putting his arms up, worried that he was soon going to join his friends.

"Lift your jacket up and turn around," Recker told him.

The kid did as was requested, revealing that he really didn't have a weapon on him. As he was spinning around, Albert came out of the office after he heard the shots. He saw Recker with a gun pointed at the remaining member of the crew.

"He one of them?" Albert said.

"Yeah. Call the police and tell them you're holding a suspect."

"You got it," Albert said, going over to the phone.

"Looks like you picked the wrong set of friends, kid," Recker said.

"They ain't my friends, really. They said they had this thing going on and it'd be easy money," he told him, shrugging.

"There's no such thing as easy money. There's your first lesson right there."

"Cops are on the way," Albert said, coming back over. "Should be here in just a couple of minutes."

"That's my cue to leave," Recker said.

"What? You have to tell the police what happened."

"Nah. You can do that for me. The two dead ones drew guns. You tell them I defended myself and shot them in self-defense. Make sure you tell them this one here wasn't armed. That's about all I can do for you, kid."

The kid shrugged, knowing he was screwed no matter what.

"Well, I gotta go," Recker said.

"Hey," Albert said, putting his hand out. "Thanks for everything."

Recker returned the handshake. "You take care."

"Don't be a stranger. You come back sometime, hear?"

Recker nodded and smiled. "I'll do that."

Recker quickly exited the store and walked down the street, staying close enough to see the store's entrance, just to make sure the third robber didn't get the jump on the elderly storekeeper before the police arrived. Three police cars came storming in only a minute later to take control of the situation. As Recker continued walking to his truck, he let Jones know the problem had been eliminated.

"Professor, situation's resolved," Recker said.

"Is there someone else with you?"

"No."

"Oh. Your use of the nickname threw me off," Jones said.

"What's the matter? Don't you like it?"

"I hadn't really given it much thought until now. Anyhow, what happened at the store?"

"Robbery thwarted, one in custody, two men down," Recker said, hurrying away at the sound of sirens.

"And Albert?"

"Safe and sound."

"Now, when you say two men down, you mean...?"

"I mean dead."

"I had an inkling that was your meaning. There was no other way to prevent it I assume?"

"If there was another way, I would've done it another way. You send me into a robbery that's about to happen with guys who have guns, what did you expect the result would be? Talk them into giving themselves up?"

"Yes, I know. It's just I wanted us to stop bad and violent things from happening and it seems as though we're just contributing," Jones said, sounding like he was having second thoughts about the whole operation.

"There's a difference. We're stopping bad things from happening to good people. The violent things are happening to the people who want it that way," Recker said.

"I suppose you're right."

"When we started, you told me sometimes you'd disagree with the way I handled things but knew I'd probably be right. These are some of those times. Trust me when I say there was no other way to handle these issues."

"I know. It doesn't always seem like the clean victory I was hoping for when I started this endeavor," the professor said.

"One thing I've learned over the years, is there is no clean victory. For anybody. Even the winners and the good people with the best of intentions wind up with blood on their hands. It's a product of the system. Be proud of what we've accomplished in a short time so far. We saved Mia from an abusive and violent ex-boyfriend; Gilbert and her boss from possible death at the hands of her husband; a store robbery that could've ended in Albert's murder if it went down differently; and a woman from being raped. Sure, a couple of people died in the process, but they weren't the people we were trying to save. They're the people who can't be saved and what we're protecting people from."

"When you put it like that it does lift my spirit's a bit. We have made a difference so far, haven't we?"

"We have. You're a big part of that. I'm the one on the street level but nothing I do is possible without you and your intel. You should feel proud of that."

9

A week had passed since the robbery attempt at Albert's went down. In that time, Recker and Jones had saved two more people from being killed, another robbery attempt, as well as an attempted arson. Recker had just arrived at the meeting spot he engineered with his contact along the Schuylkill River. He walked along the trail until he saw the statue, then waited along the metal railing by the river. He checked the time on his phone. He was about ten minutes early. Though it was a little cold, it was basically a pleasant day since the sun was out, so he didn't mind the wait so much. Fifteen minutes went by until his visitor finally arrived. Recker was leaning on the railing and looking at the river when the man put his hands on the railing next to him.

"You're looking healthy," the man said by way of a greeting.

"You look the same as when I saved you from that mob hit man in Sicily."

The man smiled, nodding. "Philadelphia, huh? Living here these days?"

"No. Told you. Cleveland."

"Oh yeah, that's right. Cleveland," the fifty-year-old former CIA agent replied, not believing it. "Just picked a neutral spot, right?"

Recker turned his head and smiled, realizing his former mentor knew him too well. "How's Boston?"

"Ahh, you know, takes a little while to get used to. The accents there drive me crazy, but what are you gonna do, you know? So what's this all about?"

"The less you know the better off you are. You're out of the game. I don't want you to get pulled back in," Recker said.

"What do you think you're doing by having me here?"

"You could've said no."

"I always had a weakness when it came to you," the man said. "I always gave you a long leash."

"Why was that?"

"Because you were a great student. And a good friend. And probably because you always reminded me of myself when I was a little younger."

They stood there for another minute, neither of them saying a word, just staring out at the water.

"They're still looking for you, you know," the former agent said.

"Figured they would be. You don't just try to terminate someone then forget about them after you've failed."

"They talked to me after London."

"When?" Recker said.

"Couple of days later. Wanted to know where I thought you might've gone. Told them I had no idea."

Recker smiled. "You always had that ability to make people believe anything you told them."

"Wasn't hard with them. I knew they were telling me some

bullshit. Said you went rogue and were doing your own assignments off the grid. I've known some agents over the years who I thought could've gone over the edge but you weren't one of them. Especially not since you had Carrie. You'd never have done that to her."

A painful look of agony overtook Recker's face as he looked down, thinking of her. "Yeah. You took a big chance helping me out like you did. I can probably never repay you for it."

"You don't have to. You've already repaid me plenty over the years."

"How you figure that?" Recker looked over at the older man.

"By being my friend. It's just a good thing you contacted me after you left that hospital in London."

"Well, I had nobody else I could contact. Nobody I trusted anyway. You were the only one I knew who wouldn't betray me."

"Never," the man said, putting his hand on Recker's shoulder. "I'm just glad I still had that guy there who took you in. He owed me a favor. Saved his mother from a rather gruesome end."

"Yeah, he told me. Sorry about blowing your hold on him over me."

"That's all right. He still owes me another one." The man laughed. "Saved his girlfriend too."

Recker looked over his shoulder, uneasy about someone else being around. "Sure you weren't followed?"

The man took a step back, faking being insulted. "Who you think you're talking to here? I know they still might be watching me in case you contact me. Took a train to New York, then hopped a different one here. We're fine."

The former agent took a large manila envelope out of his pocket and handed it over to Recker. Recker quickly opened it and took a peek inside, seeing a picture of Jones.

"That the guy you're looking for?"

"That's him." Recker nodded.

"What makes you think he can help you?"

"I hear he's good with computers."

"Yeah, if you can find him. Even the NSA doesn't know where he is. You know he's good when he disappears even from them."

"That's why I want him. I hear he can bypass just about anything," Recker said.

"Assuming you can find him. And assuming he's willing to help you."

"I can be convincing."

"What makes you think you can even find him?"

"I have a couple of leads to check out."

"Like what?"

"You know I can't tell you."

"You know you don't need him," his friend said. "Give me a couple of weeks. I'll find the name of that son of a bitch that killed…"

Recker shook his head. "I know you would. But I don't want to put you in danger. You've already done enough. If you go poking around and asking questions then they're gonna know what you're doing. There's no other reason you'd be doing it other than helping me. They'd kill you for sure."

"Let me take that chance."

"No, I can't let you do that. Not with having Jenny and the kids. You have a life with them to look forward to. You gotta put them first. Definitely before me," Recker said. "Don't worry about me. I'll find what I'm looking for."

"I know you will. If you ever need anything else, don't hesitate to call me."

"I will."

The two former agents shook hands and went their separate ways. Recker walked back to his truck and sat in it as he opened the envelope and started reading its contents. It was a report about Jones, including a small picture of him, as well as his background information. It listed his real name and everything he did for the NSA, as well as his personal information from his time before being employed by the agency. The report had him as being missing and a red alert was listed for him, the NSA still looking for his whereabouts. Everything Jones had told Recker was down there in the report. He'd been truthful about everything. No discrepancies that Recker noticed. He continued reading the report for half an hour, rereading it several times until he was sure he'd looked over every inch of it to make sure he didn't miss anything. Once Recker was satisfied that he'd looked over the report long enough, he put the information back in the envelope. After reading Jones' information, and seeing that it was as he said it was, Recker felt a little better about his situation. That small nagging feeling in Recker's gut that said maybe Jones was another in the line of people who would betray him started to fade away.

Seeing as how Jones didn't have any other assignments for him at the moment, Recker drove back to his apartment to relax for a little while. He had an average-sized place, nothing too big since he was usually on a job and not here that often. Since Recker tried to avoid most people, he chose an apartment that had its own entrance. He had the upstairs apartment in a two story building. It was a one bedroom place that he had minimally furnished, just a bed, a TV, a couple of couches and a few tables. He had a corner desk in the living room with a couple of laptops on it in case he needed to work away from the office. It was comfortable enough for him, though for the average person, it probably would've seemed a little cold and impersonal. There wasn't even a single picture on the wall.

Recker didn't get too many days off since Jones could give him an assignment at a moment's notice, but he never really minded, at least not yet. Since he had nothing else of much interest in his life, work was really all he had. At least until baseball season arrived. The nation's pastime was one of the few things in life that he really enjoyed. It didn't matter what team, there was nothing quite like watching a baseball game. It was one of the only things that really relaxed him and got his mind off his troubles. Since he traveled so much over the years, he didn't really have a favorite team; he was mostly just a fan of the game. But since he was now in Philadelphia, and it seemed as though he might be there a while, maybe he'd throw in with the hometown team. He sat at his desk for a couple of hours, searching through the MLB website, reading stories, and getting ready for the upcoming season.

About halfway through the afternoon, though, his day off was cut short. Jones had called him and asked him to come to the office as quickly as possible. He sounded like it was an emergency. Recker figured it was another murder in the making that he'd have to stop. Since he had no external ties to slow him down, he was out of the apartment in just a couple of minutes. After making the half hour trek to the office, once he entered, he could see by the expression on Jones' face the seriousness of the matter.

"From your voice it sounded pretty urgent," Recker said. "Who's getting knocked off and when?"

"The urgency is immediate as you have correctly surmised. It is not a murder, however."

"Then what is it?"

"A kidnapping," Jones' face betrayed his fear.

"Who is it?"

Jones stopped his typing and looked at Recker stony faced. "It's a child. A little girl."

"What do you have?"

"A little girl named Mara Ridley was taken sometime this morning."

"Where?"

"Happened at their home on Spruce Street," Jones said.

"What happened?"

"As far as I can tell, Mara's parents went to work, left Mara in the care of their nanny, as is per their usual, then around ten o'clock someone knocked on the door and forced their way in and took Mara."

"The police in on it?"

"No, they've been instructed to keep the police out or they'll kill Mara immediately and won't even bother asking for money. They are complying with that request."

"How'd you pick up on this?" Recker looked over Jones' shoulder at the information on screen.

"A few minutes after it happened, they called Mr. Ridley on his cell phone. He is a financial analyst and apparently couldn't get to his phone so the kidnapper left a message. That's how the system picked up on it. Take a listen," Jones said, playing the voicemail.

"Mr. Ridley, as of ten minutes ago, we're now in possession of your lovely daughter. Call your home to verify what I say. Our terms for you getting her back are that we want one million dollars in cash three days from now. If you call the police, the FBI, or involve anyone else in this, trust us that we'll know. If you call the authorities, we won't call again, we won't negotiate, and you won't see your daughter alive again. We'll just send her home in a box... in pieces. If you value her life, don't play games with us," the kidnapper said.

"He's using plural, so it's not a one-man operation," Recker said. "What do his parents do?"

"Father's a financial analyst. Mother's an executive for a large drug company."

"They have the ability to pay?"

"Yes. They have a million dollar home, a large bank account, and sizable assets in a brokerage account."

"Well if they don't have a million in their bank account, it's gonna take time to sell off their assets," Recker said. "They haven't contacted police?"

"No. I've tapped into their phone logs and engineered my way into their computer with a virus, one that won't harm them, and they've done as requested and not contacted anyone."

"Only child?"

"Yes. As soon as Mr. Ridley heard the message he called home, though call logs indicate he didn't speak to anyone. He then called his wife and the two of them raced home." Jones was staying calm.

"Nanny was most likely tied up until they got there. How old is the girl?"

"Four."

"Any security cameras on site?"

"If only it were that simple. They do but the house completely lost all power five minutes before the kidnapping."

"If they're true to their word that they'll know if the Ridley's contact anyone, then that must mean they either have the house under surveillance or they have their phones tapped or both."

"You don't think they're bluffing?"

"Maybe. But when a child's life is at stake… you don't take chances."

"Through the spyware I installed on their computer, it appears that Mr. Ridley has already sold some of his assets."

"Stocks?"

"Yes. Sell order's already gone through. It'll take a few days to settle into his account though," Jones said.

As Jones feverishly continued typing away, trying to find out all he could about the family, Recker leaned back in his chair and put his hand on his forehead, thinking of the possible scenarios.

"Can you pull up pictures of the area?" Recker said.

"Thanks to our friend, Google, yes we can. What are you looking for in particular?"

"Anything in the area where someone could see the house if possible."

"You mean a lookout?"

"Yeah."

Jones did a three-sixty with the pictures of the area, but it didn't appear to do much good. Recker sighed, not satisfied with their findings. "I was hoping for an empty building, an office, or an apartment or something," Recker said, sounding frustrated. "Just other homes across the street."

"Well, on the outside at least. Let me verify that none of those are vacant."

"I'm gonna go there and take a look around and talk to them."

"Are you sure that's wise?" Jones asked, concerned about his presence there.

"I'll just walk around the area first and gauge the situation."

"I'll keep digging and let you know if I find anything of value. I'll have to figure out a way to talk to them somehow."

"How about by phone?"

"I thought you just said their phones might be tapped?"

"The far side drawer there." Jones pointed.

Recker went to the last drawer at the end of the desk and opened it, revealing five phones. "What's this?"

"Prepaid cell phones," Jones said. "I figured we should stock up on some in case of emergencies. If you could somehow get one of them to one of the Ridley's, that would solve the issue of potential phone tapping."

"You know, you're sneakier than you appear," Recker joked.

Jones went into another drawer and took out a small square device and held it in his hand. "Here, you might need this."

"What is it?" Recker asked, taking it from his hand.

"It's a listening device. If you touch base with Ridley, convince him to put this on his phone, and if the kidnappers call, we can hear their conversation."

Recker put the device in his pocket, then grabbed one of the phones from the drawer. He then left the office in order to go to the Ridley residence. He drove half an hour to get there and found an empty parking spot along the street on the same block as the Ridley house. He got out of his truck and milled around on the sidewalk, not getting too close to the house yet. At first, he just wanted to get a sense of the surroundings and see if he could notice anyone else that might've been eyeballing the house besides him.

He walked down the street, past the Ridley house, glancing in cars as he passed them by to see if anyone was in them. Once he walked a couple of blocks, he came back up the street, taking notice of nearby buildings and windows, not to mention the rooftops. He didn't notice anything suspicious, but he couldn't be positive. He didn't want to just go up to the Ridley house and have alarm bells start sounding if someone was watching.

He figured he'd do the next best thing to avoid suspicion. He went door to door, pretending to put something in the mailbox, hoping to pass for a salesman or marketer of some kind. He didn't knock on any doors or talk to anybody. This way, if someone was watching him, if he went to every house, they wouldn't suspect him of helping the Ridley's. Once he got to the house, he knocked very loudly and hit the buzzer on the door. He then put the phone down on the ground in front of the door and walked away. Recker walked a couple of blocks until he came to a coffee house and went inside, where he called the phone that he just dropped off.

"Hello?" the man's voice hesitantly answered.

"Mr. Ridley?"

"Yes. Who's this?"

"A friend."

"Are you one of the ones who has Mara?"

"No. I'm here to help you get her back. Meet me down the street at the coffeehouse. I don't want to be seen around your house in case they have someone watching," Recker told him.

"How do I know you're not setting me up for something?"

"The only thing I want is to help get your daughter back."

"They said no cops," Ridley said.

"I'm not a cop."

"Then who are you? How would you know about this if you're not working with them?"

"Come meet me and I'll explain it to you."

"Why do I need to? As soon as I give them the money, they'll give me Mara back anyway," Ridley said.

"That's a very big leap of faith you're taking. Putting a lot of trust in the words of criminals who just abducted your daughter."

"What other choice do I have?"

"Let me help. Maybe I can find them and get Mara back before you give them the money," Recker said.

"What if it goes wrong and they do something to her? I can't take that chance. If it was my life, maybe, but not with hers."

"What happens if you give them the money, then after they have it, they kill the both of you?"

"Why would they do that?"

"Because you didn't involve police or anybody on the outside," Recker said. "They could kill anyone with knowledge of the kidnapping after they get the money and the police would never know there was one."

Ridley was silent for a few seconds, thinking about the situation. He didn't know what to do. All he wanted was for Mara's safe return. He initially thought as long as he paid the money, they would give her back. But if the stranger he was talking to was to be believed, after the kidnappers got the money, they might kill her anyway.

"Where are you again?" Ridley said finally agreeing to a meeting

"Coffee house down the street."

"When?"

"Now."

"How will I know you?"

"I'll know you," Recker said. "As soon as you walk in, turn to your left. I'm the third table."

"I'll be there in a few minutes."

Ridley wasted no time in getting there. He didn't even tell his wife what he was doing. He just told her he was going to get a coffee, not wanting to either upset her or get her hopes up. He walked the couple of blocks to the coffee shop, taking about ten minutes to get there. Ridley walked in and immediately looked to his left, seeing a man in a black trench coat sitting by himself and drinking a coffee, three tables down. Ridley cautiously approached the table, not quite sure what he was getting into, and nervous that the man wasn't really there to help him. Recker saw him as soon as he walked in the building and took a sip of his coffee as Ridley reached the table. Ridley moved a chair out and sat down, waiting for the other man to say something. Recker could see the fear in his eyes as he sat across from him. Not of him, though. Fear of losing his daughter.

"If you're not working with them, how do you know what's happening?" Ridley said, breaking the silence.

"I have resources that alert me to difficult problems where the police are not concerned."

"I don't really understand what that means."

"I know, but I don't really have time to explain it to you. The longer we sit here the longer it takes me to find your daughter," Recker said.

"Why do you want to help? What's it gonna cost me?"

"Nothing. I don't want anything from you."

"Then why would you be doing this?"

"I'm already employed by a public security firm. I go to work when things get tough,"

"What if they followed me here?"

"They would probably think you're getting coffee. There's no cops, we're not next to a window, you're fine. Besides, I canvassed the neighborhood and didn't see anything out of the ordinary."

"So they're not watching?" Ridley shook his head.

"Well, I can't guarantee that they're not so we'll just go under the assumption that they are just to be safe."

"So what are you gonna do?"

"First, do you have any idea who might be behind this?"

"No," Ridley answered with another head shake. "No one."

"Friends? Relatives? Co-workers? Anybody who's threatened you before? Anything?"

Continuing to shake his head, Ridley couldn't think of anyone. "My wife and I have banged our heads against the wall all day trying to think of something. Neither of us can come up with anyone."

"There has to be a connection somewhere. Neither of you are famous so it's not like they saw you on TV or something. Somewhere along the way, someone became aware of your situation and thought it'd benefit them."

"But who?"

"Anyone come to the house in the last couple of months to do work on it? Cable guy, electrician, anybody?" Recker asked.

Ridley leaned on the table with his hand over his mouth, racking his brain to remember. "Not that I recall."

"Difficult clients? Anybody unhappy with your work and maybe threaten you or anything?"

"No. Nothing."

"Recognize the guy's voice on the phone? The one that left the message."

"No," Ridley said, shaking his head.

"Involved in anything political? Maybe your views on something pissed someone off?"

"No. My wife and I work, then we come home to our family. No outside clubs or anything like that."

"Personal grudges, affairs, angry relatives that have been locked up or anything?"

Ridley shook his head again, "still nothing. Like I said, we've been over this all day, we can't come up with anything."

"What about the nanny?"

"Meghan? What about her?"

"What do you know about her? How long has she been working for you?"

"You don't think she's mixed up in this, do you?" Ridley looked shocked at the thought.

"I don't know. I'm just trying to find a connection or a link somewhere. If it's not with you, maybe it's with her."

"She's a sweet girl. I can't imagine she'd be mixed up in something like this."

"Maybe she is and doesn't know it," Recker said patiently. "Maybe it's someone from her past or background who knew her and found out who she was working for and thought it'd be an easy score."

"I hadn't thought about that. I just assumed it was because of us."

"Well, it might be. We have to consider all the possibilities though. How do her and Mara get along?"

"Great," Ridley shrugged. "She's great with Mara, and Mara loves her."

"Does she take Mara out sometimes for any reason?"

"Yeah, occasionally, you know, the park, toy store, bookstore, just walk around the block, things like that."

"How'd you hire her?"

"She was recommended by friends of ours. She watched their child for a few months last year and they told us she was great with kids."

"So she hasn't been with you that long?" Recker asked.

"Uh, no, about eight or nine months I'd say."

"Who watched Mara before her?"

"Well, my mother watched Mara during the day for the first couple of years, then she got sick and passed away. Then we hired a woman who worked for us for about six or eight months," Ridley said.

"What happened with her?"

"Well, we thought she might've been stealing things. Nothing big, just small things. We thought she might've been taking things and selling them. And we got the feeling she wasn't being honest. You know, if I gave her twenty dollars to take Mara out, I thought she might've been spending like five of it and pocketing the rest."

"So you fired her?"

"Well, it was nothing heated or anything like that. We just told her we didn't think it was working out and wanted to go in a different direction. Plus Mara didn't really like her that much."

"What's her name?"

"Deanna Ambersome."

"Have her address or phone number?" Recker had his phone out ready to take on the details.

"Uh, not on me, no. I can get it though. I think we have it back at the house."

"OK. I want you to go back home and get her information for me. When you get it, you call me on the phone I gave you with the number that's in there."

"You don't want me to just go get it and come back?"

"No. Coming back here again would be suspicious if someone's watching. Just use the phone I gave you. It's not traceable and they don't know you have it. If you think of anything else, no matter how small or trivial, I want you to contact me."

"OK," Ridley said. "What are you gonna do now?"

"Now I'm gonna do some background investigation."

"On Meghan and Deanna?"

"It's a start."

"Will you let me know if you find anything?"

"You'll hear from me. Just keep doing what you were doing like I wasn't involved."

"Should I let my wife know?"

"That's up to you. There's one more thing," Recker said, digging into his pocket, taking out the listening device and showing it to Ridley.

"What's that?"

"It's a listening device. Put it on your phone when you get home. When the kidnappers call again, we'll be able to hear what they say. We also might be able to get a line on where they're calling from."

"I just can't believe this is happening. You hear about things like this... but you never dream it'll be you," Ridley said, taking the square device out of Recker's hand.

"I'll get her back for you. You weren't picked at random. Someone knows something or is involved somehow. I'm gonna find out who."

10

Recker and Jones spent most of the night finding information on both Meghan Carkner and Deanna Ambersome. They worked up until midnight before calling it a night. The following morning, Recker got back to the office about five. He figured he would've beat Jones in. He was surprised that when he got there, Jones was already knee deep in work.

"And here I thought I was gonna beat you in for once," Recker said.

"Perhaps if I had actually left, you would've accomplished your goal."

"You mean you've been here working all night?"

"Well, I went on the couch for two or three hours." Jones' baggy eyes told the story just as well as words.

"I thought when we left last night that you were leaving right after me?"

"That was my intention. But I just couldn't tear myself away. There's a little girl's life that may be at stake. Me losing a few hours of sleep is hardly significant compared to that. I can always catch up after this case is over. Besides, that was one of the reasons I got the couches in here. Long nights are inevitable sometimes."

Recker nodded, agreeing, and understanding his point. He wound up only sleeping about three hours himself. He was hoping that he'd be able to turn the tables on Jones and give him the information this time.

"Find out anything yet?"

"Indeed, I have," Jones said, turning around. "I've cross checked everything I've been able to get my hands on to verify what Mr. Ridley told you about them not having problems with anyone. As far as I can tell, that's completely accurate. He was also correct in that they've had no work done in their home that I can find."

"So that leaves us the nannies?"

"Meghan Carkner, twenty-four years old, college graduate in education from Temple."

"Any sketchy characters in her family tree?"

"None that I can find. Mom, dad, brother, none have ever had any brushes with the law, other than the odd speeding ticket," Jones turned back to his screen.

"How about a boyfriend?" Recker said, looking for an angle.

"Currently single. No exes that would seem to fit the profile."

"Why do I get the feeling you're saving the best for last?"

"Because I am." Jones smiled.

"Deanna Ambersome, twenty-eight years old. Before she became a nanny for the Ridley's, she worked in retail and was fired from two different employers after she was found stealing merchandise."

"That would jive with what the Ridley's thought about her and why they fired her. That doesn't really prove anything, though,"

Recker said. "It's a long leap from stealing merchandise where you work to kidnapping somebody's child."

"Her family background would make her a more convincing candidate, however."

"What you got?"

"Mom's been in and out of jail several times for both drug possession and intent to sell. Dad's currently in prison for armed robbery."

"Sounds like a model family."

Jones put his hand up to continue. "Wait, it gets better. She currently has a boyfriend who's been in jail twice, once for assault and once for a home invasion."

"Home invasion? Small jump from that to kidnapping," Recker thought they might finally be on to something.

"There's also a brother. He's also been in jail once for burglary."

"The family that crimes together."

Recker sat on the edge of the desk and batted his eyes around the room, letting all the information that he just heard sink in. Jones swiveled his chair around to face his partner.

"What are your thoughts?" Jones wondered.

"I'd say we definitely have a couple of good suspects. The background is there."

"So, Deanna was upset at being shown the door and sought to get even somehow?"

"Sounds about right," Recker said.

A painful look took over Jones' face as he tried to understand the motivations. "Even if that's the case, why take a little girl? I mean, she has nothing to do with anything. Why do you put her in harm's way to get back at the parents, even if you feel they wronged you in some way?"

"You're trying to think like a normal, logical, caring person.

These people aren't any of those things. Remember what I told you. Mara and Deanna didn't really hit it off, anyway. The child means nothing to her. She has no attachment to her. If they did this, she doesn't really care what happens to her at this point. It's just a means to make money and get back at the people who fired you," Recker said. "Can you work your magic to find out where all those people are at right now?"

Jones turned back to the computer and started pounding away on the keyboard again. "Working on it as we speak."

While Jones was busy trying to dig up their addresses, Recker went over to the gun cabinet. He opened it and examined his choices. He pulled out two pistols and an assault rifle, plus plenty of ammunition for each. He set them down on the desk as Jones continued to work his magic.

"Got it," Jones excitedly said.

"Where are they?"

"Looks like Deanna and her boyfriend are currently renting a three bedroom twin home in Frankford."

"I'll send the address to your phone," Jones said, looking at the weapons on the desk. "Do you really think you'll need all that?"

"Like I always say, I like to be prepared. If they're there, and Mara's there, they may not want to go away quietly. And I'm not leaving until I have that child," Recker replied.

"Should I accompany you as backup?"

Recker smiled at the notion, but didn't think Jones would be much help if a gunfight broke out. He'd probably be more of a liability than not, as it'd be one more person Recker would have to look after.

"You'll be better off here. Besides, if they're not there, that'll take you out of the game for a little while. You're of more use right where you're at. I can handle whatever's there." Recker smiled at him by way of encouragement.

Recker grabbed his guns, putting the pistols in their holsters, while putting the rifle in a bag to conceal it. He checked his phone on the way to the parking lot for directions. Ambersome and her boyfriend had a house rented on Bermuda Street. He drove a little faster than usual, wanting to get there as quickly as possible, just in case Mara was there and arrived just over twenty minutes later. He found the address and parked along the street a few houses down. He got out of his truck and hid the rifle inside his trench coat. He stood a few houses away from Ambersome's address, waiting to see if he noticed any activity in the building. It was a two story, brick lined building with a covered porch. There were two white chairs just in front of the window. It seemed to be a decent area, all the homes appeared well kept, no shuttered or abandoned houses that Recker could tell. He waited about ten minutes without seeing any movement from in or around the house. Assuming he wasn't likely to see anything else, Recker started walking toward the house. He got to the porch and put his left foot on the first step leading up to it, putting his right hand on the pistol inside his coat. He turned his head slightly, trying to hear anything from inside the house. He picked his head up when the door to the neighboring house swung open, a woman stepping onto her porch. Recker sized her up for a minute to make sure she wasn't a threat. She appeared to be in her fifties, and had a newspaper in her hand as she sat down on her rocker. The woman looked at the stranger stepping onto the neighbor's porch and wondered what he was up to. He looked like a cop, so she didn't say anything to him. Now fully on the porch, Recker stood next to the window out of sight, and carefully looked inside.

"Nobody's home," the neighbor finally said.

Recker looked over at her, then back inside the window again. Satisfied that he was leveling with her, he stopped looking through the window and walked over to the small metal fence that separated the two porches. "You know the people that live here?"

"Yeah. You a cop?" she asked.

"Do I look like one?"

"Yeah."

"Then there's your answer," Recker said.

"Which one you looking for?"

"Deanna and her boyfriend,"

"What do you want them for?"

"Routine investigation. Their names have come up as suspects in a case I'm working on and I need to talk to them."

"Good luck with that. They ain't been here in at least a couple of weeks," she said.

"Really? How many people have been living here?"

"Just Deanna and her boyfriend. Her brother comes around a lot too."

"You know where they might've gone?"

The woman shook her head, "no idea. Me and them weren't friends. I'm glad they haven't been around. Maybe their lease ran out, not sure."

"Why is that? They cause a lot of trouble?" Recker wondered.

"Nothing too bad. Just a lot of small stuff, you know? Music too loud, parties late at night, that sort of thing. Actually, now that I think about it..." She hesitated.

"What's that?"

"A few weeks ago, just before they disappeared, I heard them talking on the porch. I was inside, but they were talking loud enough for me to hear."

"What were they talking about?"

"I'm not sure. Seemed like a big disagreement at first, but the boyfriend smoothed it over."

"What were they saying?"

"Couldn't hear everything clearly, but the boyfriend said something like, 'if we do this right and pull it off, we'll never have to worry about money again'. Sounded like they were gonna rob a bank or something."

"Well, I got a warrant here to search the house, so I'll be in there for a little while," Recker told her.

"They didn't really rob a bank, did they?" The woman looked worried.

"No. Something a lot worse."

Recker didn't say another word and kicked the door open. Before entering, he looked back at the neighbor and smiled.

"Aren't there supposed to be a lot more of you during these searches?" the woman said. "On TV, there's always like ten or fifteen guys looking through houses."

"We're a little shorthanded today," Recker said. "Couple of the guys called in sick."

Recker went inside and started turning the place inside out. It was already a little messy, a few dirty clothes on the floor and whatnot. He threw the cushions off the couches, looked through cabinets and closets, searched all the rooms, looking for any piece of evidence he could find that would indicate where the suspects had gone off to. He spent an hour in the home, going through each room several times, just in case he missed anything the previous time. Unfortunately, he wasn't able to find a single shred of evidence of where they were going. Not a piece of paper, not a receipt, no credit card statements, nothing at all. Recker sighed and shook his head, frustrated that he wasn't able to find anything. Standing in the middle of the living room, he let Jones know of his findings.

"Professor, just got done tossing the place," Recker said.

"And how did you fare?"

"Came up empty. They were either very careful, or just lucky, that they didn't leave anything behind."

"Or they didn't yet know where they were going," Jones said. It was a fair point.

"Kidnapping a child and asking for ransom isn't something you do on a whim. You need a plan. A good one. And it needs to be in place before everything unfolds."

"I'll start checking former addresses on my end. They didn't, by chance, leave any computers behind, did they?"

"No."

"Too bad. If they had, I could've searched through their history and possibly come up with their current location from there."

"No such luck," Recker said. "We'll have to do some more digging. What about cell phones?"

"I've already checked into that. It appears they've smartly gone with the prepaid variety. Even if they hadn't, the signals bounce off towers, I wouldn't be able to get an exact location anyway, just a general area."

"Better than anything we got right now. What about credit cards? Can you track them?"

"Yes, I could. But that would presume they had them and were using them."

"So they're not?"

"They have them, though they're currently over their spending limits," Jones said.

"So I take it that they're not using them."

"That would be correct."

"I don't suppose the boyfriend or brother have current jobs, do they?" Recker asked, not confident about the answer.

"They do not. At least, not of the legal variety."

"Man, we're really striking out here."

"Why don't you come back to the office and we'll figure out a plan from there?"

Recker did as Jones wished and went back to the office, where both of them worked the computers, shuffling back and forth between several computers at a time. Once they found the former addresses of Ambersome, her boyfriend, and her brother, Recker went to each location, hoping to turn up one of them. Since posing as a cop worked the first time, he played the part again, hoping it'd work just as well. He spent most of the day checking out the addresses, driving all over the city. Just like the first time, though, each one turned up nothing of value. Each house was occupied by either new tenants or homeowners, none of whom knew the current whereabouts of the people who lived there before they did. The cop routine worked again as well, somewhat surprisingly to Recker.

After exhausting the search of their former addresses, Recker and Jones spent the rest of the night in the office, still continuing their search. Once again, they worked right up until midnight. This time, neither one of them left to go home. They both took up residence on one of the couches to get a few hours of sleep. Recker woke up around five from the sound of the door closing. It was Jones with a couple of cups of coffee, fresh from the neighborhood convenience store. Recker sat up on the couch as Jones handed him his cup, taking a few minutes to fully wake up.

"What time'd you get up?" Recker asked.

"About four."

Recker shook his head. Jones had beaten him again. Jones sat down at the desk and started to work, still trying to find any connection to their suspects. A few minutes later, Recker joined him at the desk, taking one of the other computers. Throughout the entire morning, anytime they came up with a lead, even the smallest of leads, Recker went out to run it down. Each time was as frustrating as the time before. Ambersome and her cohorts didn't seem to be the type of criminals who'd excel at covering their tracks since it wasn't their usual type of crime, but they appeared to be doing a masterful job at it. Recker got back to the office at noon, and he wasn't in the greatest of spirits. Jones picked up on his mood as soon as he walked in and attempted to lift it. He called him over to the desk immediately to see what he picked up on.

"This just came in about five minutes ago," Jones said, playing an audio file. "It's from the device Mr. Ridley put on his phone."

"Have you got the money yet?" The same voice as before.

"I've only got some of it," Ridley said. "The rest is gonna take a couple more days."

"Your daughter doesn't have a couple more days!"

"Please, I'm trying to come up with it quickly. It takes time though. I don't just have that much money in the bank. It takes a couple of days to sell everything and get the money in my account."

"I don't wanna hear excuses. You have until five o'clock tomorrow night. If you don't have it by then, you might as well start making reservations for the cemetery, cause that's where your daughter will end up!"

"Please, no! I've done as you've asked. I haven't brought in cops or anything. Please, just don't hurt her."

"No more excuses."

Nothing but silence came after that. "Is that it?" Recker said.

"Yes." Jones smiled. "But it was enough for me to get a small trace on it."

"You got their location?" Recker said, surprised, hope in his voice.

"No. Not quite. It wasn't long enough for me to do that. I can tell that it's somewhere in the city though."

Recker slumped into a chair, dejected. "That really doesn't tell us anything then. We already knew that. We're not any closer to finding her than we were two days ago."

"Don't lose faith, Michael. Us getting frustrated won't help get Mara back," Jones said.

"I know. Time's running out, though. You able to turn up anything else?"

"Not so far."

Ten more minutes went by, Recker contemplating their options. He had an idea that might work. He'd need the cooperation of some unlikely people who might not be all that willing to help.

"If the Ridley's don't come up with that money by tomorrow, what do you think will happen?" Jones said, thinking aloud.

"Depends on the kidnappers. If they're greedy and want all of it, they might be willing to wait an extra day or two for Ridley to get it. Or, if they're getting jumpy and just want to move on, they might just tell him to bring what he's got and be done with it. Or, there's a third option."

"Which is?"

"They could not bother with it anymore and cut bait," Recker said.

"You mean they could kill Mara?"

Recker nodded. "It's a possibility."

"We can't let that happen."

"Or there's another option," Recker said.

"Which is?"

"Even if Ridley doesn't have the money, we tell him to tell them that he does. Then when he makes the exchange, I take out whoever's there."

"That could be risky."

"Could be. They might not bring Mara to the exchange site in case they expect funny business. If she's at another location, and the cash doesn't show up, they might cut their losses and go."

"Which do you think would be the best way to go?"

"To find her before any of that takes place," Recker said.

"Then we'll have to bear down."

Then, Recker decided to blurt out what he was thinking. "There's one other thing we can try."

"What's that?"

"Remember what I told you before? All this computer stuff is great, but sometimes it doesn't beat intelligence on the street and having contacts."

"How does that come into play now?"

"I'll use the contacts I have to find her."

"Are you referring to Mr. Gibson and Jeremiah?" Jones said, a tone of disbelief in his voice.

"They know the streets. They might know something. That's not all. Tyrell also knows Vincent, he's a major player in the northeast. If they're in his territory, he might know something about it or where they're at."

"You're taking a very big leap of faith, don't you think?"

"No. Not a leap of faith. A leap of desperation," Recker said. "We're running out of leads and we're running out of time. So is Mara. I'm willing to do just about anything at this point to find out where she is. Even if that means conversing with the underworld."

"You actually think they'd be willing to help?"

Recker shrugged. "Only one way to know… ask."

11

Recker and Jones deliberated the merits of asking the gang leaders to assist in their search of Mara Ridley. They would almost certainly want something in return for their help, assuming they would be willing to begin with. If they did, they'd have to deal with that when the time came. Deanna Ambersome, her boyfriend, Derrick, and her brother, Marcus, had effectively disappeared. They had to utilize all available options that they had at their disposal. Recker took out his phone and called Gibson.

"Hey, need you to do me a favor," Recker said.

"What? You need a tank? A bazooka?" Gibson said sarcastically. "How about an F-15?"

"Could you get me one?"

"No, I can't get you a plane!"

"Never hurts to ask."

"So, whatcha want?" Gibson said.

"I need to meet with Jeremiah and Vincent,"

"At the same time?!" Gibson was shocked at the request.

"Doesn't have to be. Separate will work."

"What do you want them for?"

"Business."

"You're gonna have to do better than that, man. They're gonna ask me and I'm gonna have to tell them something. Me saying 'business' ain't gonna get it done," Gibson said. "They're not gonna meet unless they got a legit reason to."

"OK, fine. There's a little girl that's been kidnapped and being held for ransom. Her life may be in danger. The exchange is supposed to go down tomorrow at five. I'd like to get to them before that."

"So what exactly do you want them to do?"

"I just wanna know if they might have any intel on what's going on or if they've heard any rumblings. If they're the kings of their turf, maybe they know something."

"I'm not sure they're gonna give two hoots about some kid missing," Gibson said.

"She's an innocent four-year-old child, Tyrell. Imagine if that was your brother missing."

"All right, man, all right. I'll put the word out. I can't guarantee anything though."

"All you can do is try."

"What time you looking for?"

"As soon as possible," Recker said.

"All right. I'll get back to you if I hear anything."

Recker put his phone down on the desk and stared at the wall, thinking about his upcoming meetings with the two crime bosses. Though he didn't know how it'd turn out, he was fairly certain the two of them would at least meet with him and hear what he had to say. Jones finished up what he was doing on the laptop before inquiring about Recker's conversation.

"What did Mr. Gibson have to say?"

"He'll put the word out and get back to me if he hears something."

"What do you think?"

"They'll agree to meet," Recker said confidently.

"What makes you so sure?"

"Curiosity. Plus, I haven't met Vincent yet, and if he's heard about me, which I'm assuming he has, he'll want to finally meet face to face."

"You think they'll help?"

"Maybe."

"You may have to sweeten the pot for them," Jones said.

"We'll see."

An hour went by and Recker had just returned to the office with a couple of sandwiches for the two of them for lunch. They ate while they worked and quickly downed the turkey club. As the last bite of the sandwich went down Recker's throat, he took a sip of his soda to wash it down. His phone started ringing, and he wiped his hands off before answering.

"What's up, Tyrell?" Recker had his fingers crossed for good news.

"You owe me for this one, you know that right?"

"I'll make it good."

"All right, Jeremiah said he'll meet with you in an hour," Gibson said.

"Where at?"

"Same place as before. You remember it?"

"I'll be there. What about Vincent?"

"I'm still waiting to hear back from him. I'll let you know."

"Thanks."

Recker hung up and immediately informed Jones that the meeting with Jeremiah was all set. Though he wasn't yet sure exactly what he was going to say to him, Recker went through a couple of different scenarios in his mind. Both positive and negative ones. Though he was accustomed to high leverage situations, Recker was still a little anxious for the hour to pass. Most of the times when he was looking for someone, it was to kill them. This time was different. This time, it was to save a life. One that he had no personal connection to, but one that he felt a certain responsibility for. Even though the Ridley's didn't initially ask for his help, with his skills and his past history, he felt he should be able to handle these types of situations.

After a few minutes, Recker left the office to drive to the meeting. He wanted to get there a few minutes early, just in case there was traffic. He got to the house about five minutes early and saw the red bandana on the boarded-up window. He started walking up the concrete path toward the door when he noticed it opening slightly. A large man appeared in the doorway, waiting for him to arrive. Once he got there, the man put his arm out, directing Recker into the living room. There, Recker saw the same table and chairs they did business at before. He took a quick look around the room and noticed Gibson was absent. Surrounded by five of Jeremiah's men, scattered throughout the room, Jeremiah was seated at the end of the table, waiting for his visitor.

"So what do I owe this pleasure?" Jeremiah asked. "Tyrell said something about a missing kid."

Recker pulled a chair out and sat down across from him. "A four year old girl was kidnapped. I'm trying to find her and bring her home."

"What's in it for you? Why do you care?"

"Let's just say I have a rooting interest in it," Recker said.

"The family hire you to get her?"

"Uh, let's just say I'm working with them."

"So is that what you're doing here? Working for the highest bidder? Mercenary? Gun for hire?"

"I'm not for hire."

Jeremiah grinned at the seemingly always coy man across from him. "Tell me about this girl you're looking for."

"Parents live on Spruce Street. Suspects are Deanna Ambersome, Derrick Ianetta, and Marcus Ambersome. All have lengthy rap sheets."

"So you can't find them and you want my help?"

"That's pretty much the size of it," Recker said.

"What makes you think I know?"

Recker shrugged. "I don't. If you've done business with them, if you know of them, if you know what happened, I just thought maybe you'd heard something."

"What makes you think I care about some high rollers on the other side of town?" Jeremiah wondered.

"Because it's not about her parents, or you, or me," Recker said, stating his case. "The only thing it's about... is the life of a four-year-old child. That should go beyond anything. Race doesn't matter, wealth doesn't matter, location doesn't matter. The only thing that matters, is that the life of an innocent little girl is in danger. That should take precedence over anything. Now, I know you got your code that you live by, just like I've got mine. But when a child's life is in danger, any child, any bravado that we imply should go right out the window."

Jeremiah was silent as he let Recker speak his mind. He put his index finger on his mouth and rubbed his lip as he listened, not taking his eyes off the former military man. "You should've went into politics. That was a nice speech."

"Only difference is I meant every word."

Jeremiah glanced around the room as he thought about it. "Only problem is that I don't know them."

"It was worth a shot."

"I'll do one for you though," Jeremiah said. "I don't know these cats, but I'll have my boys put the word out on the streets."

"I'd appreciate that," Recker said.

Jeremiah nodded to one of his men to come over. "Start putting the word out to the boys and see if they know anything about a missing kid from Spruce. What were the names again?"

"Deanna and Marcus Ambersome, and Derrick Ianetta," Recker said.

"See if anyone knows them," Jeremiah told one of his soldiers. "If any of my boys know them or know where they're at, then I'll let you know."

"Good enough for me."

"I want something in return though."

Recker was starting to get up, but sat back down, anticipating a favor request might be coming. "What do you want?"

"Information."

"About what?"

"You," Jeremiah told him. "You played sly with me before about what you were doing here. I wanna know why you're here. You do that, I'll consider us even."

"There's only so much I can say."

"Tell me what you can."

"I've been hired by a private security firm to provide protection to certain individuals that they feel need it," Recker explained.

"Like this kid?"

Recker shrugged. "They tell me the assignment, I go do it."

"That's all there is to it?"

"That's it."

"So how do I contact this security firm? Maybe I'd like additional protection," Jeremiah said.

Recker smiled. "Not quite how it works. You don't hire them. They find their own clients."

"Or clients with criminal records?"

"That too." Recker grinned. "We good now?"

Jeremiah nodded. "Yeah. Yeah, we're good. For now."

Recker left the house and went back to his truck. He called Jones to let him know how the meeting went. After his conversation with the professor was over, he started driving back to the office. He'd only driven for a couple of minutes when his phone rang again. Stopped at a red light, he answered it.

"Tyrell?" he greeted. "Missed you at Jeremiah's."

"Yeah, well, I was busy setting other things up for you."

"Oh yeah?"

"Vincent agreed to meet with you," Gibson confirmed.

"Well that's good news."

"Yeah, well, we'll find out whether it's good or not when you're finished."

"Where and when?" Recker asked.

"There's a diner in the northeast in Mayfair called Pete's Place."

"Do all the diners in this city have first names?"

"What?"

"Nothing. What time?"

"They said now."

"I'm on my way."

"I'll give 'em the heads up," Gibson said.

Recker changed his course and drove the half hour to the diner. It wasn't a big place, and it didn't appear to be that busy since the parking lot was half empty. As Recker walked toward the entrance, it appeared that one of Vincent's men was standing guard at the door. If not, it'd be the first time he ever recalled a guard at the door of a diner. He certainly had the scowl of a mob henchman.

"You the man meeting Vincent?" the man asked.

"Maybe," said Recker.

The man put his hand out. "Need your iron."

Recker balked at the request and took a step back, ready for action if that's how the guy wanted to play it. "I don't hand my guns over to anybody."

"You'll get them back when you're finished."

Recker contemplated whether he wanted to comply with the request.

"Nobody sees the boss who's packing," the man said.

After a minute of deliberating, Recker thought it was best to agree. If time wasn't of the essence, and it wasn't regarding the life of a child, he might've just decided to take off. But now wasn't the time to balk and run. Recker reached inside his coat and handed his Sig over.

"And the other one," the man said, holding his hand out.

Recker grinned. "What makes you think there's another one?"

The man looked at him funny, like he thought he was some kind of sucker or something. "The other one."

Recker reached back into his coat and pulled out his Glock, handing it to the burly man.

"They'll be here when you come out." The guard held both guns in one hand.

As soon as Recker entered the diner, he was met by another man. This time it was Jimmy Malloy, Vincent's right-hand man and second in command. He didn't say a word to Recker, instead, just holding his arm out to guide Recker along. Malloy led him down to Vincent's table, a booth in the corner by the window. Vincent was about what Recker expected. He appeared to be in his mid-forties with short brown hair, and starting to go bald in front. Dressed in a suit, sans the tie, he looked the part of an organized crime leader. He was having a plate of spaghetti, soup on the side, as Recker sat down across from him. Vincent continued eating for a minute, looking at his companion as he did so.

Vincent wiped his mouth with a napkin before starting to talk. "So you're the man I've been hearing about," he said, smiling as if he just opened a present at Christmas.

"Could be."

"So you're Recker. I have the feeling you know more about me than I do of you."

"Possible."

"What's your first name?"

"Michael."

"Which nickname do you prefer? The man with the trench coat, trench coat man, or the latest one I read about, what was it... The Silencer?"

Recker smiled.

"I prefer The Silencer," Vincent said. "It's catchy, has a good ring to it." Vincent put his hand up and looked disgusted about something. "Where are my manners? Here I am eating in front of you and I didn't even offer you something. Would you like something? Soup, sandwich, some pasta?"

"I'm good. I've already eaten."

"Are you sure? They do serve a very good soup here."

"I'm fine."

"Sorry about having to take your guns, but it's for my own protection. I always do that when I'm meeting people I don't know for the first time."

"It's OK. I don't need them to kill," Recker said. "Just makes it easier and quicker."

Vincent grinned at his confidence and ate another forkful of his spaghetti before continuing. "So what brings you here to me?"

Recker cleared his throat before answering. "There's a four-year-old girl that was kidnapped a couple of days ago. I'm trying to find the people who took her before something bad happens."

Vincent nodded as he chewed his food. "Admirable of you. Why? What are the circumstances?"

"Kidnappers are looking for a million dollars by tomorrow at five o'clock."

"Do the parents have the capability of paying?"

"Not in the timeframe they're looking for," Recker said. "In any case, even if they can, I'm not sure they'll hand the girl over."

"So you think they might kill the girl either way?"

"I think it's possible. And I'd rather find them before we have the chance of finding out."

"Considering I haven't heard of this, I'm assuming the authorities have been left out of this arrangement?"

"Yes."

"I'm unclear what you think I can do for you," Vincent said, wiping his mouth with a napkin.

"I heard you were in charge of this territory. They might be in this area. They used to rent a house down in Frankford. Maybe you heard about it, or know where they might be."

"What makes you think I'm not involved in some way?"

"I don't know. I guess I just figured someone like you wouldn't stoop low enough to kidnap a child for ransom," Recker said.

"You're an intriguing man, Mike." Vincent fixed him with a stare. "You don't mind if I call you Mike, do you? What drives you to do this?"

"Do what?"

"This thing you're doing. Helping people. So far, I've read about you stopping rapists, murderers, robberies, even an arson."

"That's my job," Recker said as plainly as he could.

"How is it that you seem to keep appearing at that exact time of need when someone's in trouble?"

"Just seems to happen that way." Recker shrugged.

"I bet. You've got some type of inside information somehow that allows you to be there. Very ingenious."

"Luck more than anything."

Vincent shook his head. "No, I don't believe that. I don't believe luck has anything to do with it. You make your own luck in this business, or any other for that matter. People like to say it's luck, whether something good or bad happens, so they don't have to take responsibility for it. But it's anything but luck. It's the choices you make that put you in that position, in that very moment, when that supposed luck occurs."

Recker nodded, agreeing with his point of view.

"You work on your own? Have a team? Or a boss?"

"Well, you have your secrets, I have mine."

Vincent smiled. "So what is it exactly that you want me to do?"

"Put the word out and see if any of your men or contacts know where they are. I'm not looking for anything except information. If you find their location, let me know, I'll take care of the rest."

"Going to kill them?"

"Unless they decide to give themselves up, I imagine that's what it'll come down to," Recker assumed.

"Why do you think I'd even be willing to help you?" Vincent forked some spaghetti.

"After meeting you, you seem like an intelligent man, well dressed, like to eat well… what I can't figure out yet, is what you're willing to do to protect yourself."

"I'm not sure I understand your meaning."

"You like having money, power, having people look up to you and fearing you. I would think someone as smart as you would understand that things like this would bring heat on you. If that kid gets killed in your territory, that's gonna bring a lot of heat from the police in this area, not to mention the bigger media presence. If you like to operate in the background, that wouldn't exactly be good for business. Plus, if something like that goes down without your knowledge, people will start questioning whether you're actually in control. That wouldn't exactly be good for your little empire, especially since you're trying to expand your power base," Recker said.

"What makes you think I'm looking to expand my power? What makes you think I'm not content with what I have?"

"You hear things. People are never content with what they have. People who have a little bit of power always want more. Human nature."

Vincent smiled, a pleased look on his face as Recker seemed to accurately describe him. "So do you have names for these people that you're looking for?" he asked, picking up his glass of beer.

"Deanna Ambersome, Marcus Ambersome, her brother, and Derrick Ianetta."

Vincent finished taking a sip from his glass and was halfway to putting it down when he heard the names. His arm froze, recognizing the last of the names, looking at Recker before turning his eyes back on his glass. Recker noticed his hesitation upon hearing the names and knew he struck a nerve.

"You know them?" Recker asked.

Vincent looked at Malloy before answering. The pleasant look on his face slowly disappeared, replaced by a look of disgust. "I know Derrick Ianetta. He's done some work for me in the past."

"You know where he's at?"

Vincent threw his hands up, "he's more of a freelancer. He's not a permanent member of my organization. He's done a few jobs for me but nothing recently. Haven't heard from him in a few months or so."

"Deanna's his girlfriend."

Vincent motioned for Malloy, sitting at a nearby table, to come over to them. "Derrick Ianetta. He kidnapped a child a few days ago and could be in the area," he said to him. "What were the others' names?"

"His girlfriend, Deanna Ambersome, and her brother, Marcus."

"Find them," Vincent said sternly.

"Yes, sir," Malloy said, leaving immediately.

"I guess I'll owe you a favor if you can find them," Recker said.

"We'll talk about that if we find them," Vincent told him. "Give me a number I can reach you in the event we do find them."

Recker grabbed one of the napkins on the table and wrote his number down on it. He slid it along the table in front of Vincent, who looked at it, then put it in his pocket. They concluded their business and Recker left the diner, making sure he picked his weapons up again from the guard at the door. He left in a better mood than he came in, sensing that they were now getting closer to finding Mara.

12

Though Recker and Jones continued their search for Mara, there really wasn't much more that they could do. They turned over all the leads that they could. Everything just came up empty. They didn't want to put all their faith in Jeremiah or Vincent, though, so they kept on plugging away. Mr. Ridley called Recker on the phone he gave him sometime during the night to ask about his progress, but Recker informed him that they hadn't found the kidnappers yet, though they were sure who was behind it. He did tell Ridley that they had a few more leads to track down and not to give up hope. The night passed, both of them sleeping in the office again. They woke up before the crack of dawn again. They passed on breakfast this time, neither having much of an appetite, knowing how high the stakes were about to become later in the day.

"I don't think I've ever rooted so hard for criminals to succeed in my life," Jones said.

Recker didn't respond to the comment, but agreed and understood the meaning behind it. A little after nine o'clock, Recker's phone rang, getting their hopes up before he saw who was calling. Hopes were quickly dashed when he saw it was Mia. Not that he was disappointed to talk to her, but he was hoping for news from one of the crime leaders.

"Hey," she said.

"Everything OK?"

"Yeah. Haven't seen or heard from you in a few days and I was thinking about you."

"Bored, huh?" he said.

Hendricks laughed. "No, nothing like that. I was just wondering if you wanted to get together for breakfast or something. I'm working the mid-shift today and just thought maybe we could get together."

"I'm sorry, I can't today. I'm not that hungry." Recker felt bad for turning her down.

"Oh." She sounded dejected. "Are you working a case?"

"Yeah." He kept it simple, not wanting to get into details.

"Maybe when it's finished then?" she said.

"Yeah, that sounds good."

"OK. I'll call you in a couple of days then?"

"Should be fine."

"OK. Talk to you then. Be careful."

"I will."

Once he saw Recker hanging up, Jones spoke up. "Are you sure it's wise to keep her involved?"

"She's not involved," Recker said.

"If she's close to you, then she's involved."

"I told you before, if something happens, it'd be good to have a nurse on our side to avoid a public hospital trip. She already knows about my past, we can trust her. Believe me, I have good instincts on who I can and can't trust."

Jones nodded. "I know. I guess I just don't want to see you get hurt again."

Recker smiled. "Professor, I didn't know you cared so much. I'm touched."

"Yes, well, let's see if we can get back to work and find Mara before it's too late."

They worked right up until noon, nothing new coming in. Recker went out to get them lunch since they were starving from missing breakfast. They got about halfway through when Recker's phone rang again. A look of hope dashed across Recker's face when he saw it was Tyrell. Maybe he had some good news for him.

"Tyrell, tell me you have something."

"Afraid not, man. Just talked to Jeremiah, and he wanted me to let you know that he came up with nothin'. He said his boys combed the streets but they have no idea where those bulls are."

Recker sighed. "I was afraid of that. Well, tell Jeremiah I said thanks for checking. I appreciate his help. You too, thanks for setting things up."

"Yeah, no sweat, man. Listen, I hope you find the girl. I really do."

"Yeah, me too," Recker said, and he meant it too.

By the sight of Recker's body language, Jones could sense that he'd gotten a negative answer from his contact. He asked the question anyway, just to be sure.

"I take it that didn't go as well as we would've hoped?"

"Yeah," Recker said, a hint of despair in his voice.

"Well, we still have Vincent."

Recker nodded, not having anything else to say.

"What do we do if Vincent doesn't find them by five?" Jones had been dying to ask but didn't want to jinx things.

"Then I'll accompany Ridley to the meeting place and try to make sure that everything goes according to plan."

"And if it doesn't?"

"Then I'll have to improvise." Recker's face was set in a hard stare.

Two more hours went by, neither man saying another word as they worried about what was about to happen in another couple of hours. A little after two thirty, Recker just about jumped off his chair in excitement when he heard his phone ringing. Since it was a number he didn't recognize, he thought it had to be Vincent.

"Hello?" Recker answered it, hoping he was right.

"Michael, good to hear your voice again," Vincent said pleasantly.

"I hope you have good news for me."

"Well, I have news. Whether it's good or not, I'll leave up to your judgment."

"OK?"

"A couple of my men have found two of them," Vincent said.

"Great. Where?"

"They're hiding out in a house over in Mayfair."

"Which ones?"

"Derrick and Deanna. I'm not sure about the other one yet."

"Question them yet?"

"We're about to go in in a few minutes. I thought I'd give you the courtesy of joining us in the discussions if you'd like," Vincent said, giving him the address.

"I can be there in twenty minutes."

Recker hung up and rushed over to the gun cabinet, eagerly trying to get himself ready.

"I take it we have good news?" Jones said, watching Recker move faster than he'd ever seen.

"Vincent found Deanna and Derrick in a house over in Mayfair. He's about to go in and question them now. I'm gonna go meet them."

"What about the brother?"

"No word about him yet," Recker said. "I'll let you know what we come up with."

Recker rushed out the door and down the steps, running to his truck with his bag of guns in hand. He peeled out of the parking lot and raced down the highway, jumping on I-95 to get there quicker. Once Recker turned onto the street, he immediately noticed Vincent's guys. They were hard to miss. There were about ten of them gathered in front of one particular house. Recker parked his truck, then walked toward the house.

"You Recker?" One of the men challenged him as he approached.

"Yeah."

"Boss is inside waiting for you."

Recker walked past the men and noticed Malloy standing in the frame of the doorway.

"You got here fast." Malloy grinned.

"I'm on the clock."

Malloy led him into the living room. Vincent was circling around Deanna and Derrick, seemingly in a calm mood. The two suspects were sitting in a chair each, side by side, their hands tied behind the backs of the chair. By the looks of it, Vincent had already done his share of interrogating the pair, as both had cuts and bruises on their faces, spots of blood on each of them. Deanna had a cut on her forehead, while Derrick had a cut above his eye and blood running down the side of his face. Recker looked at Vincent's hand and didn't notice any cuts or abrasions on it, leaving him to believe he wasn't the one who worked the two over. He glanced down at Malloy's knuckles and noticed they were red and had traces of blood on them.

"Mike, nice to see you." Vincent fake greeted him like an

unwelcome guest at a dinner party. "You're just in time. We were just about to get to where they were hiding the child."

"She's not here?" Recker said.

"No. We've already searched through the house. The child isn't here, nor is the third member of their little group."

"Please Mr. Vincent, we didn't mean nothin'. We were just lookin' for a quick, easy score," Ianetta interrupted.

"You disrespected me by bringing unwanted and unneeded attention by this little stunt of yours," Vincent responded. "If you wanted money, you should've come to me and I might've been able to give you a job or something. Instead, all you've done is bring down the heat."

"Where's the girl?" Recker said.

Ianetta spit in Recker's direction, sure that this man had something to do with his current predicament. Vincent looked to the ground, displeased at Ianetta's behavior. He gave a nod to Malloy to continue roughing up their guests. Malloy came over and gave Ianetta a backhand across the right side of his face, before nailing him with a right across on the other side of his face. Vincent grabbed his underling's arm to prevent any further damage at the moment and stepped forward, standing in front of the captured man.

"This man is my guest and he will be treated with dignity," Vincent said. "You will not disrespect him in my presence and be uncourteous."

Ianetta spit out some blood and a tooth and took a deep breath. "I'm sorry."

"Where's your brother, Deanna?" Vincent asked very politely.

She hesitated before answering, "I'm not sure."

Malloy looked to his boss before acting. Then he got the signal and backhanded her across the face, then came across the other side with the open side of his fist. After roughing her up, he took a step back to let Vincent continue talking.

"I'm not sure what you think you have to gain by this, but I assume you know that you're not leaving here until we get the information we want."

Deanna looked over at Ianetta, who nodded at her to tell their captors whatever they wanted to know. Since Ianetta had done work for Vincent, and was familiar with him, he knew what he was capable of. The best they could hope for now was just to be able to leave the house with their lives intact.

"Promise me you won't kill him," Deanna said.

Vincent paced a few steps before turning back to answer her. "I give you my word. I will not lay a hand on him."

Even though he reassured them they wouldn't kill her brother, she still was hesitant about giving up his location.

"Tell him!" Ianetta yelled, knowing what would happen if they didn't.

"Marcus is with the girl in a house on Devereaux," Ambersome said through tears and gritted teeth.

"I'm assuming he's armed?" Recker asked.

"What do you think?"

"Address?"

"6249." She sighed, knowing she had lost.

"Is he alone?"

She clenched her jaw tighter, not wanting to say another word.

"The man asked you a question," Vincent added.

"Yes. He's alone." Ambersome only answered reluctantly when Malloy stepped forward again.

Vincent immediately looked at Recker. "You go get the girl. We'll stay here with them."

Recker looked at the two sitting in the chair, then back toward Vincent. He nodded his head, knowing the probable fate that loomed over the two prisoners. He raced out of the house and got in his truck, zooming down the road to get to Devereaux Street, which wasn't too far away. While he was on the way to get Mara, Vincent still paced around the room, as Malloy got in a few more shots at the faces of both Ambersome and Ianetta.

"Please stop," Ambersome mumbled, just able to get her mouth open.

"I give you my word, Mr. Vincent, I'll never do anything like this again." Ianetta was trembling, barely able to open his eyes, and at some stage had pissed his pants.

"You see, the problem is, examples sometimes need to be made to keep the masses in line," Vincent said, stirring their fears.

"No. No," Ianetta said.

"Sometimes you need to do things that you really don't want to do to show that you're still in control. That you still have a tight grasp on things." He noticed the stain on Ianetta's pants and put a gloved hand to his nose.

"You're still the boss."

"Deanna, I'd like to offer you my condolences." He turned to the woman.

"Why?"

"Losing a brother is not an easy thing to live with," Vincent said.

More tears started rolling down Ambersome's face. "You told me you wouldn't kill him."

"And I will keep that promise. I will not kill him. Neither will any of my associates. But my friend, the one that just left here, you see, I didn't offer the same promise in regards to him. I'm quite certain he will kill your brother."

"Nooo!" she yelled.

"The only decision I have to make now is whether you two will be joining him."

"No. No. You know I can help you, Mr. Vincent." Ianetta pleaded one last time for his life.

"I really don't think you can, Derrick. You've become a liability that I can't trust."

Without saying another word, he looked at Malloy, then left the room. He heard Ambersome crying as he left, her knowing what their fate was. Malloy moved around to the front of them to ask them a final question.

"You want to see it coming?" Malloy asked the pair.

"Whatever," Ianetta said. "Just hurry up and…"

Malloy interrupted his sentence and didn't wait for an answer, quickly pulling his gun up and putting a bullet in Ianetta's forehead before he even knew what was happening. He moved over to his girlfriend's chair, though she was too busy crying to respond. She was looking down, not wanting to see the final blow coming. Malloy gently put the gun to the side of her temple and squeezed the trigger. The force of the blast knocked her chair over and onto the floor. He motioned to the others to follow him outside to rejoin the boss. Vincent was waiting on the porch as the others came out, looking up at the sky.

"Something wrong, Boss?" Malloy asked.

"Nothing, Jimmy. Nothing at all. Beautiful day out, don't you think?"

Malloy grinned. "A little chilly, but not too bad a day."

Vincent nodded. "Yes, not a bad day at all."

Once Recker arrived at Devereaux Street, he parked a few houses down, quickly getting out of his truck. He went around the back of one of the neighboring houses, carefully going from house to house, hopping some fences and ducking behind some large obstacles, making sure he wasn't seen, until he got to the one Marcus Ambersome was in. He quietly maneuvered to the back door of the house. Recker wiggled the handle of the door to see if it was locked. After a minute, he was able to pick the lock and slowly opened the door, hoping it didn't creak and give him away. The door led into the basement on the raised home. Recker quietly walked inside and started searching the room. Mara wasn't there. Recker assumed she must've been upstairs in one of the bedrooms. He went over to the stairs, standing at the bottom and looking up to where they led, up to a closed door. He climbed them and stood on the top step, putting his ear to the door to see if he could hear any voices. He clenched his grip on his gun a little tighter as he heard footsteps coming closer. Someone was walking back and forth past the door, apparently mumbling to themselves. After a couple of minutes, Recker figured it must've been Ambersome. It seemed as though he was trying to call his sister and getting frustrated that he wasn't able to get through. Recker waited about ten minutes before making his move, just to make sure there were no other people in the house. Satisfied that Marcus was alone, since he heard no other voices or movements, Recker decided it was time to act. He waited a few more minutes until Ambersome paced by the door again and then he would strike. Once Ambersome walked by the door to the kitchen, Recker waited for him to come back. As soon as he heard him walk by, Recker threw open the door and hit Ambersome in the back of the head, knocking the kidnapper to the floor. In one motion, Ambersome hit the floor, rolled over, and reached for his gun, which was tucked inside the front of his pants.

"Don't do it!" Recker shouted, having the drop on him.

Ambersome didn't listen and tried to pull his gun out, giving Recker no choice in his response. Recker pulled the trigger on his Sig Sauer, firing two shots into Ambersome's chest. Ambersome immediately slumped down further on the floor, the life evaporating from his body. Recker walked over to Ambersome's body and kicked his gun away from him. The bedrooms were upstairs and Recker ran up them to check for Mara. The first bedroom he checked was on the right. He opened the door and there she was. Just sitting on the floor in the corner with her knees up to her chest. Recker smiled at her and put his gun away. He walked into the room, trying not to frighten her any more than he knew she already was.

"Mara, my name's Michael," he softly told her. "I'm here to take you back to your mommy and daddy."

"Where are they?"

"They're waiting for you at home. I'm gonna take you there."

"Are you sure?" The little girl sounded understandably wary.

"Positive," he smiled. "Maybe if you're good, we can stop for an ice cream or milkshake on the way."

"Chocolate?" Mara asked, perking up.

"Whatever you want."

"OK."

"I'm gonna pick you up, OK? There's something downstairs that I don't want you to see."

"OK."

Recker picked her up and went downstairs, shielding her eyes so she didn't see the dead body on the floor. He carried her all the way to his truck, putting her in the front seat. He didn't have a car seat for her, so at least by having her next to him, he could keep his eyes on her and talk to her. Before starting the car, he called Mr. Ridley and let him know that he had Mara safe and sound. He put Mara on the phone with him so her mother and father could hear her voice again and know she was all right. After a couple minutes, Mara handed the phone back.

"I promised Mara I'd stop on the way for a chocolate milkshake," Recker said. "Other than that, we'll be right there."

"I don't know how to thank you," Mr. Ridley said through gentle sobs in the background.

"There's no need."

Recker did as he promised and stopped to get Mara a chocolate milkshake, the biggest one they had. After that, he drove right to Spruce Street, the Ridley's waiting on the steps leading up to their front door. Recker pulled up right in front of their house into an empty spot. The Ridley's eagerly rushed over to the truck to see their daughter. Recker unlocked the door so they could open it. Her parents pulled her out of the truck and hugged her. Recker got out and walked around to the front of the truck and watched them, relieved that it was a happy ending. Mr. Ridley pulled himself away from his family to approach Recker.

"I don't know what to say."

"Nothing needs to be said," Recker said.

"While we were waiting, my wife and I were talking, we wanted you to have some kind of reward."

Recker put his hand out to prevent him from going any further. "I don't need any reward. Getting her home back to you safe and sound is reward enough."

With tears in his eyes, Ridley smiled and nodded. "You know, I never did get your name."

"It's not important. Your family's waiting for you," Recker told him, nodding in their direction.

With his work done, Recker drove back to the office. On the way, he called Vincent, just to let him know how it all turned out and to thank him for his help. It was a brief conversation as Vincent said he had other business to attend to, but he was glad to help. Once Recker got back to the office, Jones was waiting for him. It was the happiest Recker had seen him look since they started their little partnership together.

"I think I might wanna take tomorrow off," Recker said.

"You really think you've earned it?" Jones just couldn't resist a little lightweight needling.

Recker laughed, knowing he was kidding.

"By all means, Mike. You've earned the day."

"I think that's the first time you've called me that," Recker said.

"Then when you get back, we have more victims that will need our assistance."

"All in a day's work, right Professor? All in a day's work."

FULLY LOADED

13

Jones had been calling Recker's phone multiple times an hour for the past two days, not getting a response to any of his calls or messages. He was beyond worried at that point. He knew something had happened. Something had to have gone terribly wrong. Whatever it was, he knew it must've been gravely serious for Recker to not get back to him. Not only that, but Recker didn't complete the assignment. In the nine months they'd been in operation, it was the first time Recker did not successfully complete the task. It was supposed to be an easy mission, at least as easy as any could be in their line of work. He was supposed to be looking after a woman who was being stalked and harassed, and had recently received a death threat. The perpetrator didn't appear to be that serious a threat, at least not for Recker. The man in question had no violent past and didn't seem to own a gun, not one that they could trace, anyway.

That's why Jones was so perplexed as to why Recker had suddenly gone missing. He couldn't find any signs that Recker willingly left town, or had been taken to a hospital, or had been taken to a city morgue. He checked patients recently admitted to hospitals, death notices, and police reports. He hacked every database he could think of that his friend might show up in. But nothing matched Recker's description or the area he was supposed to be in. It was almost midnight, and Jones was close to calling it a night. He glanced at his phone again, thinking if he should give it one more try before shutting everything down for the night. He dialed Recker's number again, growing even more worried with each unanswered ring.

"Michael, if you get this, please call me," Jones said in his message. "It's been a few days since I've heard from you and I'm... I'm just worried about you."

Jones put the phone in his pocket, knowing his message was likely to go unanswered, just as the previous twenty had. His eyes happened to glance over to Recker's gun cabinet and a sense of sadness came over him as he started to think about the possible reasons his friend hadn't contacted him. Most of them involved Recker's death. Jones had tried to think positively, and mostly had for the past several days, but now the realization was starting to settle in that Jones had seen him for the last time. Jones shut off the lights and laid on the couch, as he so often did when he was in the middle of a case, so he could get an early start in the morning.

When Jones woke up, he decided to retrace his steps, everything he'd done up to that point, just in case he missed or overlooked something. At nine o'clock, he tried Recker's phone again, not bothering to leave a message this time when it went to voicemail. He put the phone down on the desk, switching his attention back to the computer screen. After a minute of working, he looked back down at the phone, contemplating the one thing he hadn't tried yet. He picked it up and scrolled through the numbers, stopping once he saw the number he was looking for. Part of him wondered why he didn't try it sooner. The other part of him said, if

Recker wasn't there, he'd be worrying another person unnecessarily. Plus, Mia's apartment wasn't anywhere close to where Recker was assigned that night. Despite his concerns, Jones figured he had to try it, as he was desperate, and out of ideas. He dialed Hendricks' number, hoping to get something, maybe even a lead he didn't have before. Maybe Recker had spoken to her about something that he wasn't privy to. After the fourth ring, Hendricks picked up.

"Hello?" she said.

"Ms. Hendricks, how are you?"

"Uh, fine, do I know you?"

"Not directly. I was wondering if you could help me with something..."

"I'm not helping you with anything until I know who you are," Hendricks scoffed.

"My name is unimportant," Jones said. "What is important is a mutual friend of ours."

"I'm sure we have no mutual friends," she said.

Just as she was about to hang up Jones said, "Michael Recker."

"I don't know anybody named that," she said. "I'm sorry. You must have the wrong number."

Hendricks then hung up, not sure what just happened. Recker had always told her not to admit to anyone about knowing him, in case his old CIA friends came looking for him. In the event someone did, he instructed her to say that she didn't know him. If they showed her proof, she was to say he used a different name. She was a little scared and shook up by the call, even though she knew the day might, and now had, arrived.

A slight grin came over Jones' face, knowing that Recker had taught her well. Though Jones always had his doubts about Recker knowing and trusting her, he always told him that she wouldn't be an issue. That she would never give him up. It appeared Recker was right, though Jones was upset that it had to come to this for him to finally believe it. Jones could've just left well enough alone, but something was tugging at him that she knew something. He didn't know how he'd break through her wall, but he had to try again and convince her that he was on the same side. He rang her number again, hoping she'd answer once more, and that she didn't ignore the phone. After a few rings, she picked up again.

"Ms. Hendricks, please don't hang up, it's imperative that I find Michael," he quickly told her.

"Why do you assume I know this person?" she said.

"Because he's told me you've become friends. He's the one who helped you with your former boyfriend, Stephen Eldridge."

"How could you know that?"

"Because I'm the one who assigned him to your case," Jones said.

"You're the employer that he talks about."

"Yes. Not that I'm trying to worry you, but I've exhausted all other options, I've been trying to locate him for the past three days and it seems he's disappeared. Do you have any idea where he might have gone? Something he mentioned to you in passing? Anything?"

"How do I know you're really his employer? How do I know you didn't just find that stuff out somehow? I mean, you could've found that out about me and just assumed he helped."

"Hmm. That is an excellent point," Jones said, smiling at her resourcefulness. "Let me think of a way to prove it to you. He's driving a black Ford Explorer, does that help?"

"What's the license plate number?"

"FMJ23..."

"Who's it registered to?" she said quickly.

"Jason Smith."

"That doesn't really prove anything. You could've found that out somehow."

"Yes, I suppose I could have. Except I'm the one who bought the truck for him and gave it to him, registering it in that name."

"Besides all that, you still haven't told me who you are."

"That is a predicament in itself. Nobody knows who I am. That's a condition I adhere to to be able to do the things I do," he said.

"Well, it's been nice talking to you, but I still don't know the guy."

"Wait," Jones said hurriedly, sensing he was about to get hung up on again. He assumed he wasn't going to get another chance after this one. "What else can I tell you?"

"Name, nickname, anything that would indicate that you really are a friend of his," she said.

"Well, there is a nickname he has started calling me."

"What is it?"

"The professor," he said reluctantly.

"The professor?"

"Yes. I know it sounds silly, but..."

"So you really are telling the truth," Hendricks said with a lighter tone to her voice. Recker always told her that if he was missing and someone came looking for him named The Professor, she could trust him. "He's been saying something abo..." she said, cutting herself off after realizing she said too much.

"Ms. Hendricks? Are you saying that Michael is there with you?" Jones said, picking up on her hint.

There was a thirty second silence as Hendricks pondered what to do. In her heart, she knew he was telling her the truth. But there was still a small piece of her who wasn't quite sure. But she also knew that she'd just given it away that he was there with her.

"Is Mr. Recker OK?" Jones said. "Please tell me something."

Hearing the concern in his voice, Hendricks finally relented, deciding that she could trust him. "Yeah. He's here," she said.

"Is he all right? What's going on?"

"He's OK now."

"Now? What do you mean, now? Was he not before?"

"He showed up at my door the other night bleeding pretty badly. He'd been shot in the shoulder and was in bad shape. He's been drifting in and out of consciousness ever since. He made me promise not to take him to the hospital, so he's been laying on my couch while I've been taking care of him."

"Is he alert now? Will he survive?"

"He's sleeping right now. It looks like he'll be OK. I did the best I could with what I have to work with. I'm not exactly set up here for a makeshift emergency room," she answered.

"Why didn't he contact me at some point while he was awake? Or if you heard his phone ringing, I've been ringing it constantly the past several days," Jones said.

"He doesn't have his phone on him. I don't know what happened to it. He didn't have it when he came. I had no way of contacting you since I didn't know your number."

"I understand. Don't do anything, I'll be there in half an hour."

"I'm not sure that's the best idea," she said.

"Half an hour," he said again.

"OK. Do you need my..." she said, stopping when she realized he hung up already. "My address. I guess not."

Just as he told her he would, Jones showed up at Hendricks apartment thirty minutes later. When Hendricks opened the door, and saw him standing there, she realized why Recker called him the professor. He looked like one to her too.

"I see now why Mike calls you that," she said. "I see the resemblance."

"Yes indeed," Jones said, not necessarily overjoyed with the reference, though it really didn't bother him.

"He's over there," Hendricks said, backing up and pointing to the couch.

"Thank you."

Jones walked past his host and went over to the couch to check on his friend's condition. Jones stood over him for a few minutes, with Mia just watching, making sure he didn't do anything to hurt Recker. Though she trusted what Recker told her about the professor, there was still a piece inside her that didn't fully trust who he was. He could've been an imposter for all she knew. Or the one who shot Recker and came back to finish the job. She knew that was unlikely, and she was just being paranoid or had watched too many thriller movies. She knew it was a ninety-nine percent certainty that the strange man in her house was the real professor, but it was still in the back of her mind.

"Do you expect him to awaken soon?" Jones said.

"Probably. He's been sleeping for a while so, yeah, he'll probably wake up soon."

"Is the bullet out yet?"

"Yeah," Hendricks said. "It's a good thing that I used to work in the ER and it's not my first time doing this sort of thing. Although it's the first time I did it here."

"I guess we're fortunate that you're well versed and experienced."

"Yeah, well, he's just lucky he came to me."

"I'm quite sure luck had nothing to do with it," Jones said, remembering Recker telling him this was one of the reasons he wanted to keep Hendricks close.

Though he always understood Recker's reasoning, he never fully grasped it until now. He was right in trusting Hendricks. Jones could see that now. He watched her as she tended to Recker, seeing the care she had for him. It was unmistakable. Either she was an extremely caring type of nurse, or she had genuine feelings for him. Jones guessed it was a little bit of both.

"Have you been with him the whole time?" Jones said.

"Day and night." Hendricks pulled a blanket over Recker's body, up to his chest.

"Good thing you've been off from work in order to take care of him."

"Would've been if I was."

"You haven't gone to work?"

"No. I called out for the entire week," she said. "Told them I had a family emergency that I had to deal with."

"That's an incredibly kind gesture on your part."

"Well, I don't know about that. He's part of the reason I even have my life right now. Without him, who knows what would've happened with Steve. I owed him for that. This is the least I could do." She wiped his forehead with a damp cloth as she spoke.

"I can see he's getting the best of care under the circumstances."

"Well, like I said, I'm not set up for major emergencies. I keep a box of basic equipment and supplies just in case. I'm doing the best I can for him."

"And you've done that."

"When he came in, he made me promise that I wouldn't take him anywhere or have someone come look at him. He said if I couldn't fix him up to just let him go. The biggest issue was the risk of infection and the amount of blood loss he sustained. It looked like he'd been bleeding for quite a while."

"Did he happen to say what happened or who shot him?" Jones said.

"Hasn't said much of anything. He's been very weak with the amount of blood he lost."

MIKE RYAN

Hendricks yawned and rubbed her eyes, the result of not getting much sleep in the few days that Recker had been in her care. Jones could see that she was exhausted. She had that tired look about her.

"You look exhausted," Jones said.

Hendricks looked at him and smiled before sitting in a chair. "Yeah. You kind of get used to it in my profession though. Long hours are part of the deal sometimes. You learn to push through it."

"Is there anything I can get you?"

"No, I'm OK. Thank you though. It's nice of you to ask," she said, smiling at him again.

Jones looked back at Recker, not sure what else he could do there. It seemed as if he was getting the best of care under the circumstances. Until he awoke, he wasn't sure there was any other reason for him to be there.

"Well, I can see you're doing everything possible for him so I won't stand in your way anymore," Jones said. "If you don't mind, I'd like to come back around lunchtime, see if he's up yet."

"That should be fine."

"Great. I'll bring lunch."

"Oh, you don't have to do that."

"On the contrary, you've done a wonderful job here, I can see you're exhausted and probably haven't had much time for yourself. It'd be my pleasure."

"OK, well, if you insist."

"Turkey BLT with french fries on the side sound good?" Jones said, knowing from her file that was one of her favorite sandwiches.

"Uh, yeah, I would actually love that. That's one of my favorites. Did you already know that somehow?" she said.

Jones allowed himself a small grin and a shrug of his shoulders. "Just a lucky guess."

Jones left the apartment and went back to the office. At least now he felt a small sense of relief. Though they still had to deal with Recker's injuries, Jones knew he was alive and would be up and around soon. The bigger issue would be in determining what happened to him. Whether getting shot was a mistake, or whether Recker was targeted somehow. Those would be questions that couldn't be answered until he spoke with Recker directly though. Finally knowing that Recker was OK, Jones was able to get some work done. It was the first time in days that he could concentrate on work without getting distracted by wondering about Recker's health.

A little after twelve, just as he said he would, Jones dropped what he was doing to go visit Recker again. He stopped for sandwiches along the way, including Hendricks' favorite. Once he got to her apartment, he saw her warm smile greeting him as he brought in bags of food, one in each hand. As soon as he stepped inside, Jones noticed Recker sitting up on the couch, looking alert and well rested.

"Well... it's good to see you've finally rejoined the ranks of the living," Jones said.

Recker smiled. "Good to see you too." Although he looked better, he still sounded weak to Jones.

"You don't seem surprised to see me."

"I've been up for a while," Recker said. "Mia told me you came by this morning. Got a sandwich there for me?"

Jones looked over at him as he put the bags down on the kitchen table. "It just so happens that I do. I was anticipating you being awake and hungry. Well, maybe hoping more than anticipating."

"He woke up about an hour after you left this morning,"

Hendricks told him. "I would've called you and let you know but you didn't leave your number."

"Oh. I didn't think about that. Ms. Hendricks," Jones said, holding her food up for her to see before setting it on the table.

"Thank you. Before we get too much further into anything, can you please stop with the Miss thing?" she said. "I hate being called Miss. Just call me Mia."

"He has a thing for proper pronunciation and pronouns," Recker said, laughing at Jones' expense.

"Very well... Mia," Jones said, blushing.

Hendricks walked over to the table and sat down, eagerly taking her turkey BLT out of its white Styrofoam container. Recker slightly lifted himself off the couch to see what she was eating.

"That a turkey BLT you got there?" Recker said.

"Yes," she said. "Quite a coincidence, huh?"

"Sure is."

"I mean, someone I don't know brings me lunch and it just so happens to be my favorite sandwich."

"Amazing how that works sometimes, isn't it?"

Hendricks shook her head and rolled her eyes. "So, what do I call you?" she said to Jones as he sat down across from her.

He looked at her, his eyes opened wide, unsure of his reply. It was like he was taken off guard with the question.

"I'm not sure that's relevant."

Jones took a small bite from his sandwich and chewed slowly, hoping that would be the end of the questions.

"Well, if we're going to be around each other, don't you think I should call you something other than The Professor? That's kind of awkward."

"I wasn't aware we were going to be seeing each other."

"Well, if you're going to visit Mike while he's in my care and eat in my apartment, I'd say that qualifies."

Jones looked to Recker for help. The wounded man gave none. "She has a point," Recker said with a smile.

"I'm very reluctant to give people my name," Jones said. "With what we do, there are a lot of complications involved."

"And here I thought there was nobody on this planet more secretive than Mike," she said.

Recker laughed. "Why don't you just tell her your name? Not like it's your real one, anyway."

Jones looked at his partner, deliberating with himself on whether he should reveal it. He finally relented, figuring it wouldn't do much harm. "Very well. You can call me David."

"David. OK. Was that so hard?" Hendricks said.

"Uh, actually it was somewhat difficult."

"David what?"

"Uh... Jones."

"Jones?"

"Originality isn't one of his strongest attributes," Recker said with a laugh.

"I can see you're getting back to your normal self," Jones said in his usual dry tone of voice.

"All it takes is the best nurse in the world."

"When did she start showing up?" Hendricks sarcastically said.

"Don't be so facetious, Ms. Hend... Mia," Jones self-corrected. "You did a fantastic job."

"It was a bullet wound to the shoulder. It's not like I performed brain or heart surgery in a dimly lit dungeon somewhere."

"Still, considering the circumstances, you should feel good about what you've done. If not for you, he'd probably be dead."

"Yeah, well, let's just not make this a regular occurrence."

14

Several more days had passed, with Recker growing stronger with each day that went by. Mia insisted that he stay at her apartment for a few more days until he was better, contrary to what Recker thought was necessary. He didn't want to stay and impose on her any longer, but she wanted to make sure there were no lingering effects. If there were, at least she'd be there to take care of it. Recker wasn't as concerned about that as he was about staying in such proximity to his undeniably attractive friend. Not that he was looking for any deeper type of relationship than they already had, but he wanted to make sure that she felt the same way. There were times that he felt she might be falling for him, though he wasn't positive. Sometimes he thought it was just in his mind. Recker was sitting on the couch reading a newspaper when Mia walked over and sat next to him.

"I switched days with another nurse, so I have a couple more days off," Mia said.

"Mia, you really didn't have to do that. I'm fine," Recker said.

"I know. I just wanna make sure. A couple more days, then I'll unlock all the doors so you can leave," she said, smiling, so he knew it was a joke.

"I've been cooped up in worse spots."

"I bet. I'll be working like ten days in a row once I go back." She shook her head and pulled a sad face. "I'm gonna be so tired."

"Anything I can do to help with that? Repay what you've done for me?"

A wicked smile overtook Mia's face that she couldn't hide, though she tried. "Uh... no. It's OK."

"What was that look for?" Recker said, seeing her face light up. "What is it?"

"It's nothing," she said, holding her hand over her mouth to hide her smile.

"No, what is it?"

"Nothing. It was a slightly inappropriate thought."

"Only slightly?"

"OK. Maybe majorly inappropriate."

"What was it?"

Her head perked up as she shook it. "Uh uh... I'll never tell."

Recker could only imagine what had been running through her mind.

"You should probably get a shower," Mia said. "It's been a few days since you've had one."

"Are you trying to suggest something?" Recker said sarcastically, sniffing his armpit.

"Well, uh, you know," Mia said playfully, laughing. "No, I'm just kidding. It'll just help you in your recovery process."

"Oh. OK."

"As your dedicated and personal nurse, would you like me to sponge bathe you?" she said with a big smile. "I'm required to ask that of all patients."

"Uh, are you, now? I... uh... think I can manage that on my

own," Recker said. He knew if he answered in any other manner that it might lead to things that they might never recover from. If only from his point of view. "Thank you for the offer though."

"Too bad. I was kind of looking forward to it," she said, getting up off the couch.

Recker watched her walk away into the kitchen, getting caught up in the moment and admiring her figure. He shook his head to break his concentration from her, trying to think of something else.

"Stop that," he said, mumbling to himself. "You know what happened the last time you fell for a girl."

"Did you say something?" Mia shouted from the kitchen.

"No. Just talking to myself."

"Oh. You OK?"

"Yeah. Fine. Just fine. I think I'll go take that shower now."

"OK. There's a blue towel in the bathroom closet for you."

"Thanks."

"If there's anything you have a problem with cause your arm or shoulder hurts, just let me know and I can help," she said innocently, without a hint of deviousness.

"I think I'll be able to manage," Recker said, pulling himself off the couch.

While Recker showered, Mia plopped herself down on the couch and watched TV for a few minutes. Her brief time to relax was interrupted only a few minutes later when there was a knock on the door.

"Who could that be?" she said, putting the remote down on the table.

She cautiously walked over to the door, unsure who would be paying her a visit. She briefly thought about informing Recker that they had a visitor, but figured she'd look and see who it was first. She looked through the peephole and was quickly reassured by the sight of the professor's presence.

"What are you doing here?" Mia said.

"I'm sorry, I probably should've called first instead of just dropping by," Jones replied.

"It's OK. Come in."

Jones did as he was directed, though he still felt badly for just coming over without warning. "It's not something I usually do, dropping by unannounced."

"David... it's fine, really," she said. "I'm not mad or upset you're here. If I was, I probably wouldn't have answered the door."

Jones took a quick glance around the apartment and was slightly surprised at the missing presence of their dangerous acquaintance.

"Where is our mutual friend?" Jones said.

"Oh, he's in the shower."

"The shower?"

"Yes. People do shower , you know. I'm sure even you do it," she said.

Jones grinned. "Yes. Of course."

Without looking too alarmed, Jones quickly looked Hendricks up and down, taking notice to whether her hair was wet, or if a sprinkle of water was still attached to any other part of her visible skin.

"You OK?" Mia said.

"Hmm? Oh, yes, I'm fine. Something was just running through my mind. Nothing to worry about."

"OK. Good. Can I get you a drink or anything while you wait for Mike?"

"Uh, yes, sure, that would be nice."

"Soda, milk, coffee, tea? Sorry, don't have anything stronger than that."

"Never touch anything stronger than that anyway," Jones smiled. "Do you have iced tea?"

Hendricks nodded. "One iced tea coming up."

Hendricks came back into the living room a minute later, a glass of iced tea in hand, sitting down across from her guest as they waited for Recker.

"So what brings you over?" Mia said.

"I just had some things to discuss with Michael."

"Why are you so formal all the time? Michael... all that Miss stuff... are you always so proper?"

"I don't know," Jones said, fidgeting uncomfortably while he sipped his drink. "Just a sign of respect, I guess."

"I guess that answer will do."

They fell into an ever-growing silence.

"So why do people call you Mia when your name is Mary? It's not in your...," Jones said, desperate to fill the quiet but stopping himself before he revealed too much.

"Not in my file?" Mia said, finishing the sentence for him.

Jones let out a grin, uncomfortable about saying more.

"So, you're the one who assigned Mike to me when I had that problem before?"

Jones made a strange face and put his hands in the air, feigning ignorance.

"I had a feeling that'd be your answer," Mia said. "Anyway, when I was a little girl and just started learning to talk, I had trouble saying Mary. I said it like Mia. So, my family started calling me that, and after a while, that's just what I preferred."

Jones nodded. "Don't like Mary?"

"Mary sounds outdated. Like I'm living in the thirties or fifties or something. Mia sounds a little more modern."

They waited about ten more minutes for Recker to show himself, continuing their stilted conversation in the meantime. When Recker did come out, he was a little surprised to see Jones sitting there. He took a seat on the same couch Mia was sitting on, though not directly next to her, so there was an open seat between them.

"Looks like you two are getting awfully chummy," Recker cracked.

"Just having an enjoyable conversation with Ms. Hendricks... I mean Mia," Jones said. "Sorry, old habits die hard."

Hendricks smiled. "It's OK. You're trying. That's the main thing."

"So what're you doing here?" Recker said.

"Just came over to see how you're doing and go over a few things," Jones answered.

"I'm assuming you two are going to need some privacy," Mia said.

"If you would be so kind," Jones nicely said.

"Sure. I have some dishes in the kitchen I have to wash, anyway."

"Thank you so much."

Recker waited until Mia left the room before he sat forward on the couch. "So what do you really want?"

"Just wondering when you were coming back to work."

"Miss me already?"

"I'm not rushing you or anything. I'm just asking so I have a time frame to work with."

"In the next couple days."

"I wasn't expecting it to be so soon."

"Well, getting into a fistfight or gun battle wouldn't be wise, but I can still talk and get things done," Recker said.

"I'm getting a little worried about your arrangement here," Jones said. "It appears you two are getting a little too comfortable with each other. I mean, you're showering here now? Are you sleeping in the same bed together as well?"

"Jones. If I didn't know any better, I'd say you're getting a little jealous." Recker was kidding but kept his serious face on.

"Oh, don't be ridiculous. You know what I mean."

"I'm getting ridiculous? You're the one bringing it up. Look, I needed a shower, she has one. That's all there is to it."

"I half expected her hair to be wet when I came in."

"Well, I was waiting ten minutes in there for her but you obviously interrupted my plans," Recker said sarcastically.

Jones gave him a stone-faced look, obviously not enjoying his friend's sense of humor. "I believe you know what I'm getting at."

"Look, nothing's happened, nothing's gonna happen. OK? You know my feelings about getting involved with someone. It's not gonna happen again. Is that plain enough for you?" Recker said.

"Yes, on your end, but what about hers?" Jones leaned back to make sure Mia wasn't listening at the door. "The more you stay here and have her take care of you, the more attached she's becoming."

"No, she's not."

"Michael, I can see it in her eyes, hear it in her voice. If you can't see that she's developing feelings for you, then I need to invest in a seeing-eye dog for you, because you're as blind as a bat."

"Interesting metaphor."

"Don't try to change the subject. Tell me I'm not right."

"Can we talk about something else?" Recker said, now keen to change the subject.

"Fine. Anything come back to you about that night yet? Who shot you for instance?"

"Yeah. I was thinking about it earlier. I remember who it was."

"Who?" Jones said eagerly.

"Don't know his name. Just what he looked like. Early thirties. White guy. Close shaved haircut. Wearing a dark brown or black suit. Had something shiny on his belt. Looked like it could've been a badge. Or part of his belt. Or something else entirely. I'm not sure about that part."

"You think it might've been a cop?"

"Could've been. Not sure."

"There's been nothing in the news or on TV or in any files that I can see that would indicate an officer involved shooting in the past week," Jones told him.

"Maybe it was off the books."

"You mean a dirty cop who didn't report it?"

"It happens."

"I don't know what the connection to you would be though. If it was a cop, don't you think they'd plaster it on the news?"

"Not if it was somebody working freelance. Are you able to get your hands on photos of them?"

"Of the cops?"

"Yeah."

"I suppose it could be done. You think you'd recognize him?"

"Yeah, I think so."

"What district should I focus on?"

"All of them," Recker answered. "Focus on the detectives or plainclothes officers. Don't worry about the patrol units."

"It'll probably take me a day or two. Three at the most."

"That's fine. I'll just be here shacking up."

"That's not funny."

Recker smiled, knowing how uptight Jones was getting on the subject. Not having the desire to revisit the conversation, Jones reached into his pocket and removed a cell phone. He handed it over to Recker.

"What's this?" Recker said.

Jones seemed puzzled by the question. "What's it look like? It's a phone."

"I can see that."

"Well, you need a new one, do you not?"

"Yeah."

"Well now you have one."

"Thanks."

"By the way, what did happen to your old one?"

"Oh. I threw it in the river." Recker said.

"What?" Jones said, not sure he heard right.

"I threw it in the river."

"Why would you do that?"

"I was shot and not sure I'd make it to Mia in time before I bled too much. In case I perished out on the street somewhere, when I was found, I didn't want someone flipping through the phone and seeing all my contact names and numbers," Recker explained.

Jones nodded. "That makes sense."

"I didn't want to give you up or put anyone else in a bad position to where they'd have to explain how they know me."

"Well thank you for that."

"Is it safe to come in yet?" Mia shouted from the kitchen. "It's getting a little boring in here."

It drew a laugh and a smile from both men in the living room. They told her it was safe to enter as they'd finished discussing everything they needed to at that point.

"I didn't rush you or anything, did I?" Mia said.

"No, no, we were all through," Jones said with a nod of gratitude.

"Good. I'd hate to rush people in *my* apartment or anything."

"You know, Ms... Mia, I hadn't realized how much of a sarcastic personality you have."

"I usually only get that way when I'm tired. Normally, I'm pretty laid back and leave the jokes to other people. When I get tired, I tend to lose my filter."

"I wasn't saying it was a bad thing. Just an observation."

"Why don't you lay down and get some sleep? Jones can keep watch over me for a few hours if you're worried about me," Recker suggested.

"Yes," a surprised Jones agreed. "An excellent idea. You could use a good five or six uninterrupted hours."

"We can just sit here and talk some more business while you sleep."

Jones didn't look like that was part of his plan for the day, though. "We can?"

"We can. There's still a few other things we can discuss," Recker mentioned, nodding his head.

"Oh yes, of course. I'd forgotten about that," Jones said, still not having the faintest idea what his friend was talking about.

"Well OK," Mia agreed. "If you're sure you won't miss me too much."

"That would be impossible," Recker smiled.

"Who said there wasn't a sweet guy underneath that rough exterior?"

"Certainly nobody I know," Jones mumbled.

Mia took up Recker's suggestion and went into her bedroom to get some sleep, closing the door behind her. Recker and Jones watched her until she disappeared.

"Cute girl," Jones stated.

"Yeah. She'll eventually make some guy happy. And he'll be lucky to have her. She's a special person."

"Almost makes you wish you were that guy?"

"Don't start with that again."

"So, what other business did we have to discuss? Or was that just a ruse to get her into bed? I mean, not with you, but on her own, alone."

Recker didn't even bother acknowledging the insinuation. "How much are you progressing with that other thing?"

"What other thing?"

"You know, the thing I asked you to check on?"

"The pictures? You just asked me a few minutes ago."

"For someone as brilliant as you are, you surely can't be this stupid."

"I'm afraid you have me for a loss. I haven't the foggiest idea what you're talking about," Jones responded.

Recker rolled his eyes, wondering how a man so intelligent could be so clueless. "The person I asked you to find nine months ago."

"Oh. Agent Seventeen," Jones said.

"That's the one. You asked me to be patient, and I have been. You said it might take you some time. And it has."

"And it's gonna take a little more."

"How much more?" Recker said, his frustration evident.

"I'm not sure yet," Jones said, sensing his impatience and trying to ease his mind a little. "Just a little more time. It won't be too much longer."

"You wouldn't be intentionally stalling, would you?" Recker said, fixing on Jones with a stare.

Jones' eyes opened wide and tilted his head back, almost pretending to be insulted. "Are you questioning my integrity?"

"I know this is a project you didn't really want to embark on or a road you didn't want me to travel down," Recker stated. "I'm just wondering if that sometimes weighs on your mind."

Jones took a few seconds before answering, carefully choosing his words. "I would be remiss if I didn't say that I was, and still am, against this personal vengeful vendetta of yours. But I told you I would help find the person responsible and I will. But it's not as easy as just opening the phone book and running your finger down halfway through the page and picking someone. It's an extremely sophisticated program that takes time to work. The last thing we need is to be discovered and have the government track it back to us, showing up at our doorstep and both of us winding up in a big, dark hole somewhere, unlikely to ever see the light of day again."

"That was a little long winded," Recker remarked.

"Perhaps so. But it was what needed to be said."

Recker nodded his head, satisfied with the answer. "OK."

It was a nice little speech Jones had laid out, but he wasn't actually being totally truthful. He was being honest when he said it'd take time, and it required constant surveillance, but he wasn't putting in a hundred percent effort on it. He was deliberately slowing down the process a little. If he'd been going full bore on the project, he'd have had it ready by now. As it stood, he was another month or two away from completing it. He was hoping that the longer he took, the calmer Recker would get about the situation, even foregoing it completely. That was obviously not happening. Jones wasn't sure he believed it was a real possibility anyway, or just some foolhardy notion he had dreamed up.

He had real reservations about it, not sure whether Recker would ever return if he went after Agent 17 once he found him. Though he wasn't positive, a part of him believed that once he had found the agent in question, Recker would go off on some mission, not having any inclination to return. Or even living after his work was done. Part of him believed that finding Agent 17 was all that Recker was living for. Once that was done, Recker would no longer have a need to keep on living. That was the part of the equation that worried Jones the most and made him slow the process down.

"Just so you're aware, I'll have to put that aside for a few days while I work on finding out who did this to you."

"You can't do two things at once?" Recker said, taking an opportunity to tease his friend.

"The program I am running requires constant supervision and occasional... maintenance, shall we say? I would not be comfortable leaving it to run unattended."

"Sounds complicated."

"It is. And I believe right now that this situation commands our full attention," Jones said. "Once this is over, I can return to it with full vigor. Agreed?"

Though he agreed, Recker's shoulders drooped a little in disappointment. "Yes."

"So, once I commence my search for this assailant of yours, what do we do with him when we find him?"

Recker didn't hesitate. "That's easy. I kill him."

"Do we need to take such... drastic actions?" Jones said, picking his words carefully.

"He tried to kill me. Yes, we need to take such drastic actions. If he tried once, he'll try again."

"What if it is a police officer?"

"Makes no difference."

"You intend to intentionally kill a member of a law enforcement agency?"

"If that's what he is. If it turns out that he is a police officer, then he's obviously on the take. It's not like I'll be taking out one of the good guys," Recker said.

"How could you possibly know that?"

"You said there's nothing in the police records that indicated one of theirs was involved in a shooting."

"That's correct."

"If a police officer doesn't report being involved in a shooting, especially one that involves me, it means they're trying to hide something. Also, they're probably involved with some shady people. The community won't miss them if they're gone. Probably be better off for it too."

"Perhaps you're right. Well, if we have nothing further to discuss, I'll start digging up the pictures from the police department's files."

"Leaving so soon?"

"Is there something else you need me here for?" Jones said.

"I dunno. Wasn't sure if you could trust me alone here. Beautiful woman sleeping alone in her bedroom. Never know what might happen."

"Oh, stop it."

15

It took Jones about two days to be able to find and pull the file and picture of every police officer in Philadelphia. Once he had everything he needed, he called Recker to come to the office to see if he could identify his assailant. Recker had concluded that it was his last day at Mia's apartment anyway as she was going back to work the following day.

"So, this is it, huh?" Mia said.

Recker smiled. "Don't say it like we're never seeing each other again. I'm not leaving the city or anything. Just going back to work."

"Yeah, I know. I guess I was just starting to get used to the arrangement. Seeing that handsome face of yours every day."

"Well, once you get out of your hellish schedule in two weeks, we'll have to visit our favorite spot again."

"Is that a date?" she said hopefully.

"Let's just call it a meeting between friends."

"I guess that'll have to do. Probably as good as I'm getting right now."

Recker moved his shoulder a little and winced, causing Mia some concern.

"Are you sure you're ready to go back to work already?"

"It's been over a week. I'm starting to get a little antsy," Recker answered.

"Just make sure you're sensible and take care of yourself."

"Don't I always?" he said with a smile.

Mia leaned in and gave him a warm hug. Recker was initially taken back by it, but quickly embraced the moment. After a minute, he innocently pulled away, not wanting to get swept away by the touch and smell of her. It was a wonderful smell. And it was too intoxicating. Like fresh coffee in the morning, urging him to sample the flavor it hinted at. Even though he'd sworn off ever falling in love again, he could see it happening with her if he let it. And it was something that he couldn't let happen. For her sake. She deserved better than a life with him.

"I guess if you need anything else, medically speaking, you'll call me?" she said.

"You'll be the first one."

"I'm sure."

"I guess I owe you some special thanks for keeping me here and patching me up," Recker said.

Mia shook her head. "Nah. I owed you. Plus, it wasn't so bad seeing you every day," she said with a smile.

"Well, I should get going."

Mia tried to give him the most pleasant face she could, complete with a smile that she forced on. The week Recker stayed with her didn't help with her growing attachment towards him. Even though she knew she shouldn't pursue a relationship with him since every time she hinted or joked about them being together, he always rebuffed it or played it off, she couldn't help but be drawn to him. She felt like there was something that he wasn't telling her. There was something in his past that he didn't want her to know about. She knew he wasn't the type of guy that could be forced into anything. She just had to hope that at some point, he would let go of whatever it was that he was carrying around inside him. Though she wasn't necessarily happy to wait, she knew it was all she could do. For now.

Once Recker got back to the office, he walked around, looking at the walls as if he hadn't seen them in a long time. Jones briefly acknowledged his presence as he typed away at one of his computers.

"I like what you've done with the place," Recker said dryly, glad to be back in the swing of things.

"You were only gone a week, Mr. Recker, not a year. It's the same exact place it's always been," Jones said seriously.

"Remind me to take you to a comedy club sometime."

"For what purpose?"

"It'll do wonders for your personality."

"Are you saying there's something wrong with it now?" he said, temporarily taking his hands away from the keyboard.

"No. Not at all," Recker replied. "So... what've you come up with so far?"

"Well, I've got ninety percent of the files downloaded so far. The other ten percent should be done by the time you're done looking at the other ones."

"Any issues?"

"No, not really. There have been a few challenges such as undercover officers who've had their files redacted or 'misplaced'," Jones said, simulating quotations in the air with his fingers. "But they were just temporary problems, nothing I couldn't work around."

"That's why you get paid the big bucks."

"Here, sit at that computer," Jones said, pointing at the desktop next to him. "The pictures will start loading in a minute. They're sorted by district. Just use the mouse to click to the next picture."

Recker did as he was told and sat down at the computer to look at the pictures. He looked at each picture intently, making sure he was positive that it wasn't the same guy before going on to the next one. He dismissed most pictures quickly since they didn't have the same features he remembered the shooter as having.

"Do you actually hope he's in there?" Jones said.

"I don't hope for anything."

"I mean, I would hate to think he's a police officer."

"Like I said before... there's bad apples in every profession," Recker said.

"Yes, I suppose."

As Recker continued looking through the photos, Jones got up and poured another cup of coffee. Well, not actually poured, as he had added a new addition to the office since Recker was gone. Jones figured since neither one of them could make good coffee on their own, he'd let a Keurig machine do it for them. All they had to do was put the pod in and voila—coffee that was worth drinking. As opposed to buying it at the convenience store or making what they passed off as coffee. Recker scrunched his eyebrows together as the strange smell permeated into his nose. It smelled good. It also broke his concentration away from the pictures he was supposed to be looking at. He turned and looked at Jones, standing by the machine and drinking his cup.

"What is that?" Recker said.

"Oh. I thought we could use a little extra help in here."

"Yeah, we sure could. That's the understatement of the year."

"Would you like a cup?"

"I think I could be persuaded into trying it out."

Jones made a cup for his partner and brought it over to the desk, sitting it down in front of him. Recker leaned forward, bringing his nose to just outside of the edge of the cup, taking a whiff of it.

"That actually smells drinkable," Recker said.

"Indeed," Jones happily exclaimed, proud of his purchase. "I don't know why I never tried this sooner."

Recker picked up his cup and took a sip, pleased at the results. "Pretty good."

"You'll notice I purchased a whole cabinet for it," Jones pointed. "Underneath are other flavors and varieties. There's coffee, tea, iced tea, hot chocolate, lemonade… I haven't even tried all of them out yet."

"I don't think I've ever seen you so happy or excited over something."

"It's quite possible. I'm just in awe of that little machine."

"Hmm."

"So how are you making out so far?" said Jones as he sat back in front of his computer

"Haven't found him yet."

Considering the Philadelphia Police Department had over six thousand officers, looking through all their photos would take some time. Jones figured he really wouldn't do much good hovering over Recker as he looked through them, so he got back to work. Recker would let him know if he found the one. Jones estimated it'd take at least a few hours to look through all of them, even more if Recker took periodic breaks in between. It wound up taking even longer than Jones had figured. Recker spent the entire day and most of the night clicking through pictures. Just to make sure he didn't skip one accidently, or mistakenly pass one, Recker looked through all the pictures twice.

Once Recker had finally completed the task, he looked up at the clock and saw it was close to nine and dark outside. He leaned back in his chair and sighed, before letting out a yawn. Jones heard the sigh and stopped his work, assuming Recker was finished.

"I take it you're done?" Jones said.

"Yep."

"From the tone of your sigh, I assume you didn't find him."

"Nope."

"Don't be discouraged, we'll find him."

"I'm not discouraged. I sighed because I just spent ten hours looking at a computer."

"Oh."

"We worked through dinner," Recker said.

"Yes, I know. If you're hungry, there's some lunch meat in the fridge."

Recker got up from the desk and walked over to the refrigerator to help himself. Jones let him eat a sandwich before burdening him with any other questions.

"So, what do you think our next move should be?" Jones said, seeing Recker take the last bite of his sandwich.

"I don't know yet."

"At least we have some answers to work with. We at least know he's not a cop. That's something."

"Yeah."

"So, if he's not a cop, then who is he?"

"There's a bigger question than that," Recker said.

"Which is?"

"Was he working on his own or did someone hire him to do it?"

"I hadn't thought of that," Jones replied.

Another serious expression came over Jones' face as a thought had come to him. It was one that scared him. Recker tilted his head as he watched him, curious about what he was thinking, obvious that something was now on his mind.

"What is it?" Recker finally said.

"A terrifying thought just occurred to me."

"You just remembered you mixed your reds and whites together with your laundry this morning?"

Jones completely brushed off the sarcastic comment with a wave of his hand and focused on his problem. "What if the man that shot you is working for the government?"

"You mean the CIA?"

"What if they've found us... found you?" Jones said.

"I think you're getting a little ahead of yourself."

"That thought hasn't crossed your mind?"

"Did a few days ago. Already dismissed it," Recker said calmly, not giving it a second thought.

"How can you be so sure?"

"If they found us, we wouldn't be having this conversation right now."

"What if they were using that woman as bait to lure us out of the shadows?" Jones said, ignoring his computer to face Recker.

"I don't think so."

"How can you be so positive?"

"Don't forget, this is the kind of work I did for them. Too many variables left to chance. They don't work that way."

Jones turned back to his screen. "I wish I was as confident."

"Trust me when I tell you it's not them. Believe me, I would know if it was."

"Well then we're back to square one," Jones said with a sigh.

"Not quite," Recker said, pulling out his new phone.

"What are you doing?"

"Have an idea."

Jones looked on inquisitively as he wondered what Recker was up to. He apparently had someone on his mind that he could call for some answers, though Jones had no idea who that person could be.

"Tyrell?" Recker said into his new phone when the dial tone stopped.

"Recker? Is that you?" Tyrell said, his voice echoing from being out on the street.

"Yeah. Who else would it be?"

"Dude, I thought you was dead."

"Why the hell would you think that?"

"It's all over the streets," Gibson said. "Hold on, let me duck inside here and get some privacy. Never know who's listening out here."

"You good?"

"Yeah. So what happened to you?" Gibson's voice was clearer, the sounds of the streets duller, more distant.

"Why do you think something happened?" Recker said.

"You got shot, then disappeared for a week. No stories, no word, nothin'. Nobody heard nothin' about The Silencer. Word on the street was that you was dead."

"How'd it get out that I was shot? Only three people other than me would know."

"Well I don't know about the other two, but I know who one of them might be."

"Who?"

"The dude that shot you," Gibson said, with a hint of pleasure at drawing out the reveal, even for a few seconds.

Surprised, Recker almost dropped the phone in shock. "You know who shot me?" Recker said, putting the phone on speaker so Jones could hear.

"Yo, it's gotta be. I hear this dude been bragging all week about taking out The Silencer. Heard he got a nice little bonus too."

"A bonus?" Jones said.

"You got me on speaker or something?"

"Yeah," Recker responded. "I wanted someone else to hear the name."

"Was that The Prof I heard?" Gibson said.

"Mr. Gibson," Jones said.

"Yo, what up Prof? Been a while, man."

"Indeed, it has."

"I need a name, Tyrell," Recker said.

"You didn't hear this from me, right?"

"You got my word."

"Aight then. The dude that's been bragging is a guy named Mario Mancini," Gibson said, keeping his voice low and quiet.

"Mancini," Recker repeated. "Don't know him."

"Yeah, well, he knows you."

"He's Italian."

"Yeah. I hear he does a lot of contract work for the Italians."

"I have no beef with the Italians. Why would they want to take me out?" Recker said.

"I dunno about that, man. All I know is what I hear."

As soon as Gibson revealed the name, Jones typed it into the database of his computer. Within a minute, the man Gibson was referring to appeared on the screen. His name and a lengthy list of criminal charges appeared next to his picture. Jones looked up from the screen toward Recker and nodded, indicating it seemed like it might be true.

"You got anything else on it?" Recker said.

"Nah, that's it. You know me and the Italians ain't that close," Gibson said in his normal street drawl. "You ain't like laid up in a hospital or something, are you?"

"Nope. Good as can be."

"Glad to hear it, man. Was worried for you."

"I'm touched Tyrell, didn't know you worried so much about me."

"You're a good dude, man, I got respect for you. I'm glad you're alright."

"Yeah. Thanks, buddy."

"I heard they were looking through all the hospitals for you," Gibson said. "That's why they think they got you. They know you'd need medical attention, and you weren't there. Figured you got dropped in the river or on a slab or something."

"Not everyone who can take out a bullet works in a hospital. I know people."

"I'm sure you do." Gibson said.

"Do me a favor?"

"Name it."

"Don't let anybody know I'm alive. If they think I'm dead, let them keep thinking it," Recker said.

"Why?"

"Cause the Italians will be getting paid a visit soon. I'd prefer to make it a surprise party."

"You got it, man. My lips are sealed. Screw the Italians anyway."

"Hey, thanks for everything."

"Ain't nothin', man. Forget it."

"No, I'll have a little something for you the next time I see you."

"Just do me one favor?" Gibson said.

"Sure."

"Whenever you have this little surprise party of yours, just let me know the place and the date."

"Why? You wanna come?"

"No way, man. Whenever it is... I wanna be as far away in the other direction as possible." He started to laugh.

Recker smiled. "I'll make sure I give you a heads up."

Once Recker hung up on a still laughing Gibson, he walked around the desk and stood behind Jones to look at the computer screen. He nodded his head upon seeing the picture of Mancini.

"That's him," Recker confirmed.

"From what I can tell, he has a long history of association with the Italians," Jones responded.

"Now we just have to figure out the connection to me."

"You've never seen him before? Come across him just in passing or something?"

Recker shook his head. "No. Maybe one of the cases we worked on had an effect on him somehow. Maybe someone he knew or was friends with or something."

"Well if he was hired by the Italians, it's likely got nothing to do with him. He's just doing what he was told."

"So, whatever it was, I did something to offend somebody high up in the food chain in their organization."

"Undoubtedly."

Recker sat down next to Jones and stared at the screen for several minutes, contemplating his next move. He had his elbows resting on his knees with his hands covering his mouth and nose as he considered his next move.

"What do you want to do now?" Jones said.

"Get some more information."

"How do you plan on doing that?"

Recker told him and for the next five minutes Jones shook his head and questioned the wisdom of his plan. Recker ignored him.

16

A couple of days had passed since they found out the identity of the man who tried to kill Recker. He had put a call out to Jimmy Malloy, Vincent's right-hand man, in an effort to see the leader of the northeast territory's crime faction. Vincent was out of town for a couple of days, but agreed to meet Recker once he returned. Recker was in the office, just about ready to leave for their meeting, when Jones entered.

"Mr. Recker, I'm surprised you're still here," Jones said. "I thought you would've been gone by now."

"In a hurry to get rid of me?"

"Not at all."

"I'm just about ready," Recker said, grabbing his guns out of the safe.

"You really think this meeting will be helpful?" Jones asked as he watched Recker getting fitted out.

"Ah, not this again. Why? You don't?"

"I'm just not sure what Vincent could tell you if he wasn't involved in the shooting in any capacity."

"These guys all know each other. You'd be surprised what they know. Besides, Vincent wants to expand his power base. If he knows I'm willing to take out some of his competition, that'll make him more likely to help me. Mutual benefit, it always works," Recker said smiling confidently.

The meeting was to happen at Pete's Place, Vincent's preferred diner for meetings. It was the same place where Recker first met Vincent. Once Recker arrived, he saw the same burly guard at the door as the first time. As he saw Recker approaching, the man put his arm up to stop Recker from going inside, recognizing him from the last meeting.

"You know the drill," the guard said.

"I thought that was only for the first-time meeting someone," Recker protested.

"Or for severe threats. I'd say you qualify."

"You do realize I could kill everyone in there without a gun?"

The guard shrugged, holding steady in his position.

Recker sighed, but figured he'd comply with the request. "Fine," he said, handing his gun over.

"And the other one," the guard said, remembering from the first time.

"Was hoping you'd forgotten about that one."

"Not likely."

Recker handed over his backup weapon, then the guard stepped aside, letting him through the door. Once inside, he was immediately greeted by Malloy, who escorted Recker to the back of the diner to Vincent's table. Vincent was ready to dig into the sirloin steak on his plate when Recker sat down across from him. Vincent looked up from his plate at his guest, giving him a grin. Then a waitress came by, putting another steak in front of Recker.

"I took the liberty of ordering for you. Please," Vincent said, putting his hand out toward the steak, hoping he'd join him for lunch. "I was happy when Jimmy told me you'd requested this meeting."

"You were?" Recker said, starting to cut into his steak. Medium rare, too much blood for him but he ate anyway not wishing to appear ungracious.

"I was. I was more than a little concerned about your well-being. I'd heard some nasty rumors that you were no longer with us."

"Seems more people know about that than they should," Recker said, swallowing the meat he was chewing.

"Well, you're a big deal. Big news like that... word gets around quickly."

"I'm sure it does."

"So what brings you here today? What can I help you with?" Vincent asked, as he forked a piece of meat into his mouth.

"What makes you think I need you to help me with anything?" Recker said.

"Isn't that why you're here?"

"Maybe I can help you with something."

Vincent chewed some more, then swallowed before he replied, matching Recker's gaze the whole time. "That would be intriguing."

"Well, the shooting is what I wanted to talk to you about."

"I had a feeling it might be," Vincent said. "You want to know who it was?"

Recker shook his head, cutting another piece of meat. "I already know who it was... Mario Mancini."

Vincent was a little surprised that he already had the name of the shooter. "You work quickly. I'm impressed. So, tell me, if you already know who it is, what do you need me for?"

"What do you know of this Mancini?"

"I know him by reputation, mostly. I know of his work. I've

seen him a couple of times at some business dealings, but I've never had direct contact with him."

"Dangerous?" Recker said.

"You would be wise to be careful with him."

"I've heard that he was hired to kill me."

"Then somebody must be anxious to have you dead," Vincent stated.

"Have you heard anything about who that someone might be?"

"Unfortunately, I have not."

"How about a guess?"

"I prefer to deal with facts rather than provide loosely based suggestions."

"Well, if Mancini works with the Italians, then who would have the authority to give him an order to take me out?" Recker said, putting down his knife and fork.

Vincent sighed, looking up at the ceiling as he thought deeply about the question, being careful as to his wording. He put his elbows on the table and rubbed his hands together before answering. "From my understanding of that organization, an order like that can only be issued by two or three people."

"And they are?"

"Marco Bellomi and his two lieutenants."

Recker watched Vincent intently as he spoke, getting the distinct impression that he was holding something back. He felt like Vincent wasn't giving him the entire truth.

"I get the feeling you're not telling me everything you know," Recker said, resuming his meal. Vincent let out a slight laugh, knowing it was tough to get something past him. He sighed once again before telling him the rest of what he knew. "In a case like yours... you have such a high profile, only figuratively speaking, but you have such a large presence that hovers over the city. You're a well-known entity, if only by name, that a kill order on you would likely only come from one man."

"Who is?"

"Marco Bellomi."

"I assumed that already. I just don't know why. I've never met him or had dealings with him."

"The question would be, why would Bellomi want you eliminated?" Vincent said.

"That's a question I've been wondering myself. Haven't come up with an answer yet."

"Just from my own personal experience with him, and from what I know, he would've only assigned that order for one reason. Possibly two."

"Which are?"

Now that they were getting to the meat of the meeting, Recker's appetite disappeared. He put down his fork again to listen carefully.

"The first would be that he feels you are a major threat to him and his organization and you're getting in his way. You've either blocked some of his deals or thinks you're a threat in a future capacity," Vincent said, using his knife to emphasize his points.

"And the second?"

"It's personal. You did something or hurt someone who is close to him. In that case, it would be a revenge killing."

"As far as I know, I haven't gotten in the way of anything, and I haven't done anything to anyone associated with him," Recker said.

"That you know of. Dig deeper. The connection is there, you just haven't found it yet. But trust me, it's for one of those two reasons."

Though Vincent hadn't really told him anything Recker didn't either already know or suspect, at least it was confirmation of it.

Vincent watched Recker closely as his guest's eyes drifted away from the table, deep in thought. He could tell by his face that Recker was having thoughts of all the carnage he could cause on his path of revenge.

"Your eyes give you away," Vincent told him.

"How's that?"

"You know the name of the man who tried to kill you and the name of the man who told him to do it."

"So?"

"Revenge is something that is in the DNA of men like you and me. You must be careful. You can't just engage in a path of destruction in hopes of avenging what was done to you."

"What do you suggest I do?"

"If you intend on killing these men, you must have a well thought out plan. A spur-of-the-moment rampage in the middle of the street may well get the job done, but you'll never live to see the end results. There's no satisfaction in that."

"I know. That's why I said that I might be able to help you," Recker said, dangling the carrot.

"And what did you have in mind?"

"As far as I know, they still think I'm dead. I would like to hit them sooner rather than later to capitalize on the element of surprise. Once they realize I'm still alive they'll be on high alert, thinking I'll return the hit."

"In all probability."

"I would like your help in finding and locating them. In return, I'll take them out and perhaps open up a larger piece of real estate for your organization to claim."

Vincent chewed slowly as he considered Recker's proposal. "That's an interesting proposition," Vincent said, placing his cutlery on the now empty plate. "The only problem I see with it is if you fail, and Bellomi knows that I helped you in trying to kill him, we'll have a very ugly and high profile war on our hands. It'll be a bloodbath."

"I won't fail," Recker said bluntly. "I have something that I still need to do after I take out these two. But I can't just let them go. If they tried once, they'll try again."

"While I do have every confidence in your abilities, Mike, taking out an organized crime boss isn't exactly child's play. Especially someone who may be looking for you. The other thing to think about is if you happen to take out Mancini first, Bellomi will know you're coming. He'll be ready and waiting."

"So, you're not interested?" Recker said, beginning to stand up.

"Well, I didn't say that," Vincent said, holding up his hand to stop Recker from leaving. "If you were to take out Bellomi, without any official help from me, it'd have to be a very smart and discreet plan. Only a handful of people could know about it, otherwise you risk word getting out."

"I agree. How many people do you trust?" Recker said.

"Very few. It would also have to be people who aren't well known in my organization. Someone like Jimmy would stick out like a sore thumb. They are already well aware of him."

"All I need is the best time and place to hit them. I'll do the rest."

Vincent rubbed his hands together as he was thinking. He was intrigued by Recker's plan, but not yet convinced of its probability of success. Recker, with his meal long since cold, had no desire to stay any longer as Vincent deliberated. With or without his help, Recker would not be stopped or dissuaded in getting revenge.

"Well, when you decide, let me know," Recker said, standing up from the table.

"I'll have an answer for you before the day is over," Vincent said, resuming what was left of his meal without looking up.

Recker left the diner, picking up his guns on the way out.

Malloy watched him exit. Once he was gone, he sat down at the table across from his boss.

"What do you think?" Vincent said as he wiped up the last remnants of his meal with a piece of bread.

"This might be what we've been waiting for," Malloy answered. "We've been talking about hitting Bellomi for almost forever, boss. I mean, this might be the perfect opportunity to expand our territory. And we don't even have to do the hit. We let Recker do it, and we're in the clear."

Vincent nodded, though he still had reservations. "We still must be cautious. If word gets out that we're staking out Bellomi territory, and then there's a hit, and Recker fails, then we'll be knee deep in it."

"But if he's successful, they'll be so disorganized and bewildered, they won't know what hit them."

"Bellomi would have to be the first target," Vincent said thoughtfully.

"What about the other guy, Mancini?"

"Ahh, small potatoes. He's just a hired gun. If Mancini gets taken out, you won't see Bellomi for two years. He'll hole himself up in some fortress somewhere Recker will never get to him. No, Bellomi has to be the first hit."

"What if we agree to Recker's terms, but with some of our own conditions?" Malloy said.

"Such as?"

"We'll provide Bellomi's location, and give him access to it, wherever it might be, but he must also take out his top two lieutenants at the same time. Cripple the organization all at once. With their leadership gone, we can take over easy."

"What about Mancini?"

"He'll be in the wind. But at that point, we'll have control over half the city. If he still wants Mancini, we'll find him for him, wherever he goes."

"I think it's looking like we might have a deal with Mr. Recker," Vincent said, smiling.

"There's always another option for him."

"Which is?"

"After he takes out the Italians, he goes down," Malloy said with no flash of emotion on his face.

"Why would we wanna kill Recker after he does a job for us?"

"He's not a part of our organization, he'll be the only one who really knows what happened," Malloy said with a shrug. "Why take chances?"

Vincent shook his head, not ready to go in that direction. "No, I don't think Mr. Recker will be a problem. At least not at this point. We've had a couple dealings with him and so far, he's been a man of his word. He's been an ally to us and I see no reason to change our opinion or dealings with him. If that should change, then we'll decide at that time. But for now, they'll be no more talk like that."

Malloy nodded, complying with his boss's wishes.

"Besides, there may very well be another time and place in which Mr. Recker's services could be very useful to us," Vincent said.

Malloy tilted his head, not understanding. "In what way?"

"This city will be undergoing major changes in the next few years. Power will be redistributed. Some major players will be long gone. We'll have control over half the city. That leaves another half of it in play."

"Meaning Jeremiah?"

Vincent nodded. "Up to now we've stayed on good terms with Jeremiah. But at some point, that very well may change. There may be a time when control of the whole city is up for grabs," Vincent said.

"And you think Recker would side with us when that day comes?"

"If we have something worth offering. I don't believe he would have any interest in any of this if he didn't have a personal stake in it, like with Bellomi. But there may be a day when we can offer him something that Jeremiah cannot, if it should ever come to that."

"Maybe we could eventually bring him into the fold," Malloy said.

"No, I don't think he's the type of guy who would join up with anyone unless it was for a specific purpose. He's a loner. Plays by his own rules. Dangerous, yes, but if handled properly, can continue to be a strong ally of ours. We must give him a long leash."

"What if he gets in our way at some point? Gets in the way of one of our deals, takes out one of our guys, or someone we have a stake in?"

"We'll give him some latitude. He's a dangerous man." Vincent smiled. "Like I said, a man like him would be an extreme asset if war ever breaks out in this city. A long-term view with him will benefit us much more than any short-term deal will. We must remain cognizant of that."

Malloy nodded, agreeing to his boss' point of view on the matter.

Once Recker got back to the office, Jones was still there working on the computer. He was about to ask him how the meeting went when Recker's phone started ringing. He was a little surprised to hear from Vincent already. He figured he would take as much time as necessary to study the situation, so Recker wasn't expecting a call until later in the evening.

"Made a decision already?" Recker said, trying to hide his surprise.

"I have," Vincent said. "I will help you find the men you seek."

"Good." Recker nodded over to Jones to let him know the answer.

"I do have some conditions attached, however."

"OK?"

"Bellomi must be your first target. If you go after Mancini first and Bellomi gets wind of it, you'll never get close enough to him."

"I can agree to that."

"Here's the real kicker. When you take out Bellomi, we want you to take out his top two aides at the same time," Vincent said.

Recker sucked in a breath and thought for a moment. "I have no quarrel with them."

"Yes, but they could always take out another hit on you, deeming you a major threat. If you want to take out Bellomi, the entire organization must be crippled, brought to its knees."

"And giving you an easier time to move in and take over?"

"Does the proposition give you pause?"

"Taking out three men at one time isn't an issue. I've done it before," Recker said with a practiced air of nonchalance.

"Now, in return for this, we'll get you access to wherever you need to be to accomplish the task. We'll monitor them and make sure they're all in one place when we contact you. You'll also have to be ready to go at a moment's notice."

"I will be."

"A thing like this, a perfect opportunity could present itself at any time, and we need to take advantage of it should it arrive."

"That's not a problem. What if it's in a small, closed off area?"

"Like I said, wherever it is, we'll get you in," Vincent said.

"What about Mancini?"

"He's not a major player, he can be gotten after the others."

"Once he hears about Bellomi, he'll go underground or out of the city," Recker noted.

"He's nothing to be concerned about. Even if he goes underground, after we take out the Italians, I'll control half the city. We'll find him and snuff him out. I'll bring him to you myself. If I get word he's left the city, I'll have someone follow him to the other side of the world and bring him back. He won't get away from us. You have my word on that."

"OK."

"So we have a deal then?" Vincent said.

"We do. You get me access... I'll take them out."

"Excellent. One other thing though. Until this happens, you're gonna need to keep a low profile. I understand that may be difficult for a man like you, but it must be done. If someone spots you on the street, or you do one of your heroic deeds that winds up in the newspaper, that'll throw everything out of whack. We'll lose the element of surprise and Bellomi will be that much tougher to get to."

"How long do you anticipate this taking?" Recker said.

"Tough to say. We have to be patient. This type of thing takes time."

"Well time is something I don't have a lot of. Neither is patience."

"I understand."

"I'll give you a week. If you can't flush him out by then, I'll do it on my own."

"That could be challenging," Vincent said, suddenly sounding unsure at the unexpected twist.

"One week," Recker repeated. "Make it happen."

As soon as Recker put his phone in his pocket, he looked at Jones, who seemed to have somewhat of a disapproving face. Jones wasn't sure they should've been aligning themselves with the criminal element of the city. Recker, though, was willing to make a deal with the devil if it led to getting the result that he wanted.

"You don't agree with this?" Recker said.

Jones stopped typing to look at his partner. "I'm just not sure throwing in with a major crime syndicate is what we signed up for. We started this to stop crimes and get criminals in jail."

"I thought we started this to help prevent innocent people from getting hurt."

"We did."

"So taking out a major crime organization wouldn't qualify?"

"But at what cost? Are we going down that same path? And besides, we're taking out one organization, just so another one can move in. That's not really eliminating anything. That's just changing the composition of the players," Jones said.

"I look at it like this. One is trying to take me out. One's willing to leave me alone. If someone tries to take you out once, they'll try again. I'm not gonna let that happen."

Jones nodded. "I understand all of that. And I'm not against you taking retribution on them, per se, I just don't know if aligning with Vincent is the right move, that's all."

"One thing I learned in the CIA is that sometimes you have to make strange bedfellows if you share a common goal," Recker said. "Sometimes you gotta put other issues aside if someone else can help you accomplish that goal."

"So you're saying you'd do anything to accomplish the mission. By any means necessary."

"Well I'm not going to go out and kill a bunch of children or anything to get what I want, but as long as nobody innocent is involved, then yeah, I'll do what I have to."

"What if after you take out Bellomi, Vincent decides you're a risk that he can't allow to walk the streets? What if he has a plan to take you out the moment you take out Bellomi?" Jones said.

"This isn't my first time doing this, David. I've been double crossed before. I would imagine at some point in my life, if I keep doing this, I'm sure it'll happen again. If Vincent decides he can't have me walking around, I'll be ready for him."

"So you don't really trust him?"

"I only really trust two people in this world right now. Mia and you," Recker said, checking his weapons. "Besides, I'm fully loaded."

"I'm going to take this as one of those times when I just have to trust that you're in the right and know what you're doing," Jones said.

17

Four days had passed since Recker made the agreement with Vincent. He had confined himself to either his apartment or the office, though he was starting to get a little antsy being so cooped up. He knew it was for the best, to make sure he wasn't spotted by any of Bellomi's soldiers and throw the plan off the rails. As far as most people knew, Recker was dead. He had to keep it that way until the plan was in action. There were only five people that knew he was still alive as far as he was aware... Jones, Mia, Gibson, Vincent, and Malloy. But if he had to stay cooped up for another week, that was likely to change. Everyone would know he was still alive because he'd go on the rampage.

Recker was in the office, sorting and cleaning out his guns, as he'd done every day for the last four days. It was just something to stop him from going stir crazy. Anything to keep him from the boredom he couldn't seem to escape. Every now and then he'd do some computer work with Jones, but that usually only lasted an hour or two at a time. He missed being out on the street.

"How long do you plan to keep this up?" Jones said.

"Not much longer. Two or three more days at the most."

"Good. Because while I appreciate your situation and am trying to be as supportive as I can, there are people out there who need our help."

"I know." Recker sighed.

"Look at this," Jones said, picking up a stack of papers from the drawer and tossing them down on the desk. "Six people that I've identified as possibly needing our assistance. And while you're stuck in here, none of them are getting the help they need or deserve."

"I know," Recker said, feeling guilty enough already.

Recker was already aware that there were people out there needing assistance. It'd been weighing on his mind. It was one of the factors, in addition to wanting revenge, that was making him want to get out of there sooner rather than later. He and Jones knew that every day they delayed getting out on the street, there was a very good likelihood that someone they might have protected, could get killed. Recker's phone rang, and he snatched it from his pocket to answer it, hoping it'd be the call he was waiting for. He was disappointed when he saw it wasn't Vincent, though not completely so, since it was Mia calling. He once again chose not to answer it, the third time in four days that she had called. The third time he chose to ignore her.

"Ms. Hendricks again?" Jones said.

"Yeah."

"Not that I'm trying to intervene in your personal affairs, but may I ask why you're choosing to ignore her calls? That's the third time I'm aware of that you've done so."

"She's gonna want to meet or something and I just can't do that right now," Recker replied.

"So why don't you just tell her you're busy with a case instead of avoiding her?"

"I dunno. Just seemed simpler this way."

The sound went off indicating he had a voice message, just like the previous three times. Just like the others, it was just Mia asking him to call her back when he was free.

"You know, it's probably a good idea to call her back before she starts worrying," Jones said.

"Why would she worry?"

Jones raised his eyebrows, looking at Recker as if he were some kind of simpleton. "Probably because you were recently shot and recovering from an injury? If you don't respond she might think something happened."

"Oh. I didn't think of that," Recker said.

"Somehow that doesn't surprise me."

Jones went back to typing with a shake of his head. Taking Jones' advice, Recker immediately called Mia back. She picked up right away, the phone not even getting to the second ring.

"I patch you up and take care of you for a week, then you leave and ignore me?" Mia said.

Recker thought she sounded angry. Understandable now he thought about it. "Uh…"

"Relax, I'm just kidding."

"Yeah, I'm sorry about that. I've just been a little busy catching up on things," Recker explained.

"I kinda figured as much."

"So. What's up?"

"Nothing. Can't a girl just call a guy to see how he's doing?"

"Uh, I guess so."

"I just wanted to make sure you were OK with your shoulder," she said after a moment or two's hesitation.

"Oh. Yeah. Yeah, it's fine," Recker said, moving it around. "A little stiff at times, but not too bad considering."

"Good. Yeah, since I haven't seen or talked to you since you left my apartment, I just wanted to say hi, see how you were and all."

"I'm good," Recker said, trying to think of something else to say. Small talk was not something he enjoyed. "Uh... how's work?"

"Busy. Yeah, really busy. They're running me around all over the place. Got like another ten days straight to go." Mia laughed.

"You'll make it through."

"So, one of the reasons I called, I'm on day shift tomorrow, would you be interested in meeting after work for dinner... maybe six or seven?" she said hopefully.

Recker was afraid she was going to ask something like that. "You know, I'd really love that, but I'm already committed to doing something tomorrow night that I can't back out of. It's for a client."

"Oh. OK. Yeah, I understand. It's fine."

It didn't sound fine to Recker, so he tried to sweeten the blow. "Otherwise you know I'd love to."

"It's fine. We can maybe make it for next week or something," Mia said, obviously disappointed. "Maybe when I get out of my nightmare work schedule."

"Definitely."

"I take it you're not taking any more time off then? Getting right back in the saddle?"

"I have to. There's some things going on that I have to be involved in," Recker told her.

"You know, you could always let the police help. That's kind of their job."

"Not for this."

They talked for a few more minutes, neither saying anything of much significance, just more small talk. Once they completed their conversation, Recker let the phone swing down in his hand, hitting his leg with it and sighing.

"I take it that didn't go so well?" Jones said.

"It went fine," Recker said tersely.

"I can tell by the tone of your voice," Jones said sarcastically.

"It's just hard saying no and disappointing her."

"Why do you think that is?"

"Geez, what are you, a shrink in your spare time? I dunno. She's just always so nice and pleasant. It'd be so much easier if she wasn't so damn friendly all the time."

"Just terrible, isn't it? It'd be more preferable if she was obnoxious or something, wouldn't it?"

"You know what I mean."

"I take it she wanted to meet for dinner?"

"Yeah, tomorrow."

"Well, if you really wanted to, you could still keep a low profile by eating at her place."

Recker gave him a peculiar look upon hearing that. "What? Weren't you the one who told me not to get involved with her?"

"Since when did you ever listen to me? I'm just fleshing out options should you prefer it."

"Well I don't prefer it. It's one thing eating a restaurant with someone, it's entirely different eating at their home."

"Too personal?"

"Yes. Besides, you were right, I don't want to give her a false hope that something could eventually happen between us."

"Did you just tell me I was right?" Jones said, almost falling out of his chair in astonishment.

"Yes, but don't let it go to your head."

"It just happens so infrequently that you admit it."

For the next few minutes, Jones watched Recker circle around the perimeter of the office, deep in thought. He said a couple of things to him, but Recker didn't hear a word of it. Jones wasn't sure what was in his mind... Vincent, Mia, Bellomi, or any combination of the three. Recker's concentration was broken when his phone rang again. He eagerly looked at the screen thinking it was Vincent, but once again, was slightly disappointed.

"Tyrell? What can I help you with?" Recker said.

"Hey, uh, it's uh, kind of hard for me to ask this..."

"Just spit it out. I won't kill you over the phone."

Gibson laughed. "Yeah right. With some of the things you're capable of, wouldn't surprise me if you could."

"I'll work on it."

"I bet. Listen, I could use a favor," Gibson said.

"*You* need a favor?"

"Yeah. You said you owe me for getting you the info on Mancini, right?"

"I did."

"Well if you help me out with this, then we'll call it even."

"You haven't told me anything yet," Recker said.

"Remember I told you before about my kid brother?"

"Yeah."

"He's getting recruited hard, man. I'm afraid he's gonna get caught up in the pressure and do something he'll regret."

"Jeremiah?"

"Nah, Jeremiah wouldn't do that. He has respect for those who wanna get out of here and do something cool with their life."

"Who is it then?"

"Just some upstart gangs trying to make a name for themselves. They're small-time, man, but they're recruiting high school kids hard, to get bigger," Gibson said. He sounded genuinely concerned and Recker knew that Gibson was keen for his brother to stay away from street life.

"Does Darnell wanna do it?"

"Of course he don't. That's why he came and told me. He don't wanna, but he's afraid that somehow he's gonna get forced into it. These are kids, man, most of them are afraid to say no to these gangbangers... afraid something will happen to them if they don't do what they want."

"Why don't you just put a stop to it?" Recker said.

"It's not that easy for me. I'm out here on the streets every day. I got no gang affiliation, no one to watch my back, if I go up against these guys... even small-timers, we both know what'll happen."

Recker nodded to himself. "Why don't you ask Jeremiah for help?"

"Because you know what happens when you ask guys like Jeremiah and Vincent for help? You're indebted to them for life. It's always hanging over your head. Right now, you're really the only other person I know I can trust this with."

"So you want me to play the bad guy?"

"No, I want you to play the tough, bad ass, mo-fo that you are," Gibson said.

"Fine. If you want my help, you got it." Recker liked Gibson and anyway, he did owe him for Mancini.

"I really appreciate that, man, I really do."

Recker could hear the relief in Gibson's voice as he spoke. "It's not gonna be for a few days though. I gotta conclude my business elsewhere first."

"You goin' after Mancini?"

"The less you know the better."

"Aight, it's cool. How long will it take, you think?"

"Give me about four or five days. Then I'll take care of Darnell's problem," Recker said.

"That's fine."

"Can he hold out that long?"

"Yeah. Thanks, Recker. It means a lot to me."

"That's what friends are for, right? Like you said... I owed you one."

As soon as he hung up, Recker slumped down into the couch and stared at the wall. Now he had one more thing on his mind to think about. Jones wondered what his last conversation was about, but figured he'd wait a few minutes until Recker had come out of whatever trance he was in. He figured Recker wouldn't hear him, anyway. Recker sat there motionless for five minutes, just staring straight ahead at the wall, running different scenarios through his mind. Once he'd exhausted his brain with all the options he had available to him, he broke from his stare and stood back up. Seeing how he was back on his feet, Jones felt it was safe to engage him in conversation.

"From the tone of your call with Mr. Gibson, I take it he needs your help with something?" Jones said.

"His little brother's getting recruited by a local gang."

"I fail to see how that has a connection with you."

"Tyrell wants my help in stopping it."

"Why doesn't he just do it himself?"

"It's not that simple. Tyrell has no gang affiliation, and everyone knows it. There's nothing stopping a gang taking out a hit on him. They don't have to fear retaliation by another gang for taking out one of theirs. If he stands up to a gang on his own, they'll take him out for sure."

"So how will it be any different for you?" Jones said.

"I don't live there," Recker said. "Besides, if it wasn't for Tyrell, who knows if we would've found out about Bellomi taking a hit out on me. I owe him for that."

Jones nodded, understanding his point. "How do you propose to manage all the tasks you've got on your plate these days?"

"I'll give Vincent two more days, then I'll do it on my terms.

After that, I'll take care of Tyrell's problem. Then after that, we'll get back to work."

"What about your other problem?"

"What other problem?" Recker said, confused.

"The Mia problem. We both know she's falling for you."

Recker threw his hands up. He had no answer. Yet. "I'll just have to play it by ear I guess."

It was a relatively quiet day for the pair for the rest of the evening. No further phone calls or situations. Recker hoped the next day would be a little livelier for him. He was anxious to get back to work. Both Recker and Jones wound up sleeping in the office, taking separate couches. Recker woke up a little after eight, finding Jones already up and typing away at a keyboard. Recker walked over to the Keurig machine to make himself a cup of coffee as he got rid of the sleep from his eyes.

"What time did you get up?" Recker said.

"A little over an hour ago."

"Don't you believe in sleeping late?"

"Maybe if there weren't so many people in need of assistance. I was telling you yesterday about the stack of cases of people who need help. The list has grown to eight now. With all these cases on my mind, I find it hard to sleep well," Jones said, stretching and yawning.

"So what are you doing about them?"

"Well, a couple of these are domestic related issues. I've sent anonymous emails to the police explaining the situations, under the disguise of a concerned friend. Hopefully that at least gets a cursory look. If nothing else, maybe it'll persuade the perpetrators to back off for a while until we can get involved."

Recker let out a deep and loud sigh, easily heard by Jones.

"What is it?" Jones said.

"People out there need help and here I am standing here drinking coffee," Recker said.

"I think it's manageable for another day or so," Jones replied, hoping to ease his frustration and to guide him away from taking matters into his own hands.

"The point is I need to be out there. I didn't survive two gunshot wounds in the last nine months just to stand here on the sidelines."

"Well, hopefully in the next few days you'll be able to."

"There's no hoping. I will be. One way or another."

Recker took a few more moments to feel sorry for himself, then shook it off and joined Jones at the desk to do some computer work.

"How's Agent 17 coming along?" Recker casually blurted out.

Jones temporarily stopped typing to think of a response, though he didn't take his eyes off his computer. He then turned to his friend to speak truthfully, hoping he didn't get a death stare, or worse, in return. "Honestly? I haven't been working on it."

"Why?"

"With everything that's been going on with you, and the cases are piling up, I haven't had time to work on it. When all this is behind us, hopefully by the end of the week, I'll be able to devote more time to it."

Jones waited for an angry response, and was mildly surprised when there was none coming. "Fair enough," Recker said, understanding it wasn't at the top of the priority list at the moment.

Jones turned back to his computer and made a face, pleasantly surprised at how that turned out. Recker, though eager to find Agent 17, completely understood that Jones was stretched thin now with him not out there on the street. Jones was trying to take care of situations remotely, and keep an eye on things from a distance, not to mention trying to find Bellomi on his own, just in case Vincent came up empty or took too much time. So Recker knew he had a lot on his plate, and finding Agent 17 was not at the top of his list for the moment. He was good with that. At least for the time being. If he asked the question in another couple of weeks, and didn't get the progress he was looking for, the response might not be so pleasant. A couple of quiet hours went by until the silence was interrupted by the sound of Recker's phone. The look of hope on his face gave away who it was.

"I hope you finally have something for me," Recker said.

"I take it the four or five days you've been underground haven't been so relaxing for you," Vincent said, drawing things out.

"Pulling the trigger relaxes me. Sitting here for a week makes me go certifiable."

"Understood."

"So do you have something?"

"It took a few days longer than I planned, but we've finally got him."

"Where?"

"Bellomi is having a meeting with four or five other men, including his top two aides at a restaurant called Vicenzio's," Vincent said. "It's downtown. A rather nice establishment come to think of it."

"How'd you find out?"

"I have sources."

"Where and when?" Recker said.

"One o'clock today. Three hours from now. Can you be there?"

"Is that even a question?"

"No, I suppose not."

"I understand the restaurant doesn't open until three. So Bellomi and his cohorts will be the only ones in the place other than restaurant personnel."

"Who are the others with him?"

"Lower level guys. Probably has business to discuss with them."

"What about guards outside?" Recker said.

"There will likely be some. How many I don't know."

"I'll have to deal with them as soon as they hear the shots."

"I'll have that taken care of," Vincent said darkly.

"How?"

"Just suffice to say that they'll be incapacitated in some manner. They'll be out of the way."

"If I'm gonna do this and put my neck out there, I need to know everything. I need to know the entire plan that way I can make alterations if something goes awry. If I don't know the plan, I won't know if something's not going the way it should."

Vincent took a second to think but quickly agreed to the request. "Very well. It's a reasonable request. You have until 1:15 to do the job. At 1:10 there will be a couple of police detectives that will be out front who will take into custody whatever guards are stationed out there."

"Convenient. How am I getting in?"

"The back door will be open for you."

"Bellomi is having a high-level meeting at a closed restaurant and is going to just leave the back door open for anybody to saunter through?"

"Not quite. There will be a guard or two," Vincent answered. "Jimmy will have them taken care of by the time you get there."

"OK."

"I would suggest you take up the uniform of the staff to get closer, but that's your business. You're enough of a pro that I don't need to tell you how to get it done. We'll get you in and make sure you have the time to do it. After that, you're on your own."

"Not a problem."

"I didn't think it would be. You have five minutes. After that, I can't protect you."

"What about those detectives out front?" Recker said, slightly concerned about them.

"You don't need to worry about them. They're on my payroll."

"Do they know what's going to happen?"

"They've been informed. They know. But they don't know who will pull the trigger and they don't need to know who. Once they hear the shots, they'll stay outside and call for backup. They will not attempt to go in alone. That will give you a couple of minutes to get out through the back door."

"Sounds all right."

"Jimmy will be out back waiting for you in a car and will drive you to wherever you wish to go from there," Vincent said.

"OK."

"Is there anything that you're not comfortable with or wish to be explained further?"

"No. It sounds fine. As long as everybody does what you say they will."

"They will. The detectives out front will do their part to make sure nobody enters that restaurant. Jimmy will have the back taken care of and will make sure there is no interference from any of the staff members that are there," Vincent said. "I cannot guarantee what the members of Bellomi's party will do once they are there. I would assume they'd all be sitting and eating, but I cannot say that with full certainty."

"OK."

"So, as I said, I will make sure you get in. After you do what you came to do, I'll make sure you have a safe passage out. The rest of what happens in between those two, well... that is up to you."

18

It didn't take Recker long to get ready. As soon as he was done with Vincent, he explained the situation to Jones.

"Are you sure you can trust him?" Jones said. "What if he goes back on his word or something isn't how he promises?"

"Then I'll deal with it."

"I hope you're right."

"I think Vincent's a man of his word," Recker said. "I think he'll do what he says he will. Right now, our interests are the same. He can be trusted on this. If his interests were conflicted, it might be different. He'll gain from this. There won't be any double cross here."

"I just hope it goes according to plan and the next time I see you isn't from a jail cell or the morgue."

"Don't be a worrywart. Besides, I've been doing this for a long time. I know when something doesn't feel right."

Recker immediately got everything he needed, guns and ammo, and started to make his way downtown. He wanted to make sure there were no holdups. He also wanted to make sure he wasn't delayed by traffic and that he got there a little early so he could scout out the building and surroundings. Recker drove downtown, parking ten or twelve blocks away. He didn't want to park too close and risk being seen. He also felt that walking would give him a better idea of what was near the restaurant in case he had to leave in more of a hurry than planned, or if Malloy wasn't waiting like Vincent said he would.

Recker knew he needed his own escape plan in the event he was left on his own. Though he still felt Vincent could be trusted and he wouldn't doublecross him, he was aware of the value of a backup plan. With all his experience, he knew sometimes things just didn't go the way they were drawn up. He always had a backup plan, a second escape route. In some instances, he had a third or fourth option. When he was with the CIA, he usually had at the very least, a day or two notice before he had an assignment. This was as short a notice as he'd ever gotten. He'd have to make the best of it as there was no way of knowing when a better opportunity would come up. Plus, he was eager to put it all behind him and move on to other things. He didn't have long to remember everything. He only had a few minutes to make note of all the streets and buildings in the area in case he had to use them if he left the restaurant in a hurry. When he was with the CIA, Recker knew of some agents who preferred to work on short notice. When they had too much time on their hands before a mission, they tended to over think things. They got over anxious and they pressed, risking the integrity of the mission. Recker wasn't one of those. He preferred having a little more time to size up every situation he got in before he was knee deep in it. He liked having all the angles covered, understanding everything that could possibly go wrong, and having a countermeasure for it.

Once Recker found the restaurant, he walked past, not wanting to stop and look too long at it in case others were also staked out in the area. He walked a couple more blocks and then turned right, doubling back to go behind the restaurant. He looked at the time and still had over half an hour to go. He found a small alley between a couple of buildings to pass the time away while still having a pretty good look at the rear of the restaurant. He eagerly watched for signs of Vincent's crew. There was no sign of them.

Once thirty minutes ticked off the clock, Recker was starting to wonder if the mission was a dud. He didn't see Malloy or Bellomi's guard at the back of the restaurant. He'd give it a little more time before chalking it up as a failure. Only a minute later, Recker saw the first thing that looked promising. The back door to the restaurant opened and a couple of menacing looking men stepping through. They stopped just outside the door on both sides of it and leaned up against the wall. It was 1:02. Recker kept watching, waiting for Malloy to show up. It didn't look like he was coming. Suddenly, one of the men fluttered to the ground like he was shot. A few seconds later, the other guard flopped to the ground as well. Neither of them were getting up. Recker didn't notice any signs of life from either of them. Recker looked up, knowing there was a sniper in the area somewhere, though he wasn't leaving the confines of his position just yet to find out where it was.

Recker looked back toward the restaurant and saw a man walking towards it. He focused in on the man, getting a better look at him. It was Malloy. Upon seeing him, Recker left the alley and walked toward the rear of the restaurant. Malloy saw someone approaching and stopped in his tracks before he realized it was Recker. Vincent's right-hand man then picked up his pace again, meeting Recker at the back door of the restaurant. They both reached it at the same time.

"Is this your handy work?" Recker said, pointing at the bodies on the ground.

Malloy smiled, looking down at the bodies, each with a neatly drilled hole in the head. "Nah. Not really my style. I prefer up close and personal."

Recker looked a little uneasy and stared at the nearby buildings, knowing if Malloy didn't do it, there was another person out there who could've had a gun aimed at him at that very second. Malloy picked up on his hesitation and momentarily looked back at the building across from them.

"Don't worry. You're not on the list," Malloy said calmly.

"Good to know."

"Think we'd double cross you?"

"There's some who thought that might've been a possibility," Recker said.

"Don't worry, you're not being set up."

"If I thought I was, I wouldn't be here."

Malloy opened his jacket, revealing a Glock pistol for Recker to use. Recker grinned, then pulled out a Glock of his own. "You didn't really think I'd come empty-handed, did you?" Recker said.

Malloy shrugged. "Just thought I'd offer."

"Thanks, but I only use my own."

Recker turned the handle of the door, but it was locked. He then turned to Malloy, who smiled and stepped in front of him.

"We got this covered," Malloy said.

He knocked on the door twice, about a second apart from each other. Immediately, the door sprung open. Malloy took a step back and put both his arms out in front to usher Recker into the building.

"Not coming?" Recker said.

"Our deal was to get you in. The rest is up to you."

Recker nodded his head.

"Besides, you were told we'd get you out of here quickly, right? I'll bring the car around and wait for you."

"Where will you be?"

"Right there," Malloy indicated, pointing to a spot three buildings down on the same side of the restaurant. "I'll wait till 1:20. If you're not here, I'll assume something happened to you."

"If I'm not there it's because I'm dead."

"Let's hope it doesn't come to that."

"It won't," Recker told him. "Do you know how many are in there?"

"Five. Bellomi, his two aides, and two of his soldiers. There's three staff workers in there. They're all clean. Two in the kitchen and the manager."

"They know what's going down?"

"The manager is receiving a nice sum for his part in today's festivities. Once he sees you, he'll head into the kitchen and make sure the kitchen workers are out of the way," Malloy explained.

"Sounds like you got it all covered."

"Almost. All except for the men with the guns."

Malloy turned his back and started walking away as Recker stepped inside the restaurant. There was a small table to his left that had a white apron laying on it. He picked it up and put it on, hoping he'd blend in with the staff. If he walked into the restaurant in his regular attire, he thought there was a good chance that Bellomi's men would identify him right away and be on guard. Of course, there was a chance of that anyway, but he figured it wouldn't hurt to try it. Even a fraction of a second could be the difference between revenge or an early grave.

Recker could hear the voices of Bellomi and his men chatting away, though he couldn't hear the specifics of their conversation. He walked over to the swinging doors that led out into the restaurant, standing just behind them, looking through the glass at his intended victims. The restaurant manager saw the back of Recker standing by the door and rushed back into the kitchen area. Recker could hear the man whispering to his workers to get out of sight. He looked back toward the kitchen and saw a silver metal tray that had a couple things on it. He picked it up, holding his gun just underneath to conceal it.

The five Italians were deep in serious discussions, not paying much attention to anything else other than each other. Recker was still looking through the swinging door window, waiting for the perfect opportunity. He looked at the time, knowing he couldn't wait much longer. It was 1:14. Vincent's detectives should've been out front right about now, rounding up Bellomi's men. He'd wait two more minutes before making his move. Hopefully, they were on time. If not, they'd be coming through the front door when they heard the commotion inside. That'd mean a couple more men that Recker would have to eliminate. Two more minutes went by, Bellomi and his men were still in the same position as they were before.

Recker had to trust that the men guarding the front of the building were already being taken care of. He couldn't quite see the front door from where he was standing, and there were no windows by the tables for him to look out of. He figured it was now or never. There was no more time to waste. The table the Italians were sitting at was in the corner of the restaurant, so he had to walk across the length of the room to get to them. He had to hope that nobody recognized him or got suspicious before he got there. He gently pushed the doors open, trying not to cause any attention on himself as he walked out. He kept the tray out in front of him, both hands underneath it, one of which had his gun firmly entrenched in it. His finger was already on the trigger in case the shooting started earlier than he planned.

Recker slowly and cautiously walked toward the table, hoping nobody would bother to look up at him. He was about halfway there. Though he wasn't nervous, he did feel a little anxious. He'd faced similar odds before so he wasn't doubting his ability to get the job done. But he was aware of the capabilities of the men in front of him. He walked a couple more feet before Bellomi disengaged from his conversation and sat back, looking at the unfamiliar server approaching them. Bellomi was a frequent visitor of the restaurant and never noticed the man before. He thought it strange the manager would have a new person working at a private function for him. With Recker's low profile, none of Bellomi's men knew him by sight. Even Bellomi didn't know him by his face. Even though he ordered the hit on Recker, nobody in his organization had ever done business with him, so none of them would know him if he was standing next to them. They only knew his reputation. That was about to change.

As Recker got to within a few feet of the table, he tossed the silver tray aside and immediately started firing. Most gunmen would've shot whoever was closest to them first. But Recker knew that the men seated with their back to him would have to take a few extra seconds to turn around. That'd give him enough time to mow them down. If he shot them first, the men facing him could get lucky enough to get a shot off at him. The two men facing him were the street soldiers that Bellomi wanted to have conversations with. Recker shot them both in the chest before they even realized what was going on. Once Bellomi's lieutenants saw the others get shot in front of them, they jumped to their feet to face their assailant. It was no use though. Recker calmly fired a couple more rounds before the men were able to reach their guns. They had just turned around when Recker fired a couple more shots, both men getting plugged in the chest. Bellomi usually carried a weapon on him just in case. He was initially a little stunned when the first two of his men went down and didn't immediately reach for his gun. As his lieutenants were getting hit, Bellomi pulled out his gun, but Recker saw him just before he was about to pull the trigger. Recker beat him to the punch, shooting Bellomi in the left shoulder, causing him to fall to the ground.

Recker quickly glanced at the door in case more of Bellomi's men were running in after hearing the shots. None were. He figured Vincent's detectives must've taken care of them by now as he was promised. Recker then turned his attention back to the victims in front of him. Bellomi was writhing around in pain, the only one of the group who was still breathing. Recker checked the others to make sure they were dead while keeping an eye on Bellomi, just in case he had any other tricks up his sleeve. Once he was done checking the pulses on the dead bodies, he walked over to Bellomi, almost standing over top of him.

"Who the hell are you?" Bellomi said defiantly.

"I'm the man you tried to kill... Mike Recker."

Bellomi's eyes widened, not believing what he was hearing. "They told me you were dead. They told me they killed you."

"Not quite."

"How'd you know I'd be here?"

"Tooth fairy," Recker said sarcastically, and with a grin. "Why'd you wanna have me killed? I never ran into you before that I know of."

Still in a considerable amount of pain, Bellomi was clutching his shoulder, feeling a shortness of breath. "You got involved in a marital dispute a month or so ago."

"Yeah, so?"

"You got into it with the husband, Tony. You roughed him up some."

"Yeah, I remember. What was it to you?"

"He's one of my men. He worked for me. He asked me if I could take care of it."

"Very accommodating of you to help," Recker told him.

"Considering the guards in front and back aren't bursting in here, I'm assuming you've already taken care of them?" Bellomi was sweating now, trembling from shock.

"Oh, they've been neutralized."

"What're you gonna do with me?" Bellomi looked worried, though he was quite certain of his fate.

"Well, looks like your organization's taken a hit here today. If I could be assured that you'd never come after me again, we might have something to discuss."

Bellomi narrowed his eyes and spoke through chattering teeth. "We both know if I get out of here that I'll come looking for you."

Recker nodded. "I know. That's why there's no other way."

Recker aimed his gun at Bellomi's chest and pulled the trigger, ending the Italian mob boss' life immediately. Recker took one more glance around the room and at the bodies on the floor, just to make sure there was nobody else there, or nothing else he was missing. With his work there done, he scurried out of the seating area and back through the hallway leading to the back door. He took a quick look in the kitchen to see if the workers were there and saw anything, but they were still out of sight. Recker then bolted out the back door. While it was in the back of his mind that he might catch a bullet from the sniper out there now that the job was done, ending any possibilities of the hit being laid at Vincent's feet, he was still relatively certain that he was in the clear. As he came out of the restaurant, Recker looked a few buildings down to his right and saw the car Malloy promised him would be there. He ran over to it, getting in the front seat as Malloy jumped on the gas pedal, flooring it.

Malloy rushed through the narrow streets, narrowly missing a few cars and what surely would've been a bad accident. But after a few minutes, they were safely on their way after taking out Bellomi's crew.

"I take it there were no problems?" Malloy said.

Recker shook his head. "No. No problems. Everything went according to plan."

"Just as we assured you it would. Nothing that happened in there could be traced back to any of us, could it?"

"Not unless they can talk from the grave."

"Not likely."

"Or your staff workers decide to talk about what happened."

"Won't happen."

"How can you be so sure?"

"Only the manager knew what had to be done," Malloy said. "And he's been generously paid for his help. He's got a four-hundred-thousand dollar mortgage that was recently paid off by an anonymous benefactor."

Recker grinned, amused by the lengths they'd go to.

After twenty minutes of driving, Recker asked Malloy to drop him off at the corner of Broad Street. He didn't want Malloy taking him to his own car, just in case he tried to follow him back home or to the office. Though he didn't know if Malloy had any plans to do so, Recker knew he could easily lose him on foot if he had to. Once he was secure in knowing that Malloy, or any other of Vincent's men, weren't following him, he'd call Jones to pick him up. He figured he could go back and get his truck later.

Recker wound up walking for over an hour before he was absolutely certain that he was in the clear. He called Jones to meet him at his location, the corner of a Chinese restaurant, to take him back to the office. Half an hour later, Jones showed up, Recker quickly getting in the passenger side of the vehicle. Jones was anxious to know what happened and instantly started peppering his friend with questions.

"You were very vague on the phone in relation to what happened," Jones said.

"Everything's been taken care of," Recker said, not eager to share the gruesome details.

"Everyone is…"

"They're all dead," said Recker, responding tersely and sending Jones an evil stare. "Bellomi, four of his men… all dead."

"Mancini?"

"He wasn't there."

"Are you OK? Hurt?"

"I'm fine."

"You seem a little tense," Jones said, making sure to keep his eyes on the road ahead.

"I just killed five people. There's nothing to be joyous or happy about."

"I thought that's what you wanted," Jones said as he drove.

"Just because you're good at something doesn't mean you have to be happy about it. Just because you do something that has to be done, even if it's against people that some would say deserved it… doesn't mean you should feel good about it. There was no other way."

"And what about Mancini?"

"I'll have to get him another time."

"I'm sure once he hears about this he'll fly the coop relatively quickly."

"No doubt about it. And he'll hear about it soon. I imagine word's just starting to get out right about now." Instinctively Recker looked at his watch.

"The press will have a field day with this story."

"Most likely the lead story on the six o'clock news," Recker said, trying to keep the guilty pangs at bay.

"This won't come back to bite you somehow, will it?" Jones said.

"No. The only way it'd come back to me is if Vincent or his cronies give me up."

"Is that something we need to be concerned about?"

"Vincent wouldn't do that. He doesn't operate that way. If he gives me up, then I give him up. He wouldn't chance it."

"Well that's good." Jones nodded his agreement with Recker's analysis.

"Kill me, maybe... not turn me in."

"Well that's not so reassuring."

"Relax. Everything will be fine."

"So what do we do now?" Jones said.

"Now we get back to work."

"I've got the list down to the three most urgent."

"That's fine. But first... first I gotta take care of Tyrell's problem."

19

Recker and Jones had just gotten back to the office and Recker immediately went over to the couch and plopped himself down on it. He let out a sigh, exhausted from the day's activities. His heart was still thumping hard and his mind was still racing going over the events in his mind. Though everything went smoothly and according to plan, he didn't take much satisfaction in it. Though he still believed what he did was necessary, it was the first time he could ever recall that he felt bothered by a killing. He was beginning to question his methods, his profession, everything he'd ever done in life. He replayed the events over and over in his mind for the next several minutes. After it was finished, his thoughts turned to the faces of some of the other people who fell victim to his hands. A montage of faces passed by in quick succession, the final one being Carrie's.

Jones walked by the couch on his way to the desk. Once he finally settled in at the computer, he looked over at his friend and could tell he was troubled by something. Recker had an unfamiliar look to him, one that Jones had never seen before. Recker had a restlessness about him, like he wasn't at peace with himself. Even though no words were coming out of Recker's mouth, his face did all the talking that Jones needed to see.

Recker didn't notice a thing going on around him. A feeling of tiredness had suddenly descended over him. He'd never felt anything like it before. When he was in the CIA, he'd heard about other agents who suddenly went off the deep end, tired of their role. He'd even seen it himself in a couple of others, when a mission required him to partner up. He saw, in their eyes, an agent who no longer had the fire to keep on going. From what he'd heard, most times the feeling came on suddenly without warning. Recker wondered if all the killings were finally starting to catch up to him. He'd always hoped it never happened to him, but if it did, he hoped the reason behind it would be something that deeply moved him. Like saving an innocent person or something. Losing his luster about his profession from killing Marco Bellomi and his thugs wasn't how he envisioned it happening, if it ever did.

Jones tried saying something a couple of times to try and break Recker free from his trance, though he had no luck in doing so. He grabbed the remote and turned on the TV, hoping the additional noise would help in awakening Recker. It made no difference though. It would've taken an F-15 dropping bombs on the office to get Recker back into the moment. The local news started playing and the lead story was what happened to Bellomi, just as Recker had suspected it would be. Though Jones hated to snap him out of his doldrums, he figured Recker would want to hear what was being said about the incident. Jones quickly got up from the desk and walked over to the couch. He was careful how he awoke Recker, hearing stories about how violent men reacted after being snapped out of whatever world they were currently dreaming about. Jones gently shook Recker on the shoulder, barely moving him, hoping it was enough to get his attention. Though Recker didn't feel Jones' touch at first, a couple more shakes was enough to finally snap him back to reality. With a glossy look in his eye, Recker turned his head toward Jones and just looked at him without saying a word. Jones still wasn't sure if he was really there but started talking anyway, hoping it would seep into his head.

"The news is on," Jones said, pointing toward the TV. "They're leading with your exploits."

Recker slowly turned his head toward the set, finally snapping out of his funk. He listened intently to the news anchor's words as they talked about the situation.

"Though the police have not confirmed reports, we have learned that the bodies of reputed mob boss Marco Bellomi and four other members of his organization were found shot to death at an upscale center city restaurant roughly half an hour ago," the anchor reported. "From what we understand, there were no witnesses to the event and the police do not have any suspects in custody at this time. This is a developing story and we will give you more information as it comes in."

Jones walked back to the desk and picked up the remote, turning the volume on the TV down to a barely audible level. He kept it on just in case they came back to the story and reported additional information. He wanted to be able to get back to it quickly if they did.

"You were right," Jones said. "They led with it."

"It's big news," Recker said, slumping back into the couch once more.

"Are you OK?"

"Yeah, I'm fine."

"It seemed as if you were somewhere else for a few minutes."

Recker struggled for a minute to find a reply, eventually managing to do so. "Just, uh, thinking about some things. Nothing important."

"Anything I can help with?"

Recker shook his head. "No."

Jones knew better than to press the issue right then. He tried a different tack.

"So what else do we do about this situation?"

"There's nothing else to do," Recker said. "It's done and over with. Now we move on."

"But…"

"Nobody knows it was me. Even if they did, they don't know where I am." He shrugged. "We move on and continue doing the job we signed up for. Nothing else to it."

"Should I continue to try to monitor police communications on the issue just in case?" Jones said, not able to shake the worry from his mind.

"I don't think it's necessary, but if it makes you feel better."

"I do believe it would."

"Then by all means."

"Do you anticipate hearing from Vincent again?"

"I don't know. Maybe he'll wonder about the details, but he knows the job is done. I don't know."

As the night wore on, Recker started formulating a plan to deal with the Darnell Gibson situation. The plan, such as it was, was simple. His idea was basically to tell the gang to stop or suffer the consequences. He fully expected he'd have to shoot at least somebody, maybe even the entire group that was there. Even though he was having the mixed emotions from his earlier killing, he knew he couldn't let that interfere with his assignments or what had to be done. He had to keep plugging along. If he didn't, if he let those other emotions slow him down, then he knew he wouldn't be in the profession much longer. His hope was that once he got a good night's sleep, assuming he could, that he would wake up in a better mood.

MIKE RYAN

Recker was planning on calling it an early night and going home around nine or so. With Bellomi out of the picture now, he didn't have to worry about being spotted by someone anymore. Just before he was about to leave the office for the night, Recker's phone started ringing. Even Jones jumped a little once he heard it, startled by the sudden noise amidst the silence. Recker looked at the caller ID and seemed a little surprised at who it was. He gave a weird glance to Jones before answering.

"Up a little past your bedtime, aren't you?" Recker answered.

The man laughed. "Amusing fellow you are."

"So what can I do for you? Or Vincent?"

"Vincent would like a meeting with you in the morning," Malloy informed him.

"What for?"

"Didn't exactly say. I think he just wants to go over certain events that may or may not have happened recently."

"What's to go over? What's done is done. Everybody did their part."

"He didn't tell me the specifics. He just wants to meet."

"Where and when?"

"Same place as usual. Nine o'clock."

"I guess that'll work."

"So you'll be there?"

"I will."

"What was that about?" Jones said as soon as Recker hung up.

"Vincent wants to meet in the morning."

"Hmm."

"My thoughts exactly."

"Taking out the only witness?"

"I don't know. I kind of doubt he'd do it in a diner he goes to frequently."

"You must be cautious."

"I will be. This ain't my first rodeo."

The following morning, Recker didn't even bother going to the office first. He got up about seven and checked in with Jones to let him know he was about to head down into the city for the meeting.

"Wait a minute, I just realized you still don't have your car," Jones stated. "You left it down there yesterday, remember?"

"I got it covered," Recker replied.

"Covered? How?"

"Don't worry about it."

"Are you taking a cab? A bus?"

"You know I don't like taking public transportation."

"I know, that's why I said it."

"Well all right then."

"The question still remains though. How exactly do you plan on getting down there if you're not using public transportation and since you haven't asked me... I assume it's someone else."

"Good deduction skills."

"You asked Mia, didn't you?"

"Now don't get your panties in a bunch," Recker said.

"You really think you should be getting her involved in this?"

"She's not involved. She's just taking me to get my car."

"When did you ask her? Last night? Late last night?"

"Yeah, I mean, she was lying next to me in my bed, so yeah, why not?" he said sarcastically.

Jones was dead silent, not knowing how to respond to his insinuation.

"I'm joking, David. I just sent her a text message a few minutes ago asking if she was available to take me. She's not working till the afternoon, so she said she could. All right?"

"You say you don't want to get involved with her but you keep bringing her closer."

"What do you want me to do? Never talk to her again? Ignore her for the rest of my life? Pretend she didn't exist?"

"Of course not."

"She's proven to be trustworthy. She has medical skills that are vital to my health in case something happens. I can't shut her out completely. If we want to have her available in emergency situations, especially me, then I need to have contact with her on occasion."

"I know that. You make it sound so businesslike."

"Because that's what it is," Recker said.

"If only I believed that. I just want you to be cautious. Your definition of contact may not jive with her vision for the two of you."

"I am. I'm not gonna get her involved in something that would jeopardize her. That includes me," Recker said.

"OK. Just let me know when the meeting's over so I know it went OK."

"Will do, dad."

"Really?"

Recker let out a laugh, in a better mood than he was the previous day. A good night's sleep seemed to help alleviate some of the feelings he had the day before. Mia was eager to spend more time with Recker, even if it was only for a few minutes, and jumped at the chance to take him somewhere. She got to his apartment about 7:45. Recker was already outside waiting for her, standing near the entrance of the parking lot.

"Going my way?" Mia pleasantly said.

Recker smiled. "I think I just might be."

"So is your truck OK?"

"Yeah, it's fine. Something came up yesterday that made me have to leave it."

"Oh. Everything OK?"

"Everything's fine."

"So this is where you live, huh? Looks like a nice apartment from the outside," she said as she pulled out of the lot.

"Yeah, it's not too bad."

"Maybe I could see the inside of it someday?"

"Maybe."

"You sure don't make things easy, do you?" she said.

"I try not to. Thanks for taking me, by the way."

"No problem. That's what friends are for, right?"

"So they say."

"After you get your car, do you wanna grab some breakfast somewhere?" she said hopefully.

"Today's a bad day. I have to meet someone at nine."

"Oh. Something important?"

"Might be." Recker nodded.

"Client or something?"

"Uh, something like that."

"Oh my gosh, I have never met anyone who tells as little information as you do," she frustratingly told him. "Do you ever just answer a question?"

"I did."

"No. You have an uncanny ability, some kind of weird magical gift, that you answer a question without really answering it," Mia said. "Every time I ask you a question, I feel like I still don't know what you said in return."

Recker laughed, knowing full well it was true. He wasn't sure, though, if it was something he just did naturally, or was a byproduct of all the years he spent in the CIA. Saying as little as possible was something that was drilled into the agents to prepare themselves against saying something that would jeopardize their missions... and their lives. Old lessons died hard. He was still in the same line of work. He just had a different employer these days.

The secrecy in his life was still there, maybe even more so nowadays. Before, he had the government behind him. Now, he was on his own, outside of Jones and Mia. Answering a question truthfully, without somehow evading it, was something he probably would never do.

"Sorry about all that," Recker said. "I know I can be a frustrating person to deal with for some people."

"It's OK. I'm not mad. I just wish you'd let me in a little. You have that wall around you that you don't let anyone penetrate."

"Habit I guess."

"But why? Why won't you let it down for anyone?" Mia said.

"If I put the wall down, then people get hurt. Innocent people. It's as simple as that."

"I've never met someone as much as you who seems like they have a whole other life inside them that they don't show."

"After you drop me off, if you would rather not see or talk to me again, I completely understand. I wouldn't bother you again," Recker said.

"Don't be ridiculous. I lo… I like you, we're friends, I just feel like there's a wall between us that I'd like to somehow bypass. After what I did for you, I feel like I should've earned a little bit of trust from you."

"I trust you completely. That's why I came to you that night to begin with. Wouldn't have done it if I didn't trust you."

"Then give me something. Something that tells me who you really are. I feel like you know everything about me, and I know nothing about you. Other than you've been shot before you met me, I feel like I know very little about you, and that I only know cause I saw the other bullet hole. Friendships, relationships, they can't just be one way. It's a two-way street. I feel like right now it's just me going down a one-way street chasing after you. And you keep turning every time I get close to you," Mia said.

"I'm sorry. I know I'm not easy. But the less I tell you, the less you know, the more you're protected."

"Protected from what?"

"People that would hurt you if they knew you knew me."

"Don't you think I should know that so I can be aware of that? I mean, would you rather me walking around blindly not knowing something could happen when we're together or something?"

Recker didn't respond for a minute. Instead, he took his time to think about what she had just said. She had a point. He knew she did. Anybody who was with him was always in jeopardy. Bad things happened to people who were near him. It was usually him dishing out the punishment, but that was a byproduct of what he did.

"You're right," Recker finally responded.

"What? I am?"

"It's probably not the best idea for us to be seen together anymore."

"What? No, that's not what I was trying to say."

"But it's true."

"Oh my God, you are so frustrating. Instead of pushing me away, why don't you just tell me what's really going on? What are you so afraid of?" Mia said.

"There's only one thing I'm really afraid of. Losing people I care about."

"So if you care about me... which I hope you do, then why are you trying to push me away?"

"I mean losing them permanently."

"Oh."

"Listen, Mia. You're a great girl. I trust you completely. I like being around you. But there's things about me that I just can't tell you."

"I know. For my own safety," she sighed. "Don't you think that my safety should be my call?"

Recker was starting to tire of the questions and the conversation in general. Doubts started seeping into his mind about whether he should tell her a few things, even if they were minor. Just to give her something. Not that he was trying to blow her off, as her concerns were legitimate, and her reasons were valid. Recker let out a couple of deep sighs, loud enough for Mia to hear him.

"What's that for? Am I annoying you?" Mia said.

Recker thought he heard her huff after she spoke. "No."

"Sorry for pestering you about it. I know whatever it is you can't talk about, you have your reasons for it, and I should respect that. If you don't feel like you can talk to me about your past, that's fine. I understand. I won't ask you again."

"I'm not mad," Recker said, gazing out the window. "You have the right to ask and wonder."

"How about we change the subject?" she said, trying to change the tense mood in the car.

"No."

"Uh... what?"

"Fine. If you want some answers about me, then I'll give them to you." Recker finally relented, even if it was against his best judgment.

"Mike, it's fine. You really don't have to. If it's something you're uncomfortable doing or just can't, then I don't want to force you."

"No, you're right. You deserve to know some things about me if you're going to be near me."

"OK?"

"There's a few ground rules," he said, looking out of the car window, still not sure this was a good idea.

"OK?"

"No follow-up questions to anything I say. I'll tell you what I can tell you and that's it."

"All right."

"I'm an ex-CIA agent. I used to work for a top secret black ops department inside the CIA in which my assignments usually had me going to foreign nations and eliminating targets that were deemed a threat to U.S. interests."

Mia couldn't believe what she was hearing. So much so that she almost lost concentration on the road. She just narrowly avoided crossing the road and having a head on collision with another car.

"Wow. I can't believe it," Mia said. "So uh... so why are you here?"

"I ended up here after something happened that jeopardized my position in the agency. That other bullet wound you saw is from them trying to take me out in London. I somehow wound up here in Philadelphia and met the professor. He gave me a job trying to help people and save them from becoming a bad statistic."

"I still don't get all the secrecy though. I'd understand if you're still an agent, but if you're not, then why all the secrets?"

"Didn't I say no follow-up questions?"

"Oh. Yeah. Sorry."

"Anyway, the reason for the secrets is that the CIA knows that I'm still alive. And I'm now a threat. They tried to take me out once. They'll do it again. Once they know my location, they will come looking for me and they will try to kill me and whoever they think I'm close to," Recker said, answering the follow-up questions that he said he wouldn't.

"Oh."

"That is why I've been trying to keep you at a distance. Because if they find me, I don't want you to get caught up in the middle of it."

"So is that how you got shot last week? The CIA?"

"No, that was something different. That was someone who felt I was stepping on their toes. As far as I know, the government still doesn't know where I am."

"Do you think they're still looking for you?" she said.

"I'm not sure. Actively searching... maybe not. But I'm sure I'm still on the radar in some way. If my name pops up on someone's computer screen, I'm sure there'll be agents here hunting me not long after that."

"So I take it that Jones was somehow involved with the CIA too?" Mia asked. She couldn't help it.

"Uh... not quite. He worked in a different agency and I never met him before I came here. He has... I don't know if I'd call it a similar story... but he has a story all his own. And that's his to tell."

"What're you gonna do if the CIA finds you?"

Recker shrugged, unsure of his answer. "I'll do what I always do. Improvise."

"How long are you planning on staying here?" Mia said.

"I don't know. I hadn't thought that far ahead yet. Right now, I'm just kind of living in the moment."

"Well if there's ever anything you need from me... anything I can do to help, all you have to do is name it."

"Mia, you've done plenty to help me already," Recker said.

"I'm sure it's hard having to do what you do... and have done. What about family? Do you have any? Wife or kids or anything?"

Recker slightly turned his head in her direction without looking at her. "No. No family. No kids."

"Wife, ex-wife, girlfriend, boyfriend, anyone?"

"No."

"Must be hard being alone all the time."

"It has its advantages," he said.

"I'm sure it does."

They drove the rest of the way continuing to talk about Recker's life and his past. He was actually finding it somewhat therapeutic talking about it. It was only the second time in his life he opened up about it. The first time was to Carrie. He just hoped that Mia wouldn't end up the same way. As long as he kept her at a distance, Recker believed he had a better chance of keeping her safe. At least, that was the belief that he was clinging to. If he lost someone else that was close to him, and it was because of them knowing him, it would send him over the edge. The rampage and carnage that would follow would be the stuff of fictional action movies.

20

Once Recker was dropped off to get his car, he immediately drove to the restaurant for his meeting with Vincent. The entire drive there, instead of wondering about what Vincent wanted, his only thoughts were of Mia and the conversation they just had. Though he still wasn't sure it was the best idea to tell her some of the things he had, he did feel a sense of relief, like a little weight had been lifted off his shoulders. He really liked her, and another time and place, he might've conveyed those feelings to her, but he had to somehow bury those feelings deeper down within himself. He said it was for her protection, but at times, he wondered if the person he was really trying to protect, was himself.

When Recker got to the diner, he approached the door, seeing the same guard standing there as the previous couple of times. He stood there looking at him, wondering if he wanted to do the same song and dance they usually did as far as giving up his guns. Recker made a disgusted face, not really wanting to take the time to go into it again at that moment, and simply removed his gun from his belt, along with his backup weapon, showing them to the guard in an unassuming manner.

"Figured I'd save us the trouble today, pal," Recker stated, handing his guns over.

The guard grinned and opened the door for their visitor, Recker instantly greeted by Malloy as soon as he walked in. Recker knew the routine by now and put his hand up to stop Malloy from going any further.

"I know the way," Recker told him, walking down to Vincent's table.

Vincent looked up at his visitor as he approached and gave him a friendly smile.

"You own a piece of this place?" Recker said. "You sure seem to visit often enough."

Vincent let out a small laugh, wiping his mouth with a napkin. "No. I just like the food."

"Fair enough."

"Can I offer you something?" Vincent said.

"No, I'm good," Recker said, not really in the mood for small talk and going through the motions.

Recker wanted to get down to business as quickly as possible so he could get out of there. He sat silently, watching Vincent take a bite of his breakfast, patiently waiting for the boss to tell him what he was there for. Vincent wiped his mouth again before beginning.

"I wanted to compliment you on your thoroughness," Vincent said. "It was pulled off with great execution, no pun intended."

"Thanks," Recker replied, not impressed by the compliment bestowed upon him. "Is that all you wanted?"

"You seem tense, impatient. Someplace else you need to be?"

"I just have a lot on my plate right now. A lot of other things to do, a lot of people that need my help."

"I can imagine. I won't keep you too long. But with an operation like this, since I wasn't there, I just like to know everything's in order."

"Everything went off without a hitch," Recker said. "No problems. Your guys did what they were supposed to do. And so did I."

"You say it without any emotion or feeling."

"Cause I'm not some gun-happy idiot who's intent on hurting people or who just likes to shoot people for the hell of it. I don't take pleasure or solace in killing people."

"But you do it, anyway."

"I do what has to be done. I do what's necessary. Nothing more than that."

"So matter of fact. You know, I'm very good at reading people." Vincent shrugged. "I think it's kind of a necessity to have that trait to be in my position. And I think I have a good read on you."

"Is that so?"

"You burst on the scene here with a lot of fanfare, helping little old ladies from getting mugged, rescuing kidnapped children, but there's a dark side to you. I'm not sure if you actually enjoy what you do or you just do it cause you're good at it."

"Wouldn't do it if I didn't want to," Recker said.

"You're very cold, calculating. Not unlike myself."

"I didn't come here to be analyzed by you."

"It wasn't intended. I was struck by your demeanor."

Recker looked over at Vincent to see if he was serious or kidding. He looked serious. "Back to business, is any of this hit going to come back to me in any way?" Recker said.

"No," Vincent said quickly. "As I said, only three people know what happened in there. You, me, and Jimmy. The detectives out front were not informed of your identity."

"Four," Recker said, picking a grape from a plate in the middle of the table.

"Come again?"

"Four people. There was the manager of the restaurant who saw my face."

"You don't need to worry about him," Vincent reassured. "I know him well. He's been paid quite well for his services, and his silence, on this. He knows if he was to cross me, he would live, or not live, to regret it. He won't be an issue."

"I'll take your word for it."

"Which brings us to our next order of business and the main reason why I asked you to come here."

"OK?"

"Our relationship going forward," Vincent said.

"What about it?"

"Well, I will obviously be expanding my territory in the coming days, weeks, months, etcetera."

"And?"

"I think up to this point we've had a very good working relationship," Vincent told him.

"You expecting that to change?"

"I don't know. We helped you find that child you were looking for, you helped us take out some of our competition, things have been good between us."

"Sounds like you're anticipating a problem," Recker said smiling.

"We'll see. What would you say about joining my payroll?"

"I've already got a job."

Vincent smiled, expecting the answer. "I already assumed that'd be your reply. Wasn't expecting anything different. Figured it wouldn't hurt to ask though."

"Never does."

"Even so, it doesn't change the fact that I don't want any troubles with you going forward. We've co-existed well up until now."

Recker took a few seconds to think about his reply, careful in how he chose his words. "I'd like to think we have a certain understanding and respect of each other's positions. I'm not really interested in your business or getting in your way of whatever it is that you decide to pursue."

"Good to know," Vincent said, smiling.

"I'd also like to think that you know how dangerous I can be and that you wouldn't really be interested in getting in my way either."

"I do and I'm not."

"But at the same time, if I have a case where I'm trying to protect someone, and the person I'm trying to protect them from is one of your men… I will put them down. And I won't hesitate in doing so," Recker told him. "And I'd hope you'd understand my position."

"And I do. I guess circumstances will dictate what my response would be, if any."

Recker nodded. "Listen, I'm not interested in your business, or slowing down your operation in any manner. Doesn't concern me in the least. If you want to take control over the city, take it over. Makes no difference to me. As long as it doesn't intersect in my business. The only issue you'll have with me is if one of your men crosses the line… rapes someone, tries to kill an innocent person, something stupid along those lines." Recker laid it out as plain as he could to diffuse any tension between them.

"If one of my men does something along those lines, then I'll kill him myself," Vincent said, balling up a fist. "I don't hurt innocent people. The only things that interest me are power and money. If someone gets in my way of pursuit of those things, well, they're probably not innocent either."

Recker nodded. "I think we have an understanding."

"I agree. Before you go, I'd just like to let you know that if you ever need something in the future, anything at all, feel free to come to me for help."

"Thanks. I appreciate that," Recker said, shaking Vincent's hand.

Recker got up from the table and was about to leave, when he remembered something, and turned back around to question the mob leader.

"Oh, and, uh... about Mancini," Recker asked.

"You don't have to worry about him," Vincent said. "I've got people out looking for him as we speak. We'll find him. You have my word on that."

"Good enough for me."

"However long it takes... a day, a week, a month, or a year, when we find him, and we will, I will personally call you myself."

"I'll take it."

Satisfied with Vincent's response, Recker walked away from the table toward the door. As he passed by Malloy, Recker slapped him hard on the shoulder, but in a playful, friendly manner.

"Take it easy, Malloy," Recker told him.

"You too," the lieutenant replied.

Malloy went down to the table where his boss was sitting and sat down across from him, anxious to know his boss' thoughts on the meeting.

"What do you think?" Malloy said.

"He won't be a problem."

"Are you sure?"

"There's always a chance for a hiccup or something to not go according to plan, but I don't foresee any issues with Mr. Recker," Vincent said. "He's only in the business of protecting what he believes is the innocent. We don't encounter very many of those in our business."

"What if one of ours steps out of line or something, something unrelated?" Malloy said.

"Well then they'll probably deserve whatever is coming to them. As I've said, I think Recker could be very valuable to us at some point down the line if we play our cards right. As I told you before, we'll give him a very long leash, if he even needs one at all. A man who can do the things that he does is a man you want in your corner if the seas get rough. And if he ever needs anything and comes to us, we'll give him whatever he wants and help him in any way that he needs."

"Whatever he wants?"

"Well, within reason." Vincent sipped on his coffee and looked out through the window.

As Recker drove away from the diner, he called Jones to let him know how it went, since the professor tended to worry about things if he wasn't in the loop.

"I take it your meeting is over," Jones said when he answered.

"Yeah."

"How did it go? Any issues?"

"No problems. He just wanted to talk about a few things," he said.

"Such as?"

"Just wanted to know how the stuff with Bellomi went down."

"That's it?"

"Yeah, and he offered me a job."

"I hope you declined."

"Well, I don't know, I might have to take a few days to think about it," Recker joked.

"Seriously?"

"No. Well, he did offer me employment, but I turned it down."

"Well thank goodness for that," Jones said. "Didn't he offer you a job before?"

"Yeah. Honestly, I think the meeting was more for his own peace of mind."

"Was he worried about something?"

"I think it was more along the lines of wanting to stay out of each other's way," Recker answered. "He's taking over a bigger part of the city, his power's expanding, we've cooperated with each other several times, I think he just wants to make sure we stay on good terms."

"Doesn't that seem somewhat peculiar for a man in his position? Wanting to stay on good terms with someone who doesn't work for him?"

"No. Vincent's a smart man. He doesn't look for problems. He doesn't want to make enemies with anyone unless it's absolutely necessary," Recker said.

"What do you plan to do now?"

"Now I take care of Tyrell's problem."

Recker drove over to the high school that Darnell Gibson was enrolled at, located in the western part of the city. He called Tyrell to let him know he would be at the school that day and to get word to his brother that the situation would be taken care of.

"Exactly where has this recruitment been taking place? Any specific spot?" Recker said.

"Uh, yeah, they're waiting until the kids get off school property," Gibson answered. "Darnell said they usually are starting on kids behind the school, off Dauphin Street. There's like duplexes and stuff back there, kids cut through between the houses sometimes, so the gang isn't out in the open."

"Dauphin, got it."

"Hey, man, are you sure you don't mind doing this?"

"I told you I'd take care of it. Consider it done."

"I can't tell you enough how much I appreciate this."

"Don't mention it. Like I said, I owed you one," Recker said. "Can you get word to Darnell to let him know I'm coming?"

"Yeah, I'll shoot him a text message."

"Just tell him to go the same way he always does. I'll be on Dauphin Street looking out for him."

"I will."

Recker had some time to kill before school let out and drove around the city for a while to pass the time away. Once the afternoon hit, he made his way down to the high school, driving around it a few times just to get a feel for the area. With twenty minutes to go until school let out, Recker drove down Dauphin Street, finding a parking spot in front of a duplex. Getting ready for the job, he reached over and opened the glove compartment, taking out one of his Glock's. He set it down on the seat and took his other Glock out of his belt, making sure both guns were fully loaded. He kept his eyes peeled for signs of gang activity, looking out the windows, as well as through the rearview mirror. Nothing appeared out of the ordinary at first, but he really didn't expect to see anything yet, anyway. Not until Darnell showed up.

Twenty minutes ticked away slowly. Recker calmly waited for his cue, not the least bit anxious or nervous about what was coming. Some men in his position got antsy when they waited for a target to show themselves, anxious to get the deed over with. That wasn't Recker though. He tried not to overthink things. He also found that the men who weren't patient, who tried to rush things, who let too many thoughts cloud their mind, they were the ones who got themselves into a sticky situation, and sometimes dead. It didn't really bother him if he had to wait five minutes or five hours. No matter how big or small the job, he didn't let it become bigger than it needed to be.

Once Recker noticed a bunch of kids walking along the sidewalk, grouped together, he knew his business was about to begin.

He took another quick look at his phone to look at the picture of Darnell that Tyrell had sent to him, just to make sure that he didn't overlook him. He took his two guns off the passenger seat and put one in his right-hand coat pocket and the other inside the belt of his pants. He kept his eyes peeled for the next several minutes trying to locate Darnell with no luck. The thought occurred to him that maybe the kid got scared of having someone else intervene on his behalf and didn't want any other trouble with the gang in case things went sideways. It wouldn't be the first time that something like that happened to Recker. And if that was the case, it wouldn't really bother him. He didn't mind helping people in need, but if they didn't want his assistance, he wouldn't beg them to let him help. He'd simply find someone who did want his help.

Before giving up on the situation though, Recker would wait it out until it was a guarantee that Darnell was a no-show. It could've been that he had to stay later for something, or maybe he still was a little scared of the impending problem, but either way, Recker had time to wait and wouldn't give up on him too early. After all, Darnell was still just a kid in high school and Recker figured a lot of things must've been going through his mind at that time.

A few more minutes went by, and less kids walked by, when Recker finally saw his target. He looked in the rear-view mirror and saw Darnell walking along the sidewalk, by himself. He looked a little antsy, constantly looking around like he was waiting for someone. As Darnell passed by each car, he crouched down a little bit to look inside, wondering if that was the car that his brother's friend was going to be in. Recker kept his eyes glued to Darnell, in case the gang showed up, but assumed by Darnell's mannerisms, that he was looking for him.

"Yo Darnell!" a voice shouted out.

Recker quickly looked out his window and stared into the

driver's side mirror, observing a young male standing by one of the duplexes. A few seconds later, Recker saw another man walking down the sidewalk toward his vehicle. Recker put his arm up like he was scratching his forehead so the man wouldn't think he was watching, but he noticed that the man had a gun tucked inside the front of his pants.

"Come on over here!" the voice shouted again.

Darnell did as he was instructed and crossed the street, walking between a couple of parked cars until he stood in front of the two gang members. Recker continued watching the threesome, not wanting to intervene yet until he was sure there weren't others lurking around somewhere. He would've been surprised if it was just the two of them there to recruit Darnell. The guy who appeared to be the leader of the group, smiling and laughing about something, put his arm around Darnell and walked him through the yard between the two duplexes. Recker was about to get out of his car when he looked through his mirror again and noticed two other youngsters crossing the street in the same direction that the others just went to.

Recker stepped out of his car and just stood there for a moment, looking casual in his movements. He closed the car door and walked over to the front of the duplex, standing by the corner and peering around. The four gang members were surrounding Darnell, though the leader was doing all the talking. It appeared to Recker that all four of them were in either their late teens or early twenties.

"This is it, man," the leader of the group said, taking a gun out of his pants. "It's initiation time."

"What's that for?" Darnell said. He sounded worried.

"You gotta earn your way into this gang, man," he said, holding the gun out for Darnell to take from him.

"I don't want that."

"You're gonna take it and go up the street and rob that liquor store that's up there. You're gonna take whatever money they got in the register and bring it back here to me. Then you'll be in."

"I keep telling you I don't wanna be a part of no gang," Darnell said.

"Yo. You ain't got no choice in this. You're gonna do it whether you like it or not. Skittles over here will go with you just to make sure you do it and don't mess it up."

"I don't wanna hurt nobody, I don't wanna rob nobody. I just wanna be left alone, man."

"Yo, you either do this or we're gonna leave you alone permanently, if you know what I mean," the kid said, getting angry, putting his hands on the collar of Darnell's shirt.

Darnell sighed, afraid he was going to be forced into it. "Why do you even want me so bad, anyway?"

"Listen, we all know who your brother is. He's got connections. He knows all the big players in this city. One day, we're gonna rise up and be the big men in this city. Pretty soon, people gonna be talking about me like they do about Vincent, Jeremiah, or them Italians that just got whacked. But to do that, I'm gonna need connections, contacts, guns, merchandise, you understand where I'm going with this? Your brother's got all those."

"So why don't you just ask him instead of getting me involved?" Darnell said.

"Because your brother thinks he's gone big time or something. I got word to him about getting my hands on some stuff, and he turned me down. So, guess what? If he knows that you threw in with us, that you're a part of this gang, he's gonna wanna help his kid brother succeed. He's gonna wanna look out for him."

Once again, the gun was pushed toward Darnell, and once again, he refused to take it. "I'm not touching that, man. I don't want no part of no gun."

Recker was proud of Darnell for sticking with his position, even in the face of extreme pressure and possible personal harm, but he could tell things were beginning to spiral out of control. He could sense that the leader of the group was losing his patience and Recker worried that he might just put a bullet in Darnell and forget about the whole thing, rather than continuing to try to convince someone to join the group who clearly wanted no part of it. Recker figured it was about time he intervened and put a stop to the situation. Before moving, he looked around to make sure nobody else was walking toward him.

With the coast clear, Recker started walking between the two duplexes, making himself quite visible for the gang to see. Startled at the stranger's presence, the gang pushed Darnell away towards the wall and put their hands on their guns so they could face their visitor head on, though they didn't reveal their weapons totally yet.

"Who the hell are you?" the leader said.

"Me?" Recker said with a slight laugh. "Oh, I'm just the neighborhood watch. Heard there was some trouble."

The leader of the group looked at him with a puzzled face, not sure if the man was serious or just plain crazy. "You tryin' to be funny or something?"

"Who me? No, I never try to be funny. Just kind of comes natural."

"Yo, I ain't got time for this shit. Get lost before something bad happens to you."

"Now you're the one who's trying to be funny," Recker said.

"Is this even for real?"

"Oh, it's for real. Darnell, you can go home."

Darnell started to leave before the gang stopped him. "Wait, wait, wait, wait, wait... you ain't going nowhere, man. Not until I say so."

Darnell looked at both sides and remained in his spot, frozen, not sure what he should do.

"You know, I heard your little speech there, and it was good," Recker stated. "But you oughtta give it up. You clearly don't have the mental capacity to one day challenge Vincent or Jeremiah, both of whom I know quite well."

"You just call me stupid?"

"No. It's just very obvious that you don't have what it takes to one day be up there with the big boys." Recker kept his eyes firmly glued to the little group, ready for any sudden movements.

"Yo, I'm about to cap your ass in a minute.," the leader threatened, losing his patience.

"Darnell, why don't you go home?"

"Yo, I already told you, I give the orders around here. He ain't going nowhere."

"Do you really want him to see what I'm gonna do to you guys?" Recker said nonchalantly.

"What you're gonna do to us?" the leader responded, his voice rising in disbelief at the audacity of the man. "You do know there's four of us, right? There's only one of you."

"I know. The odds are in my favor," Recker said, getting a laugh out of the gang. Recker even got a smile out of their hilarity over the situation.

"Yo man, you're crazy," the leader said. "I almost hate to kill you."

"I'm gonna reach into my pocket for something," Recker said, putting his hand up. "It's not a gun so don't shoot or anything."

The leader of the gang was so captivated by Recker's outlandishness that he was willing to wait a few extra minutes before killing him. He just had to see what kind of craziness Recker was going to pull out of his pocket. Recker took out some keys, the keys to his car. He tossed them over to Darnell, getting a confused look from each member of the gang, unsure what the guy was doing. Darnell himself wasn't even sure what was going on.

"That's the keys to my car. It's the black Ford Explorer to the left. I want you to go sit in the passenger seat until I get back. I'll drive you home. This'll only take a few more minutes," Recker said.

Darnell looked at the gang, hesitating about moving without their permission.

"Go on," Recker said, louder this time. "You don't need their approval."

Darnell did as Recker asked and quickly shuffled away from the confrontation, running toward the black SUV. The gang didn't even try to stop him this time.

"That's all right," the leader said. "After we kill you, then we're gonna take your car. Thanks for pointing out which one it was."

"Are you guys really gonna make me kill you?" Recker said.

"Dude, this guy gets crazier by the minute," the leader said to one of the others.

"If you leave Darnell alone, and you ask me really, really nicely, I might be able to put you in touch with Jeremiah or Vincent. Maybe they could use you somehow. I kind of doubt they'd stoop to hiring you idiots but you never know."

"You know Vincent and Jeremiah?"

"Sure do. Knew the Italians too. Well, that is until I took them out."

"You took out the Italians?"

"Sure did. I don't mind saying it since you're not gonna be around to tell anybody," Recker said bluntly. He couldn't see the point in beating about the bush.

While they seemed a little off guard and not watching him very carefully, Recker quickly removed his gun from his pocket, along with the one from his belt. He stood there with a gun firmly entrenched in both hands, dropped down to his side as he waited for someone to make the first move. Recker was done talking at that point and was just ready to finish the job.

"Looks like we're doing this old west style," Recker said.

The leader of the group wasn't looking quite as confident as he was before, but he still wasn't ready to back down. He wasn't even sure the man was telling him the truth about everything. He could've just been saying it hoping that they'd back down.

"Yo, I don't believe none of that shit you just said," the leader said. "I don't believe you took down the Italians all by yourself."

Recker just shrugged, unconcerned. "Suit yourself."

"Yeah, whatever man. You stand there all cool and calm and badass like you think you're The Silencer or something? You know the guy that goes around helping people and shit."

"That's because I am The Silencer," Recker said, sounding to himself like he was in a movie or something.

Recker could see it in the eyes of the four gang members, that they weren't quite as confident as they were before. Doubt had crept into their minds. Before, they thought he was just some idiot who happened to stumble upon them. Now, they knew they were in a lot of trouble, numbers or not. Unless he wasn't really who he said he was, but they were all pretty sure he wasn't bluffing now. There was a certain confidence about him, a swagger that most men wouldn't have.

"I'm not gonna stand here all day," Recker told them, eager to get it over with. "I got things to do."

"You might be The Silencer, but it don't change the fact that we still got the numbers," the leader said, trying to look tough by puffing himself up. "Still four of us and only one of you."

"And like I said earlier... odds are still in my favor."

Another minute went by, filled with silence, none of the gang members too eager to take the first shot. Recker's reputation on the streets had grown steadily since his name first got thrown in the paper, and since then, a lot of things had been attributed to him, some of which were true, but some not. There were some killings that people assumed he was involved with, even if he wasn't, and some made up stories about him that made his legend and street rep grow even further. Nobody was too anxious to meet and do battle with him. Even though the numbers were on the gang's side, Recker was an intimidating presence standing there. Not so much him physically, since he was just an average-looking kind of guy, but the bodies that had piled up behind him over the months that he'd been there did all the talking that was necessary.

"Like I said, I got things to do, so I'll give you gentlemen till the count of five, then I'm just gonna start shooting," Recker said.

Recker wasn't bluffing, and though he didn't really like shooting first, it didn't bother him too much if he did. Especially when dealing with the deplorable or the morally corrupt, he usually just felt that they had it coming to them. He didn't owe them the right to shoot first. He thought sometimes people got too wrapped up over who took the first shot, like the good guy can only shoot if he's shot at first. He thought that was nonsense. Especially when you're dealing with those of questionable character. This wasn't the movies. Who shot first didn't matter. The only thing that mattered, was who shot last, and who walked out alive. And that would always be him. Recker counted to five under his breath and then brought his guns up, ready to fire.

"Well, if you insist," Recker whispered.

He aimed for the leader of the group first, as Recker believed he was the most dangerous of the four. He also seemed to have his gun in the best position to fire back. Recker fired his Glock, hitting the leader of the gang square in the chest, knocking him onto his back. He quickly fired at the other two members on the end, shooting simultaneously with both hands, hitting them both, though not fatally in either case. The fourth member of the group got his gun out and took a shot at Recker, though he missed. Recker did not, though. With the other three on the ground, he took aim at the final member of the gang still standing and unloaded two shots with the gun in his right hand, killing the man instantly. Recker slowly walked over to the group laying on the ground, three of them writhing in pain from their injuries. They were still breathing, and it was possible that they could've still survived if they were quickly taken to a hospital. Recker couldn't allow it, though. Even if they were patched up, he knew they'd come right back to the street and start recruiting kids to their gang and terrorizing the neighborhood. Without thinking about it too much more, Recker raised his gun, and quickly put one more shot in each of the three remaining gang members.

Recker stood over the dead bodies for a minute, just to make sure there wasn't a speck of life left in any of them. He was slightly startled though when he heard movement just around the corner to the back of the duplexes. Thinking he might have more trouble, like maybe there were more members of the gang, he cautiously walked over to the corner of the house, clinging to the wall. He peeked around the corner and saw a group of what appeared to be normal, everyday citizens walking closer. Not noticing a gun in plain sight, Recker walked out into the open in front of the approaching group. He wasn't sure exactly what to expect and kept his guns firmly in his hand, ready to fire again if necessary, though looking at the age of the crowd, he didn't really expect it to be. There were seven of them. Five of them appeared to be well into their sixties, and possibly beyond that. Only two of them looked young enough, probably in their forties, to give him a hard time.

"Can I help you people?" Recker said.

The youngest of the group, a forty-year-old homeowner that owned a house a few doors down, spoke up. "Yo, you're The Silencer, I heard you!" he yelled in excitement.

Recker grinned, still not sure what the group was after. One of the elder statesmen of the group spoke up.

"Forgive the excitement of my friend here, but we saw what was going on from the window of the house next door," the man said.

"Oh," Recker said, worried about what he might have to do.

"Don't worry, we just wanted to come over as a group and say thank you for taking out those thugs. They've been terrorizing this neighborhood for months, recruiting the kids in the area, robbing businesses, stealing from people, even beating up people who are just walking down the street."

Recker relaxed slightly, knowing now that the group didn't pose any sort of threat. "Why haven't you done something about it?" he said.

"We reported everything to the police. They took in the reports and you see them patrol the neighborhood every now and then, but," the man shrugged, "I guess they just couldn't find them. I don't know. Most of us are too old to do anything about these young bucks. Maybe in my younger days I could give them a thumpin', but not now."

"Well, I guess you won't have to worry about them anymore," Recker said.

"I know. It's a shame what it had to come down to, but, it is what it is, I guess."

"Are these the only ones or are there more of them floating around somewhere?"

"These four are the main ones," the man said, looking down at the bodies. "I think there's two or three more but once they get wind of this, I suspect they'll be scarce around here from now on.

They all took their cues from that one there anyway," he said, pointing to the leader. "With him gone, the other ones won't come back."

Recker nodded slightly, satisfied that his work there was done. "Well, I'm gonna have to get going. The police will probably be here soon enough."

"We understand. Thank you again."

"Oh, and uh, I'd appreciate it if you didn't tell the police I was here," Recker said.

"Man, I didn't see nothin'," one of the younger men said happily.

Then the elder man spoke up again. "I suppose it was probably another gang that did it. I don't know though, none of us really saw what happened. We just heard the shots," he said with a smile.

Recker returned the smile, knowing that he didn't have anything to worry about with these people. Even if they did tell the police it was him that killed the gang, it really wouldn't have changed anything. The only issue would be if they described his face, and the police got a sketch on him, but even then, Recker was confident in his ability to elude authorities, whether they recognized his appearance or not. And public opinion would be on his side, glad that he rid the world of a bunch of thugs, so he wouldn't have to worry about every Tom, Dick, and Harry being on the lookout for him every time he crossed the street.

Before Recker turned to leave, the elderly man stuck his hand out, hoping to shake The Silencer's hand. Recker tucked his gun back in his coat pocket and returned the handshake. Then, out of the corner of his eye, Recker turned and saw Darnell approaching.

"I thought I told you to stay in my car," Recker told him.

"Well, I heard the shots a few minutes ago," Darnell replied. "I figured if you were still alive that you would've been back by now. I was getting worried that you were dead."

"Not likely."

"Thank you again," the elderly man said.

"My pleasure."

"Bless you, young man," an older woman said, walking over to Recker to give him a hug and kiss on the cheek.

Recker almost blushed at the welcome he was receiving. "Thank you, ma'am."

"You make sure you take care of yourself."

"I will," Recker said with a wave.

Recker began to leave and started walking toward Darnell, putting his arm around him.

"I'll drive you home," Recker said.

"Thanks. For everything." Darnell said.

Recker stopped walking and took his arm off Darnell, turning back toward the group of people.

"If you guys ever need anything, a group like this comes back, or if you have any other problems that the police can't solve, you guys let me know and I'll come back," Recker said, loud enough for them all to hear.

"How will we know how to get in touch with you?" the elderly man said.

"You just get the word out, I'll hear it. I'll hear it."

"Bless you, brother, bless you."

21

Recker and Darnell talked about the kid's future on the short drive back to the Gibson home. Recker found out a little about what Darnell liked to do in his spare time and what his hopes were for the future. Just listening to him talk, Recker liked him. For a teenager, he had a pretty good head on his shoulders. It was actually good for him to listen and talk to someone in depth that wasn't involved in the usual business that he was wrapped up in.

"I can't thank you enough for what you did back there for me," Darnell said.

"You already did."

"It's tough, you know? Even though you know there's something that you don't wanna do. Even though you know something's wrong. One bad choice and things go bad. Changes everything."

"All it takes is one bad decision to steer your life in the wrong direction," Recker said.

"I know. That's why I told my brother about all this. That's a life that's not for me. I don't want any part of it."

"You're a smart kid."

They sat in silence at a red light for a moment.

"Am I ever gonna see you again?" Darnell said.

"Probably not."

Recker looked over at the young man who nodded back at him.

Once they pulled up to Darnell's house, Recker saw Tyrell sitting on the front steps of the row home, waiting for them. The two brothers hugged for a moment before Tyrell told his little brother to go inside where their mother was waiting for him. Once Darnell was out of sight, Tyrell walked over to Recker's car to thank him once again. They shook hands as Tyrell spilled his emotions out.

"Just wanna thank you again, man," Tyrell began.

"You already did. So did he. Multiple times."

"I know, but," Tyrell said, stopping as he started to choke up. "That's my little brother, man. You know what I mean?" he said, his voice pitched higher than normal.

Recker could see that he was deeply affected thinking about what could've happened. "There's nothing more important than family."

"I promised my mother that he wouldn't turn out like me. That he wouldn't be out here in the streets fighting for survival. That he'd use those brains of his to get out of here and make something good with his life."

"Seems like you're doing a pretty good job so far," Recker said.

"I just hope I can keep it up. There's a lot of distractions out here, bad things, bad people. A lot of things that can go wrong and push him off the wrong track."

"Well, we'll just have to make sure we keep him on the right one."

"We?" Tyrell said.

"Darnell seems like a good kid. We talked on the way over here about what he wanted to do with his life. We'll make sure it happens for him."

"Recker, man, I appreciate everything you've done for him so far, for me, but I can't ask you to do any more for him. He's not your blood, you don't have to do that," Tyrell said.

"I came to this city to help people. To make sure bad things didn't happen to good people. Darnell's a part of that. Because he's your brother, if some people know that, there's a chance he might be targeted more than some."

"I know it."

"So we'll have to make sure that doesn't happen. And because he's your brother, he'll have me watching over him from a distance," Recker said.

Recker could see that Tyrell was genuinely touched by the gesture he made of helping to keep his brother safe. Tyrell wanted to say something profound, something that could express how much that meant to him, other than just a simple thanks. But there were no words powerful enough to express his gratitude. And Recker didn't need them. He could see that Tyrell was deeply moved by his offer and that was enough for him.

After dropping Darnell off, Recker went straight back to the office, immediately getting pestered by Jones the moment he walked in. Jones dropped everything he was working on, curious about what happened with the Gibson situation.

"Judging by the fact that I don't see any blood, I take it everything went off smoothly," Jones noted.

"Was there ever a doubt?" Recker said.

"Am I going to see another news story shortly?"

"Uh... I hadn't thought about it."

"Oh dear," Jones said, walking back to his computer to analyze it. "How many bodies will I be looking for?"

Recker looked away, hesitating slightly before answering. "Four," he said, mumbling slightly, hoping Jones would drop the subject.

"Four dead bodies. I can't see how that won't be a lead story on any telecast."

"Well... had to be done I suppose," Recker said, not the slightest bit of worry in his voice. "They had Darnell cornered between two duplexes. I had to intervene in the way that I did. They were trying to give him a gun and partake in a robbery."

"I'm not questioning your decision making. I'm just concerned that there's a lot of dead bodies piling up lately. And high-profile cases at that," Jones said.

"This won't come back to us. Four gang members dead will just look like a normal gang killing."

"That very well may be. But it doesn't disguise the realities."

"What exactly are you concerned about?" Recker said. "None of this is going to come back to us. Nobody even knows we exist."

"For the moment, nobody knows we exist."

"You expect that to change?"

"When there are high-profile events, such as mob murders, gang killings, dead bodies being dropped in the middle of the street, those are highly publicized situations that bring a lot of attention on an area. A lot of attention brings on more scrutiny. By everyone. Police, federal authorities, public, attention that we don't need or want," Jones explained.

"I think you're exaggerating a little bit."

"Am I? Let's take you for example."

"Me?"

"Yes. You're a known quantity now. People are on the lookout for you," Jones said, clicking around his keyboard.

"You mean the CIA?"

"No, I mean the regular public."

"I don't follow you," Recker said.

"Well, while you are out hobnobbing with organized crime leaders, taking out rival competition and eliminating gang members without a care in the world as to who knows your identity, I'm here at my computer analyzing the ramifications of every action you take," Jones said, a note of aggravation rising in his voice.

"What do you want me to do? Work in a box? Put a bag over my head when I go out?" Recker said sarcastically.

"I would just like you to be a little more careful as to when and where you do things, as well as who you interact with. I started this operation with the intention of you being as invisible as possible. And now you're as well known as the mayor."

"I'm not known," Recker said.

"Oh really?"

"Uh, no," Recker said not very confidently. He got the feeling he was about to be proven wrong.

Jones instantly turned to his computer and started typing. Recker wasn't sure if he was now ignoring him or what. Jones pulled up several websites that he had been monitoring lately and summoned his partner over to look at them with him.

"I want you to look at this," Jones said.

"What's all this?" Recker said, sitting down next to his employer, looking at the screen.

"These are all websites and blogs that have been started within the last year with the same purpose. Would you like to know what that purpose is?"

"Uh, I have a feeling you're about to tell me."

"These are all websites and blogs analyzing the moves and actions of one man. The Silencer. You," Jones told him.

Recker put his hand over his mouth as he folded his arms and faked a cough, carefully looking at Jones.

"These few on the left here are basically harmless, they just find mentions about you in the paper when it's suspected you had a hand in something," Jones said.

"And those?" Recker said, pointing to the other sites.

"Oh. Those are bloggers who are obsessed with finding out who The Silencer actually is. Some of them have actually interviewed people who are believed to have been helped by you... all in the interest of finding out your true identity."

"Any of them actually dig up anything of consequence?"

"Thankfully, no. They've got a general description of you but that's basically it."

"So, what's the problem?" Recker said.

"The problem is that their hobby is you. I've been monitoring all of them remotely and right now they're not a danger. But that can, and at some point, will change. They've all got their theories about who you are or who you've been. Some think you're a government agent, some think you're former military, some think you're just a modern-day vigilante. The problem is that all of them are out to prove that their theories are true."

"And they're not likely to stop?"

"It doesn't appear so at the moment. They're going to keep digging. And eventually, they'll talk to the wrong person who might actually know something and then they'll know something."

Recker grinned and shook his head. "Doesn't really change anything, David. Can't work in a box. If you want me to be out there helping people... I can't always do it in the shadows."

"I know that. I just would like you to be a little more careful as to how you work."

"What're you really concerned about?" Recker said, sensing there was more to it than Jones was revealing.

"What do you mean?" Jones replied as he typed away on the computer. "I've already told you."

"All this concern can't just be about a few bloggers and websites speculating about me. You had to know things like this would pop up occasionally. A man with your background with the NSA, able to do the things that you can do with a computer, hacking government infrastructures, stealing money out of criminal bank accounts without it getting traced to you, alternating plane itineraries in a computer to make it seem like they stopped somewhere that it didn't, changing identities without breaking a sweat."

"What are you getting at?" Jones said.

"That I highly doubt someone with your capabilities would really be worried about a few homemade websites, mom's basement bloggers and conspiracy theorists," Recker said. "We both know you can hack into their computers and see everything they're working on any time you feel like it. I really doubt you feel threatened by them. And I'm sure someone as smart as you had already accounted for things like this to happen. So why don't you tell me what you're really worried about?"

As Jones thought about what Recker just said, he pushed his chair away from the desk and turned to face him. Wanting to be candid with his friend, he articulated in his mind what he wanted to say before it came out in a way that he didn't intend. Recker was right. He had other worries on his mind, much bigger concerns than he had let on.

"You are completely correct," Jones said.

"About which part?"

"All of it."

"Well that's good to know," Recker said.

"You're right, the blogs and websites are things that I had

accounted for when planning all this. They're not really an issue, I can handle them from learning too much."

"What is it then?"

"The problem is that as your reputation grows, the more people that inquire about who or what you are, the closer you are, we are, to having to close down operations and open up somewhere else."

"You're trying to tell me something without really trying to tell me something," Recker said. "So why don't you stop beating around the bush, stop speaking gibberish, and tell me what the real problem is?"

Jones sighed, trying to slow his mind down and speak calmly. "The real problem is that you're no longer a myth or an urban legend or some kind of modern day Robin Hood who helps the weak against the powerful."

"Still not seeing it," Recker told him.

"I guess what I'm saying, in as plain of a language as I can say it, is that The Silencer is now on the radar of the federal government."

Though Recker finally understood what Jones was trying to say, he didn't seem as worried about it. It might've been because he truly didn't care, or maybe it was because he knew that it would eventually happen. He really didn't believe that a man who operated behind the scenes such as he did would just go unnoticed forever. A man who was as dangerous as he was, who did the things that he did, wouldn't eventually get the attention of higher authorities outside of the local police department. Jones studied his face for a few seconds, unsure why he seemed as calm and unfettered as he was. It wasn't quite the reaction he was expecting. Though he wasn't exactly sure what reaction he'd get, silence and calm was at the bottom of his list.

"You're taking this awfully well," Jones said.

"You haven't really told me the extent of the problem yet. What exactly are we talking about?"

"Right now, the police have sent a rough sketch of you along with the file they have on you, which admittedly isn't much, to the local FBI field office to see if they have any additional information they can provide."

"How long ago was that?"

"Request went in yesterday. I'm monitoring the situation as we speak."

"Anything with the CIA yet?" Recker said.

"Not as far as I can tell."

"Then we don't have anything to worry about yet."

"I don't see how you can be so cavalier about this." Jones said, genuinely perplexed. "Do you not understand that in the logical progression of things, the CIA is probably next in line to get your information. Surely someone there will recognize you."

"Well, just slow down a minute. Take a step back and relax."

"How can you be so calm and relaxed about your cover possibly being blown?"

"First off, have you seen that sketch they have of me? Doesn't look anything like me," Recker said, trying to add a touch of humor to the situation. "Nobody's gonna make me from that. Second, anything the local police or the FBI have on me makes no difference. Even if I walked into a police district tomorrow and confessed to everything, once they type my name into their computer, nothing will come up."

"You make the FBI sound like a bunch of bumbling idiots," Jones said.

"My cover goes so deep that the only time you should worry is if my fingerprints or DNA wind up in the CIA Director's office."

"I'm very aware of your status, Mike. But the CIA is only one step away from the FBI. Don't you think that if the FBI comes up with nothing that they might bump it up the food chain?"

"No."

"How can you be so sure?"

"Because I used to work for them. Believe me, the CIA and FBI don't play well together. They might as well be two different countries. Them working together is like the United States and China becoming allies," Recker said, using both hands as props. "If the FBI asks the CIA for information, they'll get the runaround for months before they're politely told to go away. The wall between those two agencies is so thick you couldn't blast your way through it even if you had a million pounds of C-4. Trust me."

"Well, I guess I'll take your word for it but it doesn't really make me feel better."

"Wasn't supposed to. Just telling you like it is."

"And you're sure that this really is nothing to worry about?"

"You don't ask the CIA for information. They ask you. Besides, you're able to hack into the servers and databases of both the FBI and CIA, can't you?"

"Yes. But like I've told you before, to do so effectively and anonymously takes time. And by the time I've done that they could already be at our doorstep," Jones said.

"The FBI will come up with blanks. The only people you should worry about coming to look for me is the CIA. And that's not gonna happen just because the crime rate of this city goes up or someone starts to get famous for helping people. It's also not gonna happen because of a nickname I've got in the newspaper or an online blog."

"Then how do you suppose you would get back into their crosshairs?" Jones said.

"My fingerprint will turn up somewhere. Get entered into some database. My face will get recognized or it'll turn up on a

CIA facial recognition software program somewhere. You've been in the CIA computers before, you know how it works."

"While yes, I have gotten into certain areas of the CIA's computers, I certainly am not foolish enough to think I've explored everything in their arsenal. The data that agency possesses, much like the NSA, is just massive. It's so enormous that the amount of information I've gleaned from their servers is such an underwhelming low percentage. It's probably in the low single digits to be more precise. And there are some things that can't really be learned from a computer or a file. Any organization or business has a certain mindset to it that can only be fully understood by working within its walls."

"I agree. So take it from me. The police sending a request to the FBI asking about me is nothing to worry about. Nothing will come of it. If you get word the CIA is involved... then it's time to worry. And we don't have to think about that now. At least... not yet."

22

A month had passed since Recker had learned that the police department sent feelers out to the FBI to see if they could assist in identifying who The Silencer was. Like he predicted, nothing had come from it so far. Jones kept close eyes on it, monitoring the situation remotely. The FBI analyzed the information they received but had no knowledge of who The Silencer was and relayed to the police department that they couldn't help them yet. Though Recker wasn't the slightest bit concerned, Jones had been sweating a little bit over it. A weight lifted off his shoulders when he saw that the FBI was no longer involved in the case.

There was still the problem with the bloggers and websites devoted to finding The Silencer or his identity, but that wasn't anything major. Instead of trying to shut them down, hoping they'd go away or not find anything, the professor instead started to intentionally feed them misinformation in order to throw them further off the tracks. None of them was even remotely close to finding anything out at that point, but Jones wanted to make sure they wouldn't even be close for a long time. He sent everyone that was on his radar emails about The Silencer, giving them bad information about where he'd been or who he'd been with, giving them false theories about Recker's back-story or who he might have been. Jones also created false documents and stories to further perpetuate the misinformation and create so many dead ends and bad leads that it would take months, maybe even a year to discern that all the information was leading nowhere.

For his part, Recker didn't really concern himself with any of that. That was more Jones' concern. Even if his identity was known, Recker was fully confident in his ability to slip into the shadows and disappear. He'd done it numerous times before. Besides, he didn't really consider the public or a blogger or the police department, or even the FBI for that matter, much of a threat. The only thing that would concern him was if a CIA operative showed up in town.

Recker just continued what he'd been doing, helping people, closing out the cases that Jones assigned to him. With him being shot and working with Vincent, they had a backlog of cases that they had to catch up on as well as new assignments that popped up by the day. Recker was completely busy every day for the past month just clearing the cases they had without even taking a day off, which was fine by him since he liked to stay busy, anyway. Downtime and relaxation wasn't his most preferred option.

After closing out the last assignment that was left on their agenda, a domestic abuse case, Recker wearily entered the office. Though he didn't relish prolonged periods of inactivity, he sure was ready for a breather. Not a long one. He didn't want a one or two-week vacation. Just a day or so to recharge his batteries a little. He'd been running around non-stop all over the city over the past thirty days. Jones, typing away at the computer as he usually was, stopped for a few moments as he watched Recker drag himself over to the couch and plop down on it.

"I guess you'll be happy to know that there's nothing else pending as far as I can see right now," Jones said, leaning back in his office chair.

"Never thought I'd see the day."

"You look tired, worn out. Go home and get some sleep."

"Maybe later. Right now, I just wanna sit here and do nothing for a few minutes," Recker said, slumping further back on the couch.

"You've certainly earned it. If you're hungry, there's a turkey sandwich in the fridge."

"That sounds good."

Recker hadn't had a thing to eat all day and was starving. He went to the refrigerator to grab the sandwich and almost devoured it in seconds once he sat back down to eat it.

"Hungry?" Jones said, astonished at how little time he took to eat most of it.

"Just a little."

"I told you to eat something this morning before you left but you didn't listen."

"Sorry, dad," Recker.

"I take it you didn't eat anything else while you were out and about."

"No. Was too busy. Nothing else on the agenda?"

"Are you bored already?"

"No. Just asking."

"Well there's a few things that I'm monitoring as we speak but nothing that's materialized into anything we need to get involved with yet," Jones said. "Just take a couple days to relax."

"I'm not good at relaxing. You know what I'm good at? Silencing problems. Shooting things."

"Yes, I'm quite aware of your prowess with the firearms."

They continued talking as Jones did his work, him not even looking at Recker as he spoke. After a few more minutes, Recker was no longer responding to him. Jones stopped typing and looked over at him, ready to admonish him for ignoring him, but found that Recker had quietly fallen asleep. A small smile crept over Jones' face as he looked at his partner passed out on the couch.

"As I said, Mike, you've earned it," Jones whispered.

Jones kept on working for another couple of hours, trying to be as quiet as possible, though he wasn't sure it made any difference. He suspected that Recker was so tired that a parade of elephants could've marched through the room and his sleeping friend wouldn't have heard a peep. The silence was interrupted, however, at the sound of Recker's phone going off. It was so quiet that Jones jumped a little in his seat at the sound of the ringer going off, breaking the silence. Recker groggily opened his eyes and instinctively reached into his pocket though he wasn't fully awake.

"Yeah?" Recker said.

"Do you always greet everyone that way?" Mia said. "Whatever happened to hi? Or hello?"

"Oh, sorry. I didn't uh... I didn't look at my phone before I answered."

"Did I wake you up? You sound like you were sleeping or something."

"Uh, no, no, I was just uh... doing something."

"I did wake you up, didn't I? Don't lie to me."

"Yeah, maybe, well, I had to get up, anyway."

"I'm so sorry, Mike, I didn't mean to wake you," Mia told him. "I know you don't sleep a lot."

"No, don't worry about it. I had to get up anyway to do some things."

"Oh yeah? Like what?"

"You know... some things," Recker said, struggling to come up with a lie.

"OK. Well I'll let you get back to sleep. Call me later when you can." Mia said, making it sound like a question rather than a request.

"No, it's OK. I'm up now. I've been sleeping all day actually, so I had to get up soon anyway," Recker told her, getting a curious look from Jones who knew he hadn't been sleeping all day. "What's the matter? Everything OK?"

"Yeah. Everything's fine. I just got home from work and realized that we hadn't talked in like two weeks," Mia said.

"Yeah, I know. Just been really busy."

"I know. That's what I figured. But I haven't seen you in like a month. I think the last time I saw you was when I dropped you off for your truck."

"Sounds about right."

"Yeah, so I have the rest of the night to myself and I wasn't really doing anything. And I know you're probably working and all but I was just wondering if you could tear yourself away for an hour or so and have dinner... with me," she said, sheepishly, like she was back in high school asking a boy out for the first time. She was trying not to get her hopes up too high so she wouldn't get disappointed when he told her no, since she figured that Recker would decline the invitation.

"Dinner?"

"Yeah. I mean, I know it's last minute and all but I just thought I'd throw it out there in case you haven't eaten yet or anything."

Recker just happened to look over at Jones who was nodding

his head in approval. Recker scrunched his eyebrows together, thinking it was strange that the professor wanted him to go.

"Tonight?" Recker said.

"Yeah, unless you already have plans. I mean, if you do, we could always make it another night."

Recker looked at Jones again, who was still nodding his head energetically in approval of the idea. Recker was unnerved, wondering why Jones wanted him to go.

"Uh, dinner... could you hold on just a second?" Recker said, putting his hand over the phone to mute it and holding it away from his body.

"Sure," Mia said.

"What are you doing?" Recker whispered.

"What?" Jones said.

"Why are you nodding your head?"

"I take it that's Mia asking you to dinner tonight?"

"Yeah."

"I think you should go," Jones said.

"You do?" Recker said, surprised.

"Absolutely."

"Why?"

"Because I think it's a good idea. She's a friend. You need to eat. That's what people do at dinner." Jones shrugged.

"Weren't you the one who told me to keep her at arm's length before? To not let her get too close?"

"I did. But it's just dinner, right?"

"Yeah."

"Then you should go and have an enjoyable time."

"I should?"

"Absolutely."

Recker thought about if for a couple seconds and then took his hand off the phone, pressing it back against his ear.

"Dinner tonight, huh?" Recker said again.

"Yep. Dinner tonight," Mia replied.

Recker hesitated, though he wasn't quite sure why. He liked Mia and liked spending time with her, though he didn't do it often. It was probably just a safety mechanism that kicked in inside him to prevent people from getting too close to him. Or him too close to them. But since Jones was giving him the seal of approval, he thought it was best for him to accept this time.

"Yeah. Yeah, I can make it tonight," Recker said.

"Really?" Mia said, not sure that she heard correctly.

"Yeah. I actually just cleared a case I was working on so I should have the night free."

"That's awesome," she said, trying very hard not to sound too excited even though she was.

She actually wanted to scream into the phone out of joy that she finally got him to accept an offer to hang out with her. She'd asked him several other times in the last couple weeks to meet her somewhere, but each time, Recker said he had work to do. Though she knew he was busy, she couldn't help but sometimes think that he just didn't want to be around her very much. Mia wasn't scared away by his work, or his past, not that she knew much of it. But the little that Recker did tell her, she wasn't frightened to be near him. She liked him and wanted to get to know him even better. But up to this point it was always a one-way street. It was always her calling him, her asking him to go out, the lone exception being when he called her to drop him off for his car. In the time that they'd known each other, that was the only time he ever called her first. There was a piece of her that wondered why she kept trying so hard to be more of a part of his life when he kept resisting. She wasn't ready to admit defeat yet and be complicit in staying inside the friend zone. She believed there was still more to their relationship, she just had to pull it out of him.

Mia picked a restaurant and they agreed to meet there in an hour. Once they finished their conversation, Recker walked over to the desk and took a seat next to Jones and just stared at him for a minute. Jones, feeling the icy stare of his partner, cleared his throat, and tried to keep on working like nothing was wrong. Finally, he moved his head slightly in Recker's direction.

"Yes?" Jones said.

"I can't figure out what your motive is," Recker said, keeping up the stare.

"My motive?"

"Yeah. Your motive, your angle, however you want to put it. Whatever the reason is that's floating around inside that head of yours as to why you want me to meet Mia for dinner."

"I assure you I have no motive," Jones said. "I just figured you're exhausted, haven't eaten much, been working almost around the clock, I thought a nice dinner with a friend would be good for you."

Recker leaned his elbow on the desk, his hand covering his mouth and his fingers rubbing against his face as he contemplated the situation. He wasn't sure that was the truthful reason but maybe it was. Maybe it was just his natural skepticism that made him think there was something else going on. Feeling Recker's stare again, Jones turned to him once more to diffuse his concerns.

"I assure you I have no other motivations or angles," Jones said. "You've been working non-stop for a month. I'm concerned about burn out for you so I simply believe a night at dinner with a friend, even an hour or two, would be good for your health. That's all there is to it."

"That's all?"

"That is all."

"So how long was I sleeping for?" Recker said.

"About three hours."

Recker checked the time, and it was just past nine o'clock. "Guess I need to clean up a little."

"Certainly wouldn't hurt," Jones said, sniffing, getting another look from Recker. "Well I was only agreeing."

Recker then washed up and went to the restaurant that Mia recommended. They both arrived at the same time, meeting by the front door. Mia gave him a hug, happy that they were actually getting a chance to spend some time together. Once they separated from their hug, Recker looked at Mia up and down and couldn't help but think how pretty she looked. She was in a nice dress that went down to her knees and was very flattering to her figure.

"I feel kind of under dressed seeing you," Recker said.

"What? You look nice," Mia replied, looking at him in his dress shirt. "Very handsome."

"You didn't have to get all dressed up or anything for me."

"I wanted to. It's been a long time since I felt like dressing up for someone so don't complain."

"I'm not complaining. Just didn't want you to go to any trouble for me."

"It was no trouble. Unless you don't like it?" Mia said, her expression becoming worried.

"No, no. You look fine. Very pretty." He smiled. He thought she looked stunningly beautiful but couldn't say it.

"Thank you," she said, returning the smile, happy that the work she put into it seemingly paid off.

They went inside and were quickly seated in the jam-packed restaurant, getting the last remaining table. While they were looking over the menus, Mia got nervous. She was hoping she wouldn't seem boring or not have anything to say, or that they wouldn't have any awkward silences. Even though this wasn't technically a date, at least from Recker's point of view, she wanted to impress him as much as possible and try to put some seeds in his mind about taking things further with her.

"So you cleared all your cases, huh?" Mia said.

"Yep."

"Nothing on the horizon?"

"Not yet."

"That's good."

Recker looked up from the menu and at Mia, realizing that she was just trying to make conversation and that he was probably making it difficult for her. "So how's everything at work?" he said.

"Good. Kind of crazy with the number of babies and pregnant women that we have right now."

Recker smiled, not really sure how to respond, and went back to the menu. The waitress came to take their order and once she was gone, they simply looked at each other for a few seconds, neither of them sure how to restart the conversation. Recker's phone then started ringing, drawing a look from Mia, upset that their dinner was being interrupted as she had a feeling their night would be cut short. Recker pulled his phone out and looked at the screen before answering, a quizzical look on his face.

"Excuse me, I really should take this," Recker said.

"Of course," Mia replied, growing more concerned by the second.

"Hello?"

"Mr. Recker," Vincent greeted.

"Can I help you with something?" Recker said, still not quite sure the reason that he would be calling.

"No. I'm the one who's helping you. I made a promise to you some time ago and I'm now fulfilling that promise. I told you I would call you personally and I am."

"Does that mean what I think it does?" he said, finally understanding the purpose of the call.

"Well, I don't like to discuss specifics over the phone. That's why I prefer meetings. Phones are unreliable. Never know who might be listening," Vincent said. "Let's just say I think you'll be very satisfied at what I have to offer you."

Recker looked away from the table for a moment, his phone still firmly pressed to his ear and cleared his throat. Mia could tell that whatever he was being told was having a profound impact on him. From the look on his face, she assumed that it was bad news.

"Uh," Recker sighed, trying to think straight. "So, uh, where and when?"

"Right now works as good as any."

"Right now?"

"Well, I've already taken the liberty of acquiring a secure establishment," Vincent said. "This isn't something I prefer to keep lingering and have to waste further time and resources on."

"I understand."

"Any good reason why you can't make it now?"

Recker looked at Mia and knew he was gonna break her heart again if he left early. He knew she'd been looking forward to this dinner for a while and the thought of disappointing her again upset him more than he thought it would have. But he also knew that Vincent wasn't going to just hold on to Mancini indefinitely for him until the time suited him better. He'd have to do what he didn't want to and let her down again.

"No. No good reason. I'll be there," Recker said.

"Excellent."

"Just name the place."

"I'll text you the address. I'll be waiting inside."

"I'll be right there."

As soon as the words left his lips, Mia closed her eyes, disappointed that he had to go. She tried to plaster a smile onto her face, but she couldn't hide the disappointment in her eyes. Right after Recker confirmed he'd be there shortly, he was almost afraid to look at Mia's face, knowing that it was sure to be a sad one.

"You have to go," Mia said, not giving Recker the chance to say it first.

"I'm sorry. It's something I have to do. It's not something that can be put off for another time."

"I understand."

"I wish I could postpone it for another day but it's just not possible," Recker said, hating the pain on her face.

"I get it. I do. You're in demand and people need you." She sighed. "It's just that we never really get to spend any time together."

"I know. And I promise I'll make it up to you soon. Maybe we can reschedule dinner for another night."

"Maybe you could leave your phone at home whenever that happens?"

"Well, I don't know about that. But I'll try to make it for a less busier time," Recker said with a smile.

She returned his smile, though only half-hearted. "Is there ever such a thing?"

Recker acknowledged with a smirk that there probably wasn't and never would be such a time. He got up and started to leave but as he walked past her, he stopped and looked down at her, putting his hand on her shoulder, sorry that he had to go. Mia looked up at him with her sad eyes, which made him feel worse.

"Just be careful, please," Mia said quietly. "You know I worry about you."

"There's no need. I'll be fine."

"Don't kill anyone if you don't have to."

Recker took his eyes off her for a second, letting them dance around as he thought about her last words, before looking back to her. Knowing what he was leaving her to do, the words really hit home with him. He tried giving her a smile, but really couldn't muster one up. He got a text message alert and looked at it, seeing it was the address that Vincent was waiting at. Recker tapped Mia's shoulder again before leaving. Mia just sighed as the waitress came over with their appetizer. Part of her felt like leaving, but she decided to suck it up and eat there by herself since she was hungry.

As soon as Recker got in his car, he plugged the address into his GPS. It was a place in South Philly he wasn't too familiar with. That had been the Italians territory, but with them out of the picture now, he assumed that Vincent was already starting to flex his muscle in the area, claiming the area for himself. Recker got to the location in a little over twenty minutes. It appeared to be a transportation business as he pulled up to the front gate, with several different sizes and types of trucks parked just inside. There was a man standing on the other side of the gate and Recker got out to identify himself. As soon as he exited his car, another man appeared from behind one of the trucks, walking toward the gate. Recker recognized that it was Jimmy Malloy. Since the two of them needed no introduction to each other, Malloy told the other man to open the gate for Recker to enter.

"Drive up to the loading dock," Malloy told him.

Recker got back in his truck and did as Malloy suggested, driving up to the main loading area. Several trucks were already parked in their designated spots, but there was one open bay, letting Recker see that the lights were on inside. He saw a couple people moving around in there, but he couldn't quite make out who it was yet. Expecting him to be coming, a side door opened to the warehouse as soon as Recker stopped and exited his car. There was a man standing by the open door, waiting for Recker to approach.

Even though he'd been anticipating this day, it didn't seem as cut and dry as it once did. His mind was much cloudier than it had been. Maybe it was just Mia's last words that she said to him before he left the restaurant, but he really wasn't as eager to get this done with as he thought he would've been. Recker walked up the metal steps and stepped through the door opening, Vincent's man closing it behind him. Only a couple seconds after entering, Vincent walked up to him, a smile on his face.

"Glad you could make it," Vincent said, shaking Recker's hand.

Recker nodded in return, not really having anything to say.

"This way," the boss said, stretching his arm out to indicate which direction they were heading.

The two walked across the warehouse area to the far corner of a room, and then down a narrow hallway where another door was located. It was a small office space with a desk and chair in the middle of it. Sitting in the chair was Mario Mancini, tied up with a gag in his mouth. It looked like Mancini had been worked over a little bit, as he had some cuts and bruises on his face to show he'd received a bit of a beating. Recker expected to be angry when he saw him again. He expected rage to overtake his body and shoot the man in revenge for trying to take him out before without any thought. But he didn't. He just didn't have an emotional reaction to seeing Mancini. Recker didn't really feel much of anything upon seeing him. He was so devoid of feeling, it was like he'd never even seen the guy before. Hearing a noise behind him, Recker turned around and saw Malloy coming through the door. Vincent motioned to his lieutenant to go over to Mancini and remove the gag from his mouth.

"Is there anything you'd like to say before this matter is concluded?" Vincent said.

"Listen, it wasn't personal. It was just a job," Mancini said, begging for his life. "You guys know how that is. If you want me to leave town, I'll never come back. I swear."

Malloy removed a gun from his pocket and placed it on the desk in front of Recker. Recker looked down at it, then back at Mancini.

"If you'd like to use that, it's absolutely untraceable," Vincent said calmly. "Of course, if you'd rather use your own, it's completely understandable."

"Please, it was just a job." Mancini begged.

As certain as Recker had been that the next time he saw Mancini that he would kill him, he now wasn't so sure. He knew it wasn't a personal thing; it was just a job that Mancini was assigned, and maybe that was what was preventing him from feeling the rage. Recker certainly knew how it was to get an assignment like that and not have any personal feeling or emotional involvement in it. Maybe if it was more personal, than Recker would've had an easier time just raising his gun up and pulling the trigger. Maybe it wasn't any of those things. Maybe it was Mia and her final words to him in the restaurant that was preventing him thus far from killing Mancini. Maybe if Mia hadn't uttered those last words to him, it'd already be done with. He wasn't sure what it was, but he just didn't know if killing Mancini was the right thing to do anymore. With the Italians gone, it wasn't likely that he would come after Recker again with the intent of killing him. Though he couldn't be completely sure of that, he was sure that was the case. Business, not personal.

After a couple of minutes, Vincent and Malloy looked at each other, unsure what the holdup was. They figured Recker would've pulled the trigger and ended Mancini's life within seconds of seeing him. Though they weren't exactly in a hurry, and were fine with giving Recker a few extra minutes, they were confused about his hesitation.

"Mr. Recker, is there a problem?" Vincent said finally.

"No. No problem."

Even though he said that there wasn't, his lack of action indicated to Vincent that there was. Recker not only hadn't yet picked up the gun off the desk, he hadn't reached for his own gun either. He'd stood in the same spot since he entered the office, barely moving an inch.

"Please, you'll never hear from me again," Mancini pleaded again. "Tell me how far away you want me to go and I'll be there. I can even leave the country if that's what you want."

Recker wasn't really swayed by anything Mancini was saying as he knew the words were only being said out of desperation and fear of being killed. It wasn't the first time that he'd heard something similar when he had a suspect or target sitting in a chair in front of him. But this was the first time he was letting the situation drag on. Unless he was interrogating someone and needed some information first, he didn't believe in prolonging someone's death. Recker looked at the gun on the desk and all that ran through his mind was Mia's words.

"Don't kill anyone if you don't have to." The words replayed in his mind several times.

Recker heard the words so clearly it was almost like she was standing in front of him while saying it. Watching him. Any other thoughts he had were being overrun by her. He sighed and closed his eyes, rubbing the inside corner of his eyes with his finger and thumb. Recker was struggling with what to do. He wasn't sure what he wanted anymore. While his initial thoughts of taking revenge had permeated his brain since the night Mancini shot him, it was no longer clear to him that it was the right thing to do. All because of a few simple words that Mia said to him in passing. He was sure if the words had never left her lips that he would've already pulled the trigger by now. Though Vincent had been patient up to that point, that patience was slowly evaporating. It'd been several minutes since he led Recker into the office and he anticipated that the deed would be over with quickly. He didn't think it'd take a man like Recker five minutes to pull the trigger on someone he wanted dead.

"Why the hesitation, Mike?" Vincent said.

Recker sighed before answering, not sure he wanted to tell the truth. He certainly didn't want to sound weak in his present company. "I guess I'm just not sure this is what I really want."

Vincent and Malloy looked at each other, both surprised at the lack of vigor of the man standing before them. With a man of Recker's stature and reputation, and with a subject who previously tried to kill him, they didn't quite understand why he wasn't jumping at the chance for retribution. Mancini's face was slowly changing with each passing minute that he still was breathing. While he was a hundred percent certain of his fate just minutes beforehand, he now was beginning to have hope that he might just live through his current predicament.

"Can I ask why?" Vincent said. "You previously expressed great interest in getting redemption on the man who tried to kill you. Why the change?"

"I guess things just change sometimes. Sometimes you think you want something and then when it happens, you come to the realization that you didn't really want it at all," Recker said.

"I didn't take you for a man who..."

"I'm not a man who can be pigeonholed or assumed anything about," Recker tersely replied, sensing they were thinking he was weak. "Don't think cause we've done business a couple times that you can take for granted that you know what I'll do or how I think."

"I'll remember that."

"My reasons for hesitating are my own and I don't feel the need to share them."

"Then I won't press you on them any further," Vincent said.

"But with that in mind, I do feel the need to remind you that I'm not that high on burning the midnight oil, as they say. I do need you to make a decision on whether you're gonna end this man's life or not so we can all move on."

Recker looked at the gun on the desk, then at Mancini, and back to the gun once more. He took a deep breath, not believing himself what he was about to say.

"Let him go," Recker said softly.

"You wish to release him?" Vincent said, a little surprised, though he could see that was the direction this confrontation was heading.

"I don't really care what you do with him. But I'm not gonna kill him. Not right now."

"I promise you'll never see me again," Mancini said, relieved at the decision.

"Very well," Vincent responded. "I can't say I quite understand your decision, but I realize you probably have your reasons for it. I respect that."

"Don't go thinking that I've gone soft, 'cause that would be an opinion that you would regret," Recker said.

"Never crossed my mind. You and soft are two words that I would never think about putting in the same sentence."

"I take it I'll have no problem leaving?"

"I'll radio the gate," Malloy said. "You won't have a problem."

"Thanks."

Recker left the office and walked across the length of the warehouse floor, wondering if he made the right decision. Once he reached the door to exit, he took a quick look back at the office, seeing Vincent and Malloy standing in the doorway, watching his every move. Recker scurried down the metal steps and wasted no time getting back in his car. He drove toward the front gate, with Vincent and Malloy moving over to the open bay, watching his car as it drove away. Malloy took a radio out of his pocket to alert them of Recker approaching.

"Recker's driving up to the gate now. Let him pass," Malloy said.

The two men stood there for another minute until Recker's car was completely out of sight. Vincent, a bit thrown off by Recker's decision, was contemplating what he wanted to do with Mancini.

"I have to say that's a decision that I did not see coming," Vincent said.

"What do you think caused him to change his mind?"

"I'm not sure. It certainly wasn't fear. He's killed plenty of others before. I can't really say I understand it. But there was something definitely tugging at him. That much was clear."

"Should I let Mancini go?" Malloy said.

"No." Vincent looked out into the night air, still going over the options in his mind.

"What do you wanna do with him?"

Vincent sighed before coming to a conclusion. "Get rid of him."

"You wanna kill him?"

"He's of no use to us. Besides, he's not one of our men. He's been on the Italians payroll. He can be buried alongside the rest of them," Vincent said coldly.

"Maybe he could be of some use to us," Malloy said. "He's a pretty good gun. I mean, it's not like he was high in their pecking order. He's basically a freelancer."

"He's a loose end that we don't need. There's nothing he can offer us that we can't already do ourselves."

"What about just cutting him loose?"

"After having him sit in that chair tied up, thanks to us, I can't say I'd ever fully trust him. Maybe he'd leave, maybe he wouldn't. Maybe he'd harbor grudges against us, maybe not. Whatever the case, he's not good enough or valuable enough to take a chance on," Vincent explained.

"OK, boss. You think Recker would be pissed off if we kill him after saying to let him go?" Malloy said.

"Well, I'd say that Mr. Recker no longer has the right to get pissed off about anything. He had his chance to extract any justice he felt was necessary on the matter. Besides, he told us to do whatever we wanted with him."

"You want me to make him disappear?"

"No. Make an example out of him," Vincent said. "Let's let everyone know who's in charge of this area now."

"You got it."

Vincent then left, walking to his own car, and getting in the back seat as he was whisked away from the area, leaving Malloy behind to do the dirty work as he often did. Malloy wasted no time in getting done what was asked of him, immediately going back to the office, where Mancini was still restrained in the chair. The worried look on Mancini's face had evaporated, believing that he was being released since Recker no longer had him on his hit list. Since he had no beef that he knew of with Vincent's organization, it didn't occur to him that they would want him eliminated as well. When Malloy entered the room again, he wasn't worried in the slightest. Mancini just assumed that he came back to let him go. It even occurred to him that Vincent might have room for him in his organization full time. Malloy cracked his knuckles one at a time as he looked at the tied-up individual sitting in front of him.

"You guys gonna let me go now?" Mancini said.

"Things are rarely that simple," Malloy said quietly.

"What do you mean? If Recker doesn't want me dead anymore then what am I still doing here?"

"You're somewhat of a loose end."

"Loose end? What are you talking about? Let me talk to Vincent."

"Vincent's no longer here."

Getting the sense that things were taking a turn for the worse, Mancini was beginning to worry again. He started breathing more heavily and sweat started rolling down the sides of his face. Since Malloy hadn't released him yet, he could only assume that his death was still being considered, if not already decided.

"Let me talk to Vincent," Mancini said, repeating his plea.

"What for?"

"I wanna work for him."

"I don't think we're hiring," Malloy said.

"I can help you guys. You know my reputation. I'm not some street thug."

Though Malloy agreed with him, and if it was up to him, he would've released Mancini and considered his request for employment. But it wasn't up to him and he wasn't about to go against Vincent's wishes on such a trivial matter. Malloy looked down at the gun that was still sitting on the edge of the desk, about to pick it up and finally finish the job that they assumed Recker would do. Mancini noticed what he was looking at and tried to think of something else he could do to stave off his impending demise. Malloy nonchalantly picked up the gun with his right hand, though he let it swing down to his side for a few moments. Mancini started squirming around in his chair, hoping to somehow wriggle himself free.

"If you guys let me go, like I told Recker, I'll go wherever you want me to go," Mancini pleaded. "Just name it and you'll never see me again. I promise I won't be a problem."

"You know, if it was up to me, I'd let you stick around," Malloy told him, raising his gun, and pointing it at his prisoner.

"C'mon, we can work this out. We can come to some sort of

agreement. I even have some money set aside. It's like a couple hundred grand. It's yours if you want it. You can have it."

"Money doesn't interest me."

Knowing his pleas were falling on deaf ears, Mancini struggled with his ties even more, desperately trying to figure out some way out of his current predicament. A painful expression came over his face as he agonized over what he could say that would impact his release. He knew Malloy was just seconds away from ending his life and would've offered anything to change his fate.

"What do you want? C'mon, there has to be something I can give you," Mancini said, tears starting to roll down his face.

"I can't think of anything," Malloy said. He got out his radio again and spoke into it. "Bring the van up."

"There in a minute," a voice said, crackling over the radio.

"Just name what you want," Mancini said, his rising in pitch with fear.

"Like I said... it ain't up to me," Malloy told him.

Malloy then pointed the gun at Mancini's head and blew a hole in his forehead, killing him instantly. For good measure, as Mancini's head slumped forward, Malloy aimed the gun at his chest and put three more holes into him. Malloy stood there for a few seconds, admiring his handy work, though a small part of him thought it was a shame that they couldn't find some use for him in the organization. He didn't usually question Vincent's judgment, though, and didn't really put much more thought into it. Malloy walked out of the office as a couple other members of the organization entered the warehouse. Within a minute, Mancini's dead body was being carried out of the office by the two men and then dumped into the van that had pulled up.

"Get this guy out of here," Malloy said.

"What do you want us to do with him?" one of the men said.

"Don't matter. Vincent wants him seen, so dump him in an alley or a street corner or something. Just make it visible."

"Got it."

"Just make sure you're out of view of any cameras or anything. Everybody should know who did it, but we don't want any evidence that leads it back to us. Vincent just wants the statement made."

23

Recker was drinking a cup of coffee and had only been in the office for a few minutes when Jones moved from around his desk and towards the TV. Recker wondered what had him so intrigued and glanced up at the set himself as Jones turned the volume up. It was a breaking news report that had a reporter on the scene of some sort of crime, complete with flashing police lights behind him as he spoke on the screen.

"Something happened," Jones said softly.

"Something's always happening," Recker said, not really interested. "Stuff goes down in this city every day. That's nothing new. And it's not changing either."

"No, this seems like something bigger."

As Jones turned the volume up and started listening to the reporter speak, it became clear that the police had discovered a body in an alleyway. Jones was glued to the screen as the reporter described the scene and the events as they knew them.

"The police received a report of a body lying in this alley behind me about one hour ago, roughly 6AM, and quickly discovered the man was already dead, and likely had been for at least five or six hours," the reporter said, all white teeth and earnest brows.

Though Jones seemed to be fascinated by the events, Recker couldn't have cared less. As he said, bad things happened every day in that city, along with every other city in the world. One more dead body really didn't concern him one way or another, unless he was somehow connected to it. Since Jones was so enthralled by it, Recker also kept listening, somewhat lackadaisically though.

"We have since learned, in just the last few minutes through a confidential source, the identity of the man," the reporter said to the camera. "Our highly trusted source says the police have already identified the body as being Mario Mancini."

Jones' eyes almost bulged out of its sockets as he heard the name announced. He looked over to Recker, who also looked stunned to hear the identity of the body. Recker himself almost dropped his cup when the reporter mentioned Mancini's name.

"I thought you told me you left him alive," Jones said.

"I did. I didn't do that," Recker said once the initial shock wore off.

"Are you sure?"

"I would think I would know if I killed somebody or not."

"Well if you didn't do it then who did? And why?"

"Well if I didn't do it then there's only one other person who would've... Vincent," Recker said.

"Why would Vincent do this?"

"Make a statement."

"About what?"

"Usually when someone takes charge of something, such as new territory in this case, the new man in charge wants to make a statement to put everybody else on notice."

"And Mancini was one of Bellomi's men," Jones said. "Make it as violent and public as possible so everyone knows who did it."

"When I left the warehouse last night, Mancini was still tied up in the office."

"Well he obviously met a very painful demise."

"Hmm."

"What is that supposed to mean?"

"Well, I did tell Vincent to do whatever he wanted with him."

"Why would you do that?"

"Well, I said I wasn't going to kill him and I told Vincent to do whatever he wanted with him."

"I would say he obviously took you up on your word. Quite literally," Jones said. "Does the location of where they dumped him have any significance?"

"No, I don't think so."

"Well then why take the trouble of moving the body?"

"If Vincent's taking ownership of that trucking business then he wouldn't want police snooping around the area. Dumping the body in a dark alley in the middle of the night eliminates prying eyes and ears. Not to mention cameras," Recker told him.

"Well this is quite a start to the day," Jones said, turning back to his computer.

"Hopefully it doesn't get any more interesting."

Recker's hope for a boring and uneventful day from that point on wouldn't come to fruition. A little over two hours later, he received a call from Tyrell. As soon as Recker saw his name on the screen, he assumed there was trouble brewing. Tyrell didn't usually call just to chitchat.

"I assume you have more business to discuss?" Recker said.

"Don't you ever just pick up the phone and say hi?" Tyrell said sarcastically.

"Uh... no."

"You know, I've noticed that about you. Half the time you pick up the phone, you lead off with a question."

"Well maybe next time you call I'll start with a riddle," Recker said. "Or maybe you'd prefer a limerick?"

"A limerick? What's that?"

"Another time. What's on your mind?"

"Your presence is being requested," Gibson said.

"Let me guess... Jeremiah?"

"You got it, bro."

"What does he want?"

"No idea. He didn't say. He just asked if you could meet him at the usual spot."

"I guess I could do that," Recker said, subconsciously nodding his agreement.

"I'll let him know."

"What time?"

"He said noon."

"I'll be there."

Recker hung up and sat in a chair blindly staring ahead, not really focusing on anything in particular. He was struggling to figure out what exactly Jeremiah could have wanted with him. Jones let him stew there for a few minutes before he spoke up.

"I heard Jeremiah's name mentioned," Jones said, getting Recker's attention. "I take it you have a meeting with him?"

"It seems so."

"What does he want?"

"Couldn't say."

"Seems odd that he'd request a meeting the very morning Mancini is found dead. And very publicly at that," Jones said. "Might not be a coincidence."

Recker shrugged, not sure if there was a connection. "I don't know. Mancini wasn't one of his men. As far as I know, Jeremiah doesn't have a beef with any of the particular parties. Really don't know what this is about."

"Well, he must be concerned about something. It certainly isn't to request your help on a matter."

"You wouldn't think so."

Recker sat there for a few more minutes, wondering if Jones was on to something. Maybe Jeremiah's meeting was somehow connected to Mancini's death. He couldn't think of why Jeremiah would be interested in it, but that could be the reason for the meeting. At least Recker wouldn't have to worry about it for long. The meeting would be in just a couple of hours and then he'd know for sure what Jeremiah wanted him for. He kept himself busy by looking over files on the computer that Jones had asked him to examine. He got so immersed in it that he almost lost track of time for when he was supposed to leave for the meeting.

"Give me a call when you're finished," Jones said as Recker reached the door.

"Yes, dad," Recker replied, closing the door behind him.

Jones rolled his eyes and shook his head, then went back to his work. He hated when Recker called him dad. Even more than the professor. At least a professor was distinguished. Recker immediately went down to the vacant, boarded-up house that was their usual meeting place. Once he got there, he sat in his car and watched the house for a few minutes. Though he didn't feel he was on as good as terms with Jeremiah as he was with Vincent, he certainly didn't feel like he was on bad terms either. He thought there was a healthy respect between the two sides. But something was tugging at him that something wasn't right with this meeting. He wasn't sure why he thought that as nothing had happened to cause any friction between them, but he couldn't shake the feeling. It could've just been his paranoia playing on him, but it was in the back of his mind that he'd need to be alert in there.

MIKE RYAN

Recker walked up to the house, seeing the same guys as usual who opened the door for him as he approached. Once inside, Recker went into the living room and saw Jeremiah sitting in a chair in the corner. He had furnished the place up a little since the last time Recker was there. Now there was a couple of beat up looking plush chairs sitting across from each other on opposite sides of the room.

"Like what you've done with the place," Recker said, looking around.

Jeremiah laughed. "Yeah. Had my interior decorator come in here and spruce the place up. Glad you like it."

"Mind?" Recker said, pointing to the other chair.

"Please do. Had it brought in for you special."

Recker took another quick look around, making sure there were no other surprises in store for him. Such as a hitman or two waiting around the corner or in another room. It was just the two of them sitting there. Which was unusual since Jeremiah, like Vincent, usually had a guard or two nearby at all times. Jeremiah sat there silently for a moment, analyzing his visitor. He noticed that Recker seemed a little skittish, not at all like the usual confident person that he'd met with before.

"Something bothering you?" Jeremiah said.

"No."

"Seem a little jumpy."

"I've had some issues lately with, let's just say, surprises," Recker said. "I don't like surprises."

"Well you can relax. Cause there ain't no surprises in here."

"Good to know. So, what'd you wanna talk about?" Recker said.

"I just thought me and you could rap awhile about some things that have been happening around here lately."

"Such as?"

"There's a lot that's been going on here, the Italians being wiped out, Marco Bellomi and his crew being killed, this cat Mancini being found this morning. Yeah, a lot been going on," Jeremiah said, not in an accusing tone, but definitely a suspicious one.

"And you're thinking what? That I did it?"

"Have to admit the thought crossed my mind."

"I'm not sure what the significance of this conversation is," Recker said. "What exactly am I doing here? What are you hoping to find out?"

"Look, man, I got respect for you. I thought you had some respect for me. This stuff going down with the Italians impacts me and my business. I need to know if you were a part of all that," Jeremiah said. "That's why it's just me and you in here. Me and you. Man to man. No second in command, no third parties, just me and you sitting down and being real with each other."

"OK. You wanna be real with each other?" Recker said.

"Yeah, I do."

"Fine. I'll be real with you. First, you answer a question for me."

"Ask."

"Why do you wanna know if I did it?"

"Because this has got Vincent's name written all over it," Jeremiah said. "I need to know if you did it, if you're working for him, if I need to be watching my back now. A lot of things need to be answered. This city went from being shared a third between three parties and now it's down to two. Me and Vincent. I need to know if he's looking to pare things down even more. Now, my question?"

"All right. Yes, I killed Marco Bellomi and his henchmen," Recker said firmly.

"And this dude that was found this morning?"

"Wasn't me. Could've been me. But I didn't do it."

"You working for Vincent now?"

"Nope."

"Then why you taking out his competition for him?" Jeremiah said.

"Didn't do it for him."

"Then why?"

"It was a personal matter."

"A personal matter? You gonna have to do better than that."

"Why? Am I on trial for something here?"

"Maybe you are."

"Fine. I'll play along. If you want the real reason, here it is. A while back ago, in the course of my own business, I interacted with someone who apparently knew Bellomi. He didn't like what I did and took a hit out on me. Someone shot me, I survived, and then I gave them what they had coming. I did it for me, on my own. I didn't do it for Vincent and I don't much care about the power play that's going on for this city," Recker explained.

"So you're not working for him then?"

"I work for me. Now and always."

"That's what I like about you, man. That's what I respect. You don't come in here and just say what you think someone wants to hear. I can always spot a master bullshitter."

"You wanted the truth. That's what I gave."

"And I believe it. Did Vincent help you carry out this revenge of yours?" Jeremiah said.

"All he did was tell me where Bellomi would be and how I could hit them. The rest was on me," Recker replied.

"Yeah, I'm sure he was anxious for you to finish the job so he could move in on their territory."

"Like I said, none of that concerns me."

"This dude this morning, Mancini, that smacks in the face of Vincent sending a message that that's his territory now and to stay out of it."

"I'll hundred percent guarantee you it was. Mancini was the guy that shot me. Vincent found him for me last night and called me, hoping I'd come kill him."

"But you didn't?"

"I declined the offer. So, I would have to assume that Vincent did the honors for me," Recker said.

"In any of your dealings with Vincent, did he say anything about moving in on me or trying to take me out?"

"Your name never came up. But it wouldn't surprise me if he eventually tried it."

"Yeah, that's what I thought."

"I would think that if he does try, that you'll have some time to prepare yourself," Recker said.

"Why you think that?"

"Vincent's a man who moves very slowly. Methodically. He's not much for rushing into things and screwing things up because he was impatient. He likes to plan and make sure when he's ready, he finishes the job."

"You think he'll wait awhile before trying to take my part of the city?" Jeremiah said.

Recker shrugged. "I don't know for sure, but I would think he's not planning it at the moment. If you look at it logically, he seemed to be content in how things were going as they were. He didn't take over Bellomi's territory until I showed up and made it easy for him."

"That's true."

"He didn't even make a move on them. He waited for the perfect opportunity, which turned out to be me, and just slid his way over," Recker said. "So while I don't think he's planning anything imminently, I wouldn't get too comfortable just yet."

"Why's that?"

"Because Vincent's a man who loves power. He used to have a

third of the city. That wasn't enough. He wanted more. Now he's got two-thirds of it. I don't know where and when, but there's gonna come a time when two-thirds isn't enough either. He's gonna want more. And you're the man he's gonna get it from."

"That ain't happening," Jeremiah said defiantly.

"Maybe so. But he's sure gonna try. Maybe this year. Maybe next year. Maybe it won't be for another five years. But the day will come."

"I'll be ready for him."

"I'm sure you will be."

"Will you look out for me if you hear anything? Pass it along."

"This is a war I got no stake in," Recker said. "I'm not choosing sides and getting stuck in the middle of you."

"But you helped him gain some power."

"No I didn't. I helped myself in avenging a vendetta. He just happened to capitalize on it. Nothing more to it than that. On the flip side, if you wanna hit him tomorrow, and I hear about it… I'm not gonna tell him about that either."

Jeremiah leaned back in his chair, his hand touching his face and fiddling with his fingers. He just stared at Recker for a minute, studying his face. Jeremiah was excellent at reading people's faces and analyzing their words. He could tell when someone was being honest with him and when someone was feeding him a pack of lies. He could handle the truth, even if he didn't like it. He could tell that Recker wasn't holding back on him or just telling him what he thought he wanted to hear.

"We good?" Recker said.

Jeremiah started nodding. "Yeah. We're good."

"Anything else you wanna talk about? These chairs are comfy," Recker said with a grin.

"Nah, that was it."

"All right then. I'll see myself out."

Recker got up and left, Jeremiah's eyes focused on him the entire time. Once he left the house, one of Jeremiah's top aides came in to ask how the meeting went.

"Whatcha want us to do with him?" the man said.

"Nothing."

"He throw in with Vincent?"

"Nah. He's staying out of it all together," Jeremiah said.

"He say anything about Vincent?"

"Oh yeah. Vincent's coming. Don't know when, but he's coming. And we'll need to be ready when he does."

"We will be."

"Might be a year or two from now. Maybe even longer. But we need to get stronger," Jeremiah vowed.

"How you wanna do that?"

"Get more eyes and ears on the street. We need to know what's going on weeks, months before it happens."

"We'll do it."

"What we need is to somehow get Recker to throw in with us. That's a man who can do some damage in a fight."

"How you propose to do that?" his aide said.

"I dunno yet. But we gotta figure out a way. He took out the Italian leadership all by himself. A man that can do that is a man we need working with us," Jeremiah said thoughtfully. "Before Vincent gets to him first."

24

Recker's phone started ringing and as soon as he saw who it was, continued to let it ring, drawing a look from Jones. They were sitting side by side, Recker's phone lying on the desk in between their computers. Jones thought it a little strange that he wasn't answering his phone, but then thought about it, and didn't think it so strange after all. He knew who it was. The only person he didn't pick up for right away was Mia. Jones figured it must've been her. Which was strange in itself considering she was a friend, but he didn't like to butt into Recker's business too often. Jones knew he had his reasons for ignoring her calls. A few seconds after the phone stopped ringing, another ringer went off, indicating a voicemail. Jones looked at the phone out of the corner of his eye as he continued typing, wondering why Recker was still not reaching for his phone.

"Are you not going to answer that?" Jones said finally.

"Answer what?"

"The phone that just rang."

"Oh. Yeah, I'll get to it," Recker said without looking up.

Though he wasn't really satisfied with his answer, Jones didn't want to press him any further. A few seconds later his phone buzzed again, this time indicating a text message. Jones stopped typing and looked at the phone again, seeing that it was still Mia. He turned to Recker, who still wasn't making a move for it.

"Is there an issue or something?" Jones said.

"With what?"

"With Mia."

"No. No issues," Recker said.

"Well then, why are you ignoring her calls?"

"I'll get to them."

"Why don't you talk to her? You know, I've noticed that you answer your phone right away for everybody except for her," Jones said, trying to catch his attention.

It seemed to have done the trick. Recker finally looked up. "Have you now?"

"I have."

"Well if it's bothering you, then next time you can answer it," Recker said.

"Did something happen at dinner the other night?"

"Nope. Nothing happened. Not a thing," Recker said, now starting to sound angry.

With the tone of his voice obvious, Jones now wanted to get to the bottom of it. "From the sound of your voice I can see there's a problem."

"You really wanna know what the problem is?"

"That's why I asked," Jones calmly responded.

"The problem is that you were right all along."

"Gratifying to know, but which part are you referring to?"

"The getting too close part. That's the problem."

"You feel you're falling for her?"

"No. But I realized that she shouldn't be around me. I'm not good for her and I can only bring her heartache," Recker said out of frustration.

"What exactly happened at dinner?"

"Nothing. Nothing happened. That's the problem," Recker said, getting more agitated as he vented. "We were there five minutes when Vincent called. She got dressed up, looked pretty, trying to have a nice evening out, and I ruined it for her. I couldn't even give her more than five minutes of my time. I'm trying to keep my distance so she doesn't think there's a chance of something happening between us."

"And you think ignoring her calls will help with that?"

"Has to. She can't get hung up on me. She deserves better. Someone that'll pay attention to her, spend time with her, appreciate all that she has to offer. That's obviously not me."

"You seem pretty strongly opinionated about this," Jones said.

"I am. If you'd have seen the disappointment in her face, you would be too."

"I'm sure she understood. She knows what you do."

"I'm sure she did understand. That's the point. I don't want her to understand. I want her to move on from me," Recker said, not letting up in his angst.

Jones wasn't used to Recker being so frank about his feelings and it took a moment for him to frame his next question. "You said she got dressed up and looked pretty."

"Yeah, so?"

"Just saying."

"Listen, just because I can see she's pretty doesn't mean something can happen. You said it from the start that you worried about her falling for me and to keep her at a distance. You were right," Recker said, although the tortured look on his face suggested that he thought otherwise.

"It's not often you tell me I'm right so often in such a short amount of time. If it wasn't at Mia's expense I would actually feel good about it."

Recker's text ringer went off one more time, once again from Mia. Jones looked at him, hoping he'd answer it this time. Though he wasn't advocating for a relationship between the two of them, he felt Recker was being a bit too hard on himself. He suspected that although Recker said he wanted to keep Mia at a distance to keep her from falling for him even more, part of him thought Recker was doing it for himself too. He thought maybe Recker seeing her dressed up in a social setting with him stirred a few emotions inside him that he didn't want awoken.

"What if it's an emergency?" Jones said, hoping to spur him into answering. "What if she's stuck on the side of the road somewhere near a dark alley in a rough part of town?"

Recker looked at him strangely. "It's the middle of the day."

"Well, the other parts could be true."

Recker sighed, knowing he had to answer. The professor was right. If she was stuck somewhere, and it was an emergency, he'd never forgive himself if something happened to her that he could've prevented. He reached for his phone and looked at the message, then listened to the voicemail that Mia left. By Recker's facial expression, Jones could tell something wasn't normal and started worrying that it really was an emergency.

"Is she all right?" Jones said.

"Yeah. She's fine. She just wanted to know if I could come see her at work."

"Oh, dear."

"No, not about that," Recker said. "She said a friend of hers is in trouble and wanted to know if I could help."

"So what are you gonna do?"

"Go find out what the problem is. That's what you pay me for, right? Help people."

"Well after you just said..."

"Forget what I just said. If Mia needs help, I'm helping."

"Oh dear," Jones said, fearful that Recker couldn't even see what was happening to himself.

He'd just spent the last few minutes venting about wanting to keep his distance from her and the minute she asked for help, he was ready to fly off to save the day. Maybe Recker was trying to deny it, but it sure seemed to Jones like, at the very least, a serious flirtation. Recker grabbed his guns and loaded up and immediately drove down to the hospital. He went up to the fifth floor and the pediatric unit, though he couldn't get in with the doors locked. He stood there at the doors, almost expecting them to just open as if by magic, not even seeing the receptionist to the left of him.

"Father or visitor?" the receptionist said.

Recker's concentration was broken, and he looked to his left, though he wasn't sure what he heard. "What?"

"Are you a father?"

"Uh... no," Recker said hurriedly to the scary proposition, looking like a deer caught in headlights.

"Then who are you here to see?" the receptionist said slowly.

"Umm, Mia. Mia Hendricks. She's a nurse. I'm a friend. She asked me to come down."

"Oh, Mia. Just one moment."

The receptionist called the nurse station inside the locked doors for Mia, who immediately came out. As soon as the doors opened, and she saw Recker, she gave him a huge smile, relieved to see him and thankful that he came. It was times like these that reminded her how nice it was to have him in her life, even if it wasn't as close as she would have liked.

"What's the matter?" Recker said.

"Let's step inside," Mia said, bringing him beyond the doors to give them a little more privacy. Once the doors closed, she told him about her problem.

"Are you in trouble again?"

"No, thankfully. It's my friend, Susan. Susan Hanley. I've known her for ten years, since college. She's one of my best friends."

"OK, what's wrong with her?"

"She's missing."

"Missing? For how long?" Recker said.

"About a week."

"Why didn't you say anything until now?"

"I just found out this morning. Her mom called me here at work and asked if I'd seen or talked to her," Mia said. "She said Susie hasn't showed up to work for three days."

"When was the last time you spoke to her?"

"About a week ago. We met for lunch."

"When you met did she sound worried about anything? Any concerns?"

"No, nothing. We just talked about the usual stuff. Work, life, relationships, you know, that sort of thing. She seemed pretty normal."

"Anybody in her life that could possibly be a danger? Boyfriend, abusive ex, friend, someone she made enemies with? Anyone?"

Mia shook her head, struggling to come up with anything. "No, not that I know of. Right now she's single."

"Have the police been notified?" Recker said.

"Susie's mom said they were called three days ago. They haven't turned up anything."

"Is she close to her parents?"

"Her dad died a few years ago, but she's very close to her mom. They talk at least every other day. That's how she knew something was wrong. They haven't talked in a week either and she said she went to Susie's apartment, but nobody was there."

Recker didn't respond and just looked away at the wall, trying to think.

"Can you please find her? I know something terrible has happened to her. I can feel it," Mia said. "I know you have your own stuff to work on but I'm just really worried about her."

Recker grinned at her and put his hand on her arm to comfort her. "It's fine. I'm glad you came to me. Of course I'll help."

Mia sighed with relief and hugged him, "Thank you."

"I'll find her," Recker replied. "What does she do?"

"She's a pediatric otolaryngologist."

"She's an ear doctor?"

"Ear, nose, and throat," Mia confirmed. "For kids."

"OK. I'll need everything you know about her. Names, addresses, work, everything you know about her. Don't leave out anything, even if you think it's small or unimportant."

"Are you going to her apartment? If so, then I wanna come with you."

"That's not a good idea," Recker said.

"She's my friend. I'll be done work in an hour."

"Mia..."

"Mike, please. I'm not gonna interfere or get in your way. I just wanna go to her apartment with you. Maybe if there's something there, I can help."

Recker looked at her, displeased, knowing it was never a good idea to let people who were personally involved get in on a case. It usually didn't turn out well. But reluctantly, he relented.

"Fine. But that's it. You're not tagging along with me anywhere else," Recker said.

"I promise. I won't bug for anything else."

"OK. Let me know when you get home and I'll pick you up and

we'll head over there together. In the meantime, I'll start working on other things."

"What are the statistics on missing persons? Are they usually found?" Mia said, fearful of what happened to her friend.

"Statistics are useless. They're about the past. All we need to worry about is the present."

"You don't think she's de—"

Recker cut her off before she got herself too worked up over what might have been possible. "Let's just worry about finding her first. Everything else will take care of itself."

Mia took out a notepad and started jotting down a few things for Recker to get started with. As Recker left with the information, Mia watched him leave as another nurse strolled by.

"Was that the new guy you've been swooning over?" the nurse said.

"Yeah, that was him."

"Still haven't corralled him yet?"

"No. He doesn't get roped in easily," Mia said with a sigh.

"What'd you say he does?"

"He's uh... kind of hard to explain. He's kind of a private security investigator."

On the way out of the hospital, Recker called Jones to let him know they had a new assignment and to give him the specifics of the case.

"Taking on cases without me now, are you?" Jones said.

"Well since you went dry, I had to get my own."

"I take it this is a result of Mia's conversation?"

"Yeah. She's pretty worried about this woman," Recker said.

"Send me her information and I should have something for you to work with by the time you get back here."

"Will do."

Recker did as was requested and texted Jones the information

Mia gave him. By the time Recker got back to the office twenty-five minutes later, the professor already had a few leads on their subject.

"Susan Hanley, thirty years old, works at a private practice," Jones read off the screen.

"Any medical issues?" Recker said.

"She's not taking any prescriptions that I can find. At least not of the legal variety."

"So we can probably focus on foul play then. Any men in her life?"

"Well, she was married for three years, but they got divorced over a year ago. They have no children and no signs of police involvement."

"Mia said she didn't seem worried about anything."

"That would seem to imply that whatever happened to her was a sudden act," Jones said, continuing to dig up information as they spoke.

"Could be work related," Recker said, thinking aloud and on his feet.

"What kind of problem could she have, being a pediatric ear, nose, and throat doctor?"

"Even bad people have kids, David."

"True enough."

"How about trying to locate a cell phone?"

"Already tried. Wherever her phone is now, it isn't active," Jones said.

"The police should already have a file on her case. Can you tap into their investigation?" Recker said.

"Yeah. I'm also going to try to find an appointment calendar for her and cross reference some of her patients to see if I can find an outlier. Hopefully she's an adopter of online appointment books and doesn't still just use the paper."

"I'll pick up Mia and head to her apartment in a few minutes to see if there's anything of note in there."

Jones suddenly stopped typing, sure his ears were deceiving him. He turned to look at Recker. "I'm sorry, did you just say you were picking up Mia?"

Recker feigned ignorance for a minute, realizing he shouldn't have said it. "Did I?"

"I'm quite certain that you did."

"Slip of the tongue," Recker said.

"Please tell me you're not really letting Mia go with you to the Hanley woman's apartment?"

"She really wanted to go and thought she might be useful."

"And you didn't see the danger in that?" Jones said.

"I'm not taking her anywhere other than that. That's it. I thought she might pick up on something that's out of place or odd. She would obviously know better than I would if something wasn't where it should be or something was missing," Recker said.

"Hmm. Perhaps you're right about that. And time is of the essence. Most missing person cases involve family members, parents, spouses, siblings, and are resolved within a shorter period of time."

"You don't think her mother would be involved, do you?" Recker said.

"I'll check into her more closely while you're gone."

Recker left the office and headed to Mia's place. She was able to leave work just a few minutes after Recker left the hospital, so she rushed home to be dressed and ready for when he got there. He got there a little early and figured she wouldn't even be home from work yet. Recker expected he might have to wait a little while and was surprised to see Mia standing in front. He pulled up to the curb, and she quickly got in.

"Waiting long?" Recker said.

"Nope. Just a few minutes."

"Didn't think you'd even be here yet."

"Got done early," Mia said.

It was a twenty-minute drive to Hanley's apartment. Recker and Mia talked about her the entire way there as he wanted to get as much information about her as he could. He liked knowing as much as he could about someone, things that really made them tick, stuff that couldn't always be found by the keystrokes of a computer.

"You don't think Susan could've just taken off for a week, do you? Just taken a vacation or something?" Recker said.

"No. No way. She wouldn't do that. Not Susie. She was committed to her job. When we met last week, she told me she had a jam-packed schedule for the next month. She's not the type of person to just blow off her commitments. She loved the kids she worked with. She'd never just abandon them like that."

"Did she ever take any kind of drugs that you know of? Even dabble a little bit?"

"No, not that I know of. I never saw any signs of that. Even when we were in college, we were roommates, and she never did anything. Never even smoked a cigarette," Mia answered. "She'd have a drink every now and then but that's about it."

"So she didn't have a Stephen Eldridge in her life?"

Mia chuckled at the suggestion but quickly blew it off. "No, she always got the nice guys. I'm the one that got stuck with the jerks."

"What about her marriage?" Recker said.

"Yeah, Dominic. He always seemed like a decent guy. I always got along with him."

"What ended things? Did it get ugly?"

"Umm, not that I know of. From what Susie told me, there were no big blow ups or fights or anything that escalated. They just kind of grew apart. She never talked badly of him, even after it ended. I think they just wanted different things," Mia explained.

"Such as what?"

"Well, she didn't want kids for one. I think that was one of their biggest issues."

"He did?"

"Yeah. Surprising, huh? Usually it's the woman that wants the family and kids. But it was reversed in their case. He was an insurance broker and worked in an office all day, and when he got home, he wanted a big family there. Susie, though, she worked with kids all day. She wanted a quiet house with just the two of them when she got home. She didn't really want a family yet."

"I guess that's a big divide," Recker said.

"Yeah. She told him that maybe in time she'd change her mind, but I think he didn't want to wait for ten years and then find out that she still didn't want kids. So I think they just sort of agreed to part ways. Everything seemed amicable and all. I think they still talked from time to time."

"Any boyfriends since then?"

"No, not really," Mia answered. "She was content just immersing herself in her work. I mean, she usually worked ten or twelve hours a day. Plus, she said that she didn't want to get involved with someone again and go through the family thing again. I think part of her felt bad for hurting Dom with not wanting kids. She didn't want to get into another relationship and have it fall apart the same way if they wanted kids too."

"She ever have any one-night stands?"

"Not that I know of. If she did, she never told me. She never seemed that interested in having a social life again, to be honest. Sometimes I had to drag her out just for lunch. Kind of like you." Mia gave Recker a sly glance to see if her comment got a reaction. It didn't.

Recker continued peppering his passenger with questions, ranging from Hanley's mother, to her friends, coworkers, casual acquaintances, patients, anyone at all who might have known her. All in the hopes of finding someone who might've had a disagreement or problem with her. The problem was there was no such person. At least none that Mia could think of. To her knowledge, everyone loved Susan. If that was true, and Recker could rule out foul play from someone she knew, it'd make it much tougher to find her. It also increased the chances of her having a bad encounter with a completely random person she didn't know. It also raised the possibility that Hanley just ditched her life behind to start anew somewhere else, even though Mia said that was something her friend would never do. But Recker knew that oftentimes, people kept secrets. And sometimes those secrets were dark. Dark enough that the people closest to them would be completely unaware of that secret life.

25

Hanley lived on the sixth floor of an apartment building in the northeast part of the city. It was a modest apartment, nothing that the wealthy would consider living in, but not a dump either. It was a well-maintained building in a pretty safe neighborhood with most of the amenities included in the rent. Once they reached the apartment, Mia worried about how they were going to get in the door.

"I don't have a spare key or anything," Mia said.

"It's all right. I don't need one," Recker said, dropping to a knee to start picking the lock.

Just as he got started, someone started walking down the hallway on the way to their own apartment. The elderly man just stopped, concerned that the pair was trying to break into the apartment.

"Uh, Mike." Mia alerted him by tapping him on the shoulder.

Recker looked over at the man and stood up, approaching the stranger, who wasn't moving. Recker reached into his pocket and pulled out a police badge, showing it to the man.

"Mike Stevens, detective from the eighth district," Recker said.

"Oh, OK," the man said, sounding relieved. "I was getting worried you were robbers or something."

Recker smiled. "No, of course not. We're investigating the disappearance of Susan Hanley and we were about to give the room another shakedown."

"Didn't give you a key or nothing?"

"Some knucklehead couldn't remember what drawer they put it in. I don't have a high patience level so I just figured I'd make my own way in. I'm a go-getter. Not much for waiting."

"That's why you get the big collars probably," the man said, eyes widening slightly.

"You're a wise man," Recker said. "Did you know Ms. Hanley?"

"I only met her a few times in passing here in the hallway," the man said. "But she seemed like a nice woman."

"Ever see anyone with her?"

"Nah. Maybe that was her problem."

"Problem? What do you mean?" Recker said.

"I don't know how to explain it... a sense of sadness or something. Like there was trouble hanging over her or something. I guess that's a weird thing to notice when you only talk to someone a minute here or a minute there but it always seemed like she was faking a smile or sighing or something."

"Makes perfect sense. When was the last time you saw her?" Recker said.

"Oh... must have been last Friday," the man said, thinking for a minute. "Yeah. Friday, it was. It was about seven, eight o'clock at night."

"Are you sure?"

"Positive. I was just getting home after going to the grocery store. It was outside, just in front of the entrance doors. I was bringing in some bags and she was walking out."

"She say anything to you?"

"Nope. Just hello as she walked past."

"How was she dressed?" Recker said.

"In a dress, heels, looked good. Like maybe she was going somewhere fancy or something."

"Like dinner maybe?"

"Could have been. Not sure."

Recker put his hand on the man's shoulder. "You've been a big help. Did you share this with any of the other detectives that were here?"

"No."

"Why not?"

"Nobody came knocking to ask. I live all the way down the hall. Guess they only talked to the neighbors," the man said. "I was thinking about maybe calling down to the district to tell all this but I wasn't sure. Guess since now you know, guess I don't have to."

"No, you did good. I'll take it from here."

"That your partner there?" the man said, pointing at Mia.

"No, friend of Hanley's. Was hoping she could help identify something in the apartment that'd give us a break," Recker said.

"Good thinking, son. Knew she couldn't be a cop, anyway. Too pretty for that."

Recker smiled as the man kept walking down the hall, passing Mia on the way. With the additional information in mind, he went back to picking the lock.

"You always carry a fake police badge on you?" Mia said.

"Sometimes. Never know when it might come in handy."

"And what if he knew it wasn't real?"

"If it's a good fake, only one person in a thousand will be able to tell the difference," Recker said. "Most people never even see one, anyway."

"What'd he say that made you smile, anyway? Couldn't quite make it out."

"Wanted to know if you were my partner."

"What's so funny about that?"

"Nothing. He said you were too pretty to be a cop," Recker said, still smiling.

A few seconds later, and Recker had successfully picked the lock, opening the door. The two of them entered quickly, closing the door behind them.

"We'll go room to room," Recker said. "Let me know if something seems out of place or anything seems missing."

"OK."

"You know what that business of her leaving Friday night was all about?"

"No idea," Mia said.

They started searching the living room, going through the couches, tables, drawers, anything that could've housed any information. Once they exhausted the living room without finding anything, they branched out into the kitchen, then the bedroom and the bathroom. They went through each room of the apartment several times to make sure they didn't miss anything. They spent an hour searching for some kind of clue that would lead to where Hanley was. It was an hour that turned up nothing. And Mia didn't notice anything that was missing or out of place. Everything seemed as it normally was. Without any leads, Recker turned to Jones, hoping he had something for him.

"I sure hope you've turned up something cause we're striking out here," Recker said.

"I'm working on a few things at the moment," Jones said over the sound of fingers on a keyboard.

"Promising?"

"Could be. Too soon to tell yet. I think I can say that it's safe to rule out her mother."

"Why's that?"

"I've listened to the voicemails that she left her daughter. If she's involved in her disappearance then she's an excellent actress. Each one becomes more and more alarming in the tone of her voice, worried that something was wrong."

"I wouldn't read too much into that. Could just be covering her tracks," Recker said.

"No, I don't think so. When did you say she was last seen?"

"Guy here says he saw her walking out of the building Friday night around seven or eight."

"He very well might've been one of the last people to see her al—" Jones said, catching himself before presuming that she was dead.

"What makes you say that?"

"Well, her phone records for one. It appears that her mother called her at 6:05. It seems as if the call was answered. Then her mother called again at 11:45 but there was no answer. It went to voicemail. And she's been calling her phone multiple times a day ever since," Jones revealed.

"What else?"

"Well I'm still going through the phone records now. I've also found her online appointment book and I'm perusing that as well. If you're done there, I could use some help in going over these. The sooner we figure it out the better chance of us finding her still in good health."

"I'm gonna drop Mia off and then I'll be there."

"Wait, where are you going?" Mia said as soon as he hung up.

"Gotta go back to the office and help the professor sort through some things."

"About Susie?"

Recker gave a slight nod. "This is all we're working on right now."

"Can I come with you?"

"No. I told you just here, and that was it."

"But it's Susie."

"Mia, you can't tag along everywhere. Besides, David's not gonna want you knowing where our office is," Recker said.

"I don't care about your office. I just—" Mia said before being interrupted.

"I know she's your friend and you're worried, but you gotta take a step back and let me handle it, OK?"

"Will you let me know if you find something?" she said, nodding sadly.

"Well… I'll keep you up to date," Recker said.

"What's that mean?"

"I'm not gonna tell you every time I turn up something. Everything I check out might not lead to anything. But if there's something concrete that tells us something, then I will definitely let you know."

"Immediately?" Mia said.

"Yeah."

Mia reached in and hugged him again. "Thank you," she said.

Once she stepped back, Recker gave her a smile. "Sure."

After leaving the apartment, Recker drove Mia back to her place and then got over to the office as quickly as possible. He got there about an hour after talking to Jones on the phone. The professor looked like he was knee deep in work as he was feverishly typing away, trying to look at several different screens simultaneously. Jones was so heavily concentrating on his work that he didn't even hear Recker come through the door. Jones finally heard footsteps coming toward him which slightly startled him and broke his concentration.

"How you making out?" Recker said.

Jones took a deep breath and leaned back in his chair, wiping his eyes as he took a well-needed break from the computer. "These are the cases I hate the most. The ones that are missing."

"Feel like you can't take a break?"

Jones looked at him and nodded, knowing he understood. "There's that race against time mentality in cases like these. Unless she ran away of her own accord then every minute that passes could be one that entails her final breath."

"Too soon to be thinking like that," Recker said, trying to remain positive.

"Is that your true thoughts or is that mostly because she's Mia's friend and you'd hate to see how it would affect her if it turns out to be so?" Jones said.

"A little bit of both I guess. What have you turned up so far?"

"Going through her phone records is an exhaustive process."

"Heavy usage?"

"Heavy isn't the word for it, Michael. Exhausting is more à propos. She used her phone for everything. Personal, business, and anything in between. She even made and took business calls at night while she was at home," Jones responded. "It seems she was never truly off. Even after a twelve-hour day, she'd go home and follow up with patients."

"Sounds dedicated," Recker said.

"Indeed. I'm trying to match phone numbers listed with their names to see if any have criminal records. I've broken it down by the numbers she called most frequently and working my way down. No luck in that regard so far."

"What about the appointment book?"

"In the same boat. Since she mostly dealt with patients who were children, I'm running background checks on all the parents to see if we get a hit on any criminal activity involving any of them," Jones said.

"Negative so far?"

"So far."

"Anything in her calendar about a late-night meeting on Friday?" Recker said.

"No, it was clear. Her last appointment last Friday was at 4:30."

"So even if we assume that lasted half an hour, and we assume she didn't stop on the way home, that she was probably home by 5:30 or so. Took her mother's call at six. Got dressed, left around seven or so. Hasn't been seen or heard from since."

"Sounds like a logical chain of events," Jones said.

"She didn't happen to get a call between when she got home and seven or so, did she?" Recker said, hoping to catch a break.

"Oh yes. She got several calls. Four to be exact. One was her mother."

"And the other three?"

"The other three were all parents of children she'd seen earlier that week. Those conversations lasted a little over five minutes each."

"So, I think it's safe to say that whatever she was doing or wherever she was going, was personal. It's a Friday night, her calendar's clear, she looks good, dressed well, she's probably going to meet someone."

"But who?" Jones said.

"That's the question."

"Maybe she got dressed up in the hopes of meeting someone. Maybe there was no one specific. Like a club or a bar or something."

"I dunno. Mia said those things weren't really her kind of scene."

"Loneliness makes people do things they normally wouldn't. Or go places they usually don't."

"You think she was lonely?"

"Impossible to say right now. It's certainly feasible. Her neighbor thinks she looks sad sometimes, she'd been divorced for a year, nobody to go home to, working twelve hours a day, plus when she gets home. It's possible, wouldn't you say?"

"Mia never got any sense that she was."

"Hanley wouldn't be the first to try and hide it by immersing herself in work. She's only human."

"Yeah, maybe," Recker said, with a knowing sigh. "We need to locate her car."

"That would be very helpful," Jones said, moving his chair around to another computer. "On this one, I have it combing through all the camera footage taken off the cameras."

"I-95 and the turnpike?"

"As well as local roads where available."

"And so far, we're batting zero on all fronts," Recker said.

"Well if you want to talk in baseball terms then there's always the bloop single, where you don't hit the ball well and should be out, but somehow it drops in a hole and you get on base."

"Let's just hope we don't get picked off first if we get on base."

Jones had enough of a break and got back to work, Recker joining him in cross-referencing names and phone numbers, along with criminal record checks. They spent the next half hour combing through the information, coming up with nothing but blanks. They were then interrupted by the beeping sound of one of the computers.

"What's that?" Recker said.

Jones slid over to the beeping computer to check. "It's done checking turnpike photos of Hanley's car. No sign of it. It'll now switch over to I-95 cameras."

Jones watched the system go through the first few photos, then went back to the phone records he was checking. After a couple minutes, Recker started moving around like he had found something.

"Hey, here's a guy. Johnathan Chychrun," Recker stated, pulling up some more information about him.

Jones swiveled his chair closer to Recker to also look at the screen, reading aloud. "One count of misdemeanor assault, one count of criminal trespass, and one count of fleeing police. All happened over ten years ago though."

"It's a place to start."

"Ten years without any criminal offenses would seem to indicate that perhaps Mr. Chychrun has turned over a new leaf."

"Could mean he just hasn't been caught," Recker said.

Jones wasn't so sure. He pulled up some of Chychrun's personal information while Recker looked deeper into the phone records to see how many times they'd conversed.

"He's married with a seven-year-old daughter," Jones stated. "It would seem that married life settled him down some."

"They talked for four minutes last Tuesday at 7:08," Recker said.

"I don't think he's the guy. If there is a guy."

"Let's keep him on the list of possibles, anyway."

"Short list so far," Jones replied.

Recker tried to dig a little deeper into Chychrun's background, not as sure as Jones that he was completely innocent. While he did think it was unlikely, he wasn't ready to close the door on it yet. Jones thought that since he was married with a child that he had given up any criminal tendencies that he once had, but Recker was not as trusting.

"He's also not going to be meeting Hanley when he's already married," Jones said.

Recker just gave him a look. "Affairs happen all the time, David."

"At seven or eight o'clock at night?"

"Didn't realize there was only a certain time for that. Maybe the wife took the kid out for an hour or so and he had to move quickly."

"No, I'm not buying it yet. Not without some evidence."

"Maybe I should talk to him," Recker said.

"How would you go about that?"

"I have a badge."

Jones rolled his eyes and mumbled, not sure that was such a good idea.

"Right now, we have no other leads. It's a place to start," Recker said.

"Agreed."

As Recker called Chychrun, under his police detective disguise, Jones kept plugging away at the computer. As Jones was doing so, he kept one ear listening to his partner's conversation to get a sense of how it was going. By the sound of it, it wasn't going so good. After five minutes, Recker came back to the desk and sighed, tossing his phone down on it.

"I take it he's not what we're looking for?" Jones said.

"I don't think so."

"Why not?"

"He said he never saw her outside of her office. He also said that on Friday night at eight o'clock, he bought a movie online for his daughter that they started watching immediately," Recker said.

"And you believe him?"

"Yeah. Yeah, I do. It's easy enough to check, right? He said he bought it through Comcast."

"Should be easy enough," Jones said.

As they continued talking about Chychrun, another alert sounded on the computer. Jones swirled his way over to it again.

"Can't be done already, can it?" Recker said.

"No, it's not. It found something."

Recker immediately rushed over to see what it was. Jones freeze framed the picture then blew it up larger so they could see it better. He zoomed in on the license plate, getting a clear picture of the letters and numbers. He then looked down at a piece of paper on the desk and compared the two.

"It's a match," Jones said. "That's her car."

"Where's that location?" Recker said.

"Getting off I-95 on exit ramp twelve. That's the airport."

"She was getting on a plane to go somewhere or she was meeting someone. What time was that?"

"10:56."

"Everything matches up so far. Now we just have to figure out where she was going from there."

"That's going to be a tall task," Jones stated. "Especially since I'm sure the police have already gotten this far. I'm sure they've already found this picture as well."

"The police have a lot on their plate. They're juggling a lot of cases at one time. We're not. Plus, we got something they don't."

"Which is?" Jones said, struggling to figure out what that could have been.

"We got Tyrell," Recker answered.

"I fail to see how that gives us an advantage."

"He knows people all over this city. If that car's not spotted by a camera anywhere else, it's parked out of sight somewhere. We're gonna need a lot of eyes open. A lot of eyes," Recker explained.

Jones raised his eyebrows and shrugged, not sure if Recker's plan would work, but figured it was worth the effort. Recker immediately called Tyrell to see if he could help him out.

"Tyrell, I need a favor," Recker told him.

"Whatcha need?"

"A friend of a friend is missing. I've got a picture of it getting off I-95 by the airport. Think you know anybody who could see if the car is still parked there?"

"Yeah, I know some people. If the money's right," Gibson said.

"If they find this car, the money will be right."

"What's the car?"

"It's a 2015 gray Honda Civic," Recker said. "I'll send you a picture."

"What time frame you want?"

"Like now."

"I'll get some people on it."

"Thanks. I guess I'll owe you another one."

"Nah. It's cool."

"If that car's not still at the airport, have them canvass nearby areas. I'm gonna be leaving here in a few minutes to check myself too," Recker said.

"I'll give everyone the heads up. Should be able to get five or six guys on it," Gibson said.

"Thanks."

Once Recker hung up, Jones couldn't help but think that the plan was a waste of time. Not because he didn't think Gibson could help, but because he assumed the police had already done it.

"I'm sure the police have already combed over the airport for her car," Jones said.

"You're assuming they've already found that picture."

"Yes, I guess I am."

"What if they haven't?" Recker said.

"I guess you're right."

"Besides, even if they did, and it's not there, maybe it's close by. Maybe in a surrounding area that they didn't check."

"That's a lot of maybe's," Jones told him.

"No, I got one more. Maybe it's worth a shot."

"A long shot."

"A shot nonetheless."

"Even if we do find the car, that's not necessarily going to tell us where Ms. Hanley is," Jones said. "I'll check flight records to see if she took an unexpected trip."

"Also, might be a good idea to check any cameras at the airport to see if she actually went inside. I'm gonna head down there to check things out for myself," Recker said.

"What good will that do? Isn't that what you called Tyrell for?"

"Never hurts to have more eyes out there. Besides, computer work is more your thing. Out in the field is mine. Call me if you come up with something."

Recker left, heading for the airport to search for Hanley's car. Jones continued the multifaceted computer work that he was doing in the hopes of finding the needle in the haystack that they were looking for. He hacked his way into the airport security cameras to look for Hanley, starting the search after eleven, knowing that her car wasn't seen until that point. Once Recker got to the Philadelphia International Airport thirty minutes later, he checked in with Jones to see if he turned up anything yet.

"How you making out, David?"

"So far, nothing else has turned up on any cameras. The rest of the I-95 scan is done," Jones answered.

"The car didn't get back on?"

"Correct. It also appears that there's no hits on any local roadway cams either."

"What about the airport?" Recker said.

"So far that's coming up nil as well."

Recker didn't respond for a minute, thinking of some alternatives that might've happened to Hanley. Jones kept typing away, waiting for a response.

"What are you thinking, Michael?" Jones said.

"Nothing good."

By the tone of his voice, Jones had been around Recker long enough to get a hint of what was on his mind. Though Recker didn't want to say it, it was clear enough to the professor what he meant.

"You don't think she's alive, do you?"

"Let's just say I have my doubts," Recker said.

"Not that I necessarily disagree, but why do you think so?"

"She leaves her apartment Friday night looking like she's going on a date, her car looks like it's headed to the airport, she didn't leave with luggage, so unless she's got some elaborate plan in mind to disappear, it's unlikely she was going anywhere."

"Could be she just picked someone up."

"But we probably would've gotten a hit on the car getting back on I-95. It doesn't really make any sense that she'd be meeting someone there," Recker said. "If I had to take a guess, I'd say she wasn't even the one driving when that picture was taken."

"If that's the case, and somebody else was driving..." Jones said, his voice faltering, stopping short of what he intended to say.

"Then she's probably dead," Recker said, completing the words that Jones couldn't manage.

"Why would someone want her dead? There's nothing in her background that would indicate any problems or red flags that I can see."

"You know as well as I do that doesn't mean much. Bad things happen to good people all the time. Might've been a spur-of-the-moment thing."

"If she is deceased," Jones said. "Let's not assume the worst just yet."

"David, she hasn't been heard from in a week. If she didn't leave this city, it's more than likely that she's no longer amongst the living."

"Let's just keep hoping for the best. In that vein, I also tapped into the police department records to get a look at the file they have for her."

"And?"

"Looks like we were both right."

"How so?"

"They did find the picture that we did and they did do a check of the airport," Jones said. "But that's as far as they've gone with it up until now. They've got at least ten other missing person cases they're working on at the same time."

"Maybe we should expand our search then," Recker replied. "Did they do any of the surrounding area?"

"It doesn't appear so."

Recker continued his conversation with Jones for a few more minutes before checking some of the airport parking garages. Gibson sent him a message saying that his guys were already on some of the other garages and terminals, the only one left available was Parking Garage D. Recker headed over for it, a lot of thoughts and scenarios running through his mind. If they did find the car, and she wasn't the one driving it, that meant she could've been anywhere in the city. And she most definitely would've been dead. Part of him hoped that Jones found her on one of the airport cameras hopping a flight somewhere. At least that would've proved she was alive and just left town, whether for a short trip or permanently. It would've been easier and less painful to explain to Mia as well. But if that wasn't the case, he knew Mia would have a hard time with it. After another hour of scouring the airport parking garages and terminals, the team had concluded that the car wasn't parked there. Recker called Gibson for an update on their next move.

"Let's search a few nearby places," Recker said. "Maybe the car was dumped there or something."

"Yeah, all right. There's some car rental places and the other side of I-95 got some hotels and stuff," Gibson said.

"All right, send your guys to the car rental spots. Me and you will take the hotels."

Gibson informed his guys to do what Recker had requested while they took the hotels in the area, each taking a different one. As they did that, Jones was coming up empty on everything he had checked. He called Recker one more time to keep him up on his progress, or lack thereof.

"Michael, I'm fairly certain she never entered the airport," Jones said.

"Didn't find any pictures I assume?"

"Not a one. The scan of the airport is complete and the car never got back on I-95, so I'm at a loss as to where its location is."

"It's gotta be here somewhere. If it's not at the airport, and it didn't get back on I-95, then it got dumped nearby," Recker said.

After another hour of searching, Gibson's teams at the car rental business reported back that they still hadn't found anything. Tyrell told them to check a few more places in the area while he continued with the hotels in the vicinity of the airport. Recker had personally checked four hotels, each one coming back as empty as the one before. He was beginning to get a little frustrated at their lack of progress. He knew the car had to be around somewhere. He just knew it. Gibson was also on his fourth hotel, the previous three also coming up with nothing.

After Gibson got to the final hotel on his list, he cruised around the parking lot, keeping a sharp eye out. He saved the biggest hotel for last, knowing he could knock the other ones out a little faster. He gave the side lot of the hotel a good once over, making sure he accounted for every car in there before moving around to the back of the lot. He turned the corner and went up and down the rows, not really having any expectations of finding the car. He assumed since they hadn't found it yet that it was not even close. But he didn't have as much invested as Recker did. Still, he was willing to keep going as long as Recker asked him to. After he cleared the first several rows, he drove along the back row, the last one that was behind the hotel. And then he saw it. A newer looking gray Honda Civic, sitting in the middle of the row, parked between two other cars. Gibson then parked his car in an open spot then walked behind the Honda, reading the license plate, and comparing it against the numbers that Recker had given him. It was a match. He immediately called Recker with the news.

"What's up?" Recker said.

"I found it."

"What?" he said, almost not believing it.

"Found it. I'm at the Grand Marx hotel, around the back."

"Be there in five," Recker told him, then calling Jones instantly. "David, Tyrell spotted the car. I'm on my way there now."

"OK. Let me know what you find when you get there so I can start running the information in the computer," Jones said.

Even though he was only five minutes away, Recker booted his car in gear and drove fast enough to get there in just over three minutes. When he pulled around the back of the hotel, he spotted Gibson still standing by the front of the car. Recker parked his truck and then met Gibson by the Honda, the two men shaking hands.

"I told the rest of the boys that we found it and to go home," Gibson said. "They still gonna expect a little something though, even though they didn't find it."

"I'll make good on it," Recker said, tapping him on the arm.

"Yeah, I know, I ain't worried about it."

The car was locked, not that it impeded Recker much. He got out one of his many gadgets and had the car unlocked in about thirty seconds.

"That must come in handy," Gibson said, admiring Recker's handiwork.

"Always have to be prepared," Recker said with a smile.

Once inside, Recker inspected both the front and back seats, as well as the glove compartment, looking for any kind of clue that would lead to Hanley's location. Her car, though, was spotless. There was no trash, no papers in the cracks of the seat cushion, nothing that would indicate any type of struggle, or even that someone else other than her was in it. Recker sighed, thinking all along that once they found the car, that would lead them closer to finding Mia's friend. But now that they had, they weren't any closer at all.

"Maybe something's in the trunk," Gibson said.

Recker agreed and popped the trunk open. Both men walked around to the back and were instantly taken aback by what they saw. They didn't need to look for any more clues now. Susan Hanley was dead. Her hands and feet were tied together, and her mouth was gagged. Recker also noticed some blood on her, though he wasn't exactly sure where it was coming from at first glance unless he moved her body around. He didn't really want to do that though, and possibly destroy, or contaminate any evidence.

"Damn," Gibson said. "That's a damn shame."

"David, you can stop what you're working on," Recker said, calling his partner.

"Why?" Jones said, fearful of the answer.

"We found Susan Hanley. She was stuffed in the trunk. She's dead."

"Our worst fears were realized. I'll call in an anonymous tip to the police department so they can close the case out."

"No, I'll figure out who did this," Recker objected.

Jones did not like that response, however. "Michael, that's not the business we're in."

"I'm in the business of helping people."

"And there's nothing more we can do for her. I'm sorry to say it, but she's gone. There's nothing we can do to change that. It's a police matter now, let them take care of it."

"I can do it better."

"Perhaps. But while you're chasing that down, three more people might get seriously hurt that you can prevent," Jones said. "As far as I'm concerned, this case is over. Don't touch anything, don't look for anyone, just let it be."

"I'm not real good at just letting things be," Recker said.

"I'm well aware. But please just listen to me on this. We're not in the revenge game."

Recker sighed, thinking for a minute, not really wanting to close the case, even if Jones was correct. But he knew that working to solve who killed her would take time, probably more time than he had to invest. It was just hard for him to let go of something like this, something that was more personal, even if it was only because of Mia's involvement in it. Jones kept telling him to not pursue it further, and after several more minutes of convincing, Recker finally agreed.

"Fine, but I want to continue monitoring it," Recker said. "If the police haven't arrested someone in the next month or two, I'm getting back in."

"Deal. Thank you. Do you want me to tell Mia?"

"No. I'll do that."

"OK. Just so you know though, we might have a new case coming. Something just popped up on my screen a few minutes ago," Jones said.

"OK. It's gonna have to wait until tomorrow though."

"Why?"

"I'm gonna need tonight off."

"That can be arranged," Jones replied, knowing what he was intending.

"I'm turning my phone off for the night. I need to take someone to dinner."

HARD TARGET

26

It'd been three months since the day Recker found the body of Susan Hanley, stuffed in the trunk of her Honda Civic. Against his better judgment, he never sought revenge or retribution for the killing of Mia's friend. Though he disagreed with the professor's feelings, he nevertheless went along with Jones' desires. Recker pledged that if the police hadn't solved the murder and arrested the culprit by this time, that he'd get back on the case to do his own justice. Unfortunately for him, his own cases seemed to be never ending and he couldn't get back to the investigation of Hanley's murder. In the last couple of months, Recker never even had more than one day off to just relax, let alone the time he'd need to look into the Hanley case.

Though he didn't know the Hanley woman personally, with her being a friend of Mia's, it ate away at Recker that a killer was out there on the loose. Mia asked him constantly if he had the time to work on her friend's death. Over the past three months, she had become increasingly frustrated over the lack of police progress on the situation. Every time she called the police to speak to the investigators, she felt like they were giving her the runaround. She felt that they were nowhere near solving the case and she was sure they were not even investigating it any more. They didn't seem to have any leads, and she wondered if they'd just moved on to other cases that they felt were more solvable. Even though she had pestered Recker at least three times a week to enquire about Hanley's case, he tried not to get too annoyed by it, even though it sometimes took his focus off the cases he was working on now. He understood how frustrated she'd become. He felt it too.

Sitting in the diner of Joe's, one of their frequent meeting places, Recker could only assume that the Hanley case would be one of the first things that Mia brought up. Though she hadn't mentioned it the day before when she asked him to meet her for lunch, he figured he was going to hear questions about it today. Since she was running a few minutes late due to traffic, she'd already texted him to let him know she'd be there soon. Sitting there by himself, though, gave Recker some time to himself to think. With all the cases he'd been working lately and how busy he was, just taking a few minutes to think was something he didn't get much time to do.

Recker looked out the window and watched a younger couple getting into their car. For some reason; possibly the woman's blonde hair that bore a striking resemblance to Carrie's, his thoughts turned back to her. He thought about a few of the good times that they'd shared together. But those thoughts quickly turned darker when he thought about that fateful night back in London. He replayed the conversation he had with Agent 17 in his mind, over and over again. Though he was looking out the window, he wasn't seeing anything. In his mind, he was picturing what Agent 17 looked like as he had that conversation over the phone. Recker clenched his jaw tighter as his body embraced the tension that was flowing through him. Then, the image he had of Agent 17 slowly faded away as Recker's mind turned to other things. He thought about the professor's software program that was supposed to be helping find and identify Carrie's killer. With how busy they'd become, Recker had put the search out of his mind as he focused on helping the people in the city he was now in. But as he sat there thinking about it, he was becoming more agitated at the fact that Jones still hadn't found Agent 17 yet. Of course, the professor could have found him already, and he just didn't want to reveal it to Recker yet with the amount of cases they had on the table. But Recker also knew that Jones was reluctant to participate in the search, anyway. He was starting to think that unless he pestered Jones continuously about it, that the professor would never make it a priority. Jones would always find a way to put it on the back burner if Recker let him. Recker thought about the last time he asked about how the search was going. It'd probably been about a month, and it was only in passing as they were in the middle of another kidnapping case. He remembered Jones not saying much about it, just indicating that they were close.

As he sat there thinking about it, he determined that when lunch with Mia was done, he was going back to the office to confront Jones about his lack of haste in finding what was so important to Recker. He would accept no excuses or delays, and he wasn't going to take no for an answer. After all, finding Agent 17 was one of the conditions Recker insisted on when he agreed to join Jones' crusade. If he didn't like Jones' answer, then Recker would seriously consider leaving on the spot to go find the one person on earth that he hated like no other.

Recker was so deep in thought that he never even saw or heard Mia sit down across from him. She hurriedly rushed into the diner and sat down, knowing that Recker usually didn't have an overabundance of time on his hands. Once she settled in, she sighed and looked at him, noticing that he was obviously somewhere else since he didn't pay her even the slightest bit of attention. Seeing that he was looking out the window, Mia glanced out herself, wondering if something was going on out there. Not noticing anything strange, she looked back at him, curious as to what was going through that mind of his. In the time that they'd known each other, she noticed that he sometimes seemed to get lost in another moment and she often wondered just where exactly his mind went. Mia cleared her throat, hoping the noise would awaken him from whatever trance he was in, but he still paid her no mind. Though part of her wasn't sure whether she should wake him, as part of her worried that in these moments of his, he was taken back to some violent moment in his life. Seeing Recker's hand resting on the table, she reached her hand across and gently placed it on top of his. Feeling her touch, his concentration was broken, and he turned to look at her, somewhat surprised to see her sitting there.

"Hey, when'd you get here?" he asked.

"Oh, like an hour ago," Mia teased.

"Really?"

"No. I just got here a minute ago."

"Oh. I didn't even notice you come in."

"Yeah, I could tell. Everything OK?" she said, sensing that he wasn't totally there.

"Yeah, yeah. Was just thinking about something."

"Anything you wanna talk about?"

"Nope."

"Thought so."

They ordered some food and spent the next few minutes small talking, neither saying anything of much substance. Mia figured she'd wait a little while until she dropped the news on him as she was sure he wouldn't like what she had to tell him. She waited until they finished eating before she spat out what was on her mind. Part of her was nervous to talk to him about it, knowing he would vehemently disapprove of her actions.

"Have you heard anything about Susie's case lately?" she said, keeping her tone light deliberately, and running her fingers through her hair as a distraction.

Recker just shook his head. "No. Nothing new. Police still don't seem to have any leads to work from."

"They don't seem to be trying very hard."

"I know it's tough for you," Recker said.

"Yeah. That's why I started doing something about it on my own."

Recker squinted his eyes slightly, unsure what she meant, but not liking the sound of it. "What exactly have you done?"

"I started looking into some things."

"Such as?"

"Just going through her contacts, appointments, and clients to see if she had a relationship with anybody outside of work. Or maybe if any of them have a particularly violent past," Mia said, squirming uncomfortably on her seat in readiness for Recker's response.

Recker made a face and sighed, clearly unhappy. "Mia, we've already done that. When we were looking for her, we checked the backgrounds of all her clients. Only a couple had any type of criminal background and those that did, were home at the time she disappeared."

"I know. That's why I dug a little further."

"You what?"

She cleared her throat as she explained. Even when Recker didn't try to be, knowing his past history, he could be an intimidating figure. And she knew he didn't approve of anything she said or was about to say.

"I started digging into the backgrounds of some of the relatives of some of her clients," Mia stated.

"Mia."

"Don't Mia me. One of my best friends, someone I've known since college, someone I was roommates with, was killed and stuffed in a car," she said, on the verge of crying. "It's been three months since she was found and nobody, including you, seems to give a damn about what happened to her. The police don't seem to care, you give me the runaround, what else am I supposed to do?"

Knowing she was frustrated, Recker tried to be patient with her. "I know you're hurt and angry, but you can't do this."

"Why?"

"To be perfectly honest, you don't know what you're doing."

"Well someone has to do something. Nobody else is."

"Let the authorities handle it."

"We both know that if they haven't found who did it by now, the odds are only going to get worse as time moves on," Mia said.

"Maybe. But you're not equipped to do this."

"Well I've already started. I can't just go on living, knowing that Susie's killer is out there roaming the streets and no one seems to care."

"I told you that I would start looking into it as soon as I got some free time," Recker said, trying hard to stay patient.

"Which is never. Mike, you never have free time. It almost takes an act of God for you to just take a few minutes to have lunch with me," she replied in frustration.

Recker looked down at the table. The comment stung a little bit even though he knew she wasn't wrong and was well within her rights to feel that way. Mia read his face and saw that she'd hurt him a little with her words.

"I'm... I'm sorry. I didn't mean that," Mia said.

"Yes you did. It's OK. You're not wrong."

"I know you're busy and you have a lot on your plate. Not that you ever talk much about what's on it. But I know you're stretched thin already and I've already asked you more than I should about it. And I know it's not your job to look into my own personal things so I'm not even going to ask you anymore."

Recker took a few seconds to think of something to try and convince her to not pursue her intentions any further.

"What do you think's going to happen if you actually find something?" Recker asked.

"If I get close enough to actually start putting some pieces together, then I'll take what I've learned to the police."

"If you get that far."

"What's that supposed to mean?" Mia wondered.

"Because you're not a trained investigator. You're not experienced in this line of work. You make one wrong move, take one wrong step, and it could be last. If you start looking into things and ruffle the wrong feathers, you might be the next one that's stuffed in the trunk of a car," Recker warned.

"I'm willing to take that chance."

"I'm not willing to let you take that chance."

"Mike, you're not gonna stop me," she told him.

"I'm not gonna let you do this and possibly get yourself killed."

"Would it really matter to you?"

Recker leaned back, trying not to let her hurtful words get to him. He knew it was more frustration and emotion talking than anything.

"You know I care about you or else I wouldn't be here," Recker said.

"I know. I shouldn't have said it. I guess I'm not feeling myself today," she sorrowfully replied.

"I promise you that I will start looking into it."

"When?"

"As soon as I get some time."

Mia rolled her eyes and sighed, weary from hearing that line before. "I know you mean well, Mike, but I don't want to wait forever for you. I'm gonna keep looking into things on my own. If you get some free time tomorrow, or next week, or next month, then great. But I can't wait for you."

Recker also sighed, knowing there was nothing he could say that was going to change her mind. They sat there for a few more minutes, mostly in silence, both of them rather uncomfortable after their exchange. Eventually, Mia excused herself, saying she had to go home and get ready for work, having the night shift. Recker wasn't sure she was being truthful or whether she was about to do something that both of them would regret by investigating on her own. Recker didn't take his eyes off her as she walked out of the diner. He watched out the window as Mia got into her car and drove away.

Recker sat there for a little while longer, just thinking about the conversation they just had. He felt like he had let Mia down. He thought he should've done what he wanted to do in the first place and bring Hanley's killer to justice. If he had, then Mia wouldn't be in the obvious amount of pain that she was. Recker didn't blame her a bit for the way she was talking or feeling. He thought back to how he felt in the days after he learned that somebody had killed Carrie. Or the pain that he was still feeling. He didn't think that losing a friend, even a close one, was comparable to losing a wife or husband, a parent, a child, or even a brother or sister. But he knew the pain could still be severe. Severe enough for someone to do something that they shouldn't. Something such as seeking revenge or trying to investigate matters on their own when they were clearly out of their element.

He knew he couldn't let her do what she was planning, at least not alone. Recker was the only one who could help her, outside of the police, who seemed to have put the case on the back burner. He was going to go back to the office immediately to let Jones know that he had to get back on the case and insist that it wasn't up for debate. He knew the professor would likely try to talk him out of it once more, but Recker couldn't let that happen again. And while he was at it, he was going to have a much sterner conversation about the whereabouts and progress, or lack thereof, about Agent 17. Recker was through waiting and getting the runaround. There was something tugging at him that Jones had already found Agent 17 and was just holding off on telling him out of fear that Recker would leave immediately.

Once Recker got back to the office, Jones could instantly tell that something was wrong. Recker had the face of someone who was about to blow his cool, a mad scowl seeming to be permanently attached. Recker walked up to the desk and stopped, not saying a word. He just stared at the professor.

"I was going to ask how your lunch was but by the look of your face I'd say it didn't go so well," Jones stated.

"We need to have a talk."

"Oh?" Jones asked, fearful of the subject they were about to embark on. "About?"

"Two different subjects," Recker answered.

"I take it one of them will involve Mia?"

"It does."

"OK, let's start with that then," Jones said. "What exactly is the problem with her?"

"She's hurting, and she's angry. It's been three months and nobody seems to give a damn that her friend was killed."

"We both know that's not the case."

"Isn't it?" Recker asked. "If you'd have let me done what I wanted to when I found her body, we wouldn't even be having this conversation right now."

"We both know that it was for the best that we left it alone."

"No, we don't know that. I don't. The police have put the case on the back burner. You told me yourself the last time you hacked into the police files the other day that they hadn't even updated the case files in a month," Recker said. "They've moved on."

"We had other cases... our own cases, to work on," Jones responded. "As I said, we're not in the revenge business."

"But we are in the helping business. And right now we need to help Mia."

"In what regards?"

"She's out there investigating on her own. She's starting to talk to people and look at things," Recker revealed, getting a sigh out of Jones who knew that was a bad idea.

"So what do you suggest?" Jones asked.

"We both know that she's not gonna let this go. And it might not be right away, maybe it'll take some time, but we both know she's intelligent, resourceful, stubborn, and persistent. Eventually, if she pursues this, and she will, she's gonna strike a nerve with someone. She'll talk to someone who knows something. And that someone will get jumpy. And that's going to put her in danger."

Though Jones empathized with Recker's position, he wasn't so sure the situation was as dire as his friend was predicting. After all, Mia wasn't a trained investigator. Jones wasn't sure she'd get far into her investigation at all.

"At the risk of sounding cold hearted and uncaring, what makes you so sure that she won't give up after a week, despondent that she's unable to turn up anything of consequence?" Jones wondered.

"Like I said, she's strong willed. She's angry, and she's hurting. That's not a good combination. Trust me, I've been there."

"Comparing the two of you is not quite the same thing. One of you is a trained assassin skilled in the art of this type of warfare and one of you is a nurse. That hardly compares."

"Maybe so. But I'm telling you, she will not let this go," Recker warned.

"I think you're being a bit presumptuous in how far she can take this and what kind of danger she uncovers. For all we know it was a completely random act of violence against Ms. Hanley, someone who she never met before that incident. Someone who could be in an entirely different state by now," Jones rebuffed.

"You don't really believe that, do you?"

"What?"

"That it was random," Recker answered.

"I really have no idea. And neither do you."

"I know it wasn't random. Whoever did it, was someone she knew."

"And how do you know that?"

"She was strangled, then shot, then stuffed in the trunk of her car. There's nothing random about that. That's at the hands of someone who's made it personal. That's someone who's angry," Recker told him. "A stranger wouldn't bother to go through the hassle of doing all those things."

"Perhaps you're right. But I don't think we can spare the time right now to look into the case. I know that's what you're suggesting," Jones replied.

"I'm not suggesting. I'm telling you. I'm back on the case."

Jones looked despondent, knowing that he was losing the argument. He knew that Recker would put Mia's interests ahead of any other cases they were working on at the moment and was worried that other people would get hurt in the meantime. Things that could have been prevented if they weren't sidetracked with personal entanglements.

"And to what end are you going to pursue this?" Jones asked.

"What do you mean?"

"Well, how long do you plan to work on this?"

"As long as it takes," Recker answered.

"And what happens if you find the person who did this? Just turn the information over to the police?"

"I'll finish the case my way."

"Which means what?"

"I'll put two bullets in their head," Recker bluntly replied. "Then it'll be over."

"That's not how we're supposed to operate."

"That's how I operate."

"And what of our other cases?" Jones wondered. "There are other people out there who need help as well."

"I can work more than one case at a time. I can help them while helping Mia at the same time."

"Would you be doing this if it was someone other than Mia?"

"Of course not," Recker responded.

"I thought so."

"Listen, she's a friend and I care about her. I'm not about to let her get mixed up in something that she's ill-equipped for and unprepared to handle. And no, it's not because I'm falling in love with her. I know that's floating around somewhere in that head of yours."

"Just making sure I know where you stand on things," Jones said.

"I would do the same thing for you if it was you in her shoes," Recker told him.

Jones knew that there was nothing he could do or say that would change Recker's mind. Though he still wasn't sure that Mia would find the danger that Recker expected her to find, Jones had never seen him so persistent on anything before. There was no talking him out of it. And he knew better than to keep trying and fighting a losing game. He did worry about what would happen if Recker did find the culprit of Hanley's murder. It was now personal to Recker, and Jones hoped that he wouldn't get careless and make a mistake that would somehow compromise the two of them or their operation.

"When exactly do you plan on starting this little side escapade of yours?" Jones asked.

"No time like the present," Recker replied.

"Very well then. I guess we need to get started then, don't we?"

27

After an hour of working to put together some information that they could go off to re-start the Hanley investigation, Recker still hadn't said anything about the lack of progress in regards to Agent 17. Though it was still eating at him, the fire inside had subsided slightly as he continued looking into the case of Mia's friend. Not that he was happy about letting it go, but he figured right now they needed all their energy focused on the other things they were working on.

Once again, he'd put it to the side for the betterment of others, even though it frustrated him. It seemed all he ever did was push it away so they could work on other things. Recker's hatred for the man who killed Carrie was still burning strong. It never waned even for a second. At some point, if he really wanted to atone for her death, he was going to have to be selfish and put his own wants and needs above those of others. Just one time.

Taking a break for a few seconds between the different cases he was juggling, Jones looked over at his friend and thought there was still something wrong. Recker looked like a man with some heavy baggage on his shoulder. From some of his facial expressions, Jones thought he looked frustrated for some reason. It appeared to him like Recker had more on his mind than he was letting on.

"So are you going to tell me about the second thing?" Jones finally asked, remembering Recker's words when he first got back to the office.

"The second thing?"

"You said we were going to talk about two different subjects but we only got around to talking about one of them."

"The other one can wait," Recker dejectedly replied.

"If you prefer... though I can tell something else is on your mind. Might be good to air it out so you can concentrate on this with a clear head."

Recker thought about it for a minute and decided Jones was right. It was time to let it out and not hold back like he had been doing.

"Fine. You wanna know what else is bothering me?" Recker said, sounding mad.

"I'm not so sure now," Jones teased, a little worried about his anger level.

"It's your commitment level."

"My commitment level?"

"Not for this. I mean that little software program of yours."

"Oh. I see."

"Are you actually even running anything? Is it even working? I mean, every time I've ever asked you about it, all you say is that it's close. Or it's not quite ready. I feel like all you're doing is feeding me a line of crap," Recker vented. "I don't think you're looking at all. Or if you are, not very hard. You never really wanted to pursue this or wanted me to pursue it. And I think you're doing everything you can to put it off and postpone it as long as possible. Well I'm tired of waiting."

"And you want an update," Jones surmised.

Recker just shook his head. "No, I don't want an update. Cause your updates are just giving me the runaround. I want to know where he is. Now."

Jones gulped and looked over at his computer, thinking carefully as to how he should respond. He knew this day would come at some point, with Recker questioning his efforts on the search. Jones just hoped the day wouldn't come for a while yet. After thinking about his different options, and the consequences of each, he thought it best to come clean with his highly dangerous partner.

"You are correct," Jones softly stated.

"About which part?"

"All of it. You're right. I've never been enthused about participating in this project. I haven't given it my best efforts, I've kept you in the dark, I've tried to stall, and for that I do apologize."

"I don't want apologies," Recker replied. "I just want you to find him. If you can't, or won't, then just say it so I can search on my own."

"No. I told you I would help you and I will."

Recker threw his hands up. "When? I don't wanna sit here and listen to you give me nonsense for another year."

"And you won't have to. I guess I've been fearful of what would happen when the day came that I could locate Agent 17 for you," Jones told him.

"I already told you what I'd do."

"Yes, I know. That's what's frightened me. In the time that we've been doing this, we've done such great things, incredibly important things. And I guess I worry that you're going to throw away all that we've accomplished in such a short time to pursue your own vendetta."

"You're right. We've accomplished a lot. And we're gonna keep on accomplishing a lot. Me finding Agent 17 is not going to change that," Recker said.

"I guess I'm not sure I believe that. Part of me has felt that once you found him, you would never come back. I know that finding him has always been your number one goal. I guess part of me was hoping, however foolish it may have been, that as time went on that you would put that part of your life behind you and focus more on this one."

"The love of my life was taken from me. There's nothing on this world or any other that would make me forget about that. And as long as he's out there, a part of me will never be totally here."

It was an emotional heart to heart talk the two men were having, one that was much needed and overdue. While they'd known each other, they avoided talking about their true feelings on the subject and danced around it as much as possible.

"And when you find him? What then?" Jones asked.

"I'll kill him. Just like I said."

"And after that?"

"I'll come back here and continue the work that we've been doing," Recker replied.

"You make it sound like it will be that easy."

"That's all there is to it. If you'd have found him when we first started this, I honestly don't know if I would've come back. But this has become like a home, at least as much as one as I've ever had. There's people I care about here. I give you my word that I will be back."

"And what if you can't come back? What if he kills you?"

"That's not gonna happen," Recker forcefully said.

"You make it sound like you're hunting someone who's blissfully unaware or some kind of pencil pusher," Jones told him. "Your adversary is someone who's just as capable as you are, just as skilled as you are, just as dangerous as you are, someone who knows the same tricks that you do. He could just as easily kill you."

"You know, if I'd found him before we started all this, before I met you, I probably wouldn't have even cared about the outcome. I wouldn't have cared if I came back. As long as he was dead... I wouldn't have cared if I joined him in the afterlife, if there is one, or buried in the ground, or whatever it is that people believe in."

"And that's the belief and attitude that concerns me," Jones said.

"But I'm not that guy now. Not with you, and Mia, and the work we've got going on here. But I still hear those words he said to me. Every day, I replay it in my mind, over and over again. Not one day since Carrie's been gone that I haven't thought about that night. Not one," Recker said, his eyes getting glossy. "I can never be truly free from what haunts me and tears me up inside until the day he's no longer breathing. I need him to see that it's me, that I'm the one that's ending his existence."

Jones could feel the pain that Recker bore. He wore it on his shoulders every day. And now that Recker was pouring his emotions out on his sleeve, Jones knew he didn't have the right to keep the secret he'd been hiding any longer. Whether he agreed with Recker's decision or not, he was clearly still hurting, and it wasn't up to Jones to prevent him from healing or seeking closure. No matter what the outcome, the decision wasn't his to make. It was Recker's. Jones would just have to hope for the best.

"I'm afraid I have something else to tell you," Jones said, his voice barely above a whisper. "I haven't been honest with you."

"I know. You already said that."

"No. There's more. I've been keeping a secret from you and

since you have... expressed your feelings so deeply to me, I feel I need to share it."

"What is it?" Recker asked.

"I've already found him."

"What?" Recker asked in disbelief.

He was sure there was no way he heard what he thought he did. There was no way Jones was saying that he'd found Agent 17. Recker was positive he was going to say another name. Someone who was possibly connected to the man he was seeking all this time.

"I've already found him. Agent 17," Jones revealed.

"When?"

"About two weeks ago."

Shocked, Recker just stared at Jones, unable to form any words that would do the situation justice. He wasn't sure whether he should feel anger at being kept in the dark for the last two weeks, whether he should be furious at the professor for not being truthful, or whether he should be happy that the only thing he'd been living for all this time was finally within reach.

For his part, Jones felt like digging a hole and crawling into it. With Recker's incredulous reaction, the professor felt horribly for not coming forward with the information sooner. He wouldn't have blamed Recker if he got up off his chair and belted him across the face. With Recker's intimidating stare, Jones had trouble looking at him, knowing how disappointed in him Recker must've been. He felt ashamed of himself for not revealing the information as soon as he learned of it.

"I'm not going to apologize for my actions," Jones stated. "Not because I'm not sorry, but because I know those words aren't good enough or strong enough to satisfy you, as they shouldn't. I just hope that you will eventually forgive me for misleading you."

Recker finally broke his stare and leaned forward, rubbing his hands together. He let his eyes dance around the room, shifting between parts of the floor and wall, thinking about the best way to express himself. He didn't want to just emotionally blow up at Jones, unable to control himself, so he just let everything sink in for a minute until he could calmly rationalize everything.

"So were you ever gonna tell me?" Recker wondered. "I mean, were you just gonna sit on this forever?"

"I don't know." Jones shrugged. "I don't know. It's something that I wrestled with every day since his name finally popped up. There were times when I was close to saying something. But then there was another case, or another lead, or another situation that needed our attention, and I just let it slip away."

Though Recker was mad, and hurt, and felt betrayed, he was willing to put all that aside for the moment. If Jones had the information he needed, then Recker would deal with it at another time. Now wasn't the time to let his focus shift elsewhere. Now, finally, was the time to deal with Agent 17. And in the end, that was all that mattered.

"So where is he?" Recker asked.

"Right at this exact moment? I don't know," Jones answered.

Recker closed his eyes and took a deep breath, trying to control his anger. He surely could have become enraged if he so desired. But he was trying to keep his cool, only for the sake of finding his target.

"You had him. And you let him go," Recker whispered.

"Only for the moment," Jones reassured. "I can go back to where I located him and retrace his steps from that moment on. I can get a read on him again."

"How long will it take?"

"Give me a day or so and I should have it," Jones confidently stated.

"One day."

"One day. You have my word… for whatever that may be worth to you at the present time."

"Where'd you find him?" Recker wondered.

"Italy."

"What was he doing there? An assignment?"

"Yes. From what I can tell he'd been there approximately three days," Jones confirmed. "I got a hit on a report he submitted that his mission was completed."

"Where'd he go from there?"

"That I don't know. Like I said, I got sidetracked with another case we were working on and I lost his movements for the time being."

"So how do you know you're gonna be able to find him again?" Recker asked.

"Because now I know what I'm looking for," Jones answered. He reached into a desk drawer and pulled out a notepad with a bunch of names on it.

"What's this?" Recker wondered.

"Those are a list of some of his aliases. I wrote them down for the purpose of tracking him again."

"What makes you think he'll use one of them again?"

"Well, considering he's not on the run like you, I'm quite certain he'll be confident enough to use one of them rather quickly," Jones replied.

For the next couple of hours, Jones focused his attention only on finding Agent 17. With them being so close to knowing his whereabouts, spending a few more days on other matters would allow the mysterious agent to further slip through their fingers. The more they let time pass, the more Agent 17 could disguise his movements. As Jones typed away, Recker hovered over him, watching closely what he did. Though Jones understood Recker's eagerness at being so close to the man who killed his girlfriend, it still unnerved him a little bit.

"Why don't you go out for a while?" Jones asked, spinning around in his chair.

"Trying to get rid of me?"

"Not at all. It's just that it's a tad disrupting to feel you breathing on my neck."

Recker took a few steps back, getting the hint. "Just a little anxious I guess."

"I quite understand."

Recker then gave Jones some space. Instead of standing right behind him and watching him closely, Recker started pacing around the room. About every twenty minutes or so, he asked Jones the same question.

"How you making out?" Recker asked repeatedly.

"The same as the last time you asked," Jones replied. "It's coming along."

"You keep saying that."

"I understand your angst over the matter, Michael. But it's only been about five hours. I'm making progress."

"Can't you make it quicker?"

"You know as well as I do that tracing the movements of someone with multiple aliases, and who technically doesn't exist, in a government program that doesn't exist… takes quite a bit of time," Jones answered. "I said it'd be about a day and it should still be that."

Recker sighed. "Fine."

"Go home, relax, see a movie, go out and about, do something. Come back tomorrow and I should have something for you."

Recker contemplated his options for a minute before finally agreeing. Although he was hesitant to leave, he figured it was better for his nerves if he did. He'd never before been so anxious to get someone's location, but then again, he never was on a mission before as personal to him as this one was. Part of him thought that if he left, something would go wrong, and they'd lose Agent 17's location for good. Recker then realized that his presence had no real bearing on whether they found the man or not since Jones was the one doing all the legwork.

"Fine. I'll go home and come back tomorrow," Recker said.

"Don't come early," Jones told him.

"Well what time would you like me to show up?"

"Early afternoon should suffice."

"You better have it by then."

28

Jones worked continuously throughout the rest of the day and night, hardly taking any breaks at all. He only slept for about four hours, knowing he was on a deadline that Recker would be strict about. He still felt badly about not telling Recker about finding Agent 17 a couple weeks before and was pressuring himself to re-find the man as quickly as possible. And that was before Recker's warning about it being ready. If he needed more time, he was sure Recker would understand, as long as it was a reasonable amount. Though he couldn't rule out bodily harm if he crossed the wrong side of Recker again. Jones was sure his friend would never do that to him, but there was a small piece of him that thought that Recker was so obsessed with finding Agent 17 that nothing was off the table with him.

Recker hadn't slept much either. Once he lay down, all he could think about was getting Agent 17 in his sights. He thought of almost every possible scenario in which their confrontation could go down. In every single one of them, the ending came with Agent 17 getting a bullet. Sometimes it was in the head, sometimes in the chest, but they all finished with Recker standing over the lifeless body of his victim.

Doing as Jones had requested, Recker spent the morning away from the office, giving the professor enough time to find their target. At least, Recker hoped he'd given Jones enough time. If Jones told him that it'd take more time, there was no telling how Recker might respond. However, he responded, it wasn't likely to be pretty. And it definitely wouldn't be calm. He wanted Agent 17's location, and he wanted it today. No more excuses.

Recker finally rolled into the office a little after two o'clock, and in his opinion, giving Jones plenty of time. Once Jones heard the door open, he looked at his partner arriving, then looked at the clock. Recker came a little later than Jones had anticipated. With how anxious Recker was, Jones envisioned him coming a minute after twelve. He figured that was Recker's definition of early afternoon.

Recker thought that he'd be able to tell by Jones' face how the search was going, without him having to say a word. But surprisingly to him, he couldn't get a read on it. Jones didn't look especially happy, indicating that he found their guy, but he didn't look stressed or worried either, indicating that he couldn't find him yet. Recker walked right up to the edge of the desk where Jones was sitting, ready to get a report.

"Well?" Recker asked.

Jones looked up at him from the computer and opened his mouth to say something, but just froze, trying to think of the best way of putting his thoughts. Since the professor didn't come right out with it, Recker assumed that he couldn't locate him.

"You didn't find him yet, did you?" Recker asked.

Jones put his index finger in the air as he replied. "I am almost there."

Recker sighed and threw his hands up in frustration. "I've heard that before."

"No, seriously, I am almost there," Jones replied, turning his attention back to the computer, resuming his typing.

"How much longer now?"

"An hour. Tops."

"One hour?" Recker asked, not convinced of the time frame.

"Guaranteed. He's back in the United States," Jones revealed. "I'm extremely close. I've tracked his last flight back here and I'm seeing where he went from there."

"What flight?"

"He landed in New York."

"New York?" Recker asked, surprised at how close they physically were.

"He's not still there though. That's what I'm currently tracking."

Not wanting to bug Jones too much and throw his concentration off since he seemed to be so close, Recker resumed his position from the previous day, pacing throughout the room as he awaited word that their target had been found. Though he wanted to ask every few minutes how it was going, Recker refrained from doing so. Even though he didn't ask the question, he looked at Jones almost constantly, trying to read his face and actions as to whether he found him yet. After almost an hour exactly, Jones suddenly stopped typing, leaning back in his chair as he stared at the screen. Recker stopped his pacing as he anxiously awaited for Jones to say something.

"I've found him," Jones looked up and said.

Recker rushed around the desk and sat down next to Jones and looked at the screen with great anticipation. "Where is he?"

"Ohio. Just outside of Columbus to be exact."

"3248 Eddington Road," Recker read off the screen. "What is that?"

"It's a residential address," Jones answered. "It appears to be where he lives."

Recker quickly turned his head toward his partner at the revelation of having Agent 17's home address.

"I would temper your enthusiasm at having a quick and clean operation," Jones warned.

"Why's that?"

Jones switched screens and pulled up a picture of a woman holding a young child.

"Who are they?" Recker wondered.

"That would be his wife and two-year-old son."

Recker stared at the picture for a few moments.

"Does that change anything?" Jones asked. He thought that once Recker saw that the man had a young family, that maybe his thoughts on the operation might change. He clearly didn't know Recker as well as he thought.

"Changes nothing," Recker replied.

"If you kill him, you would tear this family apart," Jones reasoned. "A child will grow up without a father and a mother will lose her husband."

"Doesn't mean anything to me."

"How can you sit there and say that?"

"He killed an innocent person. And he did it happily. I'm not letting him off the hook for that just because he's married with a child," Recker answered. "He'll be lucky if I don't do to him what he did to me."

Taking a few seconds to think about his statement, Jones became horrified at the meaning, if he was correct in his assessment.

"Please tell me that doesn't mean what I fear it does," Jones stated.

Recker shrugged. "I dunno. You tell me."

"I hope that wasn't an indication that you would consider killing his wife and child."

Recker squinted his eyes like he was thinking, then shook his head. "I wouldn't kill a child."

Jones let out a sigh of relief. "Thank goodness for that. I would hope not. I thought I knew you better."

"The woman's another story," Recker said.

"Michael, I know you're consumed with rage at this man and I'm honestly not saying you're wrong in feeling that way. But you cannot kill innocent people just to satisfy your thirst for revenge," Jones pleaded. "She's an innocent woman who's probably blissfully unaware of her husband's dealings. You cannot let her take the fall for his perceived mistakes."

Recker leaned back and put his hand on his chin as he thought about it. Trying to think about it more calmly, he agreed with Jones' position. Regardless of his feelings for Agent 17, no matter how angry he was, no matter what he said or thought, he wouldn't knowingly kill an innocent person. As he was aware from his own time in the agency, he knew that the agent's wife most likely had no idea what was going on. No, he wasn't going to put anyone else's life in jeopardy. There was only one person who was going to pay the price and one person only.

"I won't take her out," Recker stated.

Jones closed his eyes and let out another sigh of relief. "Thank you for that."

"He's as good as dead though."

"I understand," Jones said.

"What's this guy's name, anyway?" Recker asked. "I'm getting tired of calling him Agent 17."

"Which one? He's got at least six names that I've identified," Jones told him.

"Whichever one he's going by right now."

"That would be Gerry Edwards."

Recker proceeded to read everything Jones had uncovered about Edwards. He read Edwards' files, reports, personal information, every assignment he'd been on, everything right down to the smallest details. He looked at several snapshots of Edwards, as well as his family. According to the reports Recker was reading, Edwards seemed to be highly thought of within the agency. He was twenty-nine years old and had been in Centurion for about three years. He'd been married for six years to his college girlfriend and had a two-year-old son. On the surface, he seemed like a normal, regular guy. If somebody was reading his information, they wouldn't see anything that would give them pause about the type of person he was. Nothing specific seemed cold or callous. But they never heard what Recker did. As Recker looked at Edwards' picture, he heard his voice again, replaying their conversation in his mind once more. He thoroughly remembered how much pleasure Edwards got out of killing Carrie. There was no sorrow or sadness in his voice. There was no sense of regret about killing an innocent person. The longer Recker stared at the picture, the hatred and rage inside him grew as well. If he had a gun within reaching distance, he'd put a bullet right through the computer screen where Edwards' picture was.

Jones was reading some of the information as well, and periodically looked at Recker. As Recker silently sat there, staring at the screen, there was an intensity about him that worried Jones. He was concerned that in Recker's quest for revenge, or justice, that there was nothing that would stand in his way. Whether it be legal or illegal, moral or immoral. Jones worried that Recker would go to any lengths to get the man he was seeking. Not only did he worry about Recker crossing the line, Jones worried that he'd obliterate the line. Jones thought that underneath that silence, Recker's blood was boiling over. In an effort to calm him down, at least on the inside, Jones started talking to him to break his concentration on Edwards' picture.

"So I take it that you'll be leaving soon to take care of this matter," Jones stated.

"Yep."

"When do you plan on leaving?"

"I'll leave later tonight or in the morning," Recker answered.

"I thought so. What else do you need from me?"

"Just to help disguise my movements."

"What did you have in mind?"

"Well, after I kill him, the CIA's gonna wind up looking into it," Recker said. "They'll look into everyone coming in or out of town. That means I have to avoid cameras."

"That would leave out planes and trains for sure."

"That'd probably be their first inquiry. And if my face pops up..."

"Unless I were to hack into the camera system and temporarily disable it," Jones mentioned.

"No, too suspicious. Then they'll know the exact times someone boarded the planes and start narrowing the list down. Everything's gotta seem natural. Can't force anything or they'll know something's not right," Recker said.

"After that your best bet is either a bus or driving down yourself. Driving down there will take about fourteen hours or so."

"More than I'd like but I think it'll be the safest way to avoid detection."

"There are cameras on the freeways too," Jones noted.

"Yeah, but my vehicle won't come up on any lists and my license plate won't get a hit."

"What about the cameras at tolls?"

"If I put on a hat and wear it down low near my eyes, it won't pick my face up clearly."

"Well if you're planning on driving, you'd probably want to leave as soon as possible."

"I'll wait until the evening rush hour is over. No sense in fighting traffic along the way," Recker replied.

They spent another hour or so going over some plans. Recker figured if he left around six that he'd get to Columbus around eight if he drove nonstop. If he floored it, he could get there by six or seven in the morning. Hopefully, he could sit outside Edwards' house before he left and Recker could get him as he left in the morning.

"Could I make a suggestion?" Jones wondered.

"As long as it doesn't involve trying to talk me out of it."

"No, I know that would be an impossible task. If you decide on killing him..."

Recker just gave him a look. "I am killing him."

"Poor choice of words, whatever you decide to do, whenever you decide to do it, please don't do it in front of or inside his house."

"Why?" Recker asked.

"For the sake of his wife and child. Regardless of their relations, no wife should walk in and see her husband murdered in their own home. No child should see their father gunned down and bleeding to death inside their home. That should be his sanctuary from the world he's about to grow up in," Jones explained.

Recker frowned, letting Jones' reasoning rattle around inside his head for a few moments. Then he nodded, agreeing to his plea.

"OK. I'll make sure they don't see it," Recker told him.

"Thank you."

"You sure do have a lot of conditions, and a lot of empathy, for these people."

"Only for the innocent, Michael, only for the innocent. That is the business we're now in, remember? Protecting the innocent."

"Yeah."

"I fully understand your reasoning for killing Edwards. I completely accept what you're about to do and have no qualms about your actions. But I will fight for the lives of those who are not connected to his dealings," Jones said. "And what do you plan to do about Mia?"

"What do you mean? What about her?"

"You did suggest that we help her with her situation."

"She shouldn't run into any problems in the time that I'm gone," Recker responded. "I won't be gone that long."

"Do you think it might be wise if you told her that you were going to look into her situation so she backs off for the time being?" Jones wondered.

"Yeah, might be a good idea at that."

Recker tried calling Mia's cell phone a few times but couldn't get through, only getting her voicemail. Though he initially thought that she wasn't being honest that she had to work, he started to think maybe she was.

"Guess she had to work after all," Recker stated.

"I wouldn't be too sure about that," Jones replied.

"Why?"

"I've uh... gotten into the hospital time clock software program that they use."

"And?"

"And she hasn't clocked in yet," Jones answered.

"Then why wouldn't she be answering me?"

Jones simply shrugged. "Maybe she's already underway in her investigation. Didn't you say she said she already started?"

"Yeah, but I didn't think she really meant anything by it. I thought it was just her way of drawing me in," Recker responded.

"It would seem you misread her."

Recker sighed, not needing any problems to pop up right now. "Ah boy."

"What do you plan to do now?" Jones asked.

"Keep calling until she picks up."

Recker did as he said he would and kept calling Mia's phone every ten minutes. After an hour of unsuccessfully trying to get a hold of her, Recker was starting to get worried. He hadn't left any messages up to that point as he tried to avoid doing that, just in case the CIA could pick up his voice through one of their voice detection programs they sometimes utilized.

"Are you sure she's not at work?" Recker asked.

"Not unless she's working for free today," Jones answered. "You could always try calling the hospital just to be sure."

"Yeah. Maybe I'll do that."

Recker then called the hospital and after a brief hold, was told that Mia wasn't scheduled to be in that day. After hanging up, he looked over at Jones and shook his head.

"She couldn't have gotten herself into any trouble already, could she?" Recker asked.

"Is that a question you want answered or are you just talking to yourself?"

"Both. I mean, what are the odds that she would've found something already that would make her not pick up the phone?"

Recker went back to repeatedly calling Mia's phone, calling it every five minutes again. Though he still wanted to avoid leaving messages, he finally relented and simply told her it was important and to call him back as soon as possible. He started pacing around the room again, his mind wandering about where she could have been. Another twenty minutes went by with still not a peep from Mia.

"Why don't you sit down?" Jones asked. "Pacing around the room isn't going to get her to call faster."

"I can't sit down."

"Can't you track her or something?"

"Possibly," Jones replied. "It'll take some time though."

Recker suddenly stopped and sat down. He put his head in his hands as he started to worry about what Mia might have gotten herself into already.

"What if she hasn't checked in by the time you want to leave?" Jones wondered.

"I'm not leaving until I know she's OK."

"You sound like a worried boyfriend."

In most circumstances, Recker might've taken offense to his implication of enhanced feelings for her. But in their current situation, he didn't pay much mind to it. He didn't even bother to reply. He looked at his phone again, thinking about calling her number one more time.

"I can't just sit here anymore," Recker stated.

"What do you plan to do?"

"I dunno. Go out and do what I do I guess."

"Where are you going to start?"

"Her apartment I guess. I'll figure out where to go from there."

"Maybe we could get Mr. Gibson involved?" Jones asked.

"Let me search her apartment first and see if I turn up anything."

Recker got up and walked over to the gun cabinet and started looking at which weapons he wanted to take with him. As soon as he picked up one of his handguns, his phone started ringing. Hoping that it was Mia, Recker rushed over to the desk to answer it. Jones, worried himself, leaned over and looked at the screen.

"It's Mia!" Jones shouted.

Recker reached across the desk to pick up the phone. "Where have you been?"

"Who taught you how to answer a phone?" she wondered.

"Are you OK?"

"Yeah, I'm fine. Why wouldn't I be?"

"Because I've been calling you for like two hours."

"Wow. You almost sound worried," Mia told him.

"I am worried."

"I didn't know you cared so much."

"Stop. You know I do," Recker said.

"I know. I'm sorry."

"Are you OK?"

"Yeah. I already said that."

"Then why haven't you been answering my calls?" Recker asked.

"I told you at the diner. I had to go to work. I'm just on my break now and saw you called."

"Mia?"

"Yeah?"

"I've already called the hospital, and they told me you weren't there and you weren't scheduled to work today," Recker revealed.

"Oh," she replied, knowing she was busted.

"Why don't you tell me where you really are?"

"I've been different places."

"So why did you tell me you had to work today when you didn't?" he asked.

"Because you wouldn't have liked it if I told you what I was really doing."

"Which was?"

"I told you I already started my own investigation into Susie's death," Mia explained.

Recker closed his eyes and sighed, afraid that was the answer he was going to get.

"I can hear you yelling under your breath," she told him.

"I'm not yelling."

"Not out loud at least."

"Mia, I'm just worried that you're gonna stumble into something that you're not prepared for," Recker said.

"I know. But I said that I wasn't waiting for anybody else anymore."

"Will you just do me a favor and step aside for a couple of days?"

"I'm not waiting anymore."

"Just for two or three days and then I promise you that I will help," he offered.

"You will? Why?"

"Because I know it's important to you and I'm worried that if I don't, then you'll get into something that you don't know how to get out of."

"What about your other cases?" Mia asked.

"I can still work my other stuff while looking into Susan's death. OK?"

"Yeah, but I've already talked to a couple people and I have some promising leads."

"Mia, please just wait a couple of days for me."

"Why do I have to wait? If you're interested in helping then why can't you get started right away?" she wondered.

"Because I have to go away for a couple of days," Recker told her.

"What? Why?"

"There's some old business that I have to finish up."

"Where are you going?" Mia asked.

"I can't really say."

"Of course you can't."

"It involves that night I told you about. When my old job tried to eliminate me."

"Oh. They found you?" she worried.

"No. But I found someone else. And it's something that I need to take care of right away."

"You are coming back, aren't you?"

"Of course I'm coming back."

"When are you leaving?"

"Tonight."

"Oh. So soon."

"Yeah. And I will be back in two or three days. Promise me you won't get into anything while I'm gone?"

"I mean, what if you don't come back?" Mia asked.

"I will be back. And when I am, I will do everything in my power to find Susan's killer. Promise me you'll wait till then?"

Mia paused, thinking of a response. "I promise I won't initiate anything."

"I guess that's as good as I'm gonna get from you," Recker replied.

"Probably."

29

Recker left Philadelphia just after seven and had been on the road for a little over five hours. For most of the drive, his mind was split between thoughts of revenge on Edwards and concern over Mia. Every time he tried to concentrate on how he'd kill Edwards, his mind would suddenly shift over to Mia's predicament. He only planned to be gone a day or two at the most, depending on how quick and easy he could get to Edwards. He assumed that Mia couldn't get into any real trouble in such a short amount of time since she just started her investigation. But then it occurred to him... what if she was further along than she let him know? Perhaps she started weeks earlier than she told him. She was already keeping it a secret from him so he wouldn't have put it past her if she started sooner than she initially told him. Recker was growing more worried that she'd get into something without him there to protect her. Figuring that Jones was still up, he called him to ask a favor.

"Hey. You weren't sleeping yet, were you?" Recker asked.

"No. I still had some things I was looking into."

"Still at the office?"

"Yes, why?"

"Just wondering."

"How are you making out so far?" Jones asked.

"Good. Should get there on time."

"Since I'm sure you didn't call to wish me pleasant dreams, what can I do for you?"

"Well aren't you cynical? Can't someone just call a friend to say hi without a reason?" Recker asked.

"Yes. But you've never done that before."

"Oh. Well, anyway, I was just calling to see if you can keep an eye on Mia while I'm gone."

"What do you mean, keep an eye on her?" Jones wondered.

"Just make sure she's not getting herself into any trouble."

"Should I follow her the entire day?"

"No. Just periodically call her. Make sure she's all right. Kind of hint at what she's doing."

"I guess I could do that. But if all you want me to do is call, then I don't see why you couldn't do that."

"Yeah, I don't think I'm high on her friend list right now," Recker said. "You're probably just as likely to draw any information out of her as I am, if not more."

"I suppose I could do that."

Jones continued working on some of the cases they'd start working on once Recker returned, assuming that he did return. There was still a part of Jones that feared that Recker wouldn't survive his encounter with Gerry Edwards. Even if Recker was successful in eliminating his target, there was always a possibility that he would get killed in his escape from the area. Jones buttoned everything up a little after two, knowing he'd have one more thing on his plate when he woke up with having to look after Mia.

Recker was right to be concerned about Mia's safety. His fears would turn out to be true as she hadn't been honest with him in regards to how far along she was with her investigation. The assumption was that she'd just started within the previous couple of days, when in reality, she was now in her fourth week. It started when she was helping Hanley's mother clean out her apartment. She found a piece of paper with a man's name and phone number placed inside a book that Susan had been reading. Joe Simmons was the name, and Mia had never heard her mention him before. Mia had gotten a hold of Hanley's appointment book and noticed that the name wasn't on it. She called the number listed on the paper but it was no longer in service. She wrestled on whether she should've handed the information over to either the police or Recker, but she figured both of them would just push her aside. Since neither of them seemed like finding Hanley's killer was high on their priority list, she was the only one who'd keep pressing to find the culprit.

It was after nine o'clock and Mia had just finished eating breakfast when she sat down to look at some of her notes. After every person she talked to, she wrote down anything of note that they might have mentioned. She checked off every single person that was listed in Hanley's appointment book and mentioned to all of them whether they knew the name of the person that she found inside that book of Susan's. Nobody indicated that they knew who Simmons was. Her phone started ringing and when she looked at the ID screen, didn't recognize the number calling.

"Hello?" she greeted.

"I hear you're looking for someone," the voice said.

"Who is this?"

"I know where you can find Joe Simmons."

"Where?" Mia excitedly asked.

"Haddix Apartments on 5th street. Second floor, room 217. Go there at twelve and I'll give you everything I have on him."

"Who are you?"

"Doesn't matter."

"Who is this Joe Simmons? How did he know Susan?" Mia wondered. "Hello? Hello?"

There was no answer. Whoever was on the other end of the phone had already hung up. Mia sat there for another hour poring over her notes, trying to piece things together the best she could. Though she was a little hesitant at meeting someone who she didn't even know the name of, she was running out of leads to run down. If Recker was still there, she might've asked him to go with her, but since he wasn't, she'd have to go it alone. As she was reading her notes, her phone rang again. She quickly jumped at the phone thinking it might've been the same guy again, but this time she recognized the number.

"Mia, how are you?" Jones asked.

"Fine. You?"

"Good."

"Mike asked you to check up on me, didn't he?" Mia asked.

"Uhh..."

"It's OK. You don't have to lie or cover for him. I know he did."

"You're right. He did," Jones replied.

"I knew it."

"So is everything alright?"

"Everything's fine. You guys are such worrywarts," Mia told him.

"Well, with good reason. You're doing something you don't have much experience in. It's more difficult that it appears on the outside."

"I've been making out OK."

"So how much progress have you made so far? Perhaps I can start running things down here on my end?"

"I don't think I need any help with anything. I've already talked to everyone on her contact list and all her clients. Even friends and family of clients," she said.

Jones tilted his head, thinking it was strange that she was so far along already. "How can you have done all that already?"

"Huh?" Mia said, worried that she said too much.

"I find it peculiar that you could have accomplished so much in such a short amount of time."

"Well, I haven't been sleeping much and I've been working around the clock."

"Considering you have a normal job, I don't see how it's possible you could have spoken to every one of her contacts so soon. Unless you've been at this much longer than we've suspected."

"No, just a couple days," Mia said.

"I may not be as adept at reading people as Michael is, but I do usually get a good impression as to when people are lying to me," Jones told her.

"Oh. Umm, I think I have someone on the other line."

"Mia?"

"Yes?"

"How long have you actually been working on this?"

"Uh... about four weeks."

"Oh dear," Jones stated.

"Everything's fine. There's nothing to worry about. Everything's fine," she reassured.

"And may I ask what you may be working on today?"

Mia wasn't sure she should tell him about the call she just received. He'd probably tell her it wasn't a good idea to go if she did. Apparently though, as Jones could attest, she wasn't a good liar. She figured she'd just kind of give a generic response without really answering the question.

"Uh... nothing," Mia told him.

"Nothing? Really?"

"I told Mike that I wouldn't initiate anything and I'm not."

Once again, Jones didn't feel like she was being truthful. "I get the sense that you're trying very hard not to tell me something."

"I don't know what you mean."

"So what do you have on your itinerary today?" Jones asked.

"Umm... nothing."

"You do realize I can check your phone logs if I have to, right?"

Mia didn't answer him and put her head down, slapping her hand against her forehead. She knew he was going to find out what she was up to whether she told him or not.

"Fine. I'm meeting someone at twelve who has some information for me," she finally relented.

"Mia... you told Mike..."

"I said I wouldn't initiate anything and I haven't. This person called me a little while ago and told me they knew something and wanted to meet. I'm just responding... not initiating."

"Semantics, Ms. Hendricks."

"Maybe."

"Who is this person that called?"

"I don't know. They didn't say."

"And you think this is wise to meet someone that you don't know who it is?" Jones asked.

"I don't know. I need answers and I'm willing to go wherever the leads take me."

"I'm not sure Michael would approve."

"Well he's not here, is he?"

"How do you know you're not walking into a trap or something? How do you know this person really has information and isn't after something else? Or maybe they just want to harm you."

"I'm sure it'll be OK," Mia replied.

"I get the feeling that nothing I can say is going to dissuade you from going."

"That's right."

"You're as stubborn as Michael."

"Everything will be fine."

"Maybe. Perhaps I should go with you," Jones offered.

"No, that's really not necessary."

"At least give me the number of the person that called you so I can look into it."

Mia hesitated, not sure that she wanted the help at the moment. While she didn't initially think anything was suspicious about the phone call from the stranger, the more she thought about what Jones said, the more doubt started creeping into her mind. After another plea from Jones requesting the number, Mia agreed and gave it to him. They kept talking as Jones punched the phone number into his system. Just as he feared, the number didn't match up to anyone.

"Did you get anything?" Mia wondered.

"As I suspected, there's no match."

"How can that be?"

"It's most likely a prepaid phone," Jones replied.

"That doesn't mean something's up or I'm in danger or anything."

"No, but just the same, I do wish you'd reconsider going. At least until Michael returns."

"I'm not waiting," she defiantly said.

"Very well. Then I will insist on accompanying you."

"I don't think you really need to."

"It would put my mind at ease," Jones told her. "If I know

you're going to this rendezvous and then I don't hear from you for a while, then my mind will wander with all sorts of terrible thoughts."

"Gee, thanks for the scare."

"Plus, Michael will never let me hear the end of it if he knows that I know that you're going to this thing and I didn't either stop you or go with you."

"So what you're really worried about is Mike giving you crap," Mia said.

"No. I care about you too."

"So have you heard from Mike since he left?" she asked. "How's his trip to Baltimore going?"

"Nice try but he did not tell you where he was going. And I can definitely say that it wasn't Baltimore," Jones answered.

"So you do know where he went."

"Yes, but I'm not at liberty to divulge that information."

"Of course you're not."

"But if you're curious as to his whereabouts, I can tell you that he's gotten there safely," Jones said.

"Is he done with whatever he was doing?"

"Not yet. He just text me a few minutes ago saying he arrived. He's not yet concluded his business."

"Why do you two always talk so cryptically?" Mia asked.

"It's for your own protection."

"That's what he says."

Mia agreed to let Jones go with her when she met the man that called her and agreed to meet at the Haddix Apartment complex. Both agreed to wait before going in until the other one arrived. Jones thought about letting Recker know what was going on but decided against it. He figured the less Recker had to worry about back in Philadelphia, the better his chances were for a successful outcome in Columbus. He didn't want Recker's mind cloudy or worried about anything other than completing what he felt he needed to do and getting back safely. If there was any trouble that arose from Mia's problem, Jones assumed he could take care of it for the time being.

Recker had just gotten to the Edwards address, a two story brick building a few miles outside of Columbus, Ohio. It was in a nice little community setting in a development with about three hundred other houses of similar stature. Recker estimated the worth of the houses to be in the four to five hundred thousand dollar range. Recker parked just up the street, still getting a good view of the Edwards house, but parking far enough away so as he wouldn't draw suspicion and be recognized. Edwards had a BMW X5 luxury crossover SUV registered to him but it wasn't parked in the driveway. There was a white Cadillac sedan still in the driveway, but that belonged to Tonya Edwards.

It was the scenario that Recker was dreading. Having to wait. With Edwards already gone, there was no telling when he might return. Recker was hoping to get to the house early enough that he could follow Edwards when he left in the morning. Now, he might have to wait all day which would delay his return to Philadelphia. It wasn't what Recker was hoping for. He hoped that he'd get there just before Edwards left and he could tail him, then kill him somewhere away from his home, then return to Philadelphia. But he realized that was the best-case scenario, not necessarily the most likely one.

As the time approached noon, Recker still hadn't observed any activity in or around the Edwards house. He figured Tonya Edwards either left with her husband or was having a quiet day at home with her son. According to their information, she didn't have a job and was a stay at home mother. Recker tried to stay busy by reading the files he printed out on Edwards. Though it wasn't complete, Jones had managed to dig up enough information about Edwards' time in the CIA, including several of his Centurion operations. Most of it seemed to be smaller assignments as the bigger missions usually were off the books or were only acknowledged by a small team of people. There was nothing in his files or reports about Recker's time in London or about Edwards killing Carrie in Florida. Not that Recker expected it to be there since those types of missions usually weren't noted anywhere except in the personal files of superiors. The CIA usually didn't chance that type of information being written anywhere within agency files for fear of leaks or hacks. Those reports were usually only handled in the files of the CIA Director or whoever was in charge of the Centurion project.

Assuming he had some time to kill, Recker started wondering what was going on back in Philly. He had sent Jones a few texts within the past half hour but didn't get a reply to any of them. Recker thought it was a little strange as Jones usually responded quickly to texts and phone calls. The professor was usually in the office and near his phone so Recker couldn't think of any reason why he would be ignoring his texts. The only thing he could think of is if something important had come up and Jones was in the field for some odd reason. Seeking to put his mind at ease, Recker tried calling Jones several times, still not getting an answer.

"Not this again," Recker whispered, not wanting to go through the same thing that he did with Mia the day before.

Recker tried calling a couple more times, each time getting a little more frustrated with each call that went unanswered. Finally, after about fifteen minutes of struggling to get through, Jones finally picked up.

"What took so long?" Recker wondered.

"I'm sorry. I just had other things I was attending to," Jones responded. "Is everything all right there?"

"Yeah. Edwards wasn't here when I arrived. Looks like I gotta wait it out for a while."

"Oh. So why are you calling then?"

"Just making sure everything's OK there," Recker answered. He thought he detected the sounds of cars and a horn in the background, making him wonder where Jones was going. "Are you driving somewhere?"

"How could you know that?" Jones asked.

"It's kind of what I do for a living."

"Indeed."

"Where are you going?"

"I'm just checking on something."

"You're a lousy liar, David. What is it that you don't want to tell me?" Recker asked.

"Well without you here, I have to go out into the field for a little bit."

Recker wasn't going to just accept that for an answer. Before leaving, they agreed to not pursue any of their upcoming cases until Recker returned. He looked at each one of the cases and remembered the names of the parties involved.

"I thought you agreed to wait till I got back?" Recker asked.

"Well, something came up that I need to check into. Shouldn't take too long."

"What case is it?"

"The uh... the Joe Simmons case," Jones said, wincing as he said it, hoping that Recker wouldn't pick up on the name.

It was a bad assumption as Recker knew the name wasn't familiar. Recker took the phone away from his ear and looked at it strangely as if he misheard the name. He knew the name wasn't among any of the cases they were beginning to look into. Even if it was a name dug up in the background, Recker didn't figure it'd be important enough for Jones to head out into the field already.

"Joe Simmons?" Recker asked. "Who's that?"

"You know, one of the cases I started working on."

"David?"

"Yes?" Jones dejectedly replied, knowing the gig was up.

"There was no Joe Simmons listed in any of the files. I checked them all before I left. So you're either making the name up to disguise something or it's something completely unrelated to any of our cases. Which is it?"

"Just let it go for now. I'll explain everything to you when you return," Jones answered.

"You really want to go this route?"

"I don't want your focus to be taken off what you're currently doing. I'll handle things here."

"There's nothing wrong with my focus. What's going on?"

"I don't want any distractions for you," Jones repeated.

"David, something's going on and I want you to tell me the truth right now," Recker tersely replied.

"Well…"

Recker didn't even let him finish, thinking he had it figured out. "It's Mia, isn't it?"

"Well…"

"Haven't even been gone one full day," Recker said to himself. "What's the problem?"

"Well, first problem is your initial estimate on how far along she was with her investigation," Jones told him.

"She didn't just start a few days ago?"

"Try four weeks."

Recker closed his eyes for a moment and sighed, afraid to hear what she'd gotten herself into. He rubbed his forehead as he waited for an explanation. "She promised she wouldn't do anything until I got back."

"Well, as she told me, she only promised not to initiate

anything. Unfortunately, she didn't promise she wouldn't respond to something."

"What happened?"

"She received an anonymous phone call to meet someone at an apartment complex to give her information on Joe Simmons," Jones explained.

"Who is this Simmons?"

"Apparently Mia found the name stuffed inside a book in Hanley's apartment when she was helping Susan's mother clean the place out."

"So she's meeting this person?"

"That would be correct."

"And I take it you're going with her?" Recker asked.

"Correct again."

"Well, thank you for that."

"I just hope we're not walking into something we're not equipped for," Jones said.

"Why do you think that?"

"I traced the number that called Mia and it came back to a prepaid phone."

"What time's the meeting?"

"In about ten minutes," Jones answered.

"I hope you're packing some iron with you."

"Though I sincerely hope it doesn't come to that, yes, yes I am."

30

Jones agreed to keep Recker updated with whatever information they learned from this anonymous meeting. Recker wasn't comfortable that they were even going to begin with, but being so far away, there was nothing he could do about it. Knowing that the two closest people he had left in his life were going to what sounded like a dangerous meeting, Recker was extremely anxious to get a call or text from Jones when it was over. Jones was right about Recker being distracted once he learned what was going on. Recker would continue staring at the Edwards house for the next half hour but his mind wasn't really there. Instead, his thoughts were turning to the situation that was five hundred miles away. He kept his phone clenched tightly in his hand as he waited for his ringer to go off. Until he got that call, his concerns over their safety was what was first on his mind.

Jones had gotten to the Haddix Apartments a few minutes before Mia did. He waited in front of the building for her until she arrived. Mia quickly peeled into the parking lot and rushed to the building where Jones was waiting. The Haddix Apartments had seen better days. It was in dire need of a facelift. Though it wasn't a slum of a building, most of the residents were in the lower income group, and quite a few were on the other side of the law. The two of them just stood there looking at the building for a minute, neither sure what they were stepping into.

"Not exactly Rittenhouse Square or Society Hill, is it?" Jones asked.

"Not exactly."

"So what do you want to do?" Jones asked, hoping she'd forget the whole thing and turn around and walk back to her car.

Mia pulled out her phone to check the time. It just turned twelve. "Well, I guess we better get up there. If we're too late, I don't know if whoever it is will wait too long."

"Maybe that's not such a bad thing."

"You don't have to come up with me if you don't want to," Mia told him.

"I'm going wherever you're going."

Even though it was still against his better judgment, Jones put his arm out to indicate he was following her lead. They walked through the front doors and saw a sketchy looking character sitting on the floor and smoking a joint. They immediately noticed the elevator right in front of them and also stairs down the hallway to both sides of them.

"Stairs or elevator?" Mia asked.

"Elevator," Jones replied. "Who knows what we might see if we take the stairs."

They stepped inside the elevator, and Mia hit the button for the second floor. They each had an uneasy feeling in their stomachs, though neither of them contemplated turning back at that point. Mia figured it was more to do with her nerves, not having to do much of this sort of work before, rather than thinking they were in any kind of danger. Jones on the other hand, was more nervous because he was afraid that they were walking into something that they weren't prepared for. And although he used to be part of the NSA, and now worked with Recker, he still wasn't used to being out in the field in these situations. His value was behind the scenes and behind a computer. Field work wasn't exactly his forte. But, with Recker absent, he really didn't have a choice.

Once the elevator doors opened, the pair stepped out into the hallway. They stood there for a moment just looking at their surroundings. They didn't see anything out of the ordinary and began walking, looking at the numbers on the doors as they passed. At the end of the hall was room 217. As they approached, they could see that the door was slightly ajar. They could see that a light was on inside and put their ear up to the door though they couldn't hear any noise. They stood there silently and motionless for a minute, waiting to hear something that would indicate somebody was in there. But there was nothing. Mia just looked at Jones and took a deep breath, ready to continue. She quietly knocked on the door, barely loud enough for even Jones to hear, let alone anyone inside. Jones stepped in front of her and pushed the door open a little farther, big enough for him to get his head through and peak inside.

"Hello? Anyone here?" Jones asked.

They didn't get a reply and Jones pushed the door open all the way, taking a quick look around the room. He looked back at Mia and nodded for her to follow him inside. As they moved throughout the room, noticing their surroundings, there wasn't much to the apartment. There was a small, beat up looking couch with a few holes in it that appeared to be at least ten or twelve years old. Right in front of that was a small card table that looked more like something for a child. Jones checked the bedroom and found a futon folded out into a bed alongside a night table with a lamp sitting on it. Mia went to the kitchen and checked the cabinets and refrigerator. If someone was living there, they didn't have a big appetite. There were only a couple of items in the refrigerator and the only thing in the cabinets were some paper plates and plastic cups. After looking in their respective rooms, Mia and Jones met back up in the living room.

"Do you think someone's even living here?" Mia asked.

"I checked the address before we left and there is a Joe Simmons that is renting the place," Jones answered.

"So was it him that called me and asked to come here? Or was it someone else who knew that he lived here?"

"I guess that's the question that needs answering. But I think we should be leaving."

"Leaving? Already? We just got here," Mia objected.

"Yes, but if the person that called you was not Joe Simmons, and he walks through that door and sees two people standing here in his apartment, I don't think I have to tell you what might happen after that," Jones told her.

"But what if it was him?"

"Then he'll call you again," Jones said, grabbing her arm.

Mia shook her arm free of Jones' grasp, wanting to stay a little longer. "No, I want to get to the bottom of this."

"Mia, we don't know exactly what we've walked into here. I think it best if we leave now."

"Well, why was the door already open?" she asked.

"I have no idea. Perhaps he forgot to close it or maybe he just stepped outside for a minute thinking he'd be back shortly. In any case, I don't think it wise for us to remain here and surprise whoever it is that returns," Jones pleaded.

"But what if this person knows what happened to Susie?"

"What if this person *is* what happened to Susan?"

Mia was starting to come around to Jones' way of thinking and figured if this person did have information for her, then he would've been there. Jones offered to do some more research on Simmons if Mia agreed to leave right then and there. The hair on the back of Jones' neck was standing up as he wasn't getting a good feeling upon being there. Something seemed wrong to him. Though Jones did a precursory check on the address of the apartment, due to time constraints, that was about as far as he got into the man's background. Since Mia's meeting was so soon, he didn't have time to further explore Simmons's history or if he had a criminal past.

"So you'll let me see where you and Mike work your magic?" Mia asked.

"No. But I promise I'll get on it right away."

"You're not gonna cut me out, are you?"

"We'll discuss it in detail once we get out of here," Jones hurriedly replied, trying to rush Mia along so they could get out of there before someone else showed up.

Jones started walking to the door, with Mia right behind him, and removed his phone from his pocket to give Recker a call and let him know what was going on. Just as they got to the frame of the door, a man jumped out from the side and struck Jones in the head with a gun. Jones instantly fell to the ground as his phone flew out of his hand across the hall. He lost consciousness and began bleeding from the top of his head.

"David!" Mia yelled, kneeling down to check on Jones' condition.

She looked up at the professor's attacker, who was simply standing there and staring down at them. He was a younger guy, mid-twenties, blonde hair, athletic build. He had a slight smile on his face, seemingly impressed by his work in striking down one of his visitors. Mia tried tending to Jones' head the best she could, though his attacker started to move her along.

"Get in," he told her, waving his gun in the direction of the apartment.

Mia slowly got up, fearful of what the man was then going to do. She retreated back into the apartment, never taking her eyes off the gun-toting stranger. With Jones still knocked out, the man grabbed the back of the professor's shirt and dragged him back inside, closing the door behind them with his leg.

"Take out your phone and throw it down on the ground," the man said.

Mia complied with the request and tossed it on the floor near the man's feet. He reached down and took the handle of his gun to smash the screen to pieces.

"You got a gun on you?" the man asked.

"No."

"Turn around."

Mia turned around and faced toward the window as the man came up behind her and started patting her down to make sure she didn't have a weapon on her. He took a couple extra liberties in squeezing and grabbing her private parts.

"All right, turn around," the man told her.

"Who are you and what do you want?" Mia nervously asked.

"Don't you know? I'm Joe Simmons."

"You're the one who called me this morning."

Simmons just smiled and nodded. "Yeah. That was me."

"Why? What do you want? Why are you doing this?"

"You're getting too close."

Mia had a feeling she knew what he meant. "You killed Susie. Didn't you?"

"A rather unfortunate event," Simmons answered.

"Why?" Mia asked. She felt like asking a million other questions but that was the only one that she could get through her lips.

"We had a date. Things started to get heated and then for some reason she started resisting. It got a little out of hand after that."

"A little out of hand? You killed her," Mia emotionally said.

"She shouldn't have slapped me like she did. Made me mad," Simmons unapologetically replied.

"You don't seem like it even bothers you in the least."

"Not the first time I've had to do something like that."

"How'd she even meet you anyway?" Mia wondered.

"My cousin was the parent of one of her patients. One day he asked if I could take the kid to see her cause he couldn't get off work. So after it was over I asked if I could take her out sometime," Simmons revealed.

"How many times did you go out with her?"

"Before I killed her? Just once. We had one date before the unfortunate mistake on her part."

Just listening to the man explain himself and keep referring to Hanley's death as an unfortunate event made Mia's blood boil. She'd never hated anyone as much as she did right at that moment. Unfortunately, there was nothing she could do about it. She wasn't armed and wasn't sure how she was going to get out of the situation.

"So how'd you find out about me?" Simmons asked. "Nobody else knew about me. Nobody else was aware we knew each other. Not even the cops. What tipped you off?"

"When I was cleaning out Susie's apartment I saw a piece of paper in one of her books. It had your name on it."

Simmons let out a slight laugh. "I knew it had to be something stupid like that. You talked to my cousin last week and when you mentioned my name, he called me to let me know. I've been keeping tabs on you for the last week."

"So what are you going to do with us?" Mia wondered, hoping not to hear what she thought she would.

Simmons shrugged, waving his gun around. "Well, unfortunately for you, you now know my secret. You know who I am, you know what happened to your friend, and I just can't let you go walking around with that kind of knowledge, now can I?"

"And if I say that I won't tell anyone?"

Simmons laughed, amused at the request. "Do I look that stupid?"

"Well, kind of," Mia joked.

"Sorry, lady. You and your friend are going to be joining your other friend in a few minutes. By the way, who is this guy?" Simmons wondered.

"Just a friend."

"You sure have a lot of friends who are gonna turn up dead."

"You don't think we came up here without telling anyone, did you?" Mia asked, hoping to delay what she hoped wasn't inevitable.

"You're lying."

Mia shrugged.

"Who'd you tell?" Simmons asked, now getting a slight look of concern on his face.

"You'll meet them soon enough. Unless they kill you before you get a chance to see their faces," Mia told him, hoping to get him nervous enough that he'd just leave.

"Sorry, I think I'm better off just blowing the both of your heads off before anyone else arrives and just blowing the scene."

Simmons raised his gun up to Mia's head, about a foot away from her forehead and was about to pull the trigger. Mia closed her eyes, not believing that she was stupid enough to put themselves in that situation. Recker was right, she thought. She wasn't trained in this sort of thing and she wasn't prepared for what might result from her asking questions. If she was going to find her way out of her predicament, she was going to have to think of something fast.

"If you kill me, there's no place on earth that you can hide from him," Mia quickly stated, almost stumbling over her words to get them out before he pulled the trigger.

"From who?" Simmons wondered.

"I told him that I was coming here," she said, breathing heavily as she tried to think.

"Told who?" Simmons angrily asked.

"If I don't make it out of here, there's nowhere that you can go that he won't find you."

"I'm not gonna ask a third time."

"The Silencer," she finally revealed.

Recker's reputation had grown so much that everyone knew his moniker. Most people thought he did good work, helping those in need. But criminals like Simmons and others of his ilk, had become deathly afraid of hearing his name. Most that had rap sheets, except for the extremely dangerous ones, hoped to never cross paths with him. Simmons could be counted among those that hoped to never find him. Though he was dangerous in his own right, after the countless stories that he'd heard over the past year involving Recker, he wasn't eager to mix it up with him.

"You know The Silencer?" Simmons asked.

Mia hesitated, hearing the worry in his voice as he said the name. "Yes."

"How do you know him?"

"I'm just a friend."

"Just a friend, huh? How do I know you're telling the truth? Maybe you're lying and just saying that," Simmons stated.

"I'm not. He already knows about you."

Simmons didn't seem to be convinced. "Yeah, well, if he knows about me then why isn't he here right now instead of you and the professor looking guy over there?"

"He was attending to something else, and I told him that I could do this and there wouldn't be any problems," Mia explained.

"Looks like you were incorrect on that one," Simmons scoffed.

"Tell me about it."

"Well if he's on my trail, then it doesn't look like I need you either way," Simmons said, raising his gun up again.

"No, please," Mia pleaded. "I can get him to back off you. But I can only do that if we walk out of here alive."

Jones began to stir and noticed that Simmons seemed to be so preoccupied with Mia that he didn't even pay any attention to him. Though he still felt a little groggy and was sure he had a concussion, he knew he had to do something if the two of them were going to walk out of there alive. He reached inside his coat pocket and withdrew the gun he took out of Recker's safe. He quickly pointed it at Simmons and pulled the trigger. Jones had fired too hastily though and didn't take long enough to aim properly. His vision was somewhat blurry, and he had more time than he thought he would. He missed Simmons completely; the bullet lodging into the wall behind him. Simmons ducked and ran over to Jones and kicked the gun out of his hand, then punched him in the face. Jones blacked out again.

With Simmons's back turned towards her, Mia rushed over to him and jumped on his back, hoping to dislodge the gun from his hand. After a brief struggle, Simmons hunched over and flung Mia over his shoulder. She landed hard on the wood floor, the back of her head striking it. She winced in pain as she grasped the back of her head. Simmons took a few steps back to make sure there was a safe distance between him and his two hostages, both of whom were still laying on the floor. He still held his gun out, taking turns at pointing to both of his would-be victims as he contemplated his next move. He wasn't completely sure that the woman in front of him was being honest that she knew The Silencer. But he thought it seemed like an odd thing for someone to blurt out, even one who was in as much trouble as she was. If she really did know him, and he killed her, Simmons knew he was as good as dead. But, if he were to take them with him to find out the truth, and they did know him, then Simmons could trade their lives for his own personal safety. And if it turned out that they didn't know The Silencer, then he could kill them at a later time. After a couple more minutes debating with himself the merits of both killing them, or taking them with him, he finally decided on what action to take.

"All right, get up," Simmons said.

Mia did as instructed and slowly got to her feet, thinking both her and Jones were as good as dead. She was a bit surprised when Simmons told them he was taking them with him.

"Get your friend up too," Simmons told her.

"He needs medical attention," Mia replied.

"He'll be fine. Whatever he needs, you can do it."

"What are you gonna do with us now?"

"I'm gonna take you with me for now. If you really do know The Silencer, then you're gonna call him and you're gonna get him off my trail," Simmons informed her.

"Well you already smashed my phone so I can't call him."

"What about his?"

Mia knelt and searched through Jones' pockets but couldn't find his phone anywhere. She thought she saw him with it but couldn't be sure of where it went to.

"I can't find it," Mia told him.

"Whatever. We don't have time right now anyway," Simmons said. "Cops are probably gonna be here soon enough. Someone probably heard that shot and called it in. We have to get going."

"So where are you taking us?"

"I'm gonna take you to a place nobody else knows about. Then you're gonna contact your friend. Wake your friend up and get him on his feet. And you better not be lying to me or else I'll kill you on the spot."

31

Recker didn't stop worrying about what Jones and Mia were doing, especially since he didn't know the exact specifics. That sinking feeling in the pit of his stomach that told him something was wrong only intensified as the time rolled by. He glanced at his phone just as the time changed to one o'clock. He started fidgeting around as he contemplated what he wanted to do. Either Jones or Mia should've checked in with him by now. With his experience, he'd attended several of these informant meetings and he never had one that lasted this long. Even if someone was late, it should've only lasted five, or ten minutes tops.

Recker now had a dilemma. Did he stay and wait for Edwards to show up? Or did he forget about him and head back to Philadelphia to check on his friends? If Jones and Mia were in trouble, they would need every second of his time that Recker could give. If Edwards didn't show up for another five or six hours, that was precious time that he wasn't sure his friends had enough of. After a few minutes of thought, there was no other decision for him to make. Even if he got back to Philadelphia and found his friends were safe, he now knew where Edwards lived. He could always come back. And if the unthinkable happened, and his friends were no longer among the living, finding and killing Edwards would be the only thing he had left.

Before leaving, he tried calling Jones' phone a couple times. He then sent him a few text messages urging him to let him know they were OK. After five minutes, he turned his attention to Mia's phone. He tried her number a few times, but hers went straight to voicemail. That was an immediate red flag as Recker knew she never turned her phone off. With her position as a nurse, she previously had told him that she never had her phone off unless it was broken somehow. Mia always kept it on in case of an emergency. Even if she was in a setting where the ringer had to be off or something, she just set it to vibrate so she could still be alerted.

Recker put his car in drive and headed back toward the highway. If he hurried, he thought he had a chance to make it back in eleven or twelve hours. But in the middle of the day, there was a good chance he'd hit some traffic on the way. If Jones and Mia were in as much trouble as Recker suspected they were, he was going to need some help before he got back. He picked his phone back up and started making some calls.

"Tyrell, I need a big favor," Recker immediately said.

"Name it."

"There's a couple people I think are in trouble. One of them's the professor."

"OK?"

"They told me they were meeting someone at the Haddix Apartment complex at twelve. They still haven't checked in yet. I get the feeling something's wrong."

"So why don't you just go there yourself?" Gibson asked.

MIKE RYAN

"I'm in Ohio right now. I'm on my way back there but I'm at least ten or twelve hours away."

"Ohio? What the hell you doing down there?"

"A story for another time. Do you think you can go there and check out the place? Do you have the time?" Recker asked.

"For you, yeah, I got the time. Haddix Apartments?"

"Yeah. You familiar with it?"

"Yeah, I been there a few times," Gibson answered.

"Well? What about it? What kind of place is it?"

"There's only two reasons most people go there."

"Which are?"

"You either looking for trouble or you running away from it."

"Crap."

"So if you haven't heard from them... they most likely found it."

"All right. How soon can you get there?" Recker asked.

"Gimme about twenty minutes. What's the room number?"

"217. Call me when you get there."

"Will do."

These were the sorts of scenarios that Recker told Jones about when they first started this operation. No matter how good Jones was with computers, like Recker said, he still needed eyes and ears out on the street. There would be times that you needed contacts, friends, people you trusted to do things that a computer couldn't. As Recker continued to drive, his worst fears were starting to flutter front and center in his mind. He couldn't shake the feeling that at least one, or even both, were dead or badly hurt. The next twenty minutes were probably the second longest of his life. The only other instance in which time seemed to go by so slowly was that night in London after Carrie was killed. In that case, it seemed like time stopped completely. The biggest difference now was that he just didn't know. Usually, the uncertainty of not knowing was almost as bad as the pain of knowing the end result. At least with Carrie, though he never had closure yet, or a sense of finality with her killer still at large, at least he had the knowledge that there was nothing else that could be done to save her. Now, he didn't know whether his friends were alive or dead. And that ate him up just as bad.

Recker kept checking the time, counting down until Gibson called. Once the twenty-minute mark was up, and still no call, Recker started worrying more. He imagined that Gibson walked in on a bloody crime scene. He quickly shook his head, trying to get the visions out of his mind and think more positively. Five more minutes passed by with still no word from Gibson. Recker had never been much of an anxious person. Never seemed to worry about much or let much bother him. But when it came to his friends, he was worried sick. As Recker sped down the road, another five minutes came and went before his phone finally started ringing.

"Tyrell, what took you so long? You said twenty minutes," Recker said.

"Man, you know Philly traffic. Took me like twenty-five minutes just to get here," Gibson responded.

"So what's the situation there? How's it looking?" Recker asked with a lump in his throat, praying he wouldn't get the answer that he feared.

"Place is empty, man."

"Empty?"

"Yeah. I mean, like, real empty. Hardly even looks like somebody lives here. If they do, they must not believe in modern technology or anything."

"Tell me what you see. Any signs of a struggle or a fight or anything?"

Gibson looked around the room but didn't notice anything.

"Nah, man. Like I said, there's not even much here to mess up. Even if there was a fight there's no way of knowing."

"Damn," Recker sighed, thinking of his next course of action.

"Hold up, there's a hole in the wall."

"What kind of hole?"

"Like a bullet hole."

"What's near it?"

"Whaddya mean, what's near it?"

"Well is there blood on the wall or floor underneath it?" Recker asked.

"Nah, nothing."

"Whoever shot it must've missed their target then."

"Anything else?"

"Not that I see. Wait a minute, wait a minute," Gibson stated, walking to the other side of the room and looking more closely at the floor and wall where Jones had been propped up.

"What is it?"

Gibson knelt by the wall and touched the red mark on the floor with his finger to analyze it. "It's blood, man."

"You notice anything else? Maybe something that was dropped by mistake, or even on purpose? Anything that seems out of place?"

"No, like I said, there ain't much here to begin with," Gibson answered, moving throughout the apartment just to double check.

"The only thing you see is the blood?" Recker asked.

"Yeah, that's it."

"How much is it? Like someone got shot?"

"Uh, no, I don't think so. It's not like a big pool or anything, more like a couple drips here or there. More like someone got busted up in the head or something. Maybe even the hand."

"Thanks Tyrell."

"No problem. I don't know what it was, but something went down here. What's the name of the dude that lives here, anyway?"

"Professor told me the name was Joe Simmons," Recker replied.

"Joe Simmons," Gibson repeated. "Joe Simmons."

"You don't know him, do you?"

"I dunno. For some reason that name rings a bell. Like I heard of him somewhere before."

"Well think. There's two lives that are hanging in the balance here."

"I'm thinking, I'm thinking."

"Yeah, well, while you're doing that, check one more thing for me?" Recker wondered.

"Depends."

"Check the parking lot and see if their cars are there?"

Since it was such a simple request, Gibson agreed and left the room to head down to the parking lot. Recker let him know the makes of Jones' and Mia's car along with the license plate numbers. Once Gibson got down to the lot and spent a few minutes checking, he spotted Jones' car. He walked behind the car and looked at the license plate, getting a match.

"I know you won't like this, but I got the professor's car here," Gibson revealed.

"What about the other one?"

Gibson walked past a few more cars then stopped, noticing a car that fit the description that Recker gave him. He went to the rear of the car and read the plate number, once again getting a match.

"There's number two," Gibson stated.

"You found it?"

"Yeah. Both here."

"Anything unusual? Unlocked, blood, anything?" Recker wondered.

"No. Both locked up tight. No sign of anything else."

"So that means they were both taken somewhere."

"That's a good sign," Gibson replied. "Means they're probably still alive. Otherwise they would've just killed them upstairs."

"Unless they killed them and were dumping the bodies somewhere."

"That's a lot of work to go through all that."

"If it's the person I think we're dealing with, then they got the history of it," Recker said.

"Whatcha mean?"

"I think they might've been meeting the person that killed that girl we found stuffed in the trunk a few months ago."

"Oh man. That's bad news then."

"I know. Anything else on the name? Remember where you heard it before?" Recker asked.

"Nah, I just can't place it. I know I never did business with him before directly or else I'd remember that," Gibson answered. "But I feel like I met him before somewhere. Maybe he was in a group and I remember the name but he wasn't like a main player."

"Well if that's the case then who would you have met in a group that would have someone like that involved?"

"Well, if I'm actually remembering right, then there's only two guys that would have a crew in a group setting that I'd have done business with."

"Let me guess... Vincent or Jeremiah?"

"That's it."

"If this is the guy we're looking for, sounds like an MO that he learned working for Vincent," Recker said.

"How you figure?"

"People that fell victim to Vincent or his crew don't always turn up at the same spot that they were killed. Sometimes they get moved or staged to a different area for whatever reasons. Jeremiah doesn't usually stage his killings. He'll just leave them where they fall."

"Yeah, yeah, that's right. Like, um, that Italian dude that shot you that wound up in that alley a few months back," Gibson said.

"Yeah."

"If Simmons's really part of Vincent's crew, I don't know how happy he's gonna be if you wind up taking him out."

"Let me worry about that."

"You need me to do anything else?"

"Not unless you can find out where Simmons might've gone," Recker responded.

"I mean, I can put some feelers out and see what happened, but I can't really promise much from that."

"Yeah, do what you can do. I appreciate it."

"You got it, bro."

As soon as he hung up, Recker knew what he had to do. He'd have to call Vincent and explain the situation and ask for another favor. Having to ask Vincent to do another thing for him wasn't the ideal scenario. Recker knew that at some point, he was going to have to repay the favors that Vincent had done for him. And however it was that Vincent wanted him to repay those favors, it wasn't likely to be something that Recker would like doing, but he would have no choice but to do it. Regardless of that, Recker didn't have any other options left. He'd have to worry about everything he owed Vincent at a later time.

There also was a different problem that occurred to Recker. And that was if Vincent was somehow involved in the disappearance of Jones and Mia. He was sure that Vincent had no idea that they were friends of his, but the thought crossed his mind, what if for some reason Vincent ordered the killing of Susan Hanley?

Recker couldn't wrap his head around why a mob boss would want someone like her killed, but he'd seen and heard of stranger things before. If that was true, then he would have also been responsible for Jones and Mia's situation right now.

If Vincent had Simmons kill the Hanley woman, and Mia somehow uncovered information that indicated such, then she'd be directly in his crosshairs. Even though it all made sense, and it certainly seemed plausible, it was still a big leap to make. Recker still wasn't sure how Hanley would be connected to Vincent to make that big of a conclusion. He figured he'd have to call and gauge Vincent's reaction to what he told him. If Vincent denied Simmons worked for him, or that he had no knowledge of anything and played dumb, then that would indicate that Vincent was involved. But if Vincent acknowledged that Simmons was one of his guys, and he seemed concerned about what was going on, then perhaps everything was being done without his knowledge.

Either way, Recker was going to have to call Vincent to find out. If he wasn't working against a time deadline, and his two friends weren't missing, then there might've been another way around it. Recker could've found out in a more discreet manner than by alerting someone he wasn't sure was innocent or not. But that wasn't the situation he found himself in and he'd just have to take his chances. The one good thing about his past dealings with Vincent was that Recker now had a direct line of communication with him. He didn't have to go through third parties or other sources to get into contact with Vincent quickly. And while he didn't have Vincent's personal number, he had Malloy's, and considering he was his right-hand man and almost always by his side, it basically amounted to the same thing. He dialed the number as he drove, getting through on the second ring.

"Recker," Malloy cautiously answered. "What can I do for you?"

"I need to talk to your boss."

"What about?"

"It's urgent," Recker answered.

"You're gonna have to do better than that."

Not wanting to reveal specifics yet, Recker thought of a generic answer while still conveying the general tone of the message. "There's a couple cases I've been working on and I need to know whether he's involved or not before I know how to proceed."

"He's not readily available right now," Malloy stalled.

"Well get him available. Cause if he's not, and one of his men is responsible for what I'm working on, then he's gonna have to worry about getting a new guy. Cause this one's gonna be dead."

Sensing the seriousness of the situation, Malloy dropped the stall tactics and thought it best to get his boss on the line. "Hold on."

It didn't even take thirty seconds before Vincent got on the other end of the phone. "Mike, what can I help you with?"

"I need answers. And I need the truth."

"Well I'll tell you what I can depending on the specifics of the question," Vincent replied, not sounding the least bit concerned or bothered.

"There was a woman doctor who was killed about three months ago," Recker explained. "She was found stuffed in the trunk of a car which was found near the airport. Do you know anything about that?"

Vincent took a few seconds to genuinely think about the question. "I seem to recall hearing something about that though I don't know too much of the specifics. Why do you ask?"

"I've been close to finding out the killer and I think he works for you. I need to know if you were involved and if the order came from you," Recker told him.

"It did not," Vincent quickly replied. "If it was someone who works for me, then it was done without my knowledge or consent."

"Which leads me to my next problem. Two more people, civilians, friends of this woman, started looking into her death on their own time."

"Let me guess… they're now in trouble?"

"They found this guy that I was looking at and now they're both missing," Recker said.

"And you're wondering if I'm involved in the death of this woman and the disappearance of her friends."

"That's pretty much it."

"Considering it's you who's asking, I'll help you out with your problem," Vincent stated. "If it was anybody else, I wouldn't give them the time of day."

"Understood."

"I will tell you with complete honesty and the utmost respect that what's happened, or happening, to these people… I have nothing to do with."

"Then that's good enough for me. I accept you for your word."

"Good. Now that that's out of the way, you said you were looking for someone who you believe is part of my crew. I'm assuming you have a name."

"I do. The name is Joe Simmons," Recker revealed.

Vincent did not immediately respond as he recognized the name instantly. He let it sink in for a minute before responding. With Vincent's hesitation, Recker assumed that he was familiar with the name.

"Considering you didn't immediately say that you had no idea who he is, I take it that you do know him," Recker said.

Vincent took another moment to respond. "Yes, Joe Simmons is one of my men."

Neither Recker nor Vincent knew what else to say after that

revelation and both stayed silent for a minute. Vincent's curiosity then took hold, wondering what Recker was planning on doing.

"How exactly do you plan to proceed now with that knowledge?" Vincent asked.

"I plan to proceed and find Joe Simmons. He doesn't happen to be with you now, is he?"

"He is not. He is called when he's needed."

"Oh."

"And if or when you do find him? What then?"

"There's a good chance I'm gonna kill him," Recker answered. "Is he a high-ranking member of your organization that you'd object to that?"

"No. He's a grunt man. He's usually used for things that might involve a little muscle. He's not involved in day-to-day matters."

"Then you won't have a problem with me killing him."

"Are you asking for my blessing in killing one of my men?" Vincent wondered.

"I just want to make sure we don't have any problems or issues that arise out of this."

Vincent took a few more seconds to think before responding, getting a little more angry about the situation, though he didn't let it show. "We will not. I'll do you one better."

"What's that?" Recker asked.

"We'll find Joe Simmons for you."

"I'm not asking you to do that."

"You don't have to. If he's done these things as you suggest he has then he's operating without my knowledge or approval on these matters," Vincent tersely stated. "And if that's the case then he's defying my wishes and orders."

"So you'll make an example out of him?"

"Think of it as you wish. Sometimes those in positions of

power must do things that will shock and awe in order to keep the rest of the herd inline."

"Well that's up to you. My main interest is getting these innocent people back safe and sound," Recker replied.

"We both have our own motives for finding him. It might help to know where you think these people have been or where they were taken."

"I believe they were taken at the Haddix Apartments. Simmons had a room there."

"I know the place. He had a room there that he used as a front in order to conduct some business dealings," Vincent explained. "When did all this occur?"

"They were supposed to meet with him about twelve," Recker answered.

"I assume you've already been there."

"I'm currently out of state. I was working on another case but I'm on my way back now. I had someone check the apartment though and there's no one there."

"I'll have someone check his home, though I'm fairly certain he wouldn't have taken them there."

"Where would he go?"

"There's a few places I can think of. How far away are you?"

"Probably about ten or twelve hours," Recker replied.

"Don't rush. We'll find him."

"What am I gonna owe you?"

"We'll talk about it another time," Vincent responded. "Let's accomplish our goal first. Once we locate him, we'll give you a call."

Recker was relieved in some fashion. At least he now knew that Vincent wasn't involved in anything, but he wouldn't feel total relief until he knew both Jones and Mia were safe and unharmed. Though he had total confidence in Vincent's ability to find his employee, he still worried about whether he'd find Simmons before he did something stupid. Once Vincent ended the conversation with Recker, he turned to his right-hand man to get the manhunt started.

"We're looking for Joe Simmons?" Malloy asked, overhearing the conversation.

"Yes."

"What for? What'd he do?"

"Recker believes he killed some doctor a few months ago and stuffed her in a trunk by the airport," Vincent explained.

"So?"

"Recker also believes her friends went looking for answers and ran into Joe a little over an hour ago and haven't been heard from since."

"Excuse me for saying so, boss, but what's that got to do with us? I mean, so what? What do we care?" Malloy wondered.

"Our reasons for caring are twofold," Vincent replied. "One, as a favor to Recker to further deepen our relationship and foster goodwill between us. As I've said before, the day will come when perhaps his services will be useful to us. And when it comes, he'll remember times like these when we helped him."

"And second?"

"Secondly, I gave explicit orders months ago that everyone was to lay low and not do anything without my orders or permission. Not one person under my command has the authority to kill anyone without my say so," Vincent angrily stated.

"I know."

"Killing is dangerous business. Kill the wrong person, at the wrong time, make careless mistakes, things have a way of unraveling and coming back to you. Unless it's under self-defense, killing is not something that's to be done haphazardly. If it's found out by the law or the public that Joe killed that woman, and then he kidnapped or killed these two people today... that's bad for our business. They'll find out his connection to me and bring unwanted attention to our operation."

"Understood," Malloy said.

"Besides all that, Joe's a minor player in our business. As I explained to Recker, sometimes examples need to be made to show that insubordination will not be tolerated or allowed. If it was someone more important in our day-to-day operations, perhaps we'd be more calculated on our decisions or even let it slide. But under the circumstances, we'll use this to further cement that my authority is not to be willfully or carelessly ignored."

32

It'd been roughly an hour since Recker and Vincent's conversation. Immediately after, Vincent sent teams of his men out into the city, scouring different buildings in search of finding Joe Simmons. Since Simmons was one of the low men on the totem pole in Vincent's business, he didn't always have steady employment from the mob boss, so he often did several things of the illegal variety on the side.

Simmons knew that if The Silencer was on his tail like Mia suggested, then he couldn't go back to his own home. He took his prisoners to a vacant one story building in the northeast part of the city that used to house several different offices. Simmons tied them each to a chair and separated them, placing them in different rooms.

"What's his phone number?" Simmons asked.

"I'm not telling you," Mia replied.

"If you value your life, you'll tell me. Otherwise, I'm just gonna wind up killing the both of you now and take my chances with him."

"That would be foolish."

"Yeah, well, wouldn't be the first time I did that.."

She was kicking herself for the situation she was now in. Not only did she put her own life in danger, she put Jones' life in jeopardy as well. In addition to that, she knew she was going to put Recker in a tough position in regards to how he was going to handle Simmons. Not to mention the fact that she felt he was going to be furious with her for making him drop whatever he was doing to come rescue her. Mia was so mad at herself that for a brief moment she felt like she deserved whatever Simmons had planned for her. Simmons took his phone out and held it out for Mia to see.

"The number?" Simmons asked again.

Mia tilted her head back, and looked away as she revealed Recker's phone number to him. Simmons gave her an evil glare, not sure she was giving him the right information.

"It better be right," Simmons told her. "If it's not, I'm not trying again."

"It's right," Mia huffed.

The number started dialing and Recker picked up after the second ring. Not recognizing the number, Recker had hoped it was one of Vincent's crew calling him with information that they'd uncovered about Simmons's whereabouts.

"Yeah?" Recker greeted.

"Is this The Silencer?"

"Who's this?"

"I have the pleasure of having two people in my company right now," Simmons answered. "I'm told they're somewhat important to you."

"You're Joe Simmons."

"That's right."

"Are they OK?" Recker asked.

"They're fine for now. You're one friend has a few knots in his head but he'll survive for the moment."

"So what do you want?"

"The girl here told me that you were on my trail," Simmons responded. "I'm willing to do some business with you."

"What do you want?" Recker repeated.

"I'll trade their lives for mine."

"How's that?"

"I'll let them go with the assurance that you forget about me," Simmons offered.

"What makes you think I can or will do that?"

"If you don't, then they're as good as dead."

"And if I agree, what makes you think I won't still come after you?"

"Because I've looked in their wallets and seen their ID's. I know who they are, and I know where they live. You come after me, I go after them," Simmons told him. "I'll even leave the city. I just want your word that you'll let me go and won't come after me."

Fearing the alternative, Recker felt he didn't have any other options but to agree to Simmons's terms. It was actually a good offer as it's probably one that Recker would've offered anyway if it meant getting his friends back unharmed. But the fact that Simmons came up with it right away and without any other strings attached basically made it a no-brainer for Recker to accept the terms.

"Well?" Simmons wondered.

"I'll agree to your conditions," Recker said. "On one condition."

"What's that?"

"I need to hear that they're still alive."

"What? Don't you trust me?"

"Not really."

"I wouldn't try to pull a fast one on you. I know you'd just come after me if I did," Simmons replied.

"I want to hear them," Recker persisted.

"Fine."

Simmons looked at Mia and put the phone up to her ear for her to talk to her friend.

"Say something," Simmons told her.

"I'm so sorry. I'm so sorry for putting you through this," Mia sobbed.

"It's alright. It's OK. I'm gonna get you out of there," Recker replied. "Does this guy know my name?"

"No, no."

"OK, good. Are you and David OK?"

Mia sniffled but kept herself together. "Yeah. Yeah, we're OK."

"All right, that's enough of that," Simmons interjected. "Everyone's OK for now."

"All right. Let them go and you have my word I won't come after you."

"Well, I'm not exactly that trusting of you either."

"What do you mean by that?" Recker asked.

"I'm not gonna just let both of them go and then hope you'll live up to the deal. I'll let one of them go now. The other I'll take with me until I'm out of the city. Once I'm out, I'll put them on a train or a bus back here."

"That's not what I just agreed to."

"Well I'm changing the deal."

"I'm not comfortable with that," Recker objected.

"Either that's the deal or I can just put a couple bullets in their heads right now and take my chances."

"If you do that, I will hunt you down until the ends of the earth. There is no place you can hide from me."

"I release one now and the other I'll send back," Simmons insisted. "Or else."

Recker just shook his head, not liking the new terms. He wasn't in much of a position to bargain though. Agreeing was his only option. "Fine. Release the girl."

Simmons just laughed. "Yeah, I knew you'd say that. No chance. She comes with me."

"Why?"

"Cause she's better company," he teased.

"Fine," Recker said, getting angrier by the minute.

There was no way Recker was just going to let Simmons take Mia out of the city and hope that he was a man of his word and send her back. Recker was going to find him before he got out of the city limits.

"So we have a deal?" Simmons asked.

"Yeah."

"I'll leave your man Jones here tied up for you. And just in case you decide that since I won't be here with him that you can just come after me first, I'm gonna make sure that's not a wise move."

"What's that supposed to mean?" Recker wondered.

"I've planted an explosive in the room that he's in. If he's still sitting there in an hour... well then, I guess he's gonna go boom," Simmons said with a laugh.

"You're bluffing."

"Maybe I am. Maybe I'm not. You really can't afford to find out though, can you?"

"You've got one hour to get your friend out of here or else this building will explode," Simmons warned.

"You gotta give me the address."

"It's a vacant office building on Knights. You find it."

Simmons then hung up and Recker shouted an expletive as he tossed the phone down on the front seat beside him. He obviously couldn't get there in an hour. He had two options at that point. Tyrell or Vincent. Since he was part of Vincent's crew, Recker figured he might've had an idea of what building he was talking about. He quickly picked his phone back up and dialed Vincent's number.

"What's up?" Malloy answered.

"Is Vincent there?"

Malloy immediately handed the phone over to his boss. "What can I do for you, Mike?"

"I just got a call from Simmons," Recker revealed.

"Oh?"

"He's holding them in a vacant office building somewhere on Knights. Have any idea where he's talking about?"

Vincent thought for a second and seemed to think he might have known where Simmons was. "Yeah, I might have an idea. There's a couple places there that could fit the bill."

"There's complications."

"There usually are," Vincent replied.

"He agreed to let the two people go if I agreed to let him out of the city," Recker told him.

"And your reply?"

"I didn't have much choice but to agree. But he's taking the girl with him and said when he's out of the city he'll send her back."

"And you don't believe him?"

"I'm skeptical."

"As well you should be."

"The guy, he's leaving there for me. But he said if I'm not there in an hour, the room he's in is gonna explode. He said he planted an explosive that'll go off in one hour," Recker explained.

"And you obviously won't be able to get there in time to save him," Vincent stated.

"Yeah."

"Say no more. We'll take it from here."

"Are you sure?"

"No need for you to worry about it anymore. It's my problem now. Your two victims will be safe and sound and Joe's not going to take anyone out of the city."

"What are you gonna do?" Recker wondered.

"That's for me to figure out. Enjoy your drive back, no need to rush and risk getting pulled over by state police or anything," Vincent said with a smile. "I'll only call you if there's an unforeseen problem. If you don't hear from me, assume everything's gone well."

"Uh... all right."

"Call me when you get back in town and we'll arrange a meeting."

"OK. I'll do that. Thanks."

"Don't mention it."

Recker wasn't sure how to feel anymore. Part of him felt like he should be relieved that Vincent assured him that he'd take over the situation from there and make sure everyone was unharmed. But part of him was still a little nervous and anxious as he was basically putting his trust, and the lives of Jones and Mia, in the hands of a crime lord. And even though Vincent had proved trustworthy in all their dealings up to that point and never gave Recker reason to doubt anything he ever told him, he was still the head of a criminal organization. No matter what, Recker was still going to worry until he saw that his two friends were safe. Or at the least heard their voices.

Vincent handed the phone back to Malloy and started to discuss their plans moving forward. Vincent was not about to let Joe Simmons out of the city. Hearing what Simmons's intentions were only affirmed to Vincent that he was making the right decision in helping Recker. If Simmons really was threatening to blow up the building one of his prisoners was in, and he was intent on taking the girl out of town with him, it was an indication to Vincent that the man was becoming unhinged. That was a lot of carnage and destruction, along with heat from law enforcement, that he wasn't authorized to unleash.

"Joe's become unglued," Vincent said. "He's threatening to take the girl out of town and blow up a building with the other guy he took if Recker's not there in an hour."

"So what do you wanna do?" Malloy asked.

"We won't let this drag on any longer. Call him and find out where he is. We'll come to him."

Malloy nodded and started dialing Simmons's number. Every time they had tried to call him previously, the call just went to his voicemail. Now they knew he was avoiding their calls and since he just called Recker, they knew his phone had to be on. Malloy kept trying but to no avail. Simmons just wasn't picking up. Vincent nodded and put his hand up for Malloy to stop trying, indicating it was OK. Vincent got out his own phone and started dialing Simmons's number. It was rare for Vincent to call any of his own men personally. It was usually Malloy that acted as the intermediary. All of Vincent's men were programmed that if he called them personally, it was extremely important, and they needed to pick up the phone immediately or else there would be consequences for them ignoring his call. After the third ring, Simmons finally picked up his phone, mostly out of fear of what would happen to him if he didn't answer his boss' call.

"Joe, we've been trying to call you for a while now," Vincent told him.

"Sorry boss, I was just in the middle of a few things."

"Oh? Anything I need to know about?"

"No, no. Nothing important. Just trying to square some things away. Did you need me for something?" Simmons worriedly asked.

"Well, as a matter of fact, that brings me to why I called," Vincent calmly stated. "I've heard some rumblings that are terribly concerning to me."

"What's that?"

"I've been told that right now you're holding two people against their will inside a vacant office building on Knights Road. Is that correct?"

"Umm...," Simmons stumbled, not wanting to lie to his leader in fear of what would happen if he did. But he also didn't want to admit the truth and have to explain himself.

"You don't have to say anything. I already know where you're at and who's with you."

Simmons took a big gulp, afraid of what he was going to hear next.

"I've also heard that you're responsible for the killing of some female doctor that was found in the trunk of a car by the airport a few months back. Is that correct?" Vincent asked.

"Mr. Vincent, I can explain."

"I don't want explanations, Joe. I also don't want apologies. It's too late for both of those things."

"I'm sorry."

"Mr. Vincent, The Silencer's on my trail, I'm just trying to somehow stay ahead of him," Simmons said.

"The Silencer, huh?"

"Yes, sir."

"What are your plans right now?" Vincent asked.

Even though Vincent already knew the situation, he was trying to play coy to get Simmons's guard down. If Simmons suspected that Vincent was also gunning for him, he'd leave town in a split second. Of course, Vincent believed he could track him down if need be, but it'd take a lot more work than planned and more effort than what he thought was necessary. It'd be much easier to bring Simmons in if he believed that Vincent was on his side. Simmons then explained the situation to his boss, telling him about his plans, his deal with Recker, even the explosive that he had planted.

"I'll tell you what, Joe. I want you to stay put and don't do anything for right now," Vincent told him.

Simmons stuttered at first, nervous about staying there with Recker on the way. "But I, uh, I… I don't know if I can handle him on my own."

"Just listen to what I tell you and you'll be fine. I'm going to send Jimmy and some other boys with him to your location. We'll set a trap for The Silencer when he gets there and we'll take him out for you. That way you never have to worry about him again and you don't have to think about leaving town."

"Mr. Vincent, thank you. Thank you. I appreciate your help," Simmons replied.

"No problem, Joe. I just wish you would've come to me sooner and we wouldn't have had to go through all this trouble. We'll take care of you though, don't worry."

"Should I get rid of these people first?"

"No. You keep them right where they are. We'll use them as part of the trap. Just keep them unharmed for now," Vincent answered.

"OK. No problem. When should Jimmy get here?"

"Give him about twenty or thirty minutes."

Simmons then proceeded to give Vincent his location, though the crime boss already had a good idea that that's where he was. Still, it avoided any possibilities of errors and lost time. As soon as Vincent got off the phone, he gave Malloy the address and told him to grab a few of his men so they could leave right away. After his conversation with his boss, Simmons was now feeling pretty confident. Even with Recker's reputation, he didn't think he could match up with all of Vincent's crew just waiting there for him. Simmons then went back into the room where Mia was.

"Looks like a change of plans, sweetheart," he said.

"What?"

"I was originally going to take you with me as an insurance policy but it looks like that won't be necessary."

"Why not? What are you gonna do?" Mia asked.

"I just talked to my boss. He instructed me to stay here and we'll deal with your friend in the appropriate manner."

"You're setting a trap for him?" she worriedly asked.

Simmons just grinned, happy at the change of plans.

"But you made a deal," Mia told him.

"Sometimes things don't work out the way you planned. Just sit tight for a while and it'll all be over soon."

Simmons then took out a white rag and shoved it in Mia's mouth, wrapping a piece of string around the back of her head to prevent her from talking and warning Recker when he arrived. Once he secured her and made sure she wasn't going anywhere, he left the room to check on his other prisoner. Mia started squirming, struggling to break free of her restraints. She tried wiggling loose, kicking her legs in the air, frantically wanting to get out from her ropes. After a few minutes she knew it was no use. She was locked in tight. Her heart sank as she thought about what Recker was about to walk into. They were being used to get to him. Though she hoped against all hope that Recker could somehow survive and fight his way through whatever obstacles he was up against, she knew it'd be tough sledding for him.

Simmons then went into the other room where Jones was sitting. The professor was sitting quietly and still, knowing that Recker was already somehow on the case. Since he told Recker he'd check in after the meeting, he figured alarm bells were going off once he never contacted him. That and the fact that Mia wasn't answering her phone either, Jones knew that he was either on the way or getting someone there in his place. Jones had a calm expression on his face and Simmons noticed that his prisoner didn't look worried. Unlike Mia, who Simmons could tell was a little upset and worried about what was happening, Jones didn't seem to have the same attitude.

"You seem awfully calm considering what's going on," Simmons stated.

"Worrying isn't going to change or alter whatever happens here," Jones replied.

"That's a very good attitude you have there. You know, in my original plan, I was thinking about putting a bomb in here. Maybe The Silencer would get to you in time, maybe he wouldn't. But there was a very good chance that you might've exploded."

"And that plan has changed?"

"I've got some friends coming. There's no need for me to be cute or play games. We're gonna have a little surprise waiting for your friend when he gets here," Simmons replied.

"You're going to ambush him?" Jones asked.

"That's what the boss wants."

"Boss? So you're not a lone wolf then. Who is your employer?"

"You think I'm dumb enough to tell you that?"

Jones shrugged. "I don't see the harm in it. I'm obviously not escaping from here to tell anyone. And if you succeed in your plan, then after you kill The Silencer, I'm quite certain you'll turn the tables on Ms. Hendricks and me so we can join him. And if you're not successful, then it won't matter because you'll be dead."

Simmons laughed, amused that his prisoner thought there was a chance The Silencer would kill them all. "There's no chance of that happening."

"Well if you're so sure of your plan, then you won't mind explaining it to me. At least give me the satisfaction of having the knowledge of what's about to happen before I go to the grave," Jones told him.

"I work for a man named Vincent."

"Vincent?"

"Yeah. You know him?"

"Well, by reputation only. What's he got to do with this?"

"He says he wants to have a little welcoming party for your friend when he gets here," Simmons said.

"And when is all this going to go down?"

"Your friend has less than an hour."

"And he said he's coming?" Jones wondered.

"Oh, he'll be here. And we'll be waiting."

Finished with their conversation, Simmons left the room to wait for his friends. Jones knew something was up. He obviously was aware that Recker couldn't get there in less than an hour. So he figured that if Recker said he could, then he must've had something planned. Could that plan involve Vincent? Although Jones was a little worried that if Simmons was Vincent's man, perhaps he reconsidered his relationship with Recker. Could be he'd decide that Recker was no longer worth keeping around. With less than an hour to go, at least his mind wouldn't have long to think about it. Whatever was going to happen, would happen soon enough.

33

Simmons rushed over to the front of the building and looked out a window. He thought he heard someone moving out there along with some muffled voices. He worried that Recker might've gotten there a little earlier than expected and before the reinforcements from Vincent arrived. Simmons looked a little to the right, past the front door, and saw a couple of familiar faces. Malloy was leading the pack. It was exactly thirty minutes since Simmons's conversation with his boss and he was sweating it out the whole time until his back up came. He hurried over to the door and unlocked it, opening it for the rest of the crew to come in. Malloy led the way, followed by four others who, judging by the scowls on their faces, didn't look too enthusiastic about being there.

"Was starting to get worried," Simmons told them. "Thought you'd already be here by now."

"We had some things to take care of on the way," Malloy replied.

"Oh. Well no big deal. As long as you beat The Silencer here that's all that really matters."

"So where are they?"

"Who?"

"The two people you're holding."

"Oh, back here."

Simmons led them through the office and down a hallway to show them his two prisoners. Mia was in an office to the left and Jones was in an office to the right directly across from her. They checked in on Mia first. As soon as Malloy saw her with the gag in her mouth, he walked over to her and undid the string that held it in place to remove it.

"What're you doing?" Simmons wondered, perplexed by his behavior.

"I don't think this will be necessary," Malloy said, dropping the rag on the floor.

"You might be sorry about that. She's a feisty one."

"Are you OK, miss?"

Mia moved her jaw around a few times then nodded. "Yeah."

"Is Vincent coming?" Simmons asked.

"He'll be here shortly," Malloy confirmed. "Where's the other guy?"

"What about her?"

"What about her?" Malloy asked.

"Well, undoing the gag, what if she calls out or something to warn The Silencer when he gets here?" he worried.

"I'm sure she won't do anything like that, will you miss?" Malloy asked her.

Mia looked at him with a painful expression and agreed, even if she wasn't sure she actually would comply with the request. "No."

"See, she'll be fine."

MIKE RYAN

Malloy told one of his men to stay in the room by the door to keep an eye on her as Simmons led them across the hallway to see Jones. He then told another of his men to go wait by the front door to keep an eye out for Vincent's arrival.

"Is he not as much trouble?" Malloy wondered, noticing that Jones wasn't as tightly restrained as the girl was.

"Nah. He's pretty mild-mannered," Simmons answered. "He seems resigned to whatever's gonna happen."

Jones recognized Malloy from the photos that he dug up of Vincent's organization for Recker when he was initially checking into them. Since they didn't seem to know who Jones was, in relation to Recker, he just played along like he wasn't familiar with any of them. Another man stayed in the room with him as Malloy and Simmons went out into the main office to wait for their boss. About five minutes later, the front door opened, with Vincent confidently walking in. A sigh of relief crossed Simmons's face, finally feeling like the situation was secure.

"Jimmy, Joe, how's everything looking?" Vincent asked.

"Everything's good," Malloy answered.

"No issues?"

Malloy just shook his head.

"Joe, I have a few more questions for you," Vincent said.

"Sure."

"On the way over here a couple things hit me out of the blue that I didn't initially think about. You talked to The Silencer on the phone, correct?"

"Yeah," Simmons replied.

"How did you get his number?"

"The girl gave it to me."

"And how did she get it?"

Simmons shrugged. "She said she knew him."

"Really?"

Simmons shrugged again. "Yeah. She had it memorized. Said they were friends."

"Well that's interesting. Wouldn't you say Jimmy?"

"Sure is," Malloy responded.

"Let's meet this girl."

"She's back this way," Simmons said, leading them back to the room she was in.

Vincent, Malloy, and Simmons stood just inside the door, looking at the tied up woman. As they continued to stand there, Mia couldn't help but feel she was in a lot of danger. She could tell by the way Simmons stood behind the others that these guys were the ones in charge of the situation now.

"Pretty girl," Vincent stated to anyone who was listening.

Vincent looked around the barren room and noticed a metal folding chair standing up against the wall in the corner. He slowly walked over to it and grabbed it before taking it over to Mia's location and setting it up a few inches away from her. He unbuttoned his coat as he sat down, wanting to have a conversation with her.

"Mia, is that right?" Vincent asked.

"Yes. Are you the one that holds his leash?"

A grin overtook Vincent's face, appreciating her feisty manner. Smiling, he looked over at Malloy and Simmons, the latter of which wasn't as amused by the comment.

"I told you she was a feisty one," Simmons said.

"I understand you know The Silencer. You're friends with him?" Vincent asked.

"I'm not telling you anything," Mia rebuffed.

Vincent made an expression that hinted at his disappointment with her answer. "That's an unfortunate response. You see, I already know that you do. Having his phone number proves that. I don't really need a confirmation from you to acknowledge that."

"Then what are you asking me for?"

"To participate in a truthful and engaging dialogue," Vincent replied. "I abhor people who lie to me. It's something that just gets under my skin and irritates me to no end. When I find people I can talk truthfully with, and feel like we're having an honest conversation, I truly appreciate their candor, even if it doesn't necessarily jive with my own views. I have a certain respect for them and feel that a bond develops between the two parties."

Mia didn't exactly know who the man was that was sitting in front of her. But there was something cold and dangerous about him. He seemed nice enough, well spoken, obviously had some degree of intelligence. But underneath all that, she could tell there was something that said he could be more ruthless and dangerous than anybody else in that room. Someone that you didn't want to mess with.

Vincent could see that she was having an internal debate as to how she should handle their conversation. He wasn't upset at her lack of trust to that point. Under the circumstances, with her being kidnapped, tied up, and whatever else Simmons had done to her, he understood her hesitancy. But he viewed her as a great resource at trying to understand Recker further. Up to that point, he knew little about Recker. He obviously knew what most people did, what was broadcast on TV, what was written in the papers, along with whatever intel he got off the street. But here sitting in front of him was someone who knew Recker personally. It was his chance to get more information about him. Something other people didn't know. And with luck, he could learn something he could use at another point in time down the road.

"So if I may ask some personal questions, just how close are you two? Friends? Girlfriend? Casual acquaintance?" Vincent wondered.

Mia took a big sigh before she revealed anything, knowing it was probably in her best interest not to dodge any more questions from him. "Uh... we're just friends."

"Nothing more?" Vincent asked, not sure that her response was accurate.

"Nothing more. We're just friends."

"OK. How may I ask did the two of you meet?"

"Um... some of those stories you read about him in the paper... I was one of them," she told him. "I was having problems with an abusive ex-boyfriend and one day Mi... he just showed up."

Vincent smiled, appreciating her resilience and restraint. He could tell that she was still trying not to reveal too much out of loyalty to Recker. It was a trait that he was fond of and one he required in his own men. Before going any further, he looked toward Malloy and nodded for him and Simmons to leave the room. After they did so, Mia started looking a little more nervous, thinking that something was about to happen to her.

"You don't need to play games with me, Ms. Hendricks. I'm fully aware of his name," Vincent said.

"You are?"

"Mike Recker. I've had the pleasure of doing business with Mike on a few different occasions."

"Oh."

"I take it you two have been friends ever since the day he helped you with your problem," Vincent assumed.

"I guess in a way."

"Not so sure?"

Mia shrugged. "I guess I try to be more friends with him than he does with me."

"Keeps you at arm's length, huh?" Vincent asked.

"Yes."

"Smart on his part."

"Why do you say that?" Mia asked.

"A man as dangerous as Mike is, someone who does the things that he does, it makes sense that he wouldn't want anybody to get too close to him. Take yourself for example. Say you two had feelings for each other and got involved, then someone like Joe out there found out about that, that would make you an appealing target to anyone who was trying to either hurt him or avoid him," Vincent explained.

"Oh. Yeah, I guess it would."

"I'm surprised that he'd still interact with you at all. I'd think that after helping you he'd just move on to his next case. Not get involved with anyone."

"I guess I kind of kept after him."

"Tell me, Mary, what is it that you do for a living?"

"Why do you wanna know?"

"Curiosity mostly."

"I'm a pediatric nurse," she told him.

"A nurse, huh?"

"Yes, why?"

"Have you always done that?" Vincent wondered.

"Well, not always. Before that I worked in an ER. But that's what I went to school for."

"I see. Good skill to have around for a man like Mike. Going to the hospital for some type of procedure for someone like him could be pretty dangerous. Never know who might show up."

"What are you getting at?" Mia asked.

"Honestly, I don't really know. I have a theory though. Hear me out and let me know what you think."

"OK."

"Several months ago, I heard Mike got shot. It was actually a man named Mario Mancini that did it. He worked for the Marco Bellomi crime family. Long story short, Mike came to me in hopes of finding Mancini, which we did. Well, I don't know if you know the results of that but both Bellomi and Mancini were widely featured on news telecasts after they turned up dead," Vincent said.

"Why are you telling me all this?"

"Like I said, curiosity. Now, I'm assuming after Mancini shot him, Mike, didn't go to a hospital. A nurse that he has as a friend, though, that might be very helpful indeed if the need should ever arise."

"Must be."

As the two of them were talking, Mia started looking more relaxed, not so uptight. But as the conversation continued, that worried look returned to her face. Vincent was pumping her for information and she could only assume that he was trying to get as much out of her as he could before he killed her. From Vincent's standpoint, he had as much information as he thought he needed. He was quite convinced that he had a good grasp on things. He figured that Recker kept a relationship with her, albeit one from not that close a distance, just in case he ever needed medical help. He thought it was a genius move and frankly one that he expected from someone who had the talents that Recker did.

Without wanting anything else from Mia, Vincent reached into his coat pocket and pulled out a small folding knife. Mia's eyes widened as she saw him remove the lethal instrument, worried that she was about to feel how lethal the object was. Seeing how scared she was becoming, Vincent sought to put her mind at ease. He leaned forward, the knife dangling off his knee.

"You can relax, Ms. Hendricks. I'm not here to hurt you," Vincent said. "You and your friend will be leaving here shortly, both of you unharmed."

Mia scrunched her face, not sure she believed him. If he was being truthful, she certainly didn't understand what was going on. "You're letting us go?"

Vincent nodded his head. "Yes."

"Not that I'm not happy or grateful, but why?"

"You see, Joe works for me, but what he did to your friend, what he's done to you is not something that I condone," he explained. "I don't wish any harm to come to you. You've done nothing wrong that I can see to be in the position you are right now."

"I thought he said you were setting a trap for Mike?"

"Well, I told him what I thought he wanted to hear in order to keep him here with you long enough for me to arrive. As I told you before, Mike and I have done some business dealings before. We have a standing arrangement of some sorts."

"So you're not gonna try and kill him?"

Vincent let out a feeble laugh. "No, trying to kill Mike would be a tall task for anyone regardless of the odds. I value the skills that Mike possesses. A man like him could be very valuable and in demand for someone in my position. Men like that, you just don't get rid of unless it's absolutely necessary. Men like Joe, however, well, they're highly replaceable. You may or may not know that Mike's out of town on business right now and he called me a little while ago and explained the situation. There was obviously no way he could get here in time to save you and your friend so he called me. And I told him I would rectify the situation. And so here we are."

Vincent then took his knife and put it between Mia's ankles and cut the rope that tied them together. He then got up and walked behind her and cut the rope that bound her hands. Once Mia's hands were free, she rubbed her wrists to try to relieve some of the pain from the pressure of the ropes. Vincent walked back in front of her as she began to stand up. Vincent put his arm up to keep her there a few more minutes.

"Am I free to go?" Mia asked.

"I'm going to ask you to remain here a little while longer," Vincent responded. "I first want to talk to the other man that was with you."

"Are you letting him go too?"

"After a brief conversation, yes. I wasn't informed of his name. Perhaps you can save me the trouble of finding out."

"Uh... David."

"David? David what?"

"Uh... Jones."

"Jones, huh?" Vincent asked, not believing that was his real name.

"Yep."

"How do you two know each other?"

"Umm... friend of the family. Yeah," Mia replied, saying the first thing that came to her.

"OK. I'm going to leave a man just outside the door. For your own protection. You're free to walk around in here if you like. I will let you know when it's safe for you to leave. Shouldn't be too long."

Mia nodded, and though she was anxious to go, figured a few more minutes wasn't too much to ask. She was just relieved that she'd be leaving at all considering a half hour previous to that she thought she was on her final breaths.

Vincent walked out of the room and closed the door behind him. He instructed one of his men to just stand there and make sure the woman didn't exit the room. Vincent stood outside the other door, thinking about how he wanted to approach Mia's friend. He took a deep breath, then walked in, grinning, and looking relaxed. Once again, Vincent looked for a chair and found one in the corner of the room. He grabbed it and walked over to

Jones, setting it up right in front of him. He then sat down about a foot away as they began to converse.

"So... Mr. Jones," Vincent said. "I've been told you have no identification on you to confirm who you are."

"Sounds as though you already know," Jones replied.

"Courtesy of your lady friend across the hall."

"Is she OK?"

Vincent nodded, "she's fine."

"Am I correct in assuming that you are Vincent?" Jones asked, even though he already knew.

"And how would you know that?"

"Well, your man told me he was waiting for you and seeing as how you have a certain presence about you it would only seem to reason that you are him."

Vincent smiled. "Very astute observation. So is Jones your real name or is it some type of alias that you and The Silencer have worked out?"

"Alias? I'm afraid I don't know what you're talking about."

"So are you telling me you don't know the identity of The Silencer?"

Jones shook his head, hopeful that he wouldn't get tripped up in a lie. "No, I don't. I only know what I read and hear. Nothing more than that."

"So you're telling me that Ms. Hendricks knows The Silencer, you know her, but yet you have no intimate knowledge of him?"

"That is correct. Mia's relationship to The Silencer is no concern of mine and whatever that relationship is... is not my business."

"And yet you accompanied her today. Why?" Vincent wondered.

"While her relationship to The Silencer is not my concern, her safety is. I was concerned about her meeting this man alone and wanted to protect her in any way I could. Obviously that did not work out as well as I would have hoped."

Vincent smiled. "Seems playing the bodyguard isn't really what you're suited for."

"Indeed."

"Exactly what is your business?" Vincent asked.

"I'm a... professor," Jones replied.

He couldn't believe he was actually using the nickname Recker had given him. But, he could see how it might fit in the eyes of other people. And if it helped to get him out of this jam, he'd be more than happy to keep on using it.

"Of what?" Vincent asked.

"History. I teach at Temple."

"So if I call down to Temple, they'll have knowledge of you?"

"Of course," Jones answered, staying strong in his bluff.

Though Vincent still wasn't sure he bought Jones' story, he didn't want to get too in depth with the questions. He was mostly trying to just scratch the surface and get whatever information he could without it sounding like an inquisition.

"So how long have you known Mike Recker?" Vincent asked.

"Who?"

"Mike Recker."

Jones answered with a slight shake of his head. "I'm afraid I don't know the name."

"And you're telling me you've never asked Ms. Hendricks who The Silencer is? Knowing full well that she probably knows his real identity."

"It's not something that really interests me," Jones stated.

"Really? Odd, don't you think?"

Jones shrugged. "I'm not much for conspiracy theories or unlocking secrets. I believe it's usually best to let things lie as they are. If things are meant to be uncovered they usually will be in due time."

"You're probably right. You're an intellectual man, Mr. Jones. I like that," Vincent grinned.

"Well, I teach so that kind of goes with the job."

"Yes, I suppose so. Not only intellectual, but fascinating."

"I don't think I've said anything that fascinating," Jones responded.

"No, it's not in what you say but how you say it. How you act. How you reply."

A more concerned look overtook Jones' face as he peered up at his visitor. He worried that Vincent had somehow figured out who he actually was. Or he'd already talked to Mia, and she gave him up. Not that he'd blame her if she did as she wasn't the most experienced at this sort of thing. He wouldn't expect her to hold up long against extensive interrogation techniques if she was exposed to them.

"And what makes you think that?" Jones wondered.

"Well, here you are sitting and talking to me calmly and rationally, seemingly knowing full well who I am. And yet you don't look concerned in the slightest," Vincent explained. "You've been beat up, knocked out, kidnapped, tied up to a chair for hours inside a vacant room and yet you don't seem rattled or fidgety. Very strange, wouldn't you agree?"

Jones simply looked down at the floor to the left of him and let a smirk emerge onto his face. He realized that Vincent was analyzing how he replied to questions more so than the words that Jones used. It was a smooth technique that Jones didn't notice at first.

"I mean, I assume that as a professor you aren't subjected to this type of behavior every week, are you?" Vincent asked.

"I would hope not."

"But you're as cool as can be like it's just another day."

"I guess I'm just a low key type of person where not much bothers me," Jones said.

"Well if this doesn't bother you, I don't know what would."

"Well, would yelling and shouting and trying to break free do me much good?"

"Not really."

"I'm not really sure I understand what you're trying to get at. Are you implying that you think I'm The Silencer?" Jones asked with a laugh.

Vincent chuckled at the suggestion. "Of course not."

"I should hope not. I mean, if I was, I probably wouldn't still be sitting here. James Bond I'm not."

"Wouldn't it be interesting if you were? No, I'm fully aware that you're not The Silencer," Vincent stated.

"May I ask you a couple of questions?" Jones wondered.

"Fire away, professor."

"What is this interest in The Silencer that you have? Do you believe I'm friends with him somehow?"

Vincent got up and walked around the room for a few moments as he pondered the question, giving it ample thought. After a minute, he stopped in back of the metal folding chair where he'd been sitting, leaning on the back of it as he looked down at Jones to answer his questions.

"My fascination with him is I guess the same as almost anyone else's. A vigilante type character who mysteriously shows up in our city... almost like out of a comic book or a movie. When not much is known about someone, you try to figure out their angle, who their associates are, what their play is, what type of connections they have," Vincent explained.

"And you think I may have some of those answers?"

"I'm not sure. And as for friends, I'm not sure a man like The

Silencer has friends. I believe he has acquaintances, business partners, perhaps a few people he's friendly with, but men like him, rarely have true friends. They can't afford it."

"Why do you say that?"

"Men who can do the things he does come from a special background. Military, government, black ops, things of that nature. It's rare for a civilian, even one trained in an organization such as mine to be able to move the way he does. He operates in the shadows, in the background, pops up out of nowhere before disappearing, helping people without wanting credit. That's a rare person," Vincent continued.

"I would have to take your word for it. I've never met someone of that background."

"That's why they don't have friends. They pick up and move at the slightest hint of trouble or of being detected. Once they're compromised, they are no longer effective. It's tough to pack up and move if you're leaving behind people you care about."

"It's a fascinating discussion but not one in which I can be of much value in, considering I have no experience in it," Jones replied.

The longer they talked, the more Vincent was convinced that Jones wasn't merely just a professor as he proclaimed. Vincent thought there was something else there. Perhaps he was a professor. But for a man sitting there tied up, something in which Vincent had a lot of experience, Jones didn't appear anxious, nervous, or fearful. Vincent had many men in that position, some of whom were dangerous in their own right, and all of them showed some type of reaction while in that chair. But not Jones. A professor who didn't exhibit one negative reaction to being there sent red flags into the air in Vincent's mind. Vincent put his hand up in the air, indicating he had more to bring to the discussion.

"I have one final thing on the subject," Vincent told him.

"OK?"

"It's my belief that a man like The Silencer can't really operate on the kind of scale that he has been without some type of help or guidance."

"Really? You mean he has a team?" Jones asked.

"In a way. Like Ms. Hendricks, a nurse who could help him in the event he's ever shot. Perhaps he has a computer genius who works magic for him..."

"Or even an intelligent professor who can help solve problems for him," Jones interrupted.

"Perhaps."

"That is an interesting theory."

"What do you think?" Vincent asked. "As a professor, do you think my theory holds any weight?"

Making a few faces as he feigned thinking about it, Jones concurred. "I believe it's possible, yes."

The conversation came to a halt and the two men just stared at each other for a minute, each apparently sizing the other one up. Jones was obviously a very intelligent man who wasn't going to be rattled or slip up in his story. Vincent didn't want to push too far as he knew that if the man before him was in The Silencer's stable, that he'd tell Recker about the questions and suspicions he had. And while Vincent sought to extract more information about Recker and his operation, he didn't want to push the boundaries just yet and risk making a new enemy. Especially when up to that point they'd had a good relationship.

"If you're done with the assertions, can I ask what you're planning on doing to us?" Jones wondered, breaking the silence after a couple of minutes.

"You will be released, Ms. Hendricks and yourself."

"Thank you."

"I would like to ask one thing of you, though," Vincent said.

"Oh?"

"As a professor, a law-abiding man as I'm sure you are, I'm asking that you don't report any of what's happened here today to the police. It'll be dealt with."

"Well, that goes against my principles," Jones expressed, trying to keep up his appearances. "I mean, the man did commit several serious crimes. How do I know he won't try again at some point? I don't want to be walking to class every day in fear that he's behind me, ready to strike or something."

"I give you my word that he'll never be an issue for you again. As I said, his crimes will be dealt with," Vincent sternly replied. "Not by a court of public opinion, though, and not by the law. It'll be dealt with by my law. And I assure you that that is far more severe."

34

Once Vincent had finished up with his interview of Jones, he had untied him and assured him he'd be leaving soon, just as he had with Mia. He still left a guard there between the two rooms even though both doors were locked. Vincent then walked out into the main part of the vacant office, ready to conclude the business they had there. Malloy looked at his boss, ready to take action once he got the word.

"Jimmy, once we all go, I want you to stay back and let Ms. Hendricks and Professor Jones out," Vincent ordered.

"You got it."

"If they need a lift or a ride anywhere, take them wherever they'd like to go."

"Right," Malloy replied.

"Wait, what?" Simmons asked, his face a picture of wide-eyed, wide-mouthed astonishment. "You're letting them go?!"

"That's right, Joe," Vincent confirmed.

"What am I missing here? They came looking for me."

"No, I'm fairly certain that whatever happened here today has come to a satisfactory conclusion."

"They're not gonna stop," Simmons objected. "They know The Silencer. I'm as good as dead if he comes after me. They're leverage for me."

"No, Joe, this ends today," Vincent repeated, nodding at Malloy.

Malloy immediately lunged at Simmons and gave him a thunderous right hook across the side of his left cheek. Simmons was surprised and stunned by the blow and instantly fell to the ground. Knowing he was in a world of trouble, he started to get back to his feet. His progress was halted though as the two men that were guarding the door rushed over to him and grabbed each of his arms as they held him in check. As Simmons was dragged back up off the floor, Malloy proceeded to rain down some more punishment on him. Blow after blow, alternating between the stomach, kidneys, and his face, it wasn't long before Simmons was in excruciating pain. As Malloy continued his assault, Vincent stepped forward, speaking to their victim as he was getting hammered with fists.

"You see, Joe, this was necessary because you put my organization in a bad light," Vincent told him. "Your actions made this a necessity because you compromised my positions."

"I'm sor...," Simmons tried to reply.

He couldn't get the rest of the words out, though, as Malloy popped him right across the jaw. With every punch, the pain that Simmons felt increased tenfold. Vincent let the action continue for a few more minutes until he felt satisfied in his own mind that Simmons had successfully gotten the message.

"You killed some female doctor that you had a crush on, or rejected you, doesn't really matter which. I gave explicit directions months ago that nobody was to be killed by one of my men in this city unless it was under my direct orders," Vincent explained to him. "Then her friends come looking for you and you kidnap them with the intention of killing them, bringing The Silencer into the equation. Did you really think I would be OK with that?"

Unable to answer with Malloy still using Simmons as a punching bag, Vincent took hold of his lieutenant's right arm. He gave Malloy a few pats on the back to indicate he was appreciative of his efforts on a job well done. Vincent, along with his men, stood over their former colleague as he writhed around in pain, coughing and spitting up blood.

"I just..." Simmons huffed, trying to catch his breath.

It felt like one or two of his ribs were fractured and he had numerous cuts on his face. His lip was busted, one of his eyes was already starting to swell up, and his nose was broken. He barely had any breath left within him to talk.

"I just," Simmons coughed. "Wasn't think... thinking," he struggled to say, spitting up more blood on the floor.

"Obviously," Vincent responded.

Malloy stood there, ready to pounce on their victim again if he was given the instructions to do so. He looked at his boss to see if he wanted him to continue pounding away, but Vincent didn't give him the green light. Instead, Vincent just stared down at the incredibly beaten man with a look of scorn and contempt. Eventually, Vincent looked over to his right-hand man and could tell that he was still itching to dish out some more punishment.

"I think our friend here has had enough, Jimmy, don't you think?" Vincent asked.

"Whatever you say, boss."

"Take him to the car."

Two of Vincent's men scraped Simmons off the floor again,

carrying him out the door and into the car that was waiting for them. Once they had gone, Vincent took Malloy's arm and led him to the far wall to discuss things further without anyone overhearing.

"Take them wherever they want to go and stay on them," Vincent told him. "Perhaps one of them goes somewhere that could give us some additional intel on where Recker sets up shop."

"Why the extra interest in Recker's activities and operations?"

"Keep your enemies close, Jimmy. Keep your friends closer. Right now he's an ally. As we both know, allegiances have a tendency to shift from time to time depending on which way the wind blows. If that should ever happen, it's best to be prepared for a worst-case scenario. And he's a man in which you need disaster plans to be made ahead of time, before the tornado strikes."

"OK. What if these two split up somewhere?" Malloy asked.

Vincent looked over to the hallway that led to both rooms that their visitors were in and debated the question. "If that happens, follow the professor. I think he's a little bit shiftier than she is. I think she was pretty much honest about her relationship with Recker. Him, on the other hand, he's a different story. I think there's much deception about him."

"I'll stay on him. What about Recker?"

"I'll call our friend in a little while and inform him that the matter's been settled. Not until you've done your part, though."

Vincent then left, followed by the man that was guarding the doors, leaving just Malloy with their two guests. Malloy waited a minute until Vincent and the rest of his crew had driven off before he let Mia and Jones out of their rooms. He unlocked Mia's door first and slowly pushed it open, seeing her pace up and down against the far wall. Once she saw the door open she stopped, wondering what was going to happen next.

"You're now free to go," Malloy told her.

"Oh. OK," Mia replied, still a bit hesitant.

"If you wait in the main office there, I'll let your friend out and then I'll take you guys wherever you'd like to go."

"Thank you," she sheepishly smiled.

As Malloy turned his attention to the other door, Mia slipped out of the room and waited in the main office. Though she had thoughts of just running out the front door as quickly as possible, it was only a fleeting thought. Jones was still in there and she couldn't just abandon him, especially after the licks he'd taken for her. As Malloy opened Jones' door, the professor was still sitting in his chair, as calm as could be. He was leaning forward with his elbows resting on his knees, and his hands clasped together.

"If you're ready we can go now," Malloy told him. "I'll take you where you need to go."

"As ready as I'll ever be," Jones replied, standing up.

Malloy held the door open as Jones walked past him. Once Jones entered the main office, Mia rushed over to him and gave him a big hug, relieved to see that he was OK, though he still had a cut on his head from the thumping that Simmons gave him. Other than that, though, he was in good shape. Jones was standing only a few inches away from where Simmons laid on the floor after his beating was administered. He looked down at the floor and noticed a small pool of blood. Knowing something must have happened, a quizzical look showed on his face. Mia noticed his strange face and looked down at the floor as well, seeing the same thing he did.

"Did something happen here?" Jones asked.

"Nothing you need to be concerned with," Malloy answered.

"It wasn't here when we came in," Mia chimed in.

"Like I said, it's nothing you need to be concerned with," he said with a smile. "Just be thankful it isn't yours."

"Whose is it?" she asked.

MIKE RYAN

"I think we should probably be going. I have a car out in front," Malloy told them, ending the questions, holding his arm out to usher them along.

Mia gave Jones a look, like she was still worried about what was to come. She still didn't feel like they were out of the woods yet. Not as long as there was a stranger, and an intimidating one at that, still hanging around. Though Vincent had kept his word up to that point, Mia still wasn't trusting of any of them. They cautiously walked out the front door, Malloy following them closely. Once they got to the car, Malloy held the back door of the car open for them to get in.

"Where can I take you?" Malloy asked.

Mia and Jones looked at each other, not exactly sure what they should say. Neither wanted to go to their house and have the man know where they lived. Although in Mia's case, it wouldn't be hard to find out, anyway. But for Jones, it was a much trickier situation. He would have to pick a completely unrelated spot or else risk giving up his role and relationship to Recker.

"Uh... if you could just drop me off at the university, that would be fine," Jones said, sticking to his cover that he just created.

Mia gave him a strange look, wondering what he was talking about. She obviously wasn't aware of the conversation he had with Vincent and had no idea about the professor identity that he was now trying to forge. Jones returned her glance and gave a slight nod with his head, trying to indicate to her to just go with whatever he was saying. He also moved his hand along the seat, trying not to be noticed by their driver, and put it on Mia's knee, tapping it a few times before putting all five of his fingers out. Although she wasn't exactly sure what he was trying to tell her, she decided she'd just roll with it. Knowing how he worked with Recker, she was confident that he had something in mind. She didn't need to know the details. She trusted him fully.

"The university?" Malloy asked. "Are you sure?"

"Yes, I know it's a little bit of a distance, but that's where I was when Ms. Hendricks met up with me this morning," Jones responded. "I'd just finished a lecture with my class and was in my office when she came over and persuaded me to join her little adventure today."

"And what about you, Ms. Hendricks? Where would you like to go?"

"Oh, you know what, might as well drop me off along with him. Like he said, I met him at the university, so my car's still there," Mia answered, playing along with the charade that Jones invented.

"If that's too far a drive, you can drop us off anywhere," Jones said. "I'm sure we can manage on our own."

"The university's fine," Malloy replied.

Malloy did as they requested and drove to Temple University, dropping the pair off near the front entrance of the campus on North Broad Street. Once Mia and Jones got out of the car, they thanked their driver for the ride and bid him adieu. As they started walking, Mia sought to clarify what Jones was doing.

"Just follow my lead," Jones stated.

"What are we doing here?"

"I told them I was a professor that taught here," he said as they walked toward the entrance.

"Why?"

"I couldn't very well tell them the truth. I can't say for certain but I get the distinct impression that they're going to attempt to follow us wherever we go."

"Oh. Why would they do that if they're letting us go?" Mia wondered.

"To attempt to find out more about Mike. There's still a lot of mystery surrounding him. They want to know how he operates, who he associates with, who else is involved," Jones explained. "They already know you're somehow involved and I believe they highly suspect that I'm somehow involved as well. I just don't believe they know how close we are or what our roles are as of yet. But that will change rather quickly if we don't lose him and lead him back to our homes."

"So I can't go back home?"

"I think they already know about you. I believe I'm the one they're interested in."

"So what are we gonna do?" Mia asked.

"We're going to lose him."

"How?"

"Very carefully."

Once Jones and Mia entered through the front doors of the campus, Jones took a quick look back to see if Malloy was starting to follow them yet. He wasn't though, as he had yet to get out of his car. Malloy didn't want to get too near them and tip them off to his presence and make them nervous. But he knew he had to move soon. With how busy of a campus Temple was, and with several exits, it wouldn't take long to lose the pair amongst the crowd. As soon as Jones and Mia walked through the doors, they made a sharp right and continued looking at the car from a window.

"How long are we gonna wait here?" Mia asked.

"Just until he moves."

"And then what?"

"Once he comes in through the front, we're gonna slip out the side and then run across the street," Jones told her.

"Why? What's there?"

"Just a café. We can then watch a little more carefully and with some distance between us. He'll wind up searching this building for us and come up empty. Then when he finally leaves, we can go back to our own places."

The Silencer Series Box Set

Just a few seconds later, everything that Jones had said, started happening. Malloy got out of his car and started walking up to the main entrance. As soon as he did, Jones hurried Mia along, rushing over to a side door. Once they exited, they clung to the side of the building, Jones peering past the corner of the building to get a look at the entrance to see if Malloy was still there. They would have to make their move quickly. North Broad Street was an extremely busy road and if they had to stand there for a few minutes to wait for cars to go by, and Malloy happened to look through a window and see them, their plan would go for naught.

"We'll wait for a red light and then dash across," Jones said.

"Ready when you are," Mia replied.

Another thirty seconds went by before the light changed to red. With the cars stopped, Jones and Mia left the side of the building and raced across the street, just ahead of a few cars that were turning onto the street. They quickly raced up the steps into the building across from the main campus and turned into the café. It was a crowded place but Mia immediately found an open table nestled right up against the window. They instantly headed for it before the seats were snatched up, giving them an excellent view of the street and Malloy's car. Mia had a few dollars on her and got each of them a coffee while they waited. Plus, after all they'd been through, they figured they could use a boost of energy from it.

"Is this what you and Mike do all the time?" Mia asked.

"Well, not quite. At least from my perspective. Mike is usually the one in the field and having to deal with all the cloak and dagger stuff," Jones told her. "It's very rare for me to be the one doing this. I'm usually in the office doing computer work, running down leads and such. Working behind the scenes."

"How do you guys do it? I mean, it's exhausting. How do you guys not break down?"

Jones smiled at her. "It's just something that you do. Every day you learn and just try to twist every situation so that it favors you. In any case, for your doubts, you appear to be holding up well."

"I guess being an ER nurse trains you to think quickly and not get rattled," she replied. "There's no time to be nervous or scared. Otherwise, people can die rather quickly."

"This isn't that much different to be honest. Mostly quick thinking, quick reactions, knowing what you can do and what you can't. One wrong turn could be your last."

"I dunno, this is different I think. Even in the ER, you're dealing with other people's lives, but you're not dealing with your own. When Simmons had us back in that building, and even in that apartment, I really thought we were going to die. I didn't think we were ever going to make it out of there alive," she said with a sense of sadness.

"One thing about this job, profession, whatever you want to call it, you can't dwell on what almost happened, or what should've happened. In the end, all that matters is what did happen and how you learn from it, how you move on."

"Even from Mike's standpoint, I can see how it can wear a person down. Doing this all day, every day, I guess I can finally see why he is the way he is sometimes. Why he sometimes seems distant."

Jones thought about continuing the conversation and replying on Recker's behalf, but decided against it. He obviously knew that the job wasn't the only reason his partner was distant at times. But Jones didn't think it was his place to tell Mia that the other part was what happened in his previous job. Or about Carrie. That was Recker's choice to tell if he ever decided to do so. Twenty minutes had passed and Mia was beginning to wonder how much time they were going to give Malloy until they moved on.

"Do you think he knows we're here?" Mia asked.

"I think we'd have seen him by now if he did."

"What's taking him so long?"

"It's a big building," Jones answered. "I'm sure he's just being thorough."

"Maybe we should go now," Mia suggested.

"No. We'll wait for him to go first."

"What if he actually is over there waiting for us? Suppose he did see us come over here."

"Well then we'll outlast him. We'll wait him out. If he's still here in another hour or two, then we'll have to assume that he knows we're still here," Jones replied. "I really don't want to leave, though, until we see him drive away."

Malloy checked the main campus, and all the buildings and doors he could access, as well as the outside perimeter of the building in his search for Jones and Mia. He looked for an hour but they had successfully evaded his pursuit. He figured they must've slipped out somewhere but continuing to look would've been a worthless cause, he thought. They could've been just about anywhere at that point. He walked back to his car to call Vincent with the news.

"Look, there he is!" Mia excitedly yelled.

"Shh," Jones replied, reminding her they were in a public place.

Malloy sat in his car for a minute, just taking one last look around before he called his boss, hoping he wouldn't get chewed out for blowing the assignment.

"Sorry, boss. I lost them," Malloy reported.

"Where?"

"Jones told me to take them to the university."

"Main campus?" Vincent asked.

"Yeah. On Broad Street. They got out, went in the main building. I tried to follow them a few minutes later, and they were gone."

"Smart. Taking you to a busy and public place. Jones' doing no doubt."

"I should've been on them tighter than I was," Malloy sorrowfully said.

"It's OK, Jimmy. I'd still call this a successful day regardless of what happened there. Get back here so we can start preparing for Recker's arrival," Vincent told him.

"I'm on my way."

Jones and Mia looked on intently as Malloy sat in his car for a few minutes. As Vincent's lieutenant drove away, the pair started to breathe a little easier, thinking that they could finally get rid of him and find some peace after a long and trying day.

"Time to go?" Mia eagerly asked.

"Now it's time to go," Jones replied.

Mia started to get up but then quickly sat back down. "Umm, one small problem that I hadn't thought about yet."

"What's that?"

"Our cars aren't here," she told him.

"I guess we'll just have to take public transportation then."

Mia nodded before realizing the next problem they had. "OK. Uh... one more thing."

"What?"

"We don't have any money."

Jones patted down his shirt and his pants. "I left my wallet in the car before going into the apartment."

"And I just spent my last couple dollars getting us coffee," Mia said.

"I guess the only other thing we can do is... well, two things."

"Which are?"

"One, call Mike."

"He's like eight or ten hours away, isn't he?" Mia asked.

"Yes."

"And the other?"

"Beg," Jones answered.

"There's one other option," Mia told him.

"Walk?"

Mia shook her head. "No. My father's wealthy."

"Yes, I know. But I don't see how that helps us now," Jones replied.

"We don't talk to each other a whole lot. But he wouldn't leave me stranded. I'll call him and tell him to send us a cab."

"Prepaid I hope."

Mia smiled. "Relax. I got this."

Mia went up to the counter and asked to use a phone, explaining the situation to the person who worked there. Sympathetic to her problem, they handed her the phone. A few minutes later, Mia returned to the table.

"How'd you make out?" Jones wondered.

"Cab will be here in about twenty minutes. He gave them his card number and told him to charge the total to him."

"Excellent. Did he wonder what the problem was or why you were here?"

"I just told him I came up here with a friend and the car broke down so we needed a lift home," Mia answered. "Like I said, we don't talk much, we don't have much of a relationship, but he'll help me out with something if I need it. Especially if it comes to money."

"Must come in handy," Jones said.

"Eh. I suppose. I only ask favors of him if it's an emergency. Other than that, I don't really need anything from him."

"Even his love?"

"To him, sending money is showing his love," Mia replied. "That's how he shows affection."

"Well I guess in this situation, we should just be thankful for that."

35

Vincent had waited a little while before calling Recker to inform him of everything that had transpired. He wanted to wait until Recker got closer to Philly until he told him that he was holding Simmons at the same warehouse where they met before, the warehouse where Recker passed on the chance of evening the score with Mario Mancini. Recker didn't need to wait the additional time, though. Not since Jones and Mia had been released.

After getting picked up by the cab near the university, Mia was dropped off first, taking her straight to her apartment. Jones instructed her not to go anywhere, except for work, until she heard from either him or Recker. Just in case Vincent had someone staking out her building, Jones didn't want her to be put in danger again until they could figure out their next steps. Jones was also fearful that someone was already there watching her apartment. Just in case that was true, and someone saw them pulling up in the cab, Jones instructed his driver to drive around aimlessly for a half hour. He periodically looked back to see if anyone was tailing them, and though he never noticed anything, he didn't want to take any chances.

Jones had the cab driver drop him off at a shopping mall so he could use an ATM to withdraw some money. If someone was tailing him, not only would he lose them in the crowd at the mall, he could take a different mode of transportation out of there. Once at the machine, he patted his back pocket for his wallet, only to remember again that he didn't have it. He usually wasn't this absent minded, but the stress of the situation must have been playing tricks with his mind. With no money in hand, he walked to the other end of the mall towards the bus stop. Noticing an increasing crowd of people, Jones assumed the next stop wasn't too far away. He didn't even care where the bus was going. He'd get off wherever it stopped then call another cab to take him to his final destination, the office. After asking a couple of people, he finally found a generous woman who gave him money for bus fare. Within five minutes, the bus rolled in and Jones boarded. It's first stop was about ten minutes away, across from a gas station and convenience store, near another strip shopping center. Once he got there, the cab ride back to the office would only be another ten or fifteen minutes away.

After an hour of successfully dodging a real, or imaginary, surveillance tag, Jones finally got back to the office. He first went inside to get a credit card to pay the cabbie, then went back inside the office. He immediately sat down at his desk and went to work on the computer. Right away, he pulled up the cameras on one of the screens that he had installed six months prior to that. He had nine cameras installed, one at each end of the building near the corners, one near the entrance of the Laundromat, two near the back entrance that led up to the office, as well as two that overlooked the entire parking lot. He scrutinized the footage for the next hour, hoping he didn't see anything out of the ordinary, or any unforeseen visitors. Luckily, it appeared to be like any other night. Quiet. Once he was satisfied that there were no more signs of trouble, he grabbed one of his backup phones out of the drawer to call Recker and let him know that he and Mia were both safe. Recker's phone was on the seat between his legs, and when he heard it ring, eagerly picked it up even though he didn't recognize the number.

"Yeah?"

"Mike, it's me," Jones replied.

"Jones, you all right?"

"I'm fine. Mia's fine too."

"Where are you?"

"I'm back at the office. Mia's at home."

Recker let out a sigh of relief, finally putting his mind at ease, knowing that his friends were safe and out of danger. "Vincent released you?"

"Yes."

"I called him to see what he could do. I knew I couldn't get there in time," Recker told him.

"Understandable."

"I wonder why Vincent hasn't called me yet," Recker stated. "He said he'd call me when everything was done. How long ago did you get out of there?"

"Probably two or three hours now. I'm sure he has his reasons. He isn't one to let much go. Very thorough."

"You talk to him?"

"Yes. Quite in depth I might add, too," Jones said.

"What about?"

"Mostly questions about you. Before he released us we had an extensive interview, mostly about my knowledge of you."

"You didn't tell him anything, did you?" Recker asked.

"Of course not. I told him I was a history professor at Temple.

I'm not sure he really believed that, but he didn't really press me too much on it."

"If he didn't press you then why do you think he didn't believe it?"

"Well, it was more how he asked than what he actually said. It was more like everything he said had a double meaning or a deeper meaning behind the actual question," Jones answered.

"He was probing you?"

"In a way, yes. He already knows you have a connection with Mia. There's no way around that. She had your phone number to contact you. There's no denying it. But I stuck to the story that I was just a friend of Mia's and didn't know you. I didn't have any identification on me for them to check so there was no way for them to prove otherwise unless I slipped up, which I did not," Jones explained.

"But he was still inferring that you knew me?"

"He definitely was. What do you think the meaning behind the questioning was? Mia said he did the same to her."

"He's digging for information on me," Recker replied.

"But why? It's not like you're an unknown to him anymore. I mean, you two have done several business transactions already."

"I'm still somewhat of an unknown to him. He knows what I do. He doesn't know how I do it, how I get my information, who else is working with me, who I know and associate with."

"So you think he wants to know all the fine details," Jones said.

"That's Vincent's MO. He needs information, craves it. He won't make a move for or against anything without having all the facts."

"You think he's planning something against you?" the professor wondered.

"No. Not right now at least. But what if something happens between us a year from now? He'll want to reach into his back pocket for that little black book of knowledge that he has on me. He'll want to know if he gets into a battle with me if I have anyone else with me so he can guard against all angles. If he thinks I'm a lone wolf and work alone, he only has to worry about the front door. If there are others, he's gotta guard the back door, side door, and every other entrance point you can think of," Recker explained.

"Well, I don't believe I was followed or they can trace me in any way. Even if they find out I'm not a professor at the university, they'll have no way of finding out my identity or where we live or work. Mia's a different story though," Jones replied. "They know her name, where she works, and if they don't know already, I'm sure they'll know her address relatively soon."

"Let me worry about that."

"What are you gonna do?"

"I'm just gonna tell Vincent straight that I won't put up with any surveillance on people I know."

"We may want to rethink that strategy."

"Why?"

"If you mention anything about me or that we've talked then he will know that we are, in fact, in cahoots as they say," Jones stated.

"Well, if they start digging around the college and find out you're not working there, then they're gonna assume that, anyway."

"I suppose I could hack into Temple's system and create an additional entry with my profile and information. I'd have to create fictional courses and students to go along with it."

"Sounds like that's gonna take a lot of time," Recker noted.

"Possibly."

"Plus, isn't that something that the university will find out rather quickly?"

"Possibly."

"Seems like a lot of effort for not much payoff then."

"We'd only need it to work for a short amount of time," Jones responded. "Just long enough for Vincent to check on my status there."

"What if he's already checked? Or what if he checks before you get that stuff into the system?"

"Then I guess I will have wasted my time."

"I don't think it's even worth the hassle," Recker told him. "If he assumes you're with me, then let him. As long as he doesn't know your real name, where you live, or where you work, it's a non-issue. Other than me, nobody else knows anything anyway."

"I suppose you're right."

"Besides, that'll take you away from other things that are more important. We need to get back to business and put this incident behind us."

"You're right," Jones agreed.

Recker continued driving, still several hours away. He wondered what Vincent was up to and why he hadn't called to deliver the news yet. In the end, it wasn't important if Jones and Mia were safe. The fact that Vincent had questioned his friends to try to find out more about their relationship to him didn't really bother Recker too much. It was something he'd expect Vincent to do at some point. It was just smart business on his part. A man in Vincent's position had to know every single detail about his friends and enemies so he could plan his next moves accordingly. As long as Vincent ended his inquisition into his friends after they were released, Recker wouldn't have a problem with it. But if he thought Mia was being followed or watched, or Jones at some point thought someone was after him, then Recker would have to lay the law down to his business acquaintance. A little after midnight, Recker's phone rang for the final time of the night. This time, it was the call he'd been waiting for all along.

"Took a while," Recker greeted.

"Yes, sorry. I hope you haven't been sweating it out all this time," Vincent replied.

"Well, I assumed since you hadn't called that all was well like you said. There were no problems?"

"Everything went down beautifully. There were no issues and your friends are now, I assume, safe and sound in their own beds."

"Thank you."

"It was my pleasure, Mike. I'm glad I could help. Just to set the record straight and before you hear it from the mouths of your friends, I just wanted to let you know that I did question them before letting them go," Vincent said.

"Question them? What about?" Recker asked, pretending like he didn't know a thing about it.

"About you. Just wondering about how they fit into your life. I hope you don't mind but I'm sure you can appreciate my position in that I need to know as much as possible about the people I do business with."

"I don't mind. In fact, I'd expect it. I could've saved you the trouble, though."

"How's that?"

"They don't. They don't fit in. First of all, I don't have friends. Can't afford to. Second, I don't know who the guy is, only that he's a friend of Mia's somehow."

"But the girl's a different story?" Vincent asked.

"She's a nurse. I figured it could be useful to know someone who could help me in the case of emergencies without needing to go to a hospital," Recker answered. "I'm sure you understand that."

"I do. And it's very smart thinking on your part."

"But she doesn't mean anything to me personally. Just someone I keep around at arm's length in case."

"Must be hard to do that with someone who's as pretty as she is," Vincent assumed.

"Doesn't mean anything to me. And I thank you for your honesty in telling me all that, but it does raise one concern for me."

"What's that?"

"Since she is a contact of mine, and I'm sure you now know where she lives and works, I can't have her feel like she's being threatened, or watched, or followed in the hopes of finding out something else about me," Recker said.

"I understand your concern. And I give you my word that, as far as I'm concerned, my enquiry into their lives and how they fit into yours is over. I give you my word that they will not be watched or followed at any time. And if you ever find that they are, it is not by my doing."

"Understood."

"Good. Now that we have that out of the way, how far out of town are you?" Vincent wondered.

"About an hour or so."

"Fantastic. Why don't you head over to the warehouse where we conducted our previous business when you get in?"

"What for?"

"Oh, I've got a little surprise for you that you may be interested in."

"I'll be there," Recker agreed.

"We'll be waiting."

After Recker put the phone down, he wondered what Vincent had in mind. Considering that's where they held Mancini for him before, Recker could only assume that they had something similar in mind once again. The only problem in Recker's mind was that he wasn't looking for anybody that would lead to such a situation again. Unless it was Simmons. The longer Recker thought about it, that was the only solution that made any sense to him. It had to be Simmons. And while he hadn't given much thought to Simmons' situation after Vincent got involved, he just assumed that Vincent either killed him or sent him packing somewhere.

Somewhat surprisingly, Recker didn't feel all that much rage toward Simmons. Was the long drive cooling off his temper? Or was it the fact that both Jones and Mia wound up being unharmed? If the situation didn't go down as it did, and Simmons had his way, then Recker's anger probably would've still been off the charts. And there was no distance that would have cooled it. For the rest of the drive, Recker's thoughts stayed with Vincent and the person that he assumed he was holding at the warehouse. Though he still didn't know what Vincent's game was. If he wanted Simmons dead, he easily could've done it himself. After all, Simmons was one of his men. He wouldn't need Recker to finish him off.

The only other reasoning that ran through Recker's mind was that it was some weird test. Did Vincent just want to see how far Recker would go to protect his friends or acquaintances? After what happened with Mancini and the fact that Recker passed up the opportunity for revenge, he wondered if Vincent was evaluating him in some form or fashion. If it turned out that Simmons was being held as a test case for Recker, he thought it might be a situation that he couldn't back down from. If things had gone down differently, and Simmons had taken Mia out of town, there was no doubt in Recker's mind that he'd hunt him down and kill him. But since things transpired differently, there was now wiggle room in Recker's mind about Simmons' ultimate fate.

If Vincent was holding his man there to see if Recker would take the bait, he thought he just might have to do it. Vincent saw him pass up the opportunity to do it once. If Recker did it twice, that might indicate weakness to the crime boss. If Recker didn't make a strong statement, he thought he might be telling everyone that it was OK to mess with people that he knew. That there would be no consequences. The longer Recker thought about it, the more convinced he became in his opinion that he'd have to swing a heavy hammer in this situation.

Whether it was real or just imagined, Recker couldn't risk a similar situation happening again. If he did nothing and let Simmons go, and word got around that The Silencer didn't retaliate for messing with his friends, then that would put Mia in even more jeopardy. Others may do the same to her or even worse without feeling at risk of Recker's wrath. Even Vincent himself may begin to think that Recker wasn't as lethal as he thought he was. Vincent might think that Recker didn't have the mean streak that most people believed he did. How he'd handle the situation, if that's what it was, was all Recker thought about for the rest of the ninety-minute drive back to Philadelphia.

Once Recker got back within the city limits, he called Vincent to let him know he was about twenty minutes away so they'd be expecting him. When Recker got to the front gates of the warehouse, he was let in without a problem or Malloy coming out to clear him. He drove up to the main building, with it looking almost exactly the same as it did the last time he was there. There was one open bay with the door open and a light on. When Recker parked, he just sat in his car for a few moments and took a deep breath, preparing himself for what he was about to walk into.

Recker got out of the car and started walking toward the side door. His legs were feeling cramped and his heart was racing as he thought about what was inside. Before he got to the steps the door opened, Malloy revealed himself within the frame of it. Malloy held the door open as Recker walked up the steps and walked inside.

"I see you guys haven't decorated much," Recker quipped.

Malloy briefly laughed before leading Recker across the floor to the side office in the back. The same one that they held Mancini in. When they got there, Malloy stopped just in front of it, letting Recker go in first. Recker instantly saw a man sitting in front of him, behind a desk and tied to a chair. Just as Mancini was before. And just like the Mancini incident, there was a gun just lying there on the desk. Recker briefly looked at him before turning his attention to the left, seeing Vincent standing there with a grin on his face.

"Hello, Mike," Vincent greeted. "Hope your drive wasn't too tiring."

"I've had worse."

"I'm sure you have."

"Who's this?" Recker asked, though he was already sure of the answer.

"That is our friend Joe Simmons."

"Looks like he's seen better days," Recker replied, noticing the numerous cuts and bruises on the man's face.

"Haven't we all?" Vincent asked, smiling.

"Why's he here?"

"Well, you see, this is an interesting predicament we've now found ourselves in."

"How so?" Recker wondered.

"The question is now what do we do with him. If we let him loose, he could always be considered a danger to you and your friends... or non-friends as they were. And for me... well, he's endangered my operations by operating outside of my guidelines that I have set forth," Vincent explained.

As they were discussing him, Simmons was wriggling around

in his chair, trying to say something. It was just muffled sounds, though, as the gag in his mouth prevented anything he said from being heard clearly. Malloy wasn't pleased with his efforts though and gave him a hard slap to the side of his head to indicate his unhappiness, quieting Simmons' movements.

"I'm honestly at a crossroads in determining the best course of action here," Vincent facetiously said.

Recker wasn't fooled in the slightest. He knew exactly what Vincent wanted. Vincent wasn't the type of man who usually struggled in making a decision. He was usually swift and decisive in determining what he wanted. Just as Recker suspected as he was driving there, Vincent was testing his resolve. He wanted to see just how cold-blooded Recker could or would be.

"Are you?" Recker asked. "I think you know exactly what you want to happen here. Seems like we were in this position once before."

"Well, circumstances are somewhat diff..."

Recker didn't see the need to listen to any more of Vincent's nonsense or games. They all knew what was supposed to happen there and Recker didn't feel like putting it off any longer. He didn't even let Vincent finish his sentence as Recker quickly reached for the gun on the desk, interrupting Vincent's thoughts. Recker pointed the gun at Simmons' chest and unloaded the clip. Pop. Pop. Pop. Pop. Pop. Pop. Six shots. Only the first one was truly needed as Simmons died after the first bullet penetrated through his body. But Recker felt like making an extra statement by emptying the gun's chamber.

Vincent and Malloy just stood there looking at the lifeless body of their former employee, somewhat stunned at the quickness and decisiveness of Recker's actions. Since Recker didn't kill the man who shot him, Vincent had reservations about whether he'd pull the trigger in this instance either. He just wasn't sure if

Recker was as vicious as his reputation seemed to entail. And though Vincent didn't have an exact preference for which way Recker would go, it would go a long way in determining how Vincent proceeded in the long run. Killing Simmons so quickly and ruthlessly seemed to enforce the notion that Recker wasn't a man to be messed with. If Recker hadn't, Vincent may have thought that perhaps he could take some liberties against him in the future if the need ever arose. Those thoughts, even if they were small in nature, had now been effectively squashed. Vincent had never seen Recker's work firsthand. He'd only heard second hand stories up until that point. But he was now satisfied that Recker was the man that he assumed him to be.

Recker didn't feel the need to stick around and admire his work any longer than necessary. He also didn't feel like sticking around to shoot the breeze or talk about what just happened either. He immediately nonchalantly tossed the gun to Malloy, who caught it in his midsection. Recker then just turned and looked at Vincent, giving him a nod before leaving the room.

"Thanks for the help," Recker told him.

"I'll put the bill in the mail," Vincent joked, getting a smile from his visitor.

Recker walked across the warehouse and out the side door on his way to his car. Vincent and Malloy emerged from the office and watched him through the open bay door as Recker drove away.

"That was quick," Malloy stated.

"Yes. Much quicker than I had anticipated," Vincent replied. "I expected there to be some conversation, some back-and-forth banter between us, but this worked out just as well."

"How you figure?"

"Each interaction we have with him reinforces our beliefs or strengthens our opinions in one way or another," Vincent explained. "After the Mancini incident, I must admit I had some doubts about him, even if they were fleeting. But this does reinforce what I've believed all along."

"Which is?"

"That he's not a man you want to cross. He's somewhat of a curiosity, don't you think?"

"In what way?" Malloy wondered.

"You saw how he acted against Mancini. Here was a man who tried to kill him, actually shot him, and he didn't seek revenge upon him. Even seemed indifferent towards his execution. Then there was tonight. Never met the man before, didn't do any actual harm to him whatsoever, but he acted quickly, decisively, ruthlessly. And with anger."

"So what's that say to you?"

"That you don't mess with the man's friends," Vincent answered. "He's more concerned with their safety and well-being than he is with his own. And that's a dangerous quality."

36

With having such a long day, Recker slept late the following morning, not waking up until eleven. After the killing of Simmons, Recker went straight to his apartment and went to bed. He sent Jones a short text message after leaving the warehouse telling him everything went well and that he'd see him later in the afternoon. Jones didn't bother inquiring into the events at the warehouse at that point, knowing there'd be plenty of time to go into it the next time Recker came into the office. He knew his partner must've been exhausted and wouldn't have been bothered if he even took the entire day off. Jones wondered about whether Recker finished his business in Ohio. Recker never mentioned whether he got the job done before returning. The professor would have felt bad if his trip had been cut short because of the predicament they put themselves in.

When Recker finally did wake up, he took a quick shower before getting on with his day. He didn't bother to eat, wanting to see and talk to Mia as quickly as possible before he did anything else. He needed to make sure she was OK. While he knew from talking to Jones that she was physically safe, Recker needed to see her with his own eyes. He needed to hear it out of her voice that there were no lasting effects. Recker once again sent a message to Jones telling him he'd be in at some point but didn't know when. He called Mia's phone a couple of times but it went straight to voicemail. He knew that she usually only turned it off when she was at work so he immediately left to go to the hospital. Knowing that she usually worked either a mid-shift or later into the night, Recker decided to wait in the cafeteria for her, knowing that she'd eventually show up when she had a break.

Recker patiently sat at a table in a corner of the cafeteria, sipping on a coffee as he calmly waited for his friend to show. After two hours of waiting, he looked at the time, but he wasn't in a hurry to leave. And he wasn't leaving until he saw her. Or until he knew she was no longer there. A lot of things went through his mind as he watched people go by. The situation Mia and Jones got themselves in the day before was the most prevalent and how close he came to losing them. He also thought about how Edwards was still out there walking around, what he did to Simmons, as well as a few fleeting glimpses of Carrie's face.

In fact, he got so lost in his thoughts that he never even saw Mia come into the cafeteria. She grabbed a few things for lunch and paid at the register. Then as she was looking for a table, she caught a glimpse of Recker sitting back in the corner. He still didn't see her and she could tell that he seemed to be in another world. Although she was happy to see him, she thought it was strange that he was there and wondered what the purpose of his visit was. She approached his table and put her tray down across from him, wondering what it was going to take for him to notice her coming. Recker's trance was broken upon seeing and hearing the tray hit the table. He looked up at her and smiled, pleased she was finally there.

"Hey," Recker happily greeted.

"Is this seat taken already?"

"Nope. Been waiting for you."

"Waiting? Why?" she asked. "How long have you been here?"

"About two hours."

"Two hours?! Why didn't you just call up and tell them to page me or something?"

Recker shrugged, not wanting to make a big deal about waiting. "I didn't want to bother you. I called your phone but since you didn't answer I figured you were here."

"Oh. Sorry, I don't have a phone right now. Mine was smashed yesterday, and I didn't get a new one yet."

"I forgot."

"Besides, it's been a pretty busy day here," she replied.

"I assumed as much. That's why I figured I'd just come down and wait for you here."

"You still should've called up."

"No big deal. I didn't mind the wait."

Mia smiled at him as she began eating. "Did you eat already?"

"Nah, this is fine," Recker replied with a shake of his head, holding his coffee up. "I'm not really that hungry, anyway."

"So what are you doing here?" Mia wondered.

"Just wanted to see you."

"Aww. You're sweet. Now what's the real reason you're here?"

Recker laughed and looked away for a moment. "Honestly, I just wanted to make sure you were OK."

"Yeah, I'm fine."

"You're sure? I know what happened yesterday must've been hard for you," he told her.

"Well, I can't say that I'm eager for it to ever happen again but I'm holding up."

"Good."

Mia looked around at the tables near them and leaned forward, making sure to keep her voice down. "What if, um, what if that guy comes back or something? What if he comes looking for me again?"

"You don't ever have to worry about him again."

"Are you sure?"

Recker nodded, "positive. He's been taken care of. He'll never be an issue for you. Forget about him."

"Now, when you say he's been taken care of, what does that mean exactly?" Mia asked, hoping it didn't mean what she thought it did.

Without coming right out and saying that he killed him, which Recker didn't want to do, he tried to think of how he could dance around the subject.

"Just means what it sounds like," Recker said. "He's gone. You don't have to worry about him. And you can rest easy, knowing that Susan's killer was brought to justice."

"By who?"

Recker and Mia's eyes locked together for a few moments. Though he didn't regret getting rid of Simmons, he was a little hesitant to come right out and tell her that he killed him. But he didn't have to. The way he was looking at her, Mia could tell that he did. If not, he would have immediately told her that someone else did. She knew that he just didn't want to admit it to her.

"Did you kill him?" she asked.

Recker sighed and looked around again as he struggled on whether he should tell her the truth. "I don't think you really need to know the particular details. Just be happy that he's gone."

Seeing that he kept avoiding the subject, Mia assumed that he just didn't want to talk about it and stopped pestering him with questions about the subject. She took a few bites of her food as she watched him rub his hands together, fidgeting around in his chair. Recker looked like he was nervous or anxious about something. She couldn't recall him ever looking like that before. Was it the questions about Simmons that he was trying to steer away from? Still, seeing him act nervous was making her a little nervous, wondering what he was doing there. Though it would've been a sweet gesture on his part to show up and just check on her well-being, it wasn't something he'd ever done before. Of course, she'd never gotten kidnapped before either.

"Is there something wrong?" Mia finally asked.

"Wrong? No, why?"

"I don't know. Just seems like you're not yourself. You seem like you're off, like you're nervous or something."

Recker shook his head. "No. I just wanted to make sure you were good."

"You could've just called for that. Why did you specifically come here?"

"Well, I got back real late last night, and I figured you were already in bed. Then when I got up, you didn't answer your phone, so I didn't want to wait until you were done work before talking to you," Recker told her.

"Are you just pumping me for information?"

"What about?"

"About what those guys did or asked."

"No, no. Only thing I'm worried about is your safety. That's it."

"You were worried about me?" she asked, never getting the feeling that he cared for her as much as she did for him.

"Of course. You weren't touched or anything were you?"

"No. I mean, Simmons slapped me in the face once or twice and grabbed my ass once, but nothing more than that."

"OK."

"It's just that...," Mia started then stopped.

"What?"

"Uh, it's nothing. Just something that the one guy said to me."

"What was it?"

"The one guy questioned me about you."

"Vincent," Recker responded.

"Yeah. I guess he wanted to see what our relationship was."

"What'd you tell him?"

"The truth. That we were just friends, and that you saved me from an abusive boyfriend once," she answered, looking sad as she played with her food.

"And?" Recker asked, concerned.

"He said something about how a man like you doesn't really have friends or anyone who's close to him."

Recker looked at her, having an idea of where she was heading. "That's sometimes true."

"And he said that it was smart of you to keep someone like me close to you," Mia said, still looking down at the table.

"And why did he say that was?"

"Cause he said that with me being a nurse that it was smart for you to keep someone like me around in case something happened to you," she explained. "Like when you were shot and came to my apartment."

Recker leaned back and put his hand on his face, running it down past his lips and chin as he thought of a reply. He could tell that she'd given it some thought, and even if she didn't believe it to be true, it at least had crept into her mind a little bit. She worried that he might have just been using her for her skills and that he didn't care about having her in his life.

"And what do you think?" Recker wondered.

Mia didn't immediately answer and just shrugged, wiping her

eye as she felt a tear start to form. "I don't know. I guess sometimes I feel like that might be true. That maybe you just keep me around because you might need me sometime."

Recker knew he had to put her mind at ease right away. He reached his hand across the table and gently grabbed hers, rubbing it slightly, not letting go of it. Once she felt his hand, she looked up at him and saw him smiling warmly at her.

"The reason I keep you around is because I want you to be in my life. Not because I need you to be," Recker told her.

"Then why do you act so carefree with me? I'll call you and you won't get back to me for three or four days. I'll ask you to dinner and ninety percent of the time you say you can't make it. I feel like you intentionally keep me at a distance."

Recker, still holding her hand, looked away as he thought of the best way to say what was in his mind. It was a topic that seemed to always pop up between them every couple of months. He could always successfully dodge away from it, but he knew that at some point, he was going to have to honestly tell her what was in his heart. And he wondered if now was the time to share that viewpoint.

"I've always felt like we shared some type of... connection or a bond," Mia told him. "Like there's something there between us. But you always just shut me out and pretend that it isn't there. Or maybe there really isn't, and it's just me hoping that there is and one day a light bulb will go off over your head and you'll see it too."

Though Recker was still hesitant to come clean about everything, he could see the pain in her eyes. Tears were forming in her eyes and he didn't want to keep putting her through the agony of not knowing exactly what their relationship was.

"Fine. I'll tell you the truth," Recker stated.

"Oh boy," Mia responded, worried. She was shaking her leg up and down as her nerves were getting the better of her as she anxiously awaited what he was about to say.

"You're right. I do push you away sometimes and sometimes I keep you at a distance on purpose."

"Why?"

"There are plenty of reasons and none are close to being anything like you're thinking."

"Just tell me and put me out of my misery."

"The real reasons are because of the man I am, the life that I lead, the things that I do, things that I've done, things in my past," he told her.

"Because of what you did in the CIA?" she asked, still not fully understanding.

"Mostly."

"But that's in the past. What's that got to do with now?"

"It's got everything to do with it," Recker huffed, still struggling with how best to describe his feelings. "Look, I like everything about you. You're pretty, smart, fearless, funny, stubborn at times... there's nothing I don't like about you. And that's what frightens me sometimes. Because I could see myself falling hard for you if I let myself."

"And you don't want that?"

"It's not that I don't want it. It's that I can't have it. I can't let it. I can't have you and you can't have me."

"But why?" Mia cried. "I still don't understand."

"Because you deserve better than me. All I can do is bring you heartache."

"You won't even give it a chance. How do you know?"

"Because I tried it once before," Recker answered, figuring it was time to reveal what he'd been hiding from her for so long. "I was engaged once."

"Oh? You've never mentioned that."

"Because it's...," Recker stumbled over his words, pain clearly still evident on his face as he thought about it. "Because it's something that I'll never get over. And it's a mistake that I'll never make again."

Mia could see how torn up Recker was over recalling his past. Though she still had trouble understanding his reasoning, she cared for him too much to not try to console him over whatever it was that still haunted him.

"What happened?" she softly asked.

Recker sighed as he began to tell his story. "A few years ago I met a woman named Carrie, and we fell in love. Without getting into every detail, I wanted to leave the CIA and settle down with her. Two years ago I was in London on an assignment. It was a setup. That scar you saw on my stomach was from that night. I was shot and bleeding badly and just walking around aimlessly until I thought of Carrie, thinking she might be in danger. So I called her to warn her and tell her what happened so she could go somewhere safe."

Mia had a feeling of what he was about to say next. She felt so badly for him as he began explaining his past. They were still holding hands, though now, she was the one rubbing his hand.

"When I called her phone, a man picked up. It was another agent. And he told me he just killed her," Recker revealed, rubbing sweat off his forehead.

"I'm so sorry, Mike."

"That's the reason why I can't let myself fall for you. I can't get involved with you and let that happen again. I won't let it. I care too much about you to let that happen again."

"But just because it happened once doesn't mean it would happen again," Mia argued.

"You don't get it. If you're with me, you will always be a target. There are people out on these streets, if they knew you were special to me, that would use you as bait in order to get to me. What you experienced yesterday would be a regular occurrence. You'd get kidnapped, followed, shot at, beat up, who knows what else? Is that what you want?"

Not knowing how to respond, Mia just looked down, obviously disappointed in what she was hearing. Recker knew he was breaking her heart, but it was something that just had to be done. For her own good.

"Listen, I'm still on the CIA's radar," Recker told her. "They're still out there looking for me. They haven't stopped looking for me and they never will. And eventually I'll pop up on one of their screens and they'll be on my doorstep. I don't want them to be at yours too."

"I understand," Mia replied, disappointment flowing from her voice.

"You deserve to be happy. You deserve someone that can make you happy. I just don't think I'm that guy."

"But you won't even give it a chance."

"If you're with me, you're always gonna have to look over your shoulder. That's not a life you should lead. That's not a life anyone should lead."

"So why do you?"

"Because it's all I know. It's who I am at this point. I can never lead a normal life even if I wanted to."

"What if you left the country?" Mia asked.

"There's nowhere you can run from these people."

"How do you even know they're still looking for you? Maybe they gave up and moved on."

"Even if they had, the things I do now still prohibit a normal life for me. I have to use different identities, stay out of view of cameras, pull a hat down over my face to avoid detection, those are things you shouldn't have to go through," Recker continued. "You should be able to come home after work and have someone there waiting for you. You should be able to look into someone's eyes when you wake up in the morning. You should be able to have a family and have kids. I can't give you any of that."

"Why does this feel like a goodbye speech?"

"I don't mean it to be."

They continued their conversation for a few more minutes, though it mostly consisted of Recker telling her why a relationship between the two of them wouldn't work. Mia couldn't help but look like she'd just been stabbed in the heart. She understood his reasoning, but it didn't help to soothe the pain. It was tough for her to understand the things that Recker had been through. It was tough for anybody who had a normal life and a regular job to get what Recker was talking about. They just couldn't comprehend what the life he led was like. Mia looked at her watch and started scurrying along.

"I'm already late. I have to go," she told him.

She had about five more minutes but she couldn't take any more of the conversation. She felt like she'd been punched in the gut, stabbed in the heart, and hit by a bus all at the same time. She gathered her stuff up and put what food remained back on the tray as she started to stand up, trying hard not to look at Recker.

"I guess I'll talk to you later," Mia said.

As Recker watched her walk out of the cafeteria, he felt terrible about making her upset. He rested his elbow on the table and put his head in his hand as he rubbed his forehead.

"This is not how I thought this was gonna go," he said to himself.

37

Recker stayed in the hospital cafeteria for another hour or so after Mia left, just thinking about everything he said, replaying their conversation in his mind. He felt like it couldn't have gone any worse. He went there to make sure she was OK, worried about her, and she left in a worse shape mentally than before Recker talked to her. He thought about waiting there the rest of the day and night until Mia was done so they could continue their conversation, so he could somehow make it right with her. Recker didn't want to leave her in such a despondent mood but he also thought that there was no way around that unless he did a complete about face in regards to what she wanted.

Eventually, he thought it was better to give her some space for a while. After their talk would she want to even be around him anymore? Instead of just sitting there doing nothing, he figured it was probably time to get back to the office and see what Jones was up to. He got back in his car and drove straight to the office without stopping.

The Silencer Series Box Set

Once he got there, he sat in the parking lot in front of the Laundromat, thinking about his options. He hadn't forgotten about Edwards. Recker wondered if the time was right to go back down there immediately and finish the job or if he should wait awhile. He wasn't even gone a day before his friends got in trouble without him there. Of course, he also realized that now that Mia's problem had been solved, there was no reason any of them should get into a situation like that again. Then there was Mia. Recker still couldn't stop thinking about her. He suddenly felt like a rush of emotions were pouring over him regarding her. Was it because her life was in danger that made him feel the things he'd been trying to bury since he'd known her? He did what he promised to himself that he wouldn't do. He let his guard down. He couldn't deny to himself any longer that he did feel an attachment toward her. But he had to fight the urge to do something about it. Recker felt strongly about not acting upon it. If they pursued a relationship, and she ended up like Carrie, he couldn't live with himself knowing another love died because of him. He sat in his car for an hour before figuring he had to get moving.

Jones noticed Recker pull into the lot via the camera feeds and wondered what he was doing, just sitting there in his car. Curiosity had gotten the better of him after his friend still hadn't exited the car after half an hour. He quickly pulled up Recker's phone records to see if he was engaged in a conversation with anybody. After seeing that he wasn't, Jones was even more perplexed than he was before. He couldn't understand what Recker was doing if he wasn't on the phone.

Once Recker finally made it up the steps and into the office, he greeted Jones and sat down at a computer. Recker put his hands on the keyboard but that's as far as he got. He sat there looking at the screen without making another move. With Mia and Edwards still on his brain, his head was in a fog. He didn't know what he was doing. He just continued to sit there for a few more minutes, his hands almost frozen on the keyboard. Jones stopped typing several times as he looked to his left, seeing that his partner seemed to be in a daze. Each time Jones looked at him, he thought, now there was a man with a lot on his brain. Recker wasn't disguising well whatever was troubling him. It was clear he had a lot eating away at him. Jones pushed his chair away from the computer and turned to face his friend, hoping he could ease his troubles away a bit. The least he could do was listen. Sometimes that was as good as anything.

"I would try to say something funny but I get the sense you wouldn't see the humor," Jones said.

Recker heard him say something, but he wasn't listening closely. "What?"

"Nothing. I was just trying to lighten the mood. Can I ask what's troubling you?"

"Nothing," Recker replied in a completely unconvincing manner.

Recker started pushing some buttons on the keyboard, but he still wasn't doing anything constructive. He was just passing time. The tone of his voice told Jones everything. With that one word, it sounded like Recker had the weight of the world on his shoulders. Jones thought he'd just leave him alone for a while to sort out his thoughts and went back to his computer. But it was still gnawing at him. He tried to think of what could have been depressing his friend so much. Then it came to him. After everything that went down the previous day, it didn't even occur to Jones to ask what happened in Ohio. He thought that must've been it and cursed himself for even forgetting about it. Either Recker killed Edwards and didn't get the satisfaction he was hoping for or he didn't kill him and was still upset about it. Pushing himself away from the computer again, Jones sought to re engage his partner in conversation.

"Can I ask about your trip to Ohio?" Jones wondered.

"What about it?"

"Did, uh, were you able to get the closure you were hoping for?"

"I did not," Recker directly answered.

Knowing he was part of the reason why Recker's plans failed, Jones felt badly about it. He thought there was probably something different he could have done to prevent the whole Simmons situation from happening.

"I'm sorry for that," Jones stated.

"It's not your fault."

Seeing that Recker still seemed angry, and whatever trance he was in, didn't seem to be going away, Jones tried to think of something to get him right again.

"Why don't you go back down there and finish what you started?" Jones told him.

"I dunno."

"It's something you've wanted for so long. Why put it off now?"

"I don't even know if it makes a difference anymore," Recker replied.

Jones leaned back in his chair, trying to analyze his friend's behavior. It was strange. Just a day before, Recker was fired up about going down to eliminate Edwards and try to get some sense of closure about everything that happened in London. And now, a day later, he didn't even seem to care. As Jones looked at him, he figured there must have been something else in play. Something else had to be bothering him to get in a mood like this. Jones was just going to have to figure out how to pry it out of Recker's lips. Then he thought about where Recker had been since he got back to town. Perhaps it was whatever happened when he met with Vincent.

"You never told me how things went with Vincent," Jones said.

"Yes I did. I sent you a text."

"Well, all you said was everything was fine. There's not a lot of details in that."

"What else do you need to know?" Recker asked.

"How about telling me what happened?"

"He said nobody from his organization would be watching for you or Mia."

"And what about Simmons?" Jones asked.

"He's dead."

"How did that happen?"

"I killed him," Recker plainly stated, without a hint of emotion.

"Oh. I see. I suppose you did what you had to do. You did what was necessary."

"Just like always."

"Is that what's bothering you? Killing Simmons?" Jones wondered.

"No."

Jones took him at his word. He didn't think a man like Simmons losing his life would be enough to drag Recker down into the dumps like this. Not that he thought killing anyone was an easy task. He'd probably begin to worry if he thought it didn't bother Recker at least a little bit, just as it did when he killed Marco Bellomi. But Simmons was not an innocent person. He was a murderer, kidnapper, as well as a host of other criminal infractions. He didn't think that was the kind of killing that would bother Recker the most. Not believing that to be the issue, Jones turned his focus elsewhere, wondering where else Recker had been. Was it something that just happened? Being fresh in Recker's mind would cause him to still be in that kind of mood, Jones thought. Seeing as how Recker took a long time to get to the office, Jones wondered what else he was doing up to that point. Considering he had yet to bring up Mia's name or ask how she was, Jones thought that maybe it had something to do with her. He thought it strange that Recker wouldn't have at least mentioned her or asked about her, unless he'd already talked to her.

"Get enough sleep today?" Jones casually asked.

"Yep."

"What else did you do today?"

"Not much," Recker answered.

"Have you talked to Mia?"

"Yeah."

"Is she OK?" Jones asked, trying to pry a more detailed answer out of him.

"I guess so."

"That doesn't sound promising."

"She's fine," Recker told him.

"Is that where you've been all day? Talking to Mia?"

"Just a little bit."

"Damn it, Mike, will you give me something at least?" Jones asked, his voice raised.

Recker just turned his head and glared at the professor, slightly annoyed by the tone of his voice. Jones could see by the evil eye he was getting that he must have struck a nerve. Whatever conversation Recker had with Mia was what was bothering him. More than Simmons, more than Vincent, more than even Edwards. That was telling to Jones. A man that Recker had been waiting almost two years to kill was taking a backseat to what Jones guessed to be an argument with a friend. Or was the friend part the issue? Jones had always known that the two had feelings for each other, though it was more obvious on Mia's part. But he could tell that Recker did too. He just was always able to push those feelings to the side.

"You know, sometimes, you just need the ear of a good friend," Jones stated. "Sometimes it helps."

Recker looked at the professor out of the corner of his eye as he thought about the proposition. Recker opened his mouth as if about to say something but then thought better of it and closed it. Venting about his feelings and opening up about his emotions wasn't one of his strengths. He just did that at the hospital with Mia and that didn't wind up going so well from his standpoint. But after thinking about it for another minute, Recker figured there was no harm in talking about it with Jones since he wasn't emotionally involved in it.

"I went to the hospital to talk with her," Recker blurted out.

"Oh? What about?"

"Just to see how she was."

"And I take it things spiraled in a completely different direction?" Jones asked.

"Yeah."

"How so?"

"I don't know. We just started talking about relationships. I don't even remember how it got to that point," Recker frustratingly said.

"What was said?"

"I told her why we could never be together. The truth."

"Everything?" Jones wondered.

"Yeah. Everything. About the CIA, about London, about Carrie, all of it," Recker revealed.

"Oh. That must have been difficult. For both of you."

"You have no idea."

"I assume she didn't take it well," Jones assumed.

"No, not so much."

"Doesn't seem like you took it very well either."

Recker finally took his hands off the keyboard, throwing them in the air as he tried to articulate his feelings.

"I don't know. It's weird. It's like, since I got back all I kept thinking about was whether she was safe, how she was doing. Like, all of a sudden I started thinking...," Recker said, stopping before he said what he was feeling.

"You started thinking of her as more than just a friend," Jones finished.

"Yeah," Recker nodded.

"I suppose it was only a matter of time."

"How's that?"

"These aren't new feelings for you. You've had them for her since you met her. You've just been able to bury them until now."

"But why are they starting now? Why does it seem like I'm unable to do it now? I don't understand," Recker said.

"Emotions are a fickle business," Jones replied. "Sometimes they creep up on you when you least want them to or expect it."

"Since I've been back, I haven't been able to block her out of my mind."

"I suspect that it's because of what happened yesterday."

"I dunno. These are situations that I've been in before."

"I would say that before now, her safety was never in question. And with what happened yesterday, your emotions came to the surface because you feared that you might lose her," Jones told him.

"Maybe."

"Perhaps you finally let yourself feel something for her, something you had successfully buried, because you worried that you'd lose her like you lost Carrie."

"But Carrie was different," Recker said. He rubbed his eyes as he felt them beginning to tear up, successfully blocking them from showing.

"Is it?"

"I was in love with Carrie. We had something special."

"And maybe you've finally let your emotions show for Mia because you feel like you could have something special with her too."

"I can't. We both know that."

"Do we?"

"C'mon, David. You're the one that initially told me to stay clear of her. You knew something like this could happen."

"All I know is that she has feelings for you. You clearly have feelings for her. What's the answer? I don't know. I'm not a love doctor. I really don't have an answer for you."

"She can't be more than a friend," Recker reinforced.

"Most people don't sit in the parking lot for an hour just thinking about a friend, do they?"

Recker looked at him, realizing he must've seen him pull up on the security cameras.

"Mike, what I do know is you're a torn individual," Jones said. "You've been beating yourself up for a long time over what happened to Carrie. And I think you've tormented yourself long enough. It's consumed every breath you've taken, every step you've walked, every plan you've made, every relationship you've encountered. Eventually you're going to have to make peace with that."

"I'm never going to forget what happened," Recker argued.

"I'm not talking about forgetting it."

"Then what are you saying?"

"At some point, eventually, you have to make peace with what happened."

"Peace with who? Edwards?"

"With yourself," Jones answered. "You've put the blame on yourself for what happened as long as I've known you."

"Because it was my fault."

"That's what I mean. Eventually, you have to move on. I'm not talking about forgetting, but moving on. You've beaten yourself up inside and let it eat at you for so long."

"What else am I supposed to do?" Recker asked.

"Forgive yourself."

"Easier said than done."

"Don't I know it."

"How'd we get to talking about this, anyway?" Recker wondered. "I thought we were talking about Mia."

"It's all connected, isn't it? Because you've never forgiven yourself or made peace with what happened in London, you've denied what was painfully obvious in your relationship with Mia. Now that her life was in danger, all those feelings for her that you locked away have managed to find their way out," Jones said.

"I can't let her love someone like me, can I? Living the way that I do, being on a CIA blacklist, that's no life for her. If they showed up here tomorrow looking for me, or us, we'd have to split in a second. I can't bring her into that, can I?"

"My honest opinion?"

"Of course."

"No, you can't. You and I have made conscious decisions that have led us up to this point. We understand the risks and understand what the consequences might be. Being romantically linked to you will cause her to become a hard target because of who you are."

"So you think I should just push her away for good?" Recker asked.

"I don't know if it needs to be that drastic of a change. As long as both of you know the boundaries and don't cross them, then I don't see the harm in continuing to know each other and be friends. The difficult part will be when you're near each other, not throwing caution to the wind, so to speak."

"If she even wants that."

"I guess the thing to do would be to throw the ball in her court and see what she wants to do."

38

For the rest of the day, Recker tried to put his thoughts of Mia out of his mind. He was deeply torn on her. On the one hand, he liked her and liked being around her. On the other hand, he knew that the deeper the attachment between the two of them grew, the more danger she would be exposed to. After a little while, Recker was successful in blocking out his feelings for her and was able to start working on some of the cases Jones had pulled up.

Both Recker and Jones worked separately for a few hours, but Jones felt there were still some questions that needed to be answered. Specifically, what Recker intended to do about Edwards. Jones was never one to advocate killing anyone, no matter what they'd done, but this was a special case. Just as he'd told Recker, he wasn't sure he would ever truly find peace within himself until all the loose ends of London had been successfully tied up. And as far as Jones could tell, the last remaining piece of London that haunted Recker was the fact that Edwards was still walking around.

"What do you intend to do about Edwards?" Jones finally asked.

"I dunno. Same as before I guess."

"You guess? This has been all that you've talked about since I've known you. Finding him. And now that you did, you don't seem to care."

"Well, the one time I left here, you and Mia had your lives put in danger," Recker replied. "I'm not gonna risk you guys just so I can settle a personal score."

"Mike, I think we can handle you being gone for a day."

Recker just shot a look at his partner, thinking he had to be kidding.

"OK, that was different," Jones quickly responded. "There was a situation that was being looked into at the same time as your departure. But that's over with now. There's nothing here holding you back."

"I guess you're right."

"And besides that, if you don't get him now while you know his whereabouts, you might never get as good a chance as you have right now."

"You're probably right but why are you pushing it so much? Since when did you become such an advocate for this? If I recall, you were against this," Recker told him.

"Yes, for a long time I was. But the more I've thought about it, like I told you, you need to find peace. You need closure. And until you've done this, you will never get it."

"Fine. Maybe I'll leave tonight then."

"After you've talked with Mia?" Jones guessed.

"Guess I'll need to find closure with her too."

"Well, before you do anything, let me make sure he's still there. I'd hate for you to go down there only to realize he's left for an assignment."

Jones immediately got back on his computer and started pulling up Edwards' information. He got back into the same screen he was on before which listed the latest assignments that had been handed to Edwards. He still had to go through a few backdoor channels just to make sure that his visit stayed in secret and didn't trip off any alarms. After about ten minutes, he had the information he was looking for.

"Oh dear," Jones stated, diverting his attention between the screen and looking at the calendar.

"What is it?" Recker anxiously asked, sliding his chair over.

"It appears Mr. Edwards has been handed a new assignment."

"Where?"

"Tough to say right now. He's got a new flight itinerary though."

"Where's he going?"

"JFK in New York."

"Where's he flying out of?" Recker asked.

"John Glenn Columbus International Airport."

"When?"

"9:30 tomorrow morning," Jones answered.

"I'll have to try and get him before he gets there. Too many cameras at the airport."

"I don't know if you'll be able to get there in time unless you leave right this second. Or, perhaps it'd be better to get him once he arrives in New York. It would be easier to get lost in the crowd there."

"More of a spotlight too. There's a heightened sense of something happening in New York. It's more laid back down in Ohio, smaller airport, I think that's the better play."

"You have to leave immediately then to give yourself enough time to make it," Jones told him.

Recker didn't have the luxury of thinking about it too much

longer. If he intended on killing Edwards before he left Ohio, he had to leave now. But it also presented an additional complication. It wasn't enough for Recker just to kill his target. He didn't want to just size him up through the scope of a sniper rifle and pull the trigger. It just wasn't enough for Edwards to be dead. Recker wanted to do it up close. He needed to do it up close. He wanted Edwards to know who was killing him. Recker concluded that if he couldn't look Edwards in the eyes as he was killing him, he'd rather pass on the opportunity and wait for another chance somewhere down the road. He thought that was the only way he'd get closure.

After taking just a minute to think about it, Recker decided now was the time. He didn't want to waste any more time doing the thing that had consumed his thoughts for too long. He quickly grabbed his duffel bag and went to his gun cabinet, putting a few weapons inside to take on his journey. Before leaving, he left a few last-minute instructions for his partner.

"If anything comes up, I don't care how urgent it is, you wait until I get back," Recker told him.

"And what if Mia somehow gets involved in another issue?"

"I'm pretty sure that's over with."

"Just throwing it out there," Jones said.

"I'm serious. Whatever it is, let it ride until I return. If Mia decides to play Sherlock Holmes again for some reason, you bring her back here and lock her in," Recker said, only half kidding.

"That would be interesting."

Recker raised his eyebrows and pointed at his friend. "I mean it."

Jones put his hand up to prevent the lecture from continuing. "You have my word. No secret missions, no anything until you return."

"I'll call you when I get there."

Recker rushed out the door and down the back steps of the office, scurrying to his car. To make it down to Ohio by the time Edwards' flight took off, he knew he'd have to step on the gas pedal. About three hours into his drive, his phone started ringing. Looking at the caller ID, it was Mia. He debated about whether he wanted to answer it at the moment, but then he thought that was something he'd done too often with her. Instead of tackling the issue head on, he skirted around it, hoping it'd just somehow go away so he wouldn't have to deal with it anymore. But he didn't want to do that anymore. He owed it to himself, and more importantly, he owed it to Mia to not dance around the subject of their relationship and feelings. Recker then used his hands-free device to answer the call.

"Hey," Recker greeted.

"Hey," she somberly returned the greeting. "Umm, I just got done work and just wanted to talk about a few things if you have the time."

"Uh, yeah, sure."

"You're not too busy or anything?"

"No. Just driving right now."

"Oh. Where you going?" Mia wondered.

"I'm just on my way to Ohio."

"Is that where you were going before my little mishap?"

"Yeah. With everything that went down I had to race back here and I never got to finish what I was working on," Recker answered.

"Oh. I'm sorry about that."

"You don't have to apologize."

"Yeah, I do. That's, um, kind of one of the reasons I wanted to call you. I just wanted to say I'm sorry about... everything."

"Mia, it's fine."

"No, I mean, you were right. With everything that we talked about earlier, I never really got to say what I wanted to say to you."

"Nothing else needs to be said," Recker told her.

"Yeah it does. I just wanted to say thank you," she said, wiping her eyes as her emotions started tugging at her. "I shouldn't have been doing what I was doing. You were right. I should've left it to you or waited for you. I didn't have any clue what was really going on and I should've listened to you. I was wrong."

"You wanted answers, and you weren't getting any. I understand how frustrating that is."

"That guy that set us free, you sent him there, didn't you?" Mia guessed.

"What makes you think that?"

"Because you were away and worried you couldn't get to us in time. So you protected us the only way you could. He's that crime boss that you mentioned before to me, isn't he?"

"That's Vincent, yes."

"Did you have to make some sort of deal with him?"

"Everything turned out fine. You don't have to worry about it."

"If you had to do something unethical, or that you didn't want to do because of my stupidity…"

"Mia, it's fine," Recker repeated. "Honest, I didn't have to ki… everything worked out."

"How long are you gonna be gone this time?"

"Well, as long as you and David stay out of trouble, just a day or two," Recker laughed.

"I'll do my best."

"That's all I can ask."

"OK, well, I guess have a good trip."

"Was there something else?" Recker asked, getting the feeling that she had other things on her mind.

"Well, I kind of wanted to go over what we talked about earlier, but since you're driving and all, I guess it can wait."

"We can talk about it now if you want. It'll help me pass the time."

"Oh. OK. Well, I'm sorry if I acted like a little school girl at the hospital," Mia said.

"You didn't."

"Yeah, well, maybe. But I thought a lot about it and I'm not gonna try and force you or push you into anything you're not comfortable with. You obviously have your reasons for whatever you decide and I'll just have to deal with it. I know I'll probably never be able to fully understand things that have happened in your life before you met me."

"I never wanted to hurt you. I tried my best to keep you at a distance because I never wanted to have this conversation with you," Recker replied. "That's probably my fault for trying to have it both ways."

"What do you mean, both ways?"

"I wanted you close, but not too close. I wanted you in my life but I just didn't do enough to make you think things would never go further with us."

"Yeah, you did. I just ignored the signs and figured I could break you down, eventually."

"Well, you're a hard person to push away. It's not easy resisting someone like you, you know. Some guy's gonna be extremely lucky to have you. In another life, maybe it would've been me. It just can't be in this one."

"I know," she sorrowfully responded, barely audible.

"But, um... if it's too much," Recker sighed. "If it's too much or too hard to continue seeing me or anything and you wanna take a break or something, then, uh, I'll understand."

"Umm, I dunno, uh, let's just see how it goes."

"So I guess we're good then?"

"Yeah. Yeah, we are. We're good," Mia said. "So maybe we'll talk again when you get back."

"Sounds like a plan."

Once the conversation ended, Recker just tossed his hand-free device on the passenger seat, clearly annoyed. He started talking to himself out loud.

"When it came to handing out the good things in life, I clearly drew the short straw. Someone up there decided I wasn't worthy of having anything good in my life for too long."

Recker allowed himself to get caught up in self pity for a little while as he continued his trek to Ohio. He never was one to get lost in regrets or what-ifs or wonder what might have been if things had gone down differently in his life. Mostly because he was basically a realist at heart. He knew that sometimes, people just got dealt a harder set of cards to deal with in life and there was no rhyme or reason to it. That's just the way it was. He never wondered before what his life would be like if he never joined the CIA or enrolled into the black ops program. But after thinking about what he lost with Carrie, and what he'd never get to have with Mia, for the first time, he started thinking about what his life would've been like if he was someone else.

Of course, he knew that by doing so, he likely never would've even met Carrie or Mia if he never joined the CIA. Everything he had done in his life had a direct impact on meeting the both of them. If he hadn't, the loss he felt with Carrie would never have been burned into his memory. And Mia wouldn't be the situation that it was. But he allowed himself to envision what life could've been like if he'd have met each of those women under different circumstances, if he wasn't the man that he was. With Carrie, he could picture himself as a family man. He saw himself coming home from work and having her there with a couple of kids running around the house. When his thoughts turned to Mia, he pictured the two of them just doing couple things, going on dates and having romantic dinners. There was a small piece of him, just for a few minutes, who wished he was someone else.

After allowing himself to dream for an hour or two about what might have or could have been, Recker finally shook free of those thoughts. It was nice while it lasted though and made the drive seem that much quicker. With those tempting thoughts now out of his system, he turned his attention back to his target. He started to envision different scenarios on how his altercation with Edwards would go down.

Recker made great time in getting back into the state, much quicker than he did the first time around. It only took him a little under thirteen hours to get there this time. As he made his way toward the Edwards home, he was a little concerned that he wasn't going to arrive before his target left for the airport. Since it was past 7am, he called Jones to see if he could help in locating him to save time.

"David, just got here, are you able to verify if he's still at home or if he left yet?" Recker wondered.

"Well, I could, but not in the timeframe that you need. It's gonna take longer than you have time for. You might be better off just heading to the airport and waiting for him there."

Recker sighed, not getting the answer that he wanted. "I was hoping it wouldn't come to that."

"Are you going to back off?"

"No. I'll make it work."

"OK. I'll do my best to start checking the airport cameras and see if I can locate whether he's there yet."

"All right. I'll put the comm in. Let me know."

Recker headed straight for the airport, hoping he'd get there before Edwards did. Once his subject checked in, and he was surrounded by a bunch of people, killing him might not be an

MIKE RYAN

option. And he was too close now to have to put it off one more time. Seeing that it was just a couple minutes before 7:30, and most people checked in about two hours before their flight, Recker thought he might've made it just in time. Before getting out of the car, he put on a blank baseball type hat, cinching it down near his eyes. He swiftly walked into the airport and immediately grabbed a newspaper in case he needed to use it as cover.

"Michael, it doesn't appear that he's there yet," Jones said.

Recker buried his head into his arm, pretending he was wiping his face to conceal him talking. "Are you sure?"

"Well, all I needed to scan was the entrance cameras. I was able to hack into them rather quickly."

"How far back did you check?"

"I went back to 6am," Jones answered. "I didn't see anyone that looked like him come in yet."

"That means he should be here any minute."

"In theory."

"What, you think he might not show?"

"I don't know. Until it happens it's never a sure thing, is it?"

Recker found a wall to lean against as he anxiously awaited for his foe to arrive. He opened up the paper to pretend he was reading it, instead peering over the top of it as he watched people enter through the front doors. After ten minutes went by, he started to get a little nervous that his target was even coming. Had Edwards got last-minute orders to change flights or not even go at all? He figured he'd wait another hour for him then he'd drive back out to his house and see if he was still there. If he wasn't in either spot, then Recker would have to regroup and come up with another plan. He was praying that it wouldn't come to that though. He was ready for it to be over now.

Luckily for Recker, if he did say a prayer, it was answered. His attention perked up at 7:50 when he saw Edwards strutting through the door. With a small bag that he was wheeling behind him, he had a confident look and walk about him, like he had no worries in the world. That was about to change if Recker had his way. He briefly replayed their conversation in his mind one more time as he watched him walk by. Recker tugged his hat down even further to prevent him from being recognized. Edwards had an arrogant look on his face in Recker's mind. Of course, that could've just been because he hated the guy.

"Jones, he's here," Recker told him. "I'll contact you when it's over."

"Please be careful," Jones responded.

Recker started following his target as he watched Edwards stop at the Starbucks. Keeping his head down to conceal his face, he took up a new position as he kept close tabs on Edwards. After his target got his coffee, he started on the move again. Before heading to the gate, Edwards made his way to the bathroom as he made a last-minute stop. Sensing that it was the best opportunity that he was going to get, Recker also made a beeline for the restroom. He cautiously opened the door, just in case Edwards had spotted him and was trying to lure him in to turn the tables on him. Luckily for Recker, he hadn't.

Edwards was at the urinal, coffee still in hand, with his back turned to the door. Recker easily could've shot him and be done with it, but it just wasn't good enough. Recker quickly knelt and looked underneath the stalls to see if anyone else was there. Seeing that they were alone, Recker walked back to the door and quietly locked it. He went over to the sink and turned the water on, pretending to wash his hands. After a minute, Edwards had finished his business and walked over to the sink. He set his coffee down on the side of the sink, not having any clue as to the identity of the man standing next to him. He turned the water on and started washing his hands, giving Recker the opportunity he was waiting for.

Recker quickly turned toward his target and put his hand on the coffee, feeling how hot it was and flipping the lid off, all within a second or two. He threw the hot coffee directly into Edwards' face, temporarily stunning him as he dabbed at his eyes. Recker grabbed the back of Edwards' head and forcefully slammed it into the sink, knocking Edwards to the ground. A big welt immediately started showing on Edwards' forehead as Recker gave him a hard kick to the face, bloodying the man's nose. Recker then picked him up and threw him into the stall door, Edwards bursting through it as his head hit the bottom of the toilet. Edwards was dazed and confused and already in a lot of pain, unable to recognize who his attacker was. Recker gave his victim another stomp to the face, making sure he couldn't get up before he unleashed some more punishment. He then straddled Edwards' body and started raining down punches in a furious manner. Alternating between his left and right hands, Recker's knuckles quickly became bloodied as he opened up cuts on Edwards' face.

After a couple of minutes, Recker stopped, taking a few moments to calm himself so Edwards could finally see who his assailant was. With cuts above both of his eyes, nose, forehead, and lip, Edwards could barely open his eyes wide enough to see out of them. But Recker tried to make it easier for him, taking off his baseball hat and tossing it on the ground. Edwards tried to make a smile and let out as much of a laugh as he could, though it caused him to start coughing up some blood. Recognizing Recker immediately, he knew he was done for. Edwards stumbled his way through a few words before his time was up.

"I knew we'd have this day at some point," Edwards said, coughing. "Didn't figure it'd go down quite like this though."

"Funny how things look from different perspectives," Recker replied. "Cause this is how I always thought it would go."

"Don't suppose begging would help?"

"Nope."

Edwards smiled again, hoping to torment his attacker one last time. "You know, thinking back, I so enjoyed killing her."

That was enough for Recker. He didn't want to hear anymore. He took out his gun from the back of his pants and pointed it at his soon to be victim. Before pulling the trigger, he had some final words of his own.

"You know, talking about different perspectives, it's funny how things work out," Recker told him. "I could've done this yesterday at your house in front of your wife and son."

Recker had almost an evil smile attached to his lips as he saw the worried look on Edwards' face. He now realized that Recker knew where he and his family lived and worried for their safety. He worried that Recker would do to his family what Edwards initiated with him.

"Please, not them," Edwards pleaded.

Recker let out a laugh and pulled the trigger of his gun, hitting the front of Edwards' thigh with his shot. Edwards screamed out in anger, wondering what Recker was waiting for in finishing him off.

"Torment me all you want, just don't kill them. I beg you," Edwards pleaded again.

"I'm not like you," Recker responded. "I don't enjoy killing. Not even you."

Recker then fired three more shots in succession, all hitting his fallen target square in his chest, instantly snuffing out whatever life remained in his helpless body. He remained standing over the dead body for another minute, just staring at the carnage that he'd just unleashed upon him. With it now over with, Recker knew he couldn't stay there any longer. Sooner or later, someone else would try coming in, and with the door locked, might inquire to someone who worked there why it wasn't open. Recker looked down and grabbed his hat, pulling it back down over his eyes as he tucked his gun away in his pants again. He exited the restroom, standing on the outside of the door for a few moments to make sure nobody else entered already. He needed to make sure he had enough time to get away. After thirty seconds elapsed without anyone coming near it, Recker quickly hurried away toward the entrance. With his hat securely pulled down near his eyes, he kept his head looking toward the floor to prevent the cameras from getting a good shot of his face.

Recker got to his car and quickly peeled out of the parking lot. He periodically checked his rearview mirror to make sure that nobody was following him. Once he was on the road for about thirty minutes, he began feeling more secure in his escape. It seemed like a clean kill without any complications that would arise from it. He had forgotten to contact Jones to let him know, so he figured he would call him so he wouldn't begin to worry.

"It's done," Recker confirmed.

"I figured as much. I kept looking at the surveillance cameras and noticed you leaving a half hour ago."

"You could make me out?"

"Well, I could just because I knew the hat," Jones answered. "But you did a good job of not letting your face show so they shouldn't be able to match it back to you."

"That's good."

"I also checked parking lot cameras just to be sure they couldn't get a shot of your license plate."

"And?" Recker wondered.

"Nothing. You're in the clear. Even if it was, I could digitally alter it."

"How could you do that?"

"Did you never wonder about when you first arrived in Philly?"

"No. What do you mean?"

"Your face was picked up by airport security cameras when we had our first talk," Jones informed him. "I had to alter and erase some of the footage so it seemed as if you were never there."

"Why? You told me you did something with the flight manifest or something."

"Just in case someone went looking at nearby airports on a hunch. They obviously knew you were on a plane somewhere. So in case they looked into every airport security system on the east coast, I had to doctor the footage."

"Oh. You never mentioned that before."

"I never thought it needed mentioning before."

"Oh. Thanks for everything."

"You're welcome."

"How's everything there?"

"Just fine. Ready to get back into the swing of things."

39

Almost the entire ride home, Recker thought about the confrontation he'd just had with Edwards. It was something he'd thought about every day for almost two years. He thought about different ways he would kill him, one of which was brutally beating him just the way he'd done it at the airport. He hoped that once it was over, a sense of relief would be lifted off his shoulders, or a bright light would suddenly shine down from the sky upon him. But it didn't happen. At least not yet. Though he did feel a small sense of satisfaction, he didn't feel anywhere near as good as he hoped he would. He was obviously glad that he found Edwards and eliminated him, but it would never bring Carrie back. What Recker lost that night in London would never return to him, no matter how many revenge killings he had. Everything was still fresh in his mind, though, and maybe in a few days or weeks, things might look much different to him. He could only hope that Jones was right in that doing this would bring the closure he needed to keep going. Hopefully, he just needed more time to get to that point.

Recker took a little extra time on the way back than he did getting down to Ohio. He didn't see the need in driving faster and risk getting stopped by the state police somewhere on the road. He finally got back to the Philadelphia area around one in the morning and went straight to his apartment to try to get some sleep. There was nothing so pressing on Jones' list of potential victims that couldn't be started the next day. After an action-packed couple of days without getting much of a chance to rest, Recker fell asleep within minutes of his head hitting the pillow.

Getting back to the office the next day around ten, Recker brought a couple of breakfast sandwiches with him. Jones was already there, hard at work as usual. The professor had his list of targets that they needed to work on and he was putting on the finishing touches to his reports, checking out some background information on the first couple of people. He took a brief break, however, when Recker handed him his food and the two men began eating at the desk.

"Just so you know, your airport situation is all over the news," Jones said.

"Figured it would be. Airport killing is a big deal."

"Yes, it is. Regardless, I'm trying to keep ahead of the situation and monitoring it to see what kind of leads they come up with."

"Anything yet?" Recker asked.

"No, not so far. You did a good job in disguising yourself so I don't expect any repercussions."

"What are they saying so far?" Recker wondered. "What are they saying he is? International hit man?"

"Hardly. They're saying he's a security consultant who had clients with ties to organized crime."

"About what I figured."

"Well, I'll keep monitoring it in any case. You certainly look a little more refreshed though," Jones told him.

"Yeah, I feel a little better."

"It's amazing what a few hours of sleep will do for you."

"Yeah," Recker replied, though still not looking pleased.

"So what's wrong?" Jones asked, sure that something still seemed to be bothering him.

"I dunno. It's just that… I don't feel all that much different than I did a few days ago."

"You mean before killing Edwards?"

"Yeah."

"Well what did you expect?" Jones wondered.

"I don't know," Recker shrugged. "I just thought maybe I'd feel… happier or something."

"Mike, you've felt a certain way for a very long time. That's been ingrained into your soul and well-being with every step you've taken. The darkness that's been milling around inside of you isn't just going to evaporate overnight. It will take time."

"Yeah, I guess."

"Believe me, it will happen. Little by little, you'll get to a better place. Eventually your mind will get to a clearer place. But it will take time. You just have to be patient with it."

"OK. I, um, talked to Mia again last night," Recker revealed.

"Oh? How did that go?"

"I guess we'll see. She wanted to apologize and thank me for the other day."

"So she isn't upset now?"

"Well I don't know about that. She seemed more understanding of my position I guess."

"What else did you say?" Jones wondered.

"I told her if what we have now is too hard for her then I'd understand if she didn't want to come in contact anymore."

"Oh. What did she say to that?"

"She said we'll see," Recker answered.

"And what do you think she'll do?"

"I really don't know."

"And what are you hoping?"

Recker just shook his head. "I really don't know that either. I just want her to be happy. And I know that won't include me."

The pair finished their conversation over breakfast and got back to work. They started analyzing each of the cases on their list and started coming up with a game plan on how to act with each of them. They only got about thirty minutes into their work when they were interrupted by the sound of Recker's phone ringing. Recker looked at the ID and was a little perplexed at the caller. He couldn't figure out what purpose they'd have for calling him now.

"Miss me already?" Recker sarcastically asked.

Malloy laughed, appreciating his sense of humor. "No, not quite. Boss wanted to talk to you. Here he is."

"Mike, how are you?" Vincent greeted.

"All right. Kind of surprised to be hearing from you to be honest."

"We've had a good relationship so far and I want to keep up the bond that we're developing."

"Sounds like you're about to drop some bad news on me," Recker guessed.

"Possibly. I'll get right to it then. Based on what transpired the other day, I've heard some rumblings that something may be going on that I wanted to alert you about."

"Which is?"

"Joe Simmons has a cousin who's apparently none too happy about his death. From what I hear, he's sworn to avenge the people that were responsible for it," Vincent revealed.

"So why don't you put a stop to it?"

"He doesn't work for me. I don't really know much about him. I don't have a file on him or anything. Like I said, he's not a part of my organization. All I know is he lives in Jersey."

"Then how do you know about him?" Recker asked.

"I have a lot of eyes and ears on the street. One of my contacts informed me that he heard about his unhappiness."

"So who's he gunning for? You or me?"

"Well, from what I understand he doesn't know of my involvement in the situation. How that is, I don't know," Vincent answered.

"So that leaves me."

"There's more."

"Go ahead."

"I've heard he's also going after your nurse friend."

"Mia?"

"From what I understand, he holds her chiefly responsible," Vincent said.

"How's he even know about all this?"

"That I don't have an answer to."

"What's this guy's name?" Recker asked.

"Jason Gallagher."

"Thanks. I appreciate you looking out."

"If you need anything else just ask," Vincent told him.

As soon as Recker put the phone down on the desk, Jones could tell that he was deeply troubled by something. Hearing Mia's name in the conversation, he had a feeling it had something to do with her, but he couldn't figure out what. Not yet. Recker stood and put both of his hands on the edge of the desk as he leaned forward, looking down as he took a deep sigh.

"What is it?" Jones hesitantly asked with great concern.

"Simmons apparently has a cousin who wants revenge for what happened to him."

"Vincent?"

"He doesn't work for Vincent," Recker replied. "He doesn't know much about the guy other than he lives in Jersey."

"How does this guy know it was you involved?"

Recker shook his head in frustration for having to deal with another problem. "I don't know."

"Is he after Vincent as well?" Jones wondered.

"No. He doesn't know about Vincent's role in it."

"That's strange."

The two men stayed silent for another minute as they deliberated on what to do next. They obviously would have to protect Mia while at the same time finding Gallagher before he had a chance to enact his plan of revenge. Then Jones made a sound and looked at Recker as if an idea just popped into his head.

"What is it?" Recker asked.

"What if Simmons called this guy before everything went down, before we met him and told him that Mia was looking for him?" Jones wondered.

"Could be."

"Or, perhaps even after Simmons took us, before Vincent arrived, maybe he called his cousin to tell him what happened?"

"Could be."

"Let me dig into Simmons' phone records and see if he placed any calls."

"Might as well check into Jason Gallagher from Jersey while you're at it."

"We should've done this before as a precaution," Jones huffed. "Just to be sure there'd be no repercussions. I don't know why we didn't."

Jones feverishly typed away, trying to get into Simmons' phone records. After a few minutes, he successfully hacked into them. He looked down the list of numbers that Simmons called and saw that he placed a call at 1:15pm, a little over an hour after the supposed meeting with Jones and Mia that resulted in their capture. Armed with that knowledge, Jones typed in Jason Gallagher's name into their database, quickly getting a hit on his name. Jones also typed in the number that Simmons called, and it came back as belonging to Jason Gallagher.

"There's the connection," Jones noted.

"After Simmons took you guys, he called Gallagher and told him what was going on," Recker assumed.

"What do you want to do now?"

"I'll go to Jersey and pay this guy a visit."

"Maybe we should call Mia and let her know to be careful," Jones said.

"I don't want to worry her if we don't have to."

"Well I don't want you traveling to New Jersey only to find out he isn't there. What if he's already on the move? Let me try pinging his cell phone."

After a couple minutes and a few shakes of Jones' head, Recker could tell that he wasn't having much luck in his endeavor.

"I'm gonna go," Recker insisted.

"Just wait," Jones replied. "Let me try a couple other things."

"Such as?"

"I can hack into the GPS on his phone if it's been enabled recently and pull up his position that way."

About five minutes passed and Jones made a few gestures to his partner indicating that it was working out.

"I got it," Jones stated.

"Great. Where is he?"

"Not in Jersey. He's on the move."

"Where?"

Jones stopped typing and turned to look at Recker. "Here."

"Here? Where? The parking lot?" Recker asked.

"Not here. Here. Philadelphia."

Recker, fearing what was about to come out of Jones' mouth next, clenched his jaws. "Where is he now?"

"I think he's heading for the hospital."

"How much time do we have?"

"None," Jones puffed. "It looks like he'll be there any minute."

Recker immediately grabbed his phone and dialed Mia's number, desperately hoping that she'd pick up. It rang several times but just went to voicemail.

"Check if she's working," Recker told his partner.

Within a couple minutes, Jones easily hacked into the hospital time management system. It was a process he'd done several times before so it wasn't much of a challenge to him since he was already familiar with it. She was scheduled to work at eleven, though she hadn't yet clocked in.

"She's not picking up," Recker worriedly said.

"I think I made a mistake."

"What?"

"I'm looking at the time stamps and locations of Gallagher's phone," Jones replied.

"What's wrong?"

"I don't think Gallagher's on his way to the hospital."

"Then where is he?" Recker asked.

Jones looked at Recker, almost afraid to deliver the news. "I think he's already been there."

"Why do you say that?"

"The time stamp on the GPS on his phone indicates he was at the hospital's coordinates at 10:45," Jones answered. "The next one at 10:55 indicates he's moving away from there."

"He was there waiting for her," Recker assumed.

"I'm afraid it looks that way. She was supposed to work at eleven. It's now 11:30, and she hasn't clocked in yet."

Recker got a maniacal look in his eyes, like he was about to rip someone's head off. Though he wasn't mad at Jones, Recker stared at him for a minute as he let the anger flow through his veins.

"How could we be so stupid?" Jones angrily asked, slapping at his keyboard out of frustration.

Recker took control of his anger, not letting it get the best of him yet, and started to think clearly about the best way to proceed.

"That hospital has security cameras," Recker stated.

"I'm on it," Jones quickly replied.

Recker took a seat again, rolling it over next to Jones as they got into the security footage. Jones rolled the cameras back to 10:30 and fast forwarded a little at a time as they looked for Mia somewhere on the screen. At 10:50, Jones paused the screen, clearly seeing Mia get out of her car after she parked in the lot. They slowly played the footage, outraged at seeing three men quickly approach her only moments after exiting her vehicle.

"What's that there?" Recker asked, pointing to something on the screen. "In that guy's hand near her back."

Jones quickly zoomed in on the object, not liking what he saw. "It's a gun."

"Can you get into her phone and see where she's at?"

Recker leaned forward and put his head in both of his hands as he rubbed his face. His mind was racing with horrible thoughts that Mia was already dead. If he lost her too, there was no telling what type of destruction was about to commence. Jones looked over at his friend and could tell he was in a considerable amount of mental anguish as he thought about Mia's fate. The news he had to tell him wasn't going to make it any better.

"I locked into her phone's GPS system as well," Jones told him.

"And?"

"It's still at the hospital."

Recker started rocking back and forth in his chair, feeling like he was about to go full bore psycho on someone. Seeking to calm his friend, Jones offered up a few solutions to quell his rage.

"If they wanted her dead yet, they probably would've done it already," Jones told him. "If they were going to kill her, they wouldn't have taken her with them."

Recker stopped rocking and looked at Jones. "They need her for something."

"Maybe Simmons told her there was a man with her. Maybe they're looking for me."

"Or Simmons told him that she was a link to me," Recker replied. "Either way, I'm the one they're getting."

"Before this gets out of hand any further, we have a valuable asset on our side," Jones said.

"I don't know if we need to get Vincent on this."

"No. I don't mean him. I mean we already have Gallagher's phone number."

"I'll call him and see what he wants," Recker said.

Recker picked up his phone and looked at the screen to see Gallagher's number. He dialed the numbers, but waited a second before hitting the call button. Recker then hit the button and anxiously waited for Gallagher to pick up. It went to voicemail though.

"Maybe he's one of those people who don't answer numbers they don't know," Recker wondered. "I'll send him a text."

"Pick up the phone idiot," Recker texted.

Almost immediately, he got a text back. "Who this?"

"Pick up and find out."

Recker's phone rang almost instantly, this time, Gallagher calling him.

"Yo, who the hell are you?" Gallagher asked.

"I hear you might be looking for me," Recker answered.

"I'm looking for a lot of people."

"That girl you just took from the hospital better be unharmed."

"How'd you know about that?"

"Doesn't matter. What does matter is what you do from here," Recker angrily told him.

"What's your interest in this?"

"Cause I'm the one that killed your cousin," Recker revealed.

"You dirty rotten son of a bitch. I'm gonna kill your..," Gallagher started to threaten.

"Enough threats. The girl has no stake in this. I'm the one that killed your cousin. You got a problem with that, then take it up with me."

"Oh, I intend to."

"Let her go and give me a time and place and I'll be there."

"Or maybe I'll just kill her right now, then come for you."

"I wouldn't do that," Recker told him, looking at the computer screen for his personal information.

"Why not?"

"Cause I see that you live in Cherry Hill. That's not too far from where I am right now. In fact, I could probably make it there before you do. You probably wouldn't want to go back there anyway, mom might not wind up looking so good," Recker warned.

Gallagher was speechless for a second, knowing that the man knew where he lived. "How do you know that?"

"Doesn't matter. What does matter is if you harm that woman with you, I will visit your home and kill every single member of your family and I'll do it without hesitation. You want retaliation for your cousin, then take it up with me."

"Fine. One hour. Mercer Cemetery in Trenton. Come alone or else I'll kill her on the spot."

Jones quickly googled Mercer Cemetery to get a look at the

layout of the area. They studied it for a few minutes before Recker decided to go.

"If I leave right now, I might be able to get there before they do," Recker said. "We're closer to Trenton than the hospital is. Those idiots shouldn't have told me a spot to meet until they got there."

"I'm assuming they didn't realize you knew their exact location," Jones replied.

"Their mistake."

"I'll keep on tracking their GPS signal but there is one other problem."

"What's that?"

"What if they meet you in the cemetery but keep Mia in the car with a guard to make sure there's no problems? If you kill the others, maybe they'll kill her regardless," Jones mentioned.

It was a situation that Recker hadn't thought of, but it certainly seemed plausible. He'd need another person with him in that event.

"I guess you're volunteering," Recker told him. "Can you still track him remotely?"

"Of course I can. Who do you think you're talking to?" Jones responded, quickly grabbing a laptop.

Recker hurried out the door once more as he seemed to do all too often the last few days. Though he had the advantage of knowing the meeting spot, he was at a disadvantage of not knowing how many men Gallagher had with him. If it was whoever could fit into one car, knowing they had Mia, he probably had no more than three or four men with him. Recker raced down route one until he got into New Jersey. They got to the cemetery in about twenty-five minutes and pulled up to the curb just down the street from it.

"There's bound to be witnesses here," Jones noted. "Too many people not to be. Plus, there's offices right across the street."

"Can't worry about that right now."

"I know. I'm just saying."

"Nobody's there yet. Looks like we beat them there," Recker said.

Recker reached toward the floor of the back seat and unzipped his duffel bag, pulling out several guns. He kept three for himself and handed one to Jones.

"You may have to use this," Recker told him, handing him the weapon.

"I know."

"You can't hesitate or we all might wind up dead."

"I'll do what has to be done," Jones confidently stated.

"I'm gonna go to the back of the cemetery and wait for them. Let me know when you first put eyes on them."

Even though Recker initially thought about going to the back and waiting, he saw a big statue near the front, easily capable of hiding him from Gallagher's view. They waited another twenty minutes, anxiously looking out for their intended victims. As Gallagher's car pulled up, Jones got out and walked to the corner of the cemetery, waiting by the brick siding. Gallagher and three men got out of the black SUV, looking like they were in a hurry. Mia did not get out with them. Jones could only assume that she was still in the car.

"Mike, they're here," Jones told him.

"Mia?"

"I don't see her."

"Check the car," Recker replied. "How many are there?"

"Four walking in now."

"This is gonna happen quick. Check the car now."

Jones scurried over to the car, but did so in a way where it didn't appear he was running right for it. He looked through the back window but couldn't see much through the dark-tinted glass. He cautiously walked around to the back window on the passenger side and peered through, still not seeing anything. Knowing he had to get in there somehow and was running out of time, he forcefully knocked on the glass. If someone was there, he figured he'd just pretend to ask for directions. He got no response though. Jones knocked once more but still heard nothing. He tried to open the doors, but they were locked.

"Mia?" Jones shouted.

He put his ear up to the window as the car started shaking slightly. Jones took a step back and looked at the car. Someone was moving in there.

"Mia, are you in there?" Jones asked again.

He put his ear up to the window again and thought he heard some muffled screams, though they were faint. Figuring they left Mia alone but tied up, Jones took a quick look around to make sure nobody saw what he was about to do. With the coast clear for the time being, Jones took the handle of the gun and smashed the driver side window open. He reached his hand in and unlocked the door, getting in the seat and quickly taking a look toward the back. There was Mia. She was on the floor of the back seat, tied up and gagged but otherwise unharmed. Jones reached back and took the gag out of her mouth.

"Are you OK?" Jones asked.

She was breathing heavily from the scare she'd gotten, but was relieved to see the professor. "Yeah, I think so."

Jones unlocked all the doors, then got out and opened the back door to help Mia get out of the car. He untied her ropes and helped her out of the car. Thrilled to see him, Mia gave him a hug so hard that it almost squeezed the life out of him.

"I'm so happy to see you," Mia said.

"We have to go to the car," Jones replied.

"Is Mike here?"

"Yes, and we're going to have to move very quickly in a minute."

"Why, what's going on?"

"You're about to hear it in a minute."

Jones took Mia by the hand and the two of them ran back toward his car. He knew they'd have to get out of there fast once the shooting started. To avoid any police entanglements, Recker would most likely be running toward the car as quickly as possible. Mia tried looking back toward the cemetery to see if she could see Recker but they were moving too quickly for her to find him.

Recker was still standing behind the ten foot high statue, out of sight from Gallagher and his men. He patiently waited there, looking to both sides of him, ready to start firing in each direction. He stuck his ear out, hoping to catch them talking or even moving closer to him.

"Where's he at?" one of the men asked.

"Spread out," Gallagher stated.

They were hoping that once they found Recker they could surround him or at least trap him, with two of them meeting him head on and the other two coming up on each side of him, leaving him nowhere to go. Recker knew one was about to come up behind him on his right and readied to fire. He moved a little closer to the corner edge of the statue as he readied to pounce on the unsuspecting man. He quietly listened for the man to step on a twig or a leaf, giving his position away.

Once he did, though, Recker knew he'd quickly have to locate the others as then bullets would start flying fast and furious in every direction. Ten seconds later, Recker heard a leaf crunching underneath a heavy foot. Giving the man a few more seconds to pass his position, Recker stepped away from the statue as he had the man in his sights. Recker calmly put his gun up to the back of the man's head and put a hole through it.

"What was that?" Gallagher worriedly asked, turning to the direction of the shot.

Almost immediately after firing the shot, Recker jumped back behind the cover of the statue, waiting for the others to come running. If he was lucky, he could gun them down rapid fire. Gallagher and the man he was with slowly started walking over, unsure what they were walking into. Knowing they were relatively close, Recker figured he could get the jump on them and surprise them. He emerged from the shadow of the statue, catching the two hoodlums completely off guard. As soon as Recker saw the outlines of the two men, he fired six shots at them in succession, not even giving them a chance to return fire. Four shots wound up hitting Gallagher, the other two hitting his friend. Both men died instantaneously.

As Recker looked at the two dead bodies in front of him, another shot rang out from the remaining crew member. The shot whizzed past Recker's head, grazing off the statue behind him. Recker dropped to a knee and quickly identified where the shot came from and located his target. Dodging another bullet in his direction, Recker returned fire with a couple shots of his own. His missed as well. Figuring he couldn't stand there all day in a shootout and wait for police to arrive, Recker took matters into his own hands. He stood and calmly started walking toward the man.

With bullets flying past him, Recker didn't even flinch. He looked and acted like he had a suit of armor on that the bullets couldn't penetrate. But just like that night in London, he believed that he was just as likely to run into a bullet as it was if he took his time. He also knew it wasn't normal behavior and thought it might intimidate whoever was firing on him, causing them to panic knowing that he was coming closer, making their aim worse as they fidgeted around with their weapon. As Recker closed in on his target, the man eventually ran out of bullets. He kept firing, though, hoping somehow a bullet would magically emerge from the chamber. Once Recker had him in his sights, he saw the worried look on the young man's face, thinking his life was soon to be over. And he was right as Recker quickly put the man out of his misery and fired two shots that hit him in the chest.

"David, pull the car down the alley," Recker told him, looking at all the dead bodies.

There was a seldom used alley to the side that led around to the back of the cemetery that Recker figured would be an easier escape path. If he just walked out the front, there were sure to be prying eyes, not only at him, but also the getaway car, putting all of them in danger of being identified. But in the back he could just climb over the short brick wall without as many eyes looking down at them. Jones did as requested, making sure that he didn't drive erratically and attract attention to the car. Recker ran toward the back of the cemetery and easily climbed over the wall. As his feet hit the ground, his gun still in hand and ready to fire in case of police. Luckily, there was nobody else back there, not even anybody walking through. Recker waited a few seconds until he saw Jones pulling up, Mia safe and sound in the back seat. She opened the back door for him as Recker quickly jumped in and sat next to her.

"Just drive like nothing happened," Recker stated. "We'll stick out like a sore thumb if we speed out of here."

Jones drove back out of the alley, slowly passing by the front of the cemetery. The three of them took a look, noticing an increasing crowd that started pouring through the front gate. Police weren't there yet, but they did detect the sound of a siren that appeared to be coming closer. Jones kept driving, a feeling of relief coming over him as he drove away.

"Once we get back to the office, I'll start to monitor the situation and see what leads they have," Jones said.

"I think I need a vacation," Mia joked, not used to as much excitement as she had experience over the past couple days.

Mia looked at Recker, so thankful for him coming after her. The feelings she had for him only intensified as she stared into his eyes, even though she knew it would never be reciprocated. She put her hand on the side of his cheek and rubbed her thumb against it as she looked at him.

"Thank you," she told him, leaning in and gently kissing him on the lips.

Recker didn't pull away even though he knew he should. After a few seconds, they mutually parted lips and Mia inched over closer to him, giving him a warm embrace as she buried her head into his chest. Recker knew it was a bad idea and simply looked down at the top of her head, leaving his hands free in the air, not wanting to caress her. But as he looked at her, he realized that this would probably be the only chance he ever had, or would permit himself to have, to be with her. He finally relented and dropped his arms, putting them around her back and holding her tightly.

Even though they were caught up in an embrace at the moment, the situation at the cemetery only reinforced what Recker believed to be true. If they were together, she'd always be a target. Though these thugs didn't know the connection between them, it was proof in his mind that it was a situation that they'd have to replay multiple times if it was known of their relationship. Mia would be used as bait to get to him. They hugged for about five minutes before finally separating. They gazed into each other's eyes for another minute, each knowing it was never going any further than what just happened. Mia was actually surprised at the amount of affection that he returned to her. But she could tell by his eyes that he was a man conflicted and she probably just caught him in a weak moment of his after the excitement of the gun battle.

Recker was a man conflicted. Though there was nothing he wanted more at the moment than to keep her in his arms, he couldn't allow himself that pleasure. Holding each other the way they just were was an intoxicating feeling, but he had to restrain himself from giving Mia the wrong impression. For her safety, he needed to keep a distance between them. He looked out the window as they drove over the bridge back into Pennsylvania, and for the second time in as many days, started to wish for a different life, a life that he could never have.

BLOWBACK

40

Langley, Virginia—A meeting had been called to discuss the killing of one of their agents, Agent 17. The Director of National Intelligence, as well as CIA Director Roberts had grown very concerned at the agency's lack of progress in finding 17's killer in the past three months. Though it had been swept under the rug in the public's eye, with 17's cover alias intact, the agency's hierarchy was starting to demand some answers. Attending the meeting were Director Roberts, his top aide, Deputy Director Tomlinson, as well as Executive Director Manning, who was in charge of the day-to-day activities of the agency. They were already in conference when Deputy Director Caldwell, who was in charge of operations and collecting foreign intelligence, came walking in. With him, was Sam Davenport, who was in charge of the Centurion Project. Roberts wasted little time in starting the questions as soon as the two visitors were seated.

"You two know why this meeting was called, right?" Roberts asked.

"Yes, sir. The death of Agent 17," Davenport said.

"I'm getting almost daily queries from the DNI as to why we still have not apprehended somebody in his death. He's killed in broad daylight, in a public airport, and three months later here we are sitting on our hands with no answers. What exactly is being done about this and why has it gotten to this point?"

Caldwell and Davenport looked at each other, unsure who should answer. Finally, Caldwell said. "As far as we can tell, there's been no international chatter indicating someone was coming for him or any type of backlash for any work he's done overseas."

"Nothing at all?"

"We've checked all our sources in every country he's been in, every assignment, but there's nothing to suggest it's an outside source."

"Outside source. Why do you phrase it like that?" Roberts said.

Caldwell looked at Davenport, expecting him to take over from there. Davenport cleared his throat and began talking. "We've come to believe it's some type of personal matter."

"Personal matter. Such as?"

"We're still digging into it."

"You're gonna have to give me something better, Sam," Roberts said. "You obviously have some type of information leading you in that direction."

"It's more theory on our part right now than actual facts."

"OK. Explain how you got there."

"As Director Caldwell said, we've checked every single assignment 17's been on, and there are no red flags, no anomalies, except for one. And it was internal."

"Internal?" Executive Director Manning asked. "You mean somebody who works for us."

"Well, worked. But yeah, that's what we think," Davenport said.

Manning looked less than convinced. "OK. So why?"

"Three years ago, 17 was part of a group of agents that participated in the elimination of one of our Centurion agents in London."

"What were the circumstances?" Roberts said, locking his fingers together as he prepared to listen.

Davenport opened one of the file folders he'd brought with him and took out papers relating to the case, passing them across the table to each man in the room. There were three sheets of paper stapled together, with information about the assignment, Recker's picture, and his bio.

"John Smith was the alias he used while with us. He was a Centurion operative who'd grown tired of his role with the agency and spilled classified information to his girlfriend at the time," Davenport said.

"It says here he was ambushed in London, but somehow survived the attack," Manning said.

"That's right. He was shot, but he killed three of our agents in the process, and wound up in a hospital. Once we got word he was there, and we arrived, he was gone."

"And you never found him again?"

"He disappeared. We didn't get another hit on him until six months later when he booked a plane ticket to Orlando, Florida."

"For what purpose?" Roberts looked confused.

"That was where his girlfriend lived and was killed," Davenport said.

"And why was she taken out? The information in this report seems sketchy and doesn't really say much."

"Smith had gone to her and told her about his role in Centurion. We thought it was a security risk."

Roberts investigative tail was up as he started grilling for answers. "Why? How do you know? And how do you know he dispensed information to her? Did you have him bugged, tailed, receive a tip, what?"

"No, Smith told us."

"He told you? He just flat out came into your office and told you?"

"Well, he said he was weary of his job and wanted to leave," Davenport said, trawling his memory. "In the course of our discussion, he indicated he had told his girlfriend certain aspects of his employment. Centurion is a top secret black ops project and cannot be revealed to anyone in any sort of fashion. So, we concluded he was becoming unstable and his girlfriend was a non-essential risk we couldn't tolerate."

Roberts held Davenport's eye for a moment. "So, you wouldn't have actually had any such information had he not walked into your office and revealed it, correct?"

"Correct."

"Now does it seem logical a man would do that if he was some sort of risk?"

"We didn't feel it was a risk worth taking."

"And how does 17 play into this?"

"17 was the agent who killed Smith's girlfriend," Davenport said as he wiped his face, a sheen of sweat forming on his forehead.

"And you think now, after all this time, Smith came back and killed him for revenge?" Manning said.

"While we have no proof at the moment, it's a working theory we're pursuing right now, yes."

"So, he just dropped out of sight for six months after London," Roberts said. "Then he popped up on the radar with a plane ticket to Florida. What happened there?"

"He never got off the plane."

"So, he probably creates a ruse to get all the attention down there while he moves in a different direction."

"We believe so."

"And Smith knows 17 killed his girlfriend because..." Manning said.

"Smith called his girlfriend to warn her but 17 answered the phone and they had a brief discussion," Davenport said, squirming in his seat.

"This sounds like it came right out of a movie or something," Roberts said. "Do you have Smith's file on you?"

"Not on me, no."

"Jeff, pull up his file."

"No problem," Manning said, typing into his laptop.

The men continued discussing the specifics of the two cases and threw some more theories into the air for a few more minutes until Manning pulled up Smith's file.

"Coming on the big screen now," Manning said.

They turned their heads to look at the monitor on the wall, a big seventy inch screen displaying Smith's personal information, as well as his Centurion assignments. They made several comments in passing as they perused the information before coming to a final conclusion after they finished.

"Looks as close to a perfect record as you can get," Roberts said. "What made you think he was a risk?"

"Just a feeling and from what he had said to me already," Davenport said.

Roberts sighed as he looked down at the desk and wiped his face with his hand, obviously distraught at what was going on.

"This is a complete mess," the director said. "So, we don't know for sure this is the work of Smith. We're just assuming it is."

"Correct," Davenport said.

"And there's no video surveillance from the airport, surrounding areas, roadways, highways, nothing to implicate him either."

"No, but that would give further credence to the theory that it's him. He'd know how to avoid all those things."

"Can I ask why I'm just hearing about this London thing three years later?" Roberts said. "Why wasn't I informed of this when it happened? Jeff, were you aware of this?"

"I was not," Manning said.

"So, who was informed of this plan, Sam?"

"I informed Director Caldwell of our intentions before it was carried out and got his approval," Davenport said. He could feel the damp patch of sweat on his back growing with every minute.

"Dean?"

"I was informed of the general circumstances, but did not review the situation in depth. I relied on the information I was given and gave the green light," Caldwell said.

"And what information was that?" Roberts asked.

"That one of our agents had revealed sensitive information to a civilian and approval was asked for to eliminate that agent along with the civilian he had contact with."

Everyone was silent for a minute as Roberts put his elbow on the table and rubbed his forehead as he looked down at the information Davenport had passed around. There was no doubt the director was obviously displeased at how the situation had been handled. After reading a few paragraphs of text, Roberts finally spoke up again.

"I'm a little bit perplexed, and perturbed, at how this entire situation has not crossed my desk before now," he said. "An agent with a near perfect record was terminated, or attempted as such, along with a United States civilian killed, within our country's borders no less, and I'm just hearing about this three years later. Jeff, how is this possible?"

"I can't say, sir. I wasn't informed of it either," Manning said.

"Sam, can you explain why this didn't go up the chain of command?"

"I asked for permission from Director Caldwell and got it. I figured it was a Centurion issue, and it was handled. Nothing else needed to be said about it," Davenport said.

"For the record, the killing of a civilian within our borders is not a pressing issue that needed to be handled immediately. At least not one who doesn't appear to be much of a threat or flight risk, as this woman was," Roberts said. "I'll give you an agent who's as skilled and lethal as Smith is, maybe there isn't time to go up the ladder. But the woman, that's gotta go across my desk. One hundred percent of the time. Understood?"

"Perfectly, sir."

"Good. Because if you had done so to begin with, I would not have authorized such an action based on the information you've acquired, which is flimsy at best."

"Understood."

"Regardless, it doesn't change the circumstances of whether Smith is responsible for 17's death," Manning said.

"Do we have any idea where Smith may be now?" Roberts said.

"Well, we believe that due to the Orlando plane ticket, he's somewhere in the United States," Davenport said. "Probably on the east coast."

Roberts put his hands together and put them over his eyes and nose as he shook his head, looking like he had a migraine coming on.

"OK, well, regardless of my feelings of what's already gone down, we need to start making some hay on this," Roberts said. "Sam, you're in charge of Centurion, it's your project, it's your men, you find where Smith is. I want you to put resources into it immediately. You'll report directly to Jeff on this and keep him updated every day on your progress, or lack thereof."

"Yes, sir."

"Once you find his location, you're to sit tight on it and bring it to my desk, is that clear?"

"Perfectly."

"If Smith's our man, and he's the one who killed 17, it's not likely he's gonna go down without a fight. We cannot afford to make a bigger mess on top of the one you've already created." Roberts said, pointedly looking around at the other men in the room.

"Can I ask another question?" Manning said. "What's the status of everyone else who was involved in the London operation?"

"In what way?" Davenport asked.

"Well are they alive, dead, what?"

"Well, the three agents who attempted to kill Smith are dead."

"Killed at the scene while trying to terminate him?"

"Correct?"

"Who else?"

"Smith's handler was in London at the time, and there was another agent who was at the girlfriend's house in Florida."

"And they're still alive?" Manning said.

"Yes."

"Hmm."

"What are you thinking, Jeff?" Roberts asked.

"Seems kind of strange. If Smith was out for revenge, don't you think he'd take everyone out, not just one?"

"Maybe the one's all he knew."

"An agent's handler is a personal connection. If he was that pissed, wouldn't you think he'd be at the top of the list?" Manning asked. "I mean, Smith would probably know how or where he could take him out if he wanted."

"The other issue is how Smith would have found out where 17

is located," Roberts said. "He didn't hit him overseas, he hit him where he lives. Somebody got him the information."

"We've checked our infrastructure and we've had no data breaches in regard to his file," Davenport said. "And he's got nobody else in the agency to turn to. We've checked to make sure nobody's made contact with him, and from what we can tell, nobody has. We've even kept tabs on his mentor who's now retired, and they've never met or made contact since all this went down."

"Well right now we're looking like world class buffoons, including me since I wasn't aware of any of this, so you better get the situation under control."

"We will. I would suggest one small thing if I could."

"Which is?"

"If we get a hit on him somewhere, I believe we should take him out immediately," Davenport said. "He's too dangerous to not act right away."

"Sam, you've already bungled one operation, don't make it two." Roberts' warning was clear. "You make a move without clearing it with Jeff or myself and you will pay for it, am I making myself clear?"

"You are."

"It's also very rare for a man, even one as skilled and talented as Smith is, to just vanish without a trace. There's always a bread crumb somewhere. We need to find it. You don't disappear without help. Someone out there knows something. Find them."

41

Recker strolled into the office a little past nine in the morning, ready to begin work on a new case. He finished his previous assignment the day before by disposing of a man who had planned on murdering his wife for insurance money. Though Recker would have preferred doing away with the man permanently, Jones persuaded him to just temporarily disable the perpetrator until police arrived. Recker left enough evidence behind that Jones had discovered which should have been enough to convict the man, without the need for further violence. As soon as Recker walked in, he noticed Jones seemed to be working rather hard, swiveling from one computer to another almost seamlessly.

"Anything on the horizon?" Recker said.

"A few promising prospects," Jones said. "Probably will take another day or two to flesh them out more until we can take action on them."

"Vacation day today then?"

"Hardly."

"Looks like you're typing away hot and heavy for something that's not imminent."

"There's something which requires immediate attention, just not regarding us," Jones said. "Well, it involves us, more specifically you, but not an upcoming case."

"Did you just speak English?"

"What I'm trying to tell you is something popped up on my Recker Radar."

"Recker Radar? Is that actually a thing?"

"It's what I named my government surveillance software program involving you."

"Oh. Interesting," Recker said. "So, you're telling me my name resurfaced somewhere?"

"It did. Approximately three weeks ago there appears to have been a high-level meeting among several high-ranking CIA officers and directors."

"So? It's common you know. It happens all the time."

"Yes, but just before the meeting, I got a hit on a memo with your John Smith alias. It came from someone named Sam Davenport and was sent to Executive Director Manning and the date was two days before that meeting."

"Was Davenport there?" Recker asked, finally concerned.

"He was as far as I can tell. That's one of the issues I was having as I cannot place exactly what this Davenport's role in the agency is."

"He's in charge of the Centurion Project."

"Then you know him?"

"I do. He's the one I initially talked to about leaving the agency. Who else was at this meeting?"

"I've confirmed Director Roberts and Deputy Director Caldwell so far. There may be more," Jones said.

"Let me see the initial memo and anything else you have."

Recker pulled up a chair next to Jones and anxiously waited for him to pull up the information. It was the first time Jones had seen a concerned look on Recker's face after informing him of a possible breach. Recker had always said he wouldn't really be worried about anyone looking for him unless it was the CIA coming. He knew they were the only ones who really had the capabilities of finding him. And if they really were looking for him, Recker knew it was only a matter of time before they found him. Jones finally pulled up the first memo and let Recker read it for himself.

To: Executive Director Manning
From: Sam Davenport

Per your request, we still have no leads into 17's death. We believe it likely to be someone with a personal connection to his past. We have several theories, though nothing concrete. We are looking into the possibility of whether it is related to a job he did that involved a former agent of ours, John Smith. I'll keep you updated.

Sam

Recker quietly sat there reading the memo, analyzing it, studying it to see if there were any hidden meanings behind any of the words as they sometimes liked to do.

"Anything else?" Recker asked after reading the memo several times.

"Yeah."

Jones brought up another memo, somewhat overlapping the first one on the screen. Recker's eyes were glued to the monitor as he began reading.

To: Sam Davenport
From: Executive Director Manning

We need further clarification on what's being done at the moment. Director Roberts is calling every day looking for answers and he's getting impatient at the lack of progress. He's called a meeting for this Wednesday at 10am with you, Director Caldwell, and myself. Bring your files and what you have on this Smith and be prepared to explain your plans going forward.

Executive Director Manning

After reading it five times, Recker leaned back in his chair, while still staring at the screen. He put his fingers over his mouth and rubbed his lips as he analyzed the memo. By his mannerisms, Jones detected something was bothering Recker.

"What is it?" Jones said. "It looks as though something's got your attention."

"I'm not sure. It's the way the second memo is worded."

"I didn't notice anything strange or out of the ordinary."

"It's the way Manning identifies me," Recker said. "He called me this Smith."

"And the significance is?"

"Well, in the grand scheme of things, I guess it doesn't make a bit of difference. But on a personal level, I always wondered just how far up the order to kill me went."

"And this helps in that?" Jones asked.

"Well, from the sound of it, it doesn't seem like Manning even knew my name."

"How can you be certain?"

"Well, he called me this Smith. It sounds like he didn't know me. Think about it, anytime a person ever says this in front of someone's name, it indicates a lack of familiarity of the subject. If he knew me, he'd just say Smith, not this Smith."

"Very astute observation, Michael."

"Which probably means the order came either from Davenport or Director Caldwell and didn't go any further up."

"Does that help us somehow?"

"If they're looking for us, doesn't help us a bit," Recker said. "But for my own peace of mind, it helps answer a question I always wondered about."

"How reassuring," Jones said.

"When was all this?"

"Looks like the meeting took place a few weeks ago. The memos aren't dated but that would place them approximately two or three days before I assume. Why would they bother with memos at all? Aren't they all located in the same building?"

"No," Recker said. "Centurion headquarters are in New York. Most black ops programs are located somewhere other than Virginia to try to operate in secrecy. Everyone knows where the CIA building in Virginia is, but it's easier to come and go without prying eyes in a completely different area. Especially a high-volume city such as New York where it's easier to blend in. Rent an office building, register a fictitious name and you're up in business."

"So, what do you propose we do about this?"

"Nothing to do yet until they show up. Just keep going about our day like normal and monitor it best we can."

"You seem pretty sure they will be here."

"Part of me has always known I couldn't run from them forever. It's the way this stuff goes. You knew it too. I guess my stunt down there in Ohio just put me back in the forefront," Recker said.

"There's always packing up and leaving."

Recker grimaced, not really keen on the idea. "We've put down roots here, made connections, friends... I don't know if it's in the cards now."

"Roots can be replanted, new connections made, and the only friend we've made here is Mia," Jones said.

"Tyrell too. Besides, I don't plan on running forever."

"So, what, you're just going to bunker down and fight like you're the last man at the Alamo?"

"Either way, this doesn't affect you. They won't find a connection between us. Whenever they find out I'm here, it'd be best if we don't get too close for a while."

"Anything that affects you, affects me," Jones said. "I can't do this on my own, and if you're gone, it would mean I have to find, train, and trust a brand-new person."

"You did it once. You can do it again."

Jones grumbled, not liking the situation one bit. "How much time do you think we have?"

"Depends. The quick version... probably a week or so. If it takes a while... few weeks, couple months at the latest."

"I suppose we both knew this would happen, eventually. I just hoped it wouldn't be for a few more years."

"Probably would have been if I hadn't taken 17 out. It would have put me back on the radar. They're looking for connections and I'm probably the only one who fits."

"Well I suppose the good news is we've got advance warning."

"I'll probably have to get word to Mia to let her know I'll be scarce for a while," Recker said.

Jones started squirming in his seat upon hearing her name, not wanting to reveal he was supposed to be meeting her for lunch. Even though Recker and Mia had a few tender moments after their little escapade in New Jersey a few months before, neither one pursued anything more serious upon their return back home. It'd actually been about two weeks since Recker had heard from Mia, which was highly unusual, considering she used to call or text him at least every other day. Jones played off his concerns by telling his partner he'd been hacking into hospital records periodically and checking Mia's time sheets. He kept telling Recker she was having a heavy workload, even working days off and overtime, which was why he hadn't heard from her much. It was an answer that satisfied Recker for the time being.

Jones was not about to be the one to inform Recker that the reason he hadn't heard from Mia was because she started dating someone else. Even though she had every right to find someone, and her and Recker weren't together, Jones still knew how Recker felt about her. He wasn't sure exactly how Recker would take the news. Maybe he'd be fine. Maybe he'd be angry. Maybe he'd get depressed. Maybe he'd be all those things wrapped up in one package. But Jones wasn't going to be the one to tell him about it. Since Recker and Mia were never together, there was no reason he should've objected to a new relationship of hers, but his feelings for her were a fickle business. Sometimes they changed with the weather and sometimes for what seemed like no reason at all. Maybe it was because Jones knew Recker really felt more for Mia than just being friends and didn't want to be the one who disappointed him, even though Recker himself said things couldn't go further with her. But what he said and what he would actually feel when she actually did move on were two different things.

The only reason Jones even agreed to meet Mia for lunch at all was because she was really persistent. She was good at it. She never did take no for an answer very well. She contacted Jones almost a week ago to ask if he could meet her for lunch. She wanted to talk to him about her new boyfriend and how to tell Recker about it, if at all. One thing Jones never imagined being when he started up this operation, was the middleman in a love triangle. He reluctantly agreed to meet Mia, mostly because he needed for Recker not to go off the deep end when he found out, and he hoped by talking with her, they could figure out the best way to break it to him.

Once noon came around, Jones started wrapping up his work on the computer. Recker was on one of the other computer stations, trying to figure out his CIA issue. His attention was diverted when he saw Jones stand, appearing like he was going out somewhere. It was pretty unusual behavior for him. Though Jones every now and then would go out for lunch, he never did when there was what appeared to be an urgent situation. And Recker figured this CIA issue could be classified as an urgent situation. Jones usually would work right through lunch and keep himself glued to his chair. So, him leaving right about now struck a chord with Recker.

"Where are you going?" Recker said.

"I have a prior engagement I have to attend."

"An engagement? What, like a party or something?"

"No," Jones said, trying to think of something else to tell him.

"Uh... then where are you going?"

"I'm meeting a contact."

"A contact? Like who?"

"Well, I can't tell you."

"Why?"

"I don't know his name," Jones said, caught in a lie.

"This is highly unusual for you, don't you think? It's usually me meeting contacts."

"Desperate times call for desperate measures."

"I didn't realize we were in desperate times," Recker said.

"Well, alarming times, how's that?"

"You want me to come along for backup?"

"No. Won't be necessary."

"You want me to monitor things from here?"

"No, I'll be fine," Jones said.

"You're being awfully cloak and dagger about this thing."

"As you know, some things have to be kept close to the vest."

"Where'd you find this contact?"

"I can't say. I'll fill you in when I get back."

"Do I have to worry? Dangerous perhaps?"

"No danger involved. It's just an exchange of information," Jones said, hoping it would be enough to quiet Recker down.

Though he wasn't really satisfied with that answer, or any of the other ones that Jones had said, Recker stopped with the questions. He realized that Jones wasn't going to tell him anything useful, so he figured it was best to just let him go. Besides, with the CIA starting to breathe down his neck, Recker didn't have time to worry about more trivial things. If Jones really needed his help, he would've asked.

When Jones got to the restaurant, Mia was already sitting and waiting. Upon seeing her, the Professor looked at his watch and hurried over to her table. Mia gave him a big smile, then stood to give him a warm hug. She had already ordered drinks for the two of them so they took their seats to look at the menu.

"Thanks for coming," Mia said.

"Sorry I'm late." Jones checked his watch. "I got caught up with things, then I hit traffic, then..."

"David, it's OK. I'm just glad you're here."

Jones lifted his drink and looked at the top of it.

"Sweetened iced tea, just the way you like it."

"You know me so well."

"Yeah, it's nice the two of us getting together like this. We should do it more often."

"Yes, I don't remember the last time we did this," Jones said.

"David, we've never done this."

"Oh, nonsense. We've had lunch together plenty of times."

"Yeah, at my apartment, or with you, me, and Mike. But never just us, out somewhere. It's kind of nice. Different."

"It is. So, should we get to the basis of this meeting?" Jones asked.

"Meeting? You make this sound so formal. Can't two friends just sit and have lunch together?"

"Indeed, they can. Our relationship, however, has never been predicated upon lunch dates or social gatherings. You indicated that you wanted advice on your situation with Michael, did you not?"

"Well, yeah."

"Well then, why beat around the bush, or dance around the subject, or pretend it's for some other reason? Friends talk about other friends, right?"

"OK," Mia said, unsure how to proceed.

She stuttered for a minute and started to say something, though no words came out of her mouth. She was very uneasy and nervous talking about the subject at all. But she knew it was better to talk it over with someone else first before approaching Recker with it. And since the only mutual friend they had was Jones, he was the only candidate for the job. Jones could see she was struggling to start the conversation, but he wasn't exactly an expert in love or relationships, so he had no idea how to help her or draw out her feelings on the matter.

"So, you're obviously aware of, uh, my... feelings for Mike," she said, stammering and taking a deep breath as if she was having a panic attack.

"Mia, you don't have to go into any kind of deep explanation of personal emotions," Jones said, trying to calm her down before she passed out or something. "I'm well aware you and Mike have an emotional attachment of sorts, but due to his... career, it is not possible to further explore those feelings you have for each other."

"OK, well, a few weeks ago I met someone."

"And?"

"Well, we went on a few dates and he now wants to date exclusively," Mia said calmly, not really believing she was saying the words.

"And your feelings are?"

"I think I might want to."

"Excellent. I think it's a fabulous idea," Jones said, without hesitation.

"You do?"

"Absolutely. You and Mike have never progressed beyond friends and I think it's time you moved on. You deserve it."

"But you don't even know who it is or what he does or anything," Mia said.

"Well who is he?"

"His name's Josh and he's a lawyer."

"Oh," Jones said, cracking a face.

"Well you don't have to say it like that. He's a really nice guy. He's not like a sleazy lawyer or anything."

"What kind is he?"

"He's a personal injury lawyer," she said. "You know, helps people who are hurt at work and the like."

"And people who spill coffee on themselves at restaurants then sue the restaurant I suppose?"

"No! At least I don't think so. Well, I dunno, but he's a really nice guy."

"Makes good money? Treats you right?"

"Yes. Well, the treating me right part. So far anyway. I'm not sure about the money. I haven't asked about his bank account, but he has his own house and a nice car so I assume he's doing all right."

"As I said, if you're happy, you have my blessings. Are you having doubts about this arrangement?"

"No. I think I want to."

"Why does it sound like you're having misgivings then?" Jones asked.

"I don't know. I guess part of me has always just been waiting for Mike to come riding in on the white horse and take me away."

"Mia, Mike doesn't own a white horse. And continually waiting for something that in all likelihood will not happen is not going to help either of you move on, especially you."

"I know." She looked downcast as she fiddled with her thumbs.

"If you really have feelings for this Josh, and you think it could possibly lead somewhere you want, then you should try to make it work."

"Should I tell Mike or no?" Mia said.

"You absolutely should tell Mike."

"You wouldn't want to kind of casually mention it to him somehow, would you?"

Jones had taken a sip of his drink, almost spitting it out at her reference. He wiped his mouth with a napkin before answering.

"No. No, I would not. I'm here for advice counseling and that is all. I'm not doing the dirty work for you."

"How do you think he'll take it?"

"Well, it sort of depends on what kind of mood he's in. There's really no way of telling in advance. If he takes it well, maybe he'll wish you well and just go back to work like it's no big deal," Jones said.

"And if he takes it badly?"

"Maybe he'll just wish you well then go back to work and shoot somebody."

42

When Jones got back to the office after his luncheon with Mia, he noticed Recker was in the same spot as when he left. Jones wondered if he even moved at all in the couple hours he'd been gone. Recker was staring hard at the computer, barely even paying any attention to Jones since he walked in.

"Have you even moved from that spot since I left?" Jones said.

Recker gave him a quick glance before returning his eyes back to the screen. "There's a lot going on."

"I don't think I've ever seen you so concerned about something before."

"I told you I would never worry until the CIA came looking. This is why."

"Just the same. I think I preferred your carefree attitude."

"So how was your meeting?" Recker asked.

"Uh... good."

"So, what are you trying to hide from me?"

"What? Hide from you?" Jones asked, trying to laugh it off. "What are you talking about?"

"Well, in all the time we've known each other, you've never been so secretive before. Now suddenly you're going off, not telling me where you're going, who you're meeting, seems kind of fishy."

"I'm just not at liberty to reveal their name."

"What was it about?"

"Just a... case."

"A case we're not on," Recker said. "Considering I finished the last one yesterday."

"Well, about the CIA problem."

"And you don't think it's worth sharing?"

Recker could tell Jones was just saying whatever popped into his mind. If it was really about a case, Jones would've just come out and said what it was about. He wouldn't have danced around the subject like he was doing. And if it was really about the CIA, it wasn't something Jones would've kept to himself. So, if it wasn't about a case, or the CIA, then it must've been something personal. Either for Recker or for Jones. With a few suspicions as to what it might've been about, Recker lobbed a few more questions at his friend, just to see how he'd handle them. After a short give and take, Recker thought he might've figured it out. At least partially.

"Is this about Mia?" Recker asked.

"What? Mia? Why would it be about Mia?" Jones asked incredulously.

"Because I haven't heard from her in a week, you're being ultra secretive, sounds like you two are planning something."

"Don't be ridiculous. What on earth would we be planning?"

"That's a good question. Why don't you answer it?"

"I can't."

"Do I have to call Mia and ask her?"

Jones suddenly looked much more pleasant. "Yes. Yes, I think you should do that."

"If I can ever get her on the phone," Recker said.

Though Jones kept buttoned up and steadfastly refused to confirm anything else, he didn't deny whatever he was hiding had something to do with Mia. For Recker it was basically a confirmation it was true. Recker grabbed his phone and made another call to Mia, once again going to voicemail. This time, he left a message.

"I guess now I know how it feels," Recker said.

"What's that?"

"Trying to call someone repeatedly and not getting an answer. I guess now I know how she's felt these past couple years when she called and I didn't answer."

"Oh. Well, turnabout is fair play as they say," Jones said.

Not having to answer any more questions, Jones sat again and got back to work. With nothing new on the CIA front, he pulled up some of the cases he'd been keeping an eye on lately. As he was working, Recker continued his CIA search, trying to glean any new information he could. After about thirty minutes, Jones made a couple of muffled sounds which distracted Recker. Since the Professor didn't say anything to him, Recker played it off and kept going about his own business. A few minutes later, Jones made the same type of noises, drawing Recker's attention again. He put his elbow on the table and rested his head on his hand staring at his partner, waiting for an explanation of his troubles. Jones didn't even seem to realize what he was doing and never took his eyes off his screen. A few more minutes went by with Recker staring and he finally got tired of waiting for an explanation.

"So, do you wanna spill it?"

Recker's voice finally broke Jones' concentration, and he looked over at his partner. "Hmm?"

"Do you wanna share what's so fascinating about whatever it is you're looking at?"

"I wish it was fascinating," Jones said. "It's more like... disturbing."

"Well, are you going to share?"

"Oh. It's one of the cases I've been monitoring. To be honest, it's one I hoped would just somehow magically go away without us having to get involved. Sadly, it doesn't seem to be the case."

"What's the trouble?"

"It's um..." Jones hesitated, rubbing his head as he thought of the best way to explain it.

Recker didn't recall a case in which Jones had trouble stating the issue before. It was his first tip-off it might be something big. "Just say it."

"Well, it's actually two people I've been keeping an eye on. I first caught wind of a text message one of them sent to the other about... children," Jones said, struggling to get the words out.

"Children? What do you mean, children? What about them?"

"One of them is a convicted child sex offender."

"What's the message say?" Recker asked.

"Well, apparently one of them has been watching an elementary school and has his eyes on a couple of kids. Some of the language they use is... well, I just can't repeat it. Not when thinking about kids. Here, you look at it."

Jones moved his chair over a little so Recker could come in and take a look at what he was seeing. Recker read the messages the two men had been sending to each other regarding the children they were seeking out. Recker had seen and heard a lot of things, and not much really bothered him. But reading what these two men were planning on doing to some small children really disgusted him.

"Who are these creeps?" Recker asked.

"Reed Laine and Sidney Bowman."

"Both convicted sex offenders?"

"Only Laine is. He is not allowed to be anywhere near a school. Bowman on the other hand, does not appear to have any kind of criminal record," Jones said, still clearly bothered by what he had picked up on.

"How do these two jerks know each other?"

"That I do not know off-hand. It appears the two somehow befriended each other somewhere along the line over the years. Maybe online, maybe in a chat room, maybe on a message board, maybe somewhere on the dark web, who knows? I do know they weren't childhood friends. They grew up in different areas, different schools, never worked together. So, my best guess is they hooked up online somewhere due to their fascination with... the kids. That seems to be the tie binding them together."

"Wonderful. Anything concrete on the time and place of what they're planning?"

"Nothing definitive as of yet."

Recker took a few steps back then walked over to his gun cabinet. He selected his two weapons, his primary and backup, as per his usual. As he closed the cabinet, he looked over at Jones, who appeared to be deep in thought. Jones was kind of staring away from the computer toward the wall, not seeming to be looking at anything in particular.

"What is it?" Recker asked.

"I was just thinking if maybe it'd be a good idea if we kept a low profile for a while."

"You mean take a vacation?"

"No. Just work more in the shadows. Relay our information to the authorities, let them handle things," Jones said. "Kind of stay quiet."

"You want us to sit on our hands while these two jerks are out there molesting kids?"

"No. Not at all. We can forward what we have to the police and let them take over the investigation."

"Why?"

"Well, with the CIA looking into your whereabouts again, I just think it may be wise to stay in the background until things blow over a little."

"David, I'm not someone who just sits on my hands very well."

"I'm aware."

"Besides, what can the police do?"

"Monitor their behavior and such."

"Yeah, monitor their behavior after they've already committed some heinous act some poor kid will never emotionally recover from," Recker said.

"I'm not saying we should do nothing."

"I know. You're just saying to let someone else do the dirty work."

"I'm just worried. If something happens, it may put you even more in the spotlight. A spotlight we don't need at the moment," Jones said. "Any type of publicity The Silencer gets at this moment may be something which draws the CIA closer to our doorstep. To your doorstep."

"You can't live in fear, waiting, wondering, hoping something doesn't happen."

"I'm not saying we should be living in fear, I'm just wanting to exercise some caution."

"Listen, I hear you and I understand your concern. But it doesn't really change anything. Do you really wanna put this in the hands of the police and take chances on the lives of children? What if the police can't act on the information you give them? Which is likely. What if they have too much on their plate and they don't get to these creeps in time? You're leaving a lot to chance."

"I know."

"And if this was some run-of-the-mill nut job and innocent children weren't at play, then maybe I'd agree with you. But I won't stand by and let children be targets. I didn't sign up for this to stand on the sidelines."

Jones nodded, completely understanding Recker's position, and actually agreeing with it. Even though he suggested caution, Jones knew his partner was right on point with his arguments and he really had no winning argument against them. Now that they were in agreement that they shouldn't do anything different than usual, Recker went back to the computer to get more information.

"Where am I gonna find these clowns?" Recker asked.

"Reed Laine lives on Washington Street and Sidney Bowman lives on Ashford."

"Do we know what school they're targeting."

"They didn't say. But, judging from where they live and the approximately to the closest school, I can take a guess," Jones said.

Recker took a final look at their addresses to memorize it before heading out to find them. He usually could commit everything to memory, but asked Jones to send him the information just in case.

"Send their pictures and whatnot to my phone," Recker said.

"Mike, if I can give some advice, please handle this as quietly as possible."

"Should I leave them tied up in the middle of a room with some porno mags taped to their chests?" he asked sarcastically.

"I'm just saying discretion is sometimes the better part of valor."

"I'll do what has to be done. No more, no less. Just like always."

Recker bid his partner goodbye and left the office to find their targets. Once he exited the office, Jones got a bad feeling about his intentions.

"Just like always. That's the part I'm worried about," Jones muttered.

As Recker drove, Jones forwarded the requested information to his phone. He sent the pictures of the two men, along with their addresses, work information, as well as DMV information on their cars. Everything Recker might possibly need to find the two as quickly as possible, he now had. Considering the two men only lived a few blocks from each other, Recker wouldn't have far to go to find either of them. Recker's first target was Laine, who was the closest. It took Recker about twenty-five minutes to reach the Laine address. Laine lived in a row home in an end unit. There was a small driveway big enough to house one car in the three-story home, though there was no car sitting there. Laine was supposed to be driving a small gray Toyota. Many owners of these homes also parked on the street by the curb due to the lack of space so Recker cruised up and down the street, and even on the connecting streets, just to make sure it wasn't nearby. But it wasn't in sight. Instead of sitting waiting for a while, Recker drove over to the address of Bowman, which was only about five minutes away. He also lived in a similar house, a row home, though his unit was in the middle. Once Recker found the address, he parked across the street. He saw a light blue Ford belonging to Bowman parked in the driveway. While Laine was single and lived by himself, Bowman was living with his parents, as the house was registered in their names.

While the thought occurred to Recker to just burst through the front door and start blasting away, he didn't want to hurt or injure innocent people, which he assumed Bowman's parents to be. Recker called Jones and asked him to run a quick background check on them just to make sure they were unaware of their son's behavior. Recker would just sit tight until Jones got back to him with the information. He also wasn't sure if the parents were even there at the moment. So, while he preferred not to wait at the moment, he figured it was the best strategy for the time being. After uneventfully sitting there for half an hour, Jones got back to him with the information he had requested.

"As far as I can tell, Bowman's parents are not connected to their son's activity in any way," Jones said.

"They don't know anything about it?"

"Well, they know their son has issues, and it looks like they've tried to get him help with psychiatrists and doctors and the like, but it doesn't appear the apple falls from the tree if you get my meaning."

"So, they don't know he's staking out schools and kids right now," Recker said.

"It wouldn't appear so."

That bit of information confirmed Recker's strategy to wait until he could get Bowman alone. Since the parents didn't seem to be involved, he was going to make sure they weren't hurt in whatever went down. Recker still wasn't sure what he was going to do, but everything going through his mind seemed to have a violent end to it. He knew it wasn't what Jones wanted, but in this case, Recker didn't see another way around it. Maybe Jones was right and they should tread carefully, but with kids involved, Recker just wasn't willing to tap dance around. He'd do what he thought was right and let the chips fall where they may.

Two more hours went by and Recker was starting to get a little antsy. Though he didn't usually get anxious over cases, when kids were involved, and not knowing exactly when the two subjects were planning on putting their plans into motion, he was ready to get moving. Fortunately, he didn't have much longer to wait. He saw the front door open, and a man came out of the house. Recker looked at his phone for confirmation it was Bowman. It was. At first glance, Bowman didn't appear to be a very threatening type of guy. He wasn't big or imposing or tough looking. He was in his mid to late forties, rim glasses, and kind of small at five feet four or five. Seeing him for the first time, you wouldn't expect him to be the type who'd have issues like this. But, as Recker was well aware, most people had secrets hidden away. He watched as Bowman locked the door to the house, walked down the steps then got into his car. As he pulled away and drove down the street, Recker followed him, keeping a safe distance behind him so Bowman wouldn't see he was being followed.

After driving for a few minutes, it became clear where Bowman was going. Once he made a left turn at the traffic light, there was an elementary school dead ahead. Bowman drove up to the edge of school property and parked just alongside the curb. It was recess and most of the kids were outside playing. Recker parked about five car lengths behind his target and just sat there watching him. As he sat there, he called Jones to let him know what was happening.

"Well, looks like we know what's on Bowman's mind," Recker said.

"Which is?"

"He just drove down to the elementary school and parked. He's watching the kids at recess."

"That is alarming, isn't it?"

"There's no use in waiting, is there?"

"We could call the police and have them run him off," Jones said.

"What for? You said he has no record. There's nothing stopping him from being near school grounds."

"I'm just searching for an alternative."

"There are no alternatives," Recker said. "You and I both know what has to be done."

Even though Recker seemed strongly in favor of capital punishment, he wasn't as sure in his own mind. It was part of why he called Jones to begin with. Part of him hoped that Jones had another solution at hand, even though Recker knew there was none. He knew what he had to do. Recker partially opened his car door, ready to unleash his brand of justice, but then thought better of it. He heard the joyful screaming of the kids playing in the background and it caused Recker to pause. He then shut his door again as he contemplated a better option. Killing Bowman near school property just didn't seem like the right move. There'd be a big commotion, along with a police presence, news cameras and reporters, and a lot of outside noise that Recker didn't think was fair to subject a bunch of young kids to seeing. Recker would have to wait and pick a better spot. As he continued thinking about his plans, his phone rang. It was Jones.

"Yeah?"

"You haven't done anything yet, have you?" Jones asked.

"No. Not yet. Why?"

"Well, as we've noted, Bowman doesn't have any type of record. It appears his family has tried to get him help for his problem."

"So? We already know all that. What's your point?" Recker said.

"My point is, you don't have to do what we both know you're planning on doing."

"I asked you for alternatives earlier. You didn't have any."

"Well, maybe if you just talked to him, let him know you're watching him, that may be enough to scare him off," Jones said.

"You really think so? People like this are sick. You really believe a good talking to is all he needs? What do you think happened when he visited the psychiatrist?" Recker asked.

"Would it hurt?"

"Well it might not hurt, but it sounds like a complete waste of time. Don't forget we got one more guy out there doing who knows what."

"Believe me, I'm well aware of that."

"You really think a little chat is going to do any good?"

"It's worth a try," Jones said.

Recker let out a little grunt, "Fine. But I'm telling you this is a waste of time."

"Noted."

Recker hung up and quickly got out of his car, not wanting to waste any more time. With his guns tucked firmly out of sight inside the belt of his pants, he closed his car door and took a look around to make sure he wasn't being watched or there was nobody nearby who could see any commotion going on. With the coast clear, Recker started walking toward Bowman's car. As he approached it, he could see Bowman was looking at the school playground through a pair of cheap looking binoculars. Seeing that made Recker even angrier and more agitated than he already was. Still unsure what he was going to do or say, Recker was just kind of making things up as he went along. He stopped when he got alongside the driver side window. Bowman didn't even realize he was there at first. Recker knocked on the window to get his attention. Startled, Bowman jumped in his seat a little when he saw the intimidating looking man standing outside his window.

"What do you want?" Bowman asked without rolling the window down.

Recker tilted his head and pointed at his ears, pretending he couldn't quite make out what Bowman was saying. Agitated, Bowman rolled his window down.

"I said, what do you want?"

"Oh, I was just wondering why you were sitting here looking at little kids," Recker said.

"Go away."

Bowman attempted to roll his window back up but Recker prevented him from doing so at first by putting his hands on the edge of the glass. Eventually though, the force of the power window made him lose his grip, and the window rolled all the way up. Rattled, Bowman reached for the ignition and turned the key in an attempt to leave the scene. Obviously, Recker's attempts for a conversation were not off to a good beginning. Though he could've just let Bowman leave since he was obviously rattled and perhaps Recker thwarted his plans, it just wasn't good enough for Recker. He reached around to his back and withdrew one of his guns and turned it around, holding it by the barrel. Recker then took the weapon and slung it to the side of his head as he viciously brought it back down like a backhanded slap, rapping it against the glass as the window shattered. Bowman stopped what he was doing and put his arms up over his head to protect himself from shards of glass cutting into his face. After a few seconds, Bowman put his arms back down, revealing his face once again to the stranger on the outside. Recker once again swung his weapon in a backhanded manner, this time forcefully hitting Bowman across the bridge of his nose, causing his head to violently snap back against the headrest. Recker then moved the gun to his left hand and reached through the window and unleashed a right cross that caused Bowman to slump across the gear lever in the middle console. Recker pulled the lock up on the inside of the door and opened it, pushing Bowman completely into the passenger seat, though half of his body was on the floor of the seat well. With Bowman in a lot of pain and holding his face due to the blood dripping down from his broken nose, Recker took control of the wheel and peeled out of the parking space.

"Who are you? What do you want?" Bowman yelled, though it was somewhat garbled as his hands were covering his mouth from still holding his nose.

"I'm just a concerned citizen," Recker said.

Recker wasn't exactly sure where he was going, figuring something would occur to him as he was driving. Or maybe, he'd see something which would just stick out to him as a good place to go. His phone started ringing again, though he didn't even check to see who it was, assuming it was Jones, and he didn't especially feel like talking to him again at the moment.

"Where are we going?" Bowman asked.

"Just shut up."

"You broke my nose."

Recker kept his eyes on the road, not feeling bothered at all. "I'm heartbroken."

"Why are you doing this to me?"

Recker didn't respond and instead focused on driving. He noticed Bowman starting to move around a little more, like he was about to get off the floor entirely and get in the seat.

"Just stay where you are or I'll break a few more things," Recker said.

He didn't feel the least bit threatened by the man, but Recker didn't want to take chances and have his passenger try something stupid. Having him kneeling on the floor kept him at a more acceptable distance. After a short drive, Recker saw a small shopping center and pulled in, parking near the outside of it, as far away from the stores as possible. It was a small center that had a grocery store, drug store, pizza shop, as well as a few other small establishments.

"Looks like this is where it ends, sonny," Recker said.

Bowman looked worried. "What are you gonna do with me?"

"Well, you and your friend Laine seem to have a little problem with looking at the kids, huh?"

"I don't know what you're talking about."

"Do I look stupid to you?"

"No."

"I've seen the messages you two creeps have sent to each other."

"It was nothing," Bowman said, shrugging his shoulders. "We were just kind of kidding around."

"You don't joke about things like that. Besides, if it was just kidding around, you wouldn't have been at the school where I found you, would you?"

"I was just taking a drive and parked for a few minutes. The kids make me feel good."

"Yeah, I bet they do." Recker felt sick to the stomach at the thought of what kind of 'good' the kids made Bowman feel.

"So, what are you gonna do?" Bowman asked, seeing the gun sitting on the seat between Recker's legs.

"Well, I'm supposed to be having a chat with you to tell you never to do it again but I have a feeling it's gonna be useless. Isn't it?"

"I'll do whatever you want."

"Yeah, I kind of figured you'd say that. Then tomorrow when I'm not around anymore you'll find yourself right back in the same situation."

"No. I swear."

Recker sighed, unsure of the point of having the conversation. He could tell it wasn't going anywhere. And like he said, as soon as he was gone, Bowman would be right back to doing the same thing. He wasn't going to change just because of a conversation with Recker. Recker wasn't sure why he even bothered to listen to Jones and try this method first. It was a complete waste of time. He should've just done what he wanted to do in the beginning. Recker grabbed the Glock from between his legs and pointed it at Bowman. Without thinking or blinking, he fired three rounds into his target's chest, killing the man instantly as his face slumped down onto the seat, his shirt soaked in blood.

He didn't want to stay at the scene very long, so Recker quickly got out of the car and started walking back to his. Luckily it wasn't too far away. It'd give him some time to calm down. Shooting someone was never a good feeling, no matter who it was, though Recker knew taking out someone like that was necessary. As he walked, he reached into his pocket and removed his phone to see who had called him. As he suspected, it was Jones. To pass the time, Recker called him back.

"You need something?" Recker asked.

"I was just calling to see how you were making out."

"Good."

"When you say good, you mean?"

"I mean it's done. Onto the next one."

"You talked with Bowman?" Jones said.

"I did. Didn't do a bit of good."

"Oh. So, what happened?"

"What do you think happened? He's dead," Recker said.

"Oh."

"I did what had to be done."

43

It'd been a few weeks since the meeting in CIA Director Roberts' office and his patience had reached its limits. He was mystified and frustrated that the agency had seemingly made no progress in that time. He had meetings lined up all day to figure out how to proceed next. Sam Davenport and his Centurion team had run out of time in his mind to find either Smith, or 17's killer, or whether or not Smith was responsible for it. He was ready to try something new. That something was someone he trusted who could bring a fresh set of eyes to the situation. Davenport and his crew obviously had no new leads and had run out of options. Roberts' first meeting was 9am with a familiar face. His intercom buzzed with a message from his secretary. It was a few minutes early, but Roberts asked her to inform him the moment his visitor arrived.

"Yes?"

"Michelle Lawson is here," his secretary said.

"Send her in."

Lawson was a bit surprised she was going to be seen so soon.

She fully expected to have to wait awhile. Not that she was unhappy about it. She was pleased she wasn't going to have to just sit and wonder why she was there for half an hour. She had no advanced warning, and she wasn't given any explanation of what she was doing there. She was told at the last minute to get to Roberts' office immediately. As soon as she opened the door, she was greeted with a smile and a handshake from the director. With his warm and pleasant disposition, she assumed she wasn't in hot water, or getting fired. It'd been a few years since her last encounter with Director Roberts. Her first, and only, meeting with him was in the same very office she was now in. Roberts asked her to sit at his desk as he walked around and did the same now.

"Good to see you again, Shelly," Roberts said.

"Good to see you too, sir. I think."

Roberts smiled. "Relax. You're not in any trouble or anything. I guess you're wondering why I called you here."

"Yeah, a little bit."

"You've done a great job with Project Specter, but to be honest, the project is probably going to be winding down in the next few years."

"Oh?" Lawson said, worried for her future.

"We've got several similar projects going on now, and in the future. We're going to need people to run those projects. And I'm going to need to appoint people I can trust to run them."

"OK?"

"I'm not promising you anything right now, but I'd like to put you in the mix for those assignments when the time comes. To do that, you need to spread your wings a little bit."

"In what way?"

"You're going to have to expand your horizons and not be just a handler. You're going to have to have more of an influence, a greater position of power and authority."

"How?" she said.

"I would like you to wrap up your work at Specter and become some sort of a freelancer," Roberts said to her. "I'd like you to work on more pressing issues and situations as they arise, then when they're over, move on to the next one. Kind of like a high leverage specialist."

"And I'd have to give up what I'm doing now?"

"Yeah, it'd be too much on your plate to do both."

"How much time do I have? When would this new position start?"

"You'd have to start immediately, such as tomorrow. How much time, well, today."

"Wow. That's quick. Not that I'm not grateful for thinking of me or for the opportunity, but why me? I'm sure there's other people who are more qualified for this," Lawson said.

"Like I said, I want someone I can trust. After the work you've done on Specter and Matthew Cain, I know I can trust you. I know you won't take shortcuts. But Cain hasn't worked for us in two years, Eric Raines is an experienced agent who doesn't need a handler with your expertise, and you need to start thinking about moving up."

"But if we ever have hopes of getting Cain back into the fold, I don't think he'll do it without me."

"You very well may be right about that. But that's a discussion for another day. If that were to ever happen, we'll deal with it when the time comes," Roberts said.

"What's the assignment you want me on?"

Roberts slid a file folder across the desk. Lawson picked it up and started looking through its contents as the director continued explaining.

"Project Centurion," Roberts said. "It was the next thing after Specter. Three months ago, one of their agents, 17, wound up dead not far from his home in Ohio inside an airport. Since then, we've still got no leads, no options, no nothing. Other than theories, which we're swimming in. John Smith, an agent Centurion leadership tried to take out several years ago is thought to be behind the killing, mostly because 17 killed his girlfriend. At least that's the theory. No proof though."

Lawson intently continued reading the file, trying to get a thorough understanding of what was going on. It was a lot of information being thrust upon her suddenly. These black ops projects were extremely secretive in nature, and nobody outside of the project, other than senior leadership, had any knowledge of any other actively running projects. It was a lot to digest in such a short amount of time.

"So, basically, at the heart of all this, my duties on this assignment would be to find 17's killer, and this John Smith, assuming that it's not the same thing," Lawson said.

"That's it. Sam Davenport, who's in charge of the Centurion Project, hasn't come up with a damn thing in a month. The DNI is pressing me for information. Information that I can't give him, because we haven't got any."

"Umm, one other thing... reading this file, I, uh... well, what exactly was the reason Smith was targeted to begin with? It's not really clear in this file."

"Apparently, Smith wanted to leave and expressed that desire, and he may or may not have divulged any details to his girlfriend. Davenport deemed that to be a security risk and sought to eliminate him," Roberts said. "This was done without my knowledge or approval. I actually just found out about Smith a month ago myself."

"May I speak freely, sir?"

"Of course."

"This case they have against Smith to begin with is rather..."

"Weak?"

"Yes."

"I agree. And if it had come across my desk at the time it happened, I would not have sanctioned or authorized any action against him. But, well, it's water under the bridge now. Now we have to clean up the mess," Roberts said.

"And what are your orders regarding Smith if I find him?"

"To do what has to be done. To grow into a leadership position, you're going to have to make the ultimate call. You understand?"

"I do. But what if I find Smith and he's not the one who killed 17?" Lawson said.

"Possibly the same thing."

"What if I could bring him back in? The case against him is weak to begin with from what I can see. He could still be a valuable asset to us if I could reach him."

Roberts chuckled and put his hand over his mouth. "It's what I like about you. Not only do you think about the improbable, you don't immediately dismiss the chances it can be done either. Not one other person has even brought up the possibility of bringing Smith back in as part of the team."

"Well, I do have a tendency to think outside the box sometimes."

"And that's why I thought of you for this. And why you need to get out from your handler shoes and expand your horizons. Do you remember the last time you were here?"

"I do."

"You came in here under difficult circumstances, and while some people would be intimidated, you fought for your beliefs. It's always stuck with me."

"It's easy to fight for something you strongly believe in. Especially when it concerns someone's life."

"But not everyone would do that."

"I also knew him. I knew he was innocent. It wouldn't be so easy or clear with someone I don't know. Someone I only know from reading a file."

"It should never be easy. Once it is, it's time to move on."

Lawson sat back in her chair and sighed deeply as she held the file folder, still reading the contents. Like Roberts suggested, this was a big opportunity for her. Hearing Project Specter was on its last legs was a bit startling, but not completely surprising. It was a project with an overabundance of issues over the years, though under new leadership, seemed to be heading back in the right direction. Unfortunately for everyone involved in Specter, though, there'd been a black cloud hanging over its head ever since their former director was indicted and found to act unethically. Several of their top agents had either retired or been transferred to other projects. Lawson moving on would be a big step up in her career. Another opportunity, at least one as strong as this one, might never come along again. The longer she thought about it, the more appealing it became. How many times in one's career does the CIA Director personally offer something like this? Probably never again. Plus, it was a good challenge. After a few more minutes of thought, her mind was pretty much made up.

"Before I make a decision, where would I work, who do I report to...," Lawson began before being interrupted.

"You'll initially work out of New York, not far from your current office. You'll have complete and total access to all Centurion's files and information. As far as who you report to, it's easy, you report to Executive Director Manning and me. That's it. This is yours, you own it, you have everything in Centurion and the agency's power at your disposal. You need something, you order it, you get it."

"And, uh, Davenport, is he going to be... well, I'm sure he's not... does he even know about this yet?"

"Not yet," Roberts said. "And as to whether he's going to be happy about you coming, no, no he won't. But that's immaterial. He'll have to deal with it."

Lawson nodded, still thinking. She knew what she wanted to do, what she thought was the right decision, but there was still something holding her back from saying the words. She never even dreamed about something like this happening, it was sort of a shock.

"Well?" Roberts asked. "What do you think?"

After a brief hesitation, Lawson agreed to the proposition. "I, uh, I accept," she said with a smile.

"Excellent. You can accompany me to my next meeting then."

"Your next meeting?"

"Sam Davenport."

"Oh. I didn't realize I'd be meeting him so soon."

Roberts grinned. "I hoped, maybe anticipated, you'd be saying yes."

"I guess I should call the office and tell them I'm being reassigned?"

"No need. I've already taken the liberty of reaching out to them. As soon as Director Hayes calls me back, I'll explain the situation to him."

Roberts left the office for a while to attend to other matters. He left Lawson behind to continue reading the file so she could get more thoroughly acquainted with the case. She had about twenty more minutes until the meeting with Davenport. Though part of her was excited about the opportunity being presented to her, she was also a little nervous. She was being given control over a top secret black ops project, and even if it was only temporary, it was still a big chance for her to show what she could do. But she also knew she was being thrust upon Davenport at the last minute, and she was taking operational control over his organization on both the Smith and 17 cases. She assumed he wasn't going to be happy at having her come aboard his operation. Lawson wasn't someone who liked conflict or enjoyed wrestling for power over people and she could only imagine how many cold shoulders or evil looks she was going to receive. Working for a black ops project herself, she knew that if someone was suddenly thrust in to take over Project Specter, they probably wouldn't be too well received either. It'd basically be a vote of no confidence on the current leadership. Otherwise, there'd be no need to bring a new person along.

After reading the file for close to half an hour, Lawson looked up at the clock on the wall and noticed it was past the meeting start time. She wondered what the hold-up was. Maybe they were prepping Davenport for her taking over control, she thought. Whatever the reason, she was getting pretty anxious to get it over with so she could start working on the assignment. A few minutes later, Director Roberts came back into the office.

"Davenport is in the conference room waiting for us. Are you ready?" Roberts asked.

"As ready as I'll ever be."

Lawson quickly shuffled the papers back inside the folder and scooped it up off the desk and scurried out of the office, closely following the director. Along the way to the conference room, she asked a few more questions, wondering about Davenport's personality.

"What kind of person is he?" Lawson asked.

"Well, a little hard-headed, probably overeager, but also someone who wants to do a good job. Not overbearing, not soft, usually even-tempered."

"Sounds wonderful."

Roberts looked back at her and smiled. "You've worked for worse."

"Good point."

"Besides, this is your operation. You don't need to take bullshit from anyone. If there's any crap that needs to be dished, I want you to be the one throwing it."

"Understood."

Roberts opened the door to the conference room and walked in, Lawson still closely following him. Already seated in the room were Executive Director Manning, Davenport, and Director Caldwell. Only Manning was aware of what was about to go down. Davenport and Caldwell were not in the loop as to the director's plans and were not given any inclination of what this meeting was about. Roberts made a quick, unfriendly type of greeting and walked around to his seat.

"Shelly," Roberts said, directing her to a chair.

Lawson sat next to Manning, as she was told. Across from her were who she assumed to be Davenport. She had seen Caldwell's picture before from other materials distributed within Specter. Since he was in charge of foreign operations, he technically had control of all secret black ops projects and was supposed to be aware of what they all were doing, though he didn't oversee the day-to-day operations of any of them. The day to day duties of Centurion were left up to Davenport. With a legal pad in front of him, Roberts briefly looked at his notes before commencing.

"I'm not gonna beat around the bush here," Roberts said. "The reason for this meeting is there's going to be a little bit of a shakeup, a little change as to the direction of Centurion. Jeff and I have talked at length about this over the past couple of weeks and we both feel, due to the lack of progress in either finding John Smith, or the killer of 17, we need to go in a different direction. From this very moment, Michelle Lawson will take over in those duties. She will have absolute power in those two cases, which may or may not be linked, and will be given complete access to Centurion offices, files, computers, etc. Sam will still have command over all other Centurion business and can focus on those other duties more thoroughly without being distracted with these other things on his plate."

"Sir, it really wasn't much of a distraction," Davenport said.

"Nevertheless, this is the decision we've made, and you'll support Ms. Lawson in whatever she needs, wants, requests, and so forth."

"Absolutely."

Lawson took turns between looking at Roberts and Davenport, who was obviously not pleased at being replaced in these matters. She imagined she'd probably feel the same way if someone was brought in above her to work on something she wasn't having much luck in.

"Dean, I don't know how well you know Shelly, but do you have any objections you'd like to raise on this?" Roberts asked.

Caldwell quickly shook his head. "No. No objections. I'm well aware of Shelly's reputation since Project Specter fell under my umbrella. I've never had the pleasure of meeting her until now, but I'm well aware of her work."

"May I ask what exactly are her qualifications for this?" Davenport said, still a little peeved about being bypassed. "How does this Project Specter compare?"

"Project Specter was the precursor to Centurion," Roberts said. "Some of what we learned from it became the basis of what Centurion was founded upon. What worked well became part of it, what didn't fell by the wayside. She's handled some of the toughest agents you can imagine."

Davenport scrunched his eyebrows together as he tried to understand what the director was telling him. "Are you saying she's just a handler?"

"Not just a handler, Mr. Davenport. She's been the handler of some of the most lethal and dangerous agents this agency has ever seen. Not to mention that she also already has experience in these types of matters. She's already been part of a team that tracked down former members of the CIA who went rogue and into hiding. Her team flushed those men out and brought them to justice."

"It was a group effort," Lawson said, almost sounding embarrassed about being thought of so highly. "Wasn't just me."

Roberts looked at her and smiled before turning his attention back to the Centurion leader. "So you see, Mr. Davenport, she's not just a handler. She has experience in these matters. And quite frankly, her agent handling days I'd say are behind her. Not that this has any importance to you, but she's moving up and could be being groomed for a leadership position in another black ops project which is in the works. She's here because she deserves it and because she's earned it."

"Understood, sir."

"Besides that, her work is exemplary. She has an outstanding attention to detail, works hard, and is very competent in her work. Something lacking at times in other individuals or agencies that won't be named at the moment," Roberts said, hinting at his obvious displeasure.

Davenport gave a single nod of his head, getting the clue that he wasn't the most popular guy in the agency at the moment. They continued talking for close to an hour, going over different strategies, as well as what had already been done so Lawson wouldn't duplicate any of their efforts. It was a tall order, but by the end of the meeting, everybody was impressed by her ideas and were sure that Lawson was up to the task.

44

Recker walked into the office and immediately headed for the coffee machine. Though he hadn't yet looked at Jones, he could almost feel the Professor's icy stare sliding down his back. Recker had already seen the morning newspaper and noticed a story on the inside detailing the murder of Sidney Bowman from the day before. Recker knew Jones was going to give him the third degree any minute. He was waiting for it. But in Recker's mind, at least the story wasn't on the front page. Not that it really deflected the heat off him anymore. As soon as the machine filled his cup, Recker grabbed it and turned around, leaning against the table. He looked over at the computer station and saw the daggers of Jones' eyes piercing a hole through him. It was the meanest, toughest, most aggravating looking face Recker could ever remember Jones having towards his actions.

"If you got something on your mind, might as well just say it," Recker said, sipping his coffee.

"Is it that you believe you're untouchable, or is it that you just don't care?"

"Neither."

"Oh really?" Jones asked. Recker had never seen him look quite so grumpy. "Knowing the CIA has once again put you on the radar, you'd think you'd act in a much more cautious manner than you do. You're reckless, like you have no care in the world."

"I told you, I'm not gonna change the way I behave or how I do business. Killing this guy isn't going to change whether or not the CIA finds me."

"Well it certainly won't hurt their chances. Did you even talk to Bowman at all?"

"Sure I did."

"I mean, did you really talk to him? Did you try to give him an out? Did you try to do things a different way? Or did you ask him one question then make up your mind it was a lost cause and just start blasting away?"

"David, it was a lost cause. People like him are sick. Talking to me isn't going to suddenly scare him straight. If you honestly believe that it would, you're living in a fantasy world," Recker said.

"I just wish you'd exercise some restraint." Jones sighed. "There's already a ton of theories floating around online about the culprit."

"Yeah? Who do they think did it?"

"Well, considering Bowman has no record and no gang affiliations, people are assuming it's not a personal vendetta. Carjacking and kidnapping seems to be the prevailing opinion so far."

"Neither of which would point to me."

"Except he was killed in a way that points to some sort of vigilante justice. There was no attempt to hide the body, or the car, or anything. And who in this city is the leader in vigilante justice?"

"Let me guess... me?"

"I wish I had a prize to offer you for your correct assessment."

"Only prize I need right now is finding the other creep," Recker said.

"Speaking of which, what are your intentions with Mr. Laine?"

"You really need to ask? You already know what my intentions are. He's gonna be joining his friend in the afterlife."

"I had a feeling that would be your response."

"Don't even tell me you're gonna try to talk me out of it. With Bowman, maybe I get it, no record or anything. Laine, though, is a different story altogether. He's got a record for this exact thing. He's not changing his ways, or finding Jesus, or becoming an altar boy, this is who he is. And he needs to be stopped. By any means necessary."

Jones didn't fight Recker's assertion. He knew he couldn't win anyway, even if he tried. But mostly, it was because in this instance, he thought Recker was right. Bowman was different, at least in his mind. He had no record, no history of violence, Jones thought there was a chance he could have been steered in a different direction with a different tactic. Laine, on the other hand, was a convicted child sex abuser, who'd also had numerous other brushes with the law and had been arrested for several other infractions. Laine was now in his mid-forties and had his first brush with the law at the age of sixteen. Jones didn't have any false beliefs about him changing his ways at this stage of the game. He knew Laine was most likely just hours away from meeting the same demise as his friend. And he wasn't going to try to fight Recker on it. The only hope Jones had was that Laine's death wasn't quite as media friendly as Bowman's was. He feared another death as public as the first one would somehow catch the attention of the CIA's radar. The only plea Jones now had was to beg Recker to keep the event as quiet as possible. At least as quiet as any death could be.

"Isn't there a way you can make it look like a robbery or something?" Jones said.

"Huh?" Recker asked, surprised at the question.

"I'd just like to keep the heat off for as long as possible. Another violent death will not help in that regard."

"Does it really matter?"

Jones shrugged. "One never knows."

"At some point the police are gonna connect the dots and figure out that these two jerks knew each other. They're eventually gonna find those text messages, same as you did. They're going to piece together that these two deaths are somehow related."

"Yes, well, anyway, I did some more digging on our friend and it looks like the reason you couldn't find him yesterday was because he has a second job."

"Which is?"

"Bouncer at a nightclub downtown."

"Guess I'm going clubbing tonight," Recker said.

"Maybe you should go home and rest up for a while."

"You trying to get rid of me?"

"Of course not. But that's the only case on our agenda right now and there's not much else for you to do that I can see."

"I can check into my old CIA friends."

"I've got a handle on it," Jones said.

"You are trying to get rid of me."

Jones was about to offer a retort but was interrupted before he could get started by Recker's phone ringing.

"Your saving grace," Recker said, waving his phone in the air. He was pleased to see it was Mia calling, since he hadn't talked to her in a while. "Hey stranger."

"Hi. I know you've been trying to check in with me lately, it's just, uh, I've been busy with work and things."

"Ah, no biggie. Everything good?"

"Yeah, everything's fine. Works busy, but normal."

"Good. Off today?"

"Uh, no. Umm, are you free today by chance?" Mia said.

"Well, looks like I might be. David's kicking me out of the office so it looks like my calendar's been cleared. Why? What's up?"

"Well, I'm about to go to lunch in about half an hour. Can you meet me at the hospital?"

"Yeah, I guess I could."

"OK. See you in a bit then."

Recker hung up and just stared straight ahead for a minute, thinking about the conversation he just had. Something seemed off about it. Mia wasn't talking like her normal self. It seemed like she had something on her mind.

"Leaving, are you?" Jones asked, overhearing the conversation.

Recker shrugged. "Looks that way."

"Well, have fun."

"You happen to know what it's about?"

"What?"

"Mia wants me to meet her at the hospital for lunch."

"And the problem is?"

"Didn't say there was a problem. Just seemed like she was talking like a person with something heavy on her mind," Recker said.

"I guess you'll know when you get there," Jones said, sounding unconcerned, though he had an idea what the subject was about.

Though Recker still was slightly concerned about Mia's tone of voice, at least he didn't have long to wait and think about it. He immediately left the office and drove down to the hospital. When he got to the cafeteria, he looked around and saw Mia already sitting at a table. It was towards the back in the corner. Recker walked around a few tables on his way and noticed a troubling look on Mia's face. She hadn't noticed he was there yet, probably because she was looking down the entire time and didn't even lift her head up once. She jumped a little when she finally noticed Recker, when he was standing right in front of her.

"Oh, I didn't even see you come in," she said.

"I'm not surprised. It didn't look like you'd see a train barreling at you."

"Huh?"

"It's nothing," Recker said. "So, what's the trouble?"

"Trouble? What makes you think there's trouble?"

"Well the look on your face for one. Looks like you're worried about something."

"Well, it's not really trouble. Umm, I just need...," Mia said, scratching the side of her neck as she stuttered and tried to think of the best way to tell him her news.

Recker reached across the table and grabbed her hand in an attempt to settle her nerves. "Mia, you can tell me anything. You know that, right?"

"Yeah. I just don't, um, I don't know how you'll take it."

"Take what? What's this about?"

"Umm, I'm, uh, kind of seeing someone."

Recker took his hand off hers and brought it back in front of him, fiddling around with his fingers as he processed Mia's news.

"Oh. Well that's, um, that's great," Recker said, faking a smile.

Mia could tell he was a little stunned by her revelation, but she knew dragging it out any longer would just make it worse.

"So, who's the lucky guy?" Recker said.

"His name is Josh. He's a lawyer."

"A lawyer?"

"Why does everyone say the same thing? What's wrong with being a lawyer? You know, David had...," she said, quickly shutting up when she realized what it was she was revealing.

"David had what?"

Mia nonchalantly shook her head as she figured how she was going to get out of the hole she just stepped in. "Nothing."

"David said the same thing? Is that it?"

Mia closed her eyes and nodded, knowing she couldn't lie to him. Even if she tried, she knew he was good at digging out the truth from people. There was no point in trying to hide it.

"You told David before me?" Recker asked.

"I just wanted to get his opinion first."

"Why?"

"Cause I wanted to see what he thought on how well you'd take it. I didn't want you to be mad or anything," Mia said.

Recker looked at a few nearby tables and the people sitting at them as he digested the news she just fed him. Mia was pleasantly surprised at how well he was taking it so far. He didn't seem angry, his face wasn't turning different shades of red, and his voice didn't indicate any level of discontent. He actually seemed somewhat indifferent to the news. As Recker thought about Mia dating someone else, one piece of him was a little sad. He wished he could've been there for her and provided her with a normal life. But he knew he couldn't and he never would. Even though he was slightly disappointed, he didn't want to show it. He didn't have the right to get mad. Not with how he always tried to keep her at a distance. He cared about her too much. It was for her own good to move on from him.

"So, how'd you meet this guy?" Recker asked.

"Uh, he was actually here for something, I think his sister had a baby, and we bumped into each other."

"And he just happened to ask you out?"

"Yeah, pretty much."

"Hmm."

"What's that supposed to mean?" Mia said.

"Nothing. So, when do I get to meet this guy?"

"What?"

"Well, we're friends, right? I'd like to meet him. I just wanna make sure I think he's right for you and all."

Mia seemed a bit taken aback by his request. She hadn't accounted for Recker wanting to meet her new beau and hadn't even thought of it for a second. She figured Recker would never want to meet someone she was dating. Unless it was to punch his lights out.

"What? What's the matter?" Recker asked.

"I, uh, just hadn't expected such a calm response out of you."

"Why? You and David thought I might go out and shoot somebody or something?"

"Umm, well, actually, we did wonder."

"I know. I sometimes have... issues. But I think it'll probably be good for you to date someone."

"You do?" Mia asked, surprised he was taking the news so well.

"Look, I think we both know the way we feel about each other, we've talked about it enough. But you also know why it's best we go in other directions. If I can't give you what you need, then you need to get it somewhere else. I understand. I get it. It's what you deserve."

"Well, I'm glad you approve."

"I do. Just as long as I meet the guy and give him my seal of approval."

"Uh, I don't know. I'm not sure it's a good idea," Mia said.

"Why? What are you afraid of?"

Mia let out a laugh. "Are you serious? What am I afraid of? Do you not know who you are?"

"OK. I know. I'm not gonna shoot him. I'm not gonna throw him off a roof or in front of a moving car. I just wanna meet him and make sure he's good enough for you."

"See, that's what I'm afraid of right there." She grinned. "You wanna make sure he's good enough for me. You're either gonna grill him, or intimidate him, or do something to scare him off."

"Mia," Recker said, putting his hands on his chest, feigning being offended. "You really think I'm gonna do something to scare this guy off?"

"Mmm, yes. Yes, I do."

"I promise you I'll be on my best behavior and I'll do nothing to embarrass you."

"I dunno. I'll think about it."

"So how long have you known this guy?" Recker said.

"You keep calling him this guy. He has a name."

"Oh. Sorry. So how long have you known this guy, Gary?"

"Josh," Mia said.

"Whatever."

"I dunno. Few weeks I guess."

"And you're getting serious about him already?"

"See, I knew you'd do this. You're already grilling me about him. It's why I was afraid to say anything to you."

"OK. OK. I'm sorry. I just wanna make sure... I guess it's just my protective nature in general, and also of you. I'm always gonna try to protect you. At least, as long as I'm in your life. I just wanna make sure you're getting into a good situation."

"I know. And that's one of the things I've always loved about you. How you look after me. But Josh is a really good guy."

"So, when do I meet him?"

Mia sighed. "I don't know. I'll see."

They continued talking for a few more minutes before they were interrupted, a voice yelling Mia's name in the distance. Recker turned his head around to see who it was, figuring it was a doctor or nurse, or maybe someone from the hospital staff. It was a younger man, though, dressed in a nice suit, in his early to mid-thirties.

"Oh my," Mia said, her mouth dropping open. "What is he doing here?"

She couldn't believe what she was seeing. Before getting up the nerve to ask Recker to lunch and spring on him the news about her new boyfriend, she had originally asked Josh to meet her. He had something come up at the last minute though and canceled on her. So, Mia figured it was as good a time as any to tell Recker about him. She never dreamed Josh would wind up coming anyway, while she was still having lunch with Recker. It was a nightmare of epic proportions. She had to have the worst luck in the world, she thought. Recker turned his head back toward Mia and gave her a little devilish smile. With the garish look on her face and how stunned she looked, he figured he had a pretty good idea who it was calling her name.

"Is, uh, this the new boy toy?" Recker asked sarcastically.

"Oh, please stop," Mia said, worrying already that she was about to have the worst moment of her life.

Recker turned his head back toward the visitor, watching his every move as he walked toward their table. Mia stood to welcome her new boyfriend, though Recker stayed seated as Josh gave her a kiss on the cheek. Josh took the seat next to Mia, who was still shocked they were all together.

"Surprised to see me?" Josh asked.

"You have no idea," Mia said shakily. "What are you doing here? I thought you said you had a last-minute appointment."

"I did. I thought it was gonna take a lot longer though. I wrapped it up fairly quickly. I figured I'd come down and surprise you."

Mia forced a smile, still incredibly uncomfortable with the two men sitting at the same table. "You definitely did."

Josh looked at the man sitting across from them and reached his hand out to introduce himself. "Hi. I'm Josh."

"Mike," Recker said, shaking hands.

"Oh. Mike. Are you the security guy she's friends with that she told me about?"

"I dunno. Am I the security guy, Mia?"

Mia put her elbow on the table and started rubbing the side of her head. "Uh, yeah, yeah. This is my friend Mike. Works in security."

"So, I hear you're a lawyer," Recker said.

"Yeah." Josh laughed. "You don't have to say it like that though. We all gotta make a living somehow, right?"

"Sure do," Recker said, disliking the man almost instantly.

"So, what kind of security work do you do? Mia said it's really dangerous stuff."

"Yeah, it can be. We do security work, investigations, you know. We take on all sorts of clients, usually those in urgent need of protection."

"Hey, if you're ever looking for a job, my firm's always looking for good investigators."

"I think I'm good where I'm at right now."

"You sure? Probably a little safer work than what you're doing now, you know?"

"Most likely. But I doubt I'd get as much satisfaction out of it," Recker said.

"Ah, you're one of those guys, huh? Live for the rush?"

Recker faked a laugh, though he wasn't amused. "No, not really."

"So, how'd you guys meet?" Josh asked. "Mia said you two are close and you've known each other a couple years. But she just won't tell me how you two met."

"I told you that his cases are classified and I can't talk about them," Mia said.

"I think I can divulge this one," Recker said, smiling at her. "Mia had an abusive ex-boyfriend that was stalking her."

"Oh wow. You never told me that," Josh said to her.

"Yeah, I was trying not to."

"So anyway, Mia's father hired me to tail her and watch over her. So that's basically how we met."

"That's great. So, you protected her against this guy and you became friends," Josh said.

"Basically."

"So, what happened to the guy? Did he go to jail?"

Recker smiled at Mia again, almost proud to recall and tell the story. "No, not quite. He had a little bit of a more... extreme end."

"Really? What happened?"

"I threw him off a roof," Recker said bluntly.

Josh laughed, thinking Recker was joking with him. By the look on his face, though, as well as the nauseated look attached to Mia's face, he quickly came to the conclusion it was no joke.

"Wait. You're joking, right?" Josh asked. "I mean, you didn't really throw him off a roof, did you?"

"Well, there's a difference of opinion amongst some of us," Recker said. "Some say he slipped. Some say he was thrown. I like to go with the latter."

"Oh. Well um... so do you usually end your cases like that?"

"Sometimes. Sometimes I just like to shoot them and be done with it."

"Oh my god," Mia whispered, low enough that nobody could actually hear her.

She closed her eyes, thinking this meeting could not have been going any worse. She put her hand over her mouth and shook her head, wondering why she deserved a fate like this.

"So uh, have you had any legal trouble in your work?" Josh said.

"No, why?"

"Oh, nothing, no reason. Just wondering."

"Interested in representing me if the need arises?" Recker asked.

"Oh, no, I'm not that type of lawyer. I do personal injury, workers' compensation, things like that."

"Oh. Mia told me you were a real lawyer."

With Recker's last line, Mia buried her head in her hands even deeper, just wanting to crawl down into a hole and hide for a while. She just wanted to be out of there and go anywhere else.

"Well I am a real lawyer," Josh said.

Recker laughed, slapping the table. "Just kidding with you, man. Of course you are."

"Oh." Josh smiled.

Mia couldn't take anymore. If she stayed there any longer with those two bantering like they were, she might've been driven crazy. Not to mention completely embarrassed. This was exactly the reason why she didn't want the two of them meeting yet. This was what she feared happening. Mia looked at her watch to end the engagement.

"Oh, look at the time. I'm late to get back," she said hurriedly, standing from her chair.

"Already?" Recker asked.

"Yes. I was only on a short lunch."

"Don't you two have to get back to work, anyway?"

"No," Recker said, shaking his head. "Remember, my calendar was clear for the day."

"Oh."

"Well if you have to go, maybe me and Josh can just keep sitting here, talking, getting to know each other."

"Uh, no, no, no, no," Mia said, flustered at another nightmarish scenario. "Uh, you have to get back to work. I know you do," she said, talking to her boyfriend.

"Yeah, unfortunately I have a few more appointments booked for the day," Josh said.

"Ahh, that's a shame," Recker said. He was enjoying himself.

"Isn't it?" Mia asked sarcastically.

"Maybe we can all get together again soon," Josh said, shaking Recker's hand as he stood.

"I'd like nothing better."

45

New York---Lawson entered the Centurion building, a six-story building located in the heart of New York City. There was a receptionist sitting at a desk in the center of the lobby. There were all glass walls dividing the lobby, coming out from the middle of both sides of the desk to the far side of each wall. There was also a glass door on the one side requiring a card to be swiped to go through it.

"Can I help you?" the receptionist asked.

"I'm here to see Mr. Davenport, please."

"And you are?"

"Michelle Lawson. I'm expected."

"Oh, yes. Just go through the door over there and up to the sixth floor, that's Mr. Davenport's office. He's expecting you. Were you given a key card?" The receptionist pointed Lawson to the correct door.

"Yes, I have it," Lawson said, rummaging through her purse to extract the card from it.

"Good. Just swipe it through the card reader attached to the door."

"Great. Thank you."

Lawson swiped her card, which was given to her at the last meeting she had at Director Roberts' office. She was a little surprised at the lack of a security guard in the building so far, but she guessed it helped with whatever their cover was. Nobody would go in there who wasn't supposed to be there, and the glass was bulletproof, so she supposed there was no need for a security presence, anyway. She got in the elevator and went up to the sixth floor, wondering what type of reception she was going to get. She assumed it'd be a little chilly as she knew Davenport wasn't exactly excited about her being there. But she wasn't there to make friends, so it didn't concern her too much. As long as she got what she needed, she wouldn't have to stay there too long. She wandered down the halls for a minute after she got off the elevator, unsure where she should've been going. She passed by a few offices, also encased in glass. She also passed by a door marked "Situation Room", which seemed to be the only door and room which couldn't be seen from the outside. Glass rooms and doors seemed to be the norm in the building, except for the Situation Room, which she could only guess was for high priority meetings or important events. A few people briskly walked past her, most not paying much attention to her. One man slowly walked past her, an open file folder in both hands as he read its contents. He briefly poked his head up and came to a sudden stop as he noticed the strange woman standing there.

"Help you?" the man asked.

"Yeah. I'm looking for Sam Davenport's office."

"Oh," he said, turning around, and pointing down the hall. "Make the first left there, his office is on the right."

"Thank you so much."

"You bet."

Lawson walked down the hall and turned left at the corner and quickly saw Davenport's office on the right. She looked at the door and saw his name written on it, though there was a woman sitting at a desk inside. It was a small room not much bigger than a walk-in closet and there was another closed door towards the middle of the room. Lawson guessed this was his secretary's office or something, or just a way to keep people from getting to Davenport he didn't want to see. Lawson went in and was immediately greeted by the woman.

"Can I help you?"

"Sam Davenport," Lawson said.

"And you are?"

"Michelle Lawson."

"One moment."

The woman held the phone and called into the office to let Davenport know he had a visitor. Once he approved it, the woman hit a buzzer located underneath the desk to unlock the door. Once it started going off, the woman directed Lawson to open the door. She barely got both feet inside the door and hadn't even gotten a chance to close it yet when Davenport hurriedly walked around his desk to greet her.

"I'd offer you something but you won't be here long enough," Davenport said, walking past her. "Follow me."

"Uh, OK," Lawson said, unsure what was going on.

Lawson followed Davenport out of the office and made a right down the hall, then walked down the end of another hallway before making a left, then down another hallway before Davenport turned into another office. He turned on a light as the two entered and removed a few books from a dust-covered desk.

"This is where you'll work out of while you're here, which I hope won't be too long," Davenport said, clearly not pleased to be seeing her.

"Looks like it's seen better days."

"Yeah, it hasn't been used for a while but it's the only office we have available right now."

"It'll do," Lawson said.

"Yeah, it's got a desk and a computer, what else do you need, right?" Davenport asked, making light of it.

"Plus, I brought my own laptop so I'll be fine," Lawson said, putting her computer bag on the desk.

"Great. Anything else you need?"

"Uh, no I don't think so. Well, I could use all the files you have on both Smith and 17, personal, work, whatever."

"Sure. I'll have my secretary bring them over and she'll give you the passwords for our software system as well," Davenport said.

"Thanks. Look, I know you're not real happy about me being here, but it wasn't my idea either."

"It's fine. All that matters is getting the job done, right?"

"Right."

With Lawson squared away, Davenport walked back out of the office, and despite his best efforts to say otherwise, she knew he wasn't happy she was there. But he was giving her what she needed, so it was the only thing that really mattered. Lawson set up her laptop and started going through some of the papers she had, Davenport's secretary coming in only a few minutes later to deliver the rest of what she needed. Lawson devoured everything available to her, studying every single piece of paper they had on both men, reading the same information several times over to get a better understanding of the agents involved. She worked right through lunch and dinner, not even paying much attention to the time, and considering she seemed to be at the very end of the building, there was no foot traffic going by to distract her. She read every report the two agents ever made, every evaluation that was done on them, looked at their physical records, read their comprehensive reports on the Centurion software program and came to one conclusion. If John Smith was 17's killer, finding him was not going to be an easy task. But she still needed more information, something she couldn't find in the reports. She walked out of her makeshift office and went down the hallway, making a few turns until she found herself back in front of Davenport's office. She wasn't even sure he'd still be in there, but once Lawson saw his secretary, figured the boss was still working. After getting clearance, Lawson was once again buzzed in. This time, Davenport was seated at his desk and didn't make a move to get up.

"Something else you need?" Davenport asked.

"I would like to talk to whoever it is you guys use to evaluate these agents."

"Why?"

"Well, it seems to be the only thing missing in those reports."

"What exactly is it you want?"

"I wanna talk to either their handlers or the psych evaluation expert you use," Lawson said.

"For what purpose? I don't understand what it's gonna get you?"

"I wanna get a deeper understanding of who these men are. There's only so much you can learn about someone from a piece of paper. I've never met them before, but the psych guy has."

"17's dead. What else do you need to learn?"

"But Smith isn't. He's out there somewhere and if I can get inside his head a little, maybe I can pinpoint where he is."

Davenport smiled, thinking she was way out of her league. "You know, no matter who you talk to, whatever you read, it isn't going to bring you closer to finding John Smith. He's a world class operator who isn't going to be found by some pencil pusher."

"That's what you think of me as? A pencil pusher?" Lawson asked.

"Look, you strike me as a nice person. Maybe you've worked on some important things and been a good handler to a few agents. But nobody outside this project is just going to waltz in here and find John Smith at the snap of their fingers," Davenport said. "You know when he'll be found? When he wants to be."

"Since we seem to be laying all our cards out on the table, perhaps you can explain to me your reasoning for trying to terminate him to begin with?"

"It's all in the reports."

"No, it's not. You really expect me to believe you tried to kill him just because he wanted to quit and go live with his girlfriend? Do I look like an idiot? Smith had an exemplary record. No verbal warnings, no written counselings, drew tough assignments, had over a ninety percent completion record, and you decided to get rid of him on a whim."

"It's in the report, I've said it before, we viewed him as a security risk," Davenport said tersely. "Yes, he was a good agent. But in our view, he was breaking down, he was starting to go haywire. He was starting to lose focus on his assignments, his mind was elsewhere, he wasn't giving everything he could in our estimation. He'd already told his girlfriend he worked for the government. It was our belief, as time went on, he'd divulge more critical information. Sure, right then, he wasn't a threat to us. But in five years, ten years, the longer he was out, the more classified information he could reveal. I decided it wasn't worth the risk so I put out the order so we would never have to worry about him. Does that satisfy you?"

"Not really. I mean, it's been what, three years now?"

"Yeah. So?"

"Well, has there ever been any indication he's leaked any secret information since he's been gone?"

"It's always easier to second guess when you don't have a foot in the game."

"Maybe so. But considering what you tried to do to him, if he hasn't told any secrets by now, I'd say the chances are good he never will," Lawson said.

"Well what difference does it make now? What's done is done."

"You're right. But I'd still like to talk to someone who's evaluated him."

Davenport didn't immediately respond, instead taking a step back as he sized up his adversary, wondering what she was up to. He knew she had something in mind she wasn't sharing. Even though Lawson was now in charge of Smith's file, he still wanted to be in the loop of what was happening. Davenport sat again as he considered her request.

"What exactly is it you're hoping to find?" Davenport asked.

"I want to see what type of mind frame he thinks Smith has."

"Well what difference would it make?"

"You said it yourself. We'll only find him when he wants to be found," Lawson said.

"And the significance to that is?"

"I'm sure a man like him still has connections, sources, he's still got his eyes and ears open as to what we're doing."

"Undoubtedly."

"So maybe we get the word out we're looking for him. That we wanna talk."

"Talk? Talk about what?"

"Correcting wrongs. Making things right again," Lawson said.

Davenport took a few seconds to analyze her words and think

them over, concluding she was crazy. He snapped up straight in his chair and leaned forward to get his point across.

"Are you seriously considering what I think you are?" Davenport asked. "Because it sounds to me like you're thinking about bringing him back in."

"Maybe. Now you understand why I wanna see and talk to the evaluator."

"You're crazy if you think Smith's ever gonna come walking through my door and work for us again."

"Well, he'd never do it for you. For someone else, maybe."

"That's just... that's..."

Lawson wasn't really interested in any of his objections though, cutting him off before he could finish whatever it was he had an issue with. "I don't really care what your thoughts are on the matter, Mr. Davenport. For the record, you've had three years to either find him or close the issue entirely. You've failed on both counts. Now, unfortunately, it's up to me to clean up the mess you created. Quite frankly, one which never should've been created to begin with. So now, are you going to give me the information I'm requesting? Or should I go over your head and call Director Roberts to get what I want?"

Davenport leaned back in his chair, a little agitated at the woman standing in front of him, taking over his case. He knew as much as he resisted though, he couldn't really fight it. This was all orchestrated by Director Roberts and Davenport knew that if Lawson wanted it, she'd get it. Director Roberts was the one who wanted this and appointed her so Davenport knew he didn't have a leg to stand on no matter what it was he objected to. Even though it was against his better judgment, Davenport lifted the phone and called down to the psych evaluator.

"Brian, I'm sending someone down to see you," Davenport said. "She wants to get information on a couple of agents. 17 and

John Smith. Director Roberts has tasked her with finding Smith so give her whatever she needs."

Davenport hung up and locked eyes with Lawson, neither of them saying a word for a minute. The Centurion director did not look the least bit pleased at having to take orders from her, believing that she didn't have a clue what she was doing.

"Thank you," Lawson said.

"You can thank me when you're finally done here."

Lawson smiled, not at all upset at Davenport not seeming to enjoy her company. "So where can I find this guy?"

"Brian Bernier. Office 508, fifth floor."

Lawson quickly turned around and stormed out of the office and headed for the elevator. As soon as she got out on the fifth floor, she could immediately tell this floor was less hectic. It was actually kind of eerie how quiet it was. As she looked up and down the hall, she didn't notice one person roaming around. The walls were painted a dark gray, the carpeting was dark, everything seemed so devoid of life. It was a complete deviation from what she found on the sixth floor, where everything seemed bright and modern. Even the lighting on the fifth floor seemed sparse, not to mention there wasn't one door or office you could see into from the outside. They were all closed off to wandering eyes. There were no glass offices or doors on this floor. In reality, the fifth floor was used exclusively for testing purposes, as well as physical and mental evaluations. It was a floor nobody ever really wanted to visit. And nobody would unless they were ordered to do so. Lawson quickly found office 508 and slowly pushed the door open, unsure what to expect. She was almost immediately greeted by a man sitting at a desk. He was an elderly man, looked slightly overweight, probably in his mid-sixties, with gray hair and glasses.

"You must be Sam Davenport's protégé," the man said.

"Well, I doubt he'd put it quite that way," Lawson said. "I'm sure he'd call me a few other things first."

The man laughed. "I'm Brian Bernier, the psych evaluator here. Sit, please."

"Thank you. My name's Michelle Lawson."

"A pleasure. I understand you're looking for information on 17 and John Smith."

"Yes. Mostly on Smith, though."

"What exactly would you like to know?" Bernier said.

"Well I've read all the reports, the ones they've written, the ones written on them, their assignments, everything. But to find Smith, I guess I'm hoping to find out what makes him tick."

"Well, 17 was a very good agent. He was confident, maybe overly so at times, a bit cocky, had a definite mean streak in him. But he always got the job done. Loved his work. Maybe too much."

"And Smith?"

"Very driven. He wanted to be the best. Professional, set in his ways, somewhat of a loner," Bernier said.

"Are you aware of what became of the both of them?" Lawson asked.

"Well I know 17 was killed in an airport in Ohio and Smith disappeared after he was scheduled to be terminated, if that's what you're inferring."

"Were you consulted before the order was given on Smith?"

Bernier didn't answer at first, instead taking a second to collect his thoughts and determining what he was willing to reveal. Lawson could tell he was beginning to hedge a little and sought to alleviate any concerns he might have had.

"I'm not here to get anyone in trouble," Lawson said. "I've been tasked by Director Roberts with finding the man who killed 17 and with finding John Smith. They may well be one and the same thing. Anything you tell me will not leave this room and anything you say will not be held or used against you in any way."

Sensing a trustworthy person sitting in front of him, Bernier finally relented and decided not to hold anything back. "I was not consulted on the Smith action."

"Are you aware of the circumstances that led to the decision?"

"They believed he became a security risk, I was told."

"And what do you think?"

Bernier once again didn't reply immediately. The strain on his face told Lawson he was hesitant to relay his true feelings on the matter. "It's not my job to make those decisions."

"It's not what I asked, doctor. In your opinion, was John Smith a security risk?" Lawson asked.

"In my opinion, no. He was not."

"Why did you believe he wasn't?"

"As I said, he was a driven man. But from my experience, agents who turn against their country are usually driven by three things: money, power, and revenge. None of those things would have described John Smith at the time."

"What did describe him?"

"Like I said, he was driven by his need to help people, help his country. Money didn't motivate him. He wasn't interested in power. And there was nothing in his life he felt the need to get revenge for."

"Did you know about his girlfriend?" Lawson asked.

"We talked about it once. He felt conflicted about his relationship with her."

"How so?"

"It was a new experience for him. His entire adult life he'd been a loner. He went from a military unit to government work, never really having any time to devote to another person. He wasn't sure he could continue having a relationship and do the job he did. He wasn't sure he could turn the switch off from violent killer to loving boyfriend then back again. He wasn't sure he could love someone, or have someone love him, while he did the things he did. He viewed himself as somewhat of a monster, someone not deserving of another's affection."

"And yet he considered leaving for her?"

"She made him feel like a normal person, like he wasn't the things he thought himself to be. The longer he was with her, the more he liked it, the more he thought he could be something else," Bernier said.

"After his girlfriend was killed, do you think he would've sought revenge on the man who did it?"

"If you're asking whether he would've sought the man responsible, then yes. He wouldn't think of it as revenge though."

"How would he look at it then?"

"He's a man who lives on principles, on his own code of conduct. He follows his own rules. He's a man who protects those who can't protect themselves. He's got a strong sense of justice. He would look at it as righting a wrong, bringing the man responsible to justice."

"That would explain it then," Lawson said to herself.

"Explain what?"

"If Smith killed 17, it would explain why he never went after anyone else who was involved. He didn't go after his handler, or anyone else he perceived to be in on it."

"Because he's not interested in revenge, per se," Bernier said. "He's mostly interested in righting wrongs, protecting others, then he is on extracting retribution. He understands the business he's in, the life he leads, that sometimes he's going to be in danger and have to defend himself. Sometimes against people he might trust. He doesn't view those others as anything other than doing what killers do. Killing an innocent civilian, though, in his mind, would be reprehensible."

"So, revealing secrets or classified information isn't something you think he'd do?"

"Not in his DNA. He told his girlfriend he worked on a secret government project he wasn't at liberty to discuss further. She never pressed him on it."

"And even with her gone and after what was done to him, he'd never go back on that?" Lawson said.

"It's been what, three years? If he hasn't done it by now, he never will."

"If he's found, do you think he could be brought back in?"

"What an interesting proposition," Bernier said. "Under the right circumstances, yes. He's still never betrayed his country, even after almost being eliminated, and his girlfriend killed. It wouldn't be easy though. It'd have to be the right person asking. As you can imagine, he wouldn't be very trusting of many people right about now."

"But you do think it's possible?"

"If you appeal to his sense of morals and he feels he can trust you, then yes, I do think it's possible."

"Where do you think a man like him would wind up after all this time?" Lawson asked.

"Hmm... interesting question. I would imagine he would hide out for a little while, lay low, try to stay out of sight for a while. But it wouldn't be for long. A man like him has a strong sense of morality, doing what's right, protecting people. I'd imagine, even if he wanted to stay hidden, he'd be drawn out by his perception of helping others. He has an unbelievable set of skills and he'd want to use them."

"Small town or a big city?"

"I would think he'd choose a big city. Plenty of opportunity to do what he does without the fear of being recognized."

"Really? You don't think he'd choose a smaller city for that purpose?"

"No. When you think about it, if he does the things he's capable of, and he unleashes the beast inside him, if he does it in a smaller town, he's going to stand out."

"But in a bigger city he can blend in," Lawson said.

"Exactly."

"Any ideas as to what city he'd choose?"

"I would say somewhere along the east coast," Bernier said.

"Why the east coast?"

"It's what he's familiar with. Centurion's in New York, his girlfriend was in Florida, if he killed 17, he was in Ohio. See the pattern?"

"Why wouldn't he go to the west coast, or even leave the country? Why would he stay here? Wouldn't he think it's more dangerous for him?"

"I don't believe he even considers the danger factor. I don't think he's concerned about being found. He's the type who believes if someone's looking for him, they'll eventually find him, wherever he may be."

"Do you think he'd be alone? Would he have help?"

"Most likely alone. If he's not, it's a small number, maybe one or two others he'd consider trustworthy enough to not turn on him. If there are others, then they're probably also on the run from something."

"Thank you, doctor, you've been a big help."

"My pleasure."

"Just one more question. Have you ever conveyed any of this to Davenport or anyone else involved in Centurion?" Lawson said.

"No."

"Why not?"

"They've never asked."

"Why do you think that is?"

"Honestly, I don't think they were ever too concerned about finding him," Bernier said. "As long as he was out of the picture, that's what was important to them."

"Why?"

"I think they realized what kind of mistake they made and any attempt to bring it into the forefront would make them look... not so good. Out of sight, out of mind."

"And the death of 17 brought it back into the limelight."

"It did."

"Anything else you'd like to add?"

"The few times I talked to Smith, he seemed like a good man. I wish you luck in your travels. If you're hellbent on finding him, I'd suggest you start by looking at cities where the crime rate has gone up, specifically murders."

46

Recker had been waiting outside of the club for several hours. He was standing across the street, leaning up against the building, just watching and waiting for his intended victim to arrive. The club didn't open until nine, but Recker got there early to conduct some surveillance and just get a general feel for the area. He saw Laine walk into the club about eight o'clock. He came back out about half an hour later to start dealing with some of the crowd as the line started forming. Judging from the amount of people waiting to go in, Recker assumed it was a fairly popular place. Though the club was located in the middle of the street, there were small walkways located on both sides of the building, leading to a larger parking lot in the back of the property.

Recker patiently waited for the right time to strike. He fielded a couple of phone calls from Jones while he waited, wanting to see if he'd done the job yet. But Recker said he was waiting for the crowd to die down a little. He also saw there were security cameras on the entrance, as well as the corner of both sides of the building.

Killing Laine might not be as easy as he thought it'd be. He could've just picked a spot somewhere and took a sniper shot at Laine from across the street, but somehow, it seemed like taking the easy way out to Recker. Anybody could do that. It took a special kind of person to kill someone up close. But he also felt as if avoiding the cameras was going to be a bit of a challenge. He didn't see a way he could've avoided them if he was going to do it there. But as he thought about it, he could sense he was getting overanxious and pressing. Two things he normally didn't do. He was usually very patient in waiting for one of his victims. But for some reason, he was trying to force this one. Maybe it was because he was feeling the CIA heat he was trying to hurry things along so he could get back to working out whether he was at risk. All he had to do was wait a few hours more until the club was closed. He already knew Laine's address. If he just waited until the business was closed, he could just follow Laine home and avoid the security cameras.

With his new plan, Recker went back to his car which was parked down the street. He still had a good view of the club and could see Laine's car as he was leaving. Once Laine got back to his house, Recker could finish him off with relative ease. It would likely be three or four in the morning once he got home and Recker wouldn't have to worry about prying eyes. He called Jones and informed him of the plan so he wouldn't bother asking him every half hour on whether the job was finished yet. Recker was parked in a metered spot and had to put some change in the machine every couple of hours as he waited. He thought about just going to Laine's house and waiting, but Recker didn't want to take the chance of his target going somewhere else first before stopping home. Then Recker might have to wait another day to finish his task. And though he was trying to be patient, he wasn't interested in prolonging this any further. He wanted it to be done tonight. Not only so he could get back to monitoring the CIA more closely, but also because every day Laine was alive, was a day a child could get hurt because of him.

Recker kept his eyes on Laine for most of the time, just in case he ducked out early. But he was still there come closing time at 2am. He stayed for half an hour after closing and most everyone else had left, though there were a few employees still there. Recker knew there was a back entrance and Laine would likely leave through there. Knowing he wasn't likely to see his target physically leave the building, Recker had to pay extra attention to the street where the cars exited. Luckily, there was only one exit. He finally saw headlights beaming across the side of the building, indicating a car was coming out. It was Laine's. Not wanting to get too close and possibly scare the man off if he noticed he was being followed, Recker kept a comfortable distance between the two of them. Especially at that time of the morning where there weren't a lot of cars out on the road, it'd be much easier to spot him if he followed too closely. Luckily, Laine appeared to be going straight home without any stops. It was about a twenty-minute drive from the club to Laine's home, which was located on a quiet suburban street.

As they pulled onto the street, Recker sped up, hoping to catch up with Laine before he actually entered the house. As he got closer, he could see he was a little too late, as Laine was already unlocking and opening the front door. Recker parked along the curb just as the door closed, making it a tiny bit tougher for him to enter. He honestly didn't feel like jumping through hoops for this assignment and decided to just be straightforward about it. Though he could've gotten in the house by some other means, it was always easier to just go in the front door. The tougher part would be whether or not Laine answered at that time of the morning, since it wasn't exactly normal to hear someone knocking at your door at 3am. But Recker didn't really care, he had a gun, he'd just start blasting away if he had to. Most people were sleeping anyway, and when they heard gunshots and woke up, he'd be long gone. But just to err on the side of caution, Recker put a suppressor on the end of his gun. It'd still make a sound, but it would be severely muted and not quite as noticeable. As Recker walked up the steps to the door, he thought about how he was going to finish the job. He could kill him the moment he saw him, but it wasn't Recker's style. He at least wanted the man to know in his final moments, why he was being killed. Recker didn't think he owed it to them, but he thought it was only fair. Recker loudly knocked on the door several times and waited a minute for an answer, though none was coming. He repeated his steps, only to get the same response. He noticed a doorbell and rang it continuously until he heard footsteps coming.

"All right, all right," Laine shouted from the inside. "What the hell do you want? It's 3am."

"I'm just here to take out the garbage," Recker said sarcastically.

Recker had been hiding his gun underneath his trench coat, firmly planted within his hand. He immediately withdrew it from his coat and pointed it at the unsuspecting man.

"Yo, man, whatever you want, just take it," Laine said, putting his hands up.

Recker didn't bother responding and instead pulled the trigger, shooting his victim in his left shoulder. Laine fell backwards, yelling in pain, and clutching at his shoulder as Recker entered his home.

"Yo, what do you want?" Laine asked.

"You hear what happened to your friend, Bowman?"

"I heard he was killed yesterday."

"Give you two guesses as to who did it." Recker grinned.

"Why? What do you got against us?" Laine asked, crawling backwards along the floor to try to escape his attacker.

"I don't like people who use children for their own pleasure."

"What're you talking about?"

"I know your record. I've seen the text messages you and Bowman exchanged. I know what you were planning."

"All right, man, I admit it. I promise I'll never do it again. I promise."

Recker was getting tired of walking and pursuing the man so he shot him in the thigh to stop him in his tracks. Laine screamed out in pain, wondering how long the man was going to torture him for.

"If you're gonna kill me, just get it over with," Laine said.

He was right. Recker didn't want to torture him while killing him. He usually only tortured people he had a personal vendetta against. He didn't even torture 17 much. Recker ended his life rather quickly for all the pain and anguish he'd caused him over the years. Recker did what he wanted and let Laine know why he was killing him, which was all he set out to do. He raised his suppressed gun at Laine's body and fired three more rounds into his chest, quickly snuffing out the remaining breaths of life within him. Not one to admire his work very much, Recker immediately turned around and walked out the door. As he walked to his car, he looked around to see if anybody was on the street, but there was no one to be seen. As he drove away, he called Jones to let him know the job was done. Jones had said he wouldn't go to bed until he heard from Recker when everything was finalized, no matter what time it was.

"David, it's done," Recker said.

"Any complications I should be made aware of?"

"No."

"Where did it happen?"

"Inside his house."

"And there were no witnesses, onlookers, anything?" Jones asked.

"No, it was a clean hit."

"Very well. I guess I shall see you in the morning then."

Recker drove back to his apartment, though he didn't go straight to bed. He was tired, but still somewhat wound up from the altercation with Laine. Though Recker believed he was completely justified in the killing and nobody would lose sleep over the death of a child abuser, it still wasn't something he could just forget in a matter of minutes. He never could. Even when he was in the CIA, he couldn't just block out someone dying and forget about it in a matter of minutes, and it hadn't changed since then. When he got home, he fixed himself a rum and coke and sat on the couch to take some steam off. He didn't bother to put the TV on, a light, or anything else to distract him. He just sat alone on the couch in the darkness, trying to sort out his thoughts. He finally slumped on the couch about 5am and drifted off to sleep.

It wouldn't be as long a rest as he was hoping for though. He initially didn't figure to get into the office until around noon, as was usually the case when he was out late on an assignment the night before. But he normally didn't have someone banging on his door in the morning either. Recker was awoken from his sleep by the thunderous pounding on his door. He reached for his gun which was still sitting on the table and slowly sauntered over to the door.

"Mike, I know you're in there. I saw your car outside," Mia yelled.

Recker took a look through the peephole, not believing what he was seeing. Though he obviously knew Mia's voice, he had no idea she even knew where he lived. She picked him up from the lot the one time he left his car downtown after taking out Bellomi and his crew, but he never told her which unit he was in. And he definitely wasn't expecting her right now. He took another look through the peephole, as the door shook from her knocks, just to make sure there was nobody with her. She seemed to be alone, so Recker finally opened the door for her. Mia barged in, not even waiting for an invitation.

"Sure, come in," Recker said.

Mia stormed into the room, looking like a ball of fire and like she had a lot on her mind. She put her hands on her hips and turned around to face her host. Recker looked at her curiously, wondering what was on her mind.

"What do you think you were doing yesterday?" Mia asked.

"What are you doing here?" Recker said.

"I wanted to talk to you."

"Ever hear of a phone?"

"No, a phone won't do for this. This needs to be done in person," she said, agitated.

"How'd you even find me?"

"I know where you live, I've been here before."

"No, you've been in the parking lot. I never told you what unit I was in."

"Well, you don't need to be a world class investigator like some people I know to figure it out," Mia said. "I looked at the names on the mailboxes in the lobby."

Recker let out a laugh, not believing her. "No, I took my name off the mailbox."

"Exactly. You have the only mailbox without a name attached to it. I assumed you'd be the only person who'd go that far."

"Hmm, not bad. But what if you made a mistake and pounded on the wrong door?"

"Then I guess I would've just used my sweet personality to

apologize." She gave him a mock smile, crinkling the corners of her eyes.

"Oh."

Mia took a quick look around the room since it was the first time she'd actually set foot in Recker's apartment, not really impressed with his décor.

"How many years have you been here?" she said.

"Uh, a few."

"And this is all you've done with it? I've seen warehouses looking better decorated than this."

"Well I'm not here much anyway," Recker said, looking around. "All I need is the basics. Got a kitchen, a couch, a TV, a bedroom, it's everything I need. I don't need fancy pictures and china and candles and all the other nonsense. I'm basically only here to sleep."

"Speaking of which, did I wake you up? You look like crap."

"Late night," he said wearily. "What time is it, anyway?"

"After nine."

"Oh. Well, I had to get up in like three hours, anyway."

"Oh. Sorry. I just figured you were up already. I assumed you were on a case or something."

"Was. Finished it last night. Late last night."

"What time'd you get to bed?"

"I think I dozed off at four or five. Something like that anyway."

"I'm sorry," Mia said, some of her bitterness fading away.

"You want a drink or something?"

"No. No. You almost made me forget what I came here for. You probably did it deliberately. Change the subject, make me feel sorry for you so I forget all about it."

Recker grinned and shrugged. "Not me. I would never."

"Yeah right."

"Don't you have work today?"

"No, I'm actually off for a day."

"Lucky you. Well, why don't you run along and spend time with your new BF," Recker said, grabbing her arm and leading her to the door.

Mia quickly shook off his grasp of her and took a few steps back, getting the urge to fight again, ready to light into him.

"No. You know how mad I am at you for yesterday?" Mia asked.

"Yesterday? What was yesterday?"

"Are you seriously gonna pretend like you don't remember what happened?"

"Refresh my memory. I barely know what day I'm in half the time. With my schedule, all the days just blend together sometimes," Recker said, playing dumb, though he knew exactly what she was referring to, buying some time so he could fashion a sarcastic reply.

"You know, lunch at the hospital, you, me, Josh. You remember, that one?"

"Oh," Recker said, tilting his head back, changing his voice slightly as he played along. "Yeah. I remember now."

"Yeah, I thought you might."

"What about it? What are you mad for? I thought we all had a great time."

Mia laughed. "Great time? Yeah right. You know how embarrassed I was sitting, listening to you?"

"Why? I thought we were all just sitting there, talking, trying to get to know each other."

"No. I know exactly what you were doing. It was the very reason why I didn't want to introduce you yet."

"Why?"

"Why? Because you were trying to make him look bad, you were trying to intimidate him, you were trying to..."

"I meant no harm," Recker said gently.

"You really think I believe that?"

"Well, I mean, he kind of seems like a... like a..."

"Like what?" Mia said, hands on hips.

"Like a tool."

"Seriously?"

"Just my opinion. I think you can do better than him."

"No. You're not playing this game with me."

"What game?"

"You're not doing this. You don't get to choose who I go out with. I was never so embarrassed as I was yesterday listening to you."

"Really? More embarrassing than being kidnapped and tied up in an empty office with a psychopath and a notorious gang and your life hanging in the balance?" Recker asked.

"That wasn't embarrassing. That was just... it was... I dunno, it was just something else." Mia stammered the words, caught off balance.

"Oh. Makes sense."

"You're gonna need to ease up on him."

"Does it really matter? It's not like I'm gonna be seeing the guy every week."

"Well, if we're still gonna be friends, then you're gonna need to get used to seeing another guy around me."

"Mia, all kidding aside, if it makes you uncomfortable being around me from now on, I'll understand. If this other relationship is something you really want, then try to make it work the best you can. If there's not room for me, I'll be OK."

"I don't want to cut you from my life. I don't. I understand things between us will never progress the way I once hoped. I'm accepting the situation. I am. But I still care about you, and I don't want to never see you again. I know we're never gonna go double dating or anything sappy, but there's no reason we can't still see each other from time to time."

Recker nodded, agreeing with her position. "OK. I promise I'll never try to intimidate him or embarrass you or anything."

"Besides, you still need me. Who else would you go to if you ever got shot again? Which is probably likely considering everything you do." Mia's lips curled up slowly into a tight smile.

"Good point. Maybe I'd just have to find myself another nurse."

"You better not."

"OK. I promise I'll be on my best behavior next time."

"That's all I ask."

~

New York---Lawson entered the Centurion offices with vigor, confident she was on the right track in finding her target. Well, maybe it was more hopefulness than confidence, but regardless of semantics, she felt like she was making headway. She felt that she had a good understanding of her subjects, how they thought, how they behaved, and where Smith might have gone. She went into Davenport's office to request a few things that she needed.

"Mr. Davenport," Lawson said.

"Mr. Davenport's in conference right now," the secretary said without looking up.

"Well, you can either buzz him to come out or I can start pounding on his door."

"Uh, just one minute."

The secretary called into the office and told Davenport that Lawson was here and insisted on seeing him immediately. Within a minute, Davenport opened the door and emerged from his office, closing it behind him as he greeted Lawson.

"I hope this is important," Davenport said. "I have critical business that I need to get back to discussing."

"I have important business that I need to discuss too," Lawson said, standing her ground.

"What do you need?"

"I need two of your analysts assigned to me for the next couple of days."

"Why?"

"I believe John Smith may be in a major city somewhere on the east coast. I need a couple of analysts to try to track him down."

"What makes you think he would be on the east coast?" Davenport asked, sounding unconvinced of her findings.

"Well, after talking to the doctor, along with my own personal observations, that's the conclusion we've come to," Lawson said.

"Sounds like a wild goose chase to me."

"Somehow, you don't surprise me."

"Fine. I'll have two analysts report to your office within half an hour."

"I'll be waiting."

Lawson then left to go back to her office while Davenport stayed stationary, thinking about whether she was as close as she believed she was and who he wanted to send to her. He then turned to his secretary before heading back to his meeting.

"Have Fulton and Rogers report to her office immediately," Davenport said.

Approximately twenty minutes later, the two analysts came to her office as she was working on her laptop.

"Ms. Lawson?" Fulton asked. "We were told to report to you."

They exchanged pleasantries and the two analysts told her about themselves. After talking to them for a few minutes and picking their brain a little, Lawson was satisfied she was getting good people she could work with. She explained the situation to them and what she was looking for.

"I would like you to start combing through airport surveillance footage," Lawson said to Fulton. "I want you to pay specific attention to two dates. The date we know Smith flew back into the country, and at the Bob Hope Airport where 17 was killed. I want you to also check out flight manifests for every flight into the country the day he was supposed to fly in."

"OK."

"Rogers, I want you to start digging into records and information for every major city on the east coast."

"What do you consider major?" Rogers asked.

"Boston, Philadelphia, New York, Atlanta, Washington, DC., Miami. Start with those first then work your way down if nothing comes of them."

"What exactly am I looking for?"

"Statistics for major crime increases in the last three years. News stories of a new gang or player in town, police requests for information regarding an individual where they don't have much,. If Smith has relocated into one of these cities, it's likely murders or major crime stats have probably gone up, and it's also likely the local police have nothing on him and have attempted to gain insight into his identity by requesting further information, either from us or the FBI."

"I'm on it."

"Thank you both. With some luck and hard work, hopefully we can pinpoint his location within a few days."

47

The Philadelphia Police Department had called a 10am press conference to discuss a string of recent murders plaguing the city. All the major news organizations were there, TV stations, newspapers, and news blogs, basically anyone who had press credentials. Though it wasn't being broadcast live on TV, the stations were just cutting up footage and highlights for their later news broadcasts; it was being streamed live on their websites. Ever since the day before when the police announced they were holding a news conference, Jones started looking into it and had a feeling that him and more specifically Recker would be the main topic. Well, more or less all Recker since he was the face of their operation. Both he and Recker were in the office watching the live stream of the event on the computer. Police Commissioner Paul Boyle stepped up to the microphone to start the conference.

"Thank you all for coming. The reason for this conference is to discuss several murders that have happened in our city recently. The last two having occurred in the past three days. We believe the deaths of Sidney Bowman and Reed Laine is the work of the man that the media and the public have dubbed The Silencer. We are releasing a picture of the man that we believe to be The Silencer and are hereby announcing him as wanted in connection with their murders. We are asking for the public's help in identifying this man so we can prevent any other incidents from happening. If you know who this man is, where he lives, or you see him walking down the street, please call the police tip line."

Boyle stepped aside as a picture of Recker appeared on a screen behind the commissioner. It appeared to be a picture from some type of security camera from the shopping center where Recker left the car and body of Sidney Bowman. It was a still shot of Recker walking away from the car. Jones glanced over at Recker, who returned his look with a shrug.

"I didn't see any cameras," Recker said.

"Obviously," Jones said. "This isn't going to help matters any."

Boyle talked about the deaths of the two men, as well as several other incidents reported to be the work of The Silencer over the past several years. He recounted not only murders, but also other minor cases they thought Recker had been involved in. After Boyle had finished his speech, he opened the floor to questions from the media.

"What makes you think the man is The Silencer?" a reporter questioned.

"This is the first actual photograph that we've gotten of him that matched up with some of the sketches that have been drawn over the past few years."

"If The Silencer did do these, what makes you think it was murder and not self-defense?"

"We have evidence that would indicate murder. I can't really get into further specifics than that."

"Doesn't Laine have a long police record?" another reporter asked.

"A man's criminal history has no bearing on whether his murder is investigated or not," Boyle said.

"Yes, but, with all due respect, every instance that you've reputed to be the work of The Silencer, innocent people have been protected, and criminals have wound up either in jail or dead."

"As I said, a victim's criminal history has no bearing on anything. The Silencer is not a member of law enforcement and is not entitled to just go shooting people at will. This isn't the wild west. We have law, we have courts, we have a justice system. We do not work outside of those controls just because we feel like it and call it justice. It's not how it works."

"But you're asking for the public's help on something they don't want to help you on," the reporter said. "I've talked to several citizens who think The Silencer is more helpful than the police are."

"Well that would be false and incorrect."

"But the public perception is, he helps the weak, the vulnerable, and the innocent. And the only people who get hurt are the criminals who are trying to capitalize or prey on them. The public supports him and believes he does what should be done and what's necessary, or does what the justice system fails to do."

"I can't help the public perception. All I can state is he's not a police officer, and he does not have justification for some of the things he does," Boyle said. "He must be held accountable the same as anyone else. It's the law."

Commissioner Boyle took a few more questions, none of which were very sympathetic to his cause of capturing or identifying who The Silencer was. As the reporters' questions indicated, the media, as well as the public, were firmly behind The Silencer. It wasn't very likely the police were going to get the kind of support they were hoping for. As the conference started to wrap up, Jones started wondering about their future.

"Should we begin packing?" he asked.

"I don't think that'll be necessary."

"Well your profile just went up five thousand percent."

"From a police standpoint, this is nothing new. I've always been on their radar. They've sent up requests to the FBI before. They're just making it public now."

"Why now after all this time?"

"I'm making them look bad I guess," Recker shrugged.

"Still, this won't make our jobs any easier."

"Wasn't easy to begin with."

"Well this won't help."

"They're grasping at straws. They're not likely to get much help from the public."

"That's a very premature assumption to make I would say," Jones said. "Your picture was just released by the police to the public and will likely be plastered on every bulletin board, bus stop, website, train station, and blog site known to mankind."

"Hate to break it to you but my face hasn't exactly been a secret for a long time," Recker said. "They've had sketches of me from almost every case I've been on since we started. From the girl I saved from getting raped at the bar, the woman I saved from her husband at the hotel, or the convenience store I saved from being robbed, they've always known what I looked like. Now they just have a physical picture."

"Still, I can't believe this won't somehow reach the ears of the CIA. This has to reach their doorstep somehow," Jones said.

"Maybe."

"For the sake of simplicity, it may be better if we start up operations in another city."

"You really wanna pick up and move?" Recker asked.

"Do I want to? No. But in the interest of self-preservation, I think it may be wise. We've always known this day may come. We always knew there could be a time when the heat became too much and it would simply be more difficult to work here. Perhaps the time has come. We've talked about this."

"I know. I just don't know if I wanna keep doing this every few years. Moving."

"Why?"

"I dunno. I feel like we've established something here," Recker said, rehashing the same conversation they had earlier.

"We've never really put down roots," Jones said. "There's nothing to prevent us from going somewhere else. Pack up the computers, load up a moving van, and we're gone. Just like that. There are other people in other cities who could use our help, just like this one."

"I know. It's just... I'd hate to lose all our contacts, friends, and have to start all over again."

"To be fair and honest, we only have one friend. And she's moving on, Mike. She's got a new relationship, she won't be around as much, there's really nothing keeping you here. You can make contacts in other places just as easily as you did here."

Recker nodded, knowing he was correct. "Yeah. Let's give it a couple weeks first and see what happens. If it looks like it's getting too hot, then we'll pack it up."

"Deal."

"Have you picked up anything in the last couple days on the CIA front?" Recker asked.

"No. It's been quiet."

∽

New York---Lawson was in her office working on some leads when Rogers came rushing in, a little out of breath. He had his laptop in hand and set it down on Lawson's desk and started typing on it.

"You're not gonna believe this," Rogers said calmly, although the speed of his entry and the glint in his eyes gave away his excitement.

He pulled up the picture of Recker off the Philadelphia Police Department's website from the photo they released of him from the press conference they had the day before. Rogers zoomed in on the picture and blew it up across the screen to get an even better look at it.

"Oh my god, it's him!" Lawson said.

"Yeah, that's what I thought."

"Where'd you get this?"

"The Philadelphia Police Department released the picture yesterday."

"Why? What happened so he'd be on their radar?"

"They're linking this man to a couple of murders that happened there within the last few days," Rogers said.

"Who were the guys he supposedly killed?"

"A couple of nobody's. One was a convicted child sex abuser, the other was a friend of his, might've dipped his toes in the same pool, just not caught yet."

"This is the break we've been looking for."

"Maybe. If the heat's on him then he might just pick up and leave," Rogers said. "Might be gone by now, anyway."

"OK. We stop everything else and concentrate on Philly," Lawson said. "We know he's there. So, let's put the pieces together and figure out what he's doing there and who he's doing it with. I'll contact the Philly police and see if I can get a look at the file they have on him."

"You got it."

Lawson immediately got on the phone and called the Philadelphia Police Department. After talking to a couple different people and being put on hold for a few minutes, she eventually was put through to Commissioner Boyle. After a quick greeting and identifying herself, she quickly got to the heart of the matter.

"I understand yesterday you held a news conference and released a picture of a suspect in some murders you've had recently," Lawson said.

"Yes, that's right."

"I believe we can help you in that regard if you're willing to reciprocate that help."

"What did you have in mind?" Boyle asked.

"We know who the man in the photo is."

"Who is he?"

"Well, first, before we get into that, I'd like to set some ground rules."

"Such as?"

"Well, I'd like to look at the file you have on him, everything you suspect him of."

"That could be arranged," Boyle said.

"Great."

"How is it that you know this guy?"

"I can't really divulge that, sir."

"C'mon, you're gonna have to do better than that. You want my cooperation? Fine. I'm willing to give it. But cooperation is a two-way street and if you want my help, then you need to fill in the dots."

"OK. I'll tell you what I can," Lawson said. "He's a former CIA agent who, due to various circumstances, is no longer with the agency."

"He went into business for himself?"

"Maybe. Kind of looks that way. There's some debate amongst some of us as to what to do with him."

"Oh, you got that too, huh?"

"What's that?"

"He's been here about three years as far as we can tell," Boyle said. "At least that's when we first started getting reports on him."

"Yeah?"

"Well, you'll see when you read his file, but so far, he's only targeted criminals. He helps the elderly, stops robberies, kills the thugs... he's a one-man task force."

"So, what's the debate?" Lawson said.

"You know how many people I pissed off in my own department with the press conference yesterday?"

"No. I guess I don't quite understand the problem."

"The problem is half my command, eighty percent of my patrol units, and sixty percent of my detectives want to leave the guy alone and let him do his thing," Boyle said. "They say he makes their job easier. They wanted me not to release anything and possibly scare the guy off and have him go to a new city."

"So, why'd you do it then?"

"Like I said in the presser, nobody's above the law. Even those who apparently are on our side. Sometimes, people trip over their halo if it falls off."

"I get your meaning."

"What's this guy's name?"

"John Smith," Lawson said.

"Really?"

"No, it really was his name with us. I don't know what he's using now."

"So, what are you guys planning on doing with him?" Boyle said.

"Well, it'll largely be up to him, assuming I get close enough to talk to him."

"You wanna talk to him?"

"Absolutely. He has a special set of skills which could be useful."

"You don't have to tell me about that. I've seen his work."

"Anyway, I can be down there tomorrow morning if that works for you," Lawson said.

"Yeah, fine."

"Can I ask one other favor of you?"

"You can ask."

"I know you just put it out there and he's your number one target, but can I ask you to back off it already?"

"Back off?" Boyle asked, surprised at the request. "You're telling me how dangerous he is, not that I need a reminder, and you want me to back off?"

"He's been missing for three years," Lawson said. "I don't want to take the chance of him feeling the walls are closing in so he flies the coop and we lose track of him again for another three years. This is the closest we've gotten to him. I don't wanna lose him now. I'm just asking, please, you don't actively pursue any leads on him until we get a team down there."

"Well, I'm not going to make any promises right now. The media and the public love his persona, so I don't even know if we're going to get any leads that are worth pursuing. I'll take it under advisement."

"Very well. I'll be down tomorrow morning."

When Lawson put down the phone, she could hardly contain her excitement. After only a few days of searching, she'd already got a line on Smith's whereabouts. It made her wonder how she could find him in a few days when the previous regime couldn't find him in three years. Then she thought about what Bernier told her and how they didn't seem to be looking for him very hard. She believed Davenport knew he'd made a colossal mistake in trying to terminate Smith and the easiest thing to do was just to sweep it under the rug. Keeping it at the forefront only reinforced what a grave error he'd made. Regardless of Davenport's reasons or ineptitude, this would be a big feather in Lawson's cap. Though she wasn't initially too sure about this assignment, she was beginning to warm up to it. She kind of liked the idea of working on specialized cases and being the big gun, brought in to save the day. Now, she just had to deliver. It was one thing to find Smith. It was another to take him out or bring him in.

Davenport was in the outside office with his secretary discussing his itinerary for the next couple of days when he noticed some activity going on in the hallways. He saw both Fulton and Rogers, analysts that he had assigned to Lawson, fly by as if they had some urgent news to share. Wondering if they'd found something, Davenport eagerly left his office and swiftly walked to Lawson's to see what the fuss was about. When he got there, Lawson and the two analysts were almost giddy and going over plans of some kind.

"From your demeanor, I take it you've caught a break," Davenport said.

"Not just a break," Lawson said. "We've found him."

"What? You found him?"

"Yes. I wish I could say it was our brilliant deductive skills, but I can't. Philadelphia police released a photo of a murder suspect."

Lawson pulled the picture up on her laptop and spun it around so Davenport could see.

"That's him," he said softly, a little stunned.

"Yes, so I'm heading down there tomorrow to talk with their police commissioner and see what they've got on him so far," Lawson said. "Maybe I can get a read on his behavior and pinpoint where we might find him."

"And your goal is to what? Take him out, have a conversation with him, what?"

"I'd like a chance to talk to him first."

It was not the answer Davenport wanted to hear. A displeased look came over his face, still believing taking Smith out was the only option. Mostly because it would look bad on him to bring back an agent who he tried to eliminate. He was worried. If Smith was brought back, Davenport would look even worse in the eyes of his superiors, and who knows, maybe even get demoted, or lose control of the Centurion Project. He wasn't about to take a chance and let that happen.

"Can we have the room, please?" Davenport asked the analysts.

Fulton and Rogers looked to Lawson, knowing there was about to be a major disagreement. Since they knew she was technically in charge of the assignment at the moment, they wanted to clear it with her first. She nodded at them to do as he asked and the two analysts went back to their own workstations.

"What exactly do you think you're doing?" Davenport asked tersely.

"I think we've already had this discussion before. I'm cleaning up your mess."

"I know what you're doing. You think if you can somehow bring Smith in you'll be a conquering hero, the white knight, or the cowboy riding into town, saving the girl, then rides back out the next day in a blaze of glory. It doesn't always work so easy."

"Why exactly are you afraid of me trying to bring him back?" Lawson said. "Afraid of how it's gonna affect your reputation? Or maybe, you'll have to answer more questions from the higher-ups on why you seemingly gave up looking for him? Or is it something else?"

"None of the above. I'm just trying to help you. I know this assignment is a big step up for you and you're being looked at for future promotions," Davenport said. "I'd hate to think you blew your big chance on some wishful thinking or some grand delusion you may have."

"So, you're just looking out for me?"

"Men like Smith cannot be rehabilitated or brought back or reconditioned. His trust is broken. Whether that's our fault isn't relevant. You want to play the good guy and make it seem like you can do something nobody else could."

"And your point?" Lawson asked, not believing a word he was saying.

"You need to be realistic. If you get close enough to talk to Smith, then you're close enough for him to put a bullet in your head. And that's the most likely scenario. If he even gets so much as a sniff of one of us nearby, his first action isn't going to be waving at you, or asking how you're doing. His first action is going to be trying to put a bullet between your eyes. And you might want to think about that possibility."

Davenport turned and left her office to go back to his as he contemplated his next move. Though Lawson knew most of what Davenport was telling her was fluff, there was one thing he said which did make sense. It was how she was going to get close enough to talk to Smith. He was right, Smith would come up shooting as soon as he knew the CIA was near him. Though she'd eventually have to figure out the answer to a tricky question, the more pressing concern was just finding him to begin with. Once Davenport got back to his office, he immediately gave his secretary a new task.

"I want you to give me a list of the closest available agents we have who are not currently on assignment," Davenport said.

"When do you need it by?"

"Within the hour. Drop everything else and get me those names as soon as possible. I may need one of them for a very urgent job."

"I'll get right on it."

Davenport went into his office and tried to get some work done, though he quickly gave up on trying to do anything. No matter what he tried to do, his mind wound up thinking about Lawson and Smith. Knowing that Lawson wasn't going to abandon her attempt in trying to recruit Smith once again back into the organization, Davenport was hellbent on making sure she wasn't successful. Whatever it took, he was going to make sure she failed. His secretary got back to him half an hour later, bringing a list of names into his office and setting them down on his desk.

"We have two agents here in New York," she said before leaving.

"Perfect. Thank you."

Once his secretary left, Davenport perused the list a little more closely. It not only had the names of the ten closest agents, it also mentioned their strengths and weaknesses in a little spreadsheet. After looking at it for a few minutes, Davenport selected the agent he thought was best suited for the job and called his number.

"Agent 23, I have a new assignment for you. It's completely off the books, there won't be a record of it anywhere," Davenport said.

"What is it?"

"You're getting two targets. I'm sending a picture of each of them to your email," he said, bringing up the pictures of Smith and Lawson on his computer screen.

"What do you want done with them?"

"Eliminate them. Both of them."

"Where will I find them?"

"Philadelphia. I want you to be there by the morning," Davenport said. "I want you to stay there until the job is done. I don't care how long it takes."

"Does it matter who gets it first?"

"Take Smith out first. He's the more dangerous of the two. Once he's out of the way, she won't be much trouble."

48

As she promised, Lawson drove down to Philadelphia the following morning and was accompanied by three other agents. It was a little after 9am, and her first stop was police department headquarters. Commissioner Boyle cleared a few minutes from his busy schedule to accommodate the CIA officials. He was under no obligation to work with them, since they had no official capacity within the United States, but he figured if he did them a favor, there might come a time when he could seek a return on the favor. It may or have been wishful thinking since the CIA was extremely guarded with their information no matter who the inquisitor was, but Boyle figured it was worth the chance. Joining the commissioner in his meeting with his guests from the CIA was Deputy Commissioner Devron King, Boyle's right-hand man.

After a brief introduction and some small talk, Boyle handed Lawson the file they'd accumulated on Smith, the man Philadelphia knew as The Silencer. Lawson eagerly read the contents of the file, trying to gain any insight she could into how he was picking his victims or what part of the city Smith was likely to be found in. She had short bursts of conversation with her guests as she read the file, trying not to get too distracted so it would make her lose focus on what she was reading.

"Just from what I'm seeing, there doesn't appear to be any similarities to any of these cases which would seem like they're related in any way," Lawson said, frustrated there wasn't an obvious lead to be had.

"Now you see the problem we've been facing for the past several years," Boyle said. "He leaves behind no traces, no evidence of any kind, nothing helpful to us."

"Then how do you attribute all these cases to him?"

"Witnesses at the scene," King said. "All the people interviewed at the scenes of these crimes described seeing the same man, similar build, same type of clothing. It's why we're fairly certain everything in this folder is his work. Stopping rape victims, robberies, possible murders, assaults, you name it, he's been there."

"How do you account for how he's been at the scene just before these crimes have happened?" Lawson said.

"We can't." Boyle shook his head. "We just don't know."

"There has to be a way he's getting there ahead of time. It can't just be luck."

"We agree. We just haven't figured out how he's doing it yet."

"He must have help," Lawson said. "He can't be working alone. There has got to be another guy. Or girl. I mean, someone has to be feeding him this information somehow."

"The only thing we can come up with is he's got some kind of underground network informing him of impending crimes. How it works exactly, we have no idea."

"Any idea of who he might be working with? He can't be doing this all himself."

King threw his arms up, indicating their lack of knowledge on the subject. "It's a little perplexing. The fact all his targets are criminals, it's kind of strange if he'd be working with other criminals to make it happen."

"Maybe whoever he's working with isn't a criminal. At least not in the way we'd view them. Looking through these cases, it doesn't seem like he sticks to any one area specifically."

"He's been all over this city," Boyle said. "Northeast, south, west, downtown, there isn't an inch of this city he hasn't covered."

"Have you gotten any tips worth acting on since you went public the other day?" Lawson said, trying to flesh out the little information she had to go on.

"Nothing worth mentioning," King said. "At least not concerning him."

"What do you mean?" Lawson asked.

"Well, over the past few years where we can definitely pinpoint he's been here, the number of anonymous tips we've received has tripled. Not necessarily about The Silencer, but about crimes in general. And many of them have been preemptive in nature."

"That's a little strange. How do you account for it?"

"We can't. We don't know how it's related, or even if it's related at all. It's just kind of an interesting sidebar."

"I have to admit our main goal in having the press conference wasn't exactly getting any type of information leading to his capture or anything," Boyle said. "We didn't expect anything of that nature to come from it."

"Then what was the reason behind it?"

"Our chief principle behind it was to bring him out into the light. A man like him works in the shadows. Our goal was to hopefully shine some light on him so his profile is raised to the point where it's uncomfortable for him to work here. Hopefully, he'd pick up and leave and go on to a new city."

"So, you have no expectations of help from the media and the public?"

"I think I explained to you yesterday about the debate The Silencer has caused within my own department," the commissioner said.

"Yes."

"Well, double that with the media and the public," Boyle said. "They view him as a modern-day Wyatt Earp, riding into town, cleaning it up, killing all the bad guys by whatever means necessary. The public will be absolutely no help. They love the guy. They view him as doing what the police won't do."

"Media too?"

"He's regular headlines for them. They wouldn't like to see him go away anytime soon. He helps sell papers. They cater to what the public wants. While there's a few who don't agree with his frontier style of justice, there's just as many if not more who agree that he's more adept at taking out the trash than we are."

"Has he ever targeted an innocent person that you can tell?" Lawson asked.

"As far as we can tell, he's never hurt anyone who did not have a criminal record," Boyle said. "And we're not talking criminal records as minor as jaywalking or loitering or something. He targets hardened criminals, those with murder, assault, armed robbery, crimes against children, against the elderly, gang bangers, you name it, he's nailed them."

"What about these last two you think he killed? I thought one of them had no record."

"He didn't. But we found incriminating text messages on his phone he'd exchanged with the other guy indicating he had some severe mental issues. He didn't have a record yet, but it looks like he was heading that way. He just hadn't been caught in the act."

"I can see why your department is split on him," Lawson said.

"Split is a bit of an exaggeration," King said. "There's probably more who view him as an asset and appreciate all the help he gives us as opposed to those who think otherwise. He's a very polarizing subject amongst us, as well as the entire city. Look, there's no doubt, while this guy's been here, crime has gone up. But there's also no doubt the number of dangerous criminals on the street have gone down. In saying that, while this guy appears to know his craft, and appears to be on our side, he's also sprung up a bunch of wannabes. Guys who don't really have any idea what they're doing."

"You mean copycats?"

"Exactly. There's been at least ten people we've identified as being disciples of his, not that he's endorsed them, but who apparently idolize him and what he seems to stand for."

"It's bound to happen," Lawson said.

"No doubt. But these copycats are dangerous. Half of them don't have the skills to do what he does and wind up dead themselves. The others are too dangerous to have a gun in their hands and target just about anything that moves, good, bad, or indifferent. So, it's not necessarily just him that's the problem. It's everything he represents. If it was just him, maybe we wouldn't be having this discussion today. But you just can't have a bunch of people running around the streets extracting their own brand of justice," King said, he seemed exasperated at the whole situation.

"Now, we've been very forthcoming and honest with you in regard to what we know and what we have," Boyle said. "I'd appreciate some honesty in return as to how you know this man as well as anything else you can tell us. Legally, you're not even supposed to be here, so you technically can't even operate within this city without someone in my department leading the charge."

"OK. I can't tell you everything," Lawson said. "But I'll tell you what I can."

"I'd appreciate it."

"I don't know what name he's using now, but when he worked for us, he used John Smith. That's what he's known as."

Boyle rolled his eyes, knowing it wasn't likely to be the man's real name either.

"He worked in foreign intelligence in secret black ops projects which required certain skills," Lawson said, continuing the briefing.

"I can imagine what those skills were," Boyle said.

"Something happened, something went wrong, something that shouldn't have, and he himself was targeted based on false information. He dropped off the grid and has been missing ever since."

"And what made him pick here to set up business?"

"We have no idea. I just took over the investigation to find him within the past week. I got information indicating he may have been in a major city on the east coast, then one of my analysts caught wind of your press conference and saw the picture you released of him, and here we are."

"So, what exactly do you presume on doing?" the commissioner said.

"Well, as you said, we can't legally act here without your knowledge and consent," Lawson said. "But you obviously have a problem on your hands regarding him and we believe we can help you with it. With your permission, we'd like to stay here indefinitely and conduct operations with the intention of finding him."

"And when you find him?"

"I would like to take him into custody and transport him back to one of our facilities."

"And what if he doesn't want to go?"

"Well, hopefully it won't come to that."

Boyle sat back in his seat, leaning against the brown leather lined chair, thinking about his options. He looked up at his deputy commissioner as he thought.

"How long do you intend to stay here?"

"However long it takes. Hopefully a few days, maybe a few weeks," Lawson said. "But if we need to stay longer, we will. We're not leaving here without him. Unless we have evidence he's gone somewhere else, in which case we'll obviously follow him."

"I'll give you permission and authority to stay and work here under one condition."

"Which is?"

"I need updates every day from you about your operations. I don't want any of my officers walking into a potential war zone because you found him, cornered him, and neglected to inform," Boyle said.

"I can agree to that."

"Would you need any further help from me?"

"No, I don't think so. If we could get a copy of these files, it's about the only thing we really need. It'll help in trying to map things out."

Boyle handed the file to his deputy commissioner and said to make a copy of everything in it to help the government agents in their quest.

"One last thing, it's kind of interesting. Not only have crimes gone up, but also way more preemptive tips have come in. Do you think there's a correlation there?" Lawson said.

Boyle threw his hands up. "Who knows? We haven't ruled it out but we have nothing to indicate it's related. Why would it be?"

"Well, if he's only targeted the so-called bad guys, and he gets wind of crimes about to happen and he can't get there, perhaps he phones it in."

"Well the increase isn't on the phone hotline," Boyle said. "It's anonymous emails coming through our system. It's skyrocketed."

"Any chance you tried to trace where those emails came from?"

"Well, the tips are routinely analyzed and matched against IP addresses from any prior messages, just to make sure we're not getting fake tips from the same address all the time."

"I take it you got nothing from them?"

"Well, some IP addresses show up a few times, but that's to be expected if it's from a higher crime neighborhood, or someone who's extra vigilant. But nothing extraordinary. So, if he's part of the increased volume of tips, we don't have any evidence to implicate him."

"Hmm. Well it was just a thought."

"Well if that's all we can do for you then I wish you luck and hopefully a quick resolution." Boyle reached out to shake hands.

Lawson reciprocated the handshake and her team left the commissioner's office, ready to embark on their mission. After getting a copy of Smith's folder, their first move was to check into a hotel and set up their operations and begin to go over plans. Based on the information in the folder, Lawson wanted to map out every location they believed Smith had ever been. They hoped, once they had done it, maybe they could discern some type of pattern leading to a consensus on his base of operations, or where he was likely to be.

It was late afternoon, and Recker walked into the office with a box of pizza for dinner. It'd been a relatively quiet couple of days since the police department's release of his picture. For his part, Recker didn't really change his behavior much. He didn't go into hiding or only go out at night time. He didn't cling to the sides of buildings or wear a hat down over his eyes. He walked around much the same as he usually did. The only difference was they had no cases to work on. Jones kept telling him things were on the horizon, he just had to flesh out the details a little more, but Recker started to get the feeling he was stalling. He had the idea

Jones was flustered by the increased activity surrounding them, both with the police and the CIA, and he was putting cases off they should've been working. Once Recker put the pizza on the table and the two men began eating, he started quizzing his friend on his suspicions.

"Seems awfully strange we haven't had any cases in the last couple days," Recker said.

"Yes, well, it happens. We've had lulls before."

"Just seems a little coincidental when it happens right after a major police news conference where they release my picture."

"Indeed," Jones said.

"Or right after we learn the CIA has put me back on their radar."

"Quite a coincidence indeed."

"David, you wouldn't be intentionally hiding cases from me, would you?"

Jones laughed, though Recker could tell a disingenuous laugh from him every time. "Don't be ridiculous."

"When things seem to get a little hot for us, you have a tendency to shut the door for a while and try to hide away," Recker said.

"Well it's a good thing one of us does. Maybe I worry too much, but you don't seem to worry enough."

"It's not that I don't worry or I'm not concerned. But I know you can't change how you act. You could hide away for a month, then the very first day you step outside, they nab you. Then what good was the month of hiding?"

"I'm not sure your analogy is valid," Jones said.

"Sure it is. You can be as careful as humanly possible and do everything you can to avoid what's coming, but it doesn't mean you can."

"So, what do you suggest? Do nothing."

"No. I suggest we do what we've been doing. Act normal. We go about our day just like always and do what you signed me up for. It doesn't mean we ignore any dangers. We'll keep monitoring them, and if something comes up which makes us have to deviate from our plans, we act accordingly. But no mass hysteria," Recker said calmly.

Jones sighed deeply, knowing his friend was probably right. He was overreacting. Jones tended to overcompensate when it looked like trouble was brewing. He was just very cautious and always preferred to err in that direction. After they finished eating, Jones finally admitted he had been intentionally pushing cases off to the side they could have been working on. It was nothing extremely urgent, such as an impending murder, or someone's life in jeopardy. If that was the case, then Jones surely would have acted upon it more swiftly.

"Well so long as it's settled, how about we look and see what's on the agenda?" Recker asked.

"Very well."

Jones walked around the desk, sat at his computer and began typing away to bring up the necessary information for Recker's next assignment. Pictures of four men came up on the screen.

"Who are these clowns?" Recker asked sarcastically.

"These clowns as you put it, appear to be a very dangerous crew."

"Crew? You mean literally?"

"Yes. It would appear they are a crew in every essence of the word," Jones said. "They've all got lengthy records and each of them are considered violent. Their last arrest was six years ago for an armed robbery of a restaurant. They were apprehended and arrested a few minutes after the event."

"So, what are they planning this time?"

"Looks like a jewelry heist," Jones said.

"Where and when?"

"David's Jewelry Store."

"Oh. Have another business you been hiding from me?" Recker cracked a joke.

Jones didn't crack a smile. "Don't be silly."

"Where is this place at?"

"On seventeenth street."

"When are they hitting?"

"The store closes at nine. The crew indicated they'd hit tonight close to closing time when there's not so many people," Jones said, checking his notes.

"How'd you get wind of it?"

"My software program picked up a set of text messages from a couple members of the group where they were talking about 'robbing them blind', as they put it. I started digging up the background info on the phone numbers, then everything just fell into place from there."

"How long ago?" Recker said.

"A few days."

"What were you gonna do if I didn't press you on this? Just let the place get robbed?"

"Of course not. I was planning on doing something," Jones said. "I just hadn't figured out what yet. Maybe send an anonymous tip to the police or something."

"Yeah, 'cause we haven't done that too much," Recker said, rolling his eyes. "You know, can they trace all those anonymous emails back to you somehow?"

"Seriously? Bite your tongue." Jones smiled. "Who do you think you're talking to? Of course they can't trace them back to me. Do you think this is the first time I've done this or something?"

"Well I just figured I'd ask. It's a cinch the CIA will be checking into it."

"No. Every anonymous email is automatically assigned a different IP address. If they check into it, they'll come up as various places throughout the city. And some outside the city I might add."

"Just thought I'd ask."

With some time to kill before the jewelry store heist, Recker and Jones went back to work for a little while. But after a few minutes, Recker remembered something he'd been meaning to bring up with his coworker. It wasn't a big deal, and with the other things on their plate the last couple of days, it didn't rate high on the priority list, but Recker did wonder about it.

"You know, it's kind of funny," Recker said.

"What is?"

"I had lunch with Mia the other day and you didn't ask anything about it."

"What's to ask? People have lunch every day," Jones said plainly, though he knew what his friend was insinuating.

"I don't."

"Well you're not normal."

"I also don't meet new boyfriends every day either."

Jones stopped typing away at the computer and pushed his seat away as he started coughing, at first forcing it before it actually became necessary.

"You alright there?" Recker asked.

"Oh yes. Just a... you know, something caught in the old pipe there."

"Shame you couldn't have been there."

"Yeah, well, you know."

"So how long were you keeping that secret from me?" Recker said.

"I wasn't keeping secrets from you."

"So, you didn't know she had a boyfriend?"

"Well, I, uh, might have heard something to that effect. But I was not keeping a secret."

"Then what would you call it?"

"I was just not sharing... news which wasn't mine to tell," Jones said, stumbling over the words.

"Wait, was it the secret meeting you had and you wouldn't tell me about?"

"Umm, possibly."

"Uh, huh."

"She merely wanted to ask my advice on how best to approach the subject with you."

"Because you're such a relationship expert?"

Jones shrugged. "When it comes to matters of the heart, I'm purely Switzerland. I'm neutral and not getting involved."

"Since when?"

"Since always."

"Yeah, OK."

"So, are you saying you actually met Mia's new boyfriend?" Jones asked.

"I did."

"Well it's a surprise she introduced you already."

Recker smiled. "Yeah, came as a surprise to her too," he said with a laugh.

"Wait, you met him by accident?"

"Apparently the guy canceled lunch, then Mia called me. Then the guy freed himself up and came over to surprise her."

"And she was surprised?"

"You have no idea."

"And though I have my own guess as to how the luncheon went, how was it according to you?" Jones said.

"I thought it went fine."

"And for them?"

"Well, I think I was a lot to take in the first time meeting me."

"You are a bit of an acquired taste," Jones said. "You have a certain disposition that may be off-putting to some people."

"So I've been told."

"And Mia was fine?"

"No, she was terrified," Recker said truthfully.

"I can imagine. I'm sure you did your best to make it as awkward as possible."

"I did not."

"Maybe one day I'll get Mia's version of the events."

"I think she's trying to burn the memory of them."

"I bet. Anyway, what did you think of her boyfriend? What was your impression of him?" Jones asked.

"I didn't like him."

"Why doesn't it surprise me?"

"No, it's not what you think. It's not because I don't want to see her with anyone else or I'm jealous or anything," Recker said.

"Then what was it?"

"I just plain didn't like the guy."

"Why?"

Recker grimaced, trying to think of the reasons behind his dislike for Mia's new boyfriend and properly explain them without sounding like a jealous ex-boyfriend. And it truly was just a general dislike for the guy. In his profession, he usually had to make quick decisions about trusting people in tight spots or high-pressure situations, and he considered himself to be a pretty good judge of character. Sometimes, first impressions were all he got from people. So, he was an experienced hand at sizing people up at first glance.

"I dunno. He just doesn't seem right for her," Recker said.

"Very astute observation," Jones said sarcastically.

"I'm not jealous. I don't have the right to be."

"Well I agree there."

"No, it's just... something seems off about him. Just personality wise."

"Does he seem shady?"

"Well, he is a lawyer," Recker said, laughing. "No, joking aside, it's not that. He might very well be a decent guy."

"I'm sure we'll find out in time."

"I think I got it," Recker said, continuing to think about it. "You know what it is? They didn't seem like they gelled. They didn't seem like they had any chemistry together."

"Well I'm sure it was awkward with having you there in the picture."

"Maybe."

"You're enough to spoil anyone's chemistry."

49

Recker had stationed himself a little way down the street from the jewelry store, just sitting in his car and watching the place for a while. He got there around seven, wanting to make sure he was there in plenty of time so he could stake the area out before the impending robbers arrived. Recker thought for a while as to how he wanted to handle the situation. He and Jones debated it for close to an hour before Recker left the office, not coming to a definite conclusion on the best way to diffuse the dangerous situation. No matter what he did, there were pluses and minuses to it. Recker figured he had two options, and both had a set of difficulties. The first option was to let them do the job and try to pick the gang off as they came out of the store. The problem with that would be if the shooting started early, and the gang got split off or separated, some of them might get away. It would mean Recker would likely have to deal with them again soon. His first choice was to eliminate them all at one time. The other problem with a shootout outside the store was that some of the gang might retreat inside if they couldn't reach their getaway car in time. It might lead to a hostage situation with whoever was working inside the store or any customers who were still left shopping.

The second option they considered was, Recker would go inside the store sometime before closing. In that scenario, he'd already be in there waiting for the crew. The danger there would be that everyone who was inside the store would be put in harm's way. Now, he could've handled it as he had in other instances, and walk inside and let the workers know what was about to go down, and take their place and wait himself. But he also figured it wasn't likely all four men would go inside to do the job. It wasn't a huge jewelry store and didn't need all four men of the crew going inside. Recker assumed at least two would go in, maybe three. Maybe the fourth would stand outside the door and be a lookout. Or if two went in, maybe one would be outside as the lookout and one would stay in their car, ready to squeal out of there in a hurry.

There was no easy answer. In every scenario Recker dreamed up, there was just as good a reason he could think of as to why he should go in a different direction. If it was just some inexperienced run-of-the-mill gang that wasn't dangerous, Recker might not have put as much thought into it as he was. He could've handled it no matter which way he chose to go. But these guys, this crew was experienced in this type of work. They'd done it before and done it well. Plus, they were known to be violent. These weren't some young kids Recker could intimidate or get the drop on because they didn't know what they were doing. This crew would likely shoot first at the earliest sign of trouble or if something didn't appear to be right or going according to plan.

After giving it ample thought and going over every different scenario he could think of, Recker finally came to a conclusion as to how to handle the situation. With how experienced this crew was, he thought it was best to wait outside for them. If he could be sure all four men would make their way inside the store, then Recker would've preferred to already be in there waiting. He could get everyone to safety first, then take his chances with the gang. But he just didn't believe more than three would walk in. In fact, the more he thought about it, the more he believed only two would go in. He tried to think of how he would handle it if he was the one robbing the store. In that case, since it wasn't a big store, and it was near closing so they wouldn't have to handle a ton of customers, Recker would only take one other person in. He'd leave one man at the door to prevent anyone from coming in, or take the chance someone would walk by and see what was going on, and he'd leave one man in the car as the driver so they could fly out of the area in a jiffy. Another problem was, Recker couldn't identify them before they actually walked into the store. They weren't likely to use any of their own vehicles, and whatever car they did use, would most likely be stolen, so he wouldn't be able to see them in advance.

It was situations like these where he wondered if it was time for a partner in the field, someone else who could handle themselves the way he could. If there was, one of them could've waited inside and dealt with whichever crew members came inside, while the other could take care of the ones on the outside. It was never something he seriously contemplated or something he even put a lot of thought into when it did cross his mind, but now he was, he wondered if it was something he should bring up with Jones. Especially with the CIA hot on their trail or more specifically, his trail. Jones really had nothing to fear from them. They didn't have anything on him. Recker was the one they were after. And though he always tried to put on a brave face and pretend he wasn't worried, he was concerned, partly about himself and partly about Jones. He worried about what would happen to him if Recker was gone. Though he suspected Jones would eventually carry on without him, it would take him some time to get things right again. With them being together the past several years, they had everything down to a science. They knew each other well and knew what each other was thinking, what they would do, in virtually every situation. If Recker was no longer there, Jones would have to find a replacement, then slowly integrate them into the business, then develop a trusting relationship, just to get back to the point they were at now. That would take years. And though it could be done, there would be a lot of people in the meantime who wouldn't get the help they could've and should've gotten.

After a few more minutes of contemplating, Recker shrugged those thoughts from his mind and got back to his current problem. If he was going to take out the entire gang after they robbed the store, he had to figure out how to take out the first two without alerting the members inside. He wasn't sure it could be done discreetly. Unless he could take them all out before going inside. That would present a whole distinct set of problems. Instead of dividing them to make the numbers smaller, he'd be taking them all on at once. But if he did it that way, it wouldn't endanger any innocent people on the inside and they certainly wouldn't be expecting it. Recker looked at the time and knew he had to stop waffling on a decision and stick to a plan. To pull this off, he was going to have to be fully committed to whatever it was he decided. Knowing time was running short, he finally decided to stick to his original plan. He'd take out whoever was left on the outside, then get the others as they came out the door. He'd have to make it work. From his vantage point, he had a good view of the front of the store, so he'd be able to easily see when the crew arrived.

As the time drew closer, Recker knew it was almost time for action. It was 8:45pm. The crew would be arriving any minute. He was well prepared in terms of firearms, as he had taken three weapons with him. He had one Glock in his hand, one in his belt, and an assault rifle strapped to his back, plus a few extra clips. If a firefight erupted, he'd be ready for it. Recker got out of his car and walked over to the other side of it, stretching his legs and getting himself ready. All the while, he kept an eye on the jewelry store so he had an idea of how many customers were inside. After ten more minutes, the crew still wasn't there yet. Although it was possible, they decided to scrap their plans, Recker still believed they'd show up. They still had five minutes, and he figured they were waiting as long as possible. Just a few seconds later a black van slowly drove past him, finding a parking spot a little up the street, not quite level with the jewelry store. Right after parking, three men spilled out of the van and ran toward the store. Recker instantly recognized the crew from the photos they had of them.

As the men approached the store, they put black ski masks on before they entered. Somewhat surprisingly, all three men entered the store. Recker assumed one of the men was standing on the inside of the door to prevent surprises and whoever was left in the van was guarding the street. Whatever the case, it made it a little easier for Recker. He knew time was short, and he had to make his first move now. Knowing the man inside the van was probably looking through the mirrors to make sure nobody came up from behind, Recker walked in the street by the cars. He got out his keys and fumbled with them in his hand to make it look like he was walking toward his car. With the van just a few feet in front of him, he put his keys back in his pocket and replaced them with a gun. As he got near the van, he could see through the side mirror that someone was still in the driver's seat. Still walking toward it, as he reached the taillights, the driver rolled his window down. Recker cautiously approached the door, knowing there was a chance the driver was waiting for him with a weapon of his own. A few inches from the door, Recker saw the left hand of the driver reach out and set it on the edge of the rolled-down window.

Once Recker got to within reach of the door, he pulled on the handle and opened the door, causing the driver to slightly lose balance. Even though the driver was waiting for him, he wasn't expecting the stranger to open the door on him. The two seconds that caused the driver to lose his balance was all Recker needed to gain the advantage. As the driver tried to steady himself and raise his own gun he had in hand, Recker pointed his weapon at the man and fired twice at point blank range. Two shots lodged firmly into the man's chest meant the crew just lost their getaway driver. Recker, while keeping one eye on the store, reached into the van and pulled out the keys from the ignition. He turned and tossed them into the middle of the street then went back towards the rear of the van. He peered around the edge, keeping his eyes centered on the entrance of the store. He thought about maneuvering a little closer to the store but wasn't sure if he'd have time before the robbers came out of the store. He didn't want to get caught out in the open without having some type of cover. At least where he was, he had the van for protection. They would be heading anyway so he figured it was best just to wait there.

Two minutes later, the three remaining members of the crew came rushing out of the store, two of them carrying a black duffel bag, presumably holding whatever jewelry, cash, and other valuables they had just pilfered. The three men planned to stagger their positioning to avoid being grouped together, with the first man getting to the truck, then the second man, then the third. As the first man got to the curb, Recker jumped out from behind the van and unloaded on the unsuspecting robber. Three shots into his chest knocked the man onto his back then Recker turned his attention to the next man who was halfway between the store and the getaway vehicle. Recker fired at the second guy, also hitting him several times in the chest and midsection. With the first two men down, he fired at the third guy, who retreated toward the store entrance. As he took another shot at the man toward the store, Recker was shocked to see the first two guys stumble back to their feet. Recker knew he hit both of them square and was stunned they weren't dead yet. As they returned fire from their respective locations, Recker took cover behind the van.

"Crap," Recker whispered to himself. "Must be wearing vests. Wasn't counting on that."

Recker put his Glock in its holster and grabbed the assault rifle from his back and spun it around to a firing position. He figured if they were wearing bullet-proof vests than he needed a little more firepower. With a few bullets from his targets glancing off the van or lodging into its metal exterior, Recker dropped down to the ground and fired his rifle at the first member of the crew. Instead of aiming at his chest, Recker fired at the man's legs, chopping him down to size as he fell to the pavement, bullets ripping into his shins. The second member of the crew started to run back toward the store entrance as well, but Recker quickly fired before he could get there, hitting the man in the back of his thighs as he crumpled to the concrete walkway. Recker looked for the third member of the crew but he was nowhere in sight. He must've retreated into the store. With the first two members of the crew seemingly down and out, Recker stood and came out from behind the van into the open. He swung the rifle onto his back again and pulled out his Glock as he walked toward the injured men on the ground. Seeing an assault rifle was still on the ground within reach of the pain riddled man, Recker kicked his gun away from him. As he stood over the fallen robber, the man could see what his shooter's intentions were.

"Please, man," the man said, holding his legs in pain.

"Today's not your day," Recker said.

Recker unloaded one round into the man's head then moved to the next member of the gang. The man was still lying face down as he was grabbing the back of his legs. The man was screaming in agony with his legs feeling like they were on fire. As Recker passed over the man on his way to the store, he didn't bother speaking to him, or letting him know what was coming. He nonchalantly fired a round into the back of the man's head, instantly silencing the man's screams of pain. Although it briefly occurred to him to just leave the two bullet-ridden bodies behind, alive, as he went after the last remaining member of the crew. He quickly dismissed the idea. These men were too unscrupulous, too violent, too much of a danger to society. Recker wouldn't lose any sleep dispatching these people to their afterlife. Once he got to the door, he tried to push it open, but it wouldn't budge. It appeared to be locked. He knew there was a good chance he was going to take some fire the minute he busted through the door. Before going in, Recker put in a new clip for his gun to make sure he was fully loaded. Sirens started wailing in the background. The police were coming. Recker figured he didn't have very long until they got there. A couple minutes at most. The smart move would've been to hike his way out of there before the cops arrived. But Recker knew there were still three people in the store who were now likely hostages, including the person who worked there and two customers. The police were qualified to handle hostage negotiations, but Recker thought if he left, there was a chance the guy might just kill one or two of them before the police got there. But once he did get inside, he didn't have a lot of time to get the job done. And he wouldn't have time to negotiate either. He thought he had maybe two or three minutes max to kill the guy and get out of there before the police swarmed the building.

The door was made of glass, making it unnecessary to have to kick it open. Recker grabbed his assault rifle and forcefully smashed it through the glass. It instantly smashed into tiny pieces as the small particles of glass fell to the ground. Gunfire erupted as the lone remaining member of the gang opened fire toward the door when the glass smashed. Recker took a small step back, knowing he was going to have to make his way inside rather quickly. Surprise was probably his best way to make entry. He saw a small kiosk near the front of the door he could take cover behind until he saw where his target was located. He dove through the newly opened door, again drawing some gunfire, and scurried along the light blue carpeted floor until he reached the kiosk. He sat on the floor with his back against the bottom of the wooden kiosk, taking a second to catch his breath and figure out what to do from there. The top of the kiosk was jewelry encased in glass, but only temporarily, as the case was immediately smashed to pieces as gunfire ripped through it. Recker put his arms over his head and ducked to protect his face from getting cut from the falling pieces of glass.

"Give it up," Recker yelled. "All your buddies are dead."

"Yeah, well, I ain't joining them," the man shouted back.

Recker took a quick look around to try to find the two customers and store worker to make sure they were safe and out of the line of fire. He couldn't initially find them though. He turned around and got on his hands and knees as he looked around the edge of the kiosk. He saw his target behind the main counter, though only the top of his head, as he was ducking behind it. Half a minute later, the man rose fully behind the counter, showing the rest of his body. Recker didn't fire though. The man was yanking at the hair of one of the customers, putting her body in front of his and holding a gun to the side of her head. She was a middle-aged woman, in her mid to late forties, and looked scared as could be. This was one of the things Recker had feared. He knew this scenario might come into play if he couldn't have gotten them all outside the store. Of course, he knew if he had waited for them inside the store, a whole other set of problems may have occurred.

But still, he hated seeing an innocent person come into the dangerous crosshairs of the two sides. Recker also rose above the kiosk and stepped away from it, slowly walking toward the counter at his target and the hostage. He aimed his gun at the man the entire time he moved closer to him.

"Let her go," Recker said.

"Yeah, right," the man said. "She's my insurance policy. She's not going anywhere."

"You got nowhere to go. I already disabled your vehicle out there so you'd have to escape on foot. Once SWAT gets here, you know there's no escape. Just make it easy on yourself."

"As long as I got leverage, I have a way of getting out of here."

"The cops are coming, they're not making any deals," Recker said.

"Unless they want bodies in here, they'll deal."

"That's not happening. Because no bodies are gonna pile up in here as long as I'm breathing."

"Well I guess I'll just have to do something about that, won't I?"

Though Recker never took his eyes off the target in front of him, he let his ears take in what was outside, listening to the sounds of the police sirens. They weren't far off. If he didn't get out of there soon, there was a chance he was going to wind up getting trapped in there himself. He knew what he had to do. He just had to make sure he had a clean shot. He had to wait until the man made his head completely visible behind the woman's face. Though Recker was an expert marksman, he didn't want to take chances with only half of the man's head as a target.

"Tell you what, why don't we switch places?" Recker asked. "Let go of the woman and take me instead."

The man laughed at the silliness of the suggestion. "Yeah right. I ain't letting go of her. Maybe if you drop your gun first, I'll think about it."

"Think of it. Having a cop as a hostage is a lot more valuable to you than these people."

"You're a cop?"

"Of course I am. Why else would I be in here? What, you think I go around getting in shootouts for kicks?"

"Where's your badge?"

"I'm undercover. I don't carry one," Recker said.

"Throw down your gun or I'll kill this woman right here."

"I wouldn't do that."

"I don't care what you would do."

With the sirens getting louder and likely getting there within the minute, Recker knew he had to make some hay, and he had to make it now. He had to come up with a new plan.

"How about this? I'll throw my gun down, then you release the woman. Then I'll give you the keys to my car and you can get out of here?" Recker said.

"Why would you do that?"

"Cause my only concern right now is saving the life of everyone in here. And I'd rather see you get away than put anyone's life in jeopardy with a police standoff."

"I dunno, man."

"C'mon, we don't have long to debate this. Listen to the sirens. The rest of the squad's right up the street and closing in fast. If you wanna get out of here, this is your ticket. You're not likely to get another chance at this."

"You're trying to pull something on me."

"I'm not trying to pull anything. I just don't want any bloodshed and I can see what's gonna happen here if you don't take this. But if you don't leave now, you'll never make it to my car in time," Recker said.

Sweat was pouring off the man's head as he contemplated the deal. Something was gnawing at him telling him something wasn't right, but in his current predicament, he really couldn't afford to be too choosy. He knew the likelihood of him getting out of the situation as is was low. As soon as the rest of the police rolled in, he knew he was going to be arrested or killed. As Recker suggested, this was his only shot at getting out of there in one piece.

"Fine. Throw your gun down," the man said finally.

Recker did as they agreed upon and gently tossed his gun down on the ground. Before making a move, he waited until the man let go of the woman hostage. As the woman slowly slid away from her captor, the man turned his attention to Recker and pointed his gun at him as he waited for him to complete his end of the deal.

"The keys?" the man said.

"I'm gonna reach inside my pocket and toss them over to you, OK?"

"Just do it slowly."

"I don't have any other weapons on me," Recker said, lying to the man. "Just the one I already put down, so take it easy."

Recker slowly moved his arm inside his coat and reached for the handle of his backup weapon. He put his left arm up to try to keep the man at ease and not tip him off that he was about to give him a surprise.

"All right, I'm just bringing out my keys now," Recker said. "I'll toss them over to you."

Seeing the man relax his gun arm ever so slightly as his elbow bent, Recker quickly withdrew his gun from its holster. As fast as possible, he immediately pointed it at the unsuspecting robber, who was caught a little off guard. Though the man still wasn't sure he trusted the cop's proposition, Recker's speed was something he wasn't quite prepared for. Assuming the man was wearing a bulletproof vest like his comrades, Recker didn't bother aiming for his chest. He didn't want to take the chance in case the guy returned fire at him. Like the other members of the crew, Recker sought to finish the man off and put an end to this standoff by taking him out with a head shot. With one quick flash, Recker withdrew his gun, pointed it at the man's head, and fired, all before the man could get a shot off himself. Recker's aim was right on target as the bullet went right through the man's forehead, though not quite on center as it caught the man a little to the left. Still, it got the job done as the man slumped to the ground and died even before the impact of hitting the carpet. With the screams of the two women customers in the store not believing what just happened, the situation was now resolved.

"Everyone all right?" Recker asked.

He got either an affirmative reply or a nod of the head from the three people who remained, still a little shaken by the events. Recker looked back toward the front door and saw the red and blue lights flashing, as well as the blaring sirens. The standoff took too long. There was no escaping now. At least not the way he came in. He quickly backtracked behind the main counter and checked on the man he just killed, just to make sure there was no mistake.

"Do you need us to stay here and get statements from us?" one of the women customers asked.

"I'm not the police."

"What? I thought you said..."

"I said what I needed to say to try to diffuse the situation," Recker said.

"Well if you're not the police, then who are you?" the store worker asked

Recker sighed as he looked around for an exit strategy. "I guess you could call me a concerned third party."

"You're not here to rob us or anything either, are you?" the woman hostage asked.

"No."

Recker continued to look around, unsure how he was getting out of this one. Several things crossed his mind, none of which had a high probability of working. He could've tossed his guns away and asked the others not to reveal his role in the shootings and pretend he was just a customer there as well, but he didn't have faith the others would keep quiet on his involvement in the killings. Not that he could blame them, he just couldn't expect them to lie about something as big as this. He could've just ran out the front door and started shooting, but it wasn't a very sensible option either. He wasn't too keen at shooting at the police, even if it was to save his own hide. For one, engaging the police was likely to be a suicide mission, considering there was probably half a dozen cars out there or on their way. But the bigger reason was, he didn't want to hurt any of them. Everything he'd done since he arrived in this city was to help people, protect the innocent. The police had the same objectives. They just went about their goals in two different ways. So essentially, they were on the same side. And if Recker was going down, he decided he wasn't taking any of them with him. He didn't figure they deserved to be on the receiving end of one of his bullets. He had to find another way.

"Are we free to leave?" the woman hostage asked.

"Just give me a minute to figure something out," Recker said.

The store worker was closely studying Recker's face and could tell by his nervous demeanor he was worried about the police outside. Seeing the man wasn't a threat to them, and seeing how he did help them and save them from being harmed and robbed, the elderly gentleman tried to find out what his problem was.

"What exactly are you afraid of, son?" the sixty-year-old man said.

Recker looked at the man and winced, not really sure it was a good idea to reveal anything to him and get him involved. But without any other good options, and with time running short, he gave a deep sigh and figured it was worth a shot or a last-ditch effort.

"Well, I'm not a so-called bad guy. I'm on the side of the good and the innocent," Recker said. "But the police and I have extremely different ways of going about the way we protect people."

"So, they'd likely lock you up, huh?"

"And throw away the key most likely."

"That's a predicament, isn't it?"

"You heard of the guy who has been running around the city the last few years? The Silencer?" Recker asked.

"The guy who goes around helping people and getting rid of thugs and criminals?"

"Yeah."

"Yeah, I've heard of him," the gentleman said.

"Well, you're looking at him."

"You're The Silencer?"

"Yes, sir, I am."

"Can we go yet?" the woman customer asked, tired of waiting for their conversation to end.

"Just hold it a cotton-picking minute," the worker said.

Recker smiled at him, thinking he seemed like an all right kind of guy.

"Hold on, we'll get you out of here, son," the worker said.

"Now I'm not going to do anything which will put you in danger, even if it means me having to stay here and take my lumps with the police," Recker said.

"No, no. Come with me. You ladies stay right there for a second," the worker said.

The elderly man led Recker into the back storeroom and to an exit door leading to the rear of the building where the trash dumpster was kept. As they walked, the police were yelling into the store via a megaphone to see what the situation was, not knowing whether any of the would-be robbers were still inside, or how much of a danger it was. Recker was about to push the door open and see what the situation was out there until the store worker stopped him.

"Just hold up there, young fella," he said. "There's an alarm box on the side here. If I don't disarm it and put the code in, there's gonna be a loud, obnoxious sound that'll be heard around the block."

The elderly man walked over to the alarm box and put the code in to disarm the door, then Recker gently pushed it open just a hair, looking out into the alley behind the store. Recker was disappointed, but not surprised, to see there were police cars lined up at both ends of the block. They would cut off his escape route and throw his plan out the window. He closed the door again, and the man put the code back in to arm the door once again. Thinking there was nothing else to do but give himself up and take his chances with the law, the store worker had one more idea to try. The man looked up at the ceiling and put his hand on Recker's forearm to stop him from going back to the front of the store.

"There's your only hope now," the man said, pointing to a ladder on the wall leading up to the circular roof hatch.

"Where's it go?" Recker said.

"Just up to the roof. The only people who use it are roofers, or the heating and air conditioning people."

"Guess it's as good a shot as any."

"Hold on, let me disarm the alarm again."

Recker scurried over to the wall and started climbing the ladder. He got about halfway up before he stopped and looked down at the elderly man.

"Hey, thanks for the help," Recker said, appreciative of the man's efforts in aiding his escape.

"No problem. Keep on what you're doing. And thanks for the assist out there."

"I'll keep a special eye out for you."

Recker continued his climb up the ladder and pushed the roof hatch open. If it'd been a little later than it was, he might've been concerned about SWAT team snipers picking him off once he got up there, but even if they'd been called, they didn't have enough time to get there already and set up. Once Recker stood on the roof and looked around, it was actually a perfect scenario. As he stood there, he wasn't visible from the street, as the edges of the store walls extended up past the rooftop, creating some cover for Recker's movements. Each store on the street had connecting walls to the business next to it so Recker quickly climbed over the wall onto the roof of the next store. He wasn't sure how far he'd have to go, or how he'd get down, but for now, it seemed like a good escape.

The jewelry store worker waited three or four minutes until him and the two female customers made their way outside into the waiting arms of the police. He figured it was what Recker needed to slip away. Once the police swept the store and started questioning everybody and figured out what happened, Recker would be long gone. Recker wasn't really concerned with anyone knowing he was there, anyway. Once Recker got to the end of the block, he used some piping, gutters, and ledges to climb himself down the side of the building. The police didn't block off the entire back alley since it'd be too long an area to partition, and instead only blocked off a few stores down from the jewelry store in both directions. Recker walked around to the front of the building and started walking back up the street to get in his car. But there was heavy police activity all around and they weren't too far from his vehicle, so he figured it was best to leave it for the time being. The last thing he needed now was to be spotted and get into a police pursuit. He'd have to come back for it another time. He called Jones to let him know the task was completed, and he needed a ride out of there.

"What was the score?" Jones said.

"Good guys four, bad guys nothing," Recker said.

50

Lawson and her team were up early to discuss their different options on finding Recker. They got started right around 6am as they gathered in one of the hotel rooms. Lawson's phone rang only a few minutes later to inform her of the details of the jewelry store incident from the night before. It was Deputy Commissioner King who told her of the incident, hoping it could maybe help them in their search for the wanted man. After a brief conversation with her counterpart, Lawson thanked him for the information then got back to her team and started brainstorming. She explained to them what happened at the jewelry store as it was explained to her.

"OK, so he's obviously getting some inside intel somehow," Lawson said. "How is he figuring out how these crimes are going to happen? He's there ahead of time, waiting for the criminals to get there. He's obviously got something in place. Some kind of system."

"Here's a far out, off the wall theory," one of her assistants said. "What if he sets up these crimes, recruits criminals to pull the job off, then stops it before it happens or just after it happens so he looks like the knight in shining armor?"

"It's an awful lot of trouble to go through without getting anything in return," Lawson said. "I mean, he's not getting money or anything from this stuff."

"He's getting notoriety. Maybe that's what he wants."

"You don't disappear from the CIA just to go to a big city and build up a reputation," Lawson said. "No, notoriety is the last thing he wants. Besides, it doesn't fit his profile. He's a low-key guy. He's not after fame or fortune. I think he genuinely is trying to do good things."

Another of Lawson's assistants chimed in with his thoughts. "Well, if it's not the notoriety, which I think we all can agree it's probably not, then we need to focus on how he's getting this information. What if all these people he's stopping are part of the same underground criminal network? They have a leader who dispatches them on these jobs and Smith has a beat on them, maybe an informant who spills what they know to him."

Lawson thought it over for a minute, but by the grimace on her face, wasn't sold on the idea. "I don't know, I have a hard time believing every crime he's stopped is from the same network. I mean, don't you think after a few times they would've shored things up if they felt there was a leak?"

"Yeah, probably."

"If the group had any brains, after the third or fourth time, they would've completely dismantled their system."

"True. That leaves only one other possibility then."

"Which is?" Lawson asked.

"He's getting the information straight from these criminals. It's not like these people are going on message boards on the internet and declaring publicly what crimes they're gonna do. He's somehow getting into their phones, their computers, their emails, something telling him what's going on."

Lawson paraded around the room as she thought. She not only believed it was as good a theory as they were going to come up with, she actually thought it might not be too far from the truth.

"OK, so let's say that's the case," Lawson said, looking around her team. "He still needs to find a way to do it. There's nothing in his background that suggests he could do something like this on his own. It can only mean he has help."

"Not only that, but it'd have to be a sophisticated system," one of the analysts said. "Unless he's just got a list of criminals and getting into their computers remotely, he'd have to come up with something very technologically advanced to pull this information out of the air."

"But you think it is possible?"

"Sure. If he's found a way to hack into the infrastructure of say... emails, for example, he could have certain words or phrases plucked out and send him an alert, or maybe even a copy of the email."

"It would require a lot of time to create a system like that," Lawson said.

"Maybe. Maybe not."

"What do you mean?"

"Well, if we do assume he's not in this alone, then it's possible his partner, or partners, are computer whizzes. Maybe, they take care of the information gathering, sorting it out, Smith goes out in the street and does what needs to be done."

"Possible."

"In any case, there are software programs already in place," the analyst said. "The NSA has been using hacking programs for emails, cell phones, computers, and surveillance systems for years. So, it's not necessarily a new concept."

"It's a new concept for someone who would now be called a civilian... albeit a very dangerous one."

"But not if he's hooked up with someone. And if this is how he's getting his info, hacking emails and such, then he's got someone with some serious skills."

"How many people outside the NSA would know how to do things like that?" Lawson said.

"There are some people who probably could. It'd take a long time to perfect a system and for it to go undetected. But there are some people, hacktivist groups, things like that who could probably create something. Or he's got someone who used to work for the NSA who's already familiar with and knows the system."

"We could be veering a little bit off course here. Let's first figure out how to apprehend Smith, then we can figure out his infrastructure afterwards."

"How about we set some type of trap for him?" the analyst asked.

"What do you have in mind?"

"If we assume we're right and he's got some type of hacking program, then let's set up some fake accounts and emails and see if we can set something up for him."

Lawson nodded, thinking it just might work. "How long would it take you to do something like that?"

"Probably a good part of the day. If his intel is as good and as deep as we think it is, you can be sure they do a good background check on their victims before they target them. We'll have to set up emails, some false identities, background info, create criminal histories and the like. It's gonna have to be detailed and look authentic," the analyst said. "Because if he's got a computer guy, and he's as good as we think he is, he's double and triple checking this stuff. They're not gonna make a move on anything until they're absolutely sure it's legit."

"OK. Do it," Lawson said. "Make it good. Take as much time as you need to get it right. Because one thing's for sure, we might not get another crack at this. If they realize it's us and we're setting a trap, the door is closing and we're never getting it open again."

~

As Lawson and her team started creating false identities and documents to set their trap, Recker and Jones continued working as they usually did, completely unaware of the impending danger they were about to face. During the early morning commute, Jones took Recker back down to the area of the jewelry store so he could pick his car back up. Once they did that, they went back to the office to figure out their next steps. Though Jones headed straight there to begin working, Recker stopped for breakfast for them both. When he got back, Jones had the television on and was watching the news. Recker didn't really need to say anything since he noticed the jewelry store in the background of the reporter who was on camera.

"I take it they're discussing last night's events?" Recker asked.

"Astute observation."

"Anything interesting?"

"I guess it would depend on your definition of interesting," Jones said.

"Was my name mentioned?"

"Oh yes. The witnesses in the store positively identified you to both the police and the media."

"Well, like I told you, without the store clerk I don't know if I would've made it out of there. That reporter could've been standing outside of the police precinct talking about my capture."

"I know. I guess it's something to be thankful for. But regardless, in the beginning of the broadcast they plastered your picture on the screen the police released the other day. You know as well as I do the CIA is getting wind of this right now."

"Probably."

"So, what do you want to do?" Jones solemnly asked.

Recker shrugged. "I don't think my position has changed any."

"You know they're coming."

"Yeah," Recker sighed.

"Then why do you insist on staying here?"

"I dunno. I guess running doesn't have much appeal to me. I've never been someone who likes to hide somewhere."

"I know that. But if we don't do something, then we both know at some point, they will find you."

"You know, when I was waiting at the jewelry store, I was thinking maybe it'd be smart if you started looking at some other candidates," Recker said.

"What?"

"Well, in case I get locked up or killed, it's gonna take a while before you can get someone else acclimated."

"Well how about if we don't let it come to that and pack up and move somewhere else?" Jones asked, pressing home his point from their previous discussions.

"David, the only one in the hot seat is me. You don't need to continually pack up and move every couple years. While I'm around, the CIA is a threat. Always will be. Do you really want to move every time there's a threat?"

"Of course not, but..."

"The more times you move, the more likely it is you're gonna make a mistake somewhere along the way."

"Well I disagree there," Jones said, trying not to boast about his skills.

"If you have to move to a new place, this isn't exactly a simple operation which can be put up and taken down at the snap of a finger," Recker said. "You have to learn the people, contacts, everything starts all over again. Mistakes will get made trying to get familiar with everything."

"Perhaps. But it's better than the alternative of just sitting here and waiting for you to get placed in a body bag."

"There's only so many times you can move."

"The world's a big place, Michael. There are infinite possibilities."

"Even if that's so, and even if the CIA never finds me, have you given thought about bringing another person on board?"

"To work alongside of us?" Jones asked, a little surprised at the question.

"Yeah."

"Hmm. It's an interesting proposition. It may have crossed my mind a time or two over the years but I can't say I have really given it much thought. Not seriously anyway."

"Maybe it's time you gave it some thought. Seriously."

"Why? Do you feel you're overworked or overwhelmed at times?"

"No, but the more people we got out there, the more people we can help," Recker said. "There are times when more bodies would make us more effective."

"But also, more people to worry about."

"We could make it work. Take tonight for instance. It was just me against four. If I had someone who could do what I do, then I could've taken two, and he could've taken two. Then the job would've been done a lot faster and I wouldn't have had to do my Houdini act at the end to escape."

"I guess there's a good point in there."

"I try to make them every now and then."

"Yes, though I wonder if you're suggesting it because you feel it's actually a good idea and you would like the help, or because you feel like your time is coming to an end and you don't want to leave me shorthanded."

Recker didn't bother to respond and just shrugged, heading over to a computer to work on some things. They had nothing else to work on according to Jones and he figured he'd try to find out anything else he could in regard to the CIA breathing down their necks. Jones periodically glanced over to his friend, a little concerned over his state of mind. He knew Recker wasn't one who scared easily, or someone who ran from a fight, but Jones just didn't get why he wasn't more interested in getting out of there with the conditions as they were. It didn't seem like Recker was giving up or anything, but Jones just felt like he should have been more willing to consider other alternatives besides staying there and slugging it out with the secretive government agency. Recker certainly didn't appear to be someone with a death wish. But his motivations for doing anything weren't always clear.

From Recker's standpoint, after hearing of the CIA coming, his first inclination was to pack up and leave the area, set up shop somewhere else and start over again. But the more he agonized over it, the more he realized he just wasn't interested in running for the rest of his life. Though he wasn't ready to leave the world yet, he just didn't want to pick up and move every time the CIA started getting close. While he was used to the cloak and dagger world he was engrossed in, he was getting to the point where he just wanted to stay in one place. He didn't want to be a nomad and move to a new city every year or two years. Recker didn't think it was much of a life, just trying to stay one step ahead of the organization that was hunting him. And since he was now back on their radar, if there was ever any doubt they'd forgotten about him, it was now gone.

Maybe if he hadn't killed 17 yet, he would've felt different. After all, for a long time, finding and killing him was the only thing

Recker was really living for. Now he had accomplished his mission, maybe Recker wasn't really living for anything. Sure, he found satisfaction in his work and helping people avoid becoming a bad statistic, but there had to be more to life than just that. Something on a more personal level. If he wasn't being hunted, maybe Mia would've been the something he needed or craved. But while the situation was the way it was, he could never put another woman's life in danger because of him. He just wouldn't. Not again.

Recker and Jones, neither of whom had much to say, worked silently for the next several hours. While Recker continued monitoring the CIA as best he could, he knew it was a losing game. There was only so much they could do from there. He knew the chances were good that he wouldn't see them until they were right on top of him. Jones was digging into the background of a few people for a few cases which were on the horizon. While he was doing that, he continued thinking about Recker's behavior and stance on not wanting to leave. Finally, he stopped working and swiveled his chair around to face his friend and pick his brain a little more.

"So, are you going to tell me what the real reason is that you don't want to leave here?" Jones said. "I know it can't be as simple as that."

"Why can't it?" Recker said, not taking his eyes off the computer.

"I don't know. Most of the time, people have more complex reasons for doing anything. It's very rarely one thing, but a mixture of thoughts that cause it."

"Maybe."

"I know you don't have a death wish. Or do you?"

Recker snickered at the suggestion. "If I had a death wish, I would've died on the battlefield last night."

"I know. If you tell me it's the honest truth that you just don't want to pick up and leave then I'll leave the subject alone. But I just don't believe it is. And considering we're in this together, and what you do affects me, I think I have a right to know the truth."

Recker sighed and finally took his attention off the computer screen. "Truthfully, I don't even know myself what the real reason is. I guess it's probably a bunch of things."

"Such as?"

"Well, part of it is the resignation that eventually they're going to find me. I mean, why keep putting it off?"

"Self-preservation is always a good reason," Jones said.

"What exactly am I preserving?"

"Your life, your work. It's a good start."

"Living on the run isn't much of a life," Recker said.

"I've never heard you talk like this before."

"I guess it's just the realization..."

"What?"

"I don't know." Recker sighed. "I guess part of me figures... I don't even know what I'm saying."

"Does this have anything to do with Mia's recent situation?" Jones said.

"Maybe a little."

After a few seconds of thinking, Jones thought he might've stumbled upon it. "Are you feeling sorry for yourself?"

"No."

"Is it about Carrie?"

"I dunno."

"Mike, you're going to have to start explaining what it is you're actually feeling."

"Explaining my feelings isn't something I'm exactly good at or used to," Recker said.

"Yes, I'm aware. But give it a try."

"I guess it's like you said, a little bit of everything. After Carrie died, the only thing that kept me going was finding the person who was responsible for it. For three years, it was my life."

"And now that's finished, you're finding it hard to have a purpose to keep going," Jones said.

"I guess so."

"Carrie's death has been avenged, Mia's moving on, and there's nothing else on a personal level to keep you moving forward."

"Yeah."

"What about the work we're doing? The people we're helping, the people who are alive and well because of you, doesn't it mean anything to you?"

"Of course it does. But there's gotta be more to life than just going around and shooting people every week, doesn't there?"

With his weary outlook, Jones could now obviously tell what the problem was. Recker needed some deeper meaning in his own life. He'd spent most of his adult life helping and protecting others so he never thought about his own needs much. Then, when he finally did and met Carrie, it was ripped away from him. He was ready to leave the life he led behind once before, and Jones surmised he might wish to do it again, or at least have a life outside of his work. But he was stuck in the neutral zone where he didn't want to be alone anymore, but he didn't want to bring someone close to him either.

"At the risk of sounding unsympathetic to your problems, Mike, at some point you're going to have to make a decision on what it is you truly want."

"Don't you ever get tired of being cooped up in here most hours of the day, seven days a week?" Recker said.

"Maybe once in a great while. But for the most part, no, it really doesn't bother me. I made the decision a long time ago when I first decided on going ahead with this operation, this would be what the rest of my life was like. And I was OK with it. I knew going into this that love or relationships would be non-existent. They would be for other people. The people I'm trying to help. I put to rest any ideas I may have ever had about leading a normal life, having a wife, having kids, buying a house, all the other normal things normal people do. I think your biggest problem is, that you had a taste of what another life could be, you liked it, and you've never let go of it."

Recker just nodded as Jones continued, not really knowing how to respond, but basically agreeing with his sentiments.

"But the life you started to build with Carrie is gone, Mike. She's gone. You've never really accepted her death. No matter what you've done, where you've gone, who you've killed, who you've met, you've never let her go. You've got to move on and accept the life you now have or choose a different path."

"I know."

"The life you had with Carrie is never coming back. You're never getting those feelings back. And unless you're planning on sweeping Mia off her feet, which I agree would be unwise, then you need to fully immerse yourself in the life we now lead and embrace it wholeheartedly."

Recker agreed with everything Jones had said to him and felt he was right on the mark. He still held on to the feelings he had when he was with Carrie and always somehow wanted those feelings to return, just not at the price she paid for them.

"I've already taken the liberty of scouting a few other cities we could relocate to if you're of mind," Jones said.

The Professor pulled out a file folder from underneath a mountain of other papers and slid it along the desk for Recker to peruse. Recker, intrigued at what Jones had come up with, curiously lifted the folder and started looking at the options.

Recker read the names aloud as he looked at the list. "Baltimore, Boston, Atlanta, Dallas, Denver, Los Angeles, Las Vegas, San Diego, Detroit, Houston."

"I figured it would be wise to leave off New York since Centurion is located there and Chicago since it's my hometown," Jones said.

"What made these cities fit the bill?"

"Large enough to blend in, and large enough to make a difference. Though if you have other suggestions or preferences, then I'm more than willing to discuss it."

"No, these are fine."

"So, does it mean you will agree to a move?" Jones asked.

"I'll consider it."

"Soon I hope."

"I don't want to move just yet."

"When?"

"Let's finish up whatever we have in the pipeline here first," Recker said. "I know you've been looking at a few things."

"So, after we clean it all up, you'll agree to go?"

Though he still didn't really want to leave, Recker begrudgingly agreed and nodded his head. "As long as everything here is finished up. And I guess I'd need to give Mia a proper goodbye."

51

Recker had called Mia and asked to meet her for lunch. It'd been a couple of days since he agreed to Jones' proposition of moving to a new city and he wanted to tell her in person he was going. He didn't want to tell her on the phone, or through a voice mail or a text message. He wanted to see her face and look into her eyes as he told her. He wasn't exactly sure how Mia would take the news, but he imagined she wouldn't be too sad or devastated considering she'd found someone new. That should've taken the sting out of it, if there was any. Recker and Jones were trying to get their last few cases squared away before Recker met Mia at the hospital.

"You know, it's probably for the best anyway that you're going far away from her," Jones said.

"Why?"

"Well, her new boyfriend for one."

"What about him?"

"Well, considering he's met you and seen your face, and the

face of The Silencer has been bandied about in the news recently, don't you think eventually he'd put two and two together?"

"Hmm. You know I hadn't really thought about it."

"Well, think about it. Considering he's a lawyer, even though not a criminal one, but still, at some point your picture will find its way in front of him. Even if he's just hobnobbing it up with other lawyers or watching TV or doing research. Somehow he'll find those pictures."

"Yeah, probably."

"Yes, and when he does, he'll have some very pointed questions for Mia, don't you think?" Jones said.

"She wouldn't tell him anything," Recker said.

"Maybe not at first. But if their relationship progresses a year or two from now and marriage is on the horizon, you really think she'd lie to him to protect you still?"

"Good point."

"And if he were to find out next week by chance, don't you think it'd put her relationship in peril, with him wondering how she knows you?"

Recker raised his eyebrows and nodded, putting his hands in the air, wondering why he was still being bombarded with questions on the matter.

"David, I already said you made a good point. I got it," Recker said.

"Well I'm just saying."

"I know. You're right. If the guy realizes who I am, then he also might start digging into things, might talk to the wrong person, then it would also put Mia in the crosshairs since she'd be the last known link to me."

"What do you think you'll say to her?" Jones asked.

"Damned if I know."

"Well you've been thinking about this for several days now, surely you must've come up with something by this time."

"Only thing I got so far is hi."

"Hi. That's it?"

"How do you come out and tell someone who saved your life and patched you up that you're moving in a week to someplace far, far, away and I can't tell her where it is for her own protection?" Recker said.

"OK, I'll help you out. How about this?" Jones said. "Say, Mia, the police are getting close to me and I have to move. How you like it?"

"And people think I'm the insincere one?"

"No good? How about this? Mia, the CIA is just about here to kill me so I have to go now."

"Who says you don't have a sense of humor?" Recker asked.

"I wasn't aware anyone said any such thing."

Recker just mumbled, unimpressed by any of the suggestions Jones had offered. Mia was a special person to him and he didn't want to be blunt or cold-blooded about it. He figured she'd still want to keep in touch somehow, either phone, or text, or email, all of which was OK with him, as long as it couldn't be traced back to his location. If anyone ever did figure out she was the last link to him, they could hack into her accounts to find him.

Once Recker got to the hospital and made his way to the cafeteria, he found their usual table in the back of it and waited for her to arrive. He was a little nervous about telling her his news. Outside of Jones, she was the only person who meant anything to him. When they first met, Recker only wanted her to remain a casual acquaintance, someone he could use in emergencies. But she obviously became so much more. She became a good friend, someone he could rely on and trust. Things which didn't come so easily to him. And he wasn't eager to let her go.

As Mia entered the cafeteria and saw her friend sitting there waiting, she could tell by his body language something was up. He just looked different. For one, he was looking down at the table and tapping his fingers on it. She could never remember a time when Recker did that. It was the first giveaway. As she approached the table, he never even lifted his head to look at her. His mind was obviously elsewhere. Instead of sitting down across from him, Mia walked up beside him and put her hand on his shoulder.

"You OK?" she asked, keeping her tone light and pleasant.

Recker's concentration was broken by her touch, and he looked up at her and smiled. "Yeah, I'm fine."

"OK. You look like something's on your mind."

"Yeah."

Concerned with what she was about to hear, Mia walked back around the table and sat across from him.

"What's the matter?" she asked.

"Nothing's the matter per se. Just some things I wanted to talk to you about."

"Oh. OK. When you asked about meeting me for lunch today it didn't sound like just a social thing."

Recker leaned his head forward and rubbed the side of his face as he tried to figure out how to begin. "Yeah, um, it's not I guess."

Seeing as how she'd never seen him so nervous before, Mia was starting to get really concerned. "Mike, you're starting to scare me, what is it?"

"I don't really know how to say it."

"Just say something."

"David was actually giving me some ideas, and at the time they seemed totally ridiculous, but now, now maybe they weren't so bad," Recker said.

"Why would David need to give you ideas on what to say? This is really bad, isn't it?"

"I guess he was right. There's really no other way around it but to just come out and say it."

Mia leaned forward, hardly able to take the suspense already. She put her elbows on the table and placed her hands on both sides of her temple as she braced herself for the news.

"Oh boy," she whispered.

"I guess I'll just say it. By the way, how's, uh, what's his name doing?" Recker asked.

"Josh? He's fine."

"Oh. Good. Everything good with you guys so far?"

"Yeah, great, like you care. Mike, will you please tell me what you have to say before I go crazy and slap you!"

In the end, he wound up just blurting it out. "I'm leaving."

Mia didn't respond at first and just continued to look at him with sort of a blank stare, like she didn't believe what she just heard. "What?"

"I'm leaving."

"What do you mean you're leaving? That's it? Leaving what? Where? When?"

"I'm leaving Philadelphia," he said.

Mia was stunned by the news. Her mouth fell open as she took her hands off her head and leaned back in her chair. She just looked at him for a minute, unsure what to say. Recker didn't quite know what else to say either and took turns between looking at her and glancing down at the table. Mia cleared her throat then coughed before coming up with something.

"Umm, when, uh, you say you're leaving, you mean, uh... for good?"

"Yeah, probably," Recker said.

Mia looked down at the table, not only stunned, but very disappointed in the news. "So, uh, when did you decide this?"

"I guess a few days ago. David and I have been talking about it for a while and it just seemed like now was the time."

"So why? Why now suddenly?" Mia asked.

"Well it's not really sudden. There's a lot of things which have gone into it."

"Mike, please don't shut me out now," she said, pleading with him. "If you're going away and leaving, probably for good, then please just be honest with me and tell me why. I mean, after all we've been through, and the things we've done for each other, just give me that much. Don't give me some crappy answer which just leaves me with more questions."

Recker looked away from her momentarily and thought about her request. Though he wasn't planning on telling her the exact truth, he figured she was right and she had the right to know.

"I'm starting to get a lot of attention here," Recker said.

"From who? The police? Because of those press conferences and pictures released of you?"

"Partly."

"You've never really concerned yourself with the police much before."

"I know. It's not just them though."

"Then what?"

"The CIA knows I'm here," he said. "They're coming for me. If they're not here already."

"What?" Mia asked, her voice raising in obvious concern of his well-being. "Umm, how do you know?"

"Well, it's complicated, but the best way I can describe it is, David built a sophisticated software program that hacks into the CIA computers and lifts information from them. Last week we found something with my name on it," Recker said.

"What was it?"

"Memos between various agencies, including the one I used to work for, and the CIA Director. They're looking into things, one of which is where I am."

"What makes you think they know where you are?" Mia said.

"Mia, these are extremely smart people who know how to find things if they look hard enough. If they haven't seen the picture of me the police have, then they will soon enough. Believe me, I used to work there, I know how it plays. If they're not already in the city, they will be quickly."

"Where would you go?"

"I don't know yet. We're still talking about it."

"Wow," Mia said, wiping her eyes as the tears started forming. "It's um, I just wasn't prepared for this."

"I know. I wanted to come tell you in person. I figured it'd be better this way."

"Well, thank you."

"Plus, it'll be easier on you this way," Recker said.

"Easier on me? How?"

"Well, with your new boyfriend. With my picture getting out there, I'm sure he'll eventually come across it, especially with him being a lawyer. It's bound to happen."

"I could handle him. You wouldn't have to worry about it."

"I know. But you shouldn't have to keep secrets or anything. It's not a good recipe for starting a relationship."

"And here I thought I was having a pretty good day." Mia laughed, trying to hide her sorrows. "I feel like you just told me my pet died or something."

"I'm sorry."

"No, it's not your fault. You obviously have to do what you feel you have to do. I just wish there was another way."

"I wish there was," Recker said.

"Will this be the last time I see you?"

Recker put his hands in the air, hoping to put a positive spin on it. "You never know. Maybe I'll be back one day."

"Can I still text you and call you or are you off limits?" Mia asked.

"My phone should be untraceable so you should still be able to."

"I guess that's something."

"Hey, a few months will go by and you'll get so busy with work and Josh you'll eventually forget what I even look like," Recker said with a smile.

"I really doubt it."

The two of them continued sitting there for another ten or fifteen minutes, reminiscing about some of the times they had shared over the past few years. Neither really wanted to be the one to end their talk first, knowing what would happen right after it. But eventually, Mia had to get back to work. Even though she was now in a relationship with another man, she'd never forget the feelings she had for him and how she hoped they'd eventually wind up together. And though she tried to tell herself she no longer had those feelings for him, they were still there. She just didn't show them anymore. As Mia stood to head back to work, Recker rose from his seat as well. They each walked around the table to the side and embraced in a big hug, Mia squeezing him tight. As Recker held her in his arms, his face drifted down to the top of her hair. He loved the scent of her perfume and wished this was a moment they would have always had. But it wasn't to be and he couldn't dwell on it anymore. As they separated, Mia gave him a final kiss on the cheek.

"I'll miss you," she said.

"Me too. You make sure you take care of yourself, OK?"

"I'll try. Who am I gonna get now to rescue me from vacant buildings and stuff?"

Recker smiled. "Well, hopefully you'll never have to worry about that stuff again."

"Yeah."

Mia smiled at him and started backpedaling, not wanting to take her eyes off him. She knew once she did, and she left the cafeteria, she most likely would never see him again. Eventually, though, she knew she had no choice but to turn around and leave. As she walked through the opened cafeteria doors, she turned around one last time and gave Recker a little wave. Recker put his hand up as well and watched her disappear as she exited the cafeteria. He couldn't help but think maybe she was the last good thing he'd ever have in his life. Wherever it was him and Jones wound up, he didn't think he'd do things like he did when he got here. It was kind of fortunate that one of their first cases just happened to involve a nurse, someone he could go to if he ever found himself hurt or injured. Whatever city they ended up relocating to, Recker didn't think he'd try to have another medically capable person on standby like he had with her. If something ever happened, he'd just try to deal with it himself, or find some underground type of doctor who'd been disbarred or did things on the side for the more criminally inclined crowd. Bringing someone decent into his world now seemed like a bad idea.

Dejectedly, Recker left the hospital and drove back to the office. Before getting there, he drove around aimlessly for a little bit, hoping to clear his mind some. Though he'd only been in town for around three years, it felt like home for him. It was the longest time he'd ever spent in one spot at any time in his life. Even when he was with Carrie in Florida, he usually would only spend a few weeks at a time there before going out on a job. He felt a little sad that he had to pick up and go somewhere else. He just hoped this wouldn't be an every other year thing with having to move. After soaking in the city streets for close to an hour, Recker finally made his way back to the office. Jones was curious how his lunch and talk with Mia went.

"So, how'd it go?" Jones said.

Recker shrugged. "I dunno. As well as can be expected I guess."

"How'd she take it?"

"She didn't break down and cry if that's what you're asking. Though it looked like she wanted to."

"I'll miss her too," Jones said. "Obviously not in the same way you will, but I'll miss her just the same."

"Yeah."

"Quite likely the last friend I'll ever have," Jones said. "Well, other than you I mean."

"Yeah, me too."

"Do you think you two will keep in touch?"

"Yeah. At first anyway. After a while, I don't know. You know what they say about friends and long-distance relationships," Recker said.

"No, I don't. What do they say?"

"They slowly drift apart. I'd imagine we'd be no different. It's tough to be a part of someone's life from a few hundred or a few thousand miles away."

"Yeah, I guess so."

"Did you give any more thought to where you wanna go?" Recker asked. "Not Houston. It's too hot. Plus, I wouldn't be able to wear my signature trench coat."

"Fine. I think we should abandon the East Coast and try the Midwest or West Coast," Jones said.

"I could agree to that. How about Detroit?"

"Why Detroit?"

"I dunno. They got a pretty big crime problem there, don't they?" Recker asked. "Seems like we'd do some good there."

"Detroit? Yes, I suppose it would work for me."

"How soon do you think it'll take to set up shop again?"

"Maybe a week, two at the most."

"Why so long?"

"Well, I need to scout locations for an office space," Jones said. "Plus, I have to change the server locations I get my information from. It takes time to do the things I do, Michael. I don't just snap my fingers and voila, magic appears. It actually takes some work and skill to do the things I do."

"I know, I know, I was just asking."

"I didn't just set up this operation in a couple days you know. It took thorough and meticulous planning."

"I bet. Speaking of new things, did you give any more thought to my suggestion of bringing on another guy?" Recker said.

"Guy? Why not a girl?"

"Just a figure of speech. Guy, girl, it, I don't care. As long as whoever's brought in can talk, shoot, and fight, and isn't a douchebag, I don't care who it is. As long as they're capable."

"I know, I was just kidding. But anyway, yes, I have given it some thought."

"And?"

"I'm not opposed to the idea. I would just like to get established somewhere else for a while before actually considering applications," Jones said. "Maybe a few months or so anyway."

"I'm surprised."

"Why is that?"

"I really didn't think you were too interested in the idea of bringing someone else on board," Recker said.

"Well, some of the points you made had some merit to them. It would make some assignments easier, as it were, but just because we might be interested in bringing someone else in, doesn't mean someone's just going to fall in our lap, just like that. It might take months or even years to find someone. I don't want to add just any old person into the fold. They have to have the right qualifications and background."

"You mean someone as loving, cheerful, and jovial as me?" Recker said with a grin.

"I don't think the world is ready for a carbon copy of you."

"That almost hurts my feelings."

"I'm sure."

"Hey, while we're on the subject of new things, how about a pet?"

"A pet?"

"Yeah, you know, something to hang around the office all day with. Something to take our mind off things every once and a while and unwind, de-stress."

"You've got to be joking."

"No, why?"

"I can barely handle you and you want to bring in an animal I have to take care of?" Jones asked.

"You don't have to by yourself. We'll all pitch in."

"What has gotten into you? First you wanna bring in another person, then you want to bring in a pet, what's next, a baby?"

"Sorry David, you're not really my type."

"Well thank goodness for that."

"So, the pet is out?"

"I really don't think we have enough time for it, do you?"

"Well, depends on what it is. Dogs are probably out. I like them, but they need more attention than other animals," Recker said. "We'd probably need something like cats, or fish, or maybe hamsters or something."

"No, no hamsters. I don't think I could work properly hearing them running around on a little wheel or whatever it is."

"Cats?"

"No, with our luck we'd wind up with one of those cats who likes to lay on your lap as you're working or lay on one of my computers or something."

"Fish?"

"I don't know, I guess I'll think about it."

"Oh, we finally found an animal you like."

"I don't dislike animals, Michael," Jones said. "I'm just not sure we can give one the attention it deserves."

"You should watch yourself, David. You're starting to sound like a grouchy old man," Recker said, grinning again.

Though Jones obviously knew Recker was kidding with the animal suggestions, or at least he hoped he was, he wasn't really enjoying this side of his friend. He preferred the violent, brooding partner he'd grown accustomed to.

"Don't you have somewhere else to go or anything?" Jones asked.

"No, not really. Why? Are you trying to get rid of me?"

"To be honest... yes."

Recker laughed, appreciating his honesty. "Well, can't get mad at you for the truth."

"Don't you have someone you could shoot or something?"

"Seriously?"

"No, not seriously."

"Oh, because I could probably go out and find someone if you really want me to," Recker said.

"I honestly have no doubts of that. But I'd really prefer if you stay out of the spotlight if possible."

"You know how I struggle with that."

"Well, hopefully it's something in which you'll improve at our next destination."

"Yeah, well, I wouldn't count on it too much if I were you."

"Believe me, I'm not."

"Ye of little faith."

"Faith can move mountains, Michael. But it can't cure someone who's gun-happy."

52

For the next several days, Jones spent a considerable amount of time trying to wrap things up in Philadelphia, while also scouting out possible locations in Detroit they could use as a base of operations. Something like what they had now was ideal, but he was open to other possibilities as well. Looking at potential offices over the internet was a bit problematic but just about possible. Thanks to the power of the internet as well as pictures of residential or commercial spaces for sale, Jones could get a decent enough handle on what was available. With the increased scrutiny, albeit more on Recker, he didn't want to take the chance of traveling back and forth to a new city and putting their plans at risk, no matter how small or remote the odds were. While he was taking care of the logistics of their planned move, Recker continued taking on a few small cases. Nothing was especially major or time absorbing, just minor things he could take care of relatively quickly.

"Did you start cleaning out your apartment yet?" Jones said.

"Have you ever seen my apartment?"

"Well you know I have. I've been in there many times."

"But have you actually looked at it?" Recker asked.

"I don't get your meaning."

"Well, if you've actually looked at my apartment, then you'd know that with the amount of stuff I have it could be cleaned out and moved in about an hour."

"An hour might be pushing it slightly," Jones said.

"Anything I need could be put in my SUV and I'd still have plenty of room to spare."

As they were discussing their moving plans, an alert came in on Jones' computer. He slid his chair over to the computer and started checking out the information as it came on screen. By his mannerisms, mumbling, and facial expressions, Recker could tell it was something big. At least bigger than the minor issues they'd been dealing with over the past week.

"What is it?" Recker asked.

"It appears we've got a hit on a potential bank robbery."

"When?"

"Looks like tomorrow around noon," Jones said.

"Nice. Haven't interrupted a good bank robbery in a long time. What kind of players are we dealing with?"

"Pulling them up now," Jones said, looking over the information before talking about it. "Looks like another four-man crew."

"Wonderful. Can't get enough of those," Recker said.

Jones was staring hard at that screen, deciphering the information. "That's not good."

"What's the matter?"

"One of the text messages I intercepted indicates they're quite willing to kill people inside. Perhaps a police matter?"

"No, I'll take care of it," Recker said.

"Are you sure? This crew looks like they're even more violent and dangerous than the last one."

"One last going away party I guess."

Jones pulled up the picture of the bank that was supposed to be hit and they started going over the background of the team behind the crime in waiting. Each member of the squad had lengthy and violent criminal histories. They were like the crew Recker took out at the jewelry store not too long ago. But the longer they looked over the impending robbery, something kept tugging at Recker that just didn't seem right.

"This doesn't feel right," Recker said.

"Why? What's the matter?"

"I dunno. It's just... it just doesn't seem like the best bank you could hit."

"Well, I'm sure they have their reasons for it," Jones said.

"I'm sure they do. It's not a large bank, it's at the end of a shopping center, it's not near a major highway," Recker said.

Jones stopped him before he could keep going. "Mike, you're thinking logically and like someone who doesn't rob banks. These people are not necessarily logical. If they were, they wouldn't do what their history says they have."

"I know. I just always try to place myself in their shoes to figure out how I would do it."

"Yes, but you also know that sometimes it's just not possible to figure out how other people's minds work."

"Yeah. Hopefully, this is the last big job we take on before we go."

"I have a feeling it will be," Jones said.

Recker and Jones spent the rest of the day multitasking. Recker began formulating a plan as to how to stop the bank robbery, while Jones continued with the impending move of their business. As Recker studied, he still found it strange how the crew was targeting that specific bank. It was a local community bank carrying a fraction of the money a few larger banks would have, several of which were only a few minutes away. But Jones was right, any bank was a target and the crew must have had their reasons for the job.

The following morning, Recker rose early, ready to tackle the day's events. For the first time he could remember, he beat Jones into the office. Jones took it as a bad omen.

"I think something is going to go horribly wrong today," Jones said.

"Why?"

"For three years I've been the first one into the office and everything has gone fine until now. Now, on one of our last days here, with possibly the most dangerous crew we've come into contact with, you break the string and mess things up by getting here first. You're putting bad voodoo on us or something."

"Really, David? Bad voodoo?" Recker asked.

"You know what I meant."

"And everything has gone fine. You really need me to go over all the times something's gone wrong? How about the time I was shot and disappeared for a few days?"

"Well, I wouldn't classify it as going wrong," Jones said. "You're still here, aren't you? Just a minor hiccup or bump in the road. But this, you're getting us off on the wrong foot today."

"I kind of doubt I'll get killed today just because I beat you into the office."

"Let's hope not."

After quelling Jones' fears and taking care of a few last-minute details, Recker grabbed some of his favorite weapons out of the gun cabinet and left the office about 10:30am. It was a half hour drive to the bank, getting him there about an hour before the job was supposed to go down, giving him ample time to wait for his targets, as he liked to do. He was in constant communication with Jones throughout the morning through the com device in his ear.

"How's everything looking so far?" Jones asked.

"Quiet. I'm just hoping nobody sees me sitting here for an hour and thinks I'm the one robbing the bank."

"That would qualify as a disaster, wouldn't it?"

Fueled by the jewelry store job, where Recker couldn't quite make up his mind on how to attack, he had already decided on a plan this time. Though he didn't think his lack of a decision at the jewelry store played any part in how things unraveled towards the end, he certainly didn't think it helped. He wasn't going to make the same mistake again here. He figured out the best strategy, and he was sticking to it. He was going to hit them as soon as he saw them arrive, hopefully killing them before they even stepped foot in the bank. The hour passed by quickly, probably because of the constant communication with Jones which kept Recker's mind off other things. As Recker looked at the time, he watched the last couple of minutes tick by until twelve o'clock hit. He did one last check of his weapons to make sure they were fully loaded, including his two handguns and his assault rifle.

Recker's eyes were diverted to the right entrance when a black cargo van pulled in and pulled up right in front of the bank's entrance.

"A van just pulled up to the bank. Think this might be it," Recker said.

"Please be careful," Jones said.

Recker jarred open his door, waiting for the bank crew to unload out of the van before he fully got out of the car, not wanting to show his hand too quickly and scare them off. Two members of the crew got out of the passenger side of the van, and with a black bag in hand, started walking toward the entrance of the bank.

"Showtime," Recker said.

He quickly got out of his car and jogged closer to the bank. Not wanting them to drive off after seeing him, Recker's first action was to shoot the tires of the van with his assault rifle to make a getaway not possible. As he scurried to the van, the driver threw a gun out the window and stuck both his hands out to indicate he was giving up. Recker thought it was a bit strange the man was giving up so quickly and without even putting up a bit of a fight. Unusual for someone with the violent background these men possessed. Recker quickly turned his attention to the men near the door, only to find they'd done the same. Their guns were on the ground, and their hands were already in the air. Recker was slightly unnerved by what was happening and took a couple of steps backwards.

"Something's not right," Recker said.

"What's wrong? What's happening?" Jones asked.

"Nothing. That's the problem. They just threw their guns down and put their hands up without even firing a shot."

"Mike, get out of there, it could be a trap."

"Yeah, I think you're right."

Just as Recker turned around and started running back to his car, sirens blared, marked and unmarked police cars raced into the shopping center from every direction. As he looked around to figure out his exit strategy among the increasing crowd, another door opened from the black van. One of the CIA assets assigned to Lawson's team took aim at Recker's chest and fired, hitting him near the shoulder. Recker grabbed at his shoulder and looked down, seeing the tranquilizer dart sticking out of it, and realized what was happening. His old friends had finally caught up with him. Breathing heavily and starting to lose consciousness, he sought to give Jones some final clarification as to what was happening so he'd know.

"David, looks like this is it," Recker said.

"Mike? Mike, what's happening?"

Recker didn't have time to respond. As soon as Jones finished, another dart made its way into Recker's chest. He dropped to a knee, feeling his last few streams of consciousness leave his body. His eyes were getting heavy and he could barely keep them open any longer. He took one last look at the black van, seeing a rifle pointed straight at him. A few seconds later, Recker finally blacked out and collapsed onto the pavement underneath him.

"Shelly, we've got him." One of the CIA officials radioed the news.

"Great, bring him to me," Lawson said.

The joint CIA/police raid was now officially over. With the police's help in securing the exits, Lawson kept her word that they'd take Recker off their hands. The men in the van took Recker's body and dragged it into the van and were gone within seconds. Jones, meanwhile, was frantically trying to figure out what had happened. While he couldn't be sure of anything yet, he could only assume Recker was trapped by either the police or the CIA. He immediately retraced everything they knew of the bank crew that turned out to be false. Unfathomably to him, someone pulled the wool over his eyes, and it quite possibly had cost Recker his freedom or his life.

As Jones panicked and started doing some computer work to figure out what happened, Recker was being taken to a facility the CIA had rented for the week. As soon as Lawson figured out how they would trap Recker, she knew they needed a secure place they could take him for the time being. Seeing as though they didn't have any nearby facilities they already owned, she found a semi-remote location in a former shipping business inside a business industrial park. It'd work perfectly since they'd only need it for a day or so.

About five hours after being taken there, Recker finally opened his eyes, only to find he was sitting with his hands behind his back and handcuffed to a chair. There was no doubt he was now in the hands of the CIA. This was their MO. Sitting by himself, tied up in an empty, dimly lit room, this was their style. After a few minutes, a door opened, and a woman started walking toward him. She sat in the empty chair a few inches across from him. It wasn't quite what Recker had expected. He figured when he was caught, assuming he wasn't shot and killed first, his final interrogation would be handled by someone he knew from Centurion.

"Hi, John. Is that what you're still going by these days or is it something else now?"

"Whatever you wanna call me is fine." Recker smiled, not seeming a bit nervous about his situation. "I can be whoever you want me to be."

"My name is Shelly."

"Nice to meet you."

Lawson returned his smile, impressed with her prisoner's calm and pleasant demeanor, who didn't seem the slightest bit anxious. "You seem awfully calm for someone in your situation."

"Well, not much else I can do right now, is there? I mean, you didn't tie my feet together, so it is theoretically possible that I could strangle you with them, but I'll wait a little while to see what you have to say first."

"Confident."

"I've done it before."

"After reading your file and your background info, it really wouldn't surprise me if you had," Lawson said.

"Considering Davenport isn't here, I assume he was bypassed, and they brought you in to find me?" Recker asked.

"Perceptive. So who were you talking to in the earpiece?" Lawson said.

"What earpiece?"

"The earpiece we found inside your ear when we grabbed you."

MIKE RYAN

"Oh, that. Yeah, I had it linked to my iPod so I can listen to some tunes while I work," Recker said, smiling. "I find music helps calms my nerves in situations like that."

"Always play it cool and calm, huh?"

"I try."

Lawson pulled Recker's phone out of her pocket and started looking through it. Luckily, Recker had gotten in the habit of deleting all his text messages and any voice mails every day, so there wasn't anything in there for her to see. Except his contact list.

"You wanna tell me who these people are?" she asked.

"No idea," Recker said.

"Who's David?"

"Uh, pizza guy. Yeah, I don't like meeting strange people so I request the same driver all the time."

"You know we can check this out, right?"

"Wouldn't get you anywhere."

"How bout Tyrell?"

"My supplier."

"Vincent? Malloy?"

"My vet and my pharmacist," Recker said.

Lawson chuckled, getting a kick out of his responses. "How about Mia? Girlfriend?"

"Just a prostitute. Gotta get your fix on somehow, you know?"

"I'm sure."

Lawson put his phone back in her pocket then pulled out a piece of paper, which was folded up. Recker wondered what she was going to try to throw on him next. She unfolded the paper and looked at it for a few seconds before talking to him again.

"So, kind of strange you have someone like Vincent in your contact list, isn't it?" Lawson asked.

"What's strange about it?"

"Someone like you doing business with a mob boss like him? I don't see the connection."

Recker smiled. "You're not supposed to."

"Tyrell Gibson. Looks like a low-level hoodlum. What's your connection to him?"

"He gets me my toys."

"Mia Hendricks," Lawson said. "You know what's strange about her?"

"You tell me."

"She's different from the others in your list."

"Oh? How's that?"

"The others have criminal backgrounds. She doesn't."

"Maybe she's better at not being caught than them," Recker said.

"Or maybe because she's a nurse. Maybe you settled down. Maybe she means more to you than the others."

"That's a lot of maybe's."

"OK, let's talk about this David fellow," Lawson said. "We can't find a last name for him, nothing comes up through his phone number, as far as we can tell, he doesn't even exist."

"Hmm... that's strange."

"Isn't it?"

"You know, this is all very enlightening, but what is it you hope to accomplish with this?" Recker said. "You know I'm not gonna tell you anything. What exactly are you fishing for?"

"I'm curious about your life for the last few years. How exactly did you come up with this system of yours? Obviously, you have some type of program pulling information from emails or texts or phones that you can act upon."

"It's really not so complicated. I'm just fighting crime wherever I find it."

"OK. Let's move on to another topic."

"Can't wait."

"Gerry Edwards. Know him?" Lawson asked.

"Is, uh, is he on television?"

"No, he's an agent of ours who was killed in an airport in Ohio."

"That's a shame," Recker said. "Dangerous profession, isn't it?"

"You wouldn't happen to know anything about it, would you?"

"Afraid not."

"And you didn't know he was the one who killed your girlfriend down in Florida a few years ago, right?"

"Oh, man, I've been looking for him too. Guess someone beat me to it."

Lawson couldn't help but smile, amused by Recker's sense of humor. She didn't figure getting any information out of him was going to be easy, but she was hoping he'd give her something, even if it was only one small thing she could run with. But Recker was an old hand at this, and he wasn't going to give them the satisfaction of learning a single thing about him since the day he left them. He knew what the plan was for him. They were going to try to learn as much about his friends as they could and possibly go after them, then wind up killing everybody they considered to be any kind of threat. He figured they'd leave Mia alone since they already had him, but Jones was another story. With his computer skills, and the fact he was already wanted by the NSA, he would likely be terminated along with Recker. The CIA wouldn't take the chance of leaving Jones alone then hoping he didn't come back for some type of revenge. Recker, though, wasn't going to give them anything on Jones, no matter what kind of technique they used on him. He knew them all and was ready for whatever they threw at him. But he was hoping to bypass all the nonsense and just go straight to the part where they killed him. He didn't want a long goodbye.

"Excuse me, you seem like a very nice person, but can we just get on with the killing," Recker said.

"What killing?"

"Mine. I hate dragging things out."

"What makes you think that's what's going to happen?" Lawson asked.

"Listen, I know the game, I know how it works. You wanna pump me for whatever information I can give and when I run dry, you finish the game. I'm not gonna play."

"Well, regardless of what you think you know, you don't. Let me explain to you exactly what's going on here. We know Gerry Edwards killed your girlfriend, Carrie. We also believe that several months afterwards you relocated to Philadelphia. How, we don't know. It is my personal belief that you hooked up with some computer geek who gets you information on what criminals or jobs to go on. I also think he found out where Edwards lived and passed the information on to you. You've been looking for him all this time then you went down there and killed him."

"Nice theory," Recker said.

"John, I know you don't trust me, and that's fine, I understand. I wouldn't trust me either in your shoes. I've looked over your package, your background, every mission you've been on, the doctors you've talked to, everyone who's ever had a connection to you since you've been in the CIA."

"And what'd you find?"

"I found someone who was wrongly terminated, attempted anyway," Lawson said. "But what you think is happening here, isn't what's happening."

Recker wasn't sure what the woman was talking about, but he was skeptical about anything she said. He figured this was the nice guy routine to get him to open up. She was good, because it almost worked. But Recker wasn't falling for it. By his facial expression,

Lawson could see he was less than impressed by anything she was saying. If she wanted him to even remotely trust her, she was going to have to make an extreme move. One that could cost her life if she was wrong about him. She got up and walked around behind Recker, just standing there for a minute. Recker was starting to feel a little uneasy, thinking this might be it. He was waiting to hear the click of a gun, or feel the sharp steel of a knife. Instead, he felt his hands become free as the rope bonding them together was untied. He brought his arms around in front of him and he rubbed his wrists as Lawson walked back around where he could see her.

"I don't want to kill you," Lawson said. "If I did, you'd be dead already."

"What makes you think you're safe enough that I won't do it to you?"

"Because I'm trusting you won't. I'm not Sam Davenport. I'm hoping that has something to do with it. And if none of that does, then there are several men outside the door who would kill you if they hear something doesn't sound right. And if none of those do it for you, then maybe your curiosity will, wondering what it is I want."

"I'm listening," Recker said, confirming that he was indeed curious.

Untying his hands was a move Recker wasn't expecting. There he was sitting in a chair without a single restraint to hold him back. Yet here was this woman talking to him like they'd known each for a long time, someone who knew what he was capable of, but didn't appear to be afraid of him in the least. It was a strange play on her part from his perspective.

"I was brought in to find you because Centurion believed you were responsible for Gerry Edwards' death," Lawson said. "After a few months of no progress, I was brought in from another agency to find you, or his killer, or both if it turned out it was you."

"Well congratulations."

"But I don't think you're a bad guy, or you're a threat, or you should've been rubbed out in London."

Recker just looked at her, wondering where she was going with this.

"I was tasked with bringing you in, one way or another. But like I said, I don't believe you're a bad guy. I don't want to bring you in dead."

"Honestly, you seem like a nice woman, but I don't wanna go back alive. Someone in Centurion will find a way to kill me anyway, or they'll stash me in some dark hole for thirty years. Neither one is an appealing proposition to me," Recker said.

"I asked Director Roberts personally if I could bring you back into the fold, if he would sign off on it, and he indicated he would," Lawson said.

Recker was a little astonished. Coming back in to work for them was literally the last thing he would have ever thought of, if he ever thought of it at all. It was so far-fetched to him he had never even considered it a possibility. Recker tilted his head back and looked away from her, thinking about what she just said. Lawson could tell he was taken aback.

"I understand you would still have trust issues," Lawson said. "We can put you in another division, another project, we can work with you to get you acclimated again."

"Why? Why go through all this trouble for me?"

"Like I said, I read your file. I didn't think what happened to you was right. And I believe you're someone who still has a lot to offer. There's a lot of things you could've done to hurt us, Centurion, the United States, but you didn't do any of them. It says a lot about you."

"I understand the way things work," Recker said, beginning to open up. "There was only one person I really had an issue with."

"Gerry Edwards?"

"Yeah. You're right. I killed him."

"How'd you find him?" Lawson said.

"That's as much as I'll reveal. What now?"

"Now I close off his file. The rest depends on you."

"And if I say no?" Recker asked.

"I'm really hoping you'll see things my way."

"I dunno. Trusting anyone within this agency is a lot to ask."

"I know. It'll be a process. But it's one I think is doable."

"What makes you think I won't say yes then when I'm in some foreign country, I won't just go off the reservation again?"

"I've thought of that," Lawson said. "There are ways around it."

Recker chuckled. "Any tracking devices you plant inside me I'll find a way to get out."

"Somehow that wouldn't surprise me."

Recker took another minute to just think about the offer just presented to him. He couldn't pretend there wasn't a piece of it that was appealing to him. Lawson struck him as being credible and believable. He was sure she was trustworthy to most other people, but for him, it wouldn't come in the matter of a few minutes. Lawson leaned forward and put her hand on one of Recker's knees. She could see he was conflicted and tried to set his mind at ease a little.

"John, you wouldn't have to run anymore," she said. "It'd be over for you."

"I don't know if I can do it anymore. That part of my life is over."

"You prefer running around in the shadows of the night, shooting low lifes, and avoiding cops?"

"It's not just that."

"Mia? This David person?"

Recker sighed, unsure he could explain it in a way that would make sense and she would understand. "It's more than that. I feel like I've made a home here. There's people here I care about. Even when I was with the agency, towards the end, I really didn't want to be there anymore."

As Recker continued to think about the offer, the less appealing it became. His heart just wasn't in doing that kind of work anymore. He knew what declining the offer meant, but he had to be true to himself and be honest with Lawson.

"Listen, I appreciate you going to the trouble of finding me and not killing me on sight, but I just can't do it," Recker said. "I think that ship has sailed. There's no going back for me now. You seem like you've been upfront with me and I'll return the courtesy. If it means you have to put me out of my misery, then you have to do what you have to do."

"So, I guess there's no way to talk you into it?"

"No. I couldn't even pretend to say I prefer my old life to now."

Lawson was disappointed in his answer as she really thought she could've convinced him to come back to the agency. She wasn't ready to give up on him though. Seeing how he hesitated a few times, and he genuinely seemed to think about it, she took it as a sign that he wasn't a completely lost cause. Working with some of the agents she had with Project Specter, she was used to dealing with rejection at first from stubborn and bullheaded agents. They continued their dialogue for several more minutes, though Lawson wasn't getting very far. Suddenly, gunfire erupted from just beyond the other side of the door. Recker and Lawson both turned their heads toward the door, startled by the development.

"Is that your team coming for you?" Lawson asked, getting her gun out.

"My team isn't violent," Recker said. "How many men you got out there?"

"Three."

The two of them stood and looked around the room to see if there was something they could get behind to protect themselves, but there wasn't. Whatever, and whoever was coming, they'd have to deal with them head on.

"You have another gun?" Recker asked.

"No."

"I hope you can use that."

"I'm adequate," Lawson said, not very confident in her abilities.

Recker looked at her, thinking they were in serious trouble. "Great."

After a few more minutes of sporadic gunfire, the guns eventually stopped. Recker and Lawson stood there waiting, hearts thumping, sweat running down the sides of their heads, wondering what was coming.

"You don't happen to want me to hang on to the gun, do you?" Recker asked.

"Not if it's friends of yours."

"Believe me, they're no friends of mine. Maybe I can hide next to the door, then when it swings open, I can jump them when they come in."

"Worth a try I guess," Lawson said.

Recker started walking toward the door when he stopped in his tracks as it suddenly burst open after being forcefully kicked in. An angry-looking man stood in the doorway with his gun pointed at the both of them alternately. Recker didn't recognize him, but he knew his type. He was a younger man, late twenties, bald head with a coarse beard, on the shorter side, wearing a brown suit. He came in so suddenly that it surprised Lawson and she couldn't raise her gun in time.

"Who are you?" Lawson asked.

"Maintenance man. Drop the gun."

Lawson did as the man directed and let the gun slip from her fingers, dropping onto the concrete floor. Recker knew what was about to happen. With his hands out to his side, he took a few steps back toward Lawson, thinking they only had one chance at surviving this.

"Which one of us are you here for?" Lawson asked.

The man just smiled. "Both."

"Who sent you?"

"Enough talk. It only prolongs the inevitable."

The man pointed at Recker, who dove back onto the ground for the gun. Their attacker quickly fired a shot at him. Lawson moved away from the action and toward the wall to get out of the line of fire. As Recker put his hands on the gun, he winced in pain as a bullet entered into his left shoulder. Recker shrugged off the pain long enough to spin around and fire a couple shots of his own. He also hit the man in his left shoulder, temporarily dropping the man to one knee. Recker continued firing, hitting his victim three more times, twice in the chest and once in the head as the man slumped to the ground, winding up flat on his back. Recker jumped to his feet and walked over to his victim to see if he was dead. Much to his satisfaction, he was. Lawson started walking over to him as Recker searched through the dead man's pockets. He pulled out some identification cards and looked at them briefly before handing them over to Lawson.

"Look familiar?" Recker asked.

"He's a Centurion agent," Lawson said. "What's he doing here?"

"Who knew you were coming?"

"The only person I told was..."

"Sam Davenport?"

Lawson looked at him incredulously, not believing Davenport would've actually tried to take them both out.

"Welcome to my world," Recker said to her. "Now you've joined the club."

"Are you OK?" Lawson asked, noticing the blood on his shirt and touching his shoulder.

"Yeah, I'll be fine."

"I'll take you somewhere to get it looked at."

"No, it's OK. Don't worry about it. I got someone."

"I'm sure you do. Oh, that's right, the nurse."

They stood there silently for a few moments, somewhat awkwardly as they figured out their next steps. Lawson was no longer in control of the situation, especially since her cohorts were now dead, and she no longer had possession of her gun. Recker realized he was now in power and the woman's fate lay in his hands. Lawson glanced down at the gun in his hands and wondered what he was going to do with her.

"So, what now?" Lawson asked.

Recker lifted his right arm and pointed the gun straight at her. After a brief second, he spun the gun around in his hand, holding the barrel of it. He then straightened out his arm and offered Lawson's gun back to her. She took it, and after pointing it at him for a split second, put it back in her holster.

"Looks like I've got a mess to clean up," Lawson said.

"How you gonna handle it?" Recker said.

"Well, I'd say Director Roberts is going to be very unhappy with a certain person who's in charge of a particular black ops program. Maybe he'll be the one who ends up in a deep dark hole somewhere."

"I wouldn't be opposed to that."

"I think it's safe to say nobody will be hearing from him for a very long time."

"And John Smith?" Recker asked.

Lawson thought for a minute before answering. She wasn't ready to give up on the thought of him eventually rejoining the agency. "As far as I can tell, Sam Davenport arranged the death of Gerry Edwards, just as he orchestrated the elimination of John Smith. He's innocent of all allegations against him and from what we've uncovered, he's not a threat at this time."

Recker gave her a wry smile. "Thank you."

"And maybe one day he'll come back into the fold. I'll continue to keep an eye on him."

"Well, you did find him once. Maybe you can do it again sometime."

Recker and Lawson shook hands, and she handed him back his phone. "You might need it," she said.

Recker then left the room and started making his way toward Mia's place so she could tend to his shoulder. One more time for old time's sake. Once he left, Lawson called Director Roberts and informed him of what happened so Sam Davenport could be taken into custody immediately. As Recker walked along the roadside, he called Jones to let him know he was OK and that he'd need a ride. When Jones finally pulled up alongside him, he had plenty of questions about his ordeal.

"Thank God, I never thought I'd see you again," Jones said.

"Had a few doubts myself."

"What happened?"

"Let's get to Mia's first and I'll tell you all about it," Recker said.

Jones called Mia to make sure she was at home, which thankfully she was after just finishing up her shift. He let her know he was bringing her a patient, which she could only guess was Recker. Once they got to her apartment, she was already waiting for them. She'd been periodically looking out the window, concerned about Recker's condition. When she noticed them pull up to the building, she saw Recker walking in, seeming normal, which relieved her worries a little. When they got to her door, they didn't even need to knock, as she swung it open for them as they got there. She immediately saw the blood on his shirt and just shook her head, at which Recker grinned.

"Will you never learn?" she asked innocently.

"Figured I'd leave you something to remember me by."

"This is a present I could've done without."

"Some things never change."

ABOUT THE AUTHOR

Mike Ryan is a USA Today Bestselling Author, and lives in Pennsylvania with his wife, and four children. He's the author of numerous bestselling books. Visit his website at www.mikeryanbooks.com to find out more about his books, and sign up for his newsletter. You can also interact with Mike via Facebook, and Instagram.

Sign up for Mike's newsletter, and receive two short stories with Recker, when he worked for the CIA as John Smith.

facebook.com/mikeryanauthor
instagram.com/mikeryanauthor

ALSO BY MIKE RYAN

The Silencer Series Box Set Books 5-8

The Silencer Series Box Set Books 9-12

The Eliminator Series

The Extractor Series

The Brandon Hall Series

The Cain Series

The Ghost Series

The Last Job

A Dangerous Man

The Crew